FRONTIER BRIDES

Four Romances Ride Through the Sagebrush of Yesteryear

COLLEEN L. REECE

BARBOUR
PUBLISHING

ISBN 1-59310-169-4

Scripture quotations are taken from the King James Version of the Bible.

Published by Barbour Publishing, Inc., P.O. Box 719, Uhrichsville, Ohio 44683, www.barbourbooks.com.

Our mission is to publish and distribute inspirational products offering exceptional value and biblical encouragement to the masses.

ecpa Member of the
Evangelical Christian
Publishers Association

Printed in the United States of America.
5 4 3 2 1

FRONTIER BRIDES

Dear Readers,

I hope you enjoy reading *Frontier Brides* as much as I enjoyed writing it.

I was born and grew up in the little mountain town of Darrington, Washington (foundation for "Hope" in the Barbour anthology *Homespun Christmas*). My parents had a deep love for reading and western history, which they passed on to my two brothers and me. I can still picture us gathered around the woodstove and devouring books by kerosene lamplight.

One Christmas, during hard times, Mom "splurged." I'll never forget Dad's joy at finding twenty Zane Grey books. The fourteen-dollar gift provided family reading enjoyment for many years.

After World War II ended, money was a little more plentiful. Our family camped all over the western states. We saw many of Zane Grey's book settings, settings so meticulously described we recognized them before seeing the "Zane Grey stayed here while writing *The Call of the Canyon*," etc., signs. Our travels and his novels influenced my desire to "someday" write Westerns containing such descriptions.

"Someday" was a long time coming. I was a school/government secretary/administrative assistant until age forty-two, when I felt called to write full-time. Now, with more than three million plus copies of my 137 books sold, I marvel. God chose an ordinary, small-town girl and accomplished extraordinary things. In response, I wrote a prayer of appreciation.

. . .the most beautiful sunset is coming tomorrow
. . .the greenest meadow is the one beyond the mountain
. . .the closest friendship waits to be formed
. . .the deepest love is still being created
. . .the best answer to my prayers is already on its way
. . .then my life will be one of hope, expectation, and joy,
and I shall be of all people most blessed.

If I Can Live Believing © 1979 by Colleen L. Reece

May *Frontier Brides* bring a smile, a tear, inspiration, and hope to each of you.

In His Service,
Colleen L. Reece

Silence in the Sage

Chapter 1

With a mighty pull on the reins and an oath, the burly stagecoach driver slowed his team to a trot, finally halting them square in the middle of the dusty West Texas road.

"What's wrong, Pete?" Gideon Carroll Scott roused from his passenger view of the familiar landscape that hadn't changed in the five years he'd been away.

"C'mon, Gideon, you haven't been gone so long you've forgotten what tricks this cursed country can play on a man, now have you?" Pete cocked his grizzled head to one side. "Hear that?"

Gideon strained his ears but heard nothing. A silence unusual to the stage route remained unbroken by even a bird's cry or rustle of a bunchgrass. Even the normally swaying bluebonnets stood still.

For a heartbeat, Gideon again became the seventeen year old about to leave for study in New Orleans, who had experienced this peculiar silence on a final ride with his brother. Cyrus, two years older, had yelled, "Take cover! Silence in the sage like this means a terrible storm is coming." He spurred his horse, and Gideon tore after him, but even the fastest horse couldn't outrun the winds that whipped around the Circle S ranch miles out of *El Paso del Norte*, the Pass of the North.

Gideon exulted in the rising wind and the flying sand, yet common sense and training brought fear as well. Too many men had lost their lives because they couldn't beat the elements.

Now the same stillness pervaded. The scent of gray-green sage intensified with the first stirrings of the wind. Lizards had long since fled to shelter. While the world seemed to wait, Gideon's heart pounded.

"We'll try for the rocks," Pete shouted over the dull roar in the distance. "Hang on." He whipped up the horses. "Giddap, you long-legged, no-good beasts!"

Gideon hastily pulled his head back inside the stagecoach. For a long way, he had ridden on top with Pete, but the rare privacy afforded by being the only coach passenger had been too enticing. He smoothed light brown hair, soon to be sun-streaked from riding and ranch chores, and took a deep breath. The reflection of excitement glowed in his Texas blue-sky eyes, and his lean body swayed with the rocking coach. Would they make the huge pile of windswept rocks before the storm hit? he wondered anxiously.

The clear summer sky darkened. Tiny grains of flying sand heralded gusts of sand-laden wind that flattened the sage and raged behind the lumbering coach. Gideon could barely see Pete's hunched shoulders and pulled-down hat, and the driver's yells blended with the growing wind.

"Made it, by the powers!" Pete drove the team behind the frail shelter provided by the rock pile. The next second, he leaped to the ground, grabbed blankets, and adroitly fastened them over the horses' heads to protect them from the blowing sand. Sweating and trembling, the steeds finally stilled beneath his strong and familiar hands.

With a soft scarf over his mouth and nose, Gideon had burrowed back against the innermost rock by the time Pete staggered toward him. "Here," he called and reached out to guide Pete in the ever-increasing storm.

"Worst thing about these storms is they come without warnin'," Pete complained as he slid his scarf over his eyes. He proceeded to lie flat on his stomach and buried his face in his crossed arms. Gideon followed suit. Flying sand still stung the inch of exposed neck between his shirt collar and low-drawn hat. Good thing he'd firmly resisted dressing in his new clerical suit for his return to San Scipio, the closest town to the Circle S. Uncomfortable but inwardly filled with the same defiant attitude toward the weather he'd had as a boy, Gideon longed to laugh at the storm and howl with the wind. Protected somewhat by the rocks, he and Pete would sensibly wait out the storm and be on their way.

"If only my New Orleans friends could see me now," he muttered. "They'd remind me that West Texas is no place for a brand-new minister!"

"Say somethin'?" Pete grunted.

"Not important." Gideon wouldn't have been able to explain if he'd wanted to. Pete's prejudices against anything except what he called a cursed land (but "wouldn't leave for a million pesos") were legendary.

Gideon sighed. All his persuading hadn't changed his friends' ideas—especially Emily Ann's—that he lived in a barren wasteland. Soft, small, and pretty, Emily Ann had tried to dissuade the young seminary student from his vow to serve in a land that needed to know God as more than a curse. Without conceit, he accepted the fact he could have married Emily Ann if he'd consented to remain in New Orleans.

Give up the rugged Guadalupe Mountains, the Pecos and Rio Grande Rivers, the deep draws that hid stray and stolen cattle, even the blazing summers and frigid winters? Life with Emily Ann and her kind offered little in comparison with home. The Circle S sprawled across a thousand acres that included everything from mountains and canyons to level grazing land.

In vain, Gideon tried to picture Emily Ann's reaction to the huge adobe home built around a courtyard in typical Mexican style. Thick walls kept out both heat and cold but kept in comfort and warmth. Bright blankets and dark polished wood, carefully tended flowers, and colorful desert paintings contrasted sharply with the restored homes in New Orleans that had escaped the devastation of the War Between the States. Gideon sometimes wondered if Emily Ann ever thought of the hardship the South had experienced. Her family had spirited her away at the first sign of trouble, and although she plaintively complained of "those cold and uncarin' Yankees," he knew she had reveled in the attention received while staying in the North. Once, she stroked the rich damask of the portieres and said, "To think that *Yankees* came down here and tried to tell us how to live!" Her silvery laughter grated on Gideon's nerves, and he bit his lip to keep from reminding her that few Southerners had been able to rebuild in the way of her wealthy family.

Gideon shook his sand-laden shoulders. San Scipio and the Circle S would seem unbearably crude to a young woman like Emily Ann. He buried his face deeper in his arms, wishing the storm would stop its roaring and go on its way. Yet wasn't this time of waiting exactly what he had felt he needed before reaching home? More than miles lay between the ranch and Louisiana. With each *clip-clop* of the horses' steady gait, Gideon became less the student and more the rangeman he had once been. At times he had to reach into his satchel and feel the reassuring crackle of his rolled diploma, the only tangible evidence that proclaimed he had completed his ministerial studies.

Now his fingers involuntarily crept to his vest pocket. Even his father would find no fault with the record his younger son had made. A clipping from a New Orleans newspaper already had creases from being unfolded and refolded. The late nights and devotion to study that enraged Emily Ann had put Gideon at the top of his class. Surely Elijah Scott would take his love-blind gaze from Cyrus at least long enough to acknowledge his achievement.

11

Don't count on it, his inner voice counseled. *Lige Scott is a great rancher, a staunch follower of the Almighty—according to what he thinks—but this love for the firstborn son is only rivaled by that of Old Testament patriarchs. In his opinion, Cyrus can do no wrong.*

Once when Gideon was a child, his mother, Naomi, tried to explain his father's feelings. "We were married for so long before we had children, Lige wondered if God were punishing him for something—don't ask me what." Her blue eyes so like Gideon's turned dreamy. "It is hard to be such a strong and powerful man like your father and yet not be able to control his own son."

"I'm his son, too," Gideon had piped in his treble voice.

"I know. So does he, when he stops to remember. We must accept him the way he is, Gideon." Naomi turned and gazed out the window. "It took strength to leave everything we knew and come to Texas after it became a state in 1845. The way was hard. Many in our party didn't make it. Every death diminished Lige, for his enthusiasm had been the driving force that encouraged friends to make the journey with us. Once we got here, he worked hard, harder than any one man should work. He stood by my bedside when Cyrus was born and watched us both nearly die. Is it any wonder he cannot see faults in the son who finally came from God?"

"But, Mother, you went through all that, too," the youthful Gideon protested. "The long trail, the hard work."

"It is different for a woman," Naomi gently said. A light her son would never forget shone in her eyes. "Women are helpmeets, companions, and strengtheners to their men. I pray that one day God will send to you a strong, true wife."

"She must be like you," Gideon sturdily maintained.

His mother ruffled the sun-streaked hair and laughed. "We hope she is much better," she teased. "Now, get about your studies. Even though he says little and expects much, your father is proud of the way you grasp learning. Besides, it will be many years before you need think of taking a wife!"

Gideon coughed against the closeness of the scarf across his face, then chuckled to himself. He could imagine the look on his mother's face if Emily Ann had been willing to visit Texas. The chuckle faded. Perhaps the response from the child that his future wife must be like Naomi had secretly built up resistance to Emily Ann.

Would the storm never end? Who could tell whether minutes had turned to hours in this poorly sheltered spot? Gideon forced himself to look again to the past to avoid the miserable present.

Born in El Paso in May 1852, Gideon was just nine years old when Texas seceded from the Union and joined the Confederate States of America in 1861. Yet those days remained clear in his mind. He had asked Cyrus, "How can part of a country just cut itself off? Isn't that like my fingers saying they won't be part of my body?"

Eleven-year-old Cyrus had ignored the question. "Father doesn't want to talk about it. He says a lot of trouble can come from what's happening." For once the careless, daring boy was cowed. "I heard him talking with Mother. He says there is going to be war."

"You mean people killing each other, like in our books?" Gideon jerked up straight. "But we're going to feel the same way."

The war years hadn't changed life drastically on the Circle S. Season followed season. Stock had to be rounded up and driven to market. Chores kept needing to be done. Yet long after the fighting ended and Congress readmitted Texas to the Union in 1870, two years after the elder Scott's native Louisiana again became part of the Union, Gideon remembered the lines that etched themselves in his father's face and aged him.

During those years, Cyrus and Gideon entered early manhood. Cyrus laughed at the idea of wanting to learn more than he already knew from books. He rode like a burr in the saddle; roped, hunted, and tracked like an Indian; gambled and drank; and yet managed to keep his father unaware of his grosser habits. Gideon sometimes wondered how Lige could fail to see the marks of debauchery when Cyrus returned from a spree with a story of being holed up through a storm or off herding cattle. Bitterly, the younger son reminded himself again and again of his father's well-known blind spot. Years of standing in Cyrus's shadow had produced a certain callousness, but his tender heart still longed for a father's approval.

Gideon's fifteenth birthday seemed a welcome harbinger, as shortly afterward a hardened-to-the-saddle traveling minister arrived in San Scipio. Never had the inhabitants of the little western town heard the Word of God preached with such power and passion. The few services made an indelible mark on a boy who had known about God since the cradle. At fifteen, Gideon came to know God and His plan of salvation through His Only Son, Jesus, as the most challenging, exciting story life offers. He said nothing to his family, but the next weeks and months of riding gave him opportunity to let the knowledge of God's goodness sink deep into his soul. On his sixteenth birthday, he dug fingernails into his callused palms, stood square in his worn boots, and told his parents, "I want to be a minister."

The tornado he expected failed to come. To Gideon's amazement, the nearest to an expression of approval Lige had ever given his son came to the seamed face. "Do you feel the Almighty is behind this, or are you just looking for a way to get off the Circle S?" Lige asked quickly but thoughtfully. A flush of pleasure and determination arose in Gideon's anxious heart.

He straightened to his full five-foot, ten-inch height, his keen blue glance never wavering. "I have to tell others what God did for all of us."

"Then go to it, Son." Lige's mighty hand crushed his son's in a grip that would have broken the bones of a lesser young man. "I need your help for a time, but I give my word. On your seventeenth birthday, if you still feel this is what God wants of you, we'll send you to New Orleans. There are still some distant relatives there, a few of whom are rebuilding. You'll be welcome." A wry smile crossed his face. "More than welcome. You'll naturally pay your way, and the money will help them."

True to his word, Gideon embarked on his new life the day he turned seventeen. To his amazement, Cyrus traveled with him. Only the night before, he confessed that he hankered to see New Orleans for himself and aimed to find a pretty little filly to bring home, if there was one who had the nerve to tackle Texas and take him on.

After some protest, Lige rolled his big eyes and agreed to the change in plans. "I reckon we can get along without you the rest of this spring and through the summer," he admitted. "Mind you, be back by fall roundup, though." His crisp order couldn't hide the pride he carried for his older son, who stood an inch taller and outweighed the stripling Gideon by fifteen pounds.

While Gideon settled into the studies that would give him the background Lige insisted he have "to be not just a parson, but a *good* one," Cyrus hit New Orleans like a cannonball. In spite of lodging with the same relatives, the brothers seldom saw each other. Spring bloomed into summer, and Cyrus played at being New Orleans's most eligible bachelor. Gideon dove into his books like a man starving for knowledge. The rare occasions when their paths crossed offered little opportunity to share more than greetings.

Suddenly Cyrus grew restless. "Can't stand this heat," he told his brother and mopped his brow. "At least in Texas when it's hot, you aren't so dripping wet all the time. Besides, I'm sick of the scent of oleander." He grinned his devil-may-care grin and added, "I'll take trail dust and the smell of sage anytime."

Instead of staying until fall, Cyrus awakened Gideon one sweltering mid-August night. Eyes red and breath foul with the fumes of brandy, he muttered, "Going home. Nothing worth staying for here," and then he lurched out. By the time Gideon came fully awake to dress and reach his brother's room, Cyrus lay passed out on his bed.

Gideon felt torn between love and disgust. Why couldn't Cyrus see what he was doing to himself? Why didn't he accept Jesus and find excitement in following Him instead of seeking it in gambling halls and who knew what other places? For a moment, he wanted to shake some sense into Cyrus, but he finally went back to bed. He regretted his decision the next morning when he went to Cyrus's room, now laid bare of all clothing and belongings.

Weeks later, Naomi wrote that Cyrus had come home "without the filly he hoped to rope" and rather quiet. Gideon suspected his brother had tarried along the way to rid himself of the marks of dissipation accumulated during his binge in New Orleans.

"Gideon?" Pete's voice interrupted his companion's reverie. "You still alive in there?" A rough hand shook his shoulder, and sand cascaded off Gideon's hat, shirt, and vest. He sat up and stamped his feet, tingling from the movement after their cramped position during the storm.

"Passed on by, didn't it?" Gideon jerked the scarf off his face and watched Pete busy himself with unmasking the team. "Arghh! Feel like I rolled in a sandbank."

"Better be thankin' that God of yours we ain't plumb smothered." Pete's weather-split lips opened in a grin. He finished with the horses, which stamped much as the men had done, obviously glad to rid themselves of their burden of sand.

Pete tossed a canteen to Gideon, then gave each of the horses water in his big, cupped hand. "Drink up. There's enough to get us to San Scipio, and we'll water down good there."

Curious at the comment about thanking God, Gideon replied, "I'll ride the rest of the way on top."

Pete just grunted, but when they got back on the road and headed through the sage toward San Scipio and home, Gideon asked, "Pete, why'd you say that, I mean, about being thankful?"

"Think preachers are the only ones who know God's ridin' the trails and watchin' over folks?" Pete shot back, then slapped the horses with the reins.

"Giddap." He swallowed some choice name for the animals and added, "I know what you're thinkin'. I ain't much, and I don't claim to be nothin' but what I am, an ornery, miserable stagecoach driver. But I reckon it's ungrateful not to be glad the Almighty's on the job."

A thrill went through Gideon. *Could he encourage the seed of faith in Pete's tough old heart?* "You know the Almighty cared enough about *all of us*," he emphasized the words, "to send His Son to die for us."

"Pretty big of Him." But Pete's voice discouraged further comment, and he gruffly added, "Save your preachin', Boy. It ain't goin' to be easy to start out in your home range." He sent a sharp glance at his passenger. "How come you didn't just stay in New Orleans? Plenty of churches there, ain't they?"

"That's why, Pete," Gideon quietly said. "San Scipio doesn't have even one, and the way I figure it, home folks have just as much right to hear the gospel as city folks." He stared unseeingly at the road ahead. "I know lots of them will think I'm just a kid. I guess I am!" He laughed, and some of his melancholy left. "Not that I'm comparing myself, but the Bible tells about a whole lot of people who spoke for the Lord when they were even younger than I. Jesus talked with the priests in the temple when He was only twelve. I'm ten years older than that."

"Didja do some preachin' for practice back there?" Pete asked. "Were you scared?"

"Scareder than the time I tangled with a polecat and had to go home and face my father," Gideon confessed.

Pete threw his head back and roared. "Son, you're gonna be all right. Just keep rememberin' who it is you're doin' this for and don't pay no mind to those who give you, uh, fits." He quickly changed the subject. "Where you goin' to start in preachin'?"

Gideon wondered at the gleam in Pete's eye but only said, "Mother wrote that Father had made some kind of arrangement for a building." His straight brows drew together. "My dream is to have a real church in San Scipio someday."

"Hmm." Pete swung the horses successfully around a bend and motioned with his whip handle. "There it is."

From their vantage point on the hill, they could see into the sleepy town of San Scipio, nestled between the rises. One long, dusty street boasted a few weathered buildings and a hitching rail, where a few lazy horses were tethered. Shade trees offered some protection from the blazing sun, and back from the main thoroughfare, several homes of varying ages and styles stood closed against the afternoon heat.

" 'Pears mighty quiet," Pete mumbled and urged the horses into a trot toward the general store, which served as a stage stop.

Why should the sleepy village cause a sense of foreboding, Gideon wondered. Or was it just the unexpected silence?

Chapter 2

The arrival of the stage seemed to wave a magic wand that brought the drowsy hamlet of San Scipio back to life. Pete threw down the mail sack, and Gideon leaped to the ground.

"Hyar!" A heavy hand fell on his shoulder.

Gideon spun around in obedience to the touch and voice of authority he hadn't known in five years. Except for a few more lines in his weather-beaten face and the glimmer of a smile so rare his younger son could count on his fingers the times he'd seen it, Lige Scott stood tall, strong, and unchanged. "Welcome home, Son."

The young minister's vision blurred. Could the approval in Lige's voice and face really be for him? He glanced around. "Mother? Cyrus?" His keen gaze caught the darkening of Lige's face.

"At the ranch. Your mother's busy killing the fatted calf."

Strange that the same parable that ran through Gideon's mind fell from Lige's lips. "And Cyrus?"

"Rounding up strays." Lige threw his massive head back, and the Scott blue eyes flashed. With a visible effort, he put aside whatever was troubling him. "I brought the wagon. Figured you'd have a lot of things that needed fetching to the Circle S."

Strangely relieved of the tension he didn't understand, Gideon laughed, and its clear, ringing sound brought an answering chuckle from Pete, who had held back from greeting Lige. "Thought for sure we'd sink when we forded the stream," he joshed as he helped the other two transfer trunks and nailed wooden boxes of books from the stage to the wagon. But when Lige and Gideon climbed into the wagon and the older man took the reins, Pete called, "Don't fergit who you're workin' for."

The horses swung into a rhythmic beat before Lige demanded, "What was Pete talking about?" Lige's long years on the range hadn't quite erased his superior feelings toward his less polished neighbors.

"Pete didn't mean anything." Gideon hated himself for his placating tone, but he couldn't help falling back into the same pattern of behavior

SILENCE IN THE SAGE

he'd used as a child to help his mother keep peace in the family. "He was just reminding me that God's my new boss."

"Huh." The grunt could have meant anything.

Gideon glanced from Lige to the road they were taking. "Why, this isn't the way to the ranch."

"Nope." Lige skillfully turned the team to the left at the end of the main street. To Gideon's amazement, he drove toward the road that wound weary miles to El Paso instead of the beaten track toward the Circle S. A quick swing to the left again, and Lige pulled in the horses. "Well, how do you like it?"

Gideon stared, closed his eyes, and blinked and stared again.

"Cat got your tongue? I asked how you like it." Lige flicked a fly off his forehead and pointed with a long, work-worn finger to a brand-new log building sitting back from the road on a little rise. "We hauled logs a lot of miles to build this, so you'd better appreciate it."

His father's grim warning lit a bonfire in Gideon's brain. "It's perfect." He scanned the building that bravely sat in its sagebrush and mesquite surroundings. Large enough to house all of San Scipio and those who ranched around it, the little wilderness church nonetheless remained small enough to be cozy.

"Dad—" Gideon couldn't go on. He barely heard his own voice using the informal name for the first time.

"I said I'd find a place for you to preach, didn't I?" Lige sounded gruffer than ever. "Well, are you going to sit there like a coyote on a rock or get down and go in?"

Gideon jumped from the wagon and walked through a welter of desert flowers someone had lovingly planted on both sides of the wide, dusty track to the door of the church. Sunflowers and bluebonnets were still damp from a recent watering; the hard clay soil around them lay dry and cracked in places. Blue mountains loomed miles away, yet in the clear air, they looked close enough to reach in minutes.

Gideon's heart swelled. He reached for the door and lifted the latch. Late afternoon sun streamed through windows that must have been hauled in from El Paso. The scent of freshly sawed wood crept into his nostrils. Peace and humility filled his soul. The silence inside the simple building bore evidence of his father's love and the devotion of a town that waited for the gospel of Jesus Christ. Young and inexperienced, could he be worthy of that devotion, worthy of his Lord?

"Well?" Lige's impatient reminder that he waited for an answer whirled

Gideon around to face his father.

"It's more beautiful than any church or cathedral I saw while I was gone." Words came faster than tumbleweeds before a wind. "All those churches and cathedrals I saw when you had me visit friends instead of coming home for holidays—why—" He choked off, and his eyes stung. "I wouldn't trade this church for all of those others put together! I'm home. *Home.*"

"Good thing." Lige frowned and turned on his heel. "We'll be dedicating this church come Sunday." He looked back over his shoulder. "Better have a rip-snorting sermon. Folks around here don't want mush." He strode out, his footsteps heavy on the hand-smoothed board floor.

Gideon smothered a laugh. Rip-snorting sermons weren't exactly what he had practiced, but if that's what San Scipio wanted, he couldn't find a better source than the Bible! He looked around the silent, waiting church once more. For the second time, a feeling of unease touched him. The church held everything he could have dreamed of and more. Indeed, he'd supposed his first services would be in some abandoned building or barn. There appeared to be no earthly reason that all was not well. Perhaps the new wrinkles in his father's face had disturbed him or the set of his jaw when he said Cyrus had gone to round up strays. Gideon sighed and carefully closed the door of the new church behind him.

The steady *clip-clop* of the horses' hooves ate up the distance between San Scipio and the Circle S. For as long as Gideon could remember, his father had always stopped the horses for a breather on top of the mesa that sloped steeply above the ranch. Today Gideon was off the wagon seat even before the horses completely stopped. A poignant feeling of never having been away assaulted him. Here he had ridden with Cyrus a hundred times. Here he had reined in the horses on the few solitary trips he made to San Scipio for supplies. A lone eagle winged high above in perfect harmony with the vast wilderness. Below, half hidden by cottonwoods planted when Lige and Naomi first acquired the small piece of land that eventually grew into the present spread, the red-tiled roof and foot-thick cream walls of the house invited weary travelers. Gideon couldn't remember a time that cowboys and cattlemen hadn't been welcome at the Circle S.

"Your mother'll be waiting," Lige reminded, and Gideon sprang back to the wagon.

"Too bad your brother isn't here." The corners of Lige's mouth turned down, and he scowled. Again Gideon had the feeling all wasn't right between father and son.

Thoughtfully, Gideon tried to turn away Lige's attention. "Coming home has taught me one thing. I never want to live anywhere else. I'll be satisfied if the good Lord provides me with a wife and kids and the chance to live here until I die."

The rustle of yellowed grass beside the wagon track and the scream of the eagle sent a chill down his spine. He sought the Lord in a silent prayer. *Dear God, when things are as near perfect as they ever will be again, please take away this awful sense that something is going to happen.*

When they descended from the mesa and drove up to the corral, Gideon felt prepared to greet his mother, who flew from the ranch house as if pursued by mountain lions. Her brown hair had streaks of gray that hadn't been there when he left, but Gideon noted her slender body hadn't changed. Neither had the blue of her eyes.

"My son." She clasped him close, then held him off to take measure with one swift glance. Gideon felt on trial for the years he had been gone and actually heaved a sigh of relief when she softly whispered, "It is well. You have kept the faith." With the lightning change of mood he knew so well, she inquired, "And how do you like your father's surprise?"

Gideon thought of the perfect church waiting for his return. "Nothing could have pleased me more." He cautiously turned to make sure Lige had taken the team and wagon on to the barn before adding in a low voice, "For the first time in my whole life, I feel Fa—Dad is proud of me."

"More than you know, especially since—"

Lige's hail stilled any confidences she might have shared. "Is Cyrus back?"

"Just in." Naomi bit her lip, and Gideon saw the familiar pleading in her suddenly serious face. Lige might deny and refuse to accept that his first-born son fell short of perfection but not Naomi. Still, for her husband's sake, she strove for harmony by cushioning the clashes that periodically came.

"What's all the shouting about?" a lazy voice drawled from the wide, covered roof extension that made a cool porch. Cyrus lounged against one side of an arched support. "Well, little brother, you ready to save everyone's souls?"

Lige growled deep in his throat as Cyrus tossed a half-smoked brown-paper cigarette to the earth and ground it with his boot heel. "Sorry, Dad. Just have to make sure Gideon remembers he's no angel, even if he is going to proclaim the good news."

Gideon hated the sarcasm that had always reduced him to a tongue-tied fool. This time he found his voice. "I never claimed to be an angel. You know that."

"Good thing." Cyrus's eyes gleamed with mischief as he gripped his brother's hand, and Gideon gave back as hearty a squeeze as he received. "Well! This boy's no tenderfoot, even if he has been living soft in the city."

"Did you find any strays?" Lige boomed, his ox-eyed gaze firmly on Cyrus.

"Some. Not as many as I expected." Cyrus shrugged. "My horse threw a shoe, and I had to come back in sooner than I planned."

"Get it fixed, and get back out into the canyons tomorrow," Lige dictated.

A wave of red ran from Cyrus's shirt collar up to his uneven hairline. "Yes, Sir!" He saluted smartly, and Gideon held his breath, but before his father could roar, Cyrus threw an arm around his brother. "Rosa and Carmelita have been cooking for days. Let's eat." He grinned at Lige the way Gideon never could do, and a reluctant smile softened their father's features.

"Give us time to wash," the head of the household ordered. "Then bring on the feast."

An hour later, Gideon sat back with a sigh of repletion. The remains of his homecoming dinner lay before him. Tamales, enchiladas, chicken, a half-dozen kinds of fruits and vegetables from the garden, and a glistening chocolate cake had been reduced to crumbs. "I haven't eaten like this since I left," he murmured.

"Temperance in all things, Brother Gideon." Cyrus pulled his face into a sanctimonious smirk. "It won't do for your congregation to know you are a glutton."

In the wave of laughter from family and servants alike, Gideon wondered how he could ever have had qualms about his return to San Scipio and the Circle S.

Not satisfied with his needling, Cyrus continued. "So, what is your text for Sunday, Brother Gideon?"

An unexplainable impulse caused him to retort, "Perhaps I'll use Cain's question, 'Am I my brother's keeper?' Genesis 4:9," he added in the spirit of fun.

A cannonball exploding in the middle of the long table couldn't have produced more devastation. Cyrus leaped to his feet, anger distorting his features. "Just what do you mean?" He glared at his brother much as Cain must have done to the ill-fated Abel. "Don't think that becoming a parson is going to make you anything except what you are, the *younger* brother." Rage tore away every shred of control. "I'll have no mealymouthed, holier-than-thou snob of a brother bossing me around!"

"I didn't mean—" Gideon couldn't believe the ugliness of his brother's discourse.

"Sit down, Cyrus," Lige commanded. He stared at Gideon. "I'll have no such talk at the table or anywhere else on this ranch. As Cyrus says, being a preacher gives you no right to make remarks about your brother."

Gideon started to protest but caught the patient and resigned shake of his mother's head and subsided, feeling the pain of injustice from Lige's remarks. *Nothing had really changed.* It didn't matter that his father had built a church. When it came to taking sides, Lige Scott would never uphold the younger brother over the elder.

So much for coming home. Perhaps Emily Ann and the others had been right when they said he should have accepted a church somewhere other than in San Scipio. Yet, as he'd told Pete, who needed Jesus more than persons like Cyrus? Jesus clearly taught He came to heal the spiritually sick, not those already in His service.

That night when all had retired and Gideon restlessly moved around his rooms, he wondered. Even his pleasure at discovering Mother had enlarged his former bedroom and cleared out rooms on either side to provide a study and sitting room dwindled at the memory of the supper table scene. As he stood for a long time looking at the brilliant, low-hanging stars in the midnight blue Texas sky, he realized there had to be more behind Cyrus's reaction than not being able to accept joking. In the past, he'd delighted in the few times when Gideon managed to get ahead of him.

As if conjured up by thinking about him, a heavy knock brought Gideon to the door.

"May I come in?" Cyrus's bold gaze took in the refurbished rooms. He raised one eyebrow. "Some accommodations. Personally, all I need or want is a place to sleep." His tone abruptly changed from indolence to vigilance. "I want to know why you said what you did at supper." He stood crouched as if posed to spring.

"First thing that popped into my mind," Gideon frankly told him, but a warning went off in his mind. *Cyrus must have some secret to seek me out like this.*

Cyrus relaxed. The smile that could charm a rattlesnake into retreating replaced the watchful gaze. "Sorry." He half closed his eyes again in the habit he had that hid any expression from others. "Like I said, I just don't want you lording it over me." He laughed. "Get it? *Lord*ing over me, although God knows, sometimes I could use a trailmate like Him, if He's everything Dad and Mother and you think He is." He gave Gideon no opportunity to reply. "If He puts up with me long enough, who knows? I might shock Him and everyone—me included—by asking Him to ride with me." The next moment, he crossed the room in long strides, his spurs clinking musically. "I'm off for a night ride. Want to come?"

Gideon's irritation melted. "Give me five minutes," Gideon told him. He threw on riding clothes and stole out after his brother in the starlight. He felt like a kid again, when he and Cyrus were supposed to be sleeping but went riding instead.

The cool night wind and the exhilaration of riding in the open country blew cobwebs from Gideon's brain and doubt from his heart. All of his love for Cyrus returned, along with an even deeper love for his brother's soul. He might have spilled out the first Scripture that came to mind, but how true it was. Ever since he first accepted Jesus, he had longed above all for Cyrus to do the same. He *was* his brother's keeper. But the night sky and the feeling God lingered close opened his heart to an enlarged truth: Every follower of the lowly Nazarene assumes keepership of all others who need to know Him. The same surety that caused him to announce on his sixteenth birthday that he must spread the gospel of Jesus Christ settled into his soul more deeply than ever.

Before they reached home, Cyrus halted his mount. He waited for his brother to pull up beside him, then addressed him in a low voice. "Gideon, no matter what happens, you'd never go back on me, would you?"

The friendly night had turned menacing. "Of course not." Gideon tried to see Cyrus's expression, but shadows and his low-pulled hat effectively camouflaged his face.

"And you'd forgive me? Seventy times seven?"

"What's this all about?" Gideon demanded sharply. His very soul chilled at some hidden meaning.

"Seventy times seven?" Cyrus repeated, then spurred his horse into a magnificent leap. "Never mind, Kid. Just testing you. . ." Cyrus's racing figure was swallowed up by the darkness.

Gideon slowly followed. Something about Cyrus frightened him. What had his brother been up to? Why should he ask such questions, request such a promise, then ride away before Gideon could answer? He had no more answers when he rubbed down his horse and slipped back into his bed.

The next morning Cyrus had returned to his old teasing self, wanting to know if "the parson" had time to help round up strays or if he planned to sleep all morning and practice his sermon the rest of the day.

Relieved but wary, Gideon rolled out, stowed away an enormous breakfast, and spent the day in the saddle. He came home stiff, sore, and convinced he'd better take it a little easier until he got his old skills back. The next day he settled with a Bible and writing materials and began making notes for the dedication sermon. How could he impress on his neighbors that his youth meant nothing, that the message he bore remained unchanged and unlimited despite the frailties of the messenger who carried it? Time spent on his knees paid off, and over the next several days, Gideon successfully balanced study, preparation, and range riding. Serving his "parish" would entail miles of hard riding to obscure dwellings; he rejoiced when he discovered he no longer felt stiff.

On Saturday night, Cyrus headed for town after being turned down by Gideon, who refused to accompany him. "Yeah, I guess it wouldn't look too good for a preacher to be part of a San Scipio Saturday night," Cyrus admitted. But he didn't heed his brother's pleas for him to stay home, either.

"Will you be there tomorrow?" Gideon asked wistfully.

Cyrus swung to the saddle. "Think I'd miss it? It's going to be better than the entertainment Blackie gets for the Missing Spur."

"I hope so." Gideon shuddered. The Missing Spur Saloon had a reputation for the so-called entertainment offered to its patrons. "How can you stand it?" he blurted out. "Why don't you find yourself a nice girl, instead of hanging around those—"

"Mind your own affairs, Parson." Cyrus's blue eyes turned icy. "If Dad asks where I am, tell him I rode into town to get a new bridle. It's true enough." He pointed to the patched-together job he'd done on his bridle and laughed mockingly. "You never would lie for me, so I won't ask you to. Just keep your lip buttoned about what you may or may not know." His horse impatiently danced, and the next instant, the two vanished except for a dust cloud kicked up behind them.

Gideon disconsolately headed for his room. Although his sermon still needed a few touches, once inside, he stood for a long moment by his deep-set window, watching the wagon track toward San Scipio and praying that somehow God would soften Cyrus's heart.

At last he went to his desk and forced himself to put personal troubles aside, losing himself in the truth of the Scriptures. For hours he considered, rejected, and, in spite of his best efforts, listened for the neigh of a horse, the jingle of spurs, or the soft footsteps that would signal Cyrus had returned.

Darkness paled. Dawn stole over the distant mountains. Gideon awakened from the uncomfortable position where he'd fallen asleep with his head on his crossed arms at the desk. Could Cyrus have sneaked in without him hearing?

In stockinged feet so as not to rouse his parents, the young minister slipped across his room, down the hall, and into Cyrus's bedroom. Yet Gideon's fingers trembled as he pushed open the door and stepped inside.

The room lay empty. The bed, neatly made.

Chapter 3

For a long time Gideon stood in the empty room and stared at his brother's unwrinkled bed. Disappointment and the nagging worry something had gone wrong swept over him. Even back in his own rooms, Gideon lay awake, wondering why Cyrus hadn't come home. He had promised not to miss the dedication of the little church and his brother's first sermon in San Scipio.

Gideon found himself defending Cyrus as he had always done. *Maybe when he reached town, his horse went lame and he stayed with friends,* he thought hopefully. Clinging to the thought of what meager comfort it offered, the troubled young minister finally managed to sleep for a few hours. He opened his eyes to a glorious summer Sunday morning and a laugh that sent relief surging through him.

"Cyrus!" Gideon tumbled into his clothes and raced to the courtyard, bright with flowers and shaded by carefully tended trees.

"Well, Parson, is your sermon ready?" Cyrus stood up from teasing a small lizard and turned his brilliant blue gaze toward Gideon.

"Ready as it will ever be." Gideon thought of the hours of prayerful study he had put into that sermon. "Glad to see you made it home. I was beginning to wonder if—"

"Shh." Cyrus furtively looked at the house, then back at his brother. "I'm sorry, but I won't be able to hear your preaching after all."

Gideon's spirits dropped. "Why not?" He stared at his brother, noting the honest regret in Cyrus's face, the misery in his eyes.

"I got word in town that—" Cyrus swallowed and shrugged. "It doesn't matter. I'm riding out as soon as the rest of you leave for church." His fingers crept to his breast pocket. Gideon could see the ragged edge of an opened letter before Cyrus stuffed it deeper in his pocket.

"When will you be back?"

"Maybe never." The somber voice stayed low, barely discernible.

"You can't mean that!" Gideon burst out. "It will kill Father. If you're in trouble, say so. You know we'll stand behind you."

Cyrus's lips twisted, then set in a grim, uncompromising line. "Not this time." He raised his voice and gave Gideon a warning look. "Well, Father, today is a proud day for the Scotts, isn't it?"

Yet Gideon saw the strong face crumple for a moment before Cyrus averted his face from Lige Scott's beaming glance. His heart felt like a cannonball in his chest. *I must find a chance to talk with Cyrus before leaving for San Scipio!*

His brother proved more clever than he. After he finished breakfast, Cyrus looked at the big clock that had traveled west with the older Scotts and then made an announcement. "Instead of riding in the buggy with you, I'll take my horse, and then I can head for El Paso after church. Talk around town is that one of the ranchers there is selling out and going back East. Maybe I can pick up a few head of prime horses."

"Not on the Sabbath," Lige ordered. "Stay in town and see the horses tomorrow."

"I reckon it won't hurt just to look at them on the Sabbath, will it?" Cyrus assumed an air of injured innocence. "The buying part can wait." He strode out without waiting for a reply.

After excusing himself, Gideon followed Cyrus outside. At the corral, Cyrus had already uncoiled his rope to lasso the horse he wanted. "Cyrus, *don't go,*" Gideon pleaded, out of breath from chasing him.

"I have to." The rope drooped from his fingers. "I'll ride out of sight, then when you're gone, I'll come back for a few belongings."

"I don't understand," Gideon cried.

"I hope to God you never do." The lariat sang and expertly dropped around a big bay's neck. Before Gideon could think of a way to stop Cyrus, his brother had saddled the bay, mounted, and ridden off with a mocking farewell wave. Shaken, Gideon wondered how he could go ahead and preach just a few hours later. He retraced his steps to the house, but instead of joining his parents, he went to his room, knelt by the bed, and stayed there for a long time, unable to pray.

When the Scotts arrived in a churchyard crowded with horses, buggies, wagons, and people on foot, a most irreverent cheer arose. A startled Gideon observed Lige's broad shoulders held straight and proud and Naomi's shy smile. Now that the day for which she'd waited so long had arrived, it seemed the most natural thing in the world to be helped down from the buggy seat and ushered into a sweet-smelling church. The absence of piano and organ did not discourage the lusty a cappella singing of familiar hymns. In this first service ever held in San Scipio in a church, ranchers and merchants, women and children raised their voices in harmony and song that lifted even Gideon's disturbed heart.

Then it was time. Clutching the pages he'd labored over so long, Gideon Carroll Scott stepped to the hand-hewn pulpit. As he looked at the first carefully written paragraph of his sermon, the words swam before him. Paralyzing fear such as he'd never known constricted his throat. To hide it, he quickly bowed his head and shot upward a frantic, desperate prayer for help. When the rustling of the congregation stilled, his mind stopped reeling. He opened his eyes and looked at the sermon, then deliberately laid it aside.

"Friends." Gideon paused and looked from one side of the packed church to the other, from front to back. Women in their best dresses held children on their laps. Men sat straight and waiting beside them. Young people eyed one another from the protection of their families. Many had grown so much in the time Gideon had been away, he could only place them by their proximity to the families he knew. Unfamiliar faces stood out like whitecaps in the gulf of waiting souls.

"Friends," he said again, "I had prepared a special sermon that seemed to be in keeping with this significant day." He held up the pages. "I can't give this sermon, at least not today. I feel that Almighty God simply wants me to share with you what He and His Son, Jesus Christ, have done for me."

Warming to the subject, Gideon told in the simplest terms possible how as a fifteen-year-old boy he had invited Jesus into his heart. Something in the way he spoke kept the congregation's attention riveted on him. Babies fell asleep in their mothers' arms. Children listened in wonder. Young and old responded to the Holy Spirit that had prompted Gideon to forsake fancy preaching and merely testify.

He went on to say how he came to know the only thing he wanted to do in life was to help others find Christ, as the traveling minister had done for him. He touched lightly on the years in New Orleans of study and preparation amid the Reconstruction efforts. He said nothing of those who wooed him, who predicted obscurity and waste in a life given to a tiny West Texas town. Instead, the great longing for his friends and neighbors to meet, know, and love the Lord rang in every word. Gideon could feel the rush of caring and ended by saying, "Not one of us can save ourselves. God in His goodness offers the only plan of salvation the world ever has known or ever will know. Will you open your hearts to His Son?"

He sat down, drained yet exultant. Here and there, faces made hard from years in a raw land trembled with emotion as tears spilled down weathered cheeks. An untrained but harmonious quartet sang the beautiful hymn "Faith of Our Fathers." A short dedicatory prayer followed, and Gideon's trial by fire ended. Handshakes that ranged from the tentative touch of the elderly to staunch grips by mighty men warmed the new preacher. Yet the knowledge that the one he most longed to bring to Jesus even now rode alone and lonely lay heavily on him. So did the guilt of carrying that knowledge.

Although Lige and Naomi didn't think anything about it when Cyrus failed to come home by Wednesday, Lige grumbled because Cyrus had missed the sermon. "Wouldn't have hurt him, and common courtesy demanded he be there," he boomed in his big voice more than once. His brow furrowed until the lines looked even deeper. "Sometimes I wish Cyrus were more like—" He broke off, as if unwilling to express even hesitant disloyalty to his firstborn.

The younger brother's heart pounded at the implied approval, but when Cyrus hadn't returned by Saturday, Gideon knew a crisis was fast approaching. Should he tell Lige the little he knew? Gideon's troubled mind queried. All he really knew was that a certain letter had reached Cyrus that evidently alarmed him into vanishing. Besides, deep in his heart, Gideon couldn't and wouldn't accept Cyrus's desertion. In spite of his faults, Cyrus loved the Circle S and had been branding calves with the S brand shortly after he learned to ride. Gideon had helped when he got old enough, but never had his heart been in it. Always, books and learning and what lay outside his own way of life lured him away from the range.

At supper Saturday evening, Lige turned to Gideon. "Do you know anything about your brother?"

The analogy of Cain and Abel returned: The Lord had inquired of Cain concerning his brother Abel's whereabouts. Unlike Cain, Gideon did not lie when he said he didn't know. He felt compelled to add, "He seemed, well, strange that Sunday morning when he rode away."

"*Strange?*" Lige's ox eyes looked more pronounced than ever.

Gideon licked suddenly dry lips. "He said he wouldn't be in San Scipio to hear me preach, but he wouldn't say why or where he was going."

Lige's heavy fist crashed to the table, and his face mottled with anger. "Why didn't you tell me this before?"

Gideon forced himself to keep his voice low, his gaze steady. "I hoped that whatever bothered him would disappear and he'd come back."

"Is that all you know?" His father's penetrating glance backed his younger son to the wall.

"Yes." Gideon would say no more; what he suspected might or might not be true. He wouldn't distress his father more by passing on suspicion. In all probability, it would only make Lige rail against him in his blind unwillingness to admit Cyrus capable of anything less than perfection.

+

Gideon's second sermon went more according to what he had prepared. After fasting and prayer, he was able to lay aside the fact of Cyrus's continued absence and concentrate.

At dawn on Monday morning, Lige rose and announced he would ride to El Paso. "Will you come with me?" he asked Gideon.

Used to being ordered and not invited, Gideon hid his astonishment and agreed. During the long ride, the intangible silence between them reminded Gideon of those eerie moments in the sage before the storm. They found the rancher who had horses to sell, and Lige discreetly led the conversation around to what buyers had been there. "One of the men from San Scipio appeared mighty interested," he said. "A little taller than my son here. Heavier, but similar coloring."

The rancher shook his head. "No one like that's been around here. I'd shore have remembered." He brightened. "Long as you're here, d'yu see anything yu like?"

Before Lige could say no, a high-stepping sorrel caught Gideon's attention. "I'd like to look at the mare," he told the rancher.

A close inspection and short ride resulted in the purchase of Dainty Bess, who had won Gideon's heart with her frisky but gentle ways.

"Yu're a good judge of horse flesh," the former owner admitted. "I'da took her back with me 'cept it's too far."

Gideon transferred saddle and bridle, attached a lead line for the horse he had ridden to El Paso, and swung aboard his new mount. "Thanks," he called. When they crossed the first hill and left the ranch behind them, he commented, "Mother will enjoy riding this horse—that is, when I'm not on her!"

"How can you be so all-fired excited over buying a horse when your brother's off God-knows-where?" Lige's criticism effectively doused Gideon's attempts at conversation. Even though he knew his father spoke from the depths of misery and concern, Gideon's old resentment returned in full force.

As much as I can and as often as my duties to the church allow, I'll try to take Cyrus's place, he vowed. He knew it wouldn't be easy. Five years had taken a toll on the range skills he once had. Sometimes he took longer doing chores or his hands proved awkward in roping. Most often Lige said nothing, yet Gideon felt the same second-best feeling he'd experienced through the years. Even if he could ride and rope and brand full-time, he'd never be Cyrus. For that, Lige couldn't forgive him.

He often felt as if the weeks following Cyrus's departure were a stack of dynamite just waiting for a spark to set it off. Once it blew, life would never be the same. To make things worse, Gideon ran into a problem with his ministry. In his naivete, he had thought all God would require of him would be to preach, visit, and comfort. He soon discovered the folly of his thinking. Time after time, he called on God to give him strength and patience with his congregation. Good folk they were, but all too human. Gideon wished he had a peso for every time he had to become a peacemaker; a sermon was sorely needed on the subject of putting aside petty differences and pride and jealousy so the Word of God could be proclaimed.

Naomi Scott proved to be a valuable ally when it came to socializing. "Just don't pay any more attention to one family than another," she quietly advised. "If you call on the Simpsons, then make sure that within a few days you also call on the Blacks, McKenzies, and Porters. Things will settle down in time, but for now everyone wants to make sure they get equal attention from the new minister." Her smile died. "And, Gideon, beware of Lucinda Curtis." Real anxiety puckered her brow. "She's spoiled and bent on getting her own way. More than one cowboy has had to leave town because of her wild tales, which," she added, "I just don't believe. Lucinda isn't that pretty, even with all her specially bought clothes and haughty ways."

Gideon sighed and ran his fingers through his now sun-streaked hair. "Why didn't they warn us in school how silly young women can be?" He laughed ruefully. "I can't physically drink gallons of lemonade or spare the time to spend afternoons in cool courtyards! Yet every unmarried female in San Scipio seems to feel such activities are part of my job. Most of them are nice enough, but sometimes I feel the way a jackrabbit must feel when being chased. As for Lucinda," he said grimacing, "she must have taken a course in tracking her prey. How she knows where I'm going to be and manages to arrive just when I'm leaving is beyond me." He thought of the tall, thin girl with the straw-colored hair and faded gray eyes that could melt with admiration or flash pure steel when crossed. "What can I do about it?"

Naomi thought for a long time, her hands strangely idle, her blue eyes deep and considering. "Perhaps you can do nothing except to be very careful. Time will take care of the problem." A dimple danced in one cheek, and her eyes sparkled. "One of these days, the Lord will send a special person into your life. Not a butterfly who knows little more than how to preen and chase, but a real woman who will love, cherish, and complete your life."

On impulse, Gideon decided to tell her about Emily Ann. "Always the Southern belle, she would have married me if I'd agreed to remain in Louisiana and take over a church. She was sure her father could arrange such a position." He laughed. "Once I saw how shallow she was inside, I dropped off her list of admirers. Wonder how many others have been on it since I left New Orleans?" He took his mother's hand. "A long time ago, I decided that until I met someone like you, I'd go it alone. Not really alone, I have my Lord. But sometime. . ." He couldn't voice the longing he felt to have a companion, one who would support and love him, bear his children, and grow old with him.

Gideon remembered that conversation, and once or twice in the next few weeks, he even hesitantly approached God about it. Although he loved his work, the natural longings for a home of his own stirred him more than at any time before. He had so much time for reflection, especially riding Dainty Bess, a sure-footed mare that needed little guidance. While he rode the range or into canyons to visit isolated ranches or for pleasure, Gideon not only came closer to God but permitted himself to dream.

Now and then he caught qualities in one San Scipio woman or another that he admired but never in Lucinda Curtis. Always courteous, he nevertheless had a hundred valid reasons for turning down the supper invitations at her home unless others would be present. The same held true for lingering after church until everyone had gone except Lucinda, who expected to be walked home. Gideon became adept at making sure a group remained to discuss music or basket dinners. He also used the distance between the Circle S and San Scipio as an excuse until it grew more threadbare than the strip of carpet in the entryway of the town's only boardinghouse.

One afternoon the young minister had just finished posting a notice on the church door about special services he planned to hold when Lucinda appeared. Trapped by his well-bred upbringing, Gideon would only politely greet the pink-gowned maiden.

"Do let us go inside. It's more comfortable."

"Why, don't you think it's nice out here?" Gideon motioned to an inviting bench he had recently placed in a shaded area. Not for a gold mine would he enter the church building and give her an opportunity to start talk as she had done with others. "I only have a little time. What can I do for you, Miss Curtis?"

"Please call me Lucinda." She blushed and looked down, but no modesty appeared in her eyes when she looked up again. "It's so much friendlier." She held out a white, well-cared-for, and obviously useless hand.

Gideon pretended not to see it and ushered her to the bench. "What was it you wanted?" He'd be hanged if he'd call her Lucinda.

"I, we, well, some of your congregation are concerned over your having to ride in from the Circle S." She lowered her lashes in an imitation of Emily Ann when she wanted her own way. "Autumn will come soon, then winter. We'd never forgive ourselves if you lost your strength from overwork."

Thunderstruck at the idea of her interference, Gideon couldn't say a word.

"Papa agrees with me, with us."

He would, Gideon thought sourly. Tom Curtis's spineless demeanor when it came to his only child was the stuff of legend in San Scipio. The storekeeper's pride and blind adoration of his child even outranked Lige Scott's.

"Anyway, when I just up and said it shouldn't happen, Papa said he'd be glad to build a room on our house just for you." She clasped her hands together and laughed, but Gideon saw the gloating triumph she couldn't hide. "You'll be like one of the family."

It took all his Christian charity not to shake her silly shoulders until she rattled like the doll she was. Gideon stood. "I'm in perfect health, Miss Curtis. Thank you for the offer." He couldn't manage to say he appreciated it. "I wouldn't even consider such an arrangement." With the cunning he'd developed against her wiles, he said frankly, "I'm sure you're aware there is already jealousy in the congregation." He forced himself to smile. "Such a move could create problems and charges of favoritism." He lowered his voice confidentially. "A young minister living in a home where there's an unmarried woman. . ." He let his voice drift off. "You can see, it just wouldn't do." Could even Lucinda Curtis swallow that serving of applesauce?

It slid down smoothly. "Oh, Reverend, why, I never once thought of that. What must you think of me?" Crocodile tears swam in her eyes. Fortunately, she didn't give Gideon a chance to reply. "We'll forget the whole thing, shall we?" She rose. "I really mustn't keep you." She gave him an arch smile. "It is so nice when a young man considers a woman's reputation."

For one moment, Gideon thought he would ruin the whole thing by laughing in her face. Instead, he told her, "A woman just can't be too careful."

Lucinda glanced at him sharply, and he wondered if she were remembering the rumors she had started about those cowboys. "Thank you, Reverend. Do you have time to walk me home?"

Not by a long shot, he wanted to tell her. Instead, he said, "No, but thanks again for your, er, concern." She picked her way across the churchyard, then stopped to wave gaily before she turned the corner. Not until he mounted Dainty Bess and got a mile out of town did he vent his anger and disgust by urging the faithful horse into a dead run.

Chapter 4

Judith Butler adjusted the mosquito netting over four-year-old Joel's small bed and swallowed hard. The small blond replica of Millicent lay in a spread-eagle position as usual. Flushed with sleep, his cheeks rosy and curly hair tangled, he tugged at Judith's heartstrings. Terror rose within her. What if she should lose him after all her struggles in the past four years to fulfill the promise she had given her dying half sister?

Judith's knees weakened, and she dropped into a shabby chair next to the sleeping boy. She rested her tired head crowned with its coronet of dark brown braids against a pale, slender hand whose calloused palm told her story of hardship. The dark brown eyes that lit with twin candles when she smiled closed. *Dear God, what am I going to do?* she silently prayed.

Only this morning her landlady had reluctantly told her she couldn't keep Joel and her much longer unless they paid something. The worn woman looked away as if ashamed to see the fear Judith knew sprang to her face.

Judith coughed as she explained, "Just as soon as I'm a little stronger, I'll be able to get work. I appreciate all you've done for us, caring for Joel when I had the fever. Please don't send us away."

The landlady's eyes filled with tears. "My dear, if I had money to buy food, I would never let you go. But with my man helpless ever since the carriage accident, I have to think of him, too. Don't you have something else you can sell?"

Judith thought of the few remaining pieces of jewelry that had brought in but a pittance when the larger pieces had been sold. The barren room she and Joel shared in the ruins of an old New Orleans house had been stripped one by one of the fine, mahogany pieces that once stood in the Butler home. Now only two cheap beds, a cracked bowl and pitcher, and little else remained. Precious Joel had made a game out of seeing their furniture go.

"It's like living in a tepee," he said with his enchanting grin, which showed small even teeth and set his blue eyes sparkling. " 'Sides, we've got you and me."

Judith's slender shoulders convulsed in a shudder. Her long illness had put a sudden end to the needlework that had supplied enough extra money to pay for their room and simple meals. Even now her hands shook so that she couldn't hold the needle. Unwilling to disturb Joel's slumbers with her agitation, Judith quietly rose and crossed the almost-empty room to kneel beside the limp curtain that sifted daylight from the single window. She unfastened the window and swung it open, hoping for a little relief from the early summer heat. A few weeks from now, it would be unbearable. Even if she could afford to stay, how could she and Joel live through another summer in this furnace of an attic? She longingly thought of her parents, both casualties of the war: her father in battle, her mother from worry and illness. The little room faded, replaced by her own merry cry and pattering feet down the steps of the beautiful home that had once been hers. . . .

"Father's come! Millie, he's here." Six-year-old Judith ran to greet him, closely followed by nine-year-old Millicent who, in spite of being older, clung to the more daring Judith and leaned on her for strength. As fair as Judith was dark, she had adored her half sister from the time their father laid the baby carefully in her arms. "A present for you, Millicent, my dear. Your own baby sister."

"I'll need my good older daughter to help me care for her," the second Mrs. Butler, who had never seemed anything but a real mother to Millie, added. She had married Mr. Butler a little over a year after his first wife died, so Millicent never knew any other mother.

Now she laughed and sped after Judith but stopped short on the wide veranda. "Why, Father, you're a *soldier!*"

"Isn't he beautiful?" Judith scampered around the tall, gray-clad man whose grim face relaxed into a smile when he caught her up in his arms. He held out his hand to Millicent.

"You're going to fight the nasty Yankees, aren't you?" Judith slid to the ground and leaned companionably against him with Millicent on his other side.

"Child, just because others don't believe as we do doesn't make them nasty," he protested. Deep lines etched his face. "I pray to God I never have to take a life. God created Northerners and Southerners alike, and He doesn't love us any more than He loves those who see things differently."

His wife joined them, fear and trouble in her pretty face, the features Judith had inherited distorted with care. "If only God would stop this awful happening." Tears sprang to her large brown eyes, but she impatiently dashed them away.

"Girls, I don't know how long I am going to be gone," Gerald Butler said somberly. "I wish I didn't have to go at all, but I must. Always remember this:

No matter how far away I am, every night just before the sun goes down and every morning when it rises, I'll be thinking of you and praying for you. Be good soldiers. Take care of your precious mama and each other."

Childish joy in his appearance fled. Judith and Millicent clasped his hands. Their mother took their other hands, and the prayer that followed burned into the children's minds, along with the special look he gave their mother before he mounted and rode off to war, his shoulders proud and square.

For a time their world of gracious living and love continued in much the same way. When the long lists of casualties began arriving, all traces of gentility faded. Gerald Butler's prayer was granted. He fell in his first battle without ever having fired a shot, his commanding officer wrote in a sympathetic letter. As life went ahead in its new order of living under Yankee control, Judith couldn't even remember when things were different. But when at last the fighting ended and troops withdrew, as great a horror as the occupation by Northern forces confronted the Butlers.

Even her great love for her daughter and stepdaughter couldn't rally Mrs. Butler enough to overcome the loss of the only man she had ever loved. Although she held on through the war, shortly afterward, she fell ill with swamp fever. A few weeks later, she died, leaving a bewildered ten and thirteen year old to face life with only God as their protector. Distant relatives offered to take the girls but not together. Older than their actual years because of the tragedies they had faced, Millicent and Judith clung more closely than ever. They unearthed the family treasures their mother had managed to secrete and keep hidden for all the long years and sought lodging with an old friend who welcomed them.

Life's cruel blows continued. When the family friend died, the girls moved on from place to place. Millicent grew thin and pale from kitchen work once done by Negro slaves. Judith sewed long hours until her small fingers sometimes bled from the coarse materials. Yet they could not and would not be separated.

Days and weeks limped into years. At seventeen and fourteen, their contrasting beauty attracted attention. Yet the modest upbringing and Christian principles instilled in them so long ago kept them aloof from the gaiety with which some tried to forget the past. Sometimes they shyly talked of the future.

"How will I know when I'm in love?" Judith demanded and bit off the thread from the seam she had just finished. Her plain dark garb worn from necessity and not choice added little to her beauty, but her fresh face and sparkling eyes needed no enhancement.

Millicent's fair face shone flower-pale against her drab clothing. "I always think that if someday someone looks at me the way Father looked at Mama just before he rode away, I'll know he loves me."

"I remember that!" Judith dropped her sewing. "I don't remember, though. Did Mama look the same way?"

"Yes." A smile curved Millicent's lips upward in the gentle way that made her resemble the Madonna Judith had seen in a painting. Her eyes held dreams and softness. "Dear Judith, how blessed we are to have such memories. God has indeed been good to us all these years." She trembled, and her smile faded. "When I think how we could have been taken away from each other, it frightens me." Her blue eyes grew feverish, and she clutched her arms together across her thin body. "I think I'd rather die than to have that ever happen."

"Silly, no one's going to separate us." Judith deliberately soothed her sister, as she had done since childhood, when she realized her own strength and Millicent's frailty. "Oh, I suppose if we get married, we might not live together, but let's marry gentlemen who will let us stay close."

Twin red spots burned in Millicent's cheeks and provided unusual color. "I'd like to see any man even *try* to separate me from my sister!"

Judith's mouth dropped open. Seldom did Millie exert herself, but she certainly sounded positive now. "Why don't we wait and worry about it when it happens?" she suggested practically. "In the meantime, there's enough light for me to whip in another seam." She bent to her work, but soon the flying needle slowed and stopped. "My idea of heaven is to never, ever have to sew another garment."

"Judith!" Millicent gasped. "Don't be sacrilegious."

She looked up in honest surprise. "God says we're supposed to ask for what we want, and I'm asking that He let me do something else when I get to heaven besides sew." She giggled, and even pious Millie couldn't resist her mirth. "Maybe all the robes of righteousness will be already made by the time I get there."

"My stars, you have funny ideas." Her sister stared at her and shook her head. "When I think of heaven, I think of God and Jesus and Father and Mother and my own mother."

"I do, too," Judith said in a small voice. "I just wish Jesus would come back soon." She threw down her sewing, and tears that had been bottled up for months fell. "Oh, Millie, will we ever really be happy again?"

The older girl knelt beside her and put both arms around her. "Life is hard, but God takes care of us, and we can be happy knowing our family is with Him. Think of all the soldiers and families who don't know Jesus, how much harder it is for them." She comforted Judith, and their mingled tears helped to wash away sad memories.

The summer of 1869 proved to be both disturbing and joyous. Judith learned that Millicent had met a dashing young gentleman who admired her and sought her out at every opportunity. *If Millie is in love, why doesn't she bring the young man to meet me?* she wondered.

"I will," Millicent promised, but she sent a sad glance around their poorly furnished abode. "It's just that we've no place, and—"

"If it's good enough for us, it should be good enough for any gentleman caller," Judith interrupted fiercely.

"Don't you see? We can't *have* gentlemen callers here without a chaperone." Millicent smiled in a way that made her sister lonely for the first time. Hot jealousy against this stranger who had come between them joined forces with the protective instinct she had always displayed toward Millie.

"It's all right, really it is," Millicent assured her. "He's tallish and as blond as I am. When he looks at me, I—" She broke off, unable to express what she felt.

"Do you feel the way Father and Mama did that day?" Judith whispered. The ecstasy in Millie's face stilled her sister's protests. "Oh, yes. If he doesn't love me, I don't know how I can go on." A dark shadow crossed her sweet face. "There are so many girls. They come and go at the place I work. Why should anyone so wonderful even look at a humble serving maid?"

"Anyone that wonderful would be bound to see past your job," Judith snapped, still troubled. "Hasn't he even asked to meet me?"

"N—no. But I've told him all about you, how clever you are with a needle and how we've stayed together all this time." Doubt crept into the blue eyes. "He just laughs and says there's plenty of time. Since I'm only seventeen and don't have a guardian, I suppose he wants to make sure I know what I want."

Judith's lips formed the question, but she couldn't quite ask, *Do you? Do you, Millie?* Instead, she held her tongue and prayed that God would care for her sister and keep her safely.

A few weeks later, Judith received the shock of her life. She came home dog-weary from hunting new quarters that might be more pleasant than those they now had. Never had she seen Millie more radiant. *"Look!"* Her sister held out her slender hand. A shiny gold ring encircled her finger.

"Millicent, you haven't, you didn't. . . *Where did you get that ring?"* Judith stared in horror, her stomach churning.

"It's my wedding ring." Happiness and regret blended in her voice. "I'm so sorry I couldn't tell you, but we, I knew how opposed you'd be to my marrying so young and especially when you haven't even met him, and—"

Judith cut through her babble. "You actually got married without ever telling me?" Suspicion crystallized. "Was this *his* idea?"

"Please don't feel badly, Dear." Even Millicent's contrite apology couldn't dim the shining radiance of her face. "Everything is going to be wonderful. I'll just be gone a few days for a short honeymoon, then we'll have a home together for always. My new husband says he will be glad to have you live with us." The sound of carriage wheels outside the window sent her scurrying to look out. She snatched a valise from the bed. "Come meet him before we go."

Judith hesitated, feeling caught in a moment somewhere between the order that had been their lives and the uncertainty ahead. "I'd rather wait until you come back," she managed.

"I understand." The sweet smile that characterized Millicent showed that she did, but her new allegiance overcame even the bonds of sisterhood. With a warm squeeze of Judith's shoulders, she sped toward the door. Her heels clattered on the staircase, and the lower door banged shut.

"What am I doing?" Judith frantically came out of the shocked trance into which she'd fallen. She raced to the window and leaned out. *"Wait!"* The word couldn't compete with the street noises and laughter of children. Millicent's face turned upward, but Judith knew she didn't look toward the window but into her new husband's face.

I must see what he looks like, she thought quickly. Judith leaned out farther but only glimpsed blond hair and the back of the man's head as he helped Millicent into the carriage.

"Wait!" she called again. "Millicent, I'll be right down!" Even as she called, she knew it was too late. The carriage wheels began to turn, and the harness jingled as her sister rode into a new life, leaving Judith behind.

It's only for a few days, she told herself again and again. She made excuses for Millie's absence, saying she had gone away with friends, yet for three nights Judith cried herself to sleep. There had to be something wrong with a man who would not only hastily marry a seventeen year old but who did it furtively and without her only close relative's knowledge. He must have known how Judith would object; perhaps he was afraid she would sway her sister against such an act. In the silence of the evenings, Judith often heard thunder in the distance that warned of a storm waiting to break. Was this small island of silence during Millicent's honeymoon also the prelude to a storm, one that would shatter Judith's world and perhaps Millie's as well?

All through those long, waiting hours beat the question, *What shall I do if she never comes back? I don't even know her husband's name!* Judith sought her Lord as never before in her young life. She stormed the very gates of heaven on Millicent's behalf and her own. She prayed for forgiveness for the hatred in her heart toward the man who had stolen Millie's love. Sometimes she even cried out for God to take her away from an uncaring world that had hurt her so deeply.

Too upset and ill to work, Judith lay on her bed listening for the sound of carriage wheels. A dozen times she leaped up and pelted to the window. When the right carriage finally came and stopped, she had fallen into a fitful sleep, her tear-stained face in the curve of one arm. Millicent found her that way, and compassion filled her. She slipped back downstairs as arranged, but with the word Judith should not be disturbed. "You can meet her tomorrow," she told her husband. "I'll stay with her tonight."

He quickly agreed, and Millie's heart swelled with love and pride in his understanding. She watched the carriage roll out of sight, thrilling that such a man had ever desired her. Then she went back to her sister, her heart filled with happy plans for the future.

"Millie?" Judith roused when Millicent reentered their room. "Is it really you? I dreamed you went off and didn't come back. I felt so alone. I didn't know what to do or where to go." She broke off. "Where is he?"

Millicent hugged her and laughed and removed a charming new hat. "We decided I'd stay here tonight. Tomorrow—" She lowered her voice to a mysterious tone. "Tomorrow we're going to see about finding a proper house. Oh, Judith, I've never been so happy in my whole life!"

Judith had never been more miserable. Yet curiosity pushed aside foreboding. "Where did you go?"

"To a wonderful inn just north of town. Then we shopped, and see?" She whirled, and her light blue summer dress flounced around her. "That's not all." She tore open a large parcel she had carried in with her. "Your favorite colors." A fluffy yellow and white dress tumbled out. "We found a shop where they sold dresses already made. It should fit. I just remembered that you're four inches taller." Millicent held the dress up to her petite five-foot, four-inch frame where it dragged on the floor.

Her troubles momentarily forgotten, Judith tried on the dress. It settled over her young body as if it had been designed exclusively to highlight her dark brown hair and eyes. "It's lovely, the prettiest dress I've had since—"

"I know." Millicent's shine dimmed. "But how glad Father and Mama would be to know we're going to be happy again." She laughed and confessed, "Don't ever tell anyone, but even on my honeymoon, I missed you so much I could hardly wait to get back to tell you how wonderful life is going to be. After tomorrow, we'll never have to worry about a place to live or having enough money to pay our way." Her sapphire eyes sparkled. "We'll wear our new dresses."

Somehow the excited girls managed to sleep a little. Judith found herself so caught up in anticipation that the little worries that pricked her heart like dressmakers' pins lost themselves. By ten o'clock, they had primped and preened until every shining hair lay in place. For the first time, Millicent wound Judith's shining braids around her head in a coronet. "The new dress needs a new hairstyle," she announced. "Besides, fourteen is no longer a child."

Judith found herself blushing up to the high lacy collar of the pretty gown. Could that really be her own image in the mirror? The girl with rosy cheeks and smiling mouth? How different from the way she had felt while Millicent had been gone! "Pooh," she told her reflection. "I worry too much." She turned toward her sister, lovely in the pale blue gown and the serenity Judith knew came from happiness. She wanted to open her heart, to confess all her doubts, yet doing so would only hurt Millie. Perhaps someday when they were both old women, they would laugh together over the younger sister's misgivings. Now they were too silly, too unreal in the clear sunny morning to utter. Not one bitter drip should be allowed to spoil Millicent's perfect day, Judith vowed with all the passion of her years. *She may never again be exactly this eager and happy.*

The thought startled her. Why shouldn't Millicent have hundreds of happy, eager days? How perfectly ridiculous to allow her own trepidation to color her judgment and imagine all kinds of ridiculous impossibilities. She twitched her skirt again and strained for the sound of carriage wheels.

They did not come.

The clock that had been in the Butler family for generations slowly ticked off the seconds, the minutes, the hours. At first Millicent laughed and admitted what a sleepyhead her husband had proven to be. He liked to stay up late and rise at his leisure. The clock ticked on, relentlessly passing noon, one o'clock, two. By three, Judith had lost interest in her pretty dress and changed. "You don't think there's been an accident," she finally said, then wished she'd kept silent.

Millicent's face turned the shade of parchment. "Surely he would have managed to send me word." She slowly rose. "We must go to where he lodges immediately."

"Wait, Millie. A carriage just stopped."

Color flowed back into her sister's face. "Thank God!" She ran to the door and flung it open. "My dear, where have you been?"

Chapter 5

J udith followed her sister to the door and glanced first at the Negro, then at Millicent, whose hand went to her throat. "Who are you, and what do you want?" she demanded.

"I have a message for the other young lady." The man held out a folded paper, turned on his heel, and hurried down the stairs.

Judith glared at his retreating back but turned back to her sister when she heard a low moan. "Millie, what is it? Is your husband hurt? Do we need to go to him?"

Millicent tottered back inside the open door and sank to a shabby settee. Every trace of color had drained from her face. She wordlessly held out the paper, and Judith grabbed it from her.

> *My dear,*
>   *New Orleans just isn't the place for me. I'm leaving for home today. I have wronged you by going through with the marriage ceremony. Forgive me, if you can.*

There was no signature.

Judith crumpled the page the way she wished she could crumple the man responsible for the devastation of her beloved sister. "How could anyone be so cruel?" Fury threatened to choke her.

"I thought he loved me." Millicent looked as if she had been stabbed.

"Quick, what is his address?" Judith sprang to the occasion. "Surely he can't have gone yet!"

The pride of her father stiffened Millie's spine. Her blue eyes flashed. "Do you think I want him to come back after this? Never!" New dignity raised her head and dried her tears.

"You don't love him any longer?" Judith's brain spun.

"Loving someone has little to do with honor and respect," Millicent quietly said as her fingers mercilessly wrung a handkerchief. "Even if he came back, this would always be between us." A little color returned to her face. "It

45

isn't even a matter of forgiving, which I could do. I'd have to, according to the Bible. But forcing him to stay when he wants to be elsewhere. . ." Her voice trailed into silence, the same silence that had hovered in the poorly furnished room while she had been away and Judith waited.

"What will we do now?" Judith asked. For the first time in her life, she felt incapable of making decisions.

Millie's lips set in a straight line. "No one knows of our marriage except we three. The family I work for granted me the time off for a rest. Tomorrow I will go back." Never had she appeared stronger. "We will go on as we have." She looked around the room and shuddered with distaste. "As soon as we're able, we will move to another part of the city and leave no address."

"But what if he should come back?" Judith cried, her heart aching at the stony look in Millicent's eyes.

"Dear sister, if he really wants to find me, he will." Long lashes swept down to hide Millie's eyes and made little dark half moons on her white cheeks. "I don't think he will, though." Her lips trembled, and she hastened to the window and looked out as if seeing far beyond the familiar street below.

Through a relentless summer and a welcome fall, there was no sign of the peripatetic bridegroom. Millicent and Judith sold a few more heirlooms and established themselves in new quarters. One autumn day, when leaves whirled before the wind, Millie told her sister she had an announcement to make. She stood by the window as she so often did.

In the silence, Judith's heart pounded for no apparent reason. What could make Millie look like that, exalted, yet despairing.

"I am with child."

At first Judith could but stare. A multitude of feelings rushed over her: shock, disbelief, even admiration that her sister could be so calm.

"You're going to have to help me," Millicent went on. "The baby will be born next spring, late April or early May. Between now and then, we must save every penny we can. No matter how hard it is, I'll never give my baby away for others to raise."

Judith ran to her and hugged her fiercely. "Of course you won't! We'll take care of the baby and—" She broke off. "Millie, don't you think you should let him know? You could send a letter to where he used to live. . . ."

Millie looked full into her sister's eyes. "No, I thought it all out before I told you. This is my child. He forfeited the right to it by leaving, even though he had no way of knowing there would be a baby." Her eyes glowed with feverish intensity. "Don't you see? He comes from a well-to-do family. Suppose he claimed the child? We have no money to fight for my baby." She caught Judith's hand and held it until the younger girl winced. "Promise that no matter what happens, you won't let him take the baby."

A warning flutter inside Judith died before her sister's agony. Making such a promise might be wrong, but Millicent's peace of mind had to be assured. "I promise." She squeezed the clutching hand. Yet another clutching hand, cold and frightening, held her heart in a grip so powerful, she wanted to cry out.

The coming of the child changed everything. They first needed to find a place where neither was known or Millicent's condition would bring shame and speculation. After much searching, they finally relocated in a drab but still respectable boardinghouse. Millie disguised herself with loose clothing and continued her maid's work. Judith sewed until her eyes burned. Babies needed things the sisters could ill afford, but little by little, a pitiful array of tiny garments lay waiting and ready. On the last day of April 1870, a frightened but determined Judith helped Millie in what fortunately was an easy birth and delivered a squalling but perfectly formed boy.

"We have no money for doctors," Millicent had insisted. "Babies come, and we can manage." All Judith's protests failed to sway her. "I'll be all right, and you're strong, almost fifteen years old."

The first weeks after her son's birth, Millicent's magnificent determination alone kept her going. She named the baby Joel Butler, and the little horde of money the girls had been able to save carried them through. A few times, Judith mentioned contacting the baby's father but found Millicent even more opposed than before. A few months later, a complete reversal occurred. For several days, Judith had been aware of the way Millie's gaze followed her whenever she was in the room. One fall evening, she quietly said, "I'm not sure if God will allow me to stay long enough to raise Joel." Her eyes held sadness but no fear. Judith noticed how frail she looked before she went on.

"All those months ago, I made you promise; now I want you to change your promise." The appeal in the thin face would have melted a heart carved from ice. "I still want you to keep my baby, Judith. But if the time ever comes that you are no longer able to do so, I release you from the promise not to contact Joel's father. There are papers hidden beneath the lining of the old trunk: the marriage lines, names, and addresses." She reached out and clung to Judith's hand. "Never read them or use the information unless you feel you have no choice but to lose Joel."

"I promise." Judith's throat felt thick. She tried to cover it by saying, "Here we are at dusk, talking gloomy thoughts!" She lit a candle, and its flickering light steadied into a glow that dispelled some of the shadows. "There, is that better?"

Millicent roused herself from her private thoughts, and they said no more. Yet the knowledge of the pact between them made Judith feel old beyond her years. Her gaze strayed toward the box they had carefully lined with soft material for a crib. He was so good, like a little golden-haired angel. He seldom cried, and his large, intelligent eyes and well-shaped head made him seem older than his few months on earth.

"Dear God," Judith whispered long after her sister slept that night. "Please, don't take Millicent. You and she and Joel are all I have left." Waves of loneliness washed through her. A few minutes later, the peace of her heavenly Father descended, and the troubled young woman slept.

As if relieved to have talked things out, Millicent rallied. She continued to work, while Judith sewed at home and cared for Joel. November and December passed. During an unusually chilly January, Millicent contracted a bad cold that kept her home. She arranged with her employer to send Judith in her place. The hardest thing was not allowing Joel to come near her lest he also become ill. By February, Millie still could not work, and a cough lingered that frightened Judith, no matter how much her sister tried to assure her. She called a doctor, who silently examined Millicent and shook his head. Judith followed him into the hall.

"I can't do anything. She let it go too long." His keen eyes bored into Judith. "You'd better contact some relatives and make arrangements for yourself and the little boy."

Somehow Judith managed to murmur her thanks and pay him as well, her heart filled with terror. If he took it on himself to let the authorities know if Millicent died, they would come and get Joel.

Millie brought it up when Judith went back into their room. Thin and wasted, she ordered her sister to get everything packed. "You don't have to tell me what the doctor said," she began. "I think I've always known how things would be. Don't cry, Judith. There isn't time. I want you to take the last of Mama's jewelry and sell it now. Sew the money into the bodice of your dress." She took a deep breath and coughed until exhausted, but her spirit permitted no giving up. "The hardest thing you've ever done is what you must do soon.

As soon as God takes me to be with Father and Mama, you must flee. Don't wait for anyone to come. When the landlady doesn't hear stirring, she will come up and find me."

"*That's horrible!*" Judith cried. "I can't do it!"

Millicent rose up on one elbow. "You must. If you love me, grant my last wish. What does it matter who buries me or where?" Fever painted red flags in the sunken white cheeks. "Don't you see? Joel will be taken from you if you don't escape with him." She panted, more beautiful in her illness than ever before. "Now go and sell the jewelry. I've remembered the name of an old friend who may take you in and never tell anyone. It's written down in the front of the big Bible." She fell back to the thin pillow, her eyes filled with pity.

"Poor Judith. So young to have all this tragedy. Please don't mourn for me. I'll be with loved ones, and soon you and my little son will come. Even if it isn't for years, it will seem in the twinkling of an eye for me." She coughed again. "Dear little sister, God will give you strength to do what you are required. He will uphold and sustain you. Now, go."

Unable to argue in the face of such courage, Judith got out the last of the jewels, donned a cloak, and hurried to the man who had purchased other items from them. Back with the money, she discovered that Millie had been doing more planning.

"Go right away and see if Mama's friend will take us, but don't say when we're coming," she ordered. "Then tell our landlady that I'm sick and we'll be moving soon. Get a drayman to come for what furniture we have left."

Again the necessity of providing for the future lent strength to the failing young woman. For several days, she kept on in spite of her obvious weakness. Not until every direction had been carried out and only a pallet on her floor remained did Millicent relax.

"It won't be long," she told Judith. "But I am so happy you will keep Joel. Remember your promise." She fell asleep with a smile on her pale lips.

All night Judith kept vigil. The light of a guttering candle showed when Millicent's earthly sleep changed. Not one tear fell. Judith had gone beyond that in the hours and days before her sister's death. She had to be strong for Joel.

After a final survey of the room, Judith left the bit of money she could scarcely afford to repay the landlady for her trouble in contacting the authorities. On a scrap of paper, she wrote, *I'm sorry it isn't more, but I must care for the child*. Once again she was glad that the room had been listed under "M. Greene," Millie's middle name. In the first rays of morning, she quietly took the sleeping child from his nest at the foot of Millicent's pallet and slipped into the mists of dawn.

Judith would never clearly remember how she and Joel existed. She stretched the bit of money in her dress while making her small charge's clothing from the leftover pieces of her sewing jobs. One by one, the familiar childhood furniture pieces vanished. Yet Joel thrived and provided joy to the girl's sad heart. While others her age danced and frolicked, she held her head high and cared for Joel. Still a child at heart in many ways, she played with him and made up games. When time permitted, she took him for walks, and although many times she ached to buy him all the things others had, he never asked for anything.

Once in awhile the old friend who now served as her landlady cared for the charming little boy while Judith delivered her work. She didn't care to allow her personal situation and business world to touch by taking him with her.

Weeks, then months, then years passed. Soon Joel would have his fourth birthday; Judith, her nineteenth. She had developed into a tall, slender young woman whose dark brown eyes still lit with twin candles when she played with Joel. Her shining coronet of dark brown braids suited her as no other hairstyle. Even Joel, who liked to brush her hair at night, thought it prettiest when coiled around her shapely head.

Because of Millicent's experience with a faithless lover, Judith almost innately distrusted men. Those she met through business who showed open admiration received instant rebuffs. Millie had been so sure of her happiness, perhaps too sure. Yet Judith could never fully regret the sad circumstances when Joel confidingly tucked his hand in hers and said he loved her.

If only she hadn't allowed herself to grow rundown by skimping on meals so she could put away extra for Joel! Suddenly Judith's secure world crashed. Sickness struck and lingered. Panicky, she tried to continue her work and could not. Even when the fever left, she crept through the days like a ghost of her former strong self. During her delirious periods, the thought hammered until she thought she would go mad. *The promise. The promise. I must keep my promise to Millicent.* Part of the time she couldn't remember what it was, and she felt too sick to care. She fought with all her remaining strength and came back from the brink of death. If anything happened to her, no one would know who Joel was! Could it be right for him to be put away and cheated out of his rightful inheritance? Over and over she considered the circumstances. If only God would help her know what to do now that she simply could not care for herself and Joel as she had done these long, hard years. . . .

Joel moved in his sleep, and Judith returned from her long mental journey to the past. She reached beneath the netting and straightened his tangle of sheets, smothering the noble brow. A wave of love stronger than any she had experienced flowed through her. She couldn't care more for Joel if he were her own son. Wasn't he her own, given to her by Millicent?

"I have to decide what to do, heavenly Father." She resumed her post at the window. "It may mean losing him, but I can't take the chance of growing ill again and not being able to provide for him." Her gaze strayed to the old trunk that held their meager supply of clothing and worldly goods. Dread filled her, yet the time had come for action. She resolutely stood and crossed to the trunk. Her hands shook so she could barely open it, but she finally lifted the lid and propped it back.

"Papers beneath the lining," she muttered. She loosened stitches so tiny as to be nearly invisible, her throat tight at the thought of Millie secreting the pages until no one would suspect the trunk contained any item but the obvious.

The few papers crackled as she withdrew them. Such a small witness to the short time Millicent had loved and rejoiced and found happiness to sustain her. Judith had to blink away the tears that persisted in coming between her and the important documents. She barely glanced at the wedding certificate. What she needed was an address, somewhere to send a letter admitting the existence of a four-year-old boy for whom she could no longer provide.

A scrawled page in the same handwriting she'd seen in the note delivered that fateful day almost five years earlier caught her attention. She snatched it up and scanned it in the fading light. "Oh, no!" She desperately pulled aside the screening curtain to get more light. Somehow moisture had seeped into the old trunk and the address was unreadable.

Judith frantically dug behind the lining for other pages but found none. She turned to the marriage lines and gave a soft cry of gladness. Clear and bright, the date of July 29, 1869, proclaimed to a more or less interested world that Millicent Butler and Gideon Carroll Scott had been united in holy matrimony.

Her gladness turned to despair. What good was a name without an address? She had no idea where this Gideon Carroll Scott lived, either while in New Orleans or when he went back to the home he mentioned in the cruel farewell note. Millicent, usually so open, had never talked about him except the times she extracted Judith's promises concerning Joel.

"Dear God, this is a mountain neither Millie nor I expected," she whispered. In spite of the warm evening, her hands felt icy and nerveless. "Now what can I do?"

Should she make inquiries in New Orleans? If so, where would she start? If she went to Millicent's employer with the story of Joel's birth, they would laugh her to scorn. Millie had been proud they had never known. Besides, opening the past might prove disastrous. What did the authorities do to young women who stole away a child, leaving no trace?

Strange that the memory of her father's words when he rode off to war came back to her now. *Every night just before the sun goes down and every morning when it rises, I'll be thinking of you and praying for you.* A passionate longing for her dead father rose within Judith. How distressed he would be to see her in such straits. Yet always he had taught that her heavenly Father loved her even more than he, although to her young heart it had hardly seemed possible.

Too weary to think longer, Judith sought out her bed. She fell asleep with a prayer for direction and guidance on her lips. Morning brought Joel to her bed in his usual whirlwind manner, and for a time she forgot their uncertain future. Yet throughout the day she found herself saying over and over in her heart and mind, *God, I am helpless. It's all up to You.*

With a round-eyed Joel beside her, Judith found the strength to delve into the depths of the old trunk. "What's this?" he asked and pointed to a slight bulge in the side. His eager fingers worked the lining loose. "Why, Judith, it's *money!*"

"It can't be," she argued, but there lay a small pouch with money in it and a paper in Millicent's fine handwriting that read, "Passage money, if ever needed." How had her sister been able to put it away from their scant income? Now if Judith only knew where to go! Or should she just give the money to their landlady and hope for the best? She rejected the idea as soon as it came. Such a temporary solution wouldn't cure their problems.

That afternoon, Judith and Joel walked through the poor neighborhood just to get away from their room. Dirty newspapers swirled in the street under horses' hooves. Perhaps she should rescue one and see if anyone needed a housekeeper, someone who would allow her to bring Joel, too. Judith managed to grab a paper slightly cleaner than the others. She idly turned the pages, pausing at one that showed a small group of men in front of a stately building. If only things had been different! She'd like Joel to go to college one day, but there seemed to be little hope unless God Himself intervened in their lives.

She started to turn the page, then stopped. A frank-faced, smiling young man stared at her from beneath the headline: WEST TEXAS MAN LEADS CLASS IN ACADEMICS. Would she ever know a young man like that? Probably not, but Joel could become one. She curiously read the words beneath the picture, wondering why anyone from West Texas would be going to school in New Orleans. The next instant, she stopped breathing, only to start again when her head spun. She closed her eyes and read the caption: Local lads found it impossible to keep up with a young ministerial student from the Wild West. Gideon Carroll Scott returns to San Scipio, Texas, for his first pastorate.

Chapter 6

The newspaper dropped from Judith's numb fingers. Blood rushed to her head as she bent to retrieve it. Her avid gaze sought out the featured picture. Was this man a scoundrel, an utterly heartless rake who broke Millicent's heart and left behind a world of trouble and misery? Impossible! And yet, how many Gideon Carroll Scotts could there be?

He had been in New Orleans all these years, hiding under the guise of one studying to be a minister! Appalled at the further evidence of his wickedness, a rush of fury sent determination coursing through Judith's veins, bringing strength to overcome the weakness caused by her illness. *Mr. Gideon Carroll Scott has a big surprise coming*, she thought with a small amount of satisfaction. She tore out the article, stuffed it in her reticule, and managed to steady her voice. "Come, Joel. It's time for us to go home."

He trotted obediently beside her, one chubby hand confidingly in hers. Now and then he pointed with the other at some wonder: an especially colorful rose, a dog on a leash, a strutting peacock on a shady lawn. His laugh rang, and his blue eyes shaped like those of the man in the newspaper shone in the sunshine. "Look, Judy."

"Yes, Dear." Preoccupation made her answer less interested than usual. When he questioningly looked up, she hastened to add, "Aren't they beautiful?" From the time Joel first walked, he had developed an inner sense that told him when his beloved Judy was troubled. Sometimes it took all her best efforts to hide her feelings so he could be the normal, happy child God had created him to be.

As soon as Joel fell asleep after their simple supper of bread and milk, Judith got out her writing materials. Page after scorching page, she wrote to the missing Gideon Carroll Scott and ended by saying she and Joel would be on their way west by the time he received her letter.

When the white heat of anger faded, reason took over. What if by some strange quirk of fate this wasn't the man who deserted Millie? "Oh, dear God," she whispered. "It must be. I asked You for help and found the newspaper. But I have to be sure. Please guide me." For a long time, she sat there thinking and listening to Joel's even breathing. At last she reluctantly tore the letter to bits. Time enough for recrimination later. Now she must make sure of her ground. She took a clean sheet of paper and wrote a simple message:

If you are Gideon Carroll Scott, who married Millicent Butler who died in early 1871, contact me.

J. Butler

She added her current address; she must stay until she received an answer. Checking to see that Joel still slept, Judith hurried downstairs and outside to post her letter to San Scipio, Texas. Surely someone there would know Gideon Scott. The paper had named it as his hometown.

She had no choice but to use a little of the designated passage money to stave off eviction until she heard from Texas. Yet, day after sweltering day passed and no message came. Judith forced herself to take up her needle and work, even when the fabric shook in her unsteady hands.

"Why d'you work so hard, Judy?" Concern shone in Joel's eyes as he leaned against her knee.

She roused from her fatigue and smiled. "Can you keep a secret?"

"Oooh, yes." His face lighted up. "Is it a nice one?"

"It's a bi-i-i-ig secret," she solemnly told him, unwilling to label what they must do next as nice. "Don't tell anyone."

"Not even God?" he anxiously asked. "We tell Him ever'thing."

"You dear!" She laid the almost-finished garment aside and pulled him into her lap, noting how worn her dark dress had become. For a moment, a vision of a fluffy yellow and white dress danced before her to be sternly put away, as the dress had been long ago. "God already knows, but we won't tell anyone else. We're going to leave here and go on a long, long trip."

"Like Mama went to heaven?" He snuggled closer to her. "That would be nice. We could see Mama and Jesus. Maybe even God."

Judith hastily corrected the impression she had given. "Not to heaven, Joel. To Texas."

"Is that close to heaven?"

Although the memory of one man's faithlessness colored her reply, Judith felt compelled to explain the situation to Joel as best she could. "I don't think so. Joel, we've never talked much about your father's family. That's because they live in Texas, and now we may get to see them. Would you like that?"

Joel's face looked puzzled, but he nodded his head.

"This is hard for me to say to you. Your mama named you after her family when you were born because your father left New Orleans and went back to Texas. I think it's time for you to know your real name: Joel Scott." Sensing that she had imparted too much information for him to process immediately, Judith returned to the details of their impending trip. "Can you imagine what Texas will look like? Think of all the cows and horses we'll see!" From her limited supply of Texas lore, she painted an exciting picture, wanting only to cry until every tear inside her washed away her misery and the need for this hateful trip.

In spite of the silence from San Scipio, she still clung to the forlorn hope Gideon might write. But as summer relentlessly continued, Judith knew they must go. With another autumn and winter just ahead, she didn't dare chance not being able to work. After a final sleepless night of prayer, she purchased passage and left New Orleans with Joel and the shabby trunk that contained little more than their well-worn clothes, the big Bible, and the precious wedding certificate.

Dust, heat, and coarse food threatened to choke Judith, but the fear of the unknown was more unpalatable. One of few women on the trip, she endured rough men who treated her kindly and palefaced men who eyed her and attempted conversation. The endless journey sometimes made her wonder if she and Joel had been crossing Texas all their lives. Overheard conversation told her how proud Texans were of their state, and she bitterly wondered why. She spoke little with her fellow travelers and reserved all her energy for Joel, who thrived on the attention after years of being so isolated. A few times she reluctantly relinquished him to a keen-eyed driver who invited "the little feller" to ride up on top with him. Joel returned big-eyed and chattering. Long-eared jackrabbits fascinated him. Tumbleweeds made him laugh with their antics. He sniffed sagebrush and said, "It tickles." Even in her misery, Judith couldn't help seeing how the little boy brought gladness to all around him. *God, may it ever be so* became her constant prayer.

Just when the exhausted young woman felt she couldn't go on another day, their driver, Pete, bellowed out, "San Scipio comin'!"

"Son Sip-yo comin'," Joel echoed.

Judith roused from her listlessness. Torrents of weakness washed through her, but she could not give up now. She instinctively turned to her source of comfort. "Dear God," she murmured so low no one else could hear, "help me to go on in Your strength. Mine is gone."

The horses topped a hill. Interested in spite of herself, Judith looked down at San Scipio, cupped between two rises. Could that be a town, the one long and dusty street with only a few buildings on each side? She leaned forward and glimpsed other buildings back from the so-called thoroughfare. The horses picked up their pace.

"Whoa, you ornery critters!" Pete stopped the stage before the building marked GENERAL STORE in faded letters on a weather-beaten board.

Judith's spirits crashed. In her need to find Joel's father, she never once thought it would be in a place like this or that places like this even existed. "Sir, isn't there a hotel?" Her voice trembled, even though she tried to keep it steady. Pete, who had leaped down and opened the door of the stagecoach, pushed his sombrero back on his head. Trouble loomed large on his unshaven face. "Naw, and the boardin'house ain't much, either."

"Wh—where can we go?"

Pete scratched his cheek. "The Curtises have the biggest place, but yu don't wanta go there." He peered at her, and his face reddened. "Beggin' yure pardon, Ma'am. But d'yu an' the little feller have kin here?"

Judith urged Joel off her lap as she considered her answer. "Gideon Scott is a relative of ours," she said somewhat awkwardly.

Glancing from Judith to Joel, enlightenment slowly came to the driver's face. "Well, by the powers, I shoulda. . ." He quickly swallowed, then mopped his face with a trail-dusty kerchief. "Stay right here." He helped them down and to a bench away from a small group of curious onlookers. Down the street Pete went in the clumsy way Judith had come to associate with Texans, who seemed more at home on horses than on foot. She vaguely wished the driver hadn't recognized Joel's lineage, but what did it matter? Before long, San Scipio and the hills and valleys would ring with shock concerning Joel's identity.

A few minutes later, Pete returned, followed by a towheaded lad who looked to be about fifteen perched behind a high-stepping horse pulling a light buggy.

"This here's Ben. He's rarin' to drive yu to the Circle S."

The Circle S?" Judith raised inquiring brows.

"Lige Scott's ranch." Pete swung the trunk expertly aboard the buggy and helped his former passengers up into it. "Good luck, Miss. You, too, little feller." He lowered his voice. "Don't pay no mind if Lige raves. It's his way." His smile warmed Judith's heart, and at that moment, she felt as if she were leaving her last friend. Her grizzled guardian angel tousled Joel's curls. "Don't yu fergit yure pardner Pete."

"I won't," the little boy promised.

"Neither will I." The grateful look Judith sent him brought an even deeper red to his windburned, leathery face. "Good-bye, and God bless you."

Ben touched the horse lightly with the reins, and the buggy rolled away. Judith didn't look back, but Joel turned around and waved to their benefactor.

"I'll just drive past the new church," Ben told his passengers. His eyes gleamed at the thought of driving this pale but pretty visitor and little boy all the way out to the Circle S. The coins Pete had given him jingled merrily in his pocket. "We got ourselves the greatest preacher there ever was."

"Oh?" Judith grasped the opportunity to learn something about Gideon.

One word of polite interest was enough to loosen Ben's wagging tongue. A straw-colored lock of hair dangled on his forehead, but it didn't slow his praise. "Gideon went to N'Orleans and studied so he could be the best preacher ever. Don't see why he needed to go, but he did. Anyway, he, oh, here's the church." Ben pulled in their horse. "Door's closed. Preacher don't stick around much; too busy out visiting folks. Here, let me help you down. You can see inside, anyway."

Judith bit back tears when she observed the faithfully cared-for flowers and the obvious love that had gone into the building. Black anger for the perfidy of the minister warred with the hatred she felt for having to expose his sin and shatter the tranquil silence that surrounded the building. Inside, the presence of God hung in the quiet air. Ben nearly burst with pride, showing the careful work put into the San Scipio church.

"We all helped," he said simply. "Sometimes when I hear Gideon preach, it makes me wonder if a feller oughtn't to get right down on his knees and thank the Almighty for bringing Gideon back when he coulda had a big city church."

Judith bit her tongue to keep from shrieking out the truth. The fall of his idol might change boyish devotion to God into bitterness. *What an awful thing Gideon has done, not just to Millicent or his congregation but to himself,* she thought. Her fingers pressed the reticule that held the creased picture of him. How like an angel he looked, how like Joel. Yet hadn't Lucifer been the fairest of all before he turned from God?

Back in the buggy, Joel fell asleep in spite of the changing country through which they passed. Ben rambled on, repeating almost verbatim Gideon's first sermon and the story of his conversation. "Pushed his notes away, he did. Just stood there and talked kinda quietlike, but you coulda heard an owl hoot a mile away, everyone was so still."

Again Judith had the feeling of wrongness. Doubt assailed her. If she had spent the last of her substance to come to San Scipio and it turned out the young minister had nothing to do with Millicent and Joel, what then?

I can always sew, she told herself, but misgivings continued to attack. Not many women in this part of the country would be in need of a dressmaker or seamstress, no matter how skilled. Perhaps that family Pete had mentioned could use her services.

She took advantage of the next time Ben stopped talking to catch his breath. "Do you know the Curtis family?"

"Huh, who doesn't? Old man Curtis is the storekeeper, 'cept his high-toned wife and daughter run him and the store, too." Ben put on a falsetto voice. " 'Oh, Mr. Curtis, you mustn't even *think* of puttin' the nicest goods out for sale! Lucinda's in des'prit need of a new gown for the ball.' "

"*Ball!* You have balls in San Scipio?" Judith forgot her troubles for a moment.

"Huh-uh." Ben grinned a comradely smile. "That's just what Mrs. Curtis called the big re-cep-tion she aimed to give for Gideon." The grin stretched into a guffaw. "Not on your tintype did it come off. Preacher up and said he'd rather just have folks come to church on Sundays, and he'd shake their hands after services."

"What did Mrs. Curtis say?"

"Not much, but Lucinda simpered around and told everyone how noble Gideon was until San Scipio wished she'd keep still."

Judith tried to fit what Ben related to the image of a young man so selfish he would marry a girl and walk out on her. It seemed impossible. Yet hadn't there been belated recognition in Pete's eyes when he glanced at Joel? Too weary to figure it out, she sighed until Ben stopped the winded horse on top of the mesa above the Circle S in the same place Lige and Gideon had rested weeks before.

"The Circle S," Ben said unnecessarily.

Restful. The word came to mind with Judith's first glance below. After the shock of San Scipio, she had feared a shack. Instead, she saw the red-tiled roof and cream adobe walls turned pure gold by the slanting sun. A feeling of coming home tore at Judith. Distant hills gave way to higher mountains. An eagle, twin to the one that winged in the sky to welcome Gideon home, cast its dark shadow over the trail ahead.

"It's so still." Judith automatically lowered her voice.

"Cyrus must not be home, or it wouldn't be."

Something in Ben's guarded voice made her inquire, "Who's Cyrus?"

"Gideon's brother, but they ain't alike." Ben miraculously stopped talking and urged the horse forward down the steep decline to the valley floor. "Circle S's the biggest and prettiest spread around. Dad says if I still want to next year when I'm sixteen, I can hire out here." His hands firm on the reins, Ben slowed the horse for a turn.

"You really love it, don't you?" Judith marveled.

Ben turned an astonished gaze toward her. "Of course I do. I was born and raised here, Ma'am." His tone said more than his words, and Judith subsided. She couldn't help but see the difference between the Circle S and other places she'd passed.

"Water and care make the difference," Ben said. Had he read her mind? "The Scotts are a hardworking outfit." He brought the light buggy to a stop in front of the house, and Judith noted the courtyard, bright flowers, and plentiful garden.

"Lige? Gideon? You've got comp'ny." Ben jumped down from the driver's seat and courteously helped Joel, who had awakened flushed and curious, and then Judith.

"Where are we, Judy?" Joel wanted to know. He rubbed the sleep from his eyes.

"We're at the Circle S, Dear. It's a big ranch." *That can't be my voice, calm and practical*, Judith thought. *Not when my stomach's going around in circles.*

"Are we going to stay here?" Joel didn't wait for an answer but ran to a nearby rosebush to sniff the flowers. Judith felt reprieved.

"Ben, who is it you've brought us?" A crisp voice with a hint of a Southern accent penetrated Judith's confusion. She turned sharply, and dust sifted from her dress. A woman, whose gray-streaked brown hair shouted middle age but whose slender figure and questioning blue gaze whispered youth, stood near the arched support that held up a wide-roofed porch. Her simple dress of blue calico matched her eyes and fitted her body well. The welcome in her eyes for any stranger reached out to Judith, adrift in a friendless land, unless she counted Pete and Ben.

"I—I am Judith Butler," she began. Her heart pounded. *How can I destroy the peace in this ranch woman's face by informing her of her son's treachery? Or will it all prove to be a terrible case of mistaken identity?* In that moment, Judith fervently hoped so. Better to have made the long trip for nothing than to bring shame to one Judith could have loved as a mother in different circumstances.

"Who are you talking to, Naomi?"

Judith knew she would never forget her first sight of Lige Scott. To her frightened vision, he loomed sky-high and desert-wide. His massive head sat square and proud on strong shoulders. Lige's blue eyes, darkened with some strange and unidentifiable emotion, stared at Judith from a network of lines in a range-hardened face. Brown hair predominantly gray successfully told the story of his hardworking life and the fight to get, hold, and expand the Circle S.

"Ben has fetched us a visitor." Naomi smiled and gracefully walked down the steps. "Her name is Judith Butler, but she hasn't told us where she comes from or why she's here."

Lige followed his wife to where Judith stood frozen. If it had seemed impossible to tell Naomi Scott why she'd come, it was preposterous to imagine accusing Gideon to this heavy-browed father. Judith couldn't move. She could not speak. She swayed from weariness, and Ben, openmouthed, steadied her. If only someone would say something, anything, to break this terrible silence before a storm Judith knew would never end.

"Judy, I like it here." Joel deserted the roses, ran from behind the buggy, and stopped between her and the Scotts. "Do you live here? Are we going to stay with you?" he asked.

Chapter 7

O h, God, not like this, Judith silently prayed, despising herself for not speaking. Now it was too late. Innocent, beautiful Joel stood smiling at Naomi and Lige, repeating his question. "Are Judy and I going to stay with you?" The look in his Scott-blue eyes and rosy face showed his eagerness.

Naomi gave a choked cry. Her face turned whiter than cotton. Lige's mighty frame jerked as if someone had shot him. Disbelief turned into anger, then fear on his face. Finally he burst out, *"Dear God in heaven, who are you, Boy?"*

Joel's mouth rounded into a little *o*. He put one finger in his mouth.

Lige fell to his knees before the child and asked again, "Who are you?" Sweat glistened in the furrows of his face.

With the sensitivity of his young years, that strange ability to know when others hurt, Joel's happiness fled. Judith suddenly found her voice. "His name is Joel Scott, Sir."

"No. *No!*" Lige stood and backed away as if pursued. But when Joel's eyes filled and he ran to Judith, the stricken man mumbled, "Forgive me, Boy." He passed one hand over his forehead. "Naomi, take them inside." Before she could comply with his order, Lige glared at the transfixed Ben. "On your way and not a word of this to anyone, you hear?"

"Yes, Sir. I mean, no, Sir." Ben almost fell over himself getting back into the buggy and turning the horse. A cloud of dust followed his rapid progress away from the Circle S and the four left behind to sort out the mystery. Someday Ben might speak of this day, but now all he wanted to do was get away as fast as he would from a threatened rattlesnake.

"Miss Butler?" Naomi Scott regained her composure, although to Judith's excited gaze, she appeared to have aged ten years in the past few moments. "Will you come in, please?" She smiled at the wide-eyed little boy who clung to his aunt's skirts, held by a tension he couldn't understand.

Judith followed the woman into a large hall with a polished dark floor and massive dark furniture. The brightness of Mexico relieved the somber mien: Colorful serapes adorned the cream plaster walls, and matching woven rugs made islands on the waxed floor.

"Oooh, pretty." Joel's love of beauty overcame his temporary shyness. He pointed to an open door leading into the flower-laden courtyard with its splashing fountain.

"Perhaps he would like to go out while we talk," Lige said hoarsely, his gaze fixed on the small boy with a strange intensity Judith couldn't translate. "May I, Judy?"

"Of course." She hugged him and watched him run into the courtyard before turning to the Scotts. "I apologize for intruding this way, but your son— he—" She swayed and would have fallen if Naomi hadn't caught her arm and led her to a settee. "Child!" The hostess in Naomi rose to the needs of a guest. "Why, you're worn out."

Naomi's kindness threatened to destroy completely what little composure Judith still possessed. "It's such a long way," she faltered. "If I could have a glass of water, please."

Naomi clapped her hands, and a smiling, dark-eyed Spanish woman in a bright, flouncy dress came into the room. "Carmelita, a cool drink for our guest, please."

Before Judith's brain stopped spinning, a tall fruit drink of unknown ingredients, an elixir to restore her spirits, turned the world right side up again.

Aware of Lige's pacing, Judith said, "I didn't want to come here, but I've been sick, and if anything happened to me, there's no one to care for Joel."

"If the boy is really a Scott—and with that face, he can't be otherwise— he will be cared for," Lige interrupted, his anger distorting his features.

Fortified by the drink and spurred by the contemptuous disbelief in Lige's voice, Judith's jaw set and her own anger flared. "Oh, he's a Scott all right."

"You have proof of this?" Naomi asked. Judith had the feeling hope still lived in the woman's heart. "When and where were you married?"

A rush of hot color stained the young woman's smooth cheeks. "Joel is not my son but my half sister's." She then forestalled the inevitable question as to why Millicent hadn't come herself. "Millie died before Joel was even a year old." She fumbled with her reticule. "I've taken care of him since."

"You aren't much more than a child yourself," Naomi observed. "How did you manage?"

"I am nineteen, Mrs. Scott." Her level gaze didn't waver. "One does what one has to do." She glanced at Lige and caught a grudging admiration in his big eyes. A moment later, the papers crackled in her fingers, but a strange reluctance made her add, "Would you like to hear the whole story?"

Naomi nodded, but Lige said nothing. Taking his silence as a consent, Judith began with the death of their parents, the unusual closeness between the sisters, and the advent of Gideon who, according to Millie, was every storybook hero rolled into one. "I couldn't understand why he wouldn't meet me," she said. Tears sparkled on her long lashes just remembering that awful time.

"Looking back, it appears he knew he couldn't get Millie any way except by marriage." She ignored a growl of protest from Lige and rushed on. "Anyway, they went away for a brief honeymoon. I'd never seen Millie so happy as when she came back wearing a pale blue dress. She had brought a beautiful gown for me, and we got ready the next morning and waited for her husband to come." Those agonizing hours returned. "He didn't even have the courage to tell Millie all his talk about making a home where I'd always be welcome was just that, talk. He sent a Negro with a message." Judith fished it out and read the words made faint by the years.

A terrible cry burst from Lige, but Judith knew she must go on. Once told, she never intended to mention that time again. "Your son might as well have put a gun to Millie's heart. Something in her died, perhaps the will to live. A few months later, she knew she was with child, and I believe she forgave everything because of the coming of her son." Judith quickly sketched in the next months, culminating with the death of her half sister.

"She made me promise I would only search for Joel's father if the time came when I could no longer care for him."

"But why?" Naomi cried. Her hands twisted, and the pain in her eyes made Judith look away. "Surely she knew that in such circumstances. . ." She couldn't go on.

"She knew her husband's family was well-to-do and feared Joel might be taken from her," Judith said in a dull voice. Would her lagging strength help her finish this ordeal?

"Did my son know about the boy?" Lige stepped closer. His eyes gleamed.

"I don't see how he could, Sir." Judith felt pity stir inside her. A man whose pride had been knifed in the way only a wayward son can do, Lige's big shoulders sagged. "We did everything possible to keep Joel's birth quiet," Judith added.

"Thank God he isn't guilty of more sins," admitted Lige, but his eyes showed that didn't lessen the magnitude of this audacious marriage and desertion. "Did he. . .do you know if he knew of your sister's death?"

Colorless, Judith shook her head. "He had no way of knowing that, I believe, because her death would not have been publicized, and Millie was known to our neighbors as Millicent Greene. When I fell so ill and didn't get my strength back, I knew I had to find him." The same fury assaulted her as when she learned of the effrontery of Millie's cowardly husband by hiding away to become a minister. "It's ironic, but the same means that alerted me to your son's whereabouts elevated him!" She intercepted the blank gaze between the Scotts but continued, "I wrote to him here in San Scipio and told him Millie died in early 1871 and asked him to contact me."

Judith heard the bellow of a terrified bullock that had escaped its master and burst into view not far from where she stood. The rage and pain resembled that in Lige Scott's voice. "Then that's why he—my son, my son!"

"Sir, I can never tell you how sorry I am to come here, but Joel must have someone in case I can't go on." Her low voice echoed in the too-silent room. Spent, Judith leaned back against the cushions of the settee.

"Then our son still doesn't know he has a child?" Naomi inquired. Her face sagged with shame. "Such a beautiful little boy to be fatherless for so many years." She patted Judith's hand. "You were right to come, my dear, although the shock is almost more than can be borne. Elijah, we will open our hearts and home to these orphaned children, both of them."

Before he could reply, two persons simultaneously entered the hall. Joel ran back in from the courtyard, his face lighted with happiness. A tall man with sun-streaked hair and an open face hurried inside. Their paths collided. A last-minute catching of the child in his arms saved Joel from a nasty fall. "Whoa, there, muchacho." The man laughed down into the child's face, then went blank with astonishment. "Why, who are you?" He whirled toward his parents and Judith.

In a sudden motion, Judith sprang to her feet and planted clenched fists on her hips. "You are Gideon Carroll Scott."

He looked amazed and set Joel down. "I don't think I've had the pleasure of meeting you, Miss."

"Nor I you." Judith clenched her teeth. "Joel, Dear, would you go back into the courtyard for just a few minutes more?" She forced a smile.

He sighed, and she knew he sensed the undercurrents that were turning the placid room into a sea of emotion. His feet dragged, and the joy of discovery he'd shown before now was sadly lacking.

"Is something wrong?" A shadow came into the young man's blue eyes. "That child, he looks so much like—"

"Why shouldn't he look like the Scotts?" Judith cried, her nerves strained to the breaking point. "He's *your* son!"

"*What?*" Gideon stepped toward her. "Are you an escaped lunatic?"

"Gideon!" Lige thundered, and Judith observed the profound change in the man. His shoulders squared. Life flowed back into his face and, with it, the darkest fury she had ever seen in a human's face.

"What's this all about?" Gideon demanded. He planted fingers in her shoulders and held fast. "How dare you come here with such a story!"

"Do you deny it?" Judith tore herself from the cruel grasp.

Gideon's face flamed until he looked like an avenging angel. "Deny it! My dear woman, you must be mad."

She lost control. "Then deny this." She snatched the carefully preserved wedding certificate and thrust it into his face. "Gideon Carroll Scott and Millicent Butler, my half sister, united in holy matrimony, July 29, 1869, in New Orleans. More like unholy matrimony." A sob escaped despite her best efforts. "You married her, carried her off for a few days, then deserted her. Your child was born the following April."

"It's a lie!" Gideon yanked the paper from her hands. His face turned ghastly. "I never even heard of a Millicent Butler, let alone married one. Father, Mother, you don't believe this woman, do you?"

"Do you deny you were in New Orleans at that time?" Judith prodded, while something inside her wished he could.

"Of course not. Cyrus and I were both there. I'd just started studying to be a minister." He looked at the wedding certificate, then started. Color poured into his face, and he squinted and peered again. "This isn't my handwriting, even though it looks like it."

"And I suppose this isn't, either." Judith produced the farewell note in its dilapidated state.

"I don't understand." Gideon went white to the lips. His eyes blazed like twin coals. Then recognition set in. "There's been a terrible mistake."

Why should her heart leap? What was this stranger to her? Judith's nails dug into her palms until they ached.

"What have you done, Gideon?" Lige marched to his son, his face a mask of stone.

"Why are you so willing to believe that I am guilty?" Gideon shouted. "I tell you, I've never seen this woman or heard of her sister." All the longing of years for his father's approval blended into his cry of despair. "If you want the truth, find Cyrus. It would be like him to marry someone using my name, and he's always been able to imitate my writing."

Crack. Lige's mighty open hand struck his younger son with such power that Gideon staggered. Bright red replaced the white of his left cheek. A suspicion of froth ringed Lige's mouth. "How *dare* you accuse your brother of your wickedness? I won't have it, do you hear?"

Gideon didn't give an inch. His eyes blazed. "Can't you even trust me until I can prove you're wrong? I have no son, and I have had no wife."

Something inside Judith turned over. If ever a voice and face proclaimed the truth, Gideon's did. Uncertainty gnawed at her. Could this young man honestly be the victim of a sadistic joke?

"Judy, are you all right?" Joel's eyes looked enormous, and he raced back inside to his sole source of comfort. "Everyone's yelling. Let's go somewhere else."

Where? rang in her brain, yet she kept her voice quiet. "If someone will drive us back to San Scipio, we'll go away. Perhaps I can find work in El Paso." *If we have money enough to get there*, she thought. Suddenly Pete's weathered face came to mind. Surely he'd help her, lend her enough to go on. Besides, God wouldn't let them down, ever.

"The child stays here." Lige, more in control than ever, belligerently stepped between Judith and the door.

"My Judy, too?" Joel rushed in where angels would have hesitated on the doorstep. He looked anxiously up at Lige.

"Of course." With a visible effort, the tall man tempered his voice. "Boy, do you like horses?"

Joel allowed himself to be sidetracked. "P'r'aps. That's what Judy says I must say when I don't know." His enchanting, innocent laugh lightened the atmosphere. He looked around the room, cocked his head at Gideon, and said, "Why do you look at my Judy so? Don't you like her?" He sat down on a stool and put one hand beneath his elbow and his chin on the supported hand. "We came such a long way. But if you don't want us, we have to go."

Naomi gave a little cry and clapped her hands. "We want you very much, Child. You're our own—" She bit off the end of the sentence and called to the maid. "Carmelita, take Miss Butler and Joel to the big room with the alcove." She then explained to Judith, "It has a small bed in the alcove for Joel and a large bed for you. I'll send up hot water immediately. Would you like supper trays instead of coming down tonight?"

Her thoughtfulness, coming so close on the cease-fire of hostilities, left Judith unsteady. "If you'd be so kind. I know Joel is exhausted."

"So are you." Naomi put a strong arm around the frail shoulders that had carried such heavy burdens for so many years. "Don't worry about anything. Whatever has happened is done and not the child's or your fault. You are welcome here, and we will talk later when all of us are less upset. Now go with Carmelita."

It seemed a long walk from the big hall to the airy rooms, but Judith rightfully attributed it to her fatigue. Even Joel acted subdued. Unused to scenes and fiercely loyal to his Judy, the little boy clung to her hand and walked sedately instead of skipping as he normally did. "We don't have to stay," he repeated after Carmelita left them. "It's nice, though." He walked to the window and looked out into the courtyard. "The flowers are pretty. Did God make them?"

"Yes, Dear." Almost too tired to respond, Judith strove to bring a more normal tone into their conversation. Time enough later to sort everything out. First she must bathe Joel, see that he ate, force food into herself, and put her charge to bed. She hadn't counted on Naomi Scott's graciousness. She herself appeared with the maids bearing hot water and supervised the filling of the tub screened off at one end of the room. She then carried Joel to her own quarters, returning later with a rosy boy in place of a dusty one. Naomi remained with them until Joel fell asleep, then personally tucked Judith into an enormous bed, plumped the pillows, and dropped an impulsive kiss on the young woman's forehead.

"Don't worry about a thing." Her gaze turned toward the worn Bible. "You're a Christian, aren't you?"

"Yes, for all my life."

"I am so glad." Naomi patted Judith's hand, then knelt by the bedside. "Our Father, we thank Thee for the gift of Thy Son. We thank Thee for sending these, Thy precious children, to us. We do not always comprehend Thy ways, but help them to know Thy loving care is around them, and grant them peace and rest. In the name of Thy Son, Jesus. Amen."

When the tears of weakness crowded Judith's eyelids, she simply squeezed Naomi's hand, which rested on hers, and listened for the closing of the massive door. She had thought she would lie awake for hours. Instead, she fell into a deep and dreamless sleep.

Judith awakened at sunrise when a cock crowed. The thick adobe walls shut out the sounds of the house, but through the open window came noises she had come to identify with life in the West. Too tired to care, she gratefully remembered Naomi's admonition to sleep as long as she could. She turned over and closed her eyes again.

"Judy, are you awake?"

She stirred from the fathoms of deep sleep to discover Joel in his night-shirt standing by her bed. Automatically, she scooted over and made room for him. The long rest had done its work well. Today might bring more problems, but at least she had survived the confrontation with Gideon.

Her heart lurched, and again she wondered why she should find it impossible to believe Gideon Carroll Scott's treachery. She considered it with part of her mind while answering Joel's chatter. Connecting such a frank-faced young man, who looked every bit the part of a man who longed to serve his God with his all, with what she knew of Millie's husband and Joel's father took more imagination than she owned. If she hadn't had the marriage certificate, the farewell note, and the young man's face stamped in miniature every time she looked at Joel, Judith could never have believed what had to be true.

"Judy. *Judy!*" Joel shook her arm hard, slid from bed, and ran to the window looking out toward the corral. "Come quick. There's a baby horse looking in our window!"

Almost as excited as the child, Judith dropped her meditations and sped across the large, richly carpeted room. *Dear God*, she prayed, *we've been in some pretty strange places, but this is the first time You've ever led us to one where we wake up and find a horse staring in at us.* Laughing at herself, she hugged Joel and said, "Let's get dressed. Who knows what's next?"

Chapter 8

From that first San Scipio sermon, Gideon loved his chosen work. He rode early and late seeking out isolated families, bringing the kind of ministry they most needed: not always a retelling of the gospel, but a living message of Jesus Christ that permitted and encouraged his participation in whatever the family might be doing. Whether rounding up strays, branding cattle, or even digging postholes, the most hated cowboy chore, Gideon had experienced the tasks on the Circle S and was an able helper.

"I never heerd tell o' no preacher doin' sich things," one grandmother protested. "Jest don't seem fittin'."

"Now, Granny." Gideon gave her the smile her Irish grandmother said warmed the cockles of her heart. "Remember how Jesus worked in the carpenter shop? I'll bet if He were to drop in, He wouldn't command you to leave bawling cows that needed herding. No, He'd take care of the work first, then have words for you of an evening, when the sun's ready to hit the bunk and let the moon have a chance to shine."

"You shore talk purty. Say, Gideon, when're you aimin' to find yourself a gal and git hitched?"

Gideon threw back his head and laughed. Mischief twinkled in his eyes. "Granny, are you proposing to me? Why, I believe you are. You're blushing all over your face."

"Go 'long with you, Gideon Scott. Don't you know a preacher's s'posed to be serious?" she scolded, even though she couldn't help laughing.

Gideon shook his head. "I find a whole lot more places in the Bible where we're told to be glad and rejoice than to go around with a face so long it's in danger of getting stepped on." He warmed to his subject. "When Jesus says He came to bring life and to bring it more abundantly, I believe that included real happiness and laughter. If more folks could see that, more of them would want to follow Christ."

"I plumb agree," the old woman said surprisingly. "There's enough miz'ry in life without it creepin' into religion."

"Good for you, Granny!" Gideon shook her hand, amazed at her hard strength and insight into things eternal. "Tell you what. First time I get to feeling bad, I'll ride back over here and let you preach me a sermon."

"I kin do it, too," she boasted, and her dark eyes sparkled. "How do you think I raised me five fine sons?"

Her question perched on Gideon's saddle horn when he turned the sorrel mare Dainty Bess toward home. Of all the horses on the Circle S, he liked her best, but he saved her for riding and chose heavier stock for working the range. From earliest dawn to last daylight, he rode and roped, talked with his heavenly Father, and prepared down-to-earth, practical sermons suited to the San Scipio area. No lofty sentiments could ease the harshness of life in West Texas in the 1870s. Gideon's prayers that incorporated pleas for today's strength and tomorrow's hope offered his widely scattered and diverse congregation a rope to which they could cling in times of trouble and happiness.

Cyrus's continued absence remained the one thorn in Gideon's side. The young minister had made surreptitious inquiries but so far had run into only dead-end trails. If a tornado had swooped down and clutched Cyrus, his disappearance couldn't have been more complete. Again and again, Gideon prayed for his brother, whose wasted, reckless life lay heavy on Gideon's soul. "Oh, God," he cried a hundred times. "Somehow, make Cyrus see and know how much he needs You." Yet weeks drifted by with no trace of the missing brother.

That one thorn also wedged itself into the new and tenuous relationship Gideon and his father had begun to develop. Gideon spent every spare minute he could find trying in some small way to replace Cyrus. Not in Lige's affections, but merely in working on the Circle S. While he would never be as proficient in range work as the superbly trained Cyrus, the long hours in the saddle plus practicing with rope and gun brought their rewards.

"Seems strange for a preacher to be practicing shooting," he told Lige one late afternoon when he had brought down a hawk threatening the baby chicks Naomi adored.

"God forbid you ever have to use that gun except in times like these." Lige nodded at the downed hawk. His face, which had grown more downcast since Cyrus rode out, turned hard. "You won't always be where you're known and have the backing of friends. Son, when that time comes, remember this: If those who test you know you can shoot and shoot well, chances are you're less likely to have to than if you never packed a gun and relied on being a preacher to protect you."

It was a long speech for his father. Gideon took a deep breath. "Thanks." The word *Dad* hovered on his lips but wouldn't come out. Not since Cyrus left had he felt he could say it, for Lige had returned to the forbidding father figure of childhood.

One morning when Gideon had ridden into San Scipio, Sheriff Collins sought him out. Long and lanky, his soft-spoken way hid iron nerves and sinews. "Heard anything of Cyrus lately?" he asked in his searching drawl.

"Why, no," Gideon said, his heart beating faster. "Have you?"

The sheriff shifted his quid and spat an accurate stream of tobacco juice into the street. "Naw. Just curious as to why he'd ride out so suddenlike." He grinned. "I consider myself a brave man, but I don't plan to ask your daddy about it."

"I don't blame you." A look of understanding passed between them. Gideon decided to lay his cards on the table. "Sheriff, it's half killing my father. You know how he is about Cyrus."

"Huh, everybody knows. Rotten shame how blind a man can be when he sets such store in his son and won't hear a thing against him." A heavy hand came down on Gideon's shoulder. "Is there anything I should know?"

"I've racked my brain over and over. All I know is that Cyrus planned to be at the church dedication. Then he rode into town, got some kind of letter, and said he was riding out." Gideon didn't add the part about Cyrus's strange talk, asking Gideon to promise he wouldn't go back on him, forgiving seventy times seven and the like. "All I could figure is that Cyrus had been gambling and someone threatened to come collect. Father hates any kind of betting. Even Cyrus couldn't get away with that." He wrinkled his forehead. "Except if that's true, why hasn't whoever wrote the letter shown up?"

The sheriff glanced both ways. No one lounged within earshot. "Something you ought to know. I saw the envelope. It came from New Orleans."

A rush of blood flowed to Gideon's head. *"New Orleans?* But Cyrus was only there that one time five years ago. He never writes letters, didn't write to me once while I was gone. Who could be trying to contact him after all this time?" The idea troubled Gideon. Surely if Cyrus had been up to his usual tricks, it wouldn't take this long for a cheated or irate gambler to trace him.

Sheriff Collins spat again. "If I were a gambling man, which I ain't, I'd bet that if I could find that letter, some of the mystery might get solved." He grinned companionably at the younger man. "Now, it's none of my affair 'less I get a complaint. Like I said, I'm just interested."

"Thanks, Sheriff." Gideon slowly walked into the general store and made his purchases, absently noting the way Lucinda Curtis bustled around and made a great show of efficiency in waiting on him. He tipped his wide hat politely and backed out, then filled his saddlebags and headed home. *Would it be wrong to search Cyrus's room?* Never had he trespassed on the unwritten law of privacy Lige established between the brothers when they were small. Did the desire to know where Cyrus had gone—and why—warrant breaking this tradition?

Anything that would straighten things out and bring Cyrus back to Lige was justified. Gideon couldn't bear seeing his father turn more and more inward with each passing day. Naomi hadn't expressed her concern verbally, but it showed in her gaze at her husband.

Rejoicing in the thickness of walls that muffled and silenced movement in other parts of the adobe ranch house, long after every light had been extinguished for the night, Gideon crept into his brother's room. Except for the clothing that Rosa and Carmelita had hung up, nothing in the room showed signs of entry. Gideon forced himself to go through each drawer of the tall chiffonier, each pocket of the clothing in the closet. Not a telltale scrap of paper showed itself. But why should it? Gideon remembered as clearly as if it had been only an hour ago how Cyrus's fingers had strayed to his breast pocket that morning in the courtyard.

"Too bad he didn't change clothes," the searcher muttered. He tried to put things together in sequence. Evidently, Cyrus had received bad news from the letter, yet it had been the night before when he demanded loyalty from his brother! Had Cyrus carried a guilty secret, perhaps for a long time, that he knew would be exposed someday but hadn't expected it to happen so soon? It seemed the only explanation. Either that or a premonition of trouble ahead so strong it forced him to ensure Gideon's support.

Gideon carefully replaced everything he had disturbed in his fruitless search. He also spent a long time praying for Cyrus before he fell asleep.

Several days later, Gideon headed for home in the late afternoon on Dainty Bess. Usually the horse whinnied when he turned her toward the ranch house and corrals, but today she stepped as lightly and smooth gaited as if they had been on the trails for an hour.

"Good girl." Gideon patted her silky mane, then relaxed in the saddle. One of her best qualities was the little guidance she needed, especially on the trail home. Gideon's mind stayed free to pursue his thoughts and dreams. When the mare stopped of her own accord on the mesa above the ranch, Gideon was roused from his comfortable slumped position in the saddle.

"Dust cloud. Wonder who's at the ranch?" Gideon waited to let Bess's heavy breathing from their climb return to normal, then headed down the trail. "It's Ben, from town. He's sure making tracks with that buggy." Gideon raised one eyebrow. The towheaded youngster's driving skill and carefulness beyond his years certainly didn't match the way that horse and carriage pelted away from the Circle S.

Dread filled Gideon. Perhaps someone in town had been hurt or needed him. Or something had happened to Cyrus. . . He touched Dainty Bess with his boot heels, scorning the spurs most cowboys used. "Hi-yi, Ben!" Bess picked up speed and flashed down the winding wagon road toward Ben. Gideon pulled her in short, and Ben stopped his panting horse. "Somebody hurt or dead?" Gideon demanded.

Ben shook his head. "Comp'ny at the ranch."

Why does the boy look so upset? Gideon wondered. A reader of faces, he saw disillusionment, anger, and the desire to get away rise in Ben's eyes. "Is something wrong?"

"Find out for yourself." Ben clucked to the horse and drove off, this time at a pace more fitting for the climb from valley floor to the mesa top.

"Something's sure eating him," Gideon commented and watched the buggy until it turned the bend and slipped out of sight. "First time he hasn't been friendly." He thought of the faithful way Ben and other young people came to church and of the high hopes he held for their salvation. He knew Ben had accepted the Lord in his heart, but so far he hadn't made it public. Gideon knew he would wait until the Holy Spirit did its work, so he didn't push. Besides, boys like Ben—and the way he'd been at fifteen—had to be *led* to the Master, never driven.

In spite of his eagerness to discover who Ben had delivered to the ranch and why it upset the boy, Gideon rubbed Dainty Bess down and watered her before going into the house. He hesitated on the cool porch, held for a moment by the same feeling he'd experienced those times before a storm. Silence, ominous and threatening, filled him with a reluctance to step across the threshold into the big hall.

To make up for his anxiety, he hurried inside, his long steps eating up the polished floor. A small blue and white and gold whirlwind raced in front of him. Unable to stop his momentum, Gideon snatched up the little boy and held him with strong arms. "Whoa there, muchacho." First he laughed, but then as he peered into the child's eyes, he felt the blood drain from his face. "Why, who are you?" He turned toward his parents. A strange young woman exploded from a settee and planted clenched fists on her hips. Travel-stained and dusty, with dark brown eyes that matched her coiled, braided hair, she glowed with an unearthly light. "You are Gideon Carroll Scott."

How could five simple words carry so much hatred and reproach? Gideon mumbled something and put down the child, who slowly went into the courtyard at the stranger's bidding. Who was she, and who was the child who looked enough like the Scotts to be one?

Ice water trickled in his veins. "Is something wrong?" Gideon asked. "That child, he looks so much like—"

Then it came. The squall Gideon had known lay waiting behind the closed ranch house door. "Why shouldn't he look like the Scotts?" Beautiful in her scorn, the young woman faced and indicted him. "He's your son."

The room spun. *Is the woman mad?* An eternity of accusations followed, along with a wedding certificate bearing his name. *Dear God, this can't be happening!* Gideon turned to his parents for comfort. *They can't believe this preposterous claim, can they?* His heart turned to a lead ball and sank to his boots. Lige believed the charge. It showed in every terrible twitch of his shaken body.

"This isn't my handwriting." He tried to defend himself. The girl produced a second piece of evidence, and light broke. *Cyrus.* Cyrus, who would stop at nothing to get what he wanted and leave others to bear the blame and shame. A flash of insight solved the strange pleas for seventy times seven forgiveness. *No, God, not this time. Let Father see what his precious older son has done.*

Gideon cried out his defense and received a blow that bruised his face but cut into his heart. Even the flicker of doubt in the woman's eyes when he proclaimed his belief that Cyrus had done this couldn't change a father's loyalty to one son at the expense of another. The temper Gideon had inherited but tried to control blazed. "Can't you even trust me until I can prove you're wrong? I have no son, and I have had no wife!" Again uncertainty showed in the watching dark eyes. Then the child called Joel ran back, frightened, needing reassurance. Gideon couldn't move, not when the stranger said they would go. Not when Lige protested. Not even when Joel asked with childish perception, "Why do you look at my Judy so? Don't you like her?" Only when Carmelita led the visitors away did strength return to Gideon's limbs and free him from the paralysis of shock.

"Father, I have never asked much from you, but I ask you now. Do you honestly believe that I am capable of marrying a woman, then deserting her?" Gideon knew his future hung in the balance. He saw doubt rise in his father's eyes. He saw the massive head begin to shake from side to side and the mouth form the word, "No." Then a transformation killed the final hope struggling for life in the young minister's breast. His mouth tasted the ashes of dishonor placed on an innocent man.

"The child is a Scott." Lige's sonorous voice rolled his verdict into the hall, where it hung in the air.

"I am not the only Scott who lived in New Orleans in the summer of 1869," Gideon said rashly, as if pouring kerosene on the fire of Lige's reactions.

"Only a sniveling coward puts blame on a man who is not here to defend himself," Lige bellowed. He raised his hand to strike again the son who dared accuse his favorite.

"No, Elijah!" Naomi planted herself squarely in front of her enraged husband. "We have never known Gideon to lie." Magnificent in her rare opposition to the lord of the household, she held him at bay in defense of her man-child. "There is more to this than we know. I feel that. Until we find the truth, we will keep the child and the young woman here."

"The truth? Woman, what more evidence do you want than a marriage certificate in your son's writing—" Gideon winced at the words *your son,* but Lige went on. "Also a note and the child himself!" Suspicion blackened his face. "Or are you also accusing Cyrus?"

"I am accusing *no one,* despite what you call evidence." Naomi didn't give an inch. Her face the color of parchment, her blue eyes shone with the fire of motherhood roused on behalf of her young. Gideon's cold heart warmed. All the adoration and love the lonely little boy had poured out on Naomi when denied his father's affection paled into insignificance when compared with what he felt for her now.

"Someday I will prove what I say is true," he promised. Before either could reply, Gideon turned on his heel and went out, his steps echoing in the hall. *How? How? How?* they mocked.

By finding Cyrus. The answer came sharp and bright as a lightning flash. He must leave San Scipio, find his brother, and for the first time in his life, force Cyrus to take the consequences of his actions.

Gideon's lips twisted bitterly in sharp contrast to their usual upward tilt. Father would rage and fume, but in the end, he'd be so glad to have his object of adulation back, the anger would dwindle and vanish. The presence of a grandson's softening influence would finish the job. Lige would cling to the boy as a second Cyrus.

"Father will also probably coerce Cyrus into marrying the woman," Gideon whispered into Dainty Bess's mane when she came at his whistle. "God forbid! Any woman who marries Cyrus will be in torment, especially one as untouched and frail as she." Yet what else could she do? Her gown bore mute witness of poverty. Her eyes showed she would never have sought out Joel's father unless she had come to the limits of her strength and ability to care for her nephew. How old was she? Eighteen? Twenty? She had cared for four-year-old Joel when little more than a child herself.

Respect stirred within him. Although he hated what she had done to his life with her false accusation, how could he help but admire a plucky girl who had become a mother by necessity? Gideon thought of the look in her eyes when she first announced him as Joel's father, something she obviously believed. Never before had he seen reflected in anyone's face the belief that he was despicable, beyond contempt.

His jaw squared. "Dear God," he breathed and swung into the saddle for a healing ride, forgetful of the fact he hadn't eaten since breakfast. "Any man who would do what she believes I did to her sister deserves that look." Shame for Cyrus and the passionate wish his brother had been different rose into a crescendo of protest. "Someday, somehow, with Your help, I'm going to prove to Father and to her I am innocent!"

Yet a jeering voice so real it rang in Gideon's ears and beat into his tired brain continued the measured cadence begun by his boot heels in the hall. Over and over the questions *How? How? How?* tormented him until he thought he would go mad.

Chapter 9

In the mysterious way Noami had always used to calm her stubborn, volatile husband, she again prevailed. Lige's first decision to disclaim Gideon as his son fell before her reason. While Gideon and Dainty Bess spent the night outdoors and an emotionally exhausted Judith slept soundly, Naomi's quiet voice and Lige's rumbling continued. Shortly before dawn, Naomi fell into a restless sleep, but Lige addressed Almighty God. Hadn't God put fathers in control of their sons? he reasoned. The Bible offered countless examples of what happened when those fathers allowed wickedness to creep into their homes. Lige therefore told God what he planned to do to straighten out the mess, then fell asleep justified.

For the sake of bright-faced Joel, whose winning ways had already softened Lige's stern outlook on life, all discussion was held in abeyance until Carmelita took the boy to the kitchen, where Rosa welcomed him with a smile and a hug. Lige waved the family into a small sitting room. "I have considered this whole unpleasant matter," he began.

Gideon made a sound of protest that died in his throat when his father glared at him. He glanced at Judith, white-faced and still. *How horrible this must all be for her,* he thought. First the long, tiring trip, then a plunge into confusion. Although she admitted she had slept, dark circles still haunted her eyes.

"Your mother has requested that I wait to pass final judgment on your actions." Lige's stony face showed doing so went against everything he believed. "Very well. You say Cyrus is somehow involved, which of course is impossible, but I will give you one month to see if you can locate and bring him back to the Circle S." A world of longing tinged his words. "Miss Butler, according to your story, you sent a letter to Gideon?"

The accused minister could keep silent no longer. "I never received a letter, but when Cyrus said he was leaving, he had a letter in his pocket." Gideon ignored Naomi's warning look. "Sheriff Collins in town said he saw a letter from New Orleans."

"Sheriff Collins?" Lige's face turned purple. "You dared discuss Cyrus with *him?*"

"Father, he asked where Cyrus had gone and brought up seeing the letter."

Cunning and pride resulted in Lige barking, "And did he say he saw the name of the person the letter was addressed to?"

Gideon's heart sank, knowing which turn the conversation had taken. "No."

"See?" Lige turned triumphantly to his wife. "Miss Butler's letter, if this were it, obviously came to Gideon."

"Then why did Cyrus open it?" Gideon demanded. "You trained us from the cradle that a sealed letter to another family member was not to be tampered with."

Lige shrugged. "Perhaps the seal had been broken."

"Then why didn't Cyrus just give me the message? Why did he ride away and say he might never come back?"

"I am not on trial here," Lige roared. "Neither is your brother. Before God, if it were not for your mother, you'd be sent packing." The veins in his neck became cords, pulsing with angry blood. "Gideon Carroll Scott, I offer you a month, for the sake of Naomi's pleading. If by that time you haven't proved to my satisfaction your innocence in this affair, San Scipio will know of your guilt. That is my promise."

Any chance of ever proving Cyrus guilty to his father seemed slim. Yet a month could change much. "I will leave today." Gideon stood, and his mouth set in a straight, grim line.

"Remember, one month. Not a day longer." The judgment followed Gideon when he stepped into the hall. Yet he was not to leave the ranch without one more disturbing interview. An hour later, he had packed what he needed, saddled Dainty Bess, and bade his mother good-bye. Lige had ridden out after delivering his ultimatum without another word to his son. Torn between what lay ahead and had been, Gideon lightly mounted Bess.

"Wait, oh, please, wait!" Judith ran toward him, casting a furtive glance back at the house. She obviously didn't want to be observed. Her dark eyes caught gleams from the sun, and she looked distraught. "Mr. Scott, I don't see how you can be innocent, but if I have falsely accused you—if indeed this brother has used your name—I hope you find him."

The unexpectedness of her seeking him out left Gideon speechless.

She stepped closer and peered up into his face. "Good-bye, Mr. Scott. May God—" She broke off as if not knowing what to say to him.

"Miss Butler, even if I can never prove it, I am not guilty in spite of the apparent evidence against me. Do you believe me?" Suddenly it seemed imperative that she do so.

"I don't know. It doesn't seem possible that you, a minister of God. . .you seem so honest and yet. . ." Her voice trailed off.

"I thank you for coming out here," he said softly. Then he touched Dainty Bess with his heels and rode away, not looking back but still able to see the troubled girl with her dark eyes that tried to look into his very soul.

Judith's slight change of manner toward him raised his spirits. So did the long, impassioned prayer he made near a big rock off the trail a few miles from the Circle S. "Dear God, You know I am innocent. You know I have no way to prove it. Your power can open doors I don't even know are there. You can uplift me and lead me to Cyrus. Surely this is why he ran away."

Gideon determinedly put aside what could happen if he caught up with his brother. By some means, Cyrus must be made to return to the ranch and clear his brother's name. Yet as the days flew into a week, then another, doubts clouded the searcher's mind. He could not find a trace of Cyrus. What if all these weeks he had lain somewhere in the canyons or over a precipice, the victim of an accident or foul play? The thought whitened Gideon's lips. He hadn't even considered such a thing, but now it seemed highly possible. Cyrus often consorted with evil men who knew he liked to carry money on him. Why hadn't he thought of such a thing before?

"Because of the way he left," Gideon told Dainty Bess. "He planned to go for some unnamed reason. I believe Judith Butler's letter forced his hand."

More days passed. By the end of the third week, Gideon daily stormed heaven. "Dear heavenly Father, ever since I gave my heart to You, I've tried to follow in the footsteps of Your Son. Where are You now? I need to find Cyrus. Only You know where he is. Why aren't You leading me to him?" Always after such a prayer, the young minister experienced pangs of guilt, but low anger also rose. He read the Bible, noted the promises, and prayed again.

Sometimes he wondered if the prayers even got beyond the wide sky above him. Bitterness as acrid as the alkali water he found in distant waterholes seeped into his soul. Was this how the Israelites felt when they wandered in the desert? Forsaken, deserted, and so alone they could barely go on?

Miles from the ranch with a few days left, Gideon turned back. He had considered vanishing the way Cyrus had done, but he rejected it as the coward's way out. Once more he would stand before his father and ask for mercy and trust. If Lige withheld it, Gideon would turn Dainty Bess back to the trails, never to return home.

✢

From the moment Gideon disappeared from sight, a time of waiting began for the Circle S, especially for Judith. She often wondered what strange impulse had caused her to seek out the young man with the sun-streaked hair and starlight in his blue eyes. At times she prayed for him in a stumbling manner that reflected her troubled mind. On one hand, there was the written evidence; on the other, there was the spirit of a man who looked into her eyes and pledged his innocence. Like a weather vane subject to each change of wind, so Judith veered from disbelief to a wavering acceptance of Gideon, the minister, as compared with Gideon, husband and father. Then again, the very beauty of his face could be what deceived Millie so thoroughly. Judith grew weary thinking of it.

In those waiting days and weeks, Joel, however, thrived as never before. Besides the love Naomi and Lige had for their new grandson, the good food and fresh autumn air bolstered the joyful child. The "baby horse" that had peeked in the window that first morning became Joel's own. In a specially designed saddle Lige proudly said he had fashioned when Cyrus was small, Joel jounced and bounced around the corral pulled by a lead rope and loved every minute. He lost some of his toddler chubbiness and gained a tanned complexion from endless hours outdoors.

"Judy, are we going to stay here f'rever and f'rever?" he anxiously asked one day when they sat together in a porch swing.

"Do you like it here that much?" She held her breath, almost hating to hear the answer she knew would come.

"Oh, yes!" His twin sapphire eyes glowed. "Gramma and Gran'pa and Rosa and Carm'lita's so nice." His joy dimmed, and he scooted closer to her. "Don't you like it, too?"

"I love it." She felt his little wiggle of joy. "I just don't know if the Scotts w—want me." Judith hated herself for the break in her voice.

Joel climbed into her lap. "Don't be sad, Judy." He stroked her now rounded cheek, a result of proper food and freedom from responsibility. "Gran'pa says if you and Gideon get married, everything will be all right."

"*What?*" She set the child farther out on her knees so she could look directly into his face. "Joel, are you making that up?"

His sensitive lips quivered. "I don't tell stories, Judy. You said God doesn't like it."

She could still scarcely believe his childish gossip. "I know, Dear, but think very hard. Did Mr. Scott really say what you told me?"

He nodded vigorously until his blond curls bounced. Anxiety still filled his eyes. "That's 'zackly what Gran'pa said. Don't you want to marry Gideon?"

"I barely know him," she retorted, then hugged Joel hard. "Don't worry about it." But she sensed the resistance in him.

"Judy, you wouldn't ever go away and leave me, would you? Not even here." He slid down from her lap and leaned against her arm. "I heard Gramma say her boy went away and left her. Not Gideon. Another boy."

"I won't leave you," she promised. Yet deep inside, the thought formed, *If this is what Elijah Scott has in mind, how can I stay?* Once the hateful idea had been so carelessly planted, Judith felt on edge. She caught the appraising looks Lige gave her now and then and appreciated the way Negro slaves must have felt on the auction block. *Sold to the highest bidder! Given in marriage to appease a powerful man who thought he could play God!* In her thoughts, Judith bitterly parodied an imaginary auctioneer.

Her turmoil continued. She wanted to ask Naomi about the diabolical plan, but she dared not. There had been no word from Gideon in the days and weeks he had been gone, and such talk would upset her more. If Naomi knew and approved of the plan, the seeds of trust growing between them would be permanently thwarted; if she didn't approve, how long could she hold out against the driving force of her husband? If only Gideon would return with Cyrus! Night after night, Judith prayed for it to happen. Nothing could be worse than this prolonged silence, not knowing what might happen next, now that Joel had innocently betrayed Lige's scheme.

The charming San Scipio area and the Circle S offered as a respite a variety of places to ride. Judith soon outgrew the capabilities of the gentle horse assigned to her and took on a trustworthy but more spirited pinto named Patchwork. By the time Joel and his pony graduated from the corral to short rides near the ranch, Judith had already explored much of the surrounding countryside. Autumn frosts had wielded their paintbrushes and left behind brilliant colors in the hills and valleys, mesas, and the deeper canyons. Joel loved to roll in piles of leaves whipped off the trees by capricious winds, but only after Judith had carefully stirred them to make sure no snakes lurked in their depths. At times, when she could put aside her fear of the future, Judith found herself laughing as she hadn't done since Millie died.

"I like you when you laugh," Joel told her solemnly, and she realized that through the years, even her best efforts to keep cheerful for him hadn't been a complete success. Now, although the strain of Gideon's return remained, the freedom given her by Naomi and Lige and the servants' eagerness to watch Joel had left its mark. Judith's favorite place to ride was the mesa top above the valley because it offered the widest view for miles around. Near the end of the fateful month of Gideon's grace, Judith found she paused there often, looking for the dust clouds that heralded riders. A few times they came, but Gideon didn't.

On the morning of the thirtieth day, Lige laid down his breakfast fork. Judith had long since learned to rise when the Scotts did and earn her keep and Joel's by working as a daughter of the house, although she was gruffly told it wasn't necessary. Joel usually awakened then, too, but this particular day, Judith had left him sleeping in his alcove.

"You know what day it is." Lige's voice sent shivers up Judith's spine that intensified when she saw that same look she had observed before, when he appeared to be measuring her.

"We know, Lige." Naomi smiled and passed freshly made apple butter to Judith for the hot biscuits Carmelita brought in. "It will be nice to have Gideon home again." She calmly ate the scrambled eggs still on her plate. "Folks have been wondering why the business you sent him on is taking so long."

Judith choked and buried her face in her napkin. When she emerged, Carmelita had gone back to the kitchen and Lige sat staring at his wife, then glanced meaningfully at Judith. She murmured a hasty, "Excuse me, please, I think I hear Joel," and escaped.

After she had helped him dress and sent him to Rosa for breakfast, she slipped out, saddled her horse as she had learned to do, and rode slowly away from the ranch. Patchwork danced a bit but settled down to her quiet command, "Steady there, Girl." The now-familiar track to the mesa top invited her, and once there, she scanned each direction. Relief filled her. No riders. Yet the day had only begun, and hours would pass before the stroke of midnight.

Twice again that day Judith saddled and rode to the mesa. Once she saw Lige's mighty horse ahead of her, and she rode behind concealing bushes until he had gone. The second time, in early evening, her sporadic vigil paid off. Dust clouds in the early blue dusk hid whoever made them, but Judith's heart thudded. Suddenly afraid of the next minutes and hours, she raced back to the corral, hastily unsaddled, left Patchwork to the ministrations of one of the hands, and ran into the house.

"There are dust clouds on the road from town. I couldn't see who or how many. . . ." She couldn't bear the unreadable expression on Lige's face, the open apprehension that shone in Naomi's eyes. "I must change my clothing." She managed a shaky smile at Joel, who sat on his grandmother's lap holding a picture book.

Why had she ever thought the waiting hard, she marveled while bathing, then donning a clean dress. Naomi had wasted no time in helping her nearly destitute guest sew a few simple house gowns and one dark dress suitable for church. Judith smoothed the pale green folds, then more firmly anchored her coronet of braids. At least the wanderer would return to a well-groomed houseguest instead of a travel-worn visitor. The irrelevant thought brought color to her face.

Before she got to the big hall the family used most often in the evenings, now warmed by logs in the enormous fireplace against the ever-colder nights, Judith peered out a window that overlooked the front of the house. Dainty Bess, a horse more worn than any she had seen, stood with drooping head. Judith then fixed her gaze on the matching figure who slid from the saddle and buried his face in the horse's mane before leading her to the corral. The fruitless journey showed in the sagging shoulders and slow steps. Judith strained her eyes, desperately hoping to see a second horse, a second tired figure, and turned away stunned to realize how disappointed she felt that Gideon had come back alone.

She slipped into the warm room, and Joel ran to her. Together they curled into a massive chair, where Judith's filmy gown made a splash of light against the tapestry. The atmosphere felt thick enough to cut. Dreading the moment when Gideon would come in, she nevertheless wanted to see him. At least the uncertainty would end.

With slow steps dragging from fatigue, Gideon faced his father, his judge. Gone forever was the boyish face Judith remembered. In its place was a strange countenance whose tired body still carried a dignity of its own that could not be denied, except by the one who refused to see it.

"*Well?*" Lige's question snapped like a whip.

"I couldn't find Cyrus."

"The month is up." Relentless, unforgiving, and self-righteous, Lige Scott folded his arms across his mighty chest. "I have done what your mother asked. Now you will do what I command."

Naomi ran to her son and wordlessly embraced him. Judith saw in her a beaten woman, at least for now. Yet she released Gideon, clapped her hands sharply, and waited until Carmelita came in. "Please take Joel to his room."

"Yes, Señora." Joel ran to her, and they disappeared. Childish laughter mixed with Carmelita's natural joy drifted back, but the lines in Lige's face did not soften.

"I have considered what God would have me do," he announced.

Judith wanted to shriek. *God! When have you ever listened to God?* Every prayer she had heard him make since she arrived was telling God how things would be, a kind of after-the-plans-formed courtesy.

"Considering all the circumstances and knowing that even as God condemned Eli for not controlling his sons, so shall he not spare fathers who permit wickedness in their family, I offer you two choices." He hesitated, and the world stood still.

"The first is to confess your sins before your congregation, to repent and seek God's forgiveness, mine, and then the people's. If they will accept it, you may continue shepherding the flock."

"You ask this of *me?*" Gideon threw off all evidence of weariness. "To stand before my people and *lie?* Father, how can you?"

Judith thrilled to his final stand for justice, but Lige's answer cut into her thoughts like a knife through a ripe peach. "It is no lie." His mighty fist crashed down on the table before him. "You had your chance to prove the falsehood against your brother. Will you accept this penance?"

"*Never!*" Gideon drew himself to full stature. "I have never lied, and I never will to save my reputation or my life."

A curious look of—was it relief?—crept into Lige's eyes. "There is a second way. The child's future must be assured. You will marry Miss Butler, become the father to Joel you should have been for years, and take the place on the Circle S of the brother you so mysteriously drove away." Lige's thundering voice cracked on the last words.

Chapter 10

At first his father's outlandish suggestion of marriage didn't register with Gideon. His brain focused on the shocking accusation that he had been responsible for Cyrus leaving. A coldness that matched West Texas in January blanketed him. The next moment, he went white-hot, grasping the full significance of Lige's decree. But before he could respond, Judith sprang up to confront her host.

"How *dare* you play God and dispose of your son's and my lives like this?" she cried. Gideon thrilled at her courage. "You think forcing us to marry will solve everything?" Her ragged laugh reminded Gideon of a dull saw pulled through hardwood. "I know nothing of this son Cyrus who ran away, but the more I hear of him, the more I believe it's possible he did just what Gideon said, married Millie under an assumed name to cover his wicked—"

"Hold your tongue, Miss Butler. You are in no position to say what will or won't be in this household." The normal timbre of his voice added a deadliness his wildest ragings never achieved. "A grandfather's claim to Joel will outweigh yours, especially when I can give the boy everything and you are obviously penniless and dependent on charity." An unpleasant smile under raised shaggy eyebrows drove home his point more clearly than the threat.

"You couldn't be so cruel as to take Joel." Judith knew she fought against terrible odds. "I wish to God I had never let you know of Joel's birth. Better for us both to have starved in New Orleans or even for him to have been taken from me than to know he must live where every thought is controlled." Her eyes blazed. "And you call yourself a follower of the meek and lowly Jesus!" The rasping laugh came again.

"Elijah Scott, I am ashamed of you." Naomi took Judith in her arms. "If you drive this girl away—and your *second* son—I will also leave and take Joel."

"*Mother!*"

"*Naomi!*"

Gideon and Lige's exclamations blended. Disbelief gave way to knowledge. Naomi Scott meant every word she said. Her set face showed this was no careless thrust meant to hold her husband at bay. She looked at him over

Judith's shoulder. "I mean it, Elijah."

"You, too, would desert me?" His face worked, an awful thing for Gideon to behold. Once he had witnessed a beaver dam crack, crumple, and fall before a relentless, flood-swollen stream. Now his father evidenced the same signs.

"First Cyrus, then Gideon, and now Naomi. What have I done to deserve such misery?" Stubborn to the end, it was apparent he could see no wrong in himself.

Gideon couldn't stand any more. His father had been driven to the dust by phantoms real and imagined, by an unreal pride in his elder son and utter faithlessness in his younger. Gideon licked dry lips and with pounding heart said, "Miss Butler, will you do me the honor of becoming my wife?"

He hadn't thought Judith could turn more pale. From the shelter of his mother's arms, Judith whipped around and stared at him. "No, oh, no!"

"Wait," he implored, conscious of Lige's open mouth and the way Naomi's arms dropped from Judith's shoulders. "It will be an empty contract shoved down our throats for Joel's sake. I knew when I came back unable to prove my innocence, I could never stay on the Circle S. God has allowed me to stand guilty in the eyes of the world and of San Scipio when they learn of this affair." He laughed bitterly. "Well, I'm through trying to preach and lead people to a God I can't trust. I'm riding away. Miss Butler, you won't be troubled with the presence of a husband, even one in name only. Don't answer now, just think about it." He turned to Lige. "Will that suit you?"

Stricken dumb by Gideon's shocking capitulation, Lige mumbled, "No need to ride off if you marry."

"There's every need," Gideon contradicted and felt his chest swell. "I wouldn't even consider such a thing if I planned to stay." He glanced at Judith, marble white and still. "Take what time you need before you answer."

"Even if she should agree, how can you accomplish this?" Naomi's eyes reflected all the doubts he felt but shoved back in favor of necessity.

"You three and Joel can go by stage to El Paso. I'll start ahead of you with Dainty Bess. We'll find a justice of the peace, and once the ceremony's over—" He shrugged, and his mouth twisted. "You'll return here, and the happy bridegroom will ride north or west or anywhere on earth that leads away from San Scipio."

Lige's stunned brain came to life. "What's to prevent you riding on and not meeting us in El Paso?"

Gideon couldn't believe what he heard. If he needed further proof his father didn't trust him, he had it in that one sentence. "It's hardly likely I'd suggest marriage if I didn't intend to be there, is it?" He swept aside any chance for an answer. "Miss Butler, just let me know if you'll be willing. I won't interfere with your life. After I'm gone for a time, you'll have no problem providing grounds for an annulment." He threw his shoulders back and walked out, little caring where he went. Had he been loco to propose marriage to this stranger? He shrugged. Why not? God wouldn't send a helpmeet for a minister whose faith had gone sour, a God who turned deaf ears to His follower's cries for help and left him to bear the stain of a sin not his own.

For three days and nights, Gideon spent little time at the ranch. He gave Dainty Bess a long rest and rode Circle S horses from early to late. He pilfered food from the kitchen after Rosa and Carmelita had finished for the day and avoided meals with the family. He grieved at the look in his mother's eyes, went out of his way to keep his distance from Lige, and hardened his heart against young Joel, who trotted after him. He observed Judith only from a distance. A few times he caught her dark and troubled gaze on him, but he only tipped his sombrero and walked on.

The fourth morning, early, he noted with satisfaction the toss of Bess's head that showed her eagerness to be out of the corral and back on the trail with her master. She came at his whistle, and he stood with one hand on her mane, his face toward the west. "It won't be long, old girl," he promised. She softly nickered and lipped the oats he held in his hand.

"Mr. Scott?"

Gideon turned. He hadn't heard Judith come up behind him. "Yes?" His muscles tensed. Something in her voice set blood racing through him.

"I–I have thought about your proposal." The rising sun lent color to her smooth cheeks and flicked golden glints into her dark coiled braids. Her hands lay clasped in front of her simple workdress. "For Joel's sake, if you meant what you said about going away and this not being a real marriage, I accept." Color richer than from the sunrise flowed into her face. "I never intended to marry, so it will impose no hardship on me to bear your name." Anguish filled her eyes. "I cannot face life without Joel, and as your father said, I have no way to care for him."

Filled with sudden pity, Gideon dared touch her hand for a moment only. "Look, Miss Butler. . ."

"Judith."

"Judith." He took a deep breath. "If the idea of this contract is repulsive to you in any way, we won't go through with it. I'll help you fight Father for the right to keep Joel and see that you find work somewhere." He watched the glad surprise that lightened her countenance give way to reality.

"I've gone over and over everything," she said simply. "I can't take the chance of falling ill again. Neither can I stay on the Circle S unless we marry, as your father wishes." Her slim shoulders shook, then squared. "I suppose in his place, I might feel the same." She managed a little smile. "It's too bad, Mr. Scott. In other circumstances, perhaps we could even have been friends."

"Then you believe in me a little?" It suddenly seemed more important than anything else in the world.

"A little."

Something within Gideon released its painful grip on his heart. He caught her hands. "Judith, if the time ever comes that I can prove my innocence, may I come back? I'm not asking any more of you than what we've agreed on," he hastily added when color rose to her hairline. "Since God has forsaken me, I need to have a dream."

"God never forsakes us, Gideon." She looked earnestly into his eyes. "Right now it seems that way to you, but no matter where you ride, remember, He's there."

He started to speak, to protest and deny, but Judith said, "Perhaps one day you will return, absolved of guilt." Her voice dropped to a whisper. "Shall we tell your fath—your parents?"

"Yes." He released her hands and followed her into the house.

Less than a week later, Judith Butler and Gideon Carroll Scott were married in a dusty El Paso office by a justice of the peace who mumbled what should have been beautiful words. Gideon thought he would scream. What a far cry from the joyous weddings he had performed! When he looked at the young woman beside him, however, an excitement he hadn't counted on shook him to his carefully polished boots. How beautiful she looked in a soft yellow and white gown, yet how little he knew of its past. Joel innocently repeated Judith's explanation about the dress.

"Judy said it came with us from New Orleans," Joel marveled. "In the bottom of the trunk. Mama brought it to Judy even before there was me, when she came home from getting married. Isn't it funny?" Pearly white teeth and a laugh like chiming bells made Joel roll with mirth. "Now Judy's getting married in the very same dress."

Had she worn it to test him? Gideon wondered. If he really had married Millicent, surely he would recognize the gown. Curse Cyrus! Not only had Cyrus ruined his opportunity to minister in San Scipio, he had blotted out all chances for a normal life. What would it be like to have Judith as his real wife, to ride and laugh and love and serve with him? The scales dropped from Gideon's inner vision. He stared at Judith and missed some of what the justice of the peace was droning.

He loved her. Of all the girls in the world, how could God allow him to meet and marry Judith Butler, whose best efforts at comforting him only came to trusting and believing in him a little?

"Place the ring on her finger and repeat after me," the official ordered.

Gideon obediently took the slim hand in his and slid on the plain gold ring he had purchased in El Paso. "I, Gideon, take thee, Judith. . ." A sudden longing to take her and ride away to a place where they could build a new life with Joel left him weak with longing, regret, and a renewed anger at Cyrus. He finished his vows, heard her low responses, and felt her hand tremble in his. Caught up in the desire for his marriage to be more than an empty contract, when the justice of the peace said, "You may kiss your bride," Gideon bent and kissed Judith full on the lips.

"Oh!" Reproach crept into her eyes, red to her face.

"Must a man apologize for kissing his wife?" Gideon recklessly whispered. Spurred by the knowledge that he was about to ride away forever, he kissed her a second time, then hurried her away from the curious eyes of the amazed witnesses. Once outside, he swung into the saddle and picked up the reins.

"Gideon, when are you coming home?" Joel called from the circle of Judith's arms.

"I don't know." His heart ached. Somehow he couldn't say the word *never.* "Father, Mother, good-bye."

Naomi's steady gaze never left her son's. "Vaya con Dios." *Go with God.*

Gideon looked at his father, stunned to see him nodding, silently adding his benediction. Last of all, he turned sideways in the saddle and faced Judith. The red lips he had kissed moved in a wordless farewell, and something in her eyes flickered, an expression he could not describe or understand.

In another moment, he would bawl like a heifer stuck in a thicket. To cover the love he knew must be shining from his face, Gideon mockingly called, "Good-bye, Mrs. Scott," and pressing his heels into the horse's sides, rode away. His added words, "God keep you, my darling," were lost in the clatter of his horse's hooves and died undelivered in the dusty air.

The tumbleweed trail swallowed Gideon as it had swallowed hundreds of pioneers before him. Old, young, wicked, misunderstood, restless, and driven, they thronged west, away from homes and families. They were a breed apart in a land that cared less about a man's past than what he would become.

Into this new world that made West Texas look tame by comparison rode Gideon, tormented by God's failure to help him and his new love for a wife he could never claim. In lonely campfires, he saw her smile; sunrise on the water brought back the dawning day when she said she would marry him. Her dark eyes stared at him from every shady trail, and her spirit rode beside him until he sought out the company of others, no matter how undesirable, to drive away memories. In the wasteland between sleep and waking when no man can control his thoughts, Gideon dreamed of a day when he could go back honorably. He awakened, haunted by the realization he had nothing to offer her even if he proved Cyrus's guilt and cleared his own name. Judith had miraculously retained her deep faith in God through everything life dealt her, whereas he, a minister, had not. His broken faith and corroding soul could never be "equally yoked" with Judith's unswerving faith.

A hundred times he told Dainty Bess, "If only things had been different, what a minister's wife she would be!" He often felt guilty for marrying her, although she had asserted she had no interest in marriage. Suppose she met someone who changed her mind? Would she feel bound by those mumbled vows and give up a chance for happiness? He writhed, jealously cringing at the thought of Judith as another man's wife.

Weeks later, he rode into the mining country of Colorado through snow that clogged the horse's hooves and slowed them until he wondered if they could make it. His present apathy left him caring little for his own life, but he pressed on because of his faithful horse. Bess deserved better than death in a blizzard because her cowardly owner holed up and froze. Now at the bottom of his stores of flour, beans, and rice, and without hope of finding fresh meat, blood rushed into his face when he reached to the very bottom of his saddlebag and found a small sack. "What on earth—" Gideon stared at the contents. *Money.* His cold, bewildered brain couldn't understand. Had some outlaw who crossed his trail and shared his grub left it there, a rude payment for kindness, stolen from some bank?

Suspicion crystallized and became belief. The odd look in Lige's face, especially just before he rode away from El Paso, provided the answer. Had Father carefully hidden the money, knowing Gideon would only find it when he had exhausted his reserves?

From despair to renewed determination, Gideon knew now he would go on. He would search and find Cyrus or somehow make the folks back home proud, the folks and Judith. For the first time in days, he permitted himself to think of her. Strange how after all this time, every meeting with her stood etched against the stormy background of their acquaintance. Most often in his thoughts, he saw her in that yellow and white dress, his unclaimed bride.

Wise in the ways of evil men, Gideon sewed his money into his clothing and kept out only enough to hire rude lodgings for the winter. He couldn't expose Dainty Bess to the freezing days and colder nights. Besides, until spring came and he could travel, it didn't matter where he stayed. Gideon settled down into his new world and became part of it.

For the first time, he patronized the gambling halls, never to bet heavily but enough to feel the deadly hold on men's hearts and souls. Was this how Cyrus had felt, urged on and radiant when winning, desperate when luck smiled on others and turned a cold shoulder on him? In an amazing streak of luck, Gideon won a sum large enough to send a gleam into the eyes of those at the table. Unwilling to become the target of men who thought nothing of killing for gold, he took advantage of an old trapper's offer to accompany him on his lines and get away from town. All winter, he remained with the mountain man but refused to go mining the next spring.

"You've been good to me," he told the bearded miner turned trapper. "Here, take this grubstake. Find yourself a mine."

"If I do, I'll find you and pay it back," the man promised. But Gideon laughed and rode away. The chances of striking it rich always loomed large in the men's minds.

He drifted north through Colorado and Wyoming, then into Montana. Spring, summer, and fall, he hired out on ranches, glad for the riding and roping. Yet in late fall, almost a year from his hasty wedding and departure from Texas, he faced himself in a bunkhouse mirror far from home and sighed. Money, he had. Comrades, as many as he would let be friends. Peace, there was none.

He scowled. *Was there no spot on earth where he could be at peace with the past?* Drifting hadn't been the answer, but neither had ignoring God. He remembered the kindliness of the trapper and the long, companionable tramps on the trap line. The next morning, he quit his job and rode south in search of another quiet winter like the year before. To his amazement, hordes of people had poured into the area.

"What's happening?" he demanded of a red-faced cowhand hitching his horse to a rail before a new saloon.

"Where yu been, Mister? Thought everyone knew about the boom." The amiable cowpoke grinned and told Gideon a miner had struck it rich nearby, bought half the town, and was "nee-go-she-ating" for the other half. "If yu want a job, his office is over there." The hand pointed to a new log building across the busy street.

Curious, Gideon ambled over and was met with a bear hug like he'd never had before. The strike-it-rich miner was the same man who had taken Gideon on his line and been grubstaked by the Texas rider. His gratitude knew no limits. He installed Gideon in the best room in the finest hotel that had sprung up and opened an account for him in the new bank that made the young man's eyes pop.

He also gave Gideon some advice. "Son, I don't know where you came from, but if you're as smart as you appear to be, you'll buy yourself a ranch somewhere, maybe Arizona. You've got enough money to stock it and hire good hands. Find yourself a pretty western gal, have some kids, be happy. Wish I'd done that."

Gideon's heart leaped at the idea of owning a ranch, but then his mind intruded. What good would it be without the wife and kids he could never have? A mocking little voice added what his heart could not, *What good without Judith?*

Chapter 11

The second winter Gideon spent in Colorado was nothing like the first. No longer a trapper's helper but a valued friend and guest in Tomkinsville, as the boom town was now called after its new owner, he spent his days playing cards in the saloon. He even picked up the coarse language of his fellow gamblers, drank for the first time in his life, and bitterly blamed God for his past. His one pleasure in his downward slide was that he now used his treacherous brother's name as his own. If anyone had told Tomkinsville that "Cyrus Scott" had once been a preacher, no one would have believed it. The few times he allowed himself to drink too much, he passionately hoped news of his tough reputation would get back to his father. If it did, Lige would admit fault in the son he had felt did no wrong.

Gideon also learned to fight and licked a half dozen cowhands known for their skill with fists. He carried his gun, remembering Lige's words that men would respect him once he'd proven himself.

Ironically, the situation Gideon had avoided like riding through a cactus patch prompted his first gunfight. A young woman named Lily, the newest of those who sang and danced in the saloon, caught his attention. Her dark eyes reminded him of Judith, and she didn't seem to belong. He befriended her, then encouraged her to leave and go elsewhere. If Lily stayed in this ungodly atmosphere, she wouldn't be able to hold out for long.

"I've got plenty of money to get you started," he told her simply. Some of the old goodness that life had erased from his face shone again. "Is Lily your real name?"

She shook her head, and red flags waved in her dusky skin.

"Good. Go to Denver or Colorado Springs or anywhere. How did you ever fall into this miserable life, anyway?"

"My parents died. I had to do something to live." Lily suddenly looked older than her seventeen years.

A pang went through Gideon. *Judith had been desperate, too, trying to earn a living for herself and Joel. What if she were forced into such work?*

Never! his mind shouted. He squared his shoulders. *Neither should this young woman.* He waited while she gave notice to the saloon owner, then escorted her to the first outgoing stage, warmed in spite of the snappy cold weather by her broken, "God bless you."

Gideon's action did not endear himself to the saloon keeper and his friends. A few days after Lily left, Sears, the biggest and meanest of them, drawled, "Too bad the rest of us ain't well heeled like Scott here. We coulda set Lily up right smart an' had us a cozy little—"

A well-placed blow cut off the suggestion. His eyes blazing, Gideon leaped from his chair at the card table and faced the foul-mouthed man. "It's men, no, *animals* like you that ruin women who have nowhere to go. You're a rotten lot!"

"An' you think *yore* better?" The humiliated Sears reached for his gun. Gideon's shot knocked it out of his hand before it ever cleared the holster.

"One more crack like that about any woman, and I'll kill you!" He backed from the saloon into black night, his gun held steady in case one of the others tried anything. Once outside, he dodged behind buildings, more afraid of himself and God than of being followed. What had he come to— Gideon Scott, whose bright and promising career had been cut off?

Revulsion filled him. His stomach heaved, and it took supreme control to keep from retching. Once he could have defended Lily by using God's Word. Now he looked down at the gun he still held. Cold sweat drenched him. Had his threat been valid? Would he have killed another human being?

Somehow he reached his hotel room and barred the door. When he lighted his lamp, the wild-eyed apparition he beheld brought his gun up until he realized he faced the mirror above the bureau.

"Who's there?" Gideon spun. The room lay silent, empty except for himself and his mirrored reflection. "Who spoke?" he demanded, wondering if he were going mad, trying to remember where he had heard those words and when.

"The prodigal son." Gideon dropped heavily onto the bed. "Luke 15. 'A certain man had two sons.' " Uncontrollable laughter shook him. "And all these years I thought the story reversed, that the elder son, Cyrus, was the prodigal!" The rest of the parable on which he had preached a half dozen sermons came back: The younger boy went to a far country, wasted his money in riotous living, and found himself in want, hungry and sick. " 'And when he came to himself, he said—' " Gideon choked. " 'Father, I have sinned against heaven.' Oh, dear God, what am I doing here?" Desolation greater than any he had known swept through him. Tonight he might have killed a man. If he kept on with the way he now lived, he couldn't avoid bloodshed. He had seen it in the eyes of the onlookers when he drew his gun with lightning speed. Every would-be gunslinger jealous of his reputation would be standing in line. Kill or be killed, the law of the frontier.

Yet unlike the repentant sinner in the parable, Gideon could not return to his earthly father. He could always return to his loving heavenly Father and find peace and a measure of comfort that might help to heal his shattered, lonely life. Before he slept, he had poured out his heart in prayer and slept as he hadn't slept since he left the Circle S. Tomorrow he would follow his benefactor's advice and ride out and find a ranch somewhere. Arizona appealed to him: plenty of land for those who were willing to work for it, defend themselves from Apaches, and dig in. Something of the range-loving boy he had been still lived inside Gideon. After a prayer of thanks to God for bringing him to himself, he slept and dreamed of a new, brighter day, one that might sometime lead to exoneration and Judith.

With a thundering knock and crashing of wood, armed, angry men stormed into his room later that night. Gideon bounded from bed, trying to make sense of the confusion. A match flared. Rude hands grabbed him. Oaths fell on his ears like hail. "Git yore pants on," he was ordered while someone lighted the lamp.

With a wrenching effort, he tore free. "I demand to know why you are here." Something in his face halted his attackers but not for long.

"Yu've got yore nerve. First you shoot up Sears in the saloon, then trail him to his shack an' knife him."

The low grumble sent horror into Gideon. He had heard of mobs who hanged accused persons first and asked questions later. "Fools," he cried. "I could have killed him when I shot him, you all know that. Why would I wait and take a chance of him getting me?" He saw uncertainty grow in some of the faces. "Do you think I'm that loco? Your friend outweighed me by at least forty pounds."

"What good is that when some jasper sticks a knife in your back?" someone called. The crowd's mood turned ugly again with "Hang him" and "String him up" heard from all corners.

"That will be just about enough of that." The quiet but deadly voice from the doorway stopped the yelling. Tomkins stood cradling a sawed-off shotgun. He patted it significantly. "This gun here's touchy, boys. Used it to stand off claim jumpers, grizzly bears, all kinds of undesirable critters." He looked at Gideon. "What's all this uproar?"

"Sears and I had an argument. He drew on me, but I beat him and shot the gun out of his hand, then came home. I don't know anything more. These, er, gentlemen seem to think I sneaked up on him and knifed him."

"You didn't, did you?" Tomkins's eyes gleamed.

Gideon shook his head, but someone cried, "He lies!"

For a single heartbeat, Gideon once more stood defying his father. The same words he used with Lige fell from his lips in a hotel room hundreds of miles away. "I have never lied, and I never will to save my reputation or to save my life. I know nothing of who stabbed Sears." He tensed, ready to spring if Tomkins didn't believe him. When the big head nodded, Gideon relaxed.

"D'yu have a knife?" an unconvinced man bellowed.

"Of course. Every rider carries a knife."

"Look like this one?" The triumphant man held out a knife, careful to touch only the tip.

Gideon shuddered at the ghastly dark stains on the blade that glinted wickedly in the dimly lit room. "It's ordinary enough to look like mine."

"Where's yore knife?" the questioner demanded.

"In my saddlebag hung on the nail in the livery stable," Gideon told him.

"Who knows it's there?" Tomkins asked with a concerned expression on his lined face.

Gideon shrugged. "Anyone who may have looked in the saddlebags." Alarm triggered inside him.

"How come yu leave yore knife there?" the persistent voice went on.

Gideon put both hands on his hips and glared. "I've never used a knife except for range work. I didn't think I'd need it here in the hotel."

"Best we mosey on down to the stable and have a look-see." Tomkins stood aside to let the others pass, then ordered, "Stop! On second thought, I'll just make sure no one decides to tamper with evidence by removing Scott's knife just as a friendly little joke." His tone left no uncertainty as to the fate of a person who tried it.

Gideon pulled on his clothes and a heavy jacket, glad his bankbook lay carefully hidden inside the jacket lining. If the worst happened, perhaps he could leap to Dainty Bess's back and ride out.

Ten minutes later, Tomkins unwillingly ordered the sheriff to lock up Gideon until the case could be looked into more thoroughly. There had been no knife in the saddlebag, and Sears lay close to death. "If he doesn't make it, you're safer here than at the hotel," Tomkins told the despairing young man. He scratched his grizzled jaw. "Don't worry. We'll get to the bottom of this, but I wish to God you'd taken my advice and got out of this place before getting yourself into trouble."

"So do I," Gideon said soberly. For a moment, he felt tempted to confess who he really was, how he'd taken his brother's name and hours before realized the dead-end trail he'd been riding. Realizing it could do more harm than good, he said nothing.

Strange how many times he had felt the silence before a storm. When Tomkinsville settled down for the rest of the night, not a dog barked. Even the light snow that had fallen earlier in the day ceased. Yet Gideon felt the same eerie sensation that preceded Cyrus's flight and Judith's arrival. Would he have another night of life? Would Tomkins's power in the boomtown be enough to sway the mob if Sears died?

"Well, God, if this is my last time to tell You I'm sorry for everything, especially for not trusting You, so be it." Gideon flung himself on the miserable excuse for a bed and hoped San Scipio would never learn what had befallen the minister they once revered.

Anxious days and high hopes followed black nights and despair for Gideon. Sears began to mend, then suffered a relapse. For three days, Tomkinsville held its breath but not its invective against the coward who had knifed him. Finally, the big man turned toward life and in a couple of weeks regained enough of his strength to respond to questions. Yet he seemed strangely reluctant to talk.

"Don't know what's got into him," Tomkins admitted with a worried frown. "Says he plans to talk when it will do the most good, at the trial." He sent Gideon a keen glance. "I'll be glad when this is all over. If you're cleared, you better skedaddle out of here. This whole thing has left a bad taste with folks. Even if you're innocent, you won't be popular in these parts." He stretched his big body. "Leastways, he didn't die. The most you can be charged with is attempted murder, which is bad enough."

After Tomkins had gone, Gideon met the Lord in prayer. "Dear God, is there a reason behind all this?" He refused to let his friend bail him out. Uncomfortable as it was, the jail offered a certain security in case Sears took a turn for the worse again.

Lulled by a sunny day that promised an early spring but had blizzards lurking up its sleeve, the citizens of Tomkinsville turned out in droves for the trial. Before going to the saloon-turned-courtroom, used because it was the largest building in town, Gideon prayed. "God, I have no defense but the truth. I commit my life into Your hands." He stopped, remembering the shock in Tomkins's face when he handed him the precious bankbook wrapped in brown paper and addressed to *Mrs. G. Scott, c/o Circle S Ranch, San Scipio, Texas*. "If anything happens, mail it."

Tomkins peered at the address. Gideon could see questions trembling on his tongue, but his loyal friend merely pocketed the package. "I'll return it after the trial," he said brusquely.

Colorado justice, often swift even when it wasn't sure, dragged while the prosecutor reached into his bag of tricks to impress the inhabitants of Tomkinsville. He painted a picture of the accused man that would have done Satan himself proud. In awful, rolling tones, he built up a setting in which Gideon, angered by his failure to kill Sears in a fair fight, vindictively followed the other man like a wolf stalking its prey. If Gideon hadn't known better, he would have been swayed by the man's false but vivid reenactment of attempted murder.

Under oath, Gideon admitted his knife had disappeared and the one used on Sears looked like it. However, he maintained that his shot in the saloon had gone exactly where he aimed it. "Sir, I've never killed a man, and I didn't mean to kill Sears."

"Then why did you say, and I quote, 'One more crack like that about any woman, and I'll kill you!' " The prosecutor fairly oozed satisfaction.

"I was angry."

"So angry you followed Sears and tried to finish the job." The prosecutor turned to the judge with a deliberate gesture. "I rest my case."

Tomkins himself had elected to defend Gideon. He grinned when he stated flatly, "I'm no lawyer, but I carry considerable weight around here." Now he leisurely stood and walked to where he could face Gideon yet not block the judge's view of his face. "How long have you known me?"

"About a year and a half."

"Tell the court under what circumstances we met."

Gideon couldn't follow the line of defense in Tomkins's thinking but obediently recited, "I came here a year ago last fall, did some gambling, and won some money. Thought I'd be better off away from town, so I went trapping with you for the winter."

"And you grubstaked me in the spring so I could go back to mining. Me, a trapper and miner who'd never had much more than the clothes on my back."

"Yes."

"Judge, this man is the real reason why Tomkinsville is booming. If he hadn't been good to a broken-down old miner, why, none of our prosperity would have come!" He waved an expansive hand. "I tried to find him and repay him after I struck it rich, but it wasn't 'til he drifted back down from Wyoming and Montana that I could locate him." He stepped closer to Gideon and clapped him on the shoulder. "Scott's no more capable of knifing anyone in the back than, than you are, Judge!"

"Prove it!" shouted the red-faced prosecutor.

"I call as my witness, Eb Sears."

Gideon gasped, as did the judge, the prosecutor, and every man present.

"Now, Mr. Sears, tell us in your own words what happened," Tomkins said, "and tell it straight."

Before he began, Sears shot an unreadable look at Gideon. "Aw, I was drunk and loud. Said some things about Lily I knew weren't true. He hit me. I got mad and drew. So did he." Sears pointed to Gideon, who silently prayed and clenched his hands into fists.

"In your opinion, did Mr. Scott try to kill you and miss, the way the prosecutor said?" Tomkins probed.

"Naw." A reluctant respect and a personal code Gideon wouldn't have expected from Sears straightened the slumping witness. "He's chain lightnin' and could shoot the eye out of a mosquito."

A little ripple of surprise ran through the room, and Gideon felt himself start to sweat. The next few moments could mean the difference between conviction and freedom.

"Mr. Sears, under oath, did Cyrus Scott knife you? You've been strangely silent ever since it happened."

Sears scratched his head. "At first, I thought so. Seemed logical. Then I started wonderin'. If he wanted to kill me, he shore coulda done it in the saloon, with everybody there havin' to testify I drew first. Naw, I don't think he knifed me."

"Do you have any idea who might have?"

Stone-cold, dead silence followed the question.

"Mr. Sears, I repeat, do you have any suspicions? Did anyone hate you enough to do this?"

Sears grunted. "I ain't the best-liked hombre in Tomkinsville." He hesitated, then said, "I've had a lot of time to think. Maybe it wasn't exactly me someone was after."

The ripple grew to a murmur, stilled when the judge banged his gavel on the bar. "Silence!"

"Just what do you mean?" Tomkins leaned forward. So did Gideon.

Sears squirmed. "I don't like accusin' anyone, but certain folks were real upset when Lily up and left."

"How do you know that?" Tomkins's voice cracked like a bullwhip.

"Lily told me." Red crawled into the tanned face. "Said when she quit, the boss ranted and raved and said he'd get even with Scott." The red deepened, but Sears looked square at Tomkins. "Maybe he saw this as a good chance. Besides, we'd had a fallin' out over the girl. I was sweet on her, and so was he, and 'til Scott came, she sorta liked me. I'da married her." He hung his head and stared at the floor. "That's why when I said all that stuff about Lily I knew wasn't true, it was 'cause I was jealous." His head snapped back up. "I shouldn't have been. Lily told me flat out Scott never asked nothin' from her, which is more than some—"

"*Liar!*" The saloon owner stood and clawed for his gun. "Too bad you didn't die when I knifed you."

"Hold it right there." A gun had miraculously sprung to the visiting judge's hand. Tomkins and the sheriff disarmed the raving man, whose tongue had been loosed by too many drinks he had served to his friends and himself, celebrating Gideon's conviction prematurely.

"Best one I ever had here." His eyes blazed hatred for both Sears and Gideon. "Those innocent types bring in customers, but she'd have come around if it hadn't been for you." He spat in their direction. "Can't tell me Scott doesn't have her waiting for him somewheres. Men don't help women like Lily unless there's something in it for them. I fixed him, stole his knife—"

The judge cut into the babbling. "Mr. Scott, you are cleared and free to go. Sheriff, lock up this murderer! He's confessed, and I sentence him to. . ."

Gideon missed the rest amid the wild cheer that shook the rafters. With Tomkins leading him, he walked out, feeling free and dirty. His sin had led to this moment, and he knew it would take a long time to rid himself of the taint of Tomkinsville.

Chapter 12

J ust before Christmas of 1876, Gideon, who had now reverted to using his own name, reined in his horse and surveyed his earthly kingdom. After traveling through much of Arizona, thrilled by its deserts and plateaus, chastened by the expanse of blue sky that make the red-rock canyons and monuments even more torrid, he had found the Double J spread not far from Flagstaff. *The name holds a certain appeal*, he ruefully admitted.

He sobered when he considered what Judith and Joel would think of Double J, surrounded by oak and manzanita, sage and pine. There were cattle enough for a good start, thanks to Tomkins. One thing Gideon had done before leaving Colorado was to seek out those whose money he had won in gambling and repay them. He would not begin his rededicated life with the Lord by building on tainted money nor under a false name. Before he left Tomkinsville, he told the whole story to his benefactor.

"You love the lass, your wife?" Tomkins shot a keen glance into his eyes.

"More than life, second only to God."

"Son, things have a way of working out. Go on out to Arizona. Get settled. Be God-fearing, honest, and work hard." Wistfulness crept into his eyes. "If I were younger, I'd go with you." But Tomkins shook his shaggy head. "Maybe one day you'll see me come riding in if my luck breaks. I've got a lot salted away, but as long as I keep finding more, I suppose I'll stay here."

"You'll always be welcome." A hard grip of hands, and Gideon rode away knowing he'd always have a friend in the man he once so carelessly helped.

Now he sat easily in the saddle and wondered what came next. He'd been from Tucson to the Grand Canyon of the Colorado River, from the White Mountains to the Mogollon Rim and into the Tonto. Yet something about the Flagstaff area held him. He thought of the group of settlers who had camped there not long before. They made a flagstaff from a pine tree and flew the American flag from it. Folks said the incident provided the name for the birth of a town.

The knowledge of men Gideon had gained both from preaching and wandering proved invaluable in selecting cowboys for the Double J. "Don't hire just anyone," Tomkins had warned. "Handpick wranglers who'll give you loyalty, not just a day's work."

Gideon heeded the advice. He never hired a hand who couldn't look him straight in the eye without wavering. He never hired a man who shifted when he spoke. He made it clear there would be no red-eye on the job, and if he heard of any man getting "likkered up" on Saturday night, that hand could pack his gear and ride out.

"Aw, Boss, what're you runnin', a Sunday school?" Gideon's foreman, Fred Aldrich, complained. "How'm I s'posed to keep a wild bunch of cowboys workin' if they can't bust loose on the weekends?"

"When you hire them, tell them what the rules are and remind them we may have a hot enough time if the Apaches hit us," Gideon told him.

Aldrich heaved a sigh clear from his dusty boot tips to the crown of the sweat-stained Stetson that shaded his keen, dark eyes. "We're gonna be the laughin' stock of all Arizony," he muttered, but faithfully carried out his orders. Because Gideon knew his standards would make it hard to get riders, he not only paid top wages but promised that any cowboy who stayed a year or more would get a bonus. The offer, a share in the Double J or a good horse and saddle, hit Arizona like a desert storm. Aldrich stuck his tongue in his cheek and solemnly confirmed the offer, sourly adding, "That's what comes of havin' a boss from Texas. Thinks his way's the only way, and shoot, he might just be right!"

Wide-shouldered, grinning cowboys, some still in their teens, came out of curiosity but stayed because of their new boss. They differed from the Texas cowboys in subtle ways. Arizona demanded more daring men because of its raw newness. It cared little for background, everything for the measure of a man. Gideon's outfit answered to names like Lonesome and Cheyenne, Kansas and Dusty. No one asked where the riders came from, and prying into a rider's past was taboo.

Gideon sometimes found this tolerance maddening, and he blew up to Aldrich one day. "Everyone knows that Stockton, who's planning to run cattle in the Tonto, is a notorious outlaw going respectable."

"Shore, Boss. Arizony's always willin' to give a man a second chance." He shrugged. "This territory's gonna be a state someday, and if it takes reformed crooks to do it, so what? Out here, long as a man's goin' straight, we figger more power to him." He half closed his eyes. "On the other hand, we also keeps our eyes peeled so he don't go back to his takin' ways, takin' other folks' property."

Gideon subsided. Who knew better than he the need for a second chance?

FRONTIER BRIDES

Although the Navajo had been put down, their final defeat coming in a fierce 1864 campaign led by the famed scout Kit Carson, the Apache had not. Small bands terrorized and raided. Cochise and Geronimo were names to respect. They led warriors against forts, towns, and lonely ranches, but the settlers were still determined to find homes. Hunted and forced farther back into the remote and seemingly impenetrable canyons, infuriated by broken treaties, the original Arizona inhabitants fought for their lives.

So far, the Double J hadn't been a target, but the threat was ever present. In some ways, Gideon pitied the Navajo and Apache. How would he feel if a horde of strangers came in and took his land? Even in the short time he had owned the Double J, he had grown to love it. With every sunrise, he looked east and thought of the past. Each sunset brought a feeling of well-being along with gloriously painted skies. He had finally conquered the poignant regret of his sins; if God had forgiven him, he had no right not to forgive himself. A desire to return to the Lord's service haunted him. Yet how could he?

That desire continued to grow. Now and then, he rode into Flagstaff on Sunday, wishing there were a church. His restlessness finally made Aldrich ask, "What's eatin' you, Boss? Yore jumpier than a fish swimmin' upstream."

Gideon took a deep breath. "Fred, what would the boys say if I invited folks out from town, anyone who cared to come, for Christmas? We could decorate and have candy for the kids and read the Christmas story out of the Bible. Sing songs, too."

Aldrich considered. "Might not be a bad idea. I reckon the boys could stand such goin's-on for once." He cocked his head to one side. " 'Tain't none of my business, but who're you aimin' on havin' read that story?"

"I thought I would," Gideon told him frankly. He looked around the large room. "Think it will hold everyone?"

"All those who'll come," Fred said cryptically. "The boys and me can stay in the kitchen if this room fills up." He grinned. "It'll be pure pleasure for us to do yore decoratin' after all the hard work we've put in this fall. By the way, Boss, now that winter's comin', what about the hands? Are you layin' them off like most of the other ranchers do?"

"Nope. Every day that's nice enough, we'll be busy working. I want this ranch house expanded. We'll add a second story—"

"Whoopee!" Aldrich's face split wide open, and he howled like a banshee. "You must be aimin' to get hitched, huh, Boss?"

Gideon's excitement died. "No."

Red faced, Aldrich broke off his rejoicing. "Sorry, Boss." He hastily stood

104

and mumbled, "I better go see what the boys are up to. Anyhow, they'll be glad to hear they won't be loafin' this winter." He backed out, obviously embarrassed.

Gideon realized the crisp air straight off the San Francisco mountains had worked through his heavy jacket. Late December was no time to dream outdoors. The boys would be waiting for him to give instructions about decorating. They'd ridden out and gathered pungent boughs, laughing and predicting how many would come out from town for "the boss's Christmas." Gideon had overheard Lonesome say, "Bet he's doin' this so we-all won't get to drinkin'. I'd sure like to wet my whistle, but I got my eye on a purty little gal in town. If I stick it out and get to be part owner of this here ranch, she's bound to see what a steady feller I am and slip into harness with me."

A roar of laughter followed Lonesome's confidence, but Gideon knew it was good-natured. The boys wouldn't admit it for a gold mine, but Aldrich had let it slip how proud they were to "help make Christmas for folks, 'specially the little ones."

"Tell them to wear their best," Gideon said. "This is their celebration, too."

Before bedtime on Christmas Eve, the ranch house smelled of fresh greens. Rude benches had been nailed together and lined the walls to give seating space. Gideon's original plan to have a service and treats for the children had met with frowning disapproval from his outfit. Aldrich reminded him, "Folks're comin' from miles around, the way I hear it."

The boys nodded solemnly, and Aldrich went on. "Seems downright unneighborly not to give 'em dinner."

"Dinner! Can we handle it?"

"Hey, Boss, when're you gonna get on to Arizona?" asked Lonesome, always the most talkative of the cowboys. "Just put the word out we'll all be havin' Christmas dinner here, and folks'll be cookin' for days ahead. Wimmenfolk like to shine, and what better place than makin' food for us pore, unfortunate cowboys?"

Gideon sensed a new camaraderie with his men. In a reckless but appreciative mood, he laughed and held up his hands in mock defeat. "All right, but be it on your heads. You'll have to help, and everyone who sticks and helps make this the best Christmas these settlers have seen in many a day gets a ten-dollar Christmas present."

"Yippee!" they chorused, but Lonesome had to have the final word. "I think I just died and went to heav'n, boys. I thought I heard the boss say ten dollars."

"Aw, you've chased so many critters and listened to them beller yore ears are as bad as yore eyesight," Aldrich told him, but the approval in his foreman's dark eyes told Gideon how far he had come with his hands.

Shortly after breakfast on Christmas Day, by buckboard and wagon, on fine horses and half-wild mustangs, the invited guests began coming. Every family brought enough food for a cavalry! Gideon started, dismayed. *What did he know about serving such a bounteous dinner?* As if reading his mind, the women shooed him out of his own kitchen and told him to go "visit the menfolk" and leave them to their work. Although he had thought his bunkhouse cook more than adequate, he revised his opinion when he saw the groaning table laden with Arizona and holiday specialties.

A billowy matron who had taken charge ordered everyone inside, shushed them, and made an announcement to Gideon. "Mr. Scott, this dinner's in honor of the Almighty's Son. It's proper and fittin' for us to give thanks." Without a pause, she bowed her head and prayed, "Lord, on this special day we give thanks for food and friends and Your goodness to us. Amen."

Gideon silently thanked God she hadn't asked him to pray. He found himself suddenly speechless at his overwhelming love for these people, longing for home and thankful. Two Christmases ago, when he had been out on the trapline with Tomkins, they'd celebrated by cooking an extra portion of rice and dried fruit to go with their venison. Last year, to his shame, he had spent Christmas gambling his life away in the saloon at Tomkinsville. His heart felt as though it were bursting. *God, thank You that at least I'm not there.*

When everyone finished eating and even the cowhands admitted that after four or five helpings, things didn't taste so good anymore, the women packed everything away. Round-eyed children sat on blankets on the floor, and Gideon knew the time had come for his "service." He refused to remember other services, the real ones when he openly preached. To do so would leave him unable to continue.

He faced his guests, noting how lone riders who had "dropped by" rubbed elbows with settlers, how former outlaws chatted with the children. In the spirit of Christmas, disagreements and differing viewpoints faded. Gideon smiled. "It's been an honor for my outfit and me to have you come." He saw the boys swell with pride. "We have a little treat for the children, but first, as has been said, it's fitting for us to recognize whose birthday this is. I thought we could sing some carols."

Never had he heard the enthusiasm with which these brave pioneers sang. "Joy to the World" literally shook the ranch house as did "Hark, the Herald Angels Sing" and "O Come, All Ye Faithful." Voices lowered on "Silent Night," and Gideon saw eyelashes blink to hide wavering emotions. When the last note died, Gideon took out his Bible. "I'd like to read from the second chapter of Luke." He steadied his voice.

" 'And it came to pass in those days, that there went out a decree from Caesar Augustus, that all the world should be taxed. . . .' " On and on went the story, unfolding with new meaning as it had for so many years. Gideon read straight through the angels' proclamation to the shepherds, " 'Glory to God in the highest, and on earth peace, good will toward men.' " The shepherds then rose and went to Bethlehem and found Mary and Joseph and the baby Jesus, not in the fine inn, but quartered in humble surroundings such as these Arizona settlers knew so well. " 'And the shepherds returned, glorifying and praising God for all the things that they had heard and seen, as it was told unto them,' " he quoted in closing.

A power greater than his own prompted him to add, "Shall we pray?" He bowed his head, and lamplight shone on his golden hair, for the winter day had been short. "Father, may we, too, glorify and praise You for all these things. In Jesus' name. Amen."

Gideon raised his head. He saw the astonishment in the faces of Aldrich, Lonesome, and many others. *What should he say?*

"Mama, is it time for the treat?" A patient child in her mother's arms broke the silence, and the crowd laughed while memories of the Christmas service retreated to the shadowy corners but remained a vivid part of the day.

"It truly is!" Gideon picked up the little girl and set her on his shoulder the way he used to do with Joel. A pang went through him, but he smiled and went to the carefully prepared little papers of candies he and the boys had painstakingly counted out and wrapped. "Merry Christmas, Honey. Come on, all you buckaroos. There's enough for everyone!" A swarm of eager but well-mannered children surrounded him. "Here, Fred, boys, help me," he called.

Five minutes later, every child had found a spot on the floor to enjoy their candy and listen to the grown-ups talk about what a wonderful day it had been. But before the gathering dispersed for home, a little group of men and women approached Gideon. "Mr. Scott, you did fine with the reading and singing and all. The praying, too. Until we can get a church and a regular preacher, would you ride into Flag on Sunday afternoons and hold meetings? Our children need to be raised by the Book, and land sakes, none of us has time during the week."

He didn't hesitate an instant. "I would be proud if you really want me." Yet to accept their genuine offer without a confession would be hypocrisy. He clenched his hands behind his back and added, "There's something you must know first. I left Texas under a black cloud, accused of something I didn't do, but I couldn't prove myself innocent."

The woman who had offered the blessing smiled until her eyes disappeared into rolls of flesh. "If the truth were to be told—which it won't and don't need to be—other folks here are ridin' under some black clouds of their own, and they may not be so innocent, either!"

The crowd laughed, and the spokesman for the impromptu committee pressed, "This is a new land, and what's gone before is gone forever. Will you hold meetings?"

"I will." Gideon straightened to full height. "And I hope every one of you will come." In a wave of laughter and anticipation, the party broke up. The boys lingered in the ranch house as if reluctant to have the day end. Gideon watched their awkward attempts at busying themselves, taking out the crude table and benches, straightening sagging boughs. Finally he said, "Before it's chore time, I want to thank you all." He took a small stack of packages wrapped and tied with string in lieu of ribbon and began to distribute them. "Merry Christmas, boys."

"Aw, Boss, the ten dollars was enough," interjected Lonesome. "Why'd you go and buy us these, anyway?" He spread out warm, lined gloves, his face shining. "I never had no gloves as good as these."

A murmur of assent rose.

To break the emotion he felt crowding him, a straight-faced Gideon told them, "You'll need them when we start building on to the ranch house!"

The outfit groaned, but Aldrich stepped forward. He carried a bulky package. "This is for you, Boss."

Gideon felt like the little girl who had received the first packet of candy. He silently untied the package that Aldrich had set on the floor.

A saddle that must have cost every ranch hand a good share of a month's wages—the saddle every rider covets and seldom owns—glistened in front of him, its silver trim beckoning his touch.

Did good old Lonesome sense Gideon's confusion? "If we'da known a present would cut off yore speech, Boss, why, we'da given it to you a couple of weeks ago when you gave Aldrich orders for us to dig holes for fenceposts!"

They trooped out, devilment clear in their lean faces, leaving Gideon only enough time to call, "Thanks," and weakly sink into a chair, then stare at Aldrich. When the door closed behind the last of the boys, he asked, "Was the saddle your idea?"

"Naw." Aldrich shook his head, and enjoyment of the situation showed plain in his eyes. "Lonesome brought it up, and the rest of the boys wished they had." His grin matched the mischief in the younger hands' faces when he added, "Glad it caught you by surprise. It woulda ruinated everythin' if you'd made some stupid remark about it bein' too much." A warning lay beneath his casual words. He headed for the door and paused with one hand on the knob. Gideon could feel something coming and tensed.

"Folks around here will respect yore mentionin' about Texas and why you left," Aldrich drawled. "Once it's been said, though, no need to talk anymore." He lifted one eyebrow and grinned again. "Merry Christmas, Boss."

"Merry Christmas." Gideon watched his foreman turn up his coat collar against the cold night air before stepping out. The latch clicked, and boot heels thudded across the porch. The silence that follows the emptying of a house when Christmas is over fell, leaving Gideon to wonder, *Surely this silence couldn't herald the coming of another storm.* He had confessed the worst, and these new neighbors cared little.

Yet within an hour, the snow came, enshrouding the Double J and obliterating all trace of the merrymakers who had come, eaten, and worshiped together, then gone back to their own homes, leaving Gideon with his memories.

Chapter 13

S pring in all its glory came to Arizona. Trees greened, budded, and burst into new life, and so did Gideon. The long winter months hadn't been idle, yet he had found time to regain his perspective. He returned to studying his Bible and, when weather permitted, rode or drove into Flagstaff to hold simple Sunday afternoon services composed of hymns, a Scripture reading, and sometimes a short lesson. Gideon always returned home more blessed than his informal congregation. If at times he longed to preach, he restrained himself. Although his bitterness against God had long since fled, he knew the time wasn't right. In the meantime, Aldrich and at least some of the boys usually came to the meetings, often slipping into the last of the benches set up in a cleaned-out barn.

"The Lord began His ministry in a stable. I reckon we can be glad to have a dry place for our meetings," folks said. They bundled in layers upon layers of clothes for the short services and grimly proclaimed that before snow flew the next fall, there'd be a regular church. The stove the barn owner generously put in kept only those in the first few rows warm.

Often while watching the snow fall, listening for the sound of laughter from the bunkhouse, Gideon felt the same uneasiness from the winter silence he'd experienced on Christmas Day. Yet as time passed, the feelings dwindled. The only unusual incident came when two of his outfit slipped the reins and came home from town bright eyed, talky, and smelling of drink.

"You know the rules, boys." Gideon faced his men, heartsick. "I won't stand for drinking."

The cowboys looked at each other, then with mutual appeal at Aldrich. The foreman shook his head, although Gideon saw how much he wanted to speak.

Lonesome took a deep breath. "Boss, we all know the rules, and these two mis'r'ble skunks don't deserve it. But yore always talkin' about how that Jesus feller in the Bible gave folks another chance if they were sorry." His keen eyes challenged Gideon. "Well, it doesn't take much to see how sorry lookin' they are." He pointed to the offenders, who sat on their bunks with heads drooping. Disarranged clothing spoke clearly that their pardners had already administered a certain amount of justice.

Lonesome went on. "We just don't want to have the Double J crew broke up." The memory of shared word and loyalty shone in his eyes and in the eyes of the others.

Gideon had the feeling he was on trial more than his men. With a quick prayer for guidance, he said, "All right. I'll let it go this one time but *never again*. If any of you ever come home drinking, pack and get your time. As for you—" He marched over to the culprits. "The offer's still good about earning a bonus, but you'll have to start your year as of right now, because I'm firing you and rehiring you this minute. Like it or lump it, and don't make me regret it."

"Fair enough." One of the cowboys held out his hand. Remorse for letting down the outfit and gladness for a second chance showed in his mighty grip. The second did the same. There might be grumbling later, but for now a sigh of relief swept through the bunkhouse, and Gideon went out feeling God had lent him for one night the wisdom of Solomon.

The threatened breakup of the Double J wove unbreakable strands that held through temptation. With an outfit so determined to stay together, any cowpoke who even thought of straying found himself promptly rounded up and brought back to the straight and narrow. No one ever mentioned the boss's handling of the winter crisis, but the long hours of spring work and the spirits of his hands told Gideon the whole story.

Spring also brought problems. Aldrich dragged in long faced and angry one sunny afternoon. "Boss, our cattle are disappearin'."

"Disappearing! How?"

"Well, it ain't four-footed critters that are responsible," the foreman said sourly. "We found signs they're bein' driven. Rustled. Plumb stole right off the Double J."

"Indians?" A chill went up Gideon's spine.

Aldrich made a rude noise. "Naw. They kill a beef, take what they want, and let the rest lay." His eyes half closed in the way they did when he considered. "How about givin' me a few of the boys to scout out Stockton's place?"

"Take anyone you need. I'll be ready as soon as you are." Gideon jumped up and reached for his hat.

"You stay here, Boss. Me and Lonesome, Dusty, and Kansas can do the job. I'd take Cheyenne, too, but he's sorer than a mule sittin' on a cactus. Toothache."

"I wouldn't think of letting you go without me, " Gideon said blandly and caught the gleam in Aldrich's eyes, although he grumbled all the way out the door. Ten minutes later, the little band had mounted and headed toward Stockton's spread.

"I thought you were sick," Gideon told Cheyenne, whose swollen jaw gave mute evidence of pain.

"Not sick enough to miss the fun." He grinned crookedly. "I'm hankerin' to see what that bunch of yahoos does when we ride in."

"Who's *ridin'* in?" Aldrich demanded. His brows drew together over keen eyes. "We're scoutin', remember?"

"Yeah," Cheyenne hastily agreed, but not before Gideon saw the exchange of glances between the cowboys.

"No gunplay," he ordered, remembering the Tomkinsville saloon.

Lonesome, who could look cherubic in feigned indignation, retorted, "Why, Boss, are you loco? Us pore old cowpokes can't hardly bear to kill a rattlesnake." His remark dropped into a silence broken only by the rhythmic beat of their horses' hooves.

"I thought Stockton was supposed to be reformed," Gideon mused aloud when they reached the borders of the former outlaw's ranch. "Why do you suspect him?"

"Suspect? We're just curious. Well, what d'you know!" Lonesome spurred his horse, and the others followed. "Funny, I'd swear that's a Double J brand on that steer." He pointed to a small bunch of cattle in a thrown-together corral. "There's another one. Mighty pee-coo-liar how they got in there, huh, Boss?"

Rage at the blatant thievery straightened Gideon's spine. His hot Texas blood boiled. "Stay here!" he ordered. Before his men could protest, he put Dainty Bess into a dead run toward the corral. Three men, none of them Stockton, leaped from their horses and faced him.

"What are you doing with my cattle in there?" Gideon yelled and pulled Bess up in front of them.

The sheer daring of his confrontation paralyzed Stockton's men. "Uh, they must have got mixed in when we brought in—"

"*Liar!*" Gideon bounded from the saddle. "Does Stockton know about this?" His voice rang in the clear air, and he read the answer in the men's faces. In a flash, Gideon leaped back onto Bess and uncoiled his lariat. Circling it over his head, he snugged it over a poorly set fencepost. "All right, Bess!" *Crash!* The post gave way and dragged behind them. A mixture of Double J stock and other brands poured out to freedom.

"Yippee-i-ay!" Lonesome bellowed, then panic clutched his voice. "Boss, *look out!*"

His warning came seconds too late. Something struck Gideon squarely in the back. He reeled in the saddle, then fell to the ground, conscious of a volley of gunfire before the world went black.

—✛—

As Judith Butler Scott in her yellow and white dress watched Gideon ride away from their wedding, something deep inside her begged him not to go. The truth she had begun to accept burst into full bloom: Gideon could not be guilty of the accusations she had made. His kisses confirmed it. Shy and reverent, they lingered on her lips and witnessed to his innocence. Blood pounded in her head. She rested her hands on Joel's shoulders for support. Would she ever see him again, this splendid man who had married her and ridden away for the sake of his family?

Somehow she pulled herself together. For Joel's sake, she must go on. Judith glanced at Lige Scott and shrank back from the naked heartbreak quickly veiled in his eyes. His two sons were both gone. He turned and looked at Joel, and Judith shivered. She must fight, or Lige would take possession of the child in an attempt to create a second Cyrus. Despair filled her and blotted out everything but the need to walk carefully, at least for a time. Yet her heart cried out for help, and the peace of God strengthened her. She could do nothing until she regained her stamina lost through sickness and worry.

The journey to El Paso had seemed endless. The journey back felt even longer. Judith had the sensation of being smothered, imprisoned. Would the Circle S swallow her and Joel?

Naomi stirred beside her, smiled, and patted Judith's hand. Her low assurance, "Things won't seem so bewildering when we get home," did much to comfort the distraught bride. As long as Naomi remained her friend, Judith could survive.

To her surprise, once they reached the ranch, Lige helped her down and said gruffly, "You're our daughter now. Naomi will see you have what you need."

His rude attempt at kindness threatened the shaky control Judith struggled to maintain. "Thank you." She blinked hard. "Come, Joel." Tired from the long journey and excitement, he trotted after her, and after a hasty wash, they both fell asleep. They didn't waken until Carmelita tapped on their door and announced supper would be ready soon.

Although for a time Judith remained on guard, as early winter came, then blizzards beyond anything she and Joel had imagined, she learned to relax. She often felt as if they'd been on the Circle S forever. Lige gave an expurgated version of Gideon's absence, merely stating he had gone away for a time. Whether he believed Gideon would return was a matter between Lige and his God. He continued to treat Judith as the daughter he had called her and frankly idolized Joel. She worried, yet perhaps someday she could. . . Every time she got that far, she put it out of her mind. Her somedays were in God's hands.

The first spring after Gideon rode away brought Joel's fifth birthday and a beautiful collie pup from his grandfather. He promptly named it Millie after asking Judith, "Would Mama like it?"

"I'm sure she would." Judith hugged him to keep her tears from showing. Yet Joel owned a more priceless possession than earthly parents. His Friend Jesus was real to the boy, an ever-present comrade of the trail. Judith often marveled at the depth of his faith and prayed it would never be tarnished.

Summer, fall, winter, and a second spring elapsed, and nothing had been heard of either Gideon or Cyrus. New patches of white marred Lige's hair. A shadow lurked in Naomi's eyes even when she smiled and played with Joel, who adored her. Because of the distance to town, Naomi and Judith continued the child's education. Lige's sad eyes brightened when he saw how quickly Joel grasped the things he learned and put them into practice. He sent away for books to fill a library, and Joel discovered new worlds beyond the borders of Texas. Best of all, he loved the Bible stories Judith read to him.

A new minister had been installed in the San Scipio church, an older man with a kindly face and a great love of the Lord. He could not preach as Gideon had, but he taught the Word of God and people liked him. Only Lucinda Curtis openly mourned "the untimely and unexplained departure of Brother Scott."

Judith never knew how Lige managed it, but her marriage to Gideon remained unknown to San Scipio. Possessed of great power because of his large holdings, he didn't hesitate to wield it in his own interests. In any event, she gladly accepted the secrecy. Most of the fold in San Scipio would have exclaimed for a day or two, then continued to welcome her, except for Lucinda. Judith dreaded the other woman's bold attempts at companionship and pleaded

Joel as an excuse to avoid the elaborate affairs given by Lucinda and her mother. Something in the washed-out gray eyes warned of a serpent's venom.

Joel's uncanny resemblance to the Scotts fed the gossip mill for a time until a drunken cowboy shot up San Scipio and turned attention toward himself. For the most part, Judith existed in a state of waiting, happy when she forgot she was Mrs. Scott, restless at other times.

Joel's growth and joy in everyone and everything on the Circle S helped her develop patience. She couldn't say what it was she waited for. Yet, how often in the evening her gaze turned west! Was Gideon somewhere beyond the horizon, struggling to patch up his life as best he could? Did he remember the woman he had married and renounced? If bright dewdrops sparkled in her lashes, no one knew but God. The love she held for her absent husband secretly warmed her. If they never met again in this life, they would in the next. She believed it with all her heart.

The summer of 1876 brought startling news to the Circle S in the form of a visitor. Tired, dusty, and determined, a big man rode in one early evening and asked to see Mrs. Scott. Rosa led him to the large room where the family gathered evenings before going to bed. The visitor looked around, noted each person present, and then strode directly toward Judith. "Mrs. Scott?"

"I am Mrs. Scott." Naomi stood, dignity in every line of her body.

"And you?" Keen eyes pierced Judith's confusion.

"I am Mrs. Gideon Scott."

"Ahh." A sigh of satisfaction lit the worn face.

"Who are you, and what do you want?" Lige put Joel off his knee and approached the man.

"I have news of your son. When have you heard from him?" The stranger's gaze bored into Lige, then turned back to Judith, ignoring Lige's strangled cry. Suddenly a great hand on his shoulder whipped him around, and Lige demanded, "What is your business here?"

"May I sit down? I've come a long way." The man didn't wait for permission but brushed dust from his pants and seated himself. "You have two sons, Cyrus and Gideon." He looked as if he were enjoying himself.

"Who are you?" Lige towered over him, but his hands shook.

"Tomkins is the name. In early winter of '74, I was running a trapline in Colorado. I'm a miner, but I was down on my luck and needed money for grub. A young feller rode in, took to gambling, and made a pile of money. He was smart enough to know it didn't make him popular, so he joined me trapping for the winter. In the spring, he grubstaked me."

"What was his name?" Lige's hands formed claws.

Judith held her breath, but let it out in a disappointed sigh when Tomkins spoke. "He called himself Cyrus Scott."

"Called himself! Wasn't that his name?" The great light of joy and hope dimmed in Lige's face.

"Turned out it wasn't. Anyway, he rode north. Said he aimed to work in Wyoming, maybe Montana." Tomkins grinned and rubbed his unshaven chin. "That summer I struck it big. Can't tell you how grateful I was to the young feller. Tried to find him and couldn't. Then just before snow flew, he came back to Tomkinsville, the boomtown that sprang up after the strike."

"Did you find out who he was?" Lige said hoarsely.

"Not then. I set him up in a hotel, put enough in the bank for him to buy a ranch, and told him to leave town." A dark cloud blackened Tomkins's face. "He hung around, though, befriended a saloon girl, nothin' more," he added when a little moan escaped Naomi's white lips. "Felt sorry for her, Ma'am. She was just a kid, so he gave her money to go away. Well, one of the bullies got likkered up, said some nasty things, and drew on my friend. Scott yanked out his gun quicker than lightning and shot the gun out of the scoundrel's hand."

He quickly sketched in the cowardly knife attack, the lynch mob, and the trial while his listeners sat wide-eyed and tense.

"Once cleared, Scott came to me and told me his story." Tomkins's gaze raked Lige. "How he got accused of something he didn't do on account of his brother."

"Gideon!" Judith's glad cry brought a smile to the leathery face.

"He rode out on the prettiest little sorrel mare I ever saw. Said he thought he'd take my advice and buy a ranch in Arizona. Oh, he gave back all the money he got gambling. Tomkinsville's still talking about it." He scratched his head. "Didn't need it, anyway. He helped me, and I saw to it he had enough for that ranch and to get it stocked. I had business down this way and thought I'd stop by. Gideon's a proud man, and he never once lied. You might keep that in mind if you're still judging him." Tomkins got up, and in spite of the Scotts' offer of hospitality, he said he'd better mosey on. He walked out, spurs clinking.

Judith roused from the shock of all she'd learned and ran after him for a private word. "Mr. Tomkins, do you know where in Arizona my husband, er, Gideon might be?"

"No, Ma'am." He shook his head. "If I did, I'd be tempted to hunt him up. Fact is, I've been considering it ever since I left Colorado. Once I get done with my business, I might just head west instead of back home."

"Take me with you," she cried.

"You love him, Lass?"

"With all my heart, more than anything except God."

"Then it's all right." Tomkins smiled at her. "When I asked him that question, he said the same thing. 'More than life, second only to God.' I told him things had a way of working out."

"Bless you!" Judith impulsively stretched and kissed the grizzled cheek. "Will you take me to find him?"

"I reckon." Dull red suffused his face, but doubt crept into his eyes. "It might be better for us to wait and see if we can smoke out where he is. Can you be patient awhile longer, Lass?"

Torn between wanting to leave immediately and the common sense of his suggestion, she reluctantly nodded.

Tomkins promised, "I'll get my transacting done, see what I can learn, and stop back in a few weeks. A big company in Houston's been pestering me to sell out my holdings. I'm considering letting them have the whole shebang. I haven't had half the fun spending my gold as I did looking for it." His eyes twinkled. "Maybe I'll retire in Arizona and see if I can find a likely partner who'll sell me half ownership in a ranch."

"Don't say anything to the Scotts," Judith warned, hating herself but knowing it had to be said. "Lige won't let Joel go easily, especially when Gideon's involved." She proudly raised her head. "I won't sneak out when the time comes, but until it does, we have to live here."

Tomkins nodded. A few minutes later, he rode away, carrying Judith's hopes and dreams in his calloused hands. When Lige threw her a questioning look as she entered the big room, she simply said, "Gideon sends his love." Blushing, she fled before he had time to respond.

Judith expected to hear from Tomkins soon. Each time Lige picked up mail in town, she anticipated a letter. None came until just before Christmas. Tomkins had fallen ill in Houston and hadn't been able to do anything about locating Gideon. He then had to hurry back to Colorado to close a deal and get the mines sold. Now winter must pass before he could do more. He regretted it but was sending out letters to different parts of Arizona where Gideon might be. He promised that even if they came to naught, he'd come and get Judith in the spring. They'd follow the sagebrush trail and find her husband if it meant visiting every ranch in Arizona!

Resigned but impatient, again Judith settled down to wait.

Chapter 14

The shooting of Gideon was followed by a burst of gunfire from the enraged Double J riders that crippled two of the rustlers and sent the third fleeing for his life. Enraged by the incident, the worthy citizens of Flagstaff, led by Aldrich, rose in mighty protest, stormed in a body to Stockton, and tersely told him to move on. "We can't prove for certain yore in on it," the foreman snapped, "but with our boss lyin' gunshot and the doc sayin' he ain't sure if he can pull him through, the Double J boys are a mite edgy."

Stockton's face showed his guilt, but he sneered and told the volunteer posse, "I've been planning to go, anyway."

"You'll stay healthier," Aldrich agreed. His fingers crept suggestively to his pistol butt. "I hear other parts of Arizony are more con-doo-sive to a long life and better for rattlesnakes."

A week later, Stockton vanished with his herd, after a few interesting riders and Aldrich, in his words, "just moseyed by to make sure none of the Double J stock took it into their heads and follered."

Gideon lay bandaged and broken. The doctor who had been summoned from Phoenix shook his head when he saw the location of the bullet. Rolling up his sleeves, he promptly called for cauldrons of boiling water and set to work. Aldrich, in a brave effort to do anything to help, followed the doctor's barked commands as if he'd studied surgery for years. When the bullet had been extracted from its dangerously close position to Gideon's spine, the foreman stumbled from the room into the waiting group of cowboys.

"Well?" Lonesome's question and haggard face bore witness to the outfit's love for the boss.

Aldrich wiped great beads of sweat from his forehead. "How the deuce do I know? Doc says he won't be able to tell for at least twenty-four hours, if then."

"How bad is it?" Dusty demanded, his face dark.

"If it had been a half inch closer to his spine, he'd have never walked again. As it is. . ." The foreman shrugged and mopped his face again.

"We should've killed them galoots outright!" Cheyenne stared at his friends.

"Naw, the boss hates killin'," Lonesome reminded. He turned back to Aldrich. "Anythin' we can do?"

"Just pray." Silence fell on the motley group, broken only when someone coughed and another shuffled a worn boot. One by one, the hands slipped out. If they followed the foreman's advice, only they and "the boss's God" would know.

For a week, Gideon's life hung in the balance. The Phoenix doctor stayed on, enlisting the help of Aldrich or one of the boys to watch while he snatched fragments of sleep. Gideon mumbled, cried out, and whispered, but loyal punchers who sat for hours by his bedside and gave him sips of water kept their mouths shut. Not even with one another would they discuss what they heard. More than once, whoever rode herd on Gideon came out of his room with a thoughtful expression on his face. The relationship between the boss and God became clearer than ever during his delirious state.

"If he dies, I'm goin' after Stockton," Lonesome told Aldrich.

The old warhorse of a foreman, aged by years of worry and danger, shook his head. "Gideon wouldn't want that." If Lonesome noticed the change of address from *the boss* to *Gideon,* he didn't let on. Instead, he reluctantly admitted, "Yeah, too bad."

Slowly the dreaded fever cooled. On the eighth day, Gideon opened his eyes, unsure of where he was. Aldrich stood bent over him. "Don't try and talk. Yore better, and I'll get the doc."

Reassured, the injured man relaxed and slept. The second time he woke, his stomach felt hollow as a log and the dizziness in his head had settled down. But not until days later, when Aldrich and Lonesome got him up and he took a few shaky steps, did he see any of them grin.

"Whoopee!" The outfit yelped and beat their hats against their jeans. "Can't keep our Texas boss down." Leaning heavily on his supporters, Gideon dropped into a chair with obvious relief, an effort almost ignored by his friends.

"Vamoose, cowpokes, and let him rest," Aldrich ordered, and the laughing bunch roared outside to let off all the steam they'd stored up during Gideon's danger.

"Your face is blacker than a midnight storm," Gideon accused his foreman. "What's eating you?"

Aldrich slowly sat down opposite him and fiddled with his hat. "I've got a kinda confession to make."

Gideon stretched and winced when the still-healing muscles pulled. How good it felt to be alive and able to walk! "Shoot."

"The night the doc said he didn't know if you'd pull through, he said we oughta notify yore next of kin. I snooped around and put some of yore mumblings together and—"

Gideon froze. "You did *what?*"

Aldrich's plaintive tone told how much he hated his confession. "I wrote to yore—to Mrs. Judith Scott at San Scipio, and told her you were lyin' here shot up."

Every nerve in Gideon's body tingled. He stared, open-mouthed, unsure whether to whoop with joy or bawl out Aldrich for interfering in what didn't concern him.

The foreman stood and regained his usual cool manner. "Just thought I'd mention it in case, uh, we get unexpected vis'tors." He clinked out before Gideon could speak.

Visitors! What if Judith and Joel should one day walk through the door of his Arizona ranch house? For the first time, he admitted the building he and his men had done that winter represented the dream they would come. He lost himself in reverie for a time, then sternly put his memories aside. Nothing had changed, except he'd gotten himself shot up, and the doc said he might never ride straight again and might walk with a limp. "Lucky at that," Doc added sourly, but Gideon just smiled. He knew the doc pretty well now, and the dedicated man would be the first to give credit to the Great Physician who pulled Gideon back from death.

He wished Aldrich hadn't told him about the letter as weeks passed and no answer came. His final hope of someday clearing himself and returning home at least for a visit flickered and went out. "Well, God, it's just us again. I'll do the best I can and trust You," he said one dusky evening when the sun's passing left trails of red and purple in the western sky. Yet he wistfully turned east and added, "But please, be with the boy—and her—and make them happy."

--+--

Hundreds of miles east of the Double J, life on the Circle S splintered with the arrival of a scrawled note. Unsigned and dirty, as if carried and passed hand to hand for weeks, the smudged name ELIJAH SCOTT with the address following was almost illegible. "What's this?" Lige demanded when Carmelita brought it to him at the supper table in early spring. He opened it, stared, and jerked as if shot. "Carmelita, where did this come from?"

Her liquid brown eyes held no guile as she said, "A man threw it from a horse and rode away, even though I called, 'Señor, do you not want to water your horse?' "

With a loud cry, Lige pushed his chair back from the table with such a mighty thrust, it overturned and crashed to the floor. He rushed to the door, yanked it open, and disappeared, leaving the door swinging. Naomi, Judith, Carmelita, and a wide-eyed Joel stared after him, then Judith came to her senses. Vaguely aware of boots pounding toward the corral, she snatched the grimy missive and read aloud.

Tell G I'm sorry. Maybe someday I'll come back. Dad, forgive. . .

The rest of the sentence was blotted, and only a sprawling *C* served as a signature.

The steady beat of hooves and a stentorian voice shouting, "Cyrus, Son, come back!" faded into eerie stillness. Naomi's lips trembled, and Judith burst out, "Thank God!" but the older woman finally cried, "God, have mercy on Elijah!"

Her own joy forgotten, Judith realized what this would mean to the stern father who had sacrificed his younger son to blind worship of the elder. Pity engulfed her and wiped away forever her anger at her father-in-law. The torment he had created for himself was punishment far beyond the laws of retribution.

Hours later, Lige returned alone. Joel lay asleep upstairs, but Naomi and Judith waited, huddled close to a blazing fire that seemed to offer little warmth.

"Was it Cyrus?" Naomi whispered.

"I don't know." Lige looked beaten, and Judith could not bear to gaze at him. The glazed eyes and the massive drooping shoulders showed more clearly than any cry of remorse the awful truth that lay ahead.

"Elijah, we must give thanks." Naomi stood and crossed to her tall husband. Judith could scarcely believe her eyes and ears. The woman who had sat crushed for hours grew in strength to meet the need. "Cyrus is alive. *Alive,* Elijah! All these months and years—" She faltered, then hope filled her face. "Don't you see? Our prayers have been answered!"

A ray of light penetrated Lige's despair, then died. "It is my fault," he said brokenly. "If I had been the kind of father I should have, Cyrus would have confessed openly." Misery returned to quench the hope. He crushed Naomi to him as if needing her physical presence, as if needing something to cling to while the world crashed around him. "And you, Judith, Daughter, your life ruined because of me. Oh, God, what have I done? Where are the sons You gave me? Cyrus, Gideon, forgive me!" He buried his face in Naomi's lap.

Judith's heart pounded. She ran to the man whose self-righteousness had caused such tragedy. "Lige, Naomi, Gideon is somewhere in Arizona. When Tomkins came last summer, he told me." She could feel bright color creeping into her face. "My life isn't ruined. *I love Gideon*. I realized it on our wedding day. Tomkins is coming back soon, and we're going west to find Gideon."

Lige raised his head. A trace of his old arrogance reared up. *"You aren't taking Joel!"*

"Yes, Lige, I am. He needs a father." Soft color mounted almost up to her coronet of braids. "I–I am sure Gideon loves me, and he will raise Joel as his own."

Lige's body went rigid, then he threw back his head and took a deep breath. "You are right, Child." He freed himself from Naomi's arms and shook himself as if coming out of a daze. "I drove my sons away. God won't allow me to destroy Joel."

Judith walked to him, took his heavy hand in her own, and gazed into his face. "Our God is a God of forgiveness. Gideon will only be glad you know the truth; I know that. You will be welcome in his home, with or without me, and Joel will always love you."

A little of the pain left Lige's eyes, but he left the room with the shambling steps of an old man who has outlived joy. Naomi ran after him and left Judith alone with the love she had openly confessed for the first time singing in her heart and in the still, spring air.

---+---

A few weeks later, Tomkins arrived. Lige Scott whitened but valiantly pulled himself together and welcomed the man who would be taking Judith and Joel with him.

"I haven't been able to find Gideon," Tomkins admitted, "but that's not surprising. Most of the messages I sent may never have reached Arizona. A man can't depend on riders who like as not take it in their heads to stop in Utah or New Mexico. We'll find him, and when we do, he's going to be one happy rancher." The miner's sally brought a blush to Judith's smooth cheeks. Yet her greatest joy came when Lige frankly told Gideon's faithful friend how he'd misjudged his son and pleaded for Tomkins to convince Gideon to forgive his father.

"Sho', he's already done that." Tomkins's hearty respect for a man who admitted his shortcomings showed in his lined face and relieved some of the suffering evident in Lige's brow. "That boy of yours is too big, or maybe it's his God that's too big, for him to hold a grudge. Better consider selling out here and heading for Arizona, Scott. Plenty of room there to leave behind troubles."

Judith saw the war that waged in Lige's heart, the leap of hope grounded by other considerations. "No, I need to stay here in case my older son comes back." The poignant admission brought tears to Judith's eyes, especially when Lige added, "Maybe someday."

"Gideon won't know me, will he, Judy?" Joel asked when she told him they were going to Arizona. "See how big I am?" He flexed his almost seven-year-old arm, and she pretended to find a muscle. "Can I take Millie? And my pony? Are Grandpa and Grandma going?" He hadn't lost his ability to ask questions.

"No, Dear. Millie needs to stay and take care of the Circle S. It's hundreds of miles, and we don't have a way to take her."

"Begging your pardon, Mrs. Scott, but there's no reason Millie can't ride along." Tomkins plunged into the conversation and received a gleeful hug from Joel. "The pony's getting too small for you, young feller. Besides, Gideon will have a real horse you can ride. I found some other folks who are heading west, so I up and bought a couple of covered wagons. We'll join with the band and be real pioneers." He cocked his head to one side. "You can take that pretty little pinto Patchwork if it's all right with the Scotts."

"Absolutely." Lige acted eager to cooperate. Judith could see the memory of his and Naomi's trek west long ago color his face and bring back life. "There's a trunk of Gideon's he might as well have, too, and my daughter will want to carry bolts of goods for clothing. Probably hard to get out there."

Judith's last sight of him was at the top of the mesa with Naomi, where she had dreamed so often. To her amazement, Tomkins had discovered that her towheaded friend Ben, who had first delivered her to the Circle S nearly three years before, longed passionately to go west and find Gideon. Now eighteen, strapping and cheery, he would drive Tomkins's second wagon.

Each day brought her closer to Arizona, closer to Gideon. If at times the thought crossed her mind he might have ridden on, she squashed it. God had worked in such incredible ways to bring them together, surely He wouldn't stop now. The dust and discomfort, storms, and threat of hostile Indians all became things she must endure.

Joel loved every minute of the long trip. He followed Ben around, rolled with Millie, and romped with others his age on the wagon train.

Some wagons turned off before the train went into Arizona. Other families saw places in New Mexico that attracted them. But Tomkins and his charges faced west, bound by a love for a young man who had captured their hearts with his sincerity and dedication. Always they asked if anyone knew of Gideon Scott. No one had heard of him until they reached Arizona.

"Gideon Scott. Hmm, name sounds famil'r," a frontiersman told them at Phoenix. He thought for a moment, his face in a dreadful scowl. Then it cleared. "Yup, he's the young feller that's set Arizony on its ear with his new-fangled idees. Won't 'low no drinkin' and ree-wards his cowpunchers by makin' them part owner of the Double J. Up near Flagstaff, he is." Dismay swept across his face. " 'Fraid I got bad news for you. He got shot up bad a few weeks ago. Can't say whether he made it. You kinfolk?"

"I'm his wife." Judith felt proud to say it out loud, and she managed to smile in spite of her stricken heart. They'd come so far. *Please, God, let Gideon be all right.*

That night Joel echoed her prayer at their nightly worship they held regardless of where they camped. "God, take care of Gideon," the child prayed, his hand warm in Judith's, and together they finished with, "For Jesus' sake. Amen."

The new and strange country they traveled between Phoenix and Flagstaff brought wondering exclamations from Joel, whose gaze riveted on strangely formed cactus, red cliffs and canyons, and a host of other exciting things. Judith barely saw them. She resented the slow, steady pace of the mules that pulled the wagon, and her mind raced ahead of them, longing for the moment they would reach the Double J. The significance of the ranch's name beat into her brain and steadied her wildly beating heart when she wondered if Gideon would truly be glad she had come. As they passed through the huddle of buildings that made up Flagstaff and forged on, Tomkins muttered that they couldn't be that far from the Double J. Judith's pale face and haunted eyes urged him on, and Ben and Joel fell strangely silent. If their beloved Gideon had died, better to find it out at the ranch than from some wagging tongue in town. The hands would allow them to camp there, regardless.

+

Why hasn't Judith answered Aldrich's letter?

The unanswered question pounded Gideon night and day. Yet days had limped into weeks that dragged by until spring slipped into the past and summer came. The doctor had been right. Gideon would always walk with a limp, and when he rode too long or too hard, his back hurt. A dream that had begun some time before of one day retracing his wild journey from El Paso to the Double J dimmed. He didn't know if he would ever be able to ride that far, even to carry the message of his Lord as he longed to do, then return to San Scipio and stay until he found Cyrus.

Sometimes he cried out to God, wondering if his father had intercepted the letter. Even though Lige believed him guilty of despicable behavior, he'd said Gideon could stay on the ranch. Surely he would respond if he knew his son lay dying.

Hope dwindled as time relentlessly rode on. More and more, Gideon relied on his heavenly Father for comfort. He would never be alone as long as the Lord traveled with him. There had to be a reason why no word came from Texas. Gideon's part was simply to trust God in all things, even when he didn't understand.

One afternoon Gideon sat astride Dainty Bess on a rise above the ranch house. Something white moved in the distance, dipped with the contour of the hills, reappeared, and was followed by a second large white shape.

"Well, I'll be. Covered wagons!" Gideon curiously watched them, then said, "Giddap, Bess. Looks like we have company." He rode to meet the wagons, idly wondering where these settlers planned to go. When, within good seeing distance, he discerned the face of the first wagon's driver, gladness filled his soul. "*Tomkins?*" Dainty Bess raced toward the billowing white wagon sail. She slid to a stop, and Gideon exploded from the saddle onto the ground to meet his old friend.

"You're a sight for sore eyes," Tomkins greeted and pounded him on the shoulder. "We heard you might be dead, and—"

A soft patter of feet interrupted him. "Gideon, you're alive." Judith ran straight to him, heedless of Tomkins's loud guffaw.

"You came." He stared at the white-faced girl clinging to his arm. "When you didn't answer Aldrich's letter. . ." He blinked to make sure she really stood there, travel stained as he had seen her so long ago, but beautiful and with a look in her dark eyes that repaid every heartache Gideon had experienced.

"I received no letter. Cyrus wrote and asked for forgiveness, but we were coming, anyway." Tears blotted out her incoherent explanation. "Oh, Gideon, God is so good." She raised her face to his.

He kissed the trembling lips and tasted salt. His arms circled her, never to let her go. "Judith, my wife." His heart overflowed. "*Thank God!*"

A second pair of arms surrounded him. He looked down. Joel's bright head rested against his jeans.

Later, there would be time to share the last weary years, Lige's remorse and repentance, and all that had separated them for so long. The silence in the sage had been broken. When storms threatened and howled above them, Judith and Gideon would face them together, united in love and blessed by faith in their heavenly Father.

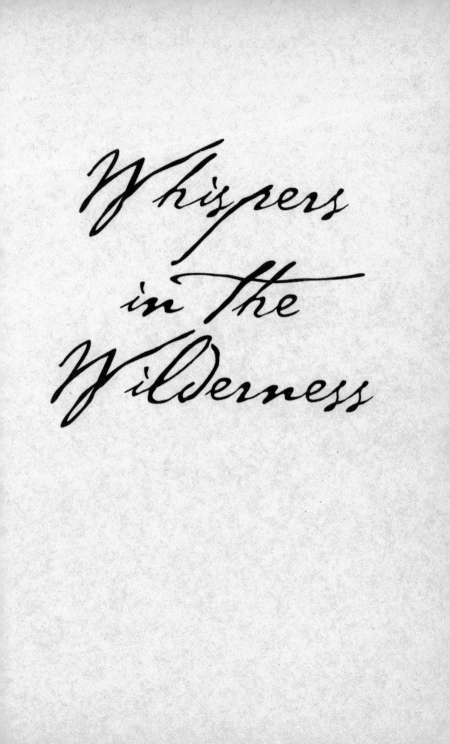

Whispers
in the
Wilderness

Chapter 1

G o or stay? Joel Scott slid from the saddle of his ebony mare, Querida, and let the reins drop. Trained to stand, she whinnied, rubbed her soft nose against his shoulder, then began to graze; the rise overlooking the Double J was no stranger to her.

A pang went through this golden-haired man with the face of an angel. How could he leave northern Arizona and all it offered? He gazed into the valley below—mute but appealing, it lay like a crumpled blanket carelessly tossed by a giant hand. Hills, valleys, forested slopes, and the distant rims of red canyons—they all wove invisible webs, as they had done eleven summers ago when Joel and his aunt ended their long search for Uncle Gideon. How quickly the years had flown! The seven-year-old boy, who had whooped with excitement when he first saw the Double J, lurked inside Joel's heart. Along with that was the awe that filled him each time he surveyed the now-expanded ranch.

Cloudless Arizona skies smiled, no bluer than the keen eyes of the motionless man. Quaking aspens with their greenish-white trunks bent toward one another and whispered wilderness gossip. Pine, cedar, and grass rustled, alive with the sheer joy of summer.

"I can't go." Joel did not realize he had spoken aloud until Querida abandoned her grazing to nuzzle his arm. He sighed and buried his face in her black mane. Even if he could bear to leave the ranch and his family, how could he part with Querida? Ten years earlier, Gideon had called his nephew to the barn. "One of the mares is ready to foal. You need to be there."

Joel wondered at the mysterious look in his uncle's face but obediently trotted after the tall man he resembled. Even now he could remember every detail of the birth, his first to witness.

"It's a filly," Gideon told the wide-eyed boy. "Male horses are colts. She's yours, Son."

"Mine?" Joel had ridden various Double J horses, but none had been his very own. He watched the filly struggle to her feet on legs that seemed too long for her body. Within a few hours, she ran about but never strayed far from her mother.

"What shall I call her?" He thought of all the black things he could: Soot, Ink, Dark Cloud. But Aldrich, longtime foreman for Gideon, shook his head. "This filly's gonna become a real pard," he told the excited boy. "Name her something special."

"What?" Joel respected Aldrich for his range lore.

Aldrich's leathery face broke into a smile, and his eyes twinkled. "Once, a long time ago, I had a pretty little filly named Querida. That's Spanish for *beloved.*" He pronounced it *Kay-reeda.*

"Querida." Joel rolled the name around on his tongue, patted his gift, and repeated, "Querida. Beloved." From that moment, the two were inseparable. By the time Querida turned five, she had reached full height and weight.

Twice, she had saved Joel from danger. Once with Joel aboard, she had outrun a visiting outlaw who had tried to buy her and had been refused. The second time was just a few months after Joel's sixteenth birthday, when Joel's foot was painfully twisted and held fast by a rock slide, trapping him. Although her eyes showed that she did not want to leave him, Querida obeyed her master's command to go home. Her arrival at the Double J, without Joel, resulted in a prompt rescue, and he loved her more than ever afterwards.

—┼—

Joel's mind returned to the present. "God, I don't know what to do." He impulsively turned to his best Friend. "You know I want to serve You—it's all I've ever wanted. To take up Uncle Gideon's work and preach." His heart glowed at the prospect.

In Flagstaff, he had already earned the nickname of the boy preacher, and it was jealously defended by Lonesome, Dusty, Aldrich, and the other Double J hands. Strangers sometimes mistakenly branded Joel as soft until a demonstration of his riding or roping would convince even the strongest nonbeliever that a man could follow God and still be a top cowboy. Talk of his talents ran second only to the ripple of shock that Gideon had caused years before when he laid down his no-drinking rule for the Double J and made it stick because of who he was and the wages he offered.

Once, a new rider asked how come young Scott could talk a bird out of its bush and still be fearless and strong.

"A lot of folks think Jesus was a tenderfoot," the young preacher shot back. "But then, a lot of folks can be wrong." His frank smile took any sting out of his words. "The hills around where Jesus lived are steep and probably as rough as some of our Arizona country. How far do you think a coddled weakling would get trying to climb them?"

The rider scratched his head and allowed that it would not be far.

Ever since his eighteenth birthday, on the last day of April, Joel found himself more introspective than ever. That day, he learned the full story of his past. Joel had always known his mama died and Aunt Judy raised him. When he inquired about his real father and why he never knew him, Gideon and Judith simply said, "When you're a man, Son, we'll tell you everything." The pain in their faces stilled his boyish questions, but the feeling of some dark secret haunted him. Two years after he and Judith came to the Double J in 1877, twin cousins came along, Matt and Millie. Judith beckoned ten-year-old Joel to see the babies and told him, "They'll be more like your brother and sister than cousins, Joel, Dear." Her dark eyes shone. "I'll need you to help me a great deal now." His childish heart swelled with the trust he saw in her face, and by the time they could toddle, Joel had the twins riding in front of him.

As if conjured up by his thoughts of them, a high-pitched cry shattered the peaceful time of contemplation. "Joel!" It echoed from a nearby cliff wall but died in the steady beat of hooves when Matt and Millie burst into sight and raced toward him. How those eight year olds could ride! Pride rose in the waiting man and chased away the need for solitude. Since April, he had mulled over the unvarnished facts of his birth. How Cyrus Scott, unworthy of the favoritism of his father, had fallen in love with pretty Millicent Butler, married her using his brother Gideon's name, then gone away without knowing of Joel's coming.

"Are you sure he didn't know about me?" Joel had demanded when the sad story ended.

"He never knew." Judith's lips trembled. "In the message I sent to him, I only said that Millie had died."

"Then he abandoned Mama but not me," Joel said, feeling somewhat relieved.

"He also said he was sorry and asked for forgiveness," Gideon put in. Longing filled his face. "I always wanted to go back, to try again to find my brother. . . ."

Did the idea begin then? Joel wondered. The passionate longing to somehow repay the wronged uncle who rode away in bitterness when his father would not believe him innocent? Months and years had passed before God's perfect timing brought Gideon and Judith together to marry and confess the love that grew during their separation.

He would be following a cold trail, common sense advised him. *With God all things are possible* (Mark 10:27), Joel's heart retorted.

Gideon could never go. A few months before Joel and Judith had come, Gideon had been shot. The doctor who had attended him had predicted that Gideon would always walk with a limp and that riding for too long or hard would result in pain. Although he managed well, a familiar grimace of pain showed Joel the folly of his uncle's attempting the kind of riding that would be necessary in traveling the path back to the past.

The second part of Gideon's dream was to return to Tomkinsville, Colorado, where he had traveled under Cyrus's name and had fallen into gambling. "There are so many I want to tell about Jesus," he said brokenly. His strong face worked, and Joel felt his own heart bound with sympathy. Joel almost cried out that he would take Gideon's place, but caution sealed his lips. Not until he received orders from his heavenly Father could he make such a commitment.

Yes, he had considered much since April. A few more days would not matter. He hailed the twins, laughingly declared their race as ended in a tie, then mounted Querida, and rode home, a chattering child on each side. But the aspens and pines and cedars continued their tattletale whispering and filled the wilderness with soft sounds, which were increased by the early evening breeze that sprang up and set the leaves to fluttering even more.

+

Day after day, Joel continued helping with the endless ranch chores, his perfectly trained body busy with his tasks and his mind free to consider. To his amazement, once the unspoken idea of retracing Gideon's journey came, it settled in like butter on a hot biscuit. Suppose he could find his real father. Surely the message his father had sent to the family's Circle S ranch showed repentance! Would not Cyrus Scott's heart be softened if the son he never knew sought him out? Finally, Joel realized why the idea appealed to him so much.

"Lord, I don't want my father to die without knowing You." He paused but refused to think of all he would leave behind if he rode away from home. "Before I go, I need to know if this is just what I want or if it's Your will."

Joel settled into a time of waiting, and the knowledge that he should go firmed. Still, he hesitated, testing himself and praying for something—anything—that would justify his decision. His answer came like a clap of thunder.

One sunny afternoon, Tomkins, who had befriended Gideon so long ago, brought Judith and Joel west, then bought into the Double J and helped it grow, rode out from his home in Flagstaff. Married to a fine woman whose husband had died on their journey to Arizona, Tomkins divided his time between the ranch and various business enterprises in town. "This state will grow," he had predicted. "It's 1888, the Indian fighting's over since Geronimo surrendered a couple of years back, and the Southern Pacific Railroad's bringing more folks in all the time. Ranching, mining, farming—Arizona's got them all."

Always cheerful and forward-looking, Tomkins had lost some of his pleasant expression this afternoon. Finally, he admitted sheepishly, "I guess my foot's getting itchy. I have a hankering to see Colorado at least once more. It was mighty good to me." A wistful look came into his keen eyes. "My wife's sister's been pestering her to visit her in California, and I've been thinking about heading east for a spell while she's gone." He lifted an eyebrow. "Only thing is, it'd be a lot more enjoyable if I had a traveling companion. What are the chances of Joel going with me?"

Thank You, Lord. Joel felt his last doubt slide away. "How are you going?"

"I'm game to just ride a horse and forget all the newfangled ways to travel," Tomkins drawled. "I reckon that Querida mare of yours can carry you to Colorado."

"And to Texas."

"Texas! Who said anything about Texas?" Tomkins's eyebrows arched like an angry cat's back.

"Texas?" Gideon's eyes gleamed, and he leaned forward. "What's on your mind, Joel?" His hands clenched and unclenched.

Joel's fiery blue gaze met his uncle's. "I want to go back to San Scipio and see my grandparents. Then, I'm going to find my father."

"You mean *try* to find him, don't you?" Judith looked shocked but sympathetic. The years had been kind to her; not a single gray hair marred the dark braids she still wore in a coronet.

"No. I'll stay until I find him."

"Impossible!" Yet, the hope in Gideon's face outweighed his words. "I tried everything. It's been fourteen years."

"Have you considered how little chance there is of your succeeding?" Judith quietly asked.

"Aunt Judy." The childish nickname came naturally. "I can't even remember the first time you taught me that God can do anything and that we must have faith." Joel straightened to his full six-foot height, young in build but with a man's steady determination in his face. "Ever since my birthday, I've known I have to find my father if he is still alive." The last words came in a whisper.

"Then you have my blessing. I only wish I were going with you," Gideon confessed. He held out a strong hand and gripped Joel's. "When you stop at the Circle S, tell Dad and Mother we already have a wing planned for them if they ever decide to sell out and come to Arizona."

"I will." As easily as that, Joel left the crossroads he had tarried beside for weeks. What lay ahead? Only God knew. He looked into Millie's and Matt's faces, quiet for once, awed by the serious grown-up talk. His gaze traveled to Gideon's face and noted the mingled fear of failure and unquenchable hope. Then to Judith, whose tranquil posture reassured him. He had known leaving would be hard, but he had not counted on its being such a wrench. All the years with Judith danced before him—the loving care, the sacrifices.

Did she sense his feelings? A small smile tilted her lips up. "God will go with you, Joel. Remember, your name means *Jehovah is the Lord*."

This brittle moment, one to treasure, was broken by Millie's plaintive, "Aren't you *ever* coming back, Joel?"

"Of course I will." He smiled at her, and her anxious look faded. Yet, when good nights had been said and Joel restlessly sought out Querida, he wondered, *How many weeks and months, even years, might it be before I return to the Double J?* He set his lips in a narrow line and vowed, "God, You have blessed my family with the means to let me go. I am going in Your name, to set things straight for Uncle Gideon and to carry salvation to those along the way. Especially to my father. Please, ride with me. No, let me ride with You—until I find my father."

News of Joel's departure created an uproar on the Double J. "Just when I'm gettin' ya to be worth somethin', you ups and rides out," Lonesome complained. Eleven years had not changed the irrepressible cowboy who now owned stock and shares in the ranch. "Dawgone, but it don't pay to invest time in a feller."

"Aw, stop your bellyachin'," Dusty called. "Everyone knows it was me who taught Joel what he knows."

"Sez who?" Lonesome ruffled like a turkey.

"Sez me."

Joel took advantage of their good-natured warfare to escape. The last thing he needed was to let the outfit know how big a lump lay in his chest. Knowing he had to go did not make it easier. Neither did uncertainty as to when he would be back. . .if ever.

From the moment Joel declared his intention to go with Tomkins, Gideon made time to spend with his nephew. With their fair heads bent over roughly drawn maps, they endlessly discussed the route that had brought Gideon from Colorado to Arizona.

"Here's a list of folks whose names I remember," the older man said, eyes filled with a reminiscent light. "People who offered a bed or a bite to eat and never asked for a peso." He laughed gleefully, and some of the lines that the years had etched disappeared from his face. "I used to hide some money where they'd find it after I left. Always felt like a kid with a new toy, thinking about the way they'd look when they found it."

He hesitated, then said, "Joel, there are two in particular I hope you can find. The girl Lily. I helped her get out of the saloon, but I didn't tell her about God." The laughter left his face, and he looked bleak. "The other one's Eb Sears."

"The man you were accused of knifing?" Joel stared.

"Yes. If he had lied, I'd have been sent to prison for a long time. Rough and mean as he was, Eb Sears must have had something good deep down, or he wouldn't have admitted he was drunk and loud, then cleared me of blame." Gideon added, "If I hadn't been so bitter against God, I'd have stayed and tried to work on that hidden good. Tell Sears where I am and that if he ever needs a job, he has one on the Double J—that is, if he will leave the bottle alone!"

⁜

A few mornings later, just after daylight but before the sun rose, Tomkins and Joel leisurely rode away from the Double J. By common consent, they halted on top of the rise and looked back. Fog wraiths hovered in the air, waiting for the sun's kiss to dissolve them. Wisps of smoke curled from the ranch house and bunkhouse chimneys. The eternal whispering of the quaking aspens trembled in Joel's ears, calling him back, pushing him on. By the time the travelers reached the high country, the green leaves would be tinged with gold, yellower than the stuff miners sold their souls to possess.

"Whispers in the wilderness," Joel said softly.

"Yeah." Tomkins relaxed in the saddle, then reminded, "It's a long way." His gaze bored into the younger man, whose fair hair showed in front of his pushed-back Stetson and contrasted sharply with Querida's shining dark hide. "It may be an even longer way home."

"I know." Yet, when the sun burst over a hill and flooded the valley with rosy light, Joel knew he would not turn back if he could. Perhaps some of his father's restless blood stirred and came to life.

With a sense of freedom, responsibility, and urgency, he anticipated what lay ahead. His vivid imagination pictured the aspen leaves whispering *hurry, hurry,* and Joel wanted to prod Querida into a dead run. For an instant, a single dark cloud appeared and blocked the sun's rays. Joel shivered. Again came that feeling of the need to hurry.

Should he tell Tomkins he could not go to Colorado, then strike out alone across Arizona, through New Mexico, and then to San Scipio? Were there forces surrounding the elder Scotts or Cyrus, if he lived, that demanded action and soon?

Do not be a fool, he chided himself. *You felt God confirming your decision to do exactly what you are doing when Tomkins suggested it. You cannot turn back now on the strength of a whim.* Yet, all that first day of travel, Joel found himself anxiously watching the southeastern sky and the giant thunderheads that gathered and attacked the earth. With the ability he had possessed since childhood to sense trouble, he prayed silently but mightily that his quest, his mission, would not fail.

No one could have been a better trailmate than Tomkins. He spoke when Joel wanted to talk, rode quietly when the younger man needed time to think, and he always recognized those times. The same qualities that Gideon had discovered in Tomkins the year they wintered together on the trapline proved strong and welcome now to Joel. Yet, a difference existed. Where Gideon had been embittered and refused to mention God, except to rail against him, Joel shared his early childhood faith. It strengthened them both. Around their nighttime campfires, when shadows hid expressions too private for anyone but God to observe, the men became partners. Joel would have trusted his life to Tomkins. He rejoiced that the older man had accepted Christ shortly after he came to Arizona. They spent hours talking of what the raw West would be like if only God were allowed to be in control, instead of greed and hatred.

Always, Joel carried Gideon's list. As they traveled, name after name received a heavy line through it. Some had moved. Others welcomed the young man with hearty approval and tales of how they discovered his uncle's money in the family Bible or under a plate. Joel's eyes opened wide at the stories. Time after time, those families, who had given what they could little afford to share and who secretly prayed for God's help, received their reward. . .and praised His name for using a passing stranger.

Tomkins's eyes glistened at the stories, and once he gruffly told Joel, "I reckon I had a part in helping answer their prayers, don't you think? If your uncle hadn't grubstaked me, I wouldn't have given him money." He cocked his head. "Wonder how the good Lord would have taken care of those folks in that situation?"

"I've decided I don't have to know *how* or *why* God does things," Joel said soberly. "Just that He does them."

Tomkins grunted, and Joel saw the approving look the other man sent toward him.

The feeling of urgency lessened a bit as they worked their way toward Tomkinsville. They had tarried along the way, and before they had reached the high country, fall had had the opportunity to paint the leaves with its frosty brush. Joel felt he had come home when they climbed the hills and saw his old friends, the quaking aspens. Now, their whispering leaves shone butter yellow, and with each passing breeze, some dropped to the ground to huddle in great golden piles. Miles of wilderness, broken only by a deserted cabin here and there, offered peace and a time to prepare for what lay ahead.

"It might be a ghost town," Tomkins muttered when they mounted the last hill from where they could look down into town. "I haven't kept in touch. Mining may be over."

Joel heard dread in his companion's voice and said nothing, but his heart thumped against his ribs. Tomkinsville represented the place where his real work must begin—the work of taking the gospel of Jesus Christ to those who most needed it and least realized their need.

"Aw, look at that!" A sigh of relief from Tomkins blended with a blast of loud music. "Still here and it sounds the same." He craned his neck, and Joel rode up beside him where the trail widened. Surrounded by snow-topped mountains, Joel's first parish waited.

Chapter 2

A tiny pulse hammered in Joel's temple. Fourteen years earlier, his uncle Gideon had ridden into Tomkinsville, sick at heart and corroded with the bitterness of false accusations. Now, Joel returned as Gideon's emissary. Another blast of raucous music desecrated the peaceful mountain air, and the young man shuddered. Flagstaff with its Saturday night cowboy sprees had been wild, but Tomkinsville roared like a wounded cougar. Would he be equal to the task that lay ahead?

He straightened in the saddle, and Querida softly whinnied. God willing, they would ride straight into the wide-open town and, if it were His plan, stir hearts for Him. Joel wondered how God felt when men invaded some of His most beautiful creations with their schemes and treachery, plotting and sin. Back home, he and Tomkins had seen mountains as high as Humphreys Peak, north of Williams, that reached well over twelve thousand feet. Crowned with early snowcaps, they glistened and shimmered in the distance, everlastingly there as a backdrop for the layers of aspens and dark evergreens that clustered at their feet. Silver waterfalls and tumbling streams fell over rocky ledges, their water so cold Joel's teeth ached when he drank. Did the inhabitants of Tomkinsville ever look up and see the beauty? Or were they too engrossed in their quest for gold and silver, gambling and drinking to raise their gaze above material things?

"First thing we should do is find a place to stay," Tomkins advised. He laughed, but Joel could see excitement in his face. "Funny, not so long ago, folks riding in would have been asking me about lodging!" He shrugged, then shamefacedly admitted, "I guess I had to come back one more time to find out how much I have back in Arizona." He fell silent.

Joel's heart beat with sympathy. What must it be like to have a wife waiting when a man came home? A rush of color streaked his tanned face. Flagstaff had lots of nice girls, but he had never seen one yet that he would want to hitch up with for life. Double harness meant two lives blended into one, each caring for the other. He had learned that from watching Gideon and Judith. They did not have to shout their love from Humphreys Peak to let people know it ran swift as a river in flood.

138

Tomkins shot him a keen glance. "Someday, Boy, you'll meet a special girl. When you do, make sure she's true and real, not just a pretty face."

Joel marveled again at the way Tomkins often seemed to read his thoughts. "I will." The idea warmed him. "I'll never marry until I know God approves." He felt he had just taken as solemn a vow as marriage itself, but his irrepressible sense of humor made him add, "I've never even courted anyone yet, so I'll hold off getting married for awhile. Besides, there's a long trail ahead."

Tomkins grinned appreciatively and reined in before the same log building that had housed his enterprises years before. No longer new, it hugged the ground firmly. The weathered logs brought a memory of Gideon returning to find that his old friend was now the big man in Tomkinsville. It was a thrilling story, one that Joel had begged to hear dozens of times—how only the inherent honesty of a loud, crude cowboy saved Gideon.

An hour later, the visitors surveyed the snug cabin Tomkins had rented at a price he snorted over and called robbery.

"You're lucky to get it at any price," the smooth-tongued gent in a funeral-black suit told them. "More and more people are coming into town all the time. Only reason I have this cabin available is that its owner took up a new residence."

Something in the man's voice sent a chill up Joel's backbone. "Where?"

"Boot Hill." A wave of the hand toward the window indicated a set-apart area with wildflowers blowing in the wind and a fresh gash in the earth. "The way I heard, he talked when he should have been listening and flashed a roll of bills that would choke a horse. Next morning, the sheriff stumbled over a body. The money hasn't shown up." He abruptly changed the subject. "Do you want it for the winter?"

Joel started to nod, caught Tomkins's warning glance, and stopped. He also saw a gleam in the agent's eyes he did not trust, and when the man asked a shade too casually, "Where did you say you were from?" Joel kept mum.

His trailmate looked squarely into the curious man's face. "We didn't say. By the way, they named this town after me some time back. I guess that's enough. We'll look over these accommodations and let you know."

Doubt replaced the suspicious gleam. The agent backtracked. "If you want the cabin for at least a month, I can let you have it a little cheaper." He named a price, still high.

Tomkins grimaced and threw down the money. "If it's dirty, we'll come back and use you for a floor mop."

Joel's mouth dropped open. He had never seen this side of his friend, not even on the long trip west with Judith years before. The minute they got outside, he burst out with, "You sure stopped him!"

Tomkins's shrewd face gave credence to his words. "Son, this is Tomkinsville." He swung onto his horse, and Joel knew that a far deeper meaning than he had suspected lay beneath the dry comment.

Their new home sat on a rounded rise out of town and far enough away to avoid some of the clamor. A view of distant peaks from the front window, the two small bedrooms with hand-hewn bedsteads, a large living room/kitchen combination, and the semiprivacy of the cabin offered all they needed.

Tomkins's eagle gaze swept over the large room. "It will do for a meeting place until we get enough folks coming to need a bigger building." He brought in a bucket of water from a nearby creek and spluttered when the icy drops hit his face. "Your turn. We don't want to meet Tomkinsville looking like two tumbleweeds."

Joel gasped when he felt the cold water on his dirty, heated skin. His teeth chattered, but he rubbed a rough towel on his face and warmed himself up. The one set of good clothes he had brought came out of his saddlebags clean but wrinkled.

"We'll find a laundry," Tomkins promised. "First, let's go get some grub." He had changed into clean pants and shirt, then bunched his trail clothes into a bundle to take with him.

Joel thought of how they had washed out their garments as best they could on their journey. Twice, a friendly rancher's wife had insisted on doing it. He swiftly made his own bundle of laundry and followed Tomkins out to the horses. "I suppose there's a livery stable here?"

"Huh!" Tomkins's eyes glowed like twin coals. "We'll keep real close watch on our horses, especially yours. No livery stable for Querida. Some of the men around here used to have taking ways and probably still do."

They found a small eating place and gorged on fresh beefsteak, mashed potatoes and gravy, corn, biscuits as light as Judith had ever made, and two pieces of apple pie apiece. Black coffee, strong enough to float a lead bar, finished off the meal.

"Well, are you ready for Tomkinsville?"

Joel took a long breath. "If it's ready for me!" he told his friend.

"Now, don't go doing anything stupid," Tomkins warned when they reached the noisy main street. They strolled along until they reached the Missing Spur Saloon. Joel's unfamiliarity with such places left him wide-eyed and wondering why Tomkins would choose a saloon as the place for making their presence known.

"There's bound to be some here who'll remember me." The answer to his unspoken question steadied Joel. "Let me do the talking." He pushed ahead of Joel and stepped inside.

The younger man's first impression mingled color and light, the reek of booze, cigarette and cigar smoke, too-loud laughter, and rough language. For a moment, he felt he had been there before. Then he realized that a replica of Gideon's descriptions, complete in every detail, lay before him. A few heads turned toward the strangers, surveyed them, then went back to their gambling and drinking.

"Don't I know you?" A burly man shouldered his way from the long bar and confronted them.

"You should. I sold you your first horse," Tomkins said.

"Well, by the powers, if it ain't Tomkins himself!" The rough face broke apart into a wide smile. "I hear tell you've been down Arizony way." He clapped Tomkins on the back. "Set 'em up, boys. This is the feller who begun what made this town famous!"

A roar of approval went up. Men crowded toward the bar, but Tomkins stopped them with the wave of a hand. "Sorry, men. I don't drink."

Guffaws replaced the cheers; scowls erased smiles.

"You ain't serious!" The burly man stared. "What'd you do, git religion?"

"That's about it." Tomkins did not move a muscle. Joel had never been prouder of his friend.

"Well, I'll be. . ." The man's jaw sagged. "What about your friend?" He turned toward Joel.

"He—"

Joel cut in, unwilling to be announced as a preacher at this particular moment. "I don't drink, either. I'm looking for a man."

Stone-cold, dead silence filled the hazy room. Tomkins's acquaintance's eyes narrowed to slits. "An' who might that man be?"

Joel sensed a certain breathlessness and rushed in where the devil himself would have hesitated. "Name of Eb Sears."

"*What!*" The thunderstruck man shook his head as if he had not heard right. "Why in tarnation does a kid like you come marchin' in lookin' for Sears?"

"He and my uncle had a mix-up years ago, and—"

"Shut up, Joel!" Tomkins seized his arm with a steel grip.

Bewildered and unsure of what he had done but instinctively knowing it was wrong, Joel felt himself propelled back toward the door. An angry buzzing, like tormented bees from a hive, followed him. Just then the door flew inward, narrowly missing Joel. A heavyset man, carrying the smell of horse, stepped inside. He raised one eyebrow curiously at the sight of a young stranger being pushed toward the door.

"Hey, Sears, the kid's lookin' for you," someone called. "Says you and his uncle had trouble years ago. Think you c'n handle him?" A roar of mocking laughter rocked the room.

Tomkins muttered something under his breath, released Joel, and took one step to the side. "Hello, Eb."

Sears shifted his astonished gaze. "Tomkins! What're you doin' back here? And who is this kid? He looks like someone I know." He glanced back at Joel. "Who's his uncle, and hadn't you better be in bed, Sonny? It's gettin' kinda late for you to be up, ain't it?"

Eager to deliver Gideon's message, Joel ignored both the fresh round of laughter and Tomkins's muttered, "Get out of here." He asked, "Remember the name Cyrus Scott?"

"Scott? Yeah, the guy they said knifed me but didn't." Sears shook himself, and his brows met in puzzlement. "I cleared him. So how come you're lookin' for me a bunch of years later?" He dropped one hand suggestively to his gun butt. Then suspicion wiped out confusion, and he jerked his revolver out of its holster.

Before it cleared leather, Sears found himself looking straight into the steady muzzle of Joel's pistol.

"Who are you, Kid?" Sears's face turned the color of old wax. "Only man I ever saw who could draw that fast was Scott."

"Put the gun on the table." Joel gestured, his face set. What a horrible way to attract the attention of Tomkinsville! He sheathed his own gun and held out his right hand. "Sears, I'm Joel Scott, Gideon Scott's nephew."

"I don't know no Gideon Scott, just Cyrus." Some of the color seeped back into Sears's ruddy face, but he didn't take the outstretched hand.

"My uncle used that name then," Joel explained. His voice sounded loud and strange in the silent room. "He has a big ranch in northern Arizona, the Double J. He got shot up years back and can't ride the way he wants to. I've come to Tomkinsville to shake your hand, tell you he's never forgotten how you told the truth and saved him, and to let you know if you ever need a riding job, there's a place for you on the Double J."

A concerted gasp ran through the room. Sears stepped back as if shocked, then stretched out his hand and grumbled, "What a way to bring friendly greetin's." He gripped Joel's hands. "We mighta killed each other."

"Naw," a heckler called while feet shifted and onlookers sat back in their chairs. "He'da bored ya, if he wanted, Eb. Young feller, where'd ya learn to shoot like that?"

"From his uncle," Tomkins interjected. He sounded delighted at the way things had turned out, but the low note in his voice told Joel he was in for it when they got home. "Well, boys, now that you've all seen what Scott can do, I'd like to invite you to see some more of his skills."

"Can he ride? Rope?" Sears shot a significant look at Tomkins. Tomkins laughed, nodded, and said loud enough for every person present to hear, "Yeah. Preach, too." His enjoyment of the situation spilled over, and his eyes twinkled. "Come out to the old Furman cabin on Sunday morning. He preaches as good as he draws a gun."

Shock, mirth, and disbelief warred in the faces of Sears and several men who crowded around him. "This kid a *preacher?* Some of the rocks you dug looking for gold musta slipped and hit you on the head," Sears pronounced solemnly.

"If you don't believe me, come see for yourself." Tomkins nudged Joel.

Joel flashed his heartwarming smile. "Sorry I had to pull a gun on you, Mr. Sears. I had to make sure you didn't kill me before I could give you Gideon's message. See, he'd been a preacher, too, but was down on his luck when he lived here. I'm taking up the work where he had to leave off."

He moved around Sears, stepped into the crisp night air, and gleefully tasted the thrill of his encounter and the openmouthed stares of the saloon patrons at this revelation. Just maybe, out of sheer curiosity, they would come to the cabin. Joel did not care why they came, just so they did.

Responsibility downed his excitement. God had placed on him a heavy duty; he must not fail. Only through strict obedience to the Holy Spirit would the gospel's message touch and perhaps change Tomkinsville.

$$\text{\Large +}$$

It did not take placards or banners to get the news out that a boy preacher had ridden into town, beat Eb Sears to the draw, invited him to ride for an Arizona cattle ranch, and would even hold a meeting the next Sunday. News ran like a spooked horse.

Tomkins said little but rounded up planks, hammer, and nails, and built some crude benches. "No telling how many folks will show up." His eyes twinkled. "Remember, I told folks you could preach as well as ride and rope and shoot." He pounded a few more nails, then eyed Joel. "I'd suggest you choose your sermon mighty careful," he added, but his eyes twinkled again.

Joel had already sensed the importance of this advice and soberly nodded his yellow head. When Tomkins refused help with his carpentering, Joel wandered off to a quiet knoll that offered as grand a view of the mountains as anything he had seen. What would appeal to the sturdy people of Tomkinsville? Certainly no watered-down message of a pallid Jesus. He closed his eyes and prayed for guidance. Warm sunlight surrounded him, and some of his feelings of inadequacy melted. Why should he fear? God had led him to this place; He would guide him.

Joel looked up at the craggy peaks above him. "I'd hate to get lost up there," he murmured, then sprang to his feet with an exultant yell. "That's it!" Thoughts raced through his brain. He pelted back to the cabin, past an astonished Tomkins. "I have my sermon," he called and bolted inside. He grabbed pencil, paper, and his worn Bible. By the time the benches stood sturdy and waiting, Joel's eyes shone and his heart thumped. "Thanks, God. This is just what's needed."

+

After the weeks on the trail, he felt a little strange when he donned his clean, pressed suit on Sunday morning. The night before, he and Tomkins scoured the cabin to within an inch of its life and arranged the benches. They had no songbooks, but Joel possessed a clear, true voice and would line out hymns if his congregation did not know them. By the appointed time, every bench groaned under the weight of ranchers and their families, curious cowboys, townspeople, and round-eyed children who always looked forward to a circuit-riding preacher.

"What a friend we have in Jesus," the people enthusiastically sang. No need for Joel to sing a line and let them repeat. "All our sins and griefs to bear." He looked into their faces and saw the marks that sin had left in many, grief in others. His throat felt tight, and his vision blurred. What a tremendous need existed in Tomkinsville! The song ended. He offered a fervent prayer, and with one accord, the people said, "Amen." Then, Joel opened his Bible.

"Our text today is from Matthew 18, verses 12 and 13. 'How think ye? if a man have an hundred sheep, and one of them be gone astray, doth he not leave the ninety and nine, and goeth into the mountains, and seeketh that which is gone astray? And if so be that he find it, verily I say unto you, he rejoiceth more of that sheep, than of the ninety and nine which went not astray.'"

He closed the Bible. "Friends, we all know that sheepherders aren't too popular around these parts." Cattlemen and cowboys snickered. "Now, when Jesus told this story, He could have just as well talked about a cow critter or a good horse. I know if I had a hundred horses and Querida strayed, I'd tackle the roughest country around to find her." He glanced out the door, open to the warm autumn air, and pointed to the mountains. Heads turned and nodded. Joel caught a spark of interest in tired eyes.

"Our Lord doesn't tell how tough that journey was. Most of us have tackled rivers in flood, blizzards, or heat that would fry a lizard. Jesus doesn't say He had to fight off wolves or a mean old bear to save that sheep. He leaves out how steep the canyons were and the times when He maybe had to carry that sheep that was struggling to get away. Living here, you can imagine how it was."

The spark of interest flared into the flame of concentration. Joel rejoiced. "What the Lord does tell us is that if the sheep gets found and brought back home where it belongs, the owner is happier over it than over all the other ninety-nine that didn't go wandering off where they didn't belong." He took a deep breath and stepped closer to his attentive listeners. "If any of you have ever had one of your children stray, you know just what the Lord means. You'd give your life in those mountains if that's what it took to bring back your child."

A subdued chorus of agreement rippled the air.

"Friends," Joel poignantly stretched out his hands, "that's just what God did. He sent His only Son, Jesus, so every one of us could be brought back from danger and have eternal life. He loved us that much. There's not a man, woman, or child here today who isn't being trailed by Jesus right now, just like that poor, lost sheep that strayed and was tracked, found, and delivered from hungry beasts and fierce storms. Unless we accept that and invite Him into our hearts and lives, why, we're worse off than that critter all alone and bleating somewhere in a dark canyon."

Joel paused, noted the wonderment in the children's faces, a mist in some of the women's eyes, the angry brushing away of a single drop on a cowboy's face. Too moved to say more, he simply said, "We will close by singing 'Praise God, from Whom All Blessings Flow.'"

The one sad note in the song and service was Eb Sears's absence. Although Joel had not expected him, he had hoped. All through the hearty handshakes and exclamations of gladness that Joel had come, the young minister silently prayed for Sears.

When the congregation poured out, leading the stampede were the few sheepish-looking cowboys who had bashfully perched as close to the door as possible. Joel's keen ears caught a little byplay from among the cowboys that sent him posthaste after the others.

Fifty feet from the cabin, Eb Sears sat on a stocky bay that casually browsed near Querida and Tomkins's horse.

"Hey, Sears, you're too late for the preachin'," one of the cowboys sang out.

"Preachin'? Oh, yeah, there was a meetin', wasn't there?" Either Sears was the finest actor west of St. Louis, or he had forgotten. Joel suspected the first.

"Thought I'd see young Scott's black horse everyone's talkin' about," Sears explained elaborately and scratched his head, a devil-may-care expression on his face.

A few laughed, but no one challenged him, and Sears added, "What's her handle?"

"Querida. It means *beloved*. She's the first horse I ever saw foaled," Joel told the big man, whose glistening eyes showed him to be a top judge of horseflesh.

"I reckon I rode out for nothin', huh. You're not goin' to sell her." The crowd lost interest and dispersed to buggies, wagons, and tethered horses.

Had Sears really come to see Querida? Joel did not think so. If he were a gambling man, he'd stake a lot that it had been the only way Sears would let himself get near a preacher, no matter how curious he might be. "No, I won't sell her, but I'm glad you came." For the second time, he shook hands with Sears, and the current that passed between them confirmed Joel's suspicions.

Chapter 3

If the gold aspens along the trails had whispered about Joel's encounter with Sears in the Missing Spur, now they sang his praises in a fluttering chorus. "Never heard a preacher preach like that" repeated itself over and over when ranchers or riders met. "That young feller talks about a God who knows Colorado and us simple folks. Never uses high-falutin' words, neither," a gnarled miner added.

Joel's second and third sermons merely added to his fame. So did the fun-loving, boyish spirit that led him into the impromptu races that Querida loved. But the test of his mettle came with the first snow.

Not everyone in Tomkinsville appreciated Joel's ministry. Business at the Missing Spur fell off when some of its patrons listened to the gospel and decided it was time to take a stand for the God who had done "a whole bunch" for them. Now, dark whispers joined the praise. Tomkins reported a growing feeling, on the part of the faithful saloon crowd, against Joel's interfering in their business.

A few days later, he stamped in out of the cold, a worried look creasing his face. "Pardner, I hate like anything to tell you, but I've got to go back to Arizona."

"Really?" Joel raised astonished blue eyes from the sermon he had been preparing and looked at Tomkins. "Is something wrong?"

"My wife's back in Flagstaff," the older man explained. "We must have got our wires crossed. I thought she'd stay longer with her sister, but she's home and lonesome." He hesitated, and Joel saw the struggle going on within him.

"It's been good to come back, but—"

"You want to get home where you belong," Joel finished. He quietly added, "I understand. When do you want to leave?"

"There's a stage going out day after tomorrow."

The words hung in the cozy cabin. Joel saw regret in the way Tomkins looked yet eagerness over seeing his wife soon. "What about your horse?"

Tomkins shrugged. "You can have him. Take him with you, or better yet,

147

sell him. He isn't my favorite. Now, if he were Querida, it would be another story." His keen gaze bored into Joel. "Do you still have plenty of money? Tomkinsville's been buzzing because you never take up an offering."

Joel flushed. "I don't need much. I'd rather the people would use their money to get a building for a church." He stretched. "I have a feeling I'll be riding on in the spring, but if there's some kind of building and folks are coming to services regularly, it shouldn't be too hard to get another preacher."

"Folks here don't want anyone but you," Tomkins said gruffly.

"I know, and it disturbs me," Joel admitted. "It's the Lord who needs to be praised, not me. Besides, I just can't help believing there's still a long trail ahead of me, and right now this is just a tarrying place." He shook with sudden melancholy. "I'll miss you, but if I had a wife back home. . ." His voice trailed off.

+

Tomkins climbed aboard the stage two days later but not before warning Joel, "Watch out for rattlers—the two-legged kind who don't have the courtesy to warn a man with their buzzing."

Joel agreed, then promptly forgot it. To his amazement, Eb Sears had dropped in to see him a time or two, although he never came to the meetings. Joel still suspected Sears had heard every word of the first sermon but did not mention it, and the big man always had an excellent reason for stopping by. Once, it was to drop off a haunch of venison he said one of the ranchers had sent. The second time, he said he had heard that Joel wanted to sell Tomkins's horse. After a lot of bargaining, Sears paid a good price for it and laconically accepted Joel's offer for a cup of coffee.

"How come you're a preacher, anyhow?" he asked over the rim of his heavy mug. "Your ridin' and ropin' and the way ya handle a gun would get ya a job on any ranch."

Joel carefully blew on his coffee to gain time to know what to tell him. Then, to his own amazement, he found himself telling his whole story to Sears, who let his coffee grow cold and grunted now and then. "So your own daddy shoved off the blame on his brother," he finally exclaimed. "Still, ya want to find him?"

A longing, greater than ever before, rose in Joel. "I have to. The note I mentioned where he asked to be forgiven shows he isn't, maybe wasn't, all bad." A somber mood crept into the little cabin; he shook it off. "Maybe, because I never knew a real father, my aunt Judith's teachings about my heavenly Father meant more. God also helped me not to be bitter, just sorry. Someday, if I can find my own father and tell him that, maybe he will contact his own parents before it's too late. It would mean the world to them. It would mean even more if he could find and accept God's forgiveness."

Sears abruptly stood. "You're all right, Kid. Just keep on tellin' folks about that God of yours." He strode to the door. "It's kinda comfortin' to think that He's trailin' after even worn-out cowpokes like me. Maybe someday I—some of us'll stop ridin' long enough to let Him catch up." The door banged behind Sears, but a flood of light and joy poured into Joel's soul.

It proved short lived. The next night, gunshots outside Joel's cabin sent him pell-mell into the night. The clatter of hooves sounded loud in his ears, then dwindled toward town. A light snow under a lopsided moon showed Querida tossing her head and dancing away from a huddled dark heap that stirred, moaned, then lay silent.

"God, what's happened?" Joel snatched the horse's reins, wondering how she had gotten loose and berating himself for not building a locked shelter for her sooner. He flipped the reins over a low-hanging tree branch and dropped to his knees beside the crumpled figure. Heavy breathing showed life, and Joel turned the body face up toward the moonlight. "Sears!" He ran his hand inside the unconscious man's jacket. His fingers came away warm with the sickening feel and smell of blood.

Every ounce of range-trained muscle and sinew worked together in a mighty burst of strength that got the far-heavier man onto Joel's shoulders and into the cabin. He staggered across the floor. Blood dripped down Sears's arm and left a ghastly red trail behind them. Once, Sears opened his eyes, but he did not speak. Then he lapsed into merciful oblivion.

Joel grabbed a knife and slit Sears's jacket. His stomach lurched when he pulled jacket and shirt open and exposed a smooth back that spurted blood. "Bullet must have gone in the front and come out here." He left Sears long enough to jerk a clean towel from a nail, fold it, and shove it against the wound with one hand. The other hand fumbled with Sears's neckerchief and pressed it against the man's chest where the bullet had entered. The towel soaked through. Joel wadded up the jacket and used it.

"God, I have to have help, or he will die. What shall I do?" He looked despairingly at the door. "If I leave him, he'll bleed to death. Please, send help!"

A minute or an eternity later, hoofbeats, then a call, "Preacher, you all right?" rang like heavenly music in Joel's ears. Two men, solid citizens who had openly proclaimed the need for a preacher in their town, burst through the still-open door. "We heard shots," one said as the second pushed past. "What's goin' on here?"

"Ride for the doctor," Joel sharply ordered. The first man bolted, and rapid hoofbeats sent thankfulness through the young preacher. "Hand me another towel. I can't get the blood stopped," Joel told the second man. Strong hands instantly snatched a towel, wadded it, and he said, "Let me." He held it ready until Joel slid his hands out of the way, then he pressed steadily. By the time the messenger returned with the doctor, the worst of the flow had been staunched.

"Looks like you've been butcherin' hogs in here," the doctor commented. "Get me hot water, clean rags." His dour face and matter-of-fact orders strangely comforted Joel. Obviously, gunshot wounds were a large part of the doctor's practice. He stitched and cleansed and bandaged but shook his head. "I don't recommend moving him far. Are you willing to keep him here? He's lost a lot of blood." The doctor looked dubious, and Joel's hopes fell again.

"He stays here." Joel motioned to Tomkins's room, then went in to make up the bed. "And he's going to make it." He folded his lips in a way that stopped possible argument, and thus began the long fight for Eb Sears's life.

It took all of Joel's prayers and the doctor's skills. For days, death lurked on the cabin's doorstep, grinning, waiting for its prey. Yet, Eb Sears's dogged determination coupled with the care he received, and he slowly began to mend.

Joel and the doctor had long since pieced together the story of the fateful night in the snow. Sears's delirium had loosed his tongue and revealed the heroism he would never have admitted to under normal circumstances. Sears had discovered a plot to murder "that interferin' kid preacher" and make it look like he had been shot during the rustling of Querida. Everyone knew of Joel's love for his horse. Nothing would be more natural than his rushing out to save the mare and being shot in the confusion.

Hoping to warn Joel, Sears sneaked out to the cabin but had arrived too late and evidently had been mistaken for the victim. Not even he knew exactly who was in on the nefarious scheme, but Tomkinsville noted the significance of certain Missing Spur habitués who mysteriously disappeared in the night. A posse rode out, but enough snow had fallen to cover tracks, and they turned back.

Joel marveled at the strange paths God used to accomplish His work. Years earlier, Sears had been felled by a jealous man who had hoped to get rid of two enemies at once. Now, he had saved Joel's life by nearly giving his own. In addition, the devotion Joel showed in his care for Sears won for him even higher esteem than all of his preaching.

A greater good came from it. The people of Tomkinsville rose in their might and declared that either the Missing Spur tone down or the town would be missing a saloon. The worried proprietor, who might or might not have been part of the plot, instituted some rules and shortened the hours the saloon stayed open. An "accidental" shooting of someone was one thing, but the deliberate planning of a murder and the resultant near killing of Sears did more to clean up the wild atmosphere of the town than Joel had even dreamed of.

⁜

Not until it was safe to leave Sears in willing, protective hands did Joel hold church again, this time in the lobby of the town's hotel. It was packed, and at the end of the service, a leading citizen announced that people were contributing money and that as soon as the weather cooperated—which might not be until spring—Tomkinsville would have its own church. He added, "With all due respect, I reckon seeing you live out what you preached and watching you take care of Eb Sears has showed us what we need to do." Joel had to bite his lip to keep from letting out a cowboy yell of happiness.

A few days later, Joel returned home to a table groaning with home-canned goods, two dressed chickens, and a bushel basket of root vegetables. "What's all this?"

Eb grinned, the first real smile Joel had seen on him since the shooting. "Folks musta thought I needed more n'r'shment than I was gettin'. They brought this over." He squirmed and winced.

"When's the boys gonna bring a wagon and haul me outa here?" His face turned dull red. "I've been clutterin' up your cabin long enough."

A wild idea popped into Joel's head and out his mouth. "Why don't you stick around, spend the winter here with me? It's lonesome since Tomkins left." He saw a wistfulness in the other man's face, quickly hidden, and blandly went on. "No one's going to be out rounding up cattle until spring, anyway."

Eb opened his mouth to speak, but Joel forestalled him. "Soon as you feel like it, there's lots you could do. I'd like to go hunting but don't know the country. Then with winter about to pounce on us, we'll need a mountain of wood."

"I'll think on it. Not sure how I'd like livin' with a preacher, even one who ain't like any preacher I ever met."

Joel wisely kept silent. Sears must have thought on it, but the subject never came up again. The minute the doctor pronounced him fit to ride, however, he took Joel on a hunting trip that ended with enough venison to provide them meat for a long time.

During the weeks together, Sears became "Eb" and "Preacher" changed to "Joel." A bond forged between the two men, and Joel learned the other side of the grudge that had caused the problem between Gideon and Sears.

"Only girl I ever cottoned to," Eb said one evening when the fire roared in the fireplace and shadows hid his face. "She liked me, too, until your uncle came. I knew I wasn't good enough for her, but I never meant bad by her." He shifted uneasily and stared into the flames. "I was aimin' to ask her to marry me, so I got sore when Gideon—Cyrus then—sent her out of town. I got drunk, which I hadn't done for a long time, made some dirty comments, and got showed up in front of everyone." He sighed. "Wonder what happened to Lily? Some lucky hand prob'ly lassoed her."

"In the spring, I'm going to Colorado Springs," Joel said quietly, aware of what it had cost this private man to share his feelings. "Gideon wanted me to especially look you up—and Lily."

Eb's big frame jerked. "Whaat?"

"That's right. He feels he missed the chance to tell you about God and won't ever be really happy until he knows you've heard it. Lily, too."

Eb's breathing quickened. "Sometimes I get tired of Tomkinsville." He leaned forward and poked at the fire, keeping his face carefully averted. "Since you're goin' to Colorado Springs, maybe I'll ride along. Not to see Lily, or anythin'," he hastily added. "When you're ridin' a horse like Querida, a feller can't be too careful."

Joel hid the twitch of his lips, but his eyes brimmed with laughter. "I'd be glad to have you. Oh, if you ever get tired enough of Tomkinsville to leave, I think you'd really like Arizona."

In the spring of 1889, over the protests of the majority of Tomkinsville, Joel and Eb Sears rode away, promising to see if a minister could be found for the little church that would be built soon. They silently halted Querida and the stocky bay that Eb rode. "Ranger's a good horse," he said, and pride shone in his eyes. "Not rustler bait like your Querida, but a good horse." He had sold the horse he bought from Joel to pay his way to Colorado Springs and to get some new clothes. "Never thought I'd wish I saved my money." He laughed, then turned the corners of his mouth down. "I guess it ain't too late. If I should take a notion to go see the Double J ranch of yours in Arizony, I don't wanta ride in lookin' like some scarecrow. Your folks'd think you took up with low comp'ny."

"They'll never think that about you, Eb," Joel said.

Admiration that had begun with the older man's willing sacrifice to save Joel and had grown during the winter months brought an unaccustomed gentleness to Eb's face, but all he said was, "Adiós, Tomkinsville. Maybe I'll see ya again and maybe I won't." He waved to the town in the valley, then rode down the trail, giving Joel a moment alone to silently bid farewell to his first parish and to offer a special prayer that the work the Lord had allowed him to begin might continue in this tiny part of the country.

—✦—

The closer they got to Colorado Springs, the quieter Sears grew. Finally, Joel demanded, "Eb, something's been eating you ever since we rode out of Tomkinsville. What is it?"

A sigh came clear from the rundown heels of Sears's boots. His face filled with misery. "What if we can't find Lily? It's been a lotta years. Or worse, what if we find her and she—" He choked on the words.

Sympathy and wonder at a love that could live for such a long time without nourishment roughened Joel's voice. "We'll find her, and she'll be the same girl you knew except now she'll be a woman—nearly thirty."

"I hope so." Sears's gloomy countenance did not lighten. "Sometimes I think I oughta stayed back there." He jerked a thumb toward the west. "Fool thing. Here I am gettin' close to forty and chasin' over the countryside like a moonstruck calf."

"Who says age has anything to do with love?" Joel flared back. "Wait 'til you get to the Double J and see Judith and Gideon. They're more in love now than when they got back together in Arizona, and that's been almost as many years since you saw Lily." He pressed his point home. "Not many men are privileged to love someone the way you've done. Honestly, even though things didn't work out the way you wanted them to, would you trade your feelings and memories?"

"Not for a gold mine." Sears's eyes flashed, then he grinned shamefacedly.

Joel threw back his head, and a clear, ringing laugh brought a reluctant smile to his partner's lips. Then Eb said, "Just ya wait. One of these days some purty little filly's gonna get ya standin' on your head, then I'll be the one to haw-haw." Anticipation stamped a boyish look on his features. "Ya still ain't said how we'll find Lily."

"Don't you think that if God brought me hundreds of miles to make sure she knows about Him, He can help us find her?"

Sears cocked his head to one side. "I don't see no signposts nailed on trees and sayin', 'This way to Lily.' " A crooked grin replaced his grumbling. "But, we ain't there yet."

Joel laughed again, but a frown puckered his forehead. He gazed unseeingly down the well-traveled road they had found when they left the trail. "I wish I could be as sure of finding my father as I am of finding Lily. Eb, if Lily's married and happy, would you consider going on to Texas with me, at least for a spell? We got along over the winter." Desire for human companionship on his uncertain journey crept into his voice.

Sears grunted. "Maybe. Watch out there, Ranger!" He swerved the bay to the side of the road to make room for a wagon coming toward them. Querida followed.

"How far to town?" Joel called when the nondescript wagon pulled abreast of them.

"Less than a mile." The driver waved and drove on.

Joel felt the stiffening go out of his knees. He had blithely promised to find Lily. *God, please help us.* Such a few words to request aid. *If only everyone realized how available God is!*

—┼—

It took time, in a town as big as Colorado Springs, to find anyone who might know Lily. Joel and Eb inquired at a couple of rooming houses, some stores, and a bank. Always the answer was, "No, don't recall a Lily." Many of those they questioned were recent arrivals.

"Try the stage line," one helpful man advised. But the old-time drivers had long since moved on, replaced by young fellows.

For five days they searched in vain, then Joel came down to breakfast in the modest lodgings they had found and announced, "We've been going at it all wrong."

"Who sez?" Sears put down a forkful of flapjacks dripping syrup.

"What we need to do is find out who the old-timers are around here." Joel attacked the steaming plate of cakes their landlady slid before him. "We'll go back to the biggest dry goods store and start there." Eb eyed him but said nothing. Thirty minutes later, they marched into the emporium. "Who's the owner?" Joel asked a clerk.

"Why, Mr. Livingston." The pale-faced young man in a store-bought suit looked surprised. "His office is up there." He waved toward a set of stairs. "Go right up."

Conscious of the clerk's stares, Joel grinned and told Eb, "Soon as we find where she is, we'll get you a suit like that jasper's wearing."

Eb just snorted and kept on climbing.

Five minutes later, a secretary, who could be a twin to the clerk, ushered them into Livingston's office. A sigh of relief escaped Joel. Good. The gray-haired man looked old enough to have settled Colorado Springs, but even thick glasses failed to hide his keen eyes.

"Sir, we're looking for a girl who came in on the stage from a mining town named Tomkinsville about thirteen years ago," Joel began. "Her name is Lily."

The man sprang from his chair; his glasses fell to the floor and shattered. "Lily! Who are you, and what do you want with her?" His hands shook, and he stared at the strangers.

A great leap of hope warmed Joel's words. "Years ago, my uncle helped her get here. My name is Joel Scott, and this is Eb Sears who used to know Lily."

Unashamed tears stood in Livingston's eyes. "Thank God you've come. If ever Lily needed friends, it's now."

Sears pushed past Joel and confronted the distraught man. His big hands worked. "Where is she?" he demanded hoarsely. "What are ya to her, and why is she needin' friends so bad?"

Livingston fumbled in his pocket and brought out another pair of glasses. He slipped them on, obviously fighting for control. "Lily is my daughter-in-law. I gave her work when she first came to town. My son fell in love with her, and they married. Last fall he was thrown and killed. Since then, Lily's changed from a happy woman to a little black shadow. Doctors say it's shock and if she doesn't come out of it soon, she'll die."

Chapter 4

N o!" Eb gave a strangled cry, then determination straightened his shoulders and snapped his head into a fighting position. Color came back to his pale face, and he wordlessly turned to Joel.

"May we see her?" Joel hesitated. "Or would it be better if you told her we were here and asked if she'd see us?"

Livingston shook his head. "She's refused to see anyone except my wife and me and the boy."

"Boy?"

"My grandson. He's five, only child she and my son could have. I think if it hadn't been for him, she'd have given up before this. But she's so tired from refusing to eat, even for Danny's sake, she can't go on much longer. Perhaps the surprise of seeing you will bring her around." He turned to Eb and held out his hands imploringly. "Forgive me for asking, but did you care for her?"

"From the first time I saw her." It came from the heart.

"Thank God." Livingston wrung Sears's hand. "Come with me."

Eb looked down at his riding garb. "Shouldn't I get some better clothes? I aimed to buy a suit."

"No, no." Livingston impatiently shook his head. He led his visitors out a private entrance, down a flight of stairs to the street, and across it. "Be what she remembers."

Joel and Eb silently followed the almost-running store owner a few blocks over to a residential area. A large, white frame house sat back in a cluster of trees. Livingston threw open the door and ushered them inside. A sweet-faced older woman rose from a low chair, her hands dripping yarn and bright knitting needles. A dark-haired, dark-eyed child solemnly looked up from his place on the floor at his grandmother's feet. Joel heard Eb's quick intake of breath and knew Danny must be the childish reflection of Lily.

"Mama, this is Eb Sears, an old friend of Lily's," Livingston explained. "The young man is Joel Scott, nephew of the kind young stranger who gave her money and sent her to Colorado Springs."

Emotion crumpled the woman's face, and she hastily said, "Danny, go to the kitchen, and ask Hannah to give you a cookie."

"All right, Grandma." The child trotted away.

For a moment, Joel became that child, being sent away while grown-ups talked. He remembered the brown faces of the Mexican servants at the Circle S and how Rosa and Carmelita welcomed a tired, uncertain little boy.

Then, Livingston said, "I'll just take Mr. Sears up first, if it's all right." He looked anxiously from Eb to Joel. "Lily won't know you, Mr. Scott."

"That's fine," Joel said, but he leaned close to Sears and whispered in his ear, "I'll be praying."

Eb gripped his hand. "Come as far as the door in case I need ya." Joel quietly followed the other two men up a flight of stairs, down a comfortable hall to an open door, then stopped. Livingston stepped through with Sears right behind.

"Lily, here's an old friend, come all the way from Tomkinsville to see you."

Joel could see every detail of the airy, wallpapered room and the slender, girlish woman who slowly rose from a rocking chair. Her dark eyes all but filled her thin face. Seldom had he encountered such gulfs of despair and sadness. *God, give Eb the right words.*

"Howdy, Lily." In the strain of the moment, all Sears's insouciance rose to sustain him. "You've been under the weather, huh?" He crossed the room with his hand held out.

She stumbled toward him. "Eb? Eb Sears?" A flicker of life stole into her eyes. "Why, after all these years! You look just the same."

"You don't," he told her frankly. "You're better lookin' now than ya were in Tomkinsville." A blush stained her pearly face, but Eb took her little white hands in his for a moment, then released them. "Sorry about your husband, Lily, but ya sure have a great little buckaroo downstairs. He's a mite puny, though. Now that spring's here, you'll need to be gettin' him out in the fresh air so he can get some color."

Joel had caught the flash of pain when Eb mentioned Lily's husband, but it disappeared into a little frown at the word *puny*. How wise of Eb to get her attention on her son and off her own problems. Concern for Danny could be the first step to her own healing.

"I brought someone you'll wanta see," Eb continued. "Joel Scott, nephew to the Scott who rode in, staked Tomkins, and sent ya out of Tomkinsville." He stepped aside, and Joel came into the pretty room.

"Lily, my uncle Gideon—who called himself Cyrus when he knew you—never forgot you or Eb." Joel quietly explained how Gideon could no longer travel long distances without pain and that he had come in Gideon's place. The growing interest in her face rewarded him. "Most of all, he wanted to tell you how much he regretted failing you."

"Failing me!" Lily backed away and sat back down in her rocker. "Cy— Gideon Scott *saved* me. If it hadn't been for him, I'd never have come here or met Dan or had little Danny or. . ." Her hands tightened on the arms of her chair.

Joel nodded, pleased with her response but noting how tired she looked. "Gideon sent you a special message, but it can wait. You need to rest. We'll come back later if you like." He held his breath.

"For supper, perhaps?" Lily looked at her father-in-law, who eagerly agreed. The three men walked out and back downstairs. Mrs. Livingston stood waiting.

"Mama, she's coming down for supper, and these men will be our guests." Happy tears filled the woman's eyes and overflowed when Livingston brokenly explained, "It will be the first time in more than a month that Lily has left her room." In a wave of thanks and more tears, Eb and Joel finally got away, promising to be back no later than five o'clock.

With one accord, they walked to the livery stable, saddled and mounted Querida and Ranger, and rode for miles, viewing Colorado Springs and the surrounding area.

When they headed back to town, Sears quietly said, "I'm still goin' to get new clothes, but no dud's trappin's. Lily ain't used to me in city clothes." He paused and waited until they reached the stable again before adding, "Joel, ya may have to go lookin' for your daddy without me." His rock-stern expression softened, and he glanced in the direction of the Livingston home. "Somehow, this feels like the end of the trail for this cowpoke. I ain't askin' anythin' of Lily 'cept to be a friend. I just feel I can help her and the buckaroo by stickin' around."

"I understand," Joel assured his friend. "The Double J will always be there no matter what happens."

"Yeah." Eb cleared his throat. "Uh, when ya said that God of yours would help us, I was leery. But we found her, didn't we?" He took a deep breath, held it, then expelled it. "If He makes her well, I'll start ridin' His trail."

"No, *no*, Eb!"

Joel's outcry froze Sears. His face hardened. "Ain't I good enough, after all ya said about Him followin' lost critters?" He laughed bitterly. "Mighta known I was playin' against a stacked deck."

"It's not that." Joel felt compelled as he had never been before. His heart burned. "Everything I said is true, but you can't bargain with God the way you'd horse trade, promising Him this if He'll do that. You know I'd give anything for you to follow the Master, but it has to be everything or nothing. Either you choose to do what you know is right and stick with it *even if Lily dies,* or it's no good, Eb."

The anger faded from Sears's face. A muscle in his left cheek twitched. "That's a mighty powerful prop'sition," he said slowly.

"It can't be any other way. Otherwise, the only reason we'd accept Christ would be for what we could get out of it."

"Isn't that what a feller does anyway?" Sears demanded. "He says yes to God so he can skitter out of gettin' punished for all the mean things he's done."

Joel never wavered. "Some folks do just that, but people who are smart give themselves because they love and appreciate what God did for them, not just to keep from getting what they deserve."

Eb grunted and changed the subject. Joel, however, noticed how thoughtful and withdrawn Eb acted while selecting his new shirt, vest, boots, hat, and pants at the emporium and while shaving, more carefully than usual. At five minutes to five, they knocked on the Livingstons' door, shiny-clean and expectant. A new dignity surrounded Sears, and Joel realized that the selflessness evident in his friend's life had changed a tough rider into a man who would put aside his own desires for the sake of another.

+

By early summer, Lily had lost much of the shadow in her eyes. Eb simply would not allow her to remain in her room and brood. Time after time, he coaxed her into walking, then riding, "Because Danny needs his mama, not just a roughneck like me," as he said.

Sometimes Joel joined them. He had faithfully delivered Gideon's message, the gospel of salvation, to Lily. In her, he found depths of bitterness that God would allow the husband she had loved to die in a senseless accident. Yet, Lily found gradual healing in the fact that God had lost His only Son— not in an accident, but in the deliberate plan to save His creation. She began to open like a tightly closed rosebud, and by the time Joel rode away in late summer, Lily and Eb both hovered on the edge of committing their lives to their Master.

Joel had intended to follow the trail to Wyoming and Montana that Gideon had taken, but the inner urgency that had prodded him, then subsided, rose sharply. On a clear summer morning, he shook hands with Sears, vaulted onto Querida's back, and turned his face toward Texas.

Well past nineteen, he no longer looked all boy. New maturity firmed his lips except when he smiled. The experiences of the past months showed in his compassionate gaze, a gaze that held more tolerance for those who slipped and fell than when he first left Arizona. Where once he would have condemned, now he stooped to lift. Yet, always in the depths of his heart, fire and ice lived side by side: the fire of his passion to find Cyrus Scott, the icy realization it might never come to pass. The thought made him tremble, and the long miles Querida carried him became hours for introspection. He had never been alone for such an extended time. First Tomkins, then Sears had provided an older and more experienced influence. Now he rode alone except for the uncanny feeling of companionship he knew must be God.

At times, Joel and Querida were tiny black dots, the only moving creatures in a vast expanse of sky and land. Then it was that Joel missed the mountains, the wilderness. How could anyone live forever in a rolling country that stretched from horizon to horizon in every direction with never having the friendly peak of a jutting mountain to offer encouragement? In sheer desperation, he sought out those riding his way, often veering from his course for the sake of hearing another human voice. After a few times, he gave this up; the naked greed in the eyes of many who he met betrayed their lust for Querida, and he slipped away.

Tired and drooping, Joel trailed into San Scipio country. He was amazed at how much he recognized and was thrilled when landmarks brought the familiar feeling he had been there before.

Almost a year after he left the Double J, the young minister and his faithful Querida, more beloved than ever after their arduous journey, *clip-clopped* into the dusty town that had changed so little that Joel blinked in astonishment. Had San Scipio been asleep these long years? No, for on closer examination, he saw signs of weathering, a few new houses. Yet, the illusion of time standing still persisted, so much so that he gasped in astonishment when he saw the church his grandfather had built now had a small, cozy cabin next to it with smoke curling from the chimney.

Tempted to stop and see who lived there, Joel shook his head. "Not yet," he told Querida. "Just a little longer, and we'll be at the Circle S." Strange that he had not said home, or was it? Most of his life had been on the Double

J. "Trot along, Querida. Maybe there will be letters from home."

In response to his voice, the black mare raised her drooping head, pricked her ears, and speeded up while Joel's keen gaze shifted from side to side in his unwillingness to miss any cherished childhood sites. Then they topped the promontory rise that overlooked the Circle S; below lay the ranch, warmed by the late afternoon sun. With a cry, Joel slid from the saddle. He raised his glance to the hills and felt a surge of strength go through him. Surely God would somehow, in some way, lead him to his father. Why else would he feel closer to that unknown man than at any other time in his life?

Stiff from long hours riding, Joel swung back into his saddle and started down to the valley. With every step Querida took, Joel relived childhood days on the Circle S. The cottonwoods he had climbed now rose tall with many years' growth. But the house looked the same—foot-thick cream walls that held heat in or cold out, depending on the season. A red-tiled roof that glistened in the sun. Joel's heart pumped. He had not sent word of his arrival, and mischief tilted his mouth skyward. He would just bet that Grandpa and Grandma would be surprised at how much he had changed from the almost seven year old who rode away atop a covered wagon. Yet, when he reached the hacienda-style house and called, "Anyone home?" Joel knew the seven-year-old boy still lived inside him.

The massive front door opened, and a man stepped out. Life's tragedies had silvered his hair, thinned him to gauntness, and carved permanent furrows in his face. But they had not been able to bow the large head or bend the shoulders that were held as erect as Joel remembered. Intent on the similarities and changes in Lige, Joel stayed in the saddle until the booming voice he would have recognized anywhere asked, "Well, are you going to sit there all day? Light down, Boy." In three giant strides, Lige reached Querida and held out his hand. His ox eyes rolled, still blue as Texas bluebonnets.

Joel dismounted, grabbed the large hand, and felt his eyes sting. He opened his mouth to speak, but a rush of flying feet halted him. A whirlwind with wiry arms and a tear-stained face caught him. "My baby!"

"Don't carry on, Naomi," Lige told his laughing, crying wife. "Let him loose long enough to look at him. He's no baby."

Joel's grandmother pulled back. Although her hair had also whitened, she looked less changed than Lige. Her eyes still snapped in the way he remembered. "Elijah Scott, it doesn't matter if he is half as tall as a mountain, this is my little boy come home." She hugged him again, announced, "Your room is ready," and fled toward the front door. "By the time you're washed up, Rosa and Carmelita will have a meal ready. You look like you could use one! There'll be hot water in your room. See that you use it. I never saw such a dusty rider." She vanished inside after her pronouncements from the porch.

"I guess Grandma will never believe I'm grown up." Joel laughed. The peppery nature that hid beneath her usual calm made him a child again. Strangely, it felt good.

"Mighty fine piece of horseflesh." Lige turned from Joel to the tired mare. "This the one you wrote about when you were a lad?"

"Yes." Joel caught the reins in one hand and headed for the corral. "I need to clean her up. She's carried me a long way."

"Better not risk Naomi's wrath," Lige suggested with the hint of a twinkle in his eyes. "I'll care for—what's her name?"

"Querida—Spanish for *beloved*."

Lige looked amused but did not say anything, just took the reins and admonished, "I'd step lively, if I were you."

Joel did. He barely wasted a glance on the large hall except to see it had not changed. The polished dark floor and furniture attested to loving care. Bright serapes on the cream plaster walls and matching, woven Mexican rugs welcomed him. So did the courtyard just outside, abloom with late summer flowers. The fountain splashed just the same as the fateful day he and Judith came to the Circle S. He started toward the large room and alcove they had used while there.

"Not there." Naomi appeared at his elbow. "You'll have Gideon's rooms." Her voice sounded choked. "You are so like him—and your father." The hand she laid on his arm trembled, but the next moment she dashed it across her eyes and crisply reminded him to hurry.

※

After his long journey from Colorado, Joel found himself content to mosey around the ranch, let Querida rest, and simply soak up the outward peace of the Circle S. Still, after a few days, his youthful resilience overcame his fatigue, and he spent hours riding with Lige. He received a visit from the San Scipio minister, a frank-faced, likable fellow who lived in the little cabin next to the church with his wife and baby.

"I'd be proud to have you preach come Sunday," the minister invited.

Joel hesitated, then caught the perceptible nod from his grandmother and Lige's quickly smothered grin. "I'd be happy to accept," he agreed.

After the visitor drove away, Joel asked, "Do they—the church—know it wasn't Gideon—" He could not go on in the face of the pain that replaced Lige's half smile and his gruff, "They know," before the big man stood and walked out.

"I had to ask." Joel stared at his hands.

"I know, Dear." His grandmother twisted her apron, then smoothed out the folds with painstaking care; Joel's heart twisted at the action. "I don't know how much you remember of that time or what Judith told you, but the Sunday after the message came from Cyrus asking forgiveness, Lige went to church alone. He wouldn't even let me accompany him. Later I learned that he courteously waited until after the sermon had ended, then told the church how unjust he had been to his younger son because of his blind love of the older. He has never mentioned his confession, but I know it must have cruelly knifed his pride." Her hands stilled, and a poignant blue light shone in her eyes. "Joel, there is no man bigger than one who will publicly admit he's wrong, even when the cost is high."

A wave of love and admiration for his grandfather tightened Joel's throat and made his heart pound. He blurted out sympathy and went to find Lige. Before the matter could be closed forever, he must again rush in where wise men would not.

He found Lige standing with one arm resting on the corral fence while he gazed toward the distant mountains. Without turning, he said, "She told you."

"Yes." Joel inhaled a blend of stable and hay odors. He wanted to cry out his feelings, but Lige had moved to some remote, unapproachable place. Joel's stubbornness rose. "Not many men would do what you did." If he lived as many years as some Old Testament patriarchs, he would never forget Lige Scott's reply.

His grandfather whipped toward him, eyes blazing with sapphire fire. "Boy, any *man* would." Lige strode away, looking even taller to Joel than ever before.

Saturday night at supper, Joel fired the first gun in a private campaign. "Why don't you sell the Circle S and move to Arizona? Gideon can't do all the riding and overseeing of the ranch he'd like to. He sure could use another good hand." He shot a covert glance at Lige and blandly continued, "Grandma, Aunt Judy really needs help with the twins." He chuckled. "Matt and Millie were eight when I left and perfect rascals. I don't know what they're like now, but they're bound to need a firm hand."

"Leave Texas?" Lige's heavy eyebrows met in a forbidding line. "Never!"

"Now, Lige," Naomi began, wistfulness at the mention of the twins softening her face. "My heart's plain hungry to see Gideon and the rest."

Lige shook his massive head as if she had hit him with a log. "You want to sell this place we've worked to build and go kiting off to Arizona? Woman, are you out of your mind?"

"No." She helped herself to more chili and passed the enormous bowl to Joel. "I just want to see my son." A spasm of pain contorted her smooth face. "We've waited here all these years hoping Cyrus would come back. He hasn't. Must I die without seeing either boy again?"

All the fight went out of Lige. He paled and, for the first time, looked old to Joel, shrunken.

"I don't mean you should sell immediately," he quickly put in. "Why don't you go to Flagstaff for a visit? See how you like the country? Your foreman's run the Circle S for years and can handle things while you're gone."

Lige straightened, and interest crept into his face. "Would you stay here while we're gone—if we go?"

A sickening flood of anguish filled Joel. How could he tell—but he had to say it. "Grandpa, I can't. Ever since I left the Double J, I've felt God had a special mission for me. That's why I'm here, as well as to see you."

Recognition, shock, hope flared in Lige's eyes. "And this mission is—"

Joel licked dry lips. His hands felt cold, his face hot. "To find my. . .my father."

Lige sucked in his breath. Naomi gave a little cry.

Joel leaned forward and planted his hands on the tablecloth before him. "I hope you'll go. There's been too many years between you and my Arizona family." His hands clenched. "Even if you stay, I'll be riding out right after I preach on Sunday."

Chapter 5

"Who am I?"

Rebecca Fairfax despairingly stretched her arms out toward the panorama before her, searching for secrets the distant wilderness might hold. How many times had she ridden to this eastern New Mexico vista in hopes it would trigger memories that tumbled in her mind, too ephemeral to hold? Some, Kit Carson and Lucien Maxwell among them, said the scene that lay before her was the grandest in New Mexico. The fan-shaped holdings of the Lazy F ranch lay between forested slopes and rolling plains where the Old Santa Fe Trail and Cimarron River wound into the blue distance. Thousands of acres, broken by a few cattle ranches, spread west past slopes that jutted sharply to glistening, white-peaked mountains. How she loved them! If only—

"Thought I'd find you here."

Vermilion, the mustang that Smokey Travis had broken and given to the girl on her eighteenth birthday just a few months before in December, shied and danced away from the man on foot who had sneaked up on them. Rebecca expertly quieted him, then turned. "What are you doing, creeping up on me, Hayes?" Her usually merry brown eyes flashed fire. Rebellious tendrils of her nut-brown hair had escaped her sombrero and curled moistly around her flushed, angry face. "I told you before to leave me alone!"

Admiration for her charm lightened Clyde Hayes's heavy, sullen face. Bold gray eyes surveyed her from dusty boot tops up her lithe, five-foot, six-inch frame. Hayes doffed his worn Stetson, exposing mousy brown hair. "It's time we had a talk," he announced.

Ugh, how I hate him, she thought. In the last year, he had turned the ranch from a place of freedom to a nightmare. Well, she would not stand for it. "I have nothing to say to you," she retorted.

"Fine way for a woman to talk about the man she's goin' to marry." Triumph leered in his eyes. "Your daddy promised you to me five years ago when I took over as foreman."

Sheer rage threatened to topple Rebecca from the saddle where she could stick like a cactus on the wildest horse. "Marry you?" She laughed scornfully and rejoiced when an ugly red crept into Hayes's face. "You're thirty-five years old, almost old enough to be my father. Even if you weren't, do you think I'd marry a man I hate with all my heart, especially since you tried to maul me coming home from the rodeo in Raton last fall?"

The red deepened. "Aw, Becky, you know I'd been drinkin' and—"

"And didn't have the decency of a rabid skunk." She dug her spurless boot heels into Vermilion's sides. He snorted, leaped, and Hayes jumped aside, but not before the stallion's shoulder caught him with a glancing blow and sent the would-be suitor flying.

Rebecca laughed again and called back over her shoulder, "Next time I'll run you down. Stay out of our way, Hayes." As soon as they reached level land, she goaded Vermilion into a dead run. Even if Hayes were mounted, he could not catch her. Not a horse for a hundred miles around equaled Vermilion.

Wind whistled past her, and if the girl's sombrero had not been firmly mashed down on her head, the hat would have gone sailing. Her laughter changed to joy, and her spirits rose, but by the time she reached the Lazy F, they drooped again. *Has Father really promised me to Hayes? If so, why?* As clearly as if it had been this morning, she remembered the day the two-hundred-pound man came. Even at thirteen, she had instinctively distrusted him, and she avoided him all she could. Perhaps the change in her father troubled her most. From the moment Hayes took over, Samuel Fairfax lost even the small amount of patience with her that he had shown before.

Now Rebecca wondered, *Does Hayes know something that would discredit Father? If not, why did he lord it over the hands until, one by one, he drove them away?*

Smokey Travis was the exception. Twenty-one, only a few inches taller than Rebecca, he had stuck. Without being vain, she knew the reason—herself. A little smile added sweetness to her lips. She did not mind having Smokey in love with her. It had changed the harum-scarum cowboy from a gambling, drinking man who kept up with the best—no, the worst—of the riders to a considerate, thoughtful protector.

Dark-haired, dark-eyed, and droll, Smokey refused to let Hayes drive him away, and when he could do so without raising Hayes's ire and ending up fired after three years of top service, Smokey unobtrusively saved the girl from encounters with the persistent foreman.

Sometimes Rebecca considered eloping with Smokey. He had never suggested it, but the way his midnight gaze followed her spoke eloquently. If she married him, she would have love and respect, not what she sensed in Hayes—his desire to possess and tame her the way she had seen him tame a wild horse.

"I'm glad he didn't get you," she whispered to Vermilion. The red stallion whinnied. "Smokey used kindness, not mastery. I wonder if real mastery actually is kindness?" She stroked Vermilion's glistening shoulder, uncoiled the lariat she always carried on her saddlehorn, and swung it in a wide loop. It dropped over the gatepost to the corral. Still in the saddle, Rebecca gave an expert tug, and the gate swung open.

"Good girl." The sound of applause from the rider perched on the fence changed her mood again. Smokey Travis's teeth gleamed white against his deeply tanned skin. His dark eyes sparkled. "Where'd you ride? I finished my chores an' looked for you." He shook his head ponderously and put on a long face. "Like looking for a white rabbit in a snowstorm." He doffed his Stetson.

Rebecca rode into the corral, slid from the saddle, and tossed Vermilion's reins to Smokey, the only cowboy the stallion would let groom him. "Will you rub him down, please, Smokey? Father will be a bear if I don't change and get to supper on time."

"How come you're so late?" Smokey cocked a laconic dark eyebrow at her.

All the girl's earlier fury returned. "Skunk Hayes followed me to the promontory."

Smokey jerked straight; his teasing fled. "What'd he want?"

A mischievous devil prompted Rebecca to say, "Me." She regretted it instantly.

Smokey's lips thinned to a slit. His eyelids half closed, and he drawled, "One of these days, me an' Hayes are going to have to have a little talk." His face turned to steel. "Even if he is the boss around here."

A little bell rang deep in Rebecca's mind but not loudly enough for her to figure out why. She grabbed Smokey's checkered sleeve and tugged. "Don't start anything. Please. He'll send you away and—"

"Would you care?" The cowboy stood bareheaded before her, face curiously still.

"You know I would." Her lips trembled. "Sometimes I feel like you're the only friend I have on the Lazy F."

"Good enough for me." Smokey relaxed and smiled at her.

She pretended not to hear his almost indiscernible "for now" when he led her horse toward the gigantic barn. Rebecca seldom allowed Vermilion the privilege of open grazing. She had seen too many avaricious riders examine her mount's every point and would take no chances on risking Vermilion's loss.

A few paces away, Smokey stopped and glanced back at her. "You know the reason you don't have all the friends you'd like, don't you?" He did not wait for her response. "Your daddy's never cottoned to us cowpokes hanging around."

Red flags waved in her face. "I don't see that it's stopped you," she shot back.

Smokey immediately reverted to his laconic self. "That's 'cause I'm the best shot, the best rider, and the best roper in northern New Mexico."

"Talk about stuck on yourself!" Rebecca made a gamin face at him. "Besides, I can outride you any day."

"Only on Vermilion," he reminded. He scratched his head. "I'll be hanged why I gave away the best horse I'll ever straddle to a braggy girl who thinks she's a real cowpoke."

Rebecca's merry trill brought a sympathetic grin to his rueful face. "Thanks for rubbing Vermilion down," she told him, then ran toward the sprawling log house a hundred yards away.

Formed in the shape of a crude "H," the weathered logs, chinked with thick adobe, had silvered with summer sun until their pale, rounded sides gleamed. Years before, when he took possession, Samuel Fairfax had wisely kept the original house and added to it. Wide porches across the front and west offered a view second only to the one Rebecca saw from the promontory. As usual, she paused and looked back, awed by the magnitude of this part of New Mexico. Could she ever live anywhere else?

Impatiently, she opened the huge front door and stepped inside. No plastered or wallpapered walls greeted her. Just whitewashed logs hung with hunting trophies and a smooth floor covered with bearskin rugs both brightened by fantastically designed Indian blankets on couches and chairs.

"Daughter?" Heavy steps from the left arm of the "H" where Samuel had his room preceded her father's entrance into the living area that took up the full front half of the crossbar. Behind it lay an enormous kitchen and Mrs. Cook's quarters.

"Cook by name, cook by trade," the round-faced woman said when she hired on at the Lazy F shortly after Samuel advertised. "Not for a bunch of roughnecks, though. It's understood that I cook for the family only, plus keep the house clean." She fondly repeated the story during Rebecca's growing-up years. Each time Mrs. Cook grew bolder, though, her boss grew more timid.

The girl loved her too much to admit she had trouble believing her father "just up and lay down and rolled over like a pup," so she merely chuckled and told Mrs. Cook how lucky they were to have her.

"There's plenty of others who'd be glad for my services," Mrs. Cook always said darkly. "Folks who won't be prying into what doesn't concern them."

Rebecca knew it would take an avalanche to uproot their cook/housekeeper, but the threat of her leaving served as an excuse not to ask about a possible Mr. Cook.

"Rebecca?" Samuel stepped into the living room and frowned with displeasure. "Why aren't you ready for supper? I won't have you at the table wearing riding clothes."

With the new awareness that had been growing since she turned eighteen, Rebecca surveyed him through the eyes of a stranger. Not quite six feet tall, he could be anywhere between forty and fifty; she had learned early not to ask questions. About 180 pounds, with not an ounce of fat, blue eyes, and graying brown hair, he wore the face of an old man on a remarkably strong and healthy body.

"I asked you a question." Not a flicker of love showed, although Rebecca knew she represented the only object in his life that could soften him.

Resentment crisped her reply. "I'd be ready if Clyde Hayes hadn't waylaid me." She ignored the storm signals that sprang to his face. "Why don't you tell him to lay off? I'm not going to marry him, ever, even if you did tell him I would." Color burned in Samuel's face at her well-placed shot, and she incredulously added, "So he wasn't lying." A pulse beat in her throat. "Father, how dared you do such a thing? He's a. . .a snake." She shuddered, as much at the look in her father's eyes as at the grim prospect of ever belonging to a man like Hayes.

"It's not for you to question your father." He retreated into the coldness that normally brought her to heel. "Hayes can run the Lazy F when I'm gone. You can't. You may as well get used to the idea."

Did she dare tell him Hayes had tried to manhandle her on the way home from Raton? She opened her mouth. . .closed it again. If he believed her, he would kill Hayes. No matter how much she hated him, she would not have blood spilled on her account. "I'll go change."

"See that you do," he told her dictatorially.

She turned toward the right arm of the "H" where the western sun sent slanting rays into her room and the storerooms. His voice stopped her in the doorway.

"I don't want you riding out with Travis again. He's in love with you, and I won't have it. Do you hear?"

Rebecca whirled. Her hands clenched into fists, and she planted her feet apart in a fighting posture. "He's the only friend I have on this ranch except Mrs. Cook. Hayes has driven away every cowboy who tried to be nice and friendly. The men barely speak to me. Do you know how it feels to be imprisoned?"

"Has Travis ever laid a hand on you?"

She hated the suspicion in his eyes. "No," she cried. *That's more than I can say for your precious Hayes.* She bit back the inflammatory words. "He respects me too much."

Her father grunted. "Go change your clothes."

Dismissed, Rebecca felt like a small child being sent to her room. She ran away from her father's presence into the haven of her bedroom and flung herself on the bed. Tears she would not shed before him came in a hot flood. How much longer could she bear his tyranny? Yet—*"Honour thy father and thy mother"* (Exodus 20:12). Where had the words come from? Rebecca believed in God. *Who could live in such a wonderful world and not believe?* But her knowledge of the Bible was vague, although she dimly remembered a woman's voice reading to her. *Had it been my mother? Do the phrases that sometimes spring into my mind have their source in the mists of my past?*

"Rebecca." The muted roar from the living room brought her to her feet. She made a hasty toilet with water, soap, and soft towels that Mrs. Cook must have fetched while Rebecca and her father argued. Then she slipped into a simple white gown, with a modest round neck, that left her arms bare below the elbows. She threw a gaily colored Mexican shawl over her shoulders, opened her door, and started toward the living room. The sound of voices halted her, but she disdainfully went on, dreading but knowing what she would find. Yes, a white-shirted Hayes, with slicked-down mousy hair and reeking to high heaven with pomade, smirked at her from the round table at one end of the living room where meals were served.

She almost fled to her room. Instead, she lifted her chin, gave the unwelcome guest who more and more frequently joined them for the evening meal a cold nod, and slipped into her chair. At least he had not held the chair for her, the lout.

All through the meal she answered in monosyllables, only when spoken to directly. Not by the flicker of an eyelash did she betray that Mrs. Cook's finest roast beef, mouthwatering rolls, and accompanying vegetables tasted like moldy sawdust to her. The moment she choked down the ambrosia pudding, she pushed back her chair.

"May I be excused, please, Father?" She rose, slim and remote in her white gown and gorgeous shawl. "Mrs. Cook promised to show me a new knitting stitch."

"Not very friendly of you to run off when I'm here," Hayes drawled.

His effrontery stung her to quick but guarded speech. She forced a brilliant smile. "But I've already seen you today, Mr. Hayes." She did not dare put him in his place by calling him Hayes as she usually did except when in the presence of her father. "Or have you forgotten so soon?" She laughed maliciously. "Father, would you believe your conscientious foreman took time to ride all the way to the promontory to talk with me instead of making sure the boys got those draws combed?" Before either man could answer the taunt, she vanished into the kitchen, eyes blazing, and carefully closed the door behind her without slamming it. "I just can't bear it," she burst out.

Mrs. Cook looked up from a pan of soapy water. Suds sparkled on her plump hands and glinted from the worn gold band on the third finger of her left hand. Her shrewd, blue eyes held welcome and sympathy. "You always have me, Child."

"I know." Rebecca crossed the kitchen and hugged the housekeeper, heedless of the flying soap bubbles that rose. "If I didn't, I. . .I. . .I'd run away with Smokey Travis!"

"Now why would you want to go and do that?" the buxom woman asked, eyebrows arching almost to her brown hair, dusted with silver that shone in the lamplight. "You're not in love with him, at least not the way you need to be when you marry." She dried her hands on a towel, hugged Rebecca, then held the girl away from her. "Child, marriage can be wonderful with the right man or miserable with—"

"Hayes." Rebecca's shoulders shook; her face whitened. "Wouldn't it be better to marry Smokey, even if I don't love him the way you say I should, than to be with Hayes? I'd rather be dead."

Mrs. Cook led her to a small table with two chairs. She gently pushed the weeping girl into one of the chairs, then billowed into the other. "And I'd rather see you dead than married to a varmint like him." Her hand, still warm from the dishwater, stroked the girl's hair. "On the other hand, it wouldn't be right or fair to Smokey for you to up and run off with him just to get away from Hayes."

Rebecca looked up and through her tears saw the puzzled expression in Mrs. Cook's face before the good woman slowly said, "I can't understand why your father's so intent about you marrying Clyde Hayes. It's almost as if our foreman knows some secret Samuel Fairfax doesn't want let out."

"Why, that's what I was thinking earlier today." Rebecca straightened and mopped her face with a handkerchief that Mrs. Cook offered her. "Smokey said something funny, too." She wrinkled her forehead, trying to remember exactly what it was. "No use. It's lost. Mrs. Cook, what would you do if you were me?"

For a long time, the housekeeper did not answer. A shadow crept into her blue eyes, darkening them. Finally she said, "First I'd ask God to help me get things straightened out; then I'd keep my eyes peeled every minute and my ears wide open. There's a lot going on around the Lazy F that I can't figure out, but I have my suspicions."

"What are they?" Rebecca leaned forward and whispered.

"It's not for me to say, at least not just yet."

Disappointed, the girl pounced on the first suggestion. "Does God help or even care about me?"

A look of reproach left her feeling scorched with shame when Mrs. Cook quietly told her, "You know better than that. If there's one thing I've taught you in all the years on the Lazy F, it's that God loves everyone and it's up to us to believe it." Her voice changed to a deceptively bland tone. "Of course, it's a lot easier to talk to Him when we know we're His children, and that only comes after we invite His Son to live in our hearts."

Longing rose in Rebecca. "I'm so tired of fighting. I wish I could, but—" A vision of the smirking Hayes danced in the warm kitchen. "He wouldn't want to live in my heart. It's too filled with hate for Hayes," she bitterly said.

"I don't like Hayes, either," Mrs. Cook admitted. "Just remember, we can despise what folks do, but God says we can't hate the miserable sinners who are trying our patience." She stood, looked at a watch she drew from beneath her apron. "Too late for the knitting lesson. Off to bed with you, Child, and don't forget to talk to God."

Rebecca did not answer. It would only hurt Mrs. Cook to know how many times her darling had talked to God and found that He did not answer. She sighed. Perhaps it would not hurt to try again. Things could not get much worse, or she would do something awful.

"God, I'm in the middle of a mess," she stated frankly when she had climbed into a nightgown and knelt by her bed. "I don't even know how to pray."

Dissatisfied but void of words, she quickly said, "Amen," and got into bed.

Her outdoor life provided exercise enough to put her to sleep immediately, but first she remembered Smokey's words. *Even if he is the boss around here.* She sat bolt upright. *Why did Smokey think Hayes was boss, not Father?*

Chapter 6

Among the hundreds of beautiful places to ride on the Lazy F, one lured Rebecca again and again. The day after her encounter with Hayes, she expertly saddled and mounted Vermilion. Warm spring sun had blossomed the range into meadows of flowers. Cottonwood and willows along the stream born in the mountains that ran through Fairfax's land and never went dry whispered secrets. In the east, the Old Trail continued its never-ending way with its sister, the Cimarron, and the sloping range smoothed into an endless prairie gray. Melting snow patches on the mountains above smiled down on the girl and her horse as they weaved their way up steep sides until they rode through groves of aspens that quivered with every breeze.

Rebecca and Vermilion emerged from the grove onto a promontory. "Whoa." She pulled lightly on the reins and wheeled the red stallion. Never did she take this particular ride without turning to look over the valley floor. The ranch in the distance looked small by comparison with the vast world spread below her.

A Mexican village she seldom was allowed to visit huddled its adobe houses together as if for protection against danger. She remembered a fiesta day, the colorful clothing, strum of guitars, and happy dancing from a year before and laughed at the way she had deliberately slipped away from home in defiance of Samuel Fairfax's orders.

"It was worth being shut up in my room for three days," she confessed to Vermilion, with a toss of her head that dislodged her sombrero and tumbled her nut-brown hair around her laughing face. The merry sparkle left her eyes. "Why doesn't Father want me to visit the village? Or ride to the neighbors?"

Vermilion shook his head, and his reddish mane brushed the girl's gloved hand.

She patted him. "I know you want to go. You're thinking about the lush green grass at Lone Man Cabin." In spite of the warm day, a shiver went through her, but she nudged Vermilion into a trot and climbed the slope to a small pass that lay above her destination. Lone Man Cabin stood in a grove of white-trunked aspens in the heart of a canyon. It had been built years before by a settler who had been killed by hostile Indians before peace came to New Mexico. A shining stream intersected the aspen grove and ran beside the dilapidated shack that, nevertheless, held a morbid fascination for Rebecca. The gobble of a wild turkey, from a thicket to her left, brought a thrill to her nature-loving heart, and she called, "Run, you white-tailed beauty!" to a graceful antelope that sprang from its grazing and bounded away at the crack of Vermilion's hooves on rock.

Minutes later, they paused by Lone Man Creek. Rebecca slid from the saddle, threw herself flat, and drank her fill of the icy water while Vermilion splashed into the stream below her, then lowered his head to drink. Satisfied, he sent up sprays of water, lunged out of the creek, and grazed, no stranger to this haunted, lovely spot.

Something about the place felt strange, not like its usual air of solitude that both fascinated and repelled the girl. She rose to investigate, walked past the cabin, and stopped short.

A fence of peeled poles, still oozing, stretched from slope to slope. A wide, closed gate kept horses and cattle from straying.

"Why, there's never been a fence here before!" Rebecca took an involuntary step toward the gate.

"Stop right there, little missy." Words harsh as the black-browed man who glided out of a clump of aspens froze her to the ground.

"Who are you, and what are you doing on the Lazy F?" she demanded, more angry than frightened. "What's this fence doing here, and why are those horses and cattle penned?"

"Beggin' your pardon, Missy, but that's my business, not yours."

"It *is* my business." Using the quick draw Smokey Travis had taught her, Rebecca pulled the small but deadly weapon she always carried and pointed it rock-steady at the intruder. "I'm Rebecca Fairfax, and this is my father's land."

A curious whistling sound alerted her, but too late. A noose sang and dropped over her head and shoulders, pinning her arms to her side with a tightening jerk that loosened her fingers until the pistol dropped. The next instant, she lay on the ground, securely bound.

The black-browed man leered down at her. "So, Missy, thought you'd hold me up, did you?" He bent, and she flinched from the smell of sweat and his whiskey breath. "Now, there ain't no use of you bellerin', so I won't gag you. Just keep your mouth shut, and you won't get hurt." He blindfolded her and laughed crudely. "My pard's pertic'ler about folks seein' his face."

Deprived of sight, Rebecca's other senses intensified. She strained her ears, trying to hear above the hard pound of her heart. *Who is the second man, the one who roped me and doesn't want to be seen?*

Hayes! The word shot into her brain like sunlight into a dark well. It drove out the fear that had paralyzed her when the evil-looking man stood over her. Bad as she suspected Hayes to be, he would not stand for any man except himself to maul her. So she lay still, motionless except for her cautious exploring fingers behind her back that tried to pick at the knots and loosen the lariat.

If I can get even one hand free, I'll snatch the blindfold off and get a good look at Hayes, she promised herself. Her plan did not work. Hayes, or whoever had tied those knots, obviously did not take chances. She could not budge them. Her mind steadied, considered, and rejected a half-dozen plans. Suddenly, hot blood pumped from her heart in a spurt of determination. She had it! Turning her head to one side, Rebecca slowly rubbed her face against the ground, flinching when dirt imbedded in her cheek but gradually working the blindfold up far enough for her to see.

She had been right. Hayes and the man who had accosted her by the fence stood several yards away in low conversation. Once, Hayes glanced at her, and she stilled and closed her eyes, praying he would not notice the position of the blindfold. He looked angry, yet something in his manner told Rebecca he was pleading with the other man. Again, she listened intensely and managed to catch a few words. ". . .didn't see me. . .you lay low. . .we'll meet. . . ."

Hayes turned abruptly and walked out of her line of vision. Rebecca did not dare move her head, but her keen ears picked up the creak of saddle leather, then guarded hoofbeats that increased into a diminishing drum. She thought of the look the black-browed man had given her and almost called out. Better to take her chances with Hayes than be left here with his partner.

"Sorry, Missy." Cold steel slipped between her wrists and cut the lariat; a rude hand snatched the blindfold from her eyes. "I didn't reckon you were really Sam Fairfax's girl." He laughed uneasily, and something flickered in his eyes. Rebecca knew he had lied. "A feller can't be too careful," he went on.

She stood and brushed debris from her riding habit. "My father will hear of this outrage," she furiously told him. She bit her tongue to keep from flinging out that she knew Clyde Hayes was involved in whatever nefarious scheme this turned out to be.

"I wouldn't say anythin' if I was you." The black-browed man opened his sheep-lined coat and showed a badge of some kind. "I've been appointed to look into the rustlin' that's goin' on, and a purty little thing like you wouldn't want to throw a hitch into my 'nvestigations, now would you?"

Not for a minute did she believe him. Yet, when Rebecca thought of the isolation, she wisely did not argue. Mrs. Cook always said there were more ways than one to skin a cat. Rebecca did an about-face and became the helpless female who is impressed with the law. "Oh, my, I can see why you couldn't have me interfering!" She gave him a dazzling smile that successfully masked her fear and disgust. "Deputy—it is *deputy*, isn't it?"

"Dep'ty Crowley." He half closed his eyes, and she saw suspicion in their murky depths.

"It's just that I got such a shock, seeing the fence and all." She nodded toward the newly erected barrier. Her frankness lightened the deputy's face, and she went on, "If I'd known you were an honest-to-goodness law officer, I wouldn't have pulled my gun." She almost choked, wondering if he would swallow that, even though what she said was true. "Is the other man a deputy, too?"

"Naw." Crowley spat a stream of tobacco juice dangerously close to his boot. "He's what you might call an intr'sted party." He pulled a plug of tobacco from his shirt pocket, cut off a quid, and stored it in his cheek.

Rebecca wanted to laugh. It made him look like a lopsided chipmunk. Instead, she delicately shuddered. "This has all been most upsetting." She managed a feeble smile that should convince the bogus deputy of her helplessness. "I suppose the corral and the horses and cattle are all part of your plan to catch rustlers?" She hoped her naïve question would disarm him.

"Uh, yeah. That's why it's 'mportant for you to keep mum." His gaze bored into her, and she suddenly felt more afraid than ever.

"I won't tell Father right away," she promised. "You'll probably get your job done soon, and then it won't matter who knows."

A hasty hand to Crowley's mouth half concealed his grin. "You're right, Missy. My job'll be done soon, and it won't matter."

Her cheek smarted from ground-in dirt, and her fingers itched to slap his leering face, but Rebecca chose the better part. "Good-bye, Mr., uh, Deputy Crowley." She turned and walked to Vermilion, who had finished grazing and now stood waiting for her. She put her left foot in the stirrup and swung her right leg across the saddle.

Crowley's voice stopped her. "Say, how about tradin' horses?" His eyes gleamed with the lust for good horseflesh that she had seen dozens of times before when rough men saw Vermilion. "This stallion's too big for such a little girl as you. Now, my mare there—" He nodded at a piebald horse Rebecca would not have ridden to an outhouse. "She's just your size."

What a credulous fool he considered her. Well, that image might just be her best protection. When he stepped in front of Vermilion, Rebecca overcame her desire to ride the man down and cried out, "Oh, be careful! Vermilion only allows me and the cowboy who broke him to handle him." The horse raised both feet in the air to prove her point, and Crowley leaped aside.

"I'd take that out of him," he muttered.

Rebecca brought her horse down and started back through the aspens. "I couldn't sell Vermilion, even to you, Deputy Crowley, but I see you know a good horse when you see one." She wanted to pointedly gaze at the corralled animals but restrained herself. Right now, getting away meant continuing the role she had chosen.

"If you ever change your mind, I'll be waitin'," he called after her.

Thoroughly disgusted, Rebecca did not answer. She used the long miles back to the ranch house to mull over everything that had happened. A half mile from home, the clatter of hooves warned that someone desperately planned to overtake her. A quick glance behind showed Hayes riding bent over the muscular neck of the racing bay he unimaginatively had christened Bay. She fought the impulse to outrun him and composed herself. A little voice inside whispered the significance of this meeting. Under no circumstances must Hayes discover that she had recognized him back at Lone Man Cabin.

"Ho, Becky." He swung up beside her and tipped his Stetson. "Have a nice ride?"

"Splendid. I went clear to Lone Man Cabin. Too bad someone doesn't build a house there. It's the prettiest place around."

"I'll start layin' the foundation tomorrow if you say the word." He pulled Bay closer and laid one hand over hers on the saddle horn where her hand rested. "Say, what happened to your face?"

Rebecca unobtrusively nudged Vermilion with her boot heel, and he danced away, leaving Hayes trying to control Bay, who feared the big red stallion along with most of the other Lazy F horses. "I hit the ground. And I told you I won't marry you."

"Girls change," he doggedly said. "How about forgiv'n' me for last fall?"

Could he really be so thick-headed he thought the only reason she hated him was because of his actions on the way home from Raton when he had been drinking? "Hayes, why don't you find a woman close to your age instead of hanging after me?" she blurted out.

His face darkened, and she knew her taunt had been a mistake. Before he could reply, she innocently asked, "Why, where's your lariat?" She pointed to Bay's saddle horn.

It distracted him, as she had known it would do. Hayes stammered and finally said, "Left it in the bunkhouse, I guess. Yeah, that's right. One of the hands sneaked it out and brought it back soaked. When I find out who, there'll be one less hand on the Lazy F."

She could not resist saying, "I thought we needed every hand we could get. I heard Father telling you to hire all the vaqueros from the Mexican village for spring roundup."

"Maybe I'll wait until after roundup." He lapsed into sullen silence, then asked, "How was everythin' at Lone Man Cabin?"

Rebecca feigned surprise. "Why? Should there be anything wrong?" She saw the quickly hidden but satisfied look in Hayes's eyes and knew it had been his idea for "Deputy Crowley" to swear her to silence about the peeled pole fence, raw in its newness.

"I just haven't ridden out there lately. Guess I should one of these days. Sometimes cattle and horses drift down the canyon by Lone Man Creek." His false laugh could not have fooled Vermilion. "Strange how dumb the critters are. They drift in but not out!"

Not so strange when they are corralled, Rebecca wanted to shout. Instead, she said, "Maybe you and some of the boys should check the canyon. I did see horses and cattle."

They reached the ranch house in time for her to escape more conversation with Hayes. As usual, Smokey Travis waited on the top rail of the corral.

"Travis, why are you sittin' there like a prairie hen on a nest?" Hayes blared, while his nondescript eyes flashed.

Dull red suffused the cowboy's brown face, and he started to speak. Behind Hayes's back, Rebecca shook her head slightly in warning. Smokey's face broke into a smile. "I'm waitin' for you, Boss, an' am glad to tell you we found most a hundred head of cattle up a draw. They must have wandered in there last fall. Anyway, we put the Lazy F brand on at least a dozen new calves and herded the whole kit and caboodle back down with the main herd." His gaze turned to Rebecca's face, and his eyes flashed.

The tension drained from Hayes's shoulders. Overbearing, even crooked he might be, but he loved the range and cattle. "That's good news." He slid off Bay, yanked off the saddle, and gave the horse a slap that sent him whinnying into the pasture nearby. "Fairfax aims to make a killin' on the roundup this spring. The more we sell, the fewer that'll fall to rustlin'."

Smokey had a coughing spell that left him red-faced and teary-eyed. "Sorry, Boss, Miss Rebecca. Must have picked up some dust in my throat." He leaped down from the fence. "I'll take care of Vermilion, if you like," he told the girl.

She started to protest and thought better of it. While she could and did perfectly groom her own horse, she knew Smokey loved Vermilion as much as she did. "Thanks, Sm—Travis," she quickly corrected. She had learned long ago that calling the cowboys by their first names made her father and Hayes furious. No use rousing their ire, especially when she had a secret. The less attention they paid her, the freer she would be to solve the mystery of Lone Man Cabin and the newly constructed fence. She burned to tell Smokey what had happened. She had promised not to report to her father about being waylaid and the developments in Lone Man Canyon but had carefully omitted any promise about not telling Smokey.

How could she get a message to him? When Father was not watching her, Hayes replaced the vigilance. Even when she did not see them, she felt their spying. Well, she could be clever, too.

After supper and dishes, while the two voices rumbled in the big living room, Rebecca covered her white gown with a long, dark cloak that hid every trace of it and allowed her to become just another dark shadow in the night. Praying for luck to find Smokey alone, she groped her way to the bunkhouse and peered in a window. She counted off the hands, from Curly the cook, to Jim, who had been with the Lazy F just a few weeks but long enough to learn that friendliness beyond a nod and "howdy" with the daughter of the house was not permitted. All accounted for—except Smokey.

An iron hand covered her lips. Another jerked her away from the window and into a clump of cottonwoods. "Who're you, an' why're you spying?" someone hissed. Rebecca found herself spun around. *God, help me,* she silently prayed. *If Father or Hayes is holding me, what will happen?*

Strong hands pulled her closer. Miserly light from the edge of the moon that rose over the mountain spilled onto the dark-clad figure, the man who held her. "Rebecca, what are you *doing* out here?"

She sagged in relief and would have fallen if not for his support. "Smokey, thank God!"

"Shh." He picked her up bodily and stepped deep into the dark shelter of the cottonwood grove. Again, he placed his hand over her lips, but gently this time. Screened by leaves filtering pale moonlight that brightened as Hayes and Fairfax stood smoking on the ranch house porch, she scarcely breathed. She could feel Smokey's deadly calm body coiled ready to spring in her defense. A lifetime later, Fairfax went inside and slammed the door; Hayes marched very close past them. Not until a light came on in the bunkhouse room, which was set apart from the long, tiered-bunk sleeping quarters of the rest of the men, did Smokey remove his hand.

"Sorry. But how'd I know you'd do such a fool thing?"

"I was looking for you," she whispered. In quick sentences, Rebecca told him what had happened from the moment she saw the fence in Lone Man Canyon until she and Hayes reached the corral.

"Why, that skunk!" Smokey shook with rage. "He roped you? I'm gonna call him out right now, and—" He tore free from her involuntary grasp and took a quick step out of their hiding place.

"Smokey, no!" Quicker than a mountain lion, she slid in front of him. "I won't have you kill because of me." She grabbed his arms with hands made strong by fear. "There's a better way to get Hayes. Don't you see? We'll watch and spy and expose his rustling, for I'm sure that's what he's doing."

"Your daddy will never believe it." He stood stock-still in her grip. Enough light sneaked past the trees to show his whitened face and inscrutable dark eyes that could dance with mischief but now looked hard and cold, relentless.

Rebecca shivered. "He will have to. I don't believe Crowley's a deputy any more than you are."

She felt Smokey give a convulsive start before he said in an odd voice, "That's—you'd better go in, Rebecca." His voice changed. "I. . .I'm glad you told me."

"So am I, Smokey. Sometimes I feel the only one who really knows or understands me is God."

He parted branches, checked both ways, then ran with her across the lighted yard to a side door in the right arm of the house where she could slip into a storeroom, then get to her bedroom, unobserved. At the doorway, he leaned down, awkwardly planted a kiss on her forehead, and said, "That's just to let you know God an' me are both on your side." Then he swung away with a remarkably light tread for a man who spent most of his waking hours in the saddle, leaving Rebecca staring after him and feeling less alone now that she had shared her heavy secret.

Chapter 7

Sometimes, Joel felt he had been riding forever. Querida scrambled up a game trail and came out on a mesa. Her owner gasped. What a view! Grand country, this New Mexican land. He had been told in Santa Fe what to expect, yet from the backbone of the tableland, between the mountains and foothills, the range curved in a half moon, walled by the Rockies. Dark, timber-sloped gullies joined cedar ridges; a bleached moon cast its pale light. No sign of human habitation for as far as Joel could see; just empty miles unrolling around him.

"We camp out again tonight, Querida." His old habit of talking to his horse and a cheerful whistle brought an answering nicker from Querida, who, freed from saddle and blanket, rolled in spring grass and then contentedly settled to graze.

A crackling fire, a meager meal of toasted biscuits and the last of his dried beef topped off by a treasured tin of peaches, brought a sigh of satisfaction. "Nothing like a meal to lift spirits. Right, old girl?"

Querida raised her head, then went back to munching.

Joel laughed, yet a certain wistfulness shone in his eyes. He washed his few eating utensils, spread blankets on the ground near his fire, and stared into the dying blaze. Now that night surrounded him, even the food could not fend off discouragement. Six months earlier, he had preached in San Scipio with startling results. Now, he rested his head on his saddle and stared at the starry sky, remembering that fateful Sabbath.

For some reason, Joel had struggled with finding a text more than at any other time he prepared a sermon. He considered and discarded a full dozen, settling on one, then another. Yet, all through his study, the words of Jesus in Matthew 5:23–24 remained present. How could he step into a strange pulpit and preach on that text? Yet, how could he deny what he felt led to say?

Refusing breakfast on the gorgeous West Texas autumn morning, he rode to town on Querida, still struggling. Early as he was, a crowd had preceded him. He remembered many of the faces and recognized others' names. One tall, thin, tired-looking woman with straw-colored hair and washed-out gray eyes approached him. She wore clothing more suitable to a young girl than to a woman nearing forty.

"You look just like your dear uncle," she gushed. "Gideon and I were sweethearts years ago." She giggled girlishly.

The grotesque sound, coming from this faded blossom trying to cling to the past, brought a startled, "Really!" from Joel.

"Oh, yes," she chortled, making no effort to lower her voice.

"I'm Lucinda—used to be Curtis. I'm sure dear Gideon has spoken of me."

Joel thanked heaven for the control he had learned over the years that now kept him from laughing at the pathetic woman. Gideon had indeed spoken of Lucinda, sharing how even though he felt sorry for her, she had made his stay in San Scipio as a preacher unbearable with her chasing.

"It's nice you could come, Miss. . .Mrs. . . ," he managed to say while she pumped his hand up and down.

"Mrs. Baker." She looked skyward and dragged a meek little man forward. "My husband, these past ten years." She gave the man no chance to speak. "Do remember me to your uncle when you see him again." With an arch smile, she took her husband by the arm. "Come along, or we won't get the front pew." He trotted obediently after her, the way a fawn followed a doe.

"Sweethearts, my eye," someone whispered behind Joel. "Leave it to Lucinda Curtis Baker to kick up a cyclone when there's no more wind than from slamming a door!"

Joel repressed a smile and greeted the next person. After folks stopped coming and every seat was filled and men were standing at the back, the San Scipio minister introduced Joel. "You all remember Gideon Scott, Elijah and Naomi's son. This is his nephew, the Scotts' grandson. I've asked him to bring the Word of the Lord to us today. Brother Joel, you have our careful and prayerful attention."

Joel found it hard to begin. His heart went out to Lige, who sat rigid at the introduction that made no mention of the long-missing real father. Yet Joel had a feeling the text that had been impressed on him was not for Lige's benefit. He opened the worn Bible that traveled on Querida wherever Joel rode. " 'Therefore if thou bring thy gift to the altar, and there rememberest that thy brother hath ought against thee; leave there thy gift before the altar, and go thy way; first be reconciled to thy brother, and then come and offer thy gift.' " He closed the Bible and leaned forward against the sturdy, handmade pulpit. "I don't know why Matthew 5:23 and 24 has driven all other Scripture passages from my mind and heart ever since I knew I would preach to you." He saw looks of surprise and exchanged glances.

"Perhaps it is because every one of us at times realizes someone, some-where, has something against us. We may have offended our brothers and sis-ters years ago and not even recognized it. Or, we may secretly know of times when we spoke unkind words that cut a tender heart." Joel continued preach-ing in a clear, simple manner, using the thoughts he felt coming. He referred to the healing that comes to both when a child of God seeks out one wronged.

He concluded, "If anything in your life is keeping your gift at the altar from being acceptable to God, make it right." He paused to be sure nothing more needed saying, then sat down.

"Let us pray," the San Scipio minister said. He offered one of the hum-blest, most beautiful prayers Joel had ever heard and followed it by leading the young guest minister to the back of the church to greet the congregation as they left.

A good half hour later, everyone except Lucinda had gone after having shaken Joel's hand and wishing him Godspeed. Even the meek Mr. Baker silently shook hands, then slipped out.

"Why, Lucinda, you're still here?" The minister turned.

Red-eyed and swollen-faced, the woman said, "I must talk with the Reverend Scott."

Joel cringed. He hated being called Reverend and set apart as some holier-than-others being. He also did not care for a private interview with the woman. Yet, none of her former kittenish attitude remained. His heart went out to her, as it did to anyone in trouble. "Tell my grandparents I'll be home soon," he said to the minister. The other man nodded and left, closing the door behind him.

"What is it, Mrs. Baker?"

Fresh tears poured. "I. . .I've done something terrible." She pressed her hands to her twisting face. "All these years, I should have spoken." The hands fell and revealed a tragic face filled with regret. "I knew, but I didn't want to. . .and then he was gone, and I hated Judith for marrying Gideon. . . ."

He could not make sense of her broken confession. "What is it you know?" he gently asked.

"Cyrus Scott. He. . .he. . ." The cloudburst came again.

Joel had always thought novels that said someone's heart stood still were the height of stupidity. Now, he experienced that very thing. He could not speak. He could not breathe. Not until hope for a long-hidden clue to his father's disappearance loosed him to action could he do more than stare at the repentant woman. "What do you know of him?" he inquired hoarsely.

She blew her nose and raised her head. Remorse lent depth to the gray eyes. "The night before he. . .he left, I saw him." Dying sobs still racked her thin frame. "I. . .I thought he was Gideon, and I called out. He was riding toward the ranch. He wheeled his horse, and when I saw who it was, I asked him to tell Gideon how thrilled the town was with his preaching." She sniffed.

"What did he say?" Joel's head spun. Had this vindictive woman held the key to Cyrus's whereabouts all these long years?

"He. . .he laughed in that hateful way he had and said he wasn't a messenger boy for his brother. When he turned back toward the ranch, he laughed again, mocking me, and said, 'Besides, I'm off to Albuquerque. Too bad I can't take Gideon with me and get him away from simpering females like you.'" Anguish filled her voice. "I made up my mind I'd die before helping him or ever telling anyone what he said." She crossed her arms over her thin chest and threw back her head. "I kept that promise until today. But when you read those verses, I knew God meant them for me." Her voice trailed to a whisper.

Hot anger over her silence melted into pity. Her eyes showed long-held pain and what it had cost her to speak. Joel put a warm, strong hand on one of her cold ones. "Mrs. Baker—Lucinda—all we can do to atone of the things we do or leave undone is to repent. That's the wonder of God's grace, that He forgives. Now, you must forgive yourself."

"Should I stand up in meeting next week and confess?"

He knew she would do it but shook his head. "No. I will tell my grandparents, but it would only cause more pain to have San Scipio hashing it over again. Tell your husband, and then accept God's forgiveness."

Something akin to glory gradually crept into her face, and when Lucinda Curtis Baker walked out of the church to her patient, waiting husband, Joel swallowed hard. Thank God for His power that had changed the foolish woman who entered church that day into the new creature who went out.

He shook his head at his musing and, with a glad heart, raced Querida back to the Circle S. His shocking announcement precipitated a crisis. Life flowed back into Lige Scott's face, and he nearly reneged on his promise to take Naomi west.

"Don't you see," he protested, "now we have something to go on, a starting place. Naomi, how can I go to Arizona when Cyrus may be alive and needing me?"

"Your younger son needs you, too, Lige," she quietly reminded. "Will you again choose Cyrus over Gideon?"

He flinched as if she had struck him, and Joel stepped in.

"Grandpa." His face shone with boyish eagerness. He gripped Lige's brawny arm. "If Cyrus is alive, I mean to find him; I vowed that when I left Flagstaff. Gideon needs you. All these years he's longed to see you and blot out the anger between you when he left. We don't know that my...my father is in New Mexico. He may have changed his mind or drifted there and gone elsewhere. Can't you trust me to seek him out?" He licked dry lips. "I believe God will help me."

The moment stretched into infinity before Lige bowed his head to a force greater than his own. "Son, I trust you. Naomi and I will catch the train from El Paso as soon as we can get there."

"Do you want me to take you?" Joel offered.

Lige shook his massive head. "No. The sooner you go, the better." He lifted both arms and let his huge hands drop on Joel's shoulders. "Go with God, Joel."

The howl of a distant coyote calling for its mate roused Joel from his reverie. He threw more wood on the fire and pulled his blankets closer against the cold spring night. The long day of riding should have left him weary. Instead, he remained sleepless, even when he closed his eyes against the display of stars hanging low in the sky. How high his hopes had been when he departed from the Circle S a few hours after Lige and Naomi boarded the stage for El Paso!

With youthful exuberance, he ignored the interminable years that stretched between Cyrus's flight from the discovery of his cruel deception and Joel's return to the ranch. He debated leaving Querida on the Circle S and going by train to New Mexico but discarded the idea immediately. He had no guarantee his father had ever reached Albuquerque or that it had not been merely a picturesque stopping place.

While Joel disconsolately reviewed the history of New Mexico, frost gathered and sparkled the range with diamond dust. Cyrus had ridden away in 1874, the same year that opened the bloodiest years of western history in eastern and central New Mexico. Between then and 1879, more desperate and vicious men than could be counted terrorized the land. Three hundred men died in the Lincoln County War that pitted rustlers, desperadoes, and cattlemen, honest and crooked, against each other. Billy the Kid boasted twenty-one killings. Sentenced to be hanged in April 1881, he killed two deputies, escaped, then was killed by Pat Garrett in July—at the age of twenty.

Geronimo, one of the last of the hostile Apache chiefs, added to the terror until his surrender in 1886. During the late 1870s, the territorial governor, General Lew Wallace, called on martial law and used troops to end the bloodbath.

Gloom dropped like a tarpaulin over Joel. Could Cyrus, with his wild love of adventure, have escaped the violence and death of those turbulent New Mexico territorial days? Or did his bones lie in some unmarked grave on the "lone prairie" along with countless others who lived and died by the sword?

In the dark hour between the waning moon and the gray dusk that heralds the dawn, when bodies and minds are at their lowest ebb, Joel Scott faced the truth. He might not be able to keep his vow. He had planned every bright bit of color concerning his father, only to have it turn to fool's gold, dross, in his hands. Most of the old-timers he talked with had never heard the name Cyrus Scott. One or two had scratched grizzled heads and admitted seeing young fellers now and then with "goldy hair and blue eyes like you'n," but they couldn't recollect any such name as Cyrus.

Joel ranged far and wide, stopping over at ranches and leaving word that if anyone knew of the man he sought, to contact Gideon Scott in Flagstaff; a reward would be forthcoming. Periodically, Joel lighted long enough to send and receive letters. So far, there had been no takers on the reward offer—just two or three false leads that roused great hope and petered out like all the others.

Joel wintered on a ranch not far from Santa Fe. He won the admiration of the hands with his range skills, the gratitude of plain folk and Mexican families with his preaching on Sundays. When spring came, they reluctantly bid him farewell.

Joel had left the Double J in Arizona in late summer of 1888. In some ways, spring 1890 found him no closer to a solution of the mystery.

Still wide awake, Joel's lips twisted in a wry grin. A few weeks from now, on April 30, he would be twenty years old. He felt at least thirty and far removed from the excited boy who set off to reclaim his father and win him for the Lord. A fierce attack of homesickness assailed him. What he would give to see the Double J, spar with Lonesome and the boys, marvel over how much Matt and Millie, the twins, had grown. When dawn broke, why should he not just saddle Querida and head west? He had acted on the advice of a cowboy from the ranch where he wintered to "ride east into as purty a country as you'll ever see" and ended up agreeing. The hand had added, "I useter work on a swell spread called the Lazy F. Wish I'd never left." Longing softened the planes of his face.

"Why did you?" Joel's keen gaze bored into the other's open, honest countenance.

"Huh, got driv' off by the owner." Amber fire flashed in the cowboy's eyes. "All I did was try an' spark the daughter." His face reddened, but he continued to look directly at Joel. "I only smiled an' talked with her a coupla times. Never even touched her. But Fairfax's foreman, Hayes, told the boss I was sweet on Rebecca. I was," he admitted. Hardness thinned his lips. "At least I didn't mean bad by her."

"Who did?"

The cowboy buttoned his lip, shook his head, then unslitted his mouth just wide enough to say, "I ain't sayin', but I sure feel sorry for any girl Hayes gets his hands on." His oblique, meaningful glance finished the story.

Joel felt pity for the unknown Rebecca and something else. "What's this Hayes like?" he demanded sharply.

"Mean. Mid-thirties. Loco over the girl. Mousy brown hair, gray eyes that make you feel like he's hidin' somethin' all the time. Big jasper, tall as you." He measured Joel with a glance. "You weigh in about 160?"

Joel nodded.

"Hayes has a good forty pounds on you." He cocked his head to one side. "If you ever just happen to mosey up that way, tell Smokey Travis howdy from Jeff."

"I will." Joel's hand shot out. But when he finished packing his saddlebags and mounted Querida, Jeff stepped closer.

"In case you should end up at the Lazy F, keep your eye peeled an' don't never let your horse run loose."

Joel's spine snapped to attention. "Hayes?"

"I never said nothin' a-tall." Jeff half closed his eyes and grinned.

"Thanks for nothin' a-tall," Joel mimicked and turned Querida in the direction the inscrutable cowboy pointed.

Mile by mile, he headed through incredible and varied country until he knew he must be near the Lazy F. The sun yawned, opened its eye a crack, and peered over a mountain. Joel still had not slept. He had to make a decision. . . go or stay. Head home in defeat and take up his lifework of preaching or aimlessly search when every clue had died. Lige and Naomi had fallen in love with the Double J, and the last thing Joel had heard was that they had ordered their foreman to sell the Circle S. Why not join them and forget the father who had never known he had a son?

Still undecided, Joel broke camp. Before he did much more riding anywhere, he needed supplies. He remembered Jeff saying a Mexican village lay on the Lazy F. He could replenish his food, get oats for Querida for a change, and look over the ranch. Time enough then to head out.

Late afternoon found him riding through range inhabited by cattle as far as he could see. Hundreds, no thousands, must be on this rolling, endless, grazing land. He finally reached the line of cottonwoods he knew bordered the stream that ran through the ranch and lay below the ranch house.

Coarse jeers and curses rent the still air, and Joel circled to avoid meeting a group of riders face to face. Something in their hard faces warned him they would not welcome a stranger. Yet, his overdeveloped sense of curiosity forced him to investigate. Admonishing Querida to silence, he slipped from the saddle and led his horse around a willow thicket.

Dear God, no! Thirty feet away, a cowboy who could not be more than a year or so older than Joel straddled a buckskin horse that nervously shifted. The man's hands were tied behind his back. With a thrill of terror, Joel saw the noose around the white-faced cowboy's neck, the big man with a taunting smile who stood with hand upraised to hit the buckskin's flank. *Hayes!* He fit Jeff's description to the last detail.

"Got anythin' to say?" a mounted rider called.

"A lot!" the doomed cowboy yelled. "Hayes knows I'm no rustler. Ask him the real reason he framed me."

"Shut up!" Hayes snatched a Colt from his holster and pointed it.

"Let him talk, Hayes." A murmur of assent ran through the assembled men, and Joel took heart. Evidently, they were not as eager for a hanging as the Lazy F foreman was.

The courageous cowboy whose life hung by a thread shouted, "Ask him about Lone Man Canyon an' a bogus deputy that calls himself Crowley an' how they roped and tied Miss Rebecca—"

In the heartbeat before Hayes moved, guilt blackened his face. The riders froze. "You lyin', thievin'—" Hayes swung his arm high, opened his palm. It exploded with a horrid crack on the buckskin's flank.

The buckskin leaped. A shot rang out and severed the tightened rope. The cowboy, still bound, fell to the ground and lay stunned.

Joel, a gun in each hand, one still smoking, stepped from the thicket and confronted the paralyzed men.

Chapter 8

Howdy, boys." Joel kept his revolvers trained square on the slack-jawed Hayes, whose face had gone a dirty yellow. "Drop the gun, Mister."

Hayes slowly let his unfired Colt drop from his fingers.

Joel shot a lightning glance toward the huddled group of staring riders, stopped at the one who had demanded that the condemned man be allowed to talk, and ordered, "You, there. Untie the boy."

"What is this, a holdup?" Hayes recovered his voice and some of his shaken arrogance. He took one step toward the newcomer.

"Don't you move." Joel's eyes flashed blue fire. He waited until the man on the ground dazedly sat up and rubbed circulation back into his wrists where the rope had cut into them. "What's your name, and what's this all about? Where I come from, we don't hang folks without a mighty good reason." The contempt in his voice sent angry red into Hayes's face and shame to the still-mounted riders' countenances.

The reprieved cowboy sprang to his feet. Tossed dark hair and scornful dark eyes highlighted his deeply tanned face. "Thanks, Stranger. I'm Smokey Travis. Clyde Hayes is foreman of the Lazy F—you musta seen the brand on a lot of cattle no matter which way you came. He's hated me an' tried to drive me away like he did every hand who's protected Miss Rebecca from him—"

"Jeff, for instance? I rode with him down Santa Fe way, and he said to tell you howdy." Joel's revolvers never wavered, but he caught the pop-eyed look on a half-dozen faces. "Now, you boys lay down your guns real nice and easylike."

A slight movement from Hayes sent steel into Joel's eyes. "I wouldn't try anything if I were you."

"Do as he says," Hayes's hoarse voice bellowed.

Joel waited until the men disarmed, then said over the pounding of his heart, "All right, let's have it." He sheathed his guns.

Smokey stepped up beside him and glared at Hayes. "He's crookeder than a mountain goat trail. Rebecca Fairfax found it out weeks ago an' told me. He's running some kind of double cross on the boss, who thinks so all-fired much of him he won't believe anything but good."

Joel's lips curled. "And the rest of these men?"

"Aw, we sure didn't know anything about a crooked deal—until just now," the cowhand who untied Smokey protested. His clear eyes attested to his honesty, but the dark faces of some of the others indicated that they had known and were neck-deep in the plot against Samuel Fairfax.

"What do you have to say?" Joel wheeled back toward Hayes.

"Lies. Travis has been a burr under the saddle ever since he rode in. I'm goin' to marry Becky, and he's jealous." Hayes spat on the ground.

"That's not what she says," said Smokey.

Joel's lips involuntarily curved upward in sympathy with Travis's mocking smile.

"It's what her daddy says that counts. Now get off the ranch. You're fired. If I ever catch you sneakin' around again, I'll run you in." Hayes stooped to pick up his Colt.

"Hold it." Like magic, Joel's revolvers sprang from his holsters in a draw so fast the crowd of men gasped. "Smokey, pitch those guns into the willow thicket. The men can get them back after we're gone."

"Just who are you, anyway, to come ridin' in where it's none of your business?" Hayes frothed at the mouth.

A slow smile of pure enjoyment crept across Joel's face. He could feel it stretch the skin across his cheekbones. "Why, saving folks is my business. I'm a preacher."

"Huh?" Hayes's exclamation mingled with Smokey's loud, "Whoopee!"

"You mean a preacher got the drop on us?" the clear-eyed cowboy demanded. "Haw, haw!" He rolled on the ground in a paroxysm of mirth.

Hayes screamed, "You're fired, too, Perkins! I knew you wouldn't last when I hired you." His colorless eyes flamed.

Perkins leaped to his feet. "Too late, Boss. I quit when Smokey said you lassoed Miss Rebecca." He looked each of the other riders in the eye. "If any of ya are men, you'll come with me." He waited a moment, but no one moved. "I'd rather ride with a herd of polecats than you. C'mon, Smokey, let's hit the trail. Half a dozen ranches around here'll be glad to get us. Preacher, how about comin' with us?"

Joel hesitated. Should he take the safer trail and leave with Smokey and Perkins? Or—he shook his head. "Jeff told me a lot about the Lazy F. I'm hankering to meet this Samuel Fairfax. Once I do. . ." He shrugged.

"Whaat?" For the third time, Joel's coolness shocked Hayes. "You think bein' a preacher's goin' to save your skin? Better get out while you can."

"You just gave me the best protection of all," Joel defied him. "Now, if anything such as an unexpected accident happens to me, Perkins, Travis, and the rest of the men will have to swear they heard you threaten my life." He strode back to Querida, calmly mounted her, and rode back to the others.

Hayes changed his tune instantly. Greed etched itself on his face and in his eyes at the sight of the black mare. "Maybe I was hasty," he half apologized. "I didn't mean anythin'." He cleared his throat with an obvious effort. "Where'd a preacher get a horse like that?" His quivering forefinger pointed straight at Querida.

"I sure didn't steal her," Joel sarcastically told him.

Smokey and Perkins went off into convulsions of laughter. Hayes glared at them but pressed his lips tight before saying, "Looks like you came a long way."

Something in his inscrutable eyes blocked Joel from frankly admitting his journey and the reason for it as he had done at other ranches. His years among rough men had not been in vain; they had given him insight into human nature. Now, he weighed Hayes and found him wanting: mean enough to be dangerous but a coward at heart. The kind of bad man without the nerve to be thoroughly bad. Followed by rustlers but never respected. Ruthless but more likely to shoot a man from ambush than meet him in a fair fight, evidenced by the way he had framed Smokey Travis on some flimsy charge, then rushed through a hanging to rid himself of a trouble spot.

"Hayes, I'm riding up to the ranch house with Travis and Perkins so they can get their gear from the bunkhouse without any interference." He lowered his voice. "I wouldn't be too anxious about following close behind if I were you." His gaze included the rest of the riders. His sunny smile flashed. "On the other hand, I guess we don't have to worry about it, do we? Smokey's horse took off for parts unknown, so he'll have to borrow yours." He thought Hayes would explode before Smokey vaulted to the saddle of Hayes's horse and rode out of sight, closely followed by Perkins and Joel.

Hidden by the willow thicket and a stand of close-growing cottonwoods, Smokey reined in Hayes's horse and motioned for his comrades to stop. His dark eyes danced, and he said in a low voice, "I'm a mighty curious galoot, an' I bet if a feller or fellers were to creep back up on them rustlers, why, it just could be interesting."

Joel slid to the ground and tossed Querida's reins to Perkins. Smokey followed suit. "Keep the horses quiet," Joel ordered.

Disappointment filled Perkins's face. "Aw, why can't I go, too?"

"We may need those horses in a hurry," Joel replied. "If you hear us yell, come running." He ignored Perkins's grunt and followed Smokey's stocky frame back to the willow thicket. A few rods away, they took cover, close enough to hear but far enough away to avoid being seen. Smokey pressed Joel's hand for silence when the crashing of brush and curses nearby told them the men were retrieving their guns.

"I'll get Travis and Perkins and that goldy-haired rider who says he's a preacher." Hayes's furious voice came clearly. Joel felt a thrill go up his spine. Without hesitation or thought of the consequences, he had rushed in to save Smokey. Now, he would have to face the consequences.

"While you're at it, I bet you'll get your hands on that black mare, too, huh, Hayes? I seen how ya looked at her."

A start went through Joel's tall frame, and only Smokey's powerful hand dragging him back down kept the sometimes reckless young minister from betraying their hiding place.

Hayes's unpleasant laugh sawed its way into Joel's brain, and his words beat red-hot and searing. "The way I see it, a dead man don't need a horse."

A burst of raucous, threatening laughter followed, then the scrambling in the brush ceased. After an altercation on who would ride double, a lot of grumbling, and Hayes's loud remarks on the subject, the steady cadence of hoofbeats faded and died in the distance.

"Thought we were goners there for a minute." Smokey sat up. "Preacher, you've gotta learn to lie still when there's danger around, no matter what." He stood, offered a hand to Joel, and sternly added, "What's your handle, any-way? Jim—that's Perkins—an' me can't keep calling you Preacher."

"I wouldn't want you to." Joel brushed leaves from his clothes, and they retraced their steps to Jim and the horses. "My name's Joel. Uh, what will Hayes do now?"

"Make up some story on why he fired the Lazy F's two best hands," Jim put in sourly. He clamped a worn Stetson down on straggling brown locks.

"Let's beat him to it." Joel bit his tongue to keep from laughing at the amazement in the cowboys' faces.

"What'd ya say?" Perkins demanded, face reddening.

"Here's what we'll do," Joel said. "The way I figure it, after what hap-pened, Hayes won't head straight for the ranch. Instead, he and his men will circle and come in later from another direction. He'll count on us being gone by the time he gets there. According to what you and Jeff said, whatever reason Hayes gives for firing you two will be swallowed whole by Fairfax." He drew his brows together. "Wonder why a man smart enough to own a spread like this doesn't have enough savvy to see through Hayes?"

"He plumb don't want to," the loquacious Jim put in. "I ain't talked much with Smokey about it, but even in the short time I've been here, it 'pears Hayes has some hold on the boss."

"Any idea what it is?" Joel mounted Querida, waited until Smokey clambered aboard Hayes's horse, and started up the trail.

"Not eggzackly, but I'm workin' on it." Jim suddenly clammed up, as if realizing how freely he'd talked to a stranger.

"What. . .uh. . .what's a preacher doing riding around in eastern New Mexico?" Smokey asked with a keen sidelong glance.

Joel deliberated for a full minute, then laid his cards on the table. "I'm looking for a man. I heard that Samuel Fairfax had been in these parts for a lot of years. Thought maybe he would have known of or have heard of my man."

"He might at that," Smokey said ponderously. "Did this feller do you wrong?"

"He doesn't even know I exist." A feeling stronger than himself prompted Joel to tell his story in a few brief sentences.

Jim, the more talkative of the two, spoke first. "That's the most peculiar tale I ever heard." He shook his head. "I never knew any Cyrus Scott." He scratched his cheek. "Never heard the name Cyrus, even."

"Smokey?"

"Naw. Beats me why you want to find your daddy, seeing he never knew you were born an' all that." He sounded doubtful.

"If he's still alive, I can't let him die without knowing about the Lord and that he's forgiven," Joel murmured.

A new constraint fell between them, broken only when Smokey pointed to the ground at a fork in the trail. "You predicted right. Hayes and the men are heading away from the ranch house." A grin split his likable face. "Whoopee! This is gonna be fun." He goaded his horse into a gallop. "Race you to the corral."

Jim followed with a yell. Querida, trained to be in front in any race, leaped forward and stretched out full length until she became a flowing machine that ate up the trail in enormous gulps. She flashed past Jim, overtook Smokey in spite of his lead, and pounded ahead of the others until Joel took pity on them and slowed her so they could catch up. Then, he leaned forward, called into her ear, "Go, Querida!" and she put on a burst of speed that brought her to the Lazy F ranch house and corral in time for Joel to slide off her back and perch on the top rail of the fence until Smokey and Jim arrived.

"Snappin' crocodiles, if Hayes ever sees that mare run, your life won't be worth a dead cactus," Jim panted, admiration written all over him.

"She doesn't even look winded," Smokey complained after keenly observing Querida contentedly munching grass, reins over her head.

A trill of laughter, sweeter than the song of a meadowlark, broke into their conversation. Joel glanced toward the ranch house about a hundred yards from the corral where he sat. A slender, running figure had covered about half the distance. Joel had seen Indian girls run with the same fleet grace. He jumped down from the fence, bared his head, and waited for the girl, who could only be Rebecca Fairfax.

Clad in boys' jeans, a blue blouse, and red kerchief, her riding boots barely touched the ground. What little hair he could see from under her sombrero curled nut brown, almost the same shade as her merry eyes. Red lips parted over even, white teeth. "Smokey Travis, whose horse—why, it's Hayes's!" Blank astonishment obliterated her smile. She raced straight to the three men, then on to Querida. "Oh, you beauty!" She whirled. Fear replaced her natural joyousness. "Jim, Smokey, what—?" A slim, tanned hand went to her throat, and her cheeks paled until the wild roses faded.

"Aw, it's nothing," Smokey mumbled.

"Don't lie to me." The brown eyes sparkled dangerously.

"Miss Fairfax?" Joel courteously began. "Is your father home?"

"Why, yes," she faltered. The fear in her eyes intensified.

"May we see him?"

"Of course, but—" She trotted alongside the men toward the ranch house.

"We'll explain everything," Joel reassured her. Some of the girl's trouble melted, and he heard her sigh of relief.

The quartet finished the walk to the large, porched, log home in silence. Joel noted the "H" shape, different from most ranch houses. They reached the bottom step, with Rebecca in the lead. The massive front door burst open. A tall man with graying brown hair and cold blue eyes stepped onto the porch. He fastened his gaze on Rebecca. "Didn't I tell you to keep away from the hands?"

"Father, something's wrong. Smokey came home riding Hayes's horse, chasing this stranger."

Joel could have sworn a look of actual relief brightened the intense blue eyes. Samuel Fairfax ignored his daughter's stumbling explanation and turned toward Joel. His mouth dropped open. He took a backward step as if hit by a battering ram.

Joel's heart leaped. This man must have somewhere encountered Cyrus! From babyhood, Judith and Gideon told him he was a replica of his father. Consternation brought Joel's spirits to earth with a resounding thud. Some tragedy lay between Samuel and the long-missing Cyrus. Could they have met, quarreled, and settled their differences in the time-honored western tradition that added bodies to Boot Hills throughout the land? It could account for Hayes's stranglehold on Fairfax. If he knew. . .

Joel's imagination ran riot.

"Who are you, and what do you want?" Fairfax demanded.

Face-to-face with a possible end to his long search, Joel could not speak. Jim Perkins mercifully introduced him.

"Boss, this here's Joel Scott, and if he hadn't come ridin' in at just the right minute, well, ol' Smokey here'd be pushin' up the daisies."

"What's that?" Fairfax roared and turned his full attention to Perkins. Yet, the pallor of his first sight of Joel remained.

"Hayes rigged up some phony evidence to show Smokey was rustlin'," Jim explained. "Even fooled me. Wasn't even goin' to let Smokey speak up in his own defense, just roped him and got ready to hang him." Memory of the tense moments brought his story alive. "Hayes slapped Smokey's horse and left Smokey danglin', but quicker than a roadrunner, Scott steps out from a willow thicket, hauls out his guns, and cuts the rope with the best shootin' I ever saw. Then he up and covers us, makes Hayes crawl, finished the party by tellin' us he's a preacher, and beats Smokey and me in a race home ridin' that black mare over there."

Fairfax ignored Jim's pointing finger, his daughter's quick gasp of horror. "Travis, if Hayes says you were rustling, you were. Now get out of here. You're fired. You, too, Perkins."

"Too late, Boss," Jim said cheerfully. "Hayes done did that. We just rode in to get our gear and 'cause Scott here said you had the right to hear what really happened 'fore Hayes comes in with his lies."

Joel grinned at his audacity but not for long. Fairfax turned back to him, accusingly. "If you're some kind of preacher, why aren't you doing your job instead of sticking your nose in where it ain't wanted?"

"I'm looking for a man," Joel said for the second time that day. "Have you ever heard the name Cyrus Scott?"

"Kin of yours?"

"My father." Joel had difficulty forming the words.

Samuel Fairfax crossed his strong arms and stared. The logs of the ranch house behind him looked no stronger than their owner. "Why come sniveling to me? What did he do. . .this. . .what's his name? Oh yes, Cyrus Scott." His face turned even stonier.

"He married my mother using his brother's name, ran out on her before she found out she would bear his child, then fled from Texas when he learned of her death." Joel did not budge an inch.

"All that?" A sardonic smile accompanied his question. "Doesn't seem to me that you or anyone would chase around trying to find a man who'd do those things."

Joel took in a deep breath, held it, then let it go before he said, "If he's dead, I want to know it. If he isn't, he needs to know he's forgiven by God and his family." Truth rang in his voice. He saw something flicker in the cold eyes and added, "So is the man who killed him, if Father died by violence. God's love covers even that."

For a moment, Samuel Fairfax stood rigid. For an eternity, he stared into Joel's eyes. Smokey coughed, and the spell broke. Fairfax unfolded his arms and said, "If this Cyrus Scott is as foolhardy as his son, he probably died years ago." His boot heel ground into the porch when he turned and went back into the house. But before he closed the door, he called, "The best thing you can do is ride out with Travis and Perkins. There's nothing on the Lazy F for you."

Was his glance at Rebecca, followed by a meaningful look back at Joel, meant as a deliberate warning? His mouth tasting like ashes, the young minister watched the door close. Its slamming sounded a death knell to his search—and his hopes.

Chapter 9

M r. Scott, I apologize for Father." A strong but shapely hand lightly touched Joel's arm and released him from his stupor.

He looked into Rebecca Fairfax's upturned face, dusky red from her efforts not to cry. Something in her troubled brown eyes reached out to him. Joel inhaled sharply; his humiliation at the hands of her father vanished. For some insane reason, he wanted to shout, to listen to his pumping heart instead of the common sense that told him to leave. He glanced at the hand still resting on his sleeve. *What would it be like to take that hand. . . and its owner. . .and ride away?*

Joel felt the blood rush to his head at the preposterous idea. He had known Rebecca Fairfax less than an hour. He ignored the little voice inside that demanded, *So what?* "It's all right, Miss Fairfax." He looked deep into her lovely eyes. "We'll meet again."

The assurance in his words set new red flags waving in Rebecca's face. "I. . .I don't see how," she faltered.

Smokey Travis and Jim Perkins had been standing silent during Joel's altercation with the owner of the Lazy F. Now, they stepped forward, Stetsons in hand. Smokey half closed his keen dark eyes and drawled, "A preacher preaches, doesn't he? If I know Samuel Fairfax, an' I do, even he won't kick up a dust storm 'cause his daughter wants to go to a meeting."

"That's how I see it, too," Jim eagerly assented, his boyish face opening into a wide grin. "Pards, we'd better get out of here." He pointed to a distant band of dark riders heading toward the ranch house. Pure devilment shone in his eyes. "But we could pervide a welcomin' committee."

"You'd better go," Rebecca told them. A shadow swept over her sweet face. "Smokey, thanks for being my friend. Good luck, Jim." But her gaze fastened on Joel. "Good-bye, Mr. Scott. God help you in your search for your father." She stepped back.

"Will you be all right?" Joel hurriedly added, "Hayes is going to be in a nasty mood."

"God and Mrs. Cook, our cook, will look after me!" Her red lips twitched.

200

"The worst Father can do is send me to my room."

"An' your window's big enough for ya to climb out if ya had to," Perkins observed.

Rebecca looked startled at the thought, then nodded.

Five minutes later, Joel on Querida, Smokey on the buckskin that had come straight back to the ranch, and Jim on a trim pinto that he said was his rode away. Rebecca waved good-bye to them from the ranch house porch.

"Kinda hate leavin' her here to face Hayes," Jim growled.

"She'll be all right. I used to think someday I'd up an' marry her," Smokey said somberly. "Get her away from Hayes."

"Why didn't you?" Joel could not keep the words back, but when Smokey's face darkened, he wished he had kept still.

"Rebecca thinks a whole lot of me, but it's like the brother she never had but should have." Smokey stared ahead at the path wide enough for them to ride three abreast. "At least I was her friend, as much as Hayes and Fairfax allowed." He turned toward Joel. "I never was good enough for her. Perkins here or the other hands aren't, either. Now, a strapping young feller like you might just—" He never finished what he started to say. His buckskin chose that moment to shy away from some real or imagined danger and execute a dance that kept Smokey busy and Joel and Jim laughing at the horse's antics.

But the young minister did not forget the gleam in Smokey's eyes. If he could win the cowboy's confidence, he would have a loyal friend for life. The same held true with Perkins, witnessed to by the way he stood up to Hayes back by the willow thicket.

"I need supplies." Joel shoved aside meditations and spoke. "I suppose I can get what I need at the Mexican village?" He intercepted the quick glance Jim sent Smokey, the lifting of eyebrows before Jim drawled, "We've seen ya ride and shoot. Can you rope?"

"A little." Joel stifled a grin, glanced around, and selected a cottonwood stump off to their left. He uncoiled his lariat from the saddle horn, swung it in a wide loop, and dropped it over the stump with an expert twist of his wrist.

"Yup, ya can rope. . .a little." Perkins waited until Joel twitched the lasso, recoiled it, and put it back in place. "Why don't you 'n' me 'n' Smokey get jobs t'gether? Like the fellers in that book."

"The Three Musketeers?" Joel's heart lifted at the thought, and a pang of lonesomeness for his comrades back on the Double J went through him. "Think anyone will hire a preacher?"

"Sure, if you're with us. Right, Smokey?"

"Haw, haw!" Smokey grabbed his hat and slapped it against his leg. His horse went into another spin.

"What's so funny, ya bowlegged galoot?" Perkins demanded as soon as Smokey got the buckskin quieted.

Tears of laughter streaming down his dark face, Smokey choked, "I reckon any rancher who sees what our new pard can do won't worry about him preaching on his own time." He wiped his eyes with a bright neckerchief. "Say, Joel, how about playing a joke on the Bar Triangle? That's the next biggest spread to the Lazy F an' always wanting good riders."

"What kind of joke?" Joel looked at Smokey suspiciously.

"We'll ride in, ask for jobs, an' not let on you're a preacher."

"Naw," Jim chimed in. "That ain't no good. When they find out, they'll think Joel's ashamed of it."

Smokey's jaw dropped. "I never thought about that." He ruefully shook his head. A moment later, his dark eyes twinkled again. "Well, how about just not telling how fast his mare is?"

Jim sat up straighter; mischief filled his lean face. "Then, when the Mexican village holds their fiesta day, Joel c'n enter his horse—what's her handle, anyhow?"

"Querida. Spanish for *beloved*."

"Kayreeda'll purely outrun ev'ry horse in New Mexico," Jim predicted.

"Not Vermilion." Smokey glared at Perkins.

Jim snorted. "Think old man Fairfax'll let Rebecca ride in any race? Not 'til all the dogies come home wearin' ribbons in their ears." He rolled his eyes.

Joel, the peacemaker, asked, "What kind of horse is Vermilion? I've yet to see an animal beat Querida, given an equal start."

"He's the purtiest, best-tamed, brightest-red mustang you ever saw," Jim admitted. "Smokey caught him an' babied him an' gave him to Rebecca on her eighteenth birthday last December." He pushed his Stetson farther back on his head. "Smokey, I'd lay even odds on Vermilion an' the black."

Smokey jealously eyed the beautiful mare. "She might win a short race, but Vermilion can't be beat in a long one."

Joel smothered a grin. The longer the race, the better Querida performed. "No sense arguing about it. When does this fiesta day come off, anyway?"

"After roundup. The whole country comes."

"Who won the horse race last year?" Joel inquired.

"Hayes." The corners of Smokey's mouth turned down. "His big bay's a grand horse." He laughed gleefully. "I did enjoy riding him today. He ain't no match for your horse or Vermilion, though. Is it a deal? We keep mum an' surprise folks at the race?"

"Why not? We won't be lying or anything."

"I wouldn't ask a preacher to lie." Smokey sent his buckskin into a run and left Joel staring after him.

"Did I say something wrong?" asked Joel.

"Don't pay no 'tention to Smokey," Jim advised. "He's taken a shine to ya, but sometimes he's plum' peecooliar about things. Love does that to some fellers." Jim shook his head and looked wise.

"Do you have a girl?" Joel asked curiously.

Perkins's blinding smile burst forth again. "Sure. Conchita's the most beautiful gal in the Mexican village. Soon's I save a little money, I'm gonna hawg-tie her an' marry her before some long-legged jasper beats me to it." A thundercloud drove away his sunny look. "An' if Hayes don't quit hangin' around her all the while he's playin' up to Fairfax, intendin' to marry Rebecca, there's gonna be trouble like you never saw."

A cold breeze of foreboding blew across Joel's heart. "You mean that rustler's actually—"

Jim nodded and looked far older than his young years. They had nearly caught up with Smokey and the buckskin, who waited for them where the road forked. "Don't say nothin' in front of Smokey," Jim cautioned in a whisper. "He hates Hayes the polecat enough already."

If ever a range were white and needing harvest for God, this wild New Mexico land fit the description! Joel silently followed his new friends. Miles later, the Bar Triangle cattle with their distinctive brand replaced the herds of Lazy F stock.

With his first view of the Bar Triangle house and outbuildings, Joel's heart beat faster. Unlike the Lazy F, the original Bar Triangle owners had built of adobe. In many ways, the main house reminded Joel of his grandparents' hacienda. Low, long, and cool, the splashing fountain in the courtyard merrily welcomed the dusty, tired riders. The owner, Ben Lundeen, practically greeted them with open arms.

"Travis, Perkins, I figured someday you'd come riding in looking for work. It's a wonder you lasted so long as you did on the Lazy F, 'specially you, Smokey. Everyone knows Fairfax don't cotton to younger riders." His firm grip and keen look measured Joel. "Who's your pard?"

203

"Joel Scott, an all-round ridin', ropin', shootin' hand, plus he's a preacher," the irrepressible Jim bragged.

"Whaat?" Lundeen's eyes bulged in his strong face. Doubt crept into his voice. "I don't know about hiring a preacher. What'll the men say?"

Quick-witted as a ground squirrel in danger, Joel replied, "Why not let them decide? Put me on for a week, then ask your outfit if they want me to stay." He glanced away from Lundeen long enough to catch Smokey's delighted grin and the way Perkins put one hand over his mouth.

"Fair enough." Lundeen nodded. "You boys know where the bunkhouse is. Go stow your gear." His eyes gleamed, and he casually added, "You can do as you like about telling the men about your interrupted necktie party."

"How'd you know?" Jim belligerently placed both hands on his hips in a fighting stance.

Again, that curious gleam filled Lundeen's eyes. "You'll find an old friend in the cookhouse. He rode in earlier today with an interesting tale for my ears only. Said he couldn't stand living with the kind of men Hayes has been hiring and that he reckoned the only two worth much wouldn't be staying."

"So, you knew all the time we were coming!" Chagrin fell on Smokey's expressive face.

"I didn't know young Scott was a preacher," Lundeen admitted. "I guess that little fact got by Curly. He spilled the other to me, and I told him to keep quiet." Trouble brooded on the lined face. "The men will hear of it soon enough. You know range talk." His gaze bored into his new riders. "It's up to Scott to prove himself."

"He will," Smokey predicted.

"Yeah, but if anythin' happens an' Joel don't stay, we go, too," Jim loyally added.

"Fair enough." Lundeen's rare smile lightened his countenance, and he looked years younger. "Go get settled." He wandered down toward the corral with them to where they had tied their horses. His steps quickened, and he headed straight for Querida. "Whose mare is this?" He stroked her soft nose.

"Mine." Pride of ownership and the long, faithful trail they had ridden together underlined the word.

"She's a beauty. You wouldn't want to sell her."

"No."

"I wouldn't, either, if I owned her." He patted Querida again, and his eyes flashed. "Good thing you're here instead of on some of the ranches. Your horse is safe on the Bar Triangle." His unspoken words, *but not on the Lazy*

F, hung in the quiet air until Lundeen said, "Tomorrow we'll see what you can do, Scott," and trailed back up to his house.

＋

It took less than a week for the Bar Triangle crew to accept Joel Scott. His range skills showed up with the best and won the respect of both men his age and much older. Lundeen just grunted at Joel's display of hard work and expertise.

True to their pact, Jim, Smokey, and Joel did not breathe a word about Querida's fleetness, even when some of the hands said a trifle too nonchalantly, "Bet she can run. Are you going to ride her in the fiesta race?"

"I might." Joel lounged on his bunk, as he had done dozens of times on the Double J. In spite of being the adopted son-of-the-house, once he had learned to ride with the outfit, he spent a lot of time in the bunkhouse and kept a bedroll there.

"Sure will be some race," some of the boys sighed enviously. "Sure hope Hayes don't win again. He wouldn't, if Fairfax'd let that girl of his ride her red horse," seemed to be the general agreed-on opinion.

"Once, when I was separatin' our cattle from the Lazy F's, I saw her racin' across the range," one cowboy said. "Never will forget it. She rode just like an Indian, bent forward in the saddle 'til her and that Vermilion looked like one critter."

"Hey, Travis, how come Fairfax's so all-fired anxious to get her hitched up with Hayes?" someone called out.

Smokey's pupils dwindled to pinpoints of blackness. "Crazy, I reckon." He breathed hard. "Beats me."

A frank-faced, young rider confessed, "I'da got me a job there in hopes of sometimes seein' the girl, but, even for that, I couldn't stomach Hayes. One of these times, he's gonna get his." Cold steel rang beneath the idle words.

Joel spent Sunday afternoon propped against an ancient oak, considering his future. He knew he had passed his trial at the Bar Triangle; he also felt at home. Yet, how could range work be related to his two missions: finding his father and preaching? A burst of song from the bunkhouse brought a sympathetic smile to his carved lips. Jim must be getting duded up to go call on Conchita. On impulse, Joel left his tree friend and ambled back to the bunkhouse. "Perkins, mind if I ride to the Mexican village with you?"

"Not atall." Jim's face was flushed with the efforts of pulling on boots shined almost as brightly as his eyes. His Sunday-white shirt and colorful scarf pleasantly added to his excited, handsome face. "Just don't ya get no ideas about her."

"I won't," Joel promised and turned to Smokey. "Are you coming?"

His friend looked up from a magazine he was reading, disgust etched into his face. "Might as well." He threw the magazine aside, stood, and stretched. "The feller who wrote the story I was reading has never been west of Boston! According to him, all us cowboys sleep in our chaps an' don't eat nothing but beef an' beans. Too bad he doesn't come out here for a spell an' see the meals Curly turns out for us poor, miserable punchers."

"Better of him if he don't come," Jim said sagely. "It'd be too bad if a feller like that got the outfit turned loose on him."

Joel laughed, but on the way to the village, he asked, "Do you think some of the men would come if I found a place to preach some Sunday?"

"They might," Smokey said after a sidelong look at Jim that Joel duly noted. "There's a padre in the Mexican village an' a little church, but not many of the ranchers go to Mass an' none of the hands." He pondered for a minute. "Now that we're on permanent-like at the Bar Triangle, ask Lundeen if it would be all right to hold a meeting there. He's honest all the way through; so's his wife. Kids are all grown and gone."

"Good idea," Jim seconded. "Maybe Rebecca Fairfax would ride over an' you could see her. . .horse Vermilion."

Joel knew exactly what Jim hinted and could not keep color from rising until he sarcastically thought, *I must be the same shade as the wonder horse they keep praising.* It made him feel hotter than ever.

"You better forget her an' keep your mind on Conchita," Smokey told him. "If you don't marry her pretty soon, I'll up an' beat you."

"She wouldn't look at the likes of ya," Jim loftily told his partner.

"Why not? I'm better looking than some people around here," Smokey retorted. "Even if I don't have a brand-new shirt an' a kerchief I could use to scare off a wild bull."

They good-naturedly wrangled all the way to the Mexican village, heaping mock insults on each other and appealing to Joel for support, and looking disgusted when he would not take sides.

The Mexican village resembled similar ones he had seen in his travels. Adobe buildings, strings of red and green peppers, the tang of dust and horseflesh, guitar music from a cantina, laughter, and the after-siesta relaxation of a Sunday.

"Conchita lives with her married sister," Jim explained when they stopped before a cream building with the inevitable red-tiled roof. Green vines grew up and over, giving an illusion of coolness Joel knew would be present even on the hottest day.

The door stood open. They dismounted and hitched their horses to a crude rail fence. Perkins's spurs jingled musically when he led the way up a path made of flat stones.

"Pard, ain't that Hayes's bay?" Smokey crouched and pointed toward a tethered horse grazing nearby, barely visible through a clump of cottonwoods.

Jim stopped in midstride. His face whitened, then a look that sent fear crawling through Joel spread across Jim's face. In the frozen second before Perkins leaped for the open doorway, a low cry came from inside the house.

Like a speeding bullet, Jim bounded inside. Smokey and Joel raced after him. The trio burst through an empty room toward the sound of a voice that pleaded, "No, no, Señor!"

"That dirty scoundrel!" Smokey choked. He and Joel crowded through the door to the small courtyard until they stood side by side with Perkins. A man with mousy brown hair stood with his back to them. An ashen-faced Mexican girl, whose disheveled dark hair and terrified eyes told the whole story, struggled in the man's arms. A ruffled white blouse sagged over one brown shoulder, and the red rose in her hair drooped in bizarre contrast to her distorted face. Hayes's fingers dug into her soft arms, and he jerked her closer. She screamed.

"Hayes!" Perkins's low, deadly voice loosened the man's hold. Hayes reached for his gun and whirled. Revolver half out of his holster, the livid-faced man faced the three men. He stared straight into Perkins's face—and saw death from the steady Colt covering him, the trigger being slowly squeezed.

Chapter 10

Horror so deep he could neither pray nor move engulfed Joel. Then, Smokey struck up Perkins's gun with one hand, while keeping Hayes covered with the Colt in his other. Perkins's shot fired harmlessly into the ceiling.

"Drop it, Hayes!" Smokey ordered.

Hayes's revolver clattered to the floor. His mouth worked helplessly; rage and wonder mingled. Long scratches on his cheeks oozed blood. He finally burst out, "You!"

"Why'd ya do it?" Jim Perkins cried. Anger still mottled his face. "The dirty skunk don't deserve to live an' ya know it! Why didn't ya let me kill him?"

Joel shrank from Smokey's bitter laugh. "Think I did it for him? Naw. He ain't worth spilling blood for." He laughed again, a wild sound that turned Hayes's face even grayer. "Besides, someday he's going to hang." He waved toward the door with his gun. "Get out, Hayes, an' don't come back here—ever. I reckon I saved your life; now I'm telling you, the next time. . ." He choked, and his dark eyes glittered.

Hayes did not say a word. He stumbled past Joel, who stepped aside from the doorway and let him go through.

Joel was sickened by the violent scene he had just witnessed, a scene that nearly led to death. His ears rang, and a few moments later, he heard hoofbeats, and he knew Hayes had fled.

"Conchita, are you all right?" The Jim who knelt by the girl bore little resemblance to the cowboy who, but for Smokey's interference, would have killed Conchita's attacker.

"Yes." She pulled her blouse back onto her shoulder. Great drops made her black eyes look like twin lakes at midnight under New Mexican stars. "He come, grab me. I fight." She extended broken-nailed hands that still trembled. "Hayes is bad." Conchita leaned against Jim.

Smokey jerked his head toward the doorway and walked out. Joel followed, conscious of shame. Not only for men like Hayes, who sank so low they made girls' and women's lives on the frontier a nightmare but for his own inadequacies. He, a minister of God, had stood speechless and power-less in the face of peril. Thank God Smokey had not.

Humbled by his lack of ability to act when necessary, a shortcoming Joel had not known he possessed, he hoarsely told his new friend, "It's a good thing you were here." He shuddered; drops of sweat sprang to his forehead. "Hayes can't help being grateful that you. . .after what he tried to do. . ."

Smokey's look of contempt stopped his stuttering. "Like I said, it wasn't for Hayes. I just couldn't stand for Jim to have a killing on his head. It would always be between him an' Conchita, for one thing. For another, Hayes's time is getting short on this range. That Lone Man Canyon business shows that." An unpleasant smile twisted his lips. He glanced back at the house, then at all sides of the wide porch where they had stopped to wait for Jim. "You look like a feller who could keep things under his hat."

"I am." Joel braced himself for the startling revelation he felt coming.

Smokey again checked to make sure they were not observed before he pulled back his vest just far enough for Joel to catch a flash of silver.

"Smokey Travis, you're a—"

"Shh. Don't tell Jim," the shorter man warned in a whisper when heavy footfalls and lighter steps announced Perkins and Conchita's arrival.

Perkins's arm lay protectively around her waist. Tearstains could not dis-guise the Mexican girl's beauty. Her eyes glowed with happiness that re-flected in her sweetheart's face. "Joel, you're a preacher. Will ya marry us?"

Jim's question drove the thought of the deputy marshal's badge that Smokey wore clean out of Joel's head. "Why, yes," he stammered. "But—"

"Pard, how can you get married?" Smokey demanded. "Where are you going to take Conchita if you do?"

A look of doubt did not change Jim's dogged determination. "We'll ride out an' find a job somewhere. Connie's willin' to work at cleanin' or cookin'." His mouth tightened. "Snappin' crocodiles, Smokey, ya don't expect me to leave her here, do ya?"

Smokey pondered. "It ain't none of my business, but if it were me, why, I'd just pack up Conchita an' her duds an' take her back to the Bar Triangle with us." A smile, singular in its sweetness, crept to his face. "Mrs. Lundeen'll take care of her 'til you get a place, especially when she hears what Hayes tried to do."

"Connie, will ya trust me an' my pards an' go?" Jim's poignant question set Joel's heart to pounding. So did the love in Conchita's liquid eyes when she said, "Yes," and pressed her face against Perkins's still-fresh white shirt. She raised her head, smiled mistily at Joel and Smokey, and ran lightly back inside.

Smokey, the coolest of the three, snickered and asked, "Do you have any money?"

"Money?" Jim stared at him.

"Yeah. Pesos, cartwheels, simoleons, good old American dollars."

"Not much." Jim spread out a pitiful array and turned deep red. "Uh, what do I need money for?"

Smokey threw his hands up in exasperation. "How're you going to get Conchita to the ranch? Does she have a horse?"

Joel laughed out loud at the comical look on Jim's bewildered face. "Don't worry. I've got plenty." He laughed again when his comrades gasped at the bills he pulled from his shirt. "Buy her a horse, Jim. Get a pack mule if you need it."

"I can't take your money," he protested.

"Call it a wedding present."

"Whoopee!" Smokey yelled. Jim rushed back inside. He returned wearing the grin Joel had come to associate with his lighthearted companion. "Connie says she doesn't need a pack mule. All she has is her clothes an' we can stow them in our saddlebags." His eyes glinted when he awkwardly added, "Thanks. . .both of ya." His face reddened. "I'm just glad we got here when we did."

"Thank God for that," Joel soberly agreed. "Wonder how Hayes is going to explain to Fairfax what happened? The Lazy F's bound to hear range gossip."

Smokey fixed a warning gaze on Joel. "You can bet your life that snake'll come up with lies enough to make himself out an angel an' the rest of us devils," he darkly prophesied. Conchita peeked out the door, and by unspoken consent, they dropped the subject. Just before dusk, the three men and a tired Conchita, unused to hours in the saddle, dismounted at the Bar Triangle.

"Pards, come with us," Jim begged. They nodded and trailed Jim and his drooping bride-to-be inside the adobe ranch house.

If Joel had ever entertained qualms about Perkins's sincerity, they vanished when Jim manfully told the surprised Lundeens, "Conchita and me aim to get married soon as I can fix a place for her. My pards and me got to her place today just in time to save her from Hayes." His eyes flashed. "Smokey said he thought you could look after her. She's willin' to work hard."

Not by a flicker of an eyelash did either Ben Lundeen or his kindly wife betray shock. Mrs. Lundeen stood, took both of Conchita's hands in her own, and said in a genteel voice, "How nice to have a girl with us again! Now that our daughter's gone, I just get hungry for another woman's company." She smiled and added, "Come, Conchita. You'll want to freshen up from your long ride."

Joel's eyes stung. The woman's acceptance and unfailing hospitality reminded him of Judith; so would she have taken in a stray.

Lundeen waited until the ladies disappeared, then inquired, "How's Hayes?"

Joel shuddered at the implication. Womenfolk in the West were to be protected and those who transgressed, punished. *God, will the day ever come when law and order other than the law of retribution rule this land?*

"Hayes'll think twice before he gets in our way again," Smokey slowly told Lundeen. His eyes shone like molten metal. "That's the second time our paths have crossed."

Joel silently added, *I pray to God there won't be another.*

✢

During the days that Joel proved himself at the Bar Triangle and settled into the outfit, Rebecca Fairfax had troubles of her own. A strange restlessness filled her, stemming from the two different versions of the attempted hanging of Smokey Travis.

Samuel made sure his daughter was present when Hayes rode in with his story of catching Smokey in the act of rustling. She noticed how he downplayed the young minister's part in it. All he said was, "Fool stranger interfered, and the men and I let Travis go after firing him and that mouthy Perkins." Yet, the girl hugged to her heart the clean blue fire of Joel Scott's eyes, his waving corn silk hair, tanned skin, and, most of all, the look in his face when he quietly said they would meet again.

How? She considered the question from her favorite range viewpoints, in her bed at night. Other comments haunted her, including Jim Perkins's laconic observation about her window being large enough to climb through if she had to.

One tense day followed another. Her father grew more taciturn and unapproachable than ever. If it had not been for the faithful Mrs. Cook, Rebecca could not have stood it. More and more, she spent free time in the kitchen, one of her few refuges away from the ever-present Clyde Hayes, who had renewed his pursuit of her, no, intensified it. Sometimes, she felt she would eventually be forced to marry Hayes simply because her father commanded it.

Yet, every time she thought of it, she cried out, "Never!" She also began to heed Mrs. Cook's lessons about trusting in the Lord and asking for His protection and help. Verses in the Bible that Rebecca had not known existed now offered comfort.

Late one Sunday night, she and her father sat reading in the big living room, a rare occurrence. Usually, if he came in before dark, Samuel buried himself in papers concerning the ranch. Tonight, she stole glances at him from behind a well-worn copy of *The Pilgrim's Progress*, a book Mrs. Cook said would help Rebecca forget her own troubles. How old and worn he looked, as if life had effectively stamped out any happiness he had ever known.

Rebecca impulsively left her chair and went to stand before him. "Father, what is it? You seem so sad." He didn't speak for such a long time that she wondered if he had heard her. When he did speak, his words left her stunned.

"Rebecca, if you don't marry Clyde Hayes, I am ruined." He spread his hands wide, expressing defeat as she had never seen him do before. His eyes pleaded. "Daughter, will you save me?"

She almost fell to her knees and promised. Then the memory of Hayes laying hands on her stilled her voice. Marriage with him would be torment until death mercifully freed her. "Father, I—"

The door flew open and slammed back against the wall with a mighty bang. Clyde Hayes strode in, glowering. Red welts stood out on his pale face, and his colorless eyes flamed with triumph. Rebecca shrank away from him.

"Hayes? What happened to you? Looks like you tangled with a wildcat."

"Might as well have." He dropped heavily into a chair without being invited. "That's what a man gets for tryin' to help a woman he don't care about."

"What are you talking about?" Fairfax dropped the book he still held.

"I rode into the Mexican village. Found Travis and Perkins attackin' the girl called Conchita. I challenged them, and they vamoosed with their tails between their legs. They sneaked back up on me, and I pulled my gun. Next thing I knew, the girl was all over me, scratchin' and spittin'. Last time I'll mix in."

Rebecca stared in disbelief. The part about Conchita scratching was obviously true. The rest she did not believe.

Neither did she believe it when Hayes contemptuously added, "That kid who calls himself a preacher was there, too. Didn't do any showin' off this time, though. Too scared, probably."

"It's an outrage when things like this go on right here on our range," Fairfax shouted. "I've a mind to get the outfit and ride down there myself." Rebecca noticed the fear in Hayes's face before he quickly said, "It ain't worth it. Besides, the girl's gone. I hid in a clump of cottonwood and watched them ride out. The men had scared up a horse for the girl, and the four of them rode off. I followed a spell, and they were headed for the Bar Triangle."

"Mighty strange they'd go that way." Samuel's eyebrows met in a frown. "The Lundeens and their ranch that's getting bigger all the time are a cactus spine in the leg, but they're decent folk. They won't put up with them."

Hayes glanced at Rebecca, whose heart nearly burst with indignation. "Oh, those men'll have some story," he carelessly said. "I just wanted you to hear what really happened."

She almost retorted, "If we want the truth, we won't get it from you," but bit her tongue and edged toward the door.

"Where are you goin'?" Hayes arrogantly demanded.

It took all Rebecca's control to say, "I rode a long way today, and I'm tired. Good night, Father, Mr. Hayes." She whipped out of the room and ran to her own.

Later, after she heard the front door close and knew Hayes had gone, she crept noiselessly down the hall and peered into the living room. Her father sat before the dying fire, graying brown head bowed as if in despair. Pity stirred her. A burning stick snapped; Samuel Fairfax groaned. Rebecca leaned forward and strained her ears to catch his low words. "God—is there no end to it?"

She wanted to go to him, but fear held her prisoner. If she did, he might ask her again to become the purchase price for his—what? Freedom? Life? Peace of mind? On hesitant feet, Rebecca stole back to her room, only to lie sleepless for hours and watch the mysterious night, shadowy and filled with uncertainty, just like her life.

Morning brought relief. No matter what, she could never marry Hayes. She avoided being alone with her father, unwilling to start another bitter argument. With Smokey no longer on the ranch to protect her, Rebecca sometimes felt herself to be a prisoner. She dared not ride far from home for fear of encountering Hayes. Not that she stood in awe of him. Vermilion could outrun Hayes's bay, and Rebecca could defend herself ably with her marksmanship. Yet, if she were forced to do so, would Father believe what she said or listen to Hayes? She could not risk finding out.

The morning after he rode in, Rebecca had privately told Hayes's story to Mrs. Cook. Her shrewd blue eyes and round face showed how little stock she put in anything Hayes said. "Looks to me like what probably happened was the other way around," she said and punched down the bread dough as if she had

Hayes on the well-floured board. "If I know folks—and I do—neither Smokey nor young Perkins would have dishonorable intentions toward any girl. As for that young preacher, I only got a glimpse of him, but what I saw is in his favor."

✛

A few days later, Mrs. Cook said, "Mrs. Lundeen sent word over there'd be a meeting on Sunday at the Bar Triangle. She invited us to come Saturday and stay over. Want to go?" Her eyes sparkled. "It's been a long time since we had a visiting preacher come through."

"I don't suppose Father will consent," Rebecca said despondently, while her heart beat fast at the idea of an outing and the chance to see Joel Scott again.

"Let me ask him," Mrs. Cook suggested.

"All right, but it won't do any good."

Rebecca's pessimism held all that day but miraculously left at supper when Mrs. Cook said, "Mr. Fairfax, the Lundeens are holding a meeting on Sunday and asked us to come over Saturday and stay. I think we should go, all of us. Rebecca needs to be with folks other than us."

Samuel laid his fork down. "You do, do you?" He frowned.

"Yes, I do. It pays a body to let the neighbors know he's friendly."

Fairfax jerked at the word "he," took a mouthful of beefsteak, chewed it thoughtfully, and swallowed. "Might not be a bad idea. I've been meaning to talk to Lundeen about roundup. This is probably as good a time as any."

Mrs. Cook reverted to her humble servant role. "Thank you, Sir." But, when she went to bring in the dessert, she lifted her eyebrows in a victory signal behind the master-of-the-house's back.

Rebecca could scarcely believe it. She wanted to mention the jaunt to her father but held her tongue. To do so might cause him to change his mind, and she simply had to go.

On Friday before the meeting, a second messenger arrived from the Bar Triangle. "There's gonna be a weddin' tomorrow night," he told Mrs. Cook and Rebecca. "Bring your fanciest clothes." He looked at the girl admiringly. "Uh, Smokey Travis sends greetin's."

"Is Smokey getting married?" Mrs. Cook gasped.

The rider shook his head. "Nope. It's that pard of his." He glanced at Rebecca again. "All the boys at the Bar Triangle are jealous. Lundeen's done fixed up a little cabin for the newlyweds." He grinned. "This is sure a big weekend for the preacher."

Before Rebecca could ask why, the rider shifted in the saddle. The girl followed his glance toward her father riding in.

"Gotta go. See y'all tomorrow." He spurred his horse and rode off with a cheerful wave and a tip of his hat to Fairfax.

"Who was that, and what did he want?" Samuel demanded sharply when he reached the house and slid from the saddle.

Mrs. Cook placidly said, "Mrs. Lundeen sent word we'd get in on a wedding as well as preaching and to bring our good clothes."

"Wedding? Whose?" The words shot like bullets out of Samuel's pinched mouth.

"Why, I don't rightly know, except it isn't Smokey Travis. Kind of sounded like it might be the young preacher himself."

Fairfax stared at her, dumbfounded. An odd look covered his face, one Rebecca had never before seen. "Scott? Who's the bride?"

"I don't know that, either," Mrs. Cook admitted. "Maybe one of the girls from the Mexican village."

Anger contorted Samuel's features. He brushed past the two women, slammed into the house, and let the door crash behind him.

"My stars," Mrs. Cook gasped. "What did I say to set him off? He sounded like he actually cared who the preacher married!"

He isn't the only one who cares, a wicked little voice inside Rebecca taunted. She raised her chin defiantly and said, "What does it matter? Come help me decide what to wear, will you, please?" Yet, all during the choosing of just the right gown and pressing and carefully packing it before the wedding, Rebecca's heart lay cold and heavy in her chest, making it hard for her to breathe and talk normally.

Chapter 11

One look into Conchita's innocent, dark eyes put to rest forever any suspicion Rebecca carried concerning the Mexican girl's reputation. An hour after the Lazy F contingent reached the Bar Triangle, the two maidens giggled and chattered as if they were long-separated sisters—especially when Conchita blushingly confessed she had been in love with "Señor Jeem" ever since young Perkins first visited the village.

Why should a great burden roll off Rebecca's shoulders? Her face rivaled the pink rose tucked in her nut-brown hair.

Later, Smokey managed to whisk Rebecca out of her father's vigilant scrutiny and whisper, "How come Hayes showed up? Did he trail you?"

Rebecca made a sound of disgust; a frown marred her pretty face. "I couldn't believe it when he said he reckoned he'd mosey along." Her eyes flashed. "I overheard Father tell Hayes privately there had better not be any trouble."

"An' what did Hayes say to that?" Smokey's intense, dark gaze never left her face.

"He told Father he wouldn't start anything but if—" She hastily swallowed Hayes's derogatory "those three snakes" and substituted, "If anyone started trouble, he'd see that he finished it." She caught Smokey's rigid arm with one hand. "For Conchita's sake and mine, keep away from him."

"I can't back away if he comes looking for me," Smokey protested. Storm signals waved in his face. Rebecca could see he was torn between wanting to please her and following the range law that demanded a man answer an insult.

She lowered her voice. "It's just that every time Hayes gets mixed up in something, Father pushes me more to marry him. I can't, Smokey, I just can't. If only we could prove how rotten Hayes is and get him sent away!"

A curious expression rested on the cowboy's lean face. "Keep holding out. Maybe one of these days, we'll nail Hayes." He grinned, and mischief lurked in his eyes. "My new pard's been looking forward to seeing you again."

Rebecca could not stop the rich blush that mantled her face. "Oh? How strange, since Jim's marrying Conchita tonight."

"My other pard. The long-legged galoot duded up ready to perform the ceremony who's leaning against the door frame an' watching us." He raised one hand, motioned Joel to join them, and whispered in a woebegone voice, "Since you only care for me like a brother, you couldn't do better than Scott. He may be a preacher, but he's a real man, too. I sneaked around an' listened while he practiced preaching. He talks 'most as well as he rides an' ropes an' shoots."

"We meet again, Miss Fairfax. I'm glad." Joel's eyes glowed like blue jewels. In spite of obvious attempts to make his blond hair lie down, it lay in waves and looked even more golden in contrast with his suntanned skin. His blinding smile set Rebecca's heart to beating.

"It's nice to be here," she said noncommittally and held out her hand. It lost itself in Joel's strong one, but she noticed he made no effort to hold it longer than courtesy allowed, unlike some riders who used introductions as an excuse for extra friendliness.

"Excuse me, but I'd better hunt up Perkins an' make sure he hasn't got cold feet." Smokey abruptly abandoned them. Rebecca found herself at a loss for words and felt horrified when she heard her own voice asking, "Mr. Scott, why did you and Smokey and Jim bring Conchita here?"

The blue gaze turned to steel. "No gentleman speaks to a lady of what would have happened to her if we hadn't arrived just when we did. Thank God we came."

His heartfelt prayer filled in all the blanks left by his refusal to discuss what she had suspected all along—that Hayes had been the villain.

A little later, Conchita confirmed it. While dressing in the beautiful white gown and Spanish lace mantilla Mrs. Lundeen had kindly lent her for her wedding, she told Rebecca in a few broken whispers how Hayes came, took her by surprise, and attacked her. "He is bad," she finished. "Señorita, never let him find you alone." It took all Rebecca could do to change the fear in the bride-to-be's eyes to the joy that rightfully belonged to her on her wedding day.

Conchita had shyly asked Rebecca to stand up with her, along with Smokey, who flanked the eager groom. Glad that she had heeded Mrs. Cook's advice not to wear white and rival the bride, Rebecca's rose pink gown swished around her ankles and made a perfect background for the dark-haired girl who turned toward Perkins in perfect trust. Quite a crowd of neighbors had ridden to the Bar Triangle for the event. Admiration of the young women's beauty rippled through the small crowd.

Rebecca could openly observe Joel throughout the simple but touching ceremony. His face shone with goodness. He spoke of the responsibility Jim and Conchita faced and the happiness they could find in one another by becoming part of God's plan for husbands and wives since time began. When he came to the question, "Do you, Conchita, take Jim. . . ," Rebecca thought, *What would it be like, promising to take a man for better and worse, in sickness and health; mutually agreeing to be his companion; promising to keep yourself for him and from all others until death?* How much love she would have to feel before consenting to such solemn, irrevocable vows!

She glanced to the side and caught Hayes's stare. How terrible to be linked with him. Not even to save her father could she face life as Hayes's wife. The curl of his lip showed his contempt for the sacredness of the vows that Conchita and Jim made before God and these people. Rebecca forced herself to look steadily at Hayes for a moment, refusing to show the fear that crawled in her veins, then she deliberately turned back to watch Jim place a simple gold band on his bride's finger and salute her with a quick, boyish kiss.

You couldn't do better than Scott. Smokey's satisfied announcement rang in her ears. Her heart fluttered, but a wave of people, determined to greet the bride, washed between them. Not until the new Mr. and Mrs. Jim Perkins fled to the privacy of the cabin that the Lundeens provided did Rebecca get to speak to Joel again. She found herself tongue-tied once more.

"They'll be happy," Joel said. He looked both ways and lowered his voice. "This is my first wedding."

"It was beautiful," Rebecca murmured, wondering how a man like this had escaped feminine wiles. Smokey had mentioned that Joel had passed his twentieth birthday a few months before this early summer wedding. "I look forward to hearing you preach tomorrow."

Humility replaced Joel's smile. "It's been some time since I gave a sermon, not since I left Santa Fe." He expertly guided her to a small bench partially secluded from the party that had spilled out of the adobe ranch house into the yard. "I know the Lord will help me give the right message, though. He always does." Moonlight silvered his fair hair.

"Mr. Scott—or do I call you Reverend?" She laughed and nervously pleated her soft pink gown.

"Just Joel, please."

Encouraged, she asked, "Would you tell me more about your search to find your father?"

One of Joel's best skills lay in his ability to paint vivid word pictures. He told the pathetic story of his mother in a way that brought a mist to Rebecca's eyes. He mentioned his long trail to find those his uncle Gideon longed to reach with the gospel for Jesus Christ. A happy laugh crinkled his face when he said, "Just today I got word from Colorado Springs that Eb Sears and Lily are going to marry. Little Danny will have a father again, but the best thing is that Eb and Lily have decided to follow the Master. Eb is going into the store with Livingston, Lily's father-in-law, who loves her and Danny and can't bear to lose them."

"A sad tale with a happy ending. Mr., uh, Joel, do you think God has a happy ending for everyone?"

He remained quiet for several moments, then slowly replied, "I believe everyone who accepts Christ and walks in His path will have the happiest ending of all—eternal life. I also feel God gives His children what He knows is best for them, although it may not be what we think will make us happy."

"Then, even if you don't find your father, you won't feel cheated?" It suddenly seemed vitally important to know. Rebecca clasped her hands, looked up at him in the moonlight, and added, "You won't feel that God let you down?"

"I'll be disappointed," the young minister admitted. "I still believe some-day I will find Father. If I don't, God must have a reason."

Rebecca felt bitterly disappointed. "Mrs. Cook always says the same thing, that God must have a reason. If this is true, why can't He let us know?" Her fingers clenched. "I've tried to trust Him, but when I see Father grow-ing old and going somewhere inside himself away from me, it's hard. I don't know how long it's been since he's laughed."

"Is Hayes responsible?"

The sympathetic question opened the floodgates. "He has to be. Father never was boisterous, but before Hayes came, he smiled and rode with me. Now, most of the time he just broods and lets Hayes run things. Run them down," she added. Her lips twisted. "Smokey said cattle are disappearing from the Lazy F. Then, that episode at Lone Man Cabin—" She put her hand over her mouth.

"It's all right. Smokey told me what happened."

Relief at having someone else know left her weak. "I promised not to tell Father, but I had to tell Smokey." A puzzled feeling went through her. "He said something funny tonight about maybe nailing Hayes."

Joel took her hand and pressed it. "Miss Rebecca, will you trust Smokey and me and most of all God? I have a feeling things will work out."

"Sometimes I don't think there is a way out," she said.

His fingers tightened. "There is always a way up." He freed her hand and smiled at her. "Now I'm getting into my sermon for tomorrow."

She felt her lips quiver into an answering smile but sobered when a heavy voice demanded, "What are you doin' out here?" Hayes stood at her elbow with a scowling Samuel Fairfax just behind him.

How much have they heard? Rebecca frantically wondered before she sprang to her feet. "I can't see that is any of your concern."

"It's mine." Fairfax pushed past Hayes and confronted her. "Get in the house." He turned a scorching gaze on Joel. "If I catch you around her again, I'll horsewhip you. Like father, like son."

Rebecca gasped at the sneer in his voice, the satisfaction on Hayes's face made grotesque by waving shadows that crossed and recrossed it with every movement of the rising breeze.

"I wouldn't try that if I were you." Joel leisurely got up, planted his feet apart, and did not give an inch.

"Who do you think you are!" Hayes fairly frothed at the mouth.

"Shut up, Hayes." Smokey Travis stepped from behind a cottonwood. His wedding clothes had been replaced by work shirt, pants, and vest. His Stetson rode on the back of his head, and moonlight glittered in his eyes.

Had he been playing watchdog? Rebecca felt herself go cold. "Father, Smokey, please. Don't spoil Conchita's wedding."

"That woman? I'm surprised even Perkins'd marry her," Hayes jeered. "But, he's no better than she is."

"Liar!" Smokey bellowed and dove headfirst into Hayes's stomach like a barreling cannonball. The unexpected attack knocked the taller, heavier man to the ground and winded him enough so that Smokey could get in a half-dozen pounding blows on Hayes's face before Fairfax could pull him off.

"Look out!" Rebecca screamed.

Hayes had recovered enough to reach for his gun, black death in his face.

Rebecca screamed again and flung herself in front of Smokey. In the same instant, Joel, unarmed, drew back one foot and sent the gun spinning. "You rotten coward!" he said.

Smokey tore free from Fairfax and towered over Hayes on the ground, nursing a bruised hand from the powerful kick. "Next time I see you, you'd better see me first, Hayes." He whipped around toward Fairfax. "If you aren't as crooked an' yellow as this coyote, you'll kick him off the Lazy F before there ain't no Lazy F left." Rage overcame caution. "While you're at it, ask him about hawg-tying your daughter at Lone Man Cabin an' having a phony deputy who calls himself Crowley make her swear she wouldn't tell you what happened."

Father, be a man, Rebecca silently prayed—in vain. Samuel licked dry lips, sent a furious glance at the huddled figure of Hayes, cursed him, and ordered, "Get back to the ranch." His daughter saw hatred beyond belief in his face, but not a word came concerning Smokey's charge.

"I told you to get in the house." Fairfax glared at Rebecca. With a little cry, she gathered her skirts around her and ran, but not before hearing Joel Scott's accusation, "Samuel Fairfax, the meanest animal alive protects its young. God forgive you for standing by and letting this vile man near the sweetest, purest girl God could create!"

His praise warmed the fleeing figure's cold heart. She slowed down before she reached the main body of merrymakers. Incredible as it seemed, they laughed, talked, and evidently had not been aware of the fight. Rebecca paused and smoothed down her hair, hoping she did not look as distraught as she felt.

"It's about time to start the shivaree," someone called. Rebecca had never been allowed to participate in the mock serenade with which cowhands often celebrated weddings. They would keep the young couple awake with their hollering, beating on pans, and demands for food.

But Rebecca could not face it now. Mrs. Cook stood a little apart, and she went straight to her. "I'm really tired. Do we have to go?"

"My stars, no, Child. Let the cowboys do the noisemaking. We'll go on to bed. You sure looked lovely tonight. That new preacher could barely stop looking at you long enough to get Jim and Conchita hitched." A wistful look that reminded Rebecca of long-forgotten feelings crept into her face. "Joel Scott would be a solid foundation a woman could build love and a home on and know they would stand."

First Smokey, now Mrs. Cook. Rebecca wondered if she had fallen into a conspiracy to throw her into Joel's arms. The idea sent a glow through her, and long after Mrs. Cook slept, Rebecca lay awake reliving those moments on the little bench until Hayes and his evil crept into her patch of Eden.

Before daybreak, shouts and hoofbeats awakened Rebecca.

"What is it?" Mrs. Cook sleepily rose on one elbow.

Rebecca ran to the window and threw it wide open. Smokey's voice cut through the murky dawn. "Roll out, men! One of the night guard just rode in, shot to pieces. The red-and-white herd in the south pasture's gone."

"Gone?" Was that Jim Perkins's voice?

"Yeah. Gone. Vamoosed. Disappeared. Every hide an' horn of them. We're riding."

"What's going on out there?" Rebecca recognized her father's bellow.

"Rustlers." Smokey's succinct reply brought action.

Ten minutes later, Rebecca had dressed, told Mrs. Cook she was going to Conchita, and joined the pale, deserted bride on the tiny porch of the cabin. Together, they watched the group of riders vanish into the predawn mists, Conchita openly crying. Rebecca's heart muscles contracted. Even the mists had not hidden a certain sunny head, bare of covering for a moment when Joel doffed his sombrero and rode away. Would there be a preaching after all? Or would some of those grim-faced riders not return? Rebecca strained her eyes until the moving black dots disappeared from sight.

"Why do men rob and kill?" Rebecca burst out. "Sometimes I hate this country."

"They have not the love of God in their hearts," Conchita sadly replied and wiped her eyes.

God. A vision of the world as it could be rose with the New Mexican sun. The day came alive in a burst of glory that failed to lift the spirits of those who watched. By mutual consent, Mrs. Cook, Rebecca, Mrs. Lundeen, and Conchita spent the waiting hours cheering one another.

"It's a shame your wedding had to be followed by something like this." Mrs. Lundeen stabbed a bright knitting needle into the ball of yarn in her lap and sighed. "Men ride off, women wait."

Conchita pressed her lips tightly together and did not answer; neither did Rebecca. Yet, time after time, one of them went for a drink of water or outside for a breath of air, but always in the direction that faced the trail that had swallowed the pursuing party.

Curly, the former Lazy F cook who now reigned in the Bar Triangle cookhouse, added fresh horror when he reluctantly crossed to the ranch house and told them that the night herder had died. "Not any older than Smokey," he said. His face contorted, and his lips thinned. He barely resembled the jolly man Rebecca remembered. "I hope they get the skunks who did this and hang them on the nearest cottonwood." His eyes slitted. "I'da gone, too, but the boy needed me worse." His shoulders sagged, and he looked straight into Rebecca's face. "Be careful, Miss," he whispered when the others considerately turned away. "Hayes didn't go with the others."

A thrill of fear shot through her. "Why not?"

"He says. . ." Curly paused. "He says Fairfax told him to keep his eyes peeled and stay here." The cook made a rude noise with his mouth.

"Do you believe him?" Rebecca demanded, hands icy with foreboding.

"Sure, just like I b'lieve the sun comes up in the west." Curly gave her another warning look and waddled back toward the bunkhouse where Hayes stood on the porch watching.

"What're you tellin' her?" Hayes held his hands menacingly close to his holsters.

"Whadda y'think I'm tellin' her?" Curly retorted. "The kid died, didn't he?"

Even with the distance between them, Rebecca could see Hayes relax. He put his hands on his wide hips and stared at her. She gave him a look of unutterable scorn and went back inside.

Yet when the men had not come back by dusk, she could no longer stand being cooped up. "I think I'll go into the courtyard," she told the others. She glanced both ways, and relieved that Hayes had ridden off earlier on some pursuit of his own, she idly walked around the flower-bright area. The perfume of roses heavily scented the evening air; the dimness before moonrise, broken only by light streaming from a few windows into the otherwise dark garden, offered respite to her aching heart. Somewhere in the vast range or forest her father, Mr. Lundeen, Smokey, and the others tracked a band of murderous rustlers who had killed once and would not hesitate to kill again. Joel rode with them, with his angelic face that could change to righteous anger, the way it had done when he defended her against her father.

Perhaps Samuel Fairfax really was not her father. If he were, how could he sacrifice her to Hayes? Or, after today, would he no longer insist she must marry against her will to save him? Surely, even though he failed to rebuke his foreman, his blind eyes must have been opened to Hayes's wickedness. Rebecca, while gazing at the splashing water in the fountain, tried to piece together the scraps of her past and Hayes's hints, the way Mrs. Cook pieced patchwork scraps until she had a complete quilt.

Lost in concentration, she forgot Conchita and Curly's warning that Hayes presented unseen danger. Suddenly, a stealthy step behind her triggered an alarm in her brain—but too late. She opened her mouth to cry out, but a rag, stuffed in her mouth, stopped her. Strong arms lifted her, too tightly for her to struggle. *God, are You there?* She clung to Joel's faith; her own was too weak to help.

Chapter 12

Fury flowed through Rebecca like floodwaters in autumn. How could Hayes dare to manhandle her like this? Now, she must put her anger to work and get out of this predicament. She had been warned against him but never dreamed he would be bold enough to snatch her out of the courtyard. She tried to think with his brain. Next would come a wild ride to some deserted cabin. She refused to consider anything further.

To her amazement, Hayes made no attempts to ride off with his captive. He merely carried her to an unlighted room at the far end of the sprawling ranch house and whispered in her ear, "Promise not to yell, and I'll take the gag off."

She nodded, eager to get rid of the rag or scarf or whatever it was that nearly choked her. Hayes set her down and yanked the gag. In a twinkling, Rebecca darted toward the door through which they had come. She had not promised not to escape.

"Here, none of that!" Her enemy caught her with strong hands that dug into her shoulders. She silently fought, but her 120 pounds, although range-trained to strength, could not overpower Hayes's 200 pounds. He forced her into a chair and tied her down, hands behind her back, feet crossed.

Rebecca's eyes had adjusted to the faint light that crept in through the window even before Hayes had carefully closed the shutters, struck a match, and lit a lantern. She saw he had brought her to a storeroom. Her lip curled. "I see you prepared for this outrage." She nodded at the lantern, strangely out of place among the neatly stacked boxes of supplies.

"It's time we had us a little talk," he announced. In the lantern light, he loomed taller and meaner than ever, and she hated the triumph flaming in his eyes. Had he looked like that the day he caught Conchita alone? Rebecca forced herself not to shudder. Once she showed fear, he became the master.

"There's nothing for us to discuss. Ever," she defied him, even while her bonds cut into her delicate wrists as she surreptitiously moved them to try to free herself.

Hayes lost any semblance of courtesy. "When you know everythin', you'll come crawlin' to me, beggin' me to marry you." She just stared at him, and he added, "Now you and me are goin' to settle things right now. When I rode into the Lazy F and saw you, I arranged with your daddy that we'd be married. I've kept my mouth shut waitin' to let you get used to the idea. No more. Samuel's actin' like he's about to go back on our deal and take what comes." Hayes fixed his gaze on Rebecca and laughed harshly. "It's been worth waitin'. You were a purty kid, but you're a better-lookin' woman. Too good for Travis or that young preacher."

She started, and he laughed again. "I saw him lookin' at you."

"Why don't you just say what you have to say and let me go?" Rebecca's brown eyes flashed fire, but she deliberately yawned. "I find this whole conversation tiresome."

Had she gone too far? In spite of her determination not to cringe, she could not help shrinking back when Hayes's long arms reached out as if he would shake the living daylights out of her.

"You and your haughty ways," he cried, keeping his voice low, which made it even more frightening. "Why, you ain't even Fairfax's kid! He picked you out of some hole-in-the-wall run by outlaws, made a deal to meet your own daddy here, then murdered him, brought you to the ranch, and claimed it with some kind of paper."

Rebecca felt the blood drain from her face. Her mind churned. "It isn't true."

"You callin' me a liar? Then listen to this. If Samuel Fairfax is so pure and lily-white, how come when I rode in and accused him to his face, he turned the color of ashes and begged me to forget it?" Passion contorted Hayes's features into those of a monster bent on devouring its prey. "He offered me the foreman's job and said someday when I married you, the Lazy F would be all mine. There, that takes some of the pride outa you, doesn't it?"

It could not be true. Yet, if Hayes was lying, why had Father given him full rein over the ranch? Why did he not question the firings and unexplained cattle losses? Fairfax was not the kind of man to take such things without protest unless, as Hayes said, he had a terrible secret he feared would be discovered. Yet, something in the whole situation smelled rottener than a dead skunk. Rebecca slowly raised her chin a notch and quietly demanded, "If you're supposed to get me and the ranch anyway, just why have you been running off cattle and horses and hiding them in Lone Man Canyon?"

Hayes's face turned dirty white in the lantern light. "Who says I did that?" he blustered. "Why would I, when it's all gonna be mine real soon?"

She went cold at his confidence, but her intense gaze never wavered from his guilty face. "I worked the blindfold free, Hayes." Her voice cracked like a teamster's bullwhip. "I saw you and confirmed what I suspected when you roped and tied me. There's not an outlaw in New Mexico who'd dare touch Samuel Fairfax's daughter." Her voice broke. Perhaps she was not his daughter at all. Much as she feared to admit it, the ring of at least some truth underscored Hayes's story.

The man's gall held. "Wives can't testify against their husbands," he gloated. "Now, when that preacher comes ridin' back in. . .if he does. . .we'll have us another weddin'." He smiled.

Rebecca wondered how a smile could look so evil. Yet, with keen insight born of desperation, she saw something else. Clyde Hayes, wicked to the core, loved her. Not in the tender, gentle way she dreamed of when she thought of love, but with a love that caused him to take risks beyond belief to possess her. A flicker of an idea tickled her mind and grew. Could she play on that feeling, change it to the kind of love that would put her happiness above his own?

She stared into his face, searching for a clue, a hint of relenting or pity. She found none.

"I won't have to make you promise not to talk about this with anyone." Hayes laughed suggestively. "Men who kill in cold blood end up danglin' from a tree limb."

"The way Smokey Travis almost did—and for nothing," Rebecca bitterly accused. "Thank God Jo—Mr. Scott came when he did."

"I'll get that preacher one of these days," Hayes threatened as he untied her. "You've got 'til noon tomorrow to make up your mind whether I spill the beans and your daddy hangs." He bowed low and mockingly, swung open the door, stepped outside, and checked the courtyard. "Sleep well, Becky." His menacing laughter followed her as she ran.

Somehow, she managed to get back into the courtyard and remain long enough to gather her wits before Conchita came looking for her. The new bride's despair drove some of Rebecca's problems away when Conchita confessed, "I fear for—the men."

"Nothing too bad could have happened," Rebecca automatically consoled, noticing how large her friend's eyes looked in her pinched face. When Conchita showed no signs of being cheered, Rebecca took a deep breath and added, "We must trust in God. He is everywhere, and He can take care of Jim and Father and the others." Joel's image sprang to mind.

At last Conchita responded. Her brown fingers pressed Rebecca's tanned hand. "Gracias." But as more endless hours limped by, the strain continued. Husbands, father, friends—somewhere in the night chasing desperadoes. How could one bear it? Yet, what could not be changed must be endured. Rebecca felt she put away the last of her childhood and became a woman during the waiting time that left her too numb to even face Hayes's revelations.

The clock struck midnight. Rebecca thought she would shriek if something did not happen soon. A faint sound in the night air brought her out of her chair. "Listen!" She threw the front door wide; the steady clatter of hooves increased. Rebecca raced into the yard, closely followed by Conchita, Mrs. Lundeen, and Mrs. Cook, who had absolutely refused to go to bed while the others watched for the men.

Aware of Conchita's hard breathing beside her that echoed her own, Rebecca held her breath when a band of horses and riders swept toward them. She frantically glanced from horse to horse, then caught her throat with one hand. "Oh, God, no!"

Three of the horses wore empty saddles. One was her father's.

-+-

Joel Scott had not been asleep when the fatally wounded night herder rode in. For hours he had lain awake wondering, *Can love come this way, in two brief encounters?* Yet, he felt he had known Rebecca Fairfax always, that she had lurked in the dim recesses of his heart until he found her in reality. Everything about her pleased him. Her merry brown eyes, which could fill with horror or pain or comfort. Her tanned skin and nut-brown hair. Her sturdy form, tall enough for the top of her head to reach his lips, as she had reached his heart.

He laughed to himself. Such flights of poetry for a range-riding preacher! Yet, the intensity of her questions, when she asked if God had happy endings for people, had shown real searching for answers about God. Suddenly, his fresh-born love gave way to a higher feeling. Joel bowed his head and prayed for the girl whose rose pink gown had been no fairer than the one who wore it. His fingers strayed to the wilted rose that had dropped from her hair when she fled from her father's wrath and the ugly scene with Hayes. He had absently picked it up when the others left and tucked it in his pocket. Now he held the crumpled flower to his nose; its perfume remained intact, as alluring as Rebecca in all her innocence.

Joel still held the rose petals when the sound of a running horse shattered the predawn. One of a grim-faced group of men, he rode away to—what? Possible death, for sure. Rustlers were not known for their willingness to be captured. Memory of Rebecca's and Conchita's fearful faces when he waved to them rode with him. "God, be with us this night," he prayed, then nudged Querida closer to Samuel Fairfax and his mount. No matter what the man hid, and Joel felt sure he had a dark secret, this was still Rebecca's father. Perhaps in the long hours ahead, a time would come when he needed a friend; Smokey, Perkins, and even Lundeen seemed to have little use for Fairfax.

Smokey spurred his buckskin up alongside Joel and mumbled low enough so Fairfax could not hear, "Do you find anything funny about Hayes staying behind an' not riding with us?"

"I do." Jim Perkins must have ears like an elephant to have heard Smokey, Joel marveled. The just-married cowboy crowded close on the other side of Smokey. "Mighty peecooliar, ain't it?" He pulled his Stetson down over his forehead, and even in the pale dawn, his usually happy-go-lucky face shone sober. "Also strange that rustlers knew just what time to steal the cattle. Word didn't get sent to folks 'round here concernin' the weddin' 'til just a few days ago."

"Then someone who knew tipped the rustlers off, told them there'd just be a few cowpokes night herding," Smokey put in. This time he did not bother to lower his voice.

"What's that you say?" Fairfax spoke for the first time since they had left the Bar Triangle. "Are you accusing someone, Travis?"

"Nope. I know what it's like to be accused an' tried an' convicted when I didn't do anything." Smokey's words dropped like a shroud over the conversation. Fairfax snorted and swung away from the other three, his back stiffer than a ramrod.

Joel saw Smokey cock his head toward Jim, lift his eyebrows, then follow the owner of the Lazy F. He prodded Querida, and Perkins's sorrel trailed after them.

"Fairfax, hold up."

The tall man reined in and glared. "What do you want?"

Smokey waited until the rest of the riders swept by before opening his coat and showing the silver badge he wore. Rays of the rising sun reflected off it.

"You? A deputy marshal?" Fairfax roared. A gray shadow crept over his face in spite of the sunlight bathing the little group huddled together.

"Shh." Smokey glanced up the trail, then back at Fairfax. "What I said last night is true. Your daughter discovered a passel of Lazy F an' other cattle an' horses all tucked away in Lone Man Canyon behind a new fence."

"Leave my daughter out of this," Fairfax ordered furiously.

"Ump-umm. Not when she ain't safe from being lassoed an' hawg-tied by crooks like Hayes an' that fake deputy Crowley."

Fairfax looked like he might explode. He licked his lips and looked sick. "I can't believe Hayes would do that! Why, when he—"

"When he thinks he's gonna get the whole kit 'n' caboodle by marryin' your daughter," Perkins tossed in.

Obviously shaken, Fairfax resorted to sarcasm. "When did you get on the side of the law, Travis?"

"About a week after Rebecca told me what happened at Lone Man," Smokey said quietly.

"I don't understand," Joel burst out. "All the time, when Hayes tried to hang you, why didn't you show your badge then?"

An unaccustomed red crept into Smokey's face. "Aw, I got so mad at Hayes, I yelled out what he had done to Rebecca instead of telling the boys I'd got myself appointed deputy marshal."

"You no-good dumbhead," Perkins yelled, face redder than Smokey's. "I oughta beat the stuffin' out of you here 'n' now."

Joel stopped impending hostilities by demanding, "Mr. Fairfax, I meant what I said last night. Your daughter needs protection from Hayes. If you won't give it, we will, but it's hard to believe you'll let that snake walk in and take over everything you own."

"I have no choice. If Rebecca ever finds out what Hayes knows, she'll never forgive me. You think I care about the ranch? I'd ride out with my daughter in the middle of the night if I didn't know Hayes would follow and spill everything. How can a man go so far wrong?" He laughed wildly and without mirth. "Every day since Hayes rode in, my life has been miserable!" His granite face worked.

"But you don't have to go on," Joel exclaimed. Pity for the hard man suffering before him reached inside the young minister and demanded his best. "No matter what you've done, God forgives—and I believe your greathearted daughter will, too."

All the fire went out of Fairfax and left him a beaten, old-looking shell of a man. "If I could believe that, I'd. . ." He shook his head. "It's too late."

"It's never too late, Man." Joel could not let this opportunity slip away, perhaps never to come again. Yet, fate thought otherwise; the swift return of one of the posse broke into the trembling moment.

"C'mon. The tracks are leadin' to Lone Man Canyon, an' if they've got provisions, the rustlers can hole up there 'til Judgment Day!"

"Are you with us, Fairfax?" Smokey half closed his eyelids. "I got a feeling we'll find some mighty interesting things in a little while. Maybe enough to put Hayes away or hang him."

Hope flared in Fairfax's eyes, making them bluer than usual; then it died. "I'm with you, but no matter what Hayes is accused of, it won't keep him from talking before he gets what's coming to him."

"Well, no," Jim Perkins drawled. A cheerful grin tilted his lips. "I don't reckon nobody's gonna believe much of what some rustler sez, right, Smokey? I know I wouldn't."

"Me, either." Smokey's dark eyes flashed. "Hayes can do all the crowing he wants an' just get in deeper. Trying to blackmail a well-known rancher on some trumped–up charge won't hold much water."

"If I thought that, I'd fall on my knees and thank God," Fairfax murmured. Joel saw that the tortured man really meant it. But his blood ran cold when Fairfax added, "He's insanely in love with Rebecca. It's the only thing that's kept him silent this long."

"If ya think you've been in misery, get it into your noggin that marryin' Hayes would put that daughter of yours in a whole lot more," Perkins snapped. "And she ain't done nothin' to deserve it, whether you have or not." He spurred his sorrel. "Now, ride!"

Querida leaped ahead. Joel glanced over his shoulder at Smokey and Fairfax. They followed and soon caught up with the rest of the Bar Triangle men.

"They got a head start," one angry cowboy said. He pointed to the beaten earth that bore mute evidence to the passing of a large herd of cattle. "Our man hadta ride clear back when he wasn't in no condition to do it. This ain't gonna be no Sunday school picnic." His face reddened. "Sorry, Joel. No offense 'ntended."

"None taken. Besides, sometimes even rattlesnakes come to Sunday school picnics." In an attempt to lighten the atmosphere, he added, "That's my sermon for the day, men, since we won't be home in time for the meeting."

"Haw haw." The cowboys and Lundeen roared. A faint smile even crossed Fairfax's set countenance, but the following hours wiped away everything except the knowledge that a hard and dangerous job lay ahead.

Lundeen was aghast when he saw the trail the rustlers had made no attempt to erase; he also advised caution. Once the posse reached the entrance to Lone Man Canyon, the men were to move softly and keep their eyes and ears wide open. "If we can sneak up on them all inside Lone Man Cabin, we'll order them out with their hands up. Wish we had a law officer with us." He sighed.

"We do." Smokey showed his badge. The others gasped, but Lundeen's face broke into a grim smile.

"All right. If they won't come out, we'll burn the shack. It's old and dry as tinder. Not even a rustler's gonna hang out in there once it starts smoking."

"Easy as fallin' off a horse," Perkins muttered. "But it won't be." His prediction came true. A lookout, at the top of a bluff above the canyon, sent a volley of shots down like hail.

"Take cover!" Lundeen bellowed.

Joel dove for shelter, heard heavy, running steps behind him, and twisted around. Fairfax almost made it to the screening underbrush; then he stumbled, fell. More shots rang out. To Joel's horror, Fairfax rose, twitched, and fell back. Heedless of his own safety, Joel leaped from cover and zigzagged the short distance to Samuel. He snatched him up, staggered under the heavier man's weight, and made it back to safety, vaguely conscious that Smokey and Jim had stepped into the open and emptied their rifles toward the unseen shooter.

"Is he all right?" Lundeen slithered across the needle-covered ground.

"I don't know." Joel gently laid down his burden, looked at the bright red stains that covered his hands, and shuddered. Samuel Fairfax lay broken, unconscious, and bleeding at his feet. If he died, anything he might have known about Cyrus Scott would die with him. A thought, so grotesque it made Joel's heart skip a beat, bored into his brain. *What if Rebecca wasn't Samuel Fairfax's daughter after all? What if Cyrus Scott had been that father and Fairfax knew it?*

An even more startling idea insinuated itself into Joel's mind. If such a thing proved to be true, Rebecca could never be his wife—she would be his sister.

Chapter 13

Lundeen examined the unconscious Samuel Fairfax with strong, sure hands, then grunted. "Ahuh. Good." He ran one finger along a shallow groove on Fairfax's head. "Creased him just enough to knock him out. Head wounds always bleed bad." He ripped his kerchief off, made a pad of it, and pressed it against the bullet wound. "Give me another scarf, someone."

Joel grabbed his from his neck and handed it over. Lundeen tore it into strips, knotted them, and wound them around Samuel's head to hold the pad in place. When he stood, his face looked stern. "All right, men, let's round up the dirty, thievin' skunks and head home. Haven't heard no more out of that sharpshooting jasper, so he's either dead or out of commission. Joel, you stay with Fairfax. It won't do for him to wake up and not know where he is. Might thrash around and start his head bleeding again. Smokey, Jim, ride with me. The rest of you scatter and surround Lone Man Cabin. By now, I'd guess that pack of coyotes are holed up in there."

Leaving their horses tied nearby, the posse slipped through the shelter of bushes and behind trees near the cabin. Joel had not realized they were so close. By almost closing his eyes and straining, he could glimpse the dilapidated shack in the distance and hear men yelling in the clear air. He divided the eternity of waiting between checking Fairfax, who had not yet regained consciousness, and the stealthy figures closing in on the cabin.

"Come out of there with your hands up!" Lundeen's stentorian yell could almost have been heard back at the Bar Triangle.

A volley of words from the cabin answered him; a hail of bullets sang past the well-concealed posse. "Let 'em have it, boys," Lundeen roared.

A burst of gunfire and a high-pitched cry from inside the cabin brought Joel to his feet. Why was he here while Smokey and Jim and the others fought the enemy to all decent people? A terrible choice loomed. If he left his post and joined the others, in all probability he would be forced to kill, something he had vowed never to do. Sweat beaded his forehead. "God, those rustlers are vile!" Yet, Jesus had died for such as them. *What had Smokey*

232

told him so long ago? He wrinkled his forehead. Oh, yes. He had been ready to leap up and pummel Hayes, but Smokey dragged him back into hiding and later warned, *You've gotta learn to lie still when there's danger around, no matter what.* Was God admonishing him to lie still now?

A low moan brought Joel to his knees beside Fairfax, whose hand went to his head. Joel caught it before he could disturb Lundeen's bandage. "The lookout creased you. Take it easy."

Samuel's blue eyes glazed with pain and something else. He reached toward Joel with shaking fingers.

The young minister had tended enough pain-racked persons to recognize distress. "You can talk later."

Samuel shook his head vehemently, then winced at the movement.

Sensing the fallen man's need to speak, Joel leaned close and stared straight into Fairfax's eyes. "Remember, whatever you've done, no matter how guilty you are, you can be forgiven."

A curious blend of shame, hope, and poignancy went through the watching eyes before Samuel mumbled, "Guilty. . .as. . .sin," then turned his head and closed his eyes.

Joel's heart felt like a rock. He had hoped beyond hope Fairfax would prove to be Hayes's victim and not criminally guilty. What chance did Rebecca have for the happy ending she had so wistfully confessed she dreamed of?

Lundeen's shout pierced Joel's thoughts. "Come out, or we'll burn you out," he bellowed. A sneering laugh and another round of shots served as an answer.

Joel's gaze fixed on a running figure, who carried a torch made from a dry, pitchy, pine branch. Smokey. "God, no!" Joel froze, unaware of his prayer.

The figure zigzagged toward the cabin, nimbly dodging bullets and using the cover of his comrades' heavy firing to near the cabin and toss his torch in a fiery arc that left it on the bone-dry roof and sent flames licking the tinderlike debris. Smokey veered to one side when the Bar Triangle men cheered. The cheers turned to dismay when a defiant shot from the cabin found its mark, and Smokey fell.

Hatred overrode all of Joel's caution. Heedless of the consequences, he leaped up and ran with all his might toward Smokey. If those murderers had killed him, Joel would personally see to it they paid—unless the posse beat him to it.

Shots, dense smoke, coughing, then a loud, "We're comin' out, hands up."

"Keep them high," Jim Perkins ordered at the top of his lungs.

By the time Joel reached Smokey, seven dark-faced men, led by the so-called Deputy Crowley, had stumbled into the open, tears streaking through the soot on their faces.

"Tie them, or better yet, hang 'em," a cowboy called.

"Naw." Smokey's voice sounded surprisingly strong for a man who had been shot. He struggled to his feet, right hand pressed over his left shoulder, left hand reaching inside his coat and flashing his badge. "We'll haul them in an' let the law take care of them."

"Smokey, you're all right?" Joel grabbed his friend's arm.

"Easy, Pard. It ain't much more than a scratch, but it's sore." He scowled at the men being bound, and a wicked glint flashed in his eyes, brighter than the sun on his badge. "Play along with me," he whispered into Jim's ear, then loudly announced, "Too bad, Crowley an' the rest of you. We know who's behind our red-an'-white herd disappearing an' ending up here." He nodded past the cabin to steers crowded behind a sturdy, new-looking fence, now roiling and bellowing from the shooting. "Yeah, you notice Clyde Hayes ain't riding with us."

"Last I saw, he was standin' on the bunkhouse porch watchin' us ride off." Perkins tightened his rope around a pasty-faced Crowley.

"It wouldn't s'prise me if he's clean outa the country by the time we come ridin' in with you fellers."

"He's just the kind who'll leave someone else to take the punishment," Joel confirmed.

"That's what he thinks," one of the rustlers snarled. "He planned the raid, told us most everyone'd be up at the marryin'. I ain't takin' the blame so he c'n go free!"

"Me, neither," another put in, and a ripple of assent flowed through the group.

Crowley broke under the pressure and to save his own skin. "Hayes said Fairfax'd started actin' funny. He was afraid the old man'd go back on his word about that daughter of his, so he hired us to steal all the cattle we could before Hayes waylaid the girl and rode off with her."

Flames danced in Smokey's eyes. "You skunk! We oughta hang you right here for being part of such a scheme." He yanked out his revolver with his right hand; blood dripped down his left sleeve. Crowley's eyes looked as if he was staring death in the face.

"Get them outa here," Smokey barked and sheathed his gun. "Somebody bandage me up an' see who's hurt or dead."

Lundeen turned doctor again, while Jim and the others finished tying the outlaws in the saddles. A few minutes later, he returned to report, "One rustler's dead. Our outfit's not even scratched 'cept for Smokey 'n' Fairfax. I sent a rider up the bluff to check on the sharpshooter." That rider returned with the news the lookout man had evidently died in the exchange of shots early in the fray.

Lundeen strode back to Samuel Fairfax, who had again drifted into unconsciousness. "Hmm. It's a long ride back. Joel, you stay with him. The rest of us'll take in our prisoners and get a wagon back here as soon as we can."

"I reckon I'll stay, too," Smokey said.

"What? Let a little scratch keep you waiting for the wagon?" Lundeen joshed in his heavy manner.

"Ump-um." Unperturbed, Smokey shook his head. "Reckon you're forgetting something—Hayes." His succinct reminder snapped the men to attention. "The way I see it, soon as you ride in an' he sees his pards all trussed up like a Thanksgiving turkey, he's going to hop on the best horse he can find an' come a-running."

"He won't come this way," Joel protested. "That would be stupid."

"Naw," Perkins butted in, lean face grim. "Smokey's right. Hayes'll figure we figure that'd be just what ya said—stupid. So he'll do a double double cross and go where he ain't s'posed to be a-tall." He looked longingly at Smokey and Joel. "Lundeen, can't I stay with my pards?"

Lundeen deliberated. "You better come with me, Perkins. Just in case any of these rustlers get some funny ideas about trying to escape. With Fairfax, Joel, and Smokey missing, it leaves us shorthanded, and we've got a herd to drive, too."

"Okay, Boss." Jim heaved a big sigh, bent toward his friends, and warned, "Keep your eyes wide open. It's gonna take time to get a wagon back here. You got plenty of water from the creek. Kinda short on grub, though." He brightened. "Hey, Boss, when we knock down that fence and start the herd toward home, want me to leave a beefsteak on the hoof behind?"

Lundeen nodded. "Hurry it up. The sun won't stick around all night, and we've got a long way to ride." The big man knelt by Fairfax, lifted an eyelid, and grunted. "He will be okay. Probably sleep and wake up a half-dozen times before we get back."

In a short time, silence replaced the cowboy yells, hoofbeats, and clouds of dust that marked the exodus of the Bar Triangle riders with their prisoners and herd.

Smokey gazed after them. "It coulda been a whole lot worse," he said significantly. He gingerly fingered his left arm. "Good thing I hit the dirt when I got winged. Say, how about some of that beefsteak? Jim hacked off a coupla hunks before he left." Smokey nodded toward the charred shack. "Lots of good embers there."

Reaction set in. Joel gulped. "I don't think I can eat anything. . .at least for awhile." He fought nausea and dropped to a downed tree trunk to hide the way his knees buckled.

"I understand." Smokey's face turned grim, and he looked older than the mountains surrounding them. "You've got to look at it this way. Let rustlers alone, an' they get bolder an' bolder. First thing you know, they start picking off honest ranchers and cowpokes, just like they did with the boy who rode out to take night watch, singing an' never knowing he'd come back all shot up." He planted both hands on his hips. "I hate killing, too. Sometimes I think a man oughta move somewhere away from every critter there is." He slowly shook his head. "Guess it wouldn't do any good. There's decent folks an' skunks no matter where you go." He grinned. "At that, let's wait awhile before we eat." He yawned. "I didn't get much shut-eye last night. Mind if I crawl under a tree an' conk out?"

"Go ahead. I'll stay with Fairfax." Joel knew he had slept even less than Smokey did, but the day's events left him wide-eyed. Besides, Fairfax might awaken and talk.

"If Hayes shows up, I'll come running," Smokey promised. "Never did sleep sound, an' since I got to be a poor, lonesome cowpoke, as Perkins calls us, I wake up real easy." He yawned again, stretched, and headed for a tall cottonwood that provided shade. Five minutes later, Joel heard snoring. He grinned. Smokey might wake easy, but he slept sounder than he admitted.

Joel gradually settled down. He drowsed until Fairfax awakened again. "Have some water." He held a canteen. Samuel drank deeply, and once more, that poignant blue light brightened his life-weary eyes. Encouraged by it, Joel asked in a low voice, "Do you want to tell me the whole story?"

Fairfax recoiled, and Joel quickly added, "About Rebecca."

The other man hesitated, then nodded. The water seemed to have cleared his mind. He brokenly began, "Rebecca's not my daughter."

Joel slowly iced in spite of the warm afternoon. What he had suspected changed to certainty. The girl he had fallen in love with must be his sister. . . and Samuel Fairfax had somehow done away with Cyrus Scott, Rebecca and Joel's father.

"I met her daddy years ago, partnered with him until he got tangled in with a band of crooked men. Hayes was one of them."

Joel's mouth dropped in astonishment, and Fairfax managed a grim laugh. "Oh, he knew me long before he came to the Lazy F. You know how he threatened to expose me. I had done nothing wrong, but I couldn't prove my innocence. Hayes only knew part of the story."

Innocence? Joel remembered the agony in Samuel's face when he had whispered, "Guilty as sin." He opened his mouth, but Samuel had already picked up the threads of his story.

Rebecca's mother had died, and her father had no choice but to keep her with him. He worshipped her, as he had worshipped her mother. "Besides, they had no kinfolk near." Fairfax reached for the canteen and drank deeply again. He glanced at the still-sleeping Smokey and lowered his voice. "When he got in so deep with the outlaw again, my pard came to me in the dead of night. He told me to take Rebecca and ride out, to get away from the breaks and head for northeastern New Mexico. Sometime before, he'd arranged to buy a ranch."

"The Lazy F." Joel could almost see Fairfax and young Rebecca fleeing in the dead of night. What must that wild journey have been like to her? His heart throbbed with sympathy.

"The Lazy F," Fairfax confirmed. He lay quietly for a moment, so still that the quivering cottonwoods' secrets traveled back and forth from leaf to leaf, as portentous as those Samuel had revealed. "The man I'd ridden with loaded me with money and gave me ownership papers to claim the ranch. I reasoned that even though he probably got it from stealing or worse, the girl should have a chance. Besides, he said he'd sneak away when he could and come. He'd be able to travel better alone than if he had Rebecca with him; she'd be the first person the outlaws would look for when they followed—and they would. He never said he helped himself to their cache, but I figured it out." Fairfax laughed grimly. "I'd found my chance to be partners, half owner of a ranch in a grand country I fell in love with years before when I rode through it. We came. Rebecca loved it, the same as me. In time, she quit asking when her daddy would come. Long before that, she'd crawled into my heart the way a son or daughter of my own would have done."

Fairfax's lips twisted. "In time, I think she forgot she wasn't mine, at least most of the time. Then, Hayes came." The man's voice changed. The look of granite returned to his face, and his eyes lost their poignant blueness. "I learned Rebecca's real daddy had been killed the very night I rode out with her! Hayes had spent all the time in between looking for me. He'd quit the gang, suspecting the truth—that I had the loot. He wandered from place to place and finally tracked me down. Said he'd swear I killed my pard to get the ranch.

"I couldn't stand for Rebecca to know her own daddy had turned outlaw or that the home she loved so much had been paid for with tainted money. I bribed Hayes to keep his mouth shut, told him he could marry Rebecca and one day own the Lazy F. He saw to it the cowboys couldn't get near her and drove them away—until Smokey came and stuck." Fairfax groaned and struggled to a sitting position, then dropped his head in his hands. "I knew she hated him, but I didn't see any other way. Then you came."

Joel held his breath and endured the searching gaze.

"You rode right in on that black horse of yours, braced me, called me, and made me look at myself. I didn't like what I saw, but I had no choice. Either I kept my word to Hayes and lost Rebecca or broke my promise that she'd marry him and lost her—forever."

"And now?" Joel leaned forward, tense as a bowstring.

"I'll go to jail, but she won't marry Hayes." Manhood flowed back into the nearly beaten man. His shoulders straightened. Some of the greatness that must once have been his came into his features. His blue eyes shone.

"That isn't necessary, Fairfax," Smokey said softly from behind them. His dark face wore a smile, blinding in its unexpected sweetness.

"What did you say?" Samuel got up from the ground, held his head, and tottered toward the cowboy. Joel's heart contracted at the look of hope that dawned in Fairfax's eyes.

"Hayes is the one going to jail for a long time, maybe forever. I've been snooping around since I got to be a deputy marshal, an' I've discovered some mighty interesting things. Such as a warrant out for the arrest of a man named Hill, who bears a curious resemblance to Hayes."

"Warrant? For what?" Fairfax shook his blood-stained head and looked bewildered.

"For the murder of Seth Foster years ago."

"Seth Foster?" Fairfax blanched and gave an awful cry. "But that's him, the man Hayes claims I killed. My pard, who bought the Lazy F under the name Samuel Fairfax!"

"Correct." Smokey grinned, took the makings from his shirt pocket, and rolled a cigarette. He stuck the brown paper cylinder into his mouth, lit it, and puffed once.

Joel felt he had wandered into a never-ending maze. Seth Foster. . . Samuel Fairfax. . .Hayes who was really Hill. He shook his head. Once, he had been caught in rolling, red floodwaters. Their turgid undercurrents had threatened to suck him under and hold him until life fled. Now he felt caught the same way, tossed by dark currents he could neither understand nor fight. "Then Rebecca Fairfax is really Rebecca Foster?"

"I took his name to claim the ranch, the way he insisted. The transaction had been through another party, one who knew nothing of Seth's real name." Fairfax clutched his head and sat back down on the ground. "Can you see why I didn't want Rebecca to know all this, when I could prove nothing except that I traveled under a dead man's name, had that man's daughter, and lived on a ranch he owned?"

A million questions danced in Joel's beleaguered brain. Yet foremost, relief underlined each. Rebecca was not his sister. Gladness like a prayer winged into Joel's heart.

"Hold the confab," Smokey warned and ran toward a vantage point to return a few minutes later wearing a broad grin. "It's okay. Thought I heard something."

"They won't get a wagon back before tomorrow," Fairfax predicted. "Did I hear something about beefsteak, or was I dreaming?"

"I fry a mean piece of meat," Smokey admitted. "Pard, you feel like eating now?" he asked Joel.

The young minister only nodded. All his questions had come down to one burning thought, something between him and Fairfax, not even to be heard by the faithful Smokey. With a keen glance, that worthy individual grinned and walked away to fry his steak.

"Mr. Fairfax, no, that isn't your name, is it?" Joel tried to find his way out of the maze. "Oh, hang it all, if you aren't Fairfax, who are you?" His voice sounded loud in his ears, but he knew it would not carry past the first tattletale cottonwood. "And what do you know about Cyrus Scott? *I have to know.*" He braced himself for the truth, prepared for anything—except Fairfax's answer.

Quietly, without fanfare, the older man stared straight at Joel. "I am Cyrus Scott, your father."

Chapter 14

I am your father," the man that Joel had known as Samuel Fairfax repeated. "God forgive me."

Faced by the shocking end of his long search, the younger man could only stare. All these weeks, the father he had sought for months, right here. "But you said he probably died years ago," Joel stammered.

The poignant light he had come to recognize but never understood crept again into the Lazy F's owner's eyes, turning them so blue, Joel wondered how he could have failed to identify this man as a Scott.

Joel felt his own eyes burn when his father said, "I tried to bury Cyrus Scott years ago after I discovered your mother died. If I'd only known about you!" The anguished cry tore into Joel's heart.

"You couldn't know. Judith was afraid you'd take me."

Cyrus flinched. "Once, I would have." He raised a shaking hand. "Can God forgive me? Can you?" His eyes looked like those of a dog Joel once rescued from a beating.

Everything the young minister believed about forgiveness battled with his long-standing hurt and anger at what Cyrus had done. He had prattled of the need to forgive without knowing the depths of his own resentment or the difficulty of doing so. Now, his father's question nailed him to the cross of memories. If he could not forgive, Cyrus would never believe God could, either.

Slowly, almost of its own volition, Joel's hand extended, and for the first time, he touched his father. . .tentatively, then with a hard grip of hands that promised much. Joel felt Cyrus's fingers tremble. A look of near-glory cut years off Cyrus's face until he resembled Gideon. Joel took a sharp breath. A flood of pent-up emotions roared through him.

"Hey, steaks are done an' burning," Smokey called.

After another mighty squeeze, the two men's hands parted. Shoulder to shoulder, they headed toward Smokey. When they reached him, Joel threw back his head and announced, "I'd like you to meet my father."

Smokey gave them an inscrutable look. "I know."

"What?" Joel leaped toward him and glared. "You know?"

240

"Sure. When I got to nosing around, I put a few facts together an' figured it out." His maddening smile drove Joel wild, especially when he added with a grin that stretched clean across his face, "The way I see it, 'til your daddy got ready to talk, it was up to me to button my lip an' keep it that way."

"Thanks, Smokey." Cyrus offered his hand to the cowboy he had driven off his ranch.

In the greatheartedness that set Smokey apart from the common herd, he responded and shook heartily before complaining, "If we don't eat, this beefsteak's gonna be tougher than saddle leather."

The three men fell to and finished every scrap of the enormous steak, then chafed at the bit until the wagon from the Lazy F arrived. Lundeen and his men had taken the two dead rustlers' horses and the one Cyrus had ridden back to the ranch with them. Now, Smokey on his buckskin and Joel on Querida trailed the team and wagon, along with Jim Perkins, who had changed horses and come back.

"I'm glad we ain't hauling Rebecca's daddy back worse hurt than he is," Smokey muttered. He cocked an eyebrow. "Say, Pard, since she won't ever love me the way a woman should, I hope you get her."

Joel marveled at the unselfish loyalty of the man whose life he had saved. "I do, too."

Smokey yawned. "Me for the bunkhouse soon as we get there." The next moment, he straightened out of his slumped position. "Dust cloud over there."

Jim glanced in the direction Smokey pointed. "So what?"

"That's the direction of the Lazy F, Dumbhead," Smokey retorted.

Perkins pulled his Stetson farther down over his eyes. "He's had just about enough time to get to the Lazy F and back."

"Who?" Joel sensed significance in the exchange. "You mean Hayes?"

Jim snorted disgust. "I ain't the only dumbhead around here even if you are a preacher." He narrowed his eyelids and cried, "Will ya look at what he's ridin'?"

Joel concentrated on the distant moving dot.

"By the powers, if that's not Vermilion!" Smokey snapped his spine straight and raced to the wagon driver. "Hayes is heading back toward Lone Man riding Vermilion. Tell the boss we're following him." He wheeled his buckskin and galloped the way they had come. "Come on, pards. We may be able to head him off. Joel, we've been wanting to see what that Kay-reeda

241

horse of yours can do. Now's the time!"

A thrill of adventure shot through Joel. Querida responded to the change of directions with her usual grace. Jim and Smokey could not have kept up if Joel had not held Querida in. She might need her magnificent reserve of strength later rather than at this moment.

Taking advantage of a line of cottonwoods in between, the three riders managed to stay out of Hayes's sight until just before they reached Lone Man. They flashed into the open, then saw Hayes look their way, check the big red stallion that fought him, and take off toward the north.

"I knew Vermilion'd never stand for that skunk," Smokey yelled. "Rebecca an' me are the only ones he takes to."

"Good." Perkins's mouth opened in a wide grin. "Ride 'em, cowboys!" He bent low over his horse's neck and urged her closer, taking care not to crowd Querida with her flying hooves.

A long, straight path lay before them, with Vermilion racing straight for the mountains. Hayes had evidently mastered the stallion temporarily and put him into a dead run.

Smokey sped up until he could shout to Joel, "We can't catch him. Maybe you can. He ain't taking time to use his rifle. He probably cleaned out all the cash an' jewels he could find at the Lazy F an' figures on hiding out. Querida, show your stuff!" He snatched the sweat-stained Stetson from his head, leaned over, and cuffed Querida's flank.

Unused to being struck, the soot-black horse whinnied in protest, gathered her muscles, and gave a mighty spring. She came down stretched out and already into the gliding run that won admiration from anyone who saw her race.

Joel heard the loud "Whoopees" from Smokey and Jim. He looked over his shoulder at them pelting along behind as fast as their mounts could carry them, then slipped into his forward thrust position and called in Querida's ear, "Go, Beloved!"

A half mile later, Joel knew he had gained on Vermilion and Hayes, but not much. Another half mile and the distance between them shrank, but infinitesimally. At the end of two miles, Querida's flowing stride narrowed the space between them until Hayes rode glancing back over his shoulder every few minutes.

Joel knew Querida and Vermilion were equally matched. Under the same conditions, the outcome of the race would be a toss-up. Today, Querida had the advantage of nearly a day's rest and grazing against the long ride

Vermilion had already made from the Lazy F.

Now, Joel came close enough to see Hayes's hate-filled face and the way he rudely raked the red stallion's sides with his spurs. "Don't do it!" he wanted to shout. Obviously, Hayes did not realize what such treatment of a high-spirited mustang would do, a horse that had never known spur or whip and had been tamed with love and kindness.

In desperate straits, with Querida closing in on him and Smokey and Jim galloping nearer all the time, Hayes lost his wits completely. He spurred Vermilion again. At the same time, he transferred the reins to his left hand and reached with his right to his rifle scabbard to jerk out his weapon.

With a horrid scream, Vermilion retaliated. Instead of running faster, he leaped into the air, whirled, and came down on stiff legs. It jolted the rifle from Hayes's hand. He snatched for it, missed, and threw himself off balance.

For the second time, Vermilion bucked, jerking the reins free of Hayes's restraining grip and getting his head between his knees. Humped like an upside down "U," the red horse came to earth in a series of bone-crunching leaps and dislodged his rider.

To Joel's horrified gaze, Hayes fell heavily—but his left ankle twisted in the stirrup. He kicked frantically, trying to free himself. Joel screamed at Querida to run; Smokey and Jim thundered behind them, too late.

Not until Vermilion worked himself free of the dragging man, did he, at Smokey's urgent whistle, halt and stand trembling while the cowboy he loved calmed him down and tethered him to a nearby cottonwood.

"Hayes?" Smokey asked, his face gray.

"Dead." Joel turned away from the man who had plotted against others, murdered Rebecca's father, and now lay at their feet, a victim of his own evil. Sick of it all, he buried his face in Querida's sweating side and stayed a long time. When he turned, he saw Jim slip a roll of greenbacks into his saddle-bag with the comment, "Reckon Fairfax'll be glad to get this."

Joel shuddered, but Smokey looked first at him, then at Jim, last of all at the red stallion that stood quietly, his nose nudging Smokey's shoulder. "We have to tell folks Vermilion threw Hayes." The gray shade had not lifted from his face. "He's no killer horse, though. An' if Rebecca knows just how Hayes died, she won't ride or trust Vermilion."

"No reason she should know, is there?" Jim's intent gaze bored into Joel.

Joel shook his head, unable to believe the docile creature that trotted after Smokey like a pet dog could have been transformed into a whirling cyclone from sheer pain and mistreatment.

"Then we don't tell her a-tall." Jim sighed. "You'll have to let Querida race Vermilion sometime, Joel, or folks won't believe she beat him."

"It wasn't a fair race," Joel quietly told them. "Vermilion had been ridden miles and miles before it began." He stared at the long, still figure covered by a tarp from Jim or Smokey's saddle. "How do we get him back? I doubt that Vermilion will stand for carrying him."

"The buckskin will." Smokey and Jim hoisted the tragic burden to the horse's broad back and secured it. "I'll ride Vermilion soon as he gets his wind."

Drained by the revelations and events of the past few days, Joel simply let the reins lie loose and left it to Querida to follow the trail home. Smokey and Jim rode behind him, but the minister who no longer felt young did not look back. Behind him lay the ghastly reminder that the wages of sin is death. Only by looking forward could he rid himself of the bloodshed and violence. No wonder Jesus wept over the world and commanded His followers to tell others of Him and free them from darkness.

–+–

Hours earlier, when the clock at the Bar Triangle struck midnight, Rebecca heard hoofbeats, and the waiting women ran into the yard. A gang of horses and riders swept toward them. Three of the horses wore empty saddles; one was Samuel Fairfax's.

"Oh, God, no!" Rebecca caught her throat with one hand. "Father?"

"He's gonna be all right, Miss Rebecca." Jim Perkins leaped from his sorrel, gathered a sobbing Conchita in his arms, and smiled at Rebecca over the bowed, dusky head.

"But where is he?" She frantically checked the group of men surrounding a sullen-faced band of bound men. "And Joel? And Smokey?"

"All right as sunshine in the mornin'." Nothing daunted Perkins for long. "Your daddy got creased, head wound. Made him too dizzy to ride. We're sendin' a wagon for him soon as it gets light. Joel 'n' Smokey stayed with him."

"You're sure Father isn't badly hurt?"

Jim shoved back his Stetson, and the light streaming from the open doors behind them shone on his face. "Lundeen says he's okay, and Lundeen knows about doctorin'—he patched up your daddy's head." The reassurance in his voice gave way to a sudden frost. "Where's Hayes? Turns out he's behind all this mess."

"I heard a horse goin' out as we were comin' in," a cowboy sang out. "Want us to go get him?"

"Naw. He won't know for sure if we're onta him." Perkins gave a mighty yawn. "It ain't long 'til daybreak. Get some shut-eye, and we'll go chasin' Hayes tomorrow." He turned Conchita toward their new home, and they walked away, his arm around her shoulders, hers on his waist.

Rebecca watched them through a mist of envy. If God ever allowed her to walk that way with Joel. . . She shook her head, and when she got back inside, went to her room, unwilling to talk even with Mrs. Cook. The shock of seeing that riderless horse and noticing Joel had not come home had unnerved her.

"God," she prayed. "You win. Even if Father is hurt worse than Jim said or if Joel never loves me, You can help me. No one else can. No matter what happens, please, accept and be with me." Surprisingly enough, she fell into such a deep sleep that she never heard when the wagon went for her father but awakened to sun streaming into the room and a feeling of hope inside her.

The hope wavered when she saw how worn her father looked, the bloody bandage around his head. Not until he held out a hand and said, "Daughter, as soon as I get cleaned up, I want to talk with you," could she believe he really would get well. Yet, the following talk—in which he freely confessed his wild youth, real identity, and how her own father had died— brought her pain beyond belief for the white-faced man who spoke, for the weak, easily led father, for the mother she could barely remember.

Cyrus finished by telling her, "Joel has forgiven me. I believe God will, too." He turned his face toward the west. "One day, we'll go find Gideon and Judith and my parents." His voice faltered, and he brushed his hand across his eyes. "Joel says they forgave me long ago. Can you? My only excuse is that I loved you as the child I longed for."

Tears gushed. She flung herself into his arms as she had longed to do since childhood. "You're the only father I've ever known. The name doesn't matter."

"Especially when it appears to me a certain young minister and newly discovered son of mine intends to convince my adopted daughter that Rebecca Scott's a much nicer name than Rebecca Foster-Fairfax!" His blue eyes twinkled, and color returned to his gaunt face.

"Rebecca, you run along now and let your daddy rest," Mrs. Cook ordered from the doorway. If she had heard Cyrus's comment, she chose to ignore it as well as the rich blush that crept into the girl's fresh face.

Banned, Rebecca fled to her room, then sallied forth to watch for Joel, Jim, and Smokey. Her heart had flip-flopped when the driver of the wagon carrying Cyrus told her sourly, "Those three took off like skeered jackrabbits after Hayes. They should be 'long most any time."

Any time stretched into hours, but at last Rebecca's peering from the window rewarded her. Three drooping horses with tired-looking riders rode into view. Conchita, who had joined Rebecca's vigil, exclaimed, "There are four horses. What—"

Rebecca did not wait for the rest of her sentence. She bounded outdoors in spite of the dress she wore in place of her usual riding clothes. She had put it on, refusing to admit even to herself how much she longed for Joel to notice and approve. "Vermilion?" She halted just outside the corral. "Smokey— what—who—?" She mutely pointed toward the tarpaulin-covered figure the men slid to the ground.

Smokey waited until they finished, then doffed his hat. "He took all the cash he could find at the Lazy F. Thought he'd get away, probably leave New Mexico territory."

"What happened to him? You didn't shoot him, did you?" Rebecca clenched her hands and looked pleadingly from Smokey to Jim to Joel. He looked at her with such compassion in his eyes that she suddenly felt afraid. "Smokey, tell me."

"Aw, he couldn't handle Vermilion. Tried to run away from Querida, who was fresh." Smokey awkwardly turned the big hat in his hands. "Vermilion threw him and he landed bad."

Relief flowed through her. "Thank God! I couldn't stand for you to have killed him." She shuddered and involuntarily looked at Joel.

A beautiful light dawned in Smokey's tired face. "We appreciate that. Now, we're three dirty tramps who need baths. If you'll excuse us, I reckon we'll see you later." He limped off, bearing evidence of long hours in the saddle. Jim followed, but Joel lingered.

"Have you talked with. . .your father?"

She smiled tremulously. "My adopted father has told me everything." She remembered Cyrus's final statement and turned rosy red.

"May I see you later?" he asked in a low tone.

"Why, of course." Her traitorous heart nearly gave her away.

"In the courtyard, perhaps?" His blue eyes so like his father's eloquently presented his unspoken cause.

"Not in the courtyard." She bit her lip. "Last night Hayes caught me there and. . .and threatened me." Later, she could tell him the whole story. Now, she moved in a daze through the hours between his homecoming and the end of the supper hour. Clad in white, a rose tucked in her hair, Rebecca glimpsed herself in a mirror, gasped, and leaned closer. Had love made her beautiful? Her usually merry brown eyes had softened; her skin glowed. The curves of her red lips looked fuller. Or had surrender to her Lord added the finishing touches?

Joel led her away from the lighted ranch house, down toward the river that rippled in the starlight. Columbine and bluebonnets bent their heads when the couple passed. A knowing moon cocked one eye and turned Joel's blond hair to glistening silver; it reflected in Rebecca's eyes.

Joel found a smooth stump, brushed it clean, and seated her. "Rebecca," he said softly. "I think I've been looking for you all my life. Could you ever care for me?"

A rush of unworthiness filled her. "I. . .I can never be good enough for you, a man of God." Her voice sounded small and forlorn in the big night. "Though now I know you're right. . .no one can live and be happy without Him." She drew in a long breath and released it. "I told Him that today before you came home." She ignored his involuntary start and quickly added, "I didn't bargain. I just. . .accepted."

"I am so glad." Joel hesitated. "Love isn't a matter of being good enough. It's sharing and growing. I love you more than anything on earth. Do you care at all?"

"I care." Her low whisper reached his ears. He caught her close, never to let her go. She nestled in his arms, heard his heart beat, and felt more protected than ever before in her life.

Later would come all the explanations, the long trip back to San Scipio and the Circle S, and a much longer trip to the Double J, their new home in Arizona. For now, green leaves fluttered above them, whispering in the wilderness their secrets of love and joy and the gospel of Jesus Christ that they would carry.

But Perkins, the incorrigible, had the last word. Walking with his new wife in the moonlight, they paused and observed the charming tableaux that Joel and Rebecca made posed under the cottonwoods. Jim tightened his arm on Conchita's shoulders and whispered, "Snappin' crocodiles, looks like we'll be havin' another weddin'. Say, Connie, how'd ya like to see Arizona? It's a shame for pards like me 'n' Joel 'n' Smokey to get broke up."

He snickered real low and added, "Besides, I bet some Arizona gal's just waitin' to meet some cowpoke like Smokey. Ain't it our duty to see she ain't disappointed?"

Conchita dragged him away and left the night to Joel, Rebecca, and the still-whispering trees.

Music in the Mountains

To the many readers of
Silence in the Sage and *Whispers in the Wilderness*. . .
and to new readers. . .
this book is gratefully dedicated.

Prologue

*Summer 1889, Double J Ranch
near Flagstaff, Arizona*

Gideon Carroll Scott slid painfully from the saddle of his sorrel mare, Miss Bess, and dropped the reins so his well-trained horse would stand. How many times in the past thirteen years had he brought knotty problems to the rise overlooking the Double J? No matter how troubled he felt, the panoramic view never failed to restore his peace: the valley, dotted with his and Judith's cattle; cedar, pine, and a lazy stream; quaking aspens whispering secrets; distant red rimrock telling nothing.

The spread was his by the grace of God and backing from a down-on-his-luck prospector Gideon once grubstaked. His partner, Tomkins, would gleefully recount to anyone who would listen how he struck it rich, purchased most of a Colorado town that later boomed, then sold out his holdings, and with Gideon purchased the now-prosperous Arizona ranch.

Gideon limped to the edge of the rise, aware as always of the twinges from a long-ago gunshot wound. The doctor had warned him too much riding would bring pain, but the blue-eyed man whose sun-streaked hair held silver threads felt glad to be alive. A quarter-inch closer, and the bullet would have severed his spine. He shivered in the warm air. God had been good.

He looked down again. From this same point, he had seen the billowing white canvas of the Conestoga wagon that brought his unclaimed wife, Judith, to find him, along with their beloved eight-year-old nephew, Joel.

Miss Bess whinnied and nudged his shoulder with her soft nose. He absently patted her shining mane. At thirty-seven, he still became misty at the memory of the mare's mother, which had faithfully carried him for so many wandering years.

Loyal Dainty Bess had braved sun and drought, blizzard and wind, bearing on her back a bitter outcast, unjustly accused of a brother's crime. From Texas to Colorado, Wyoming to Montana, and finally to Arizona, she had carried Gideon. Even the filly she left as her legacy could never take her place, although Miss Bess had proven herself as steadfast as her mother.

Gideon turned his back on the ranch and mounted, only to silently survey the sapphire sky. If anyone had told him all those years ago the day would come when he would wait for a stage bringing the father who drove him away, he'd have laughed in their face. A trained minister, Gideon had nonetheless worn the brand of his brother's cowardice, a brand etched on his heart by his father.

"It's all behind me," he told the tiny white cloud that scooted by. "God, only You and Judith know how much it meant when my brother Cyrus sent a note asking forgiveness and confessing his guilt. I wonder. . ." He sat so still, Miss Bess tossed her head. "Will Joel find his father someday? Or does Cyrus lie somewhere beneath the dust of the tumbleweed trail?" Longing swelled within him. Not just for the coming reunion with his father and mother whom he hadn't seen in fifteen years, but for the soul of his beloved elder brother. It had taken a long time, but with God's help, Gideon had forgiven Cyrus. Now all he wanted was to know if his older brother lived and, if so, to have him find Christ.

As he turned toward home, he was met by his nine-year-old twins racing toward him on their ponies. Millie led, as usual, with Matt just a few paces behind. How they could ride!

"I won," Millie cried, her dark brown eyes glowing like her mother's. Her long, dark brown braid was all that distinguished her from her twin.

"Aw, you got a head start." Matt brought his dancing pony to a stop. "Dad, Mother says for you to hurry or—"

"Or you'll be late picking up Grandpa and Grandma," Millie finished. A frown marred her smooth tan forehead. "I don't see why you're going and we can't."

Matt couldn't resist the urge to crow. "Anyone almost ten like we are should know. Or didn't you listen when Mother said Dad had waited a lot more years to see them than we have?"

Millie pouted a bit and threw a disdainful look at her twin. "You're so smart. I bet you don't know why Dad really wants to go by himself." She looked mysterious.

"Neither do you. You're just mad 'cause you can't go."

With the sunny quirk that kept Millie from being obnoxious when she didn't get her own way, she grinned and admitted, "So? You want to go to Flagstaff, too." She dug her heels in her pony's sides and headed for the two-story weathered ranch house, calling over her shoulder, "Race you home!"

Matt couldn't resist her challenge. He and his pony pelted after the jean-clad figure bent low over her racing steed. "Hurry up, Dad!" he called back.

Gideon breathed easier. When his prying daughter proclaimed she knew his reasons for leaving his family behind, he felt his heart bounce. He and Judith had agreed the twins need not know how deep or bitter the chasm had been between Gideon and his parents. Their quick loyalty would color their love for their grandparents and the long-missing uncle. Gideon had never lied. He merely said there had been trouble and misunderstanding. Now that Joel had grown up and ridden back over the trails Gideon traveled many years earlier, ending up at the Circle S ranch near San Scipio, Texas, outside of El Paso, the elder Scotts decided to visit. "We might even talk them into selling the Circle S and living out here," he promised.

The twins could barely wait, but Millie disconsolately said, "I wish Joel were coming with them." She sighed. "I know he's gone to look for his father, but I miss him. He's been gone forever."

"Not forever," her more methodical twin put in, his dark eyes teasing. "Just a year."

"That's forever." Millie sighed clear down to her boots. "Why didn't he stay here with us?"

Clear-eyed Judith tenderly smoothed her daughter's rumpled hair back from her face. The years had been kind. No trace of white lightened her dark brown braids, still worn in a coronet. Happiness with the husband she once took highlighted her still-beautiful face. "Joel went on a mission," she explained. "People your father knew a long time ago needed to hear about Jesus."

"And Dad couldn't go, so our big brother went," Millie supplied. "Except he's really our cousin, isn't he?" She didn't wait for her mother's nod. "I still call him brother, and so does Matt."

"He's the best brother in the whole world," Matt declared. Tired of inactivity, he leaped to his feet. "C'mon, Millie, let's go see what Lonesome and Dusty and the rest of the outfit's doing." They left with a familiar whoop that boded no good for any of the hands too busy to talk with them.

Now Gideon prodded Miss Bess into a gallop as he rode into the corrals. Tossing her reins to Matt, who actually had outdistanced his sister, he advised, "Take care of her, will you?"

"Sure, Dad." Pride showed in every inch of his face, but he offered generously, "You can help me, Millie. Dad has to get cleaned up, and so do we."

"Thanks," Gideon called, then swung toward the house in a long lope.

The time-silvered logs little resembled the Mexican adobe home and court-yard of his youth. How would Dad and Mother like it? A prayer of longing filled him. *Please, God, let all be well and according to Your will.* He slipped inside and upstairs, hearing Judith's gentle laugh from the kitchen mingled with Millie's higher-pitched voice. Evidently the lure of grooming Miss Bess had failed to soothe the sting of a loss to her twin. A little later, Gideon ran downstairs, soap-and-water fresh, new riding outfit pressed and impressive. "How do I look?" he demanded.

"Like a happy rancher welcoming his parents to the Double J." Judith smiled from the doorway, and he felt the thrill that never failed to come when he saw her and remembered the long months when time and circumstances had separated them.

"I am, Judith. This has been one of my dreams. Now if only. . ." He swallowed. Sadness must have no place on this special day, not even the poignant longing to know about Cyrus.

"Vaya con Dios." Judith Butler Scott lifted her face for the kiss he always bestowed even when leaving for a short time. He saw the goodness, the love, and the tears she tried to hide. For a moment, Gideon held her close to his heart, then walked slowly out and climbed into the buggy his longtime foreman Fred Aldrich had waiting. He had started on his journey to weave threads from the past into the tapestry of the present.

—+—

Lige Scott turned from the stage window to the wife who had loved him so many years. His blue eyes that often looked steel hard now resembled the soft Arizona dawn. "We're almost there." Thin, gaunt, silver of hair, and furrowed of face, still the mighty head and shoulders remained erect, unbowed by his once-blind love for his older son or his unjust accusations for the younger. Time had mellowed his heart, but true repentance for accusing Gideon of Cyrus's actions had won forgiveness from his heavenly Father. The past few years, letters had flown between Texas and Arizona. Now at the urgent prodding of the golden-haired Joel, the boy preacher who had chosen to follow in his uncle's footsteps, and of white-haired Naomi, with the snapping blue eyes and patient spirit, only minutes remained until they reached their destination.

"Naomi, has he really forgiven me?"

The same love that strengthened her through all his headstrong years of serving the Almighty according to the gospel of Elijah Scott shone in her face. "Oh ye of little faith! Gideon and Judith's letters told you that. So did Joel when he came."

The giant pioneer's mouth worked. "I haven't deserved it."

Her work-worn hand, beautiful in its mute witness of a life lived in service to God and others, gently rested on his massive, calloused paw. "Elijah, if any of us got what we deserved, God wouldn't have sent His Son to take our punishment so we could one day live with Him."

"I know. It's just that for the first time in my life, I'm afraid." The whisper barely reached her straining ears.

"I believe Gideon has forgiven you with all his heart," she told the troubled man. His convulsive grip of her hand threatened to crush bones, but a tremendous sigh heaved from the cavern of Lige's chest, and he said no more.

The long journey drew to a close. The stage slowed at the driver's bellow, "Whoa, you miserable critters!" Lige held tight rein on his desire to leap out and find his son and helped Naomi from the conveyance. He reached strong arms to accept the trunks and bags the driver pitched down. Back turned to Naomi, his keen ears caught her cry, "Gideon!"

Lige shot a prayer toward heaven. His first look into Gideon's eyes would tell him what he must know. He felt suspended in judgment between heaven and earth. Then he turned to meet his wronged son.

The steady blue eyes that had accused him in memory for fifteen years held nothing but love.

Great tearing sobs rose within him. Lige opened both arms, heedless of staring passengers and curious bystanders. "My son, my son!" Unashamed tears poured.

"Dad, welcome home."

The next instant, Lige caught Gideon in an embrace that wordlessly said what he could not. Yet the hard muscles that encircled him confirmed what the blue eyes had spoken, forgiveness surpassed only by God's gift to the world.

Another cry from Naomi opened the closed circle. Yet even the moment she had longed for ever since her younger son rode away failed to quench her indomitable spirit. "Land sakes, what's all this sniveling about? We're here, aren't we, and right glad of it."

Laughter rumbled in Lige's throat and gratefulness for the release from emotions far deeper than he had ever expected. He held Gideon away. " 'Cept for some silver in your hair, you don't look any older."

"Judith and the twins are waiting," Gideon said quietly. "Mother, Dad, thank God you've come." His voice broke, and he led them to the buggy. After helping Lige load their belongings, Gideon turned the horses toward the Double J.

＋

Summer 1890, Colorado Springs, Colorado

Eb Sears let the white pages of a just-delivered letter drift to the carpeted floor of his living room. The stocky man's big frame shook. "Dear God, is this the answer?" He thought of the recent months when his wife, Lily, had reverted to the listless woman he and Joel Scott had found more than a year before. It was then Joel had shared his message of salvation.

A wide smile crossed the weathered face as he thought of Joel. Eb looked older than his late thirties but still vulnerable as far as Lily and her six-year-old son, now his cherished stepson, were concerned. "Still hard to believe what crooked paths You took to make me listen," he told God. "First off, Gideon sends his son to tell me any time I want a job in Arizona, one's waitin'." He shook his thatch of coarse hair. "Good thing, too. All the time he took care of me after I got shot made me see what he preached in Tomkinsville was true."

So much had happened since Joel rode away in search of his father. Eb and Lily both accepted the Lord and found love for one another. Her first husband's parents, who kept her when he died, had met with a fatal accident, leaving Lily bereft. A few weeks earlier, she had cried out, "Eb, can't we sell the store and go away? I don't want to live here anymore."

A million prayers followed and then today. . . Eb reread the missive from Gideon Scott, a man he once despised.

> We're still hoping you and Lily and young Danny will come to the Double J. Tomkins and I are expanding our holdings, and there's plenty of room in this wild land for us all. I've never forgotten that you could have let me hang for a crime I didn't commit. Joel sent word you and Lily had given your lives to God. Eb, you'll never regret it.
>
> My parents have decided to sell out in Texas and stay here. The best news of all is that Joel located Cyrus, has fallen in love with his adopted daughter, Rebecca, and hopes to come west soon.
>
> Why don't you join them? Flagstaff needs more Christian settlers and ranchers. I can't ride as long and far as I'd like. The bullet one of Zeke Stockton's men put in me saw to that. I haven't told Judith, but

rumors have it Stockton didn't go straight after we released him; that he's in up to his sombrero with one of the worst bands of outlaws and rustlers in the Tonto, where he built a home.

We need you, Eb. Will you come? Of course, if Lily won't leave Colorado Springs, I'll understand.

The scrawled signature, *Gideon Scott*, sent a wave of longing through Eb. More convinced than ever that God had nudged Gideon into writing at just this time, Eb bounded into the bedroom where Lily sat looking out the window. "How would you like to go to Arizona?" he asked.

The dark-eyed, dark-haired child who sat leaning against her rocker leaped to his feet. "Daddy, Daddy, can I have a pony?"

"I wouldn't be surprised." Eb caught Danny up and hugged him. He couldn't love the boy more if Danny were his own. "Well, Lily?"

A faint color stained her thin white cheeks. With an obvious effort, she stood and ran to him. "I'm ready to leave tomorrow." The strength of her arms surprised him.

"Whoa, there," Eb told them when Danny squealed and clapped his hands. "First we have to sell the store and house, then get outfitted. Gideon suggests we travel by way of Texas and meet up with Joel."

Lily stiffened in his arms. He glanced at her in dismay and said, "Run along, Buckaroo. Your mother and I have some talkin' to do."

"We're going to Arizona, we're going to Arizona," Danny chanted into her face.

"Is somethin' wrong?" He held her out from him and peered anxiously into her face.

Dread had replaced her eagerness, and she drooped in his arms. Past thirty, to her husband she looked no older than she had at seventeen, although thinner and more worn. "Eb, will I be welcome?" A slight red crept into her cheeks, and her dark eyes misted.

"Welcome! I should smile." He stared at her, unable to believe his ears. "Why, just read this." He spread the pages before her and pointed out the places where Gideon so warmly encouraged them to come. "Why should you—?"

Her head rested on his broad chest. How easily she tired. "They all know I sang in the Missing Spur."

Understanding filled him, and his arms tightened. "You were an innocent kid who had to eat, and you did nothin' ever to be ashamed of," he told her fiercely. "Think Gideon would have staked you and got you away if he hadn't known you were just plain good all the way through?" He picked her up, crossed to the rocker, and cradled her as if she were a baby. " 'Sides, even if you hadn't been good—and you were—remember what Joel said? Jesus ain't carin' about the past. Once we give Him us, why, that's all that matters." He stilled the rocker. "Lily, Girl, if God kept count of all our sins, we'd all be goners, 'specially me."

She burst into healing tears, the first that had fallen since the double funeral. "It's just that I want you and Danny to be proud of me. Gideon married a real lady, and I'll bet Joel will, too."

The big man who found it hard to open his heart took a deep breath, then slowly released it. "I loved you from the minute I saw you. Nothin' ever changed that. Nothin' ever will. You know Gideon and Joel. Reckon they'd ever get hitched to anyone not just as lovin' and carin'?"

"N—no." She nestled closer in his arms.

Danny burst back in, putting an end to confidences. When he ran to them, trouble sponged all the joy from his face. "Mama, you're crying. Don't you want to go to Arizona?" With an obvious effort, he swallowed and said, "We c'n stay here; just don't cry."

He looked so forlorn standing there that Eb shifted Lily and put Danny on his knee. "Son, Mama's crying 'cause she's happy. We'll go to Arizona as soon as we sell our holdin's."

"God'll help us," Danny confidently told them. He slid down and trotted to the door. "Better get packed. God does things real fast!"

The young boy's prophecy came true. In less than a week, the Searses had buyers for both store and house. They joyously thanked their heavenly Father and rejoiced that the good prices would allow them to purchase land in Arizona. Recent telegrams convinced them not to go by way of Texas. Since Joel's ever-growing caravan now planned to go by Conestoga wagon, Lily's frail constitution would be pushed to the utmost.

Instead, Eb purchased passage by stage. They would travel straight through to Arizona and be there long before Joel's wagon train arrived. The little family knelt together and asked God's help for a safe journey. As they walked away from the house that had never really felt like home, Danny expressed their feelings aptly. " 'Bye, house. We won't never see you no more 'cause we're off to Arizona." He tugged at Eb's sleeves. "Don't forget my pony."

Eb, who had never been out of Colorado, looked down at the child. "I won't, Son." His gaze met Lily's, and a slow smile crept to his lips. "It won't be long 'fore we're all fat and sassy." He knew his laughing words conveyed what his grateful heart could not.

Chapter 1

Summer 1890, Circle S Ranch, San Scipio, Texas

Hey, Boss, what's eatin' Smokey?" Bowlegged Jim Perkins shoved his sweat-stained Stetson far back on his head and cocked an eyebrow. Joel Scott tore his blue gaze from the stubborn canvas he'd finally secured over the hoops of the Conestoga wagon. This hospital on wheels would soon make the long journey to Flagstaff, Arizona, and his uncle Gideon's Double J ranch. His tousled golden hair formed a skewed halo around his rugged, tanned face, which could look younger than twenty and older than the steeply sloping mesa above the Circle S. "Is something eating him?"

"Is somethin' eatin' him!" Jim, just a few years older than his new boss, rolled his eyes toward heaven. "Snappin' crocodiles, if yu ain't deaf, dumb, and blind!" He removed his hat, slapped it against his dusty jeans, and crammed it back on his head. "Haw, haw, bein' in love's made yu plumb loco." When a wave of red swept into Joel's face, the clear-eyed, lovable cowboy went on.

"Now some folks can handle love and dooty all at the same time. Take me, f'r instance. Do I let my purty little wife, Conchita, keep me from my chores? Ump-umm." The teasing gave way to a warm glance. "Have to admit, it makes comin' home and findin' her waitin' real good." With his lightning ability to change moods, he added, "When're yu and Rebecca gettin' hitched?"

Joel completed his struggle with the billowing white top that gave covered wagons the nickname *prairie schooners.* The same glow he'd seen in Jim's eyes brightened his own into twin lakes. "We decided to wait until we get to the Double J. Samuel, I mean, Cyrus said he knew the folks would be pleased."

"I don't know. Our little jaunt woulda made an awful nice honeymoon." Jim grinned. "Come to think of it, that's just what Connie 'n' me will have."

Now came Joel's turn to tease. Although his faith in God and ability to clearly present his Master's message of hope and salvation had earned him the title of boy preacher, he could hold his own with his sometimes cantankerous, always alert companions. "Of course you won't want to let sparking interfere with your dooties." He carefully mimicked Jim's pronunciation.

"No more than your spoonin' under the New Mexico and Arizona stars," Jim shot back. "Now gettin' back to Smokey—"

"I honestly haven't noticed a thing," Joel confessed. His strong hands stilled. "Everything's happened so fast since the showdown with Hayes. Finding out Samuel Fairfax is really my father, Cyrus, and no kin to Rebecca; getting him fit enough to bring back here from the Lazy F; selling the ranch and all the horses and cattle except what we're driving to Arizona. . . ." He paused, looking troubled. "You don't think Smokey's regretting leaving New Mexico, do you? He could have stayed on the Lazy F as foreman. Lundeen of the Bar Triangle was glad to expand and all but begged Smokey to stay."

"Naw, that ain't it a-tall," Jim disagreed. A wise look crept into his far-seeing eyes. "I kinda got a hunch, and if it's what I think, he'll get worse or better." He grinned tormentingly at his boss, sauntered off, and left Joel with the urge to throttle him.

"He and Smokey are no different from Lonesome and Dusty back home," he muttered. A thrill of anticipation assaulted him. If all went well, the caravan would start their drive to the Double J in just a few days. He forgot all about Smokey Travis's possible problems in the excitement and need to remember a hundred details.

✦

Inside the sprawling adobe home, Cyrus Scott gazed about with mingled emotions. The thick walls, impervious to heat and cold, had housed him for twenty-four careless years. *If only I could relive them,* he thought desperately. Not only those first years of his life but many more had been wasted because of his rebellious desire to ride the range, take what he wanted, and let the other fellow be hanged. In the time since he'd been shot, Cyrus had had ample time to consider the results of his actions. If he hadn't secretly married Millicent Butler, using his younger brother's name, he wouldn't be lying here filled with dread at meeting Gideon again after sixteen long, empty years. Although Joel repeatedly had assured him he'd been forgiven years before, Cyrus still had his doubts.

Joel. A smile of pride crept over the tired face as gratitude filled him. Had any man ever had such a son? He scoffed at the idea. How many young men would take up a work begun by another, travel back over untamed trails, and right wrongs with the sword of truth?

"Father?" A soft voice interrupted his musings, and he turned his graying head. Rebecca, the girl entrusted to his care and whom he loved more than any daughter, stood near. Her merry brown eyes sparkled, and an errant ray of sun through the window gilded her nut-brown hair. Soon she would be his daughter by law. What a pair she and Joel would make! They were both dedicated to the Lord Cyrus had only begun to know personally, although he'd been taught about God and Jesus since the cradle.

"You should see the wagon!" She clapped her hands, and a rich smile curved her lips. "The bed must be ten feet long and a good four feet wide. We'll put in feather ticks, and you can ride on top of them comfortable as a king." Her laugh rang like a string of silver bells on a horse's harness. "Joel just got the canvas on—it's been waterproofed for days—and the sides slide up so you can have fresh air and see out." She stepped closer, and he saw the little gold sparkles that danced in her eyes when she got excited. "You really are well enough, aren't you? We don't have to go yet."

"Well enough!" Rotund Mrs. Cook, fresh-faced and motherly, marched into the room. "If he gets any better, I won't be able to keep him from mounting a horse and setting off alone." With the familiarity of years as Cyrus and Rebecca's cook and housekeeper, she frankly stated her opinion whenever it suited her.

"I'm so glad you're going with us!" Rebecca hugged her friend and adviser.

"And where else would I be if I didn't? Think I'd let you two head off to Arizona and leave me behind to miss all the fun?" Her hands worked as she talked, twitching the sheets and pillows, smoothing the light blanket over her employer's feet.

"Let's see." Rebecca ticked off on her fingers. "There'll be we three; Joel, Jim, and Conchita, that's six. Curly, who straight out and said he'd be glad to 'mosey along' and help with the cookin'. I wasn't sure he'd leave the Bar Triangle and Lundeen." Her eyes filled with mischief. "I think he figures he'd be lonesome without Mrs. Cook."

Cyrus laughed, but the worthy woman's mouth turned down, although a twinkle in her eyes belied her true feelings. "More'n likely he's trying to show folks he's a better cook than I am. Well, we'll see. I never did cook for the hands, as you well remember, and I don't intend to start now. Let Curly feed them."

"But we're the hands," Rebecca laughingly protested. "Think I'm going to ride in the wagon with Father? Vermilion's just hankering for the chance to help drive the herd, and so am I. Smokey said. . ." She broke off. "Have either of you noticed how quiet Smokey is lately?"

Mrs. Cook snorted. "As if a body didn't have enough to do with packing and planning. You do run on, Child." She started for the door. "If you think something's wrong, why don't you just up and ask him?" She went out and closed the door behind her.

"Well?" Cyrus looked at his daughter who glanced down at the cook's parting shot.

"I don't think I can." Confusion showed in her blooming face, and she bit her lip. "Smokey's too bighearted to have bad feelings toward Joel, yet once he cared for me. I always felt toward him like a sister."

Cyrus warmed to her confidences. In all the years he'd lived under a cloud, she hadn't been able to get through his bullheaded determination to run her life. He couldn't remember a time when she'd talked with him as she did now. "Rebecca, I wouldn't worry too much about Travis. Right now, he's probably doing a lot of thinking, maybe just adjusting his feelings toward you. I'm sure Smokey never felt he had a chance. He was simply your good friend when you needed one badly. Once we get to Arizona, why, he'll meet a girl and fall in love with her. He loves Joel like a brother, and not just because Joel saved his life. Don't fret about it. Just be the same friend you've always been."

"Thank you, Father." She stooped and kissed him, and Cyrus felt a drop fall to his cheek. With light steps, she crossed the room. "Rest as much as you can. It's a long way to Arizona."

And to Gideon and Dad, he mentally added.

In spite of the increasing last-moment preparations, Joel managed to keep an eye out for his pard Smokey. He saw nothing amiss and wrote off Perkins's croakings as a wild imagination. Rebecca said nothing more as she was caught up with household duties, along with the others.

Handsome, dark-eyed, dark-haired Smokey Travis faithfully performed every job given to him. A top hand, he had stayed on the Lazy F for three years, far longer than most of the cowpunchers who'd been driven away by the merciless Hayes, usually for daring to be pleasant to Rebecca. Time and again, the good-natured Smokey with his droll sense of humor swallowed Hayes's goading or blunted it with a grin. His keen eyes saw danger in

Cyrus's association with a foreman he obviously disliked but kept on.

"Doggone it, something's gnawing on me," he admitted one afternoon. Chores done, Jim had sought Conchita, and Joel and Rebecca had drifted off together. Even Curly had deserted and dared approach Mrs. Cook in the kitchen. Smokey heard them wrangling and grinned. Then the smile faded from his pleasant lips. He headed for the corral and talked to the horses. Vermilion, the red mustang he'd caught and tamed for Rebecca's eighteenth birthday the previous December, nickered and raced toward him. The buckskin Smokey usually rode followed.

"How about you, Kay-reeda?" Smokey called to the shining black mare that had carried Joel on the long trek from Arizona.

Querida tossed her mane and edged closer. Beloved by name, beloved by her owner, she and Vermilion offered a sight that made the horse-loving cowboy's eyes glisten. "Someday we'll put you in a real race," he promised. His lean face glowed at the prospect. "That other time was no contest." Memories of the desperate race to catch the crooked Hayes galloped through his mind, a race that ended in tragedy for the thieving foreman, but in freedom for Rebecca and her father.

The red stallion turned and nudged Querida, who whinnied softly. Thunderstruck, Smokey slapped his knee. "Well, I'll be! That's it." Relief spilled into laughter. "I'll be switched if I don't have a case of the two by twos."

The buckskin nuzzled his shoulder, and he talked to her the way he'd done many times during lonely night watches. "You know that ark Joel talks about. Two by two, that's how they came. An' that's how it's getting around here." His laughter died as suddenly as it had come. When had gladness for his pards become tarnished with a longing to possess what they did? Smokey forgot the Circle S and the upcoming trip and daydreamed against the fence. Someday he'd like to have a spread of his own, a little place where he could bring a girl as sweet and charming and good as Conchita or Rebecca. "Never was good enough for Becky," he muttered, his gaze toward the west and new beginnings. "Joel's just what she needs, an' am I ever glad he came lookin' for his daddy. I wonder. . ." The patient buckskin never learned what it was her rider wondered. A hail from the house cut into Smokey's soliloquy, and with a final pat, he headed where duty called.

Yet once the idea had been planted, Smokey began to look forward to Arizona. He only grinned when Perkins solemnly told him Arizona girls were said to be fighting wildcats. "I've wrangled with wildcats before," he loftily told Jim. "The secret to it's all in knowing how to handle them an' never letting them get the best of you."

His loyal, heckling friend shook his head disbelievingly. "Aw, you ain't never even seen the kind of wildcats that live in Arizona." To prove his point, that night when everyone gathered for supper, he innocently asked Joel, "What's it really like where yu come from? Now that it's gonna be our home, mebbe we'd better know what to expect."

Joel leaned back in his chair, eyes half closed. "It's different from Utah or Colorado, New Mexico or Texas. There's a kind of music in the Arizona mountains and canyons."

"Music?" Rebecca's eyes looked like big brown saucers. "You mean singing?"

"That's only part of it," he eagerly told her and the others. "Although more and more God-fearing families are coming to add their voices to the good old hymns. Arizona's music is more than that. It's bawling cattle and whispering aspens. It's thunder, lightning, rain, hail. Shouting riders and quiet nights. The rattle of a snake giving a warning or the snarl of an angry bobcat or mountain lion. The growl of a bear protecting her cubs, the sound of snow falling from a cabin roof or tree branch." Sadness shadowed his youthful face. "It's the sound of rifles and Colts in the hands of those who prey, those who defy them; the sizzle of a red-hot branding iron, the scream of an eagle or wild horse." His gaze rested on Rebecca's brown head. "It's the croon of a mother tending a sick child, the sound of children laughing in a meadow of blowing flowers, the rumble and roar of floodwaters pounding through the echoing canyon. It's also a whisper in the wilderness, the voice of God pleading with hearts to receive Him."

Smokey silently stood and slipped out. Why should his eyes sting and the very soul within him cry out to be part of the music in the mountains? His stomach felt hollow and empty, although supper had been ample and he'd eaten prodigiously. From force of habit, he turned toward the corral, cut out the buckskin, and rode into the summer night. Plenty of music here, too, if a man considered the chirp of crickets and crying nightbirds' music. Straight to the promontory that overlooked the Circle S he rode, never knowing that first Gideon, then Judith, and later Joel had sought out the same spot.

Under the Texas sky, Smokey Travis realized the longing within him had a deeper meaning than he had thought. While he still clung to his dream of a wife and someday kids of his own, he had been stirred to the depths of his being by Joel's words and the reverence in his voice.

He drew a long, quivering breath. He could still see the look on his friend's face, the radiance and the shining goodness mingled with humility.

"That Trailmate of his must make him like that," Smokey pondered. "Wonder if a plain old cowpuncher like me could ever get that way?" He shrugged off the idea. Life on the frontier trying to survive, homeless, without folks, hadn't been easy. He had seen the worst and the best, falling somewhere between them. Skilled with horse, rope, Colt, and rifle, something had held him back from following the downward path that ended in debauchery. He'd seen too many who took it. Smokey had also avoided women; that is, until he met Rebecca Fairfax. He had been glad he could look her square in the eye without stains on his soul. He still was. No matter what the future held, her girlish innocence had fostered in the trailhand the knowledge that unless he found another as clean and high-spirited, he must ride alone.

At last they were ready. On Saturday, the eight who would share the hardships and joys of the trail gathered in the partially dismantled home. Many precious belongings must remain, but Cyrus had selected the choicest of the blankets, pictures and hangings, and the carved candlesticks and other special items his mother cherished. Already they lay packed into a second wagon, where Rebecca and Mrs. Cook would sleep. Curly had surprised them by claiming experience and insisting he would drive one of the wagons. Mrs. Cook looked at him suspiciously, but his usual jolly manner hid any devious scheme he might be concocting. Jim and Conchita had a small "honeymoon wagon," and he, Joel, and Smokey would take turns driving it while the others managed the herd. At the last minute, a surprisingly generous offer from the Circle S buyer had further depleted the cattle. The two men with the help of an insistent Rebecca and Conchita could handle them, with Curly helping stand night guard.

"I think it is fitting that we rest on the Sabbath and begin our journey the next day," Cyrus told them. "Besides, I'd like to hear Joel preach."

A slow color spread over the young minister's face, but his blue gaze never wavered. "I'd be happy to preach," he told them simply.

The next day, they met in a shady grove that offered protection against the scorching sun. Dressed in clean but plain clothing, they sang the beloved old hymns Joel had said were part of the music of Arizona. Now that the time had come, there was no looking back. Ahead lay adventure, challenge, life.

And love? Smokey wondered. *Will Arizona fill the hole inside me?* Would its wind and storm and battering rain that brought years-old seed alive and blooming until the desert lay carpeted with flowers satisfy his inner restlessness? He thought of the red-rock canyons Joel described. Of the icy, rushing streams; the snowcapped mountains; the Mogollon [muh-gee-yohn] Rim and Tonto Basin, wild as the day they were created and filled with dark, silent men who kept apart from those not of their own. Surely somewhere he would find what he sought.

Smokey jerked his attention back to Joel, whose face glowed with an inner light. Still caught up in his daydreams, the cowboy let his tanned hands gently rest on his knees. He heard Joel say he would read from 1 Kings 19:11–12. The next moment, the words snatched Smokey's full attention.

> "And he said, Go forth, and stand upon the mount before the Lord. And, behold, the Lord passed by, and a great and strong wind rent the mountains, and brake in pieces the rocks before the Lord; but the Lord was not in the wind: and after the wind an earthquake; but the Lord was not in the earthquake:
> And after the earthquake a fire; but the Lord was not in the fire: and after the fire a still small voice."

Joel paused. Smokey stared at him with unseeing eyes. How many times had he stood on mountains and felt the ground slide beneath his feet, not from earthquakes but from loose shale. The sensation of having the earth on which he stood quivering, breaking free, brought terror. How many windstorms had he breasted, exultant, glorying in the gale that wreaked havoc in forests and shrieked across the land! He had seen fire in all its mad beauty, devouring the prairie, greedily taking the grass that cattle and horses and deer needed to survive. And the lightning strikes that toppled and turned giant trees to ugly black snags, reminders of the forces of unleashed nature.

Smokey marveled, recalling certain phrases from the Scripture reading. *The Lord was not in the wind. . .not in the earthquake. . .not in the fire. . .after. . .a still small voice.* His heart and mind rebelled. The God he knew was in all those things. Although he'd not put it into words, Smokey felt no one could witness the things he had seen and not know Someone stood behind them.

He didn't hear the rest of Joel's sermon. If all his years of finding the Creator in dust and wind, cyclone and blizzard, thunder and lightning meant nothing. . . He struggled to understand. Why would a God so great He could inspire followers to become His messengers, as Joel Scott had done, whisper in a still small voice? Wouldn't He shout from the tallest peak, proclaim His majesty in a booming voice magnified by canyon walls?

Strangely disappointed, Smokey left the service feeling emptier than ever.

Chapter 2

R ebecca, are you sure you don't want to change your mind about going with the herd?" Joel anxiously surveyed his fiancée, whose tumbled brown curls formed a halo around her laughing face. "The Southern Pacific will get you and Cyrus to Arizona a whole lot faster than our wagon train."

She looked surprised. "We settled that a long time ago. Father will be fine, and I wouldn't miss this trip for all the trains in the West. Soon wagon travel will be a thing of the past. I want to be able to tell our children their parents once pioneered, just as their grandparents did." A lovely color came into her face.

"That's what I wanted to hear," Joel admitted. After glancing both ways to make sure the cottonwood grove was deserted, he passionately took Rebecca in his arms. "If I live to be a hundred, I'll never stop thanking God for leading me to you—and to Dad," he said softly as he rested his chin on top of her shining head.

"Only a hundred? Piker!"

He tilted her head back with one forefinger and kissed her. Rebecca's arms stole up and around his neck, and for a long, precious moment, they stood together, welded by love and hope for the future.

A dozen yards away, Smokey turned from the charming scene. A familiar pang went through him. Would he ever get used to seeing Joel and Rebecca or Jim and Conchita kissing without wishing for a girl of his own?

Don't be a fool, he told himself. *You aren't an old man at twenty-one. There's plenty of time, an' remember what Jim said about Arizona girls.* He stifled a laugh and was about to sneak off, unwilling to be caught spying on his boss and friend, but then he stopped in his tracks. "Not my fault if every time I turn around, I fall over them, is it?" he demanded of the empty sky. Smokey snorted, called himself a fool again, and went back to the last-minute jobs. They'd be leaving within an hour. Gladness filled him, and his dark eyes sparkled. Would Arizona prove to be as grand and wild as Joel described?

"It'll have to go some to beat New Mexico," the lithe rider decided aloud. "Leastways, the parts I've ridden." He thought of the fan-shaped scene visible from the Lazy F: forested slopes, rolling plains, the old Santa Fe Trail, the Cimarron River. Thousands of acres with only a few cattle ranches, spreading west like a lava flow past slopes that rose into jutting snowcapped peaks. "Kit Carson, Maxwell, and other old-timers were right," he mused. "They called it the grandest sight in New Mexico. Maybe I should have taken Lundeen up on his offer. Foreman of the Lazy F, pretty fine-sounding. Wonder if it's too late? I helped Joel get his daddy home to Texas. I could go back."

He shook his dark head, and a poignant light crept into his dark eyes. Joel Scott and Jim Perkins were the best pards he'd ever had. He'd trail along to Arizona with them. If he didn't like it, he could move on. "Anyway, I guess I have to learn more about that Trailmate of the boss's," he muttered half under his breath.

"What're yu mumblin' about?" Perkins, whose face looked mischievous all the time and downright devilish most of the time, grinned and raised one eyebrow.

"Just thinking. Mostly about how some fellers get to drive a wagon with a pretty little filly next to them an' other poor cowpokes are left to eat dust and nurse bad-tempered critters," Smokey shot back.

"Hey, Pard, yu c'n drive Connie part of the time if yu like, if yu promise not to tell her ever'thin' yu know about me." Jim grinned again.

"Huh, why would I want to ride with an old married woman, even one as good-looking as Conchita?" Smokey glared at his bosom buddy. Some impulse made him add, "You just wait 'til we roll into Arizona. Why, I'll bet Joel's uncle Gideon's told all the gals from Flag to Phoenix I'm coming." Smokey closed his eyes and let his face relax into a smile. "I can see it now. A great big parade with girls in fluffy dresses an' a band; there's probably a banner saying, 'Here comes Smokey Travis, the best doggone cowpuncher in Texas, New Mexico, an' all of Arizona.'" He opened his eyes.

"Yu con-ceited rooster," Jim told him disgustedly. "Yu'll be lucky if one girl's there, let alone a whole herd of 'em." His face brightened. "'Course, if she's like Connie or Becky, yu only need one." He pounded his sparring partner on the back until Smokey told him to lay off, they had work to do.

One of the decisions Joel had made about the trip was for each of them to have an equal voice in all decisions. They had spent hours poring over maps. Cyrus proved invaluable in their plans because of his earlier wanderings. He didn't know Arizona, but he'd ridden through much of New Mexico.

Joel remembered a surprising amount from when he and Judith crossed with Tomkins, even though he'd been young. Smokey, Jim, and Curly added their two cents.

"The way I see it," Smokey said in one of their sessions, "it's roughly 450 miles from the Circle S to Phoenix; after that, there's another 150 on to Flagstaff and the Double J. That's 600 miles. Now allowing for heat an' dust an' cranky cows, we'll do good if we make 15 to 20 miles a day."

"Yu mean I got thirty or forty days to sit next to Connie?" Jim gleefully asked, and his handsome wife blushed like a late summer rose.

"Yeah, an' thirty or forty nights to take turns singing to the herd," Smokey reminded.

Jim's chagrin was painted all over his weathered face. "Aw, I never thought of that."

Rebecca spoke up, her eyes like brown stars. "I thought the early pioneers always made at least twenty miles a day."

"Ump-umm," Curly disagreed, his jolly face set in concentration. "The pioneers usually had oxen or mules. We're using horses."

"Father, why didn't the earlier pioneers use horses?" Rebecca wanted to know.

Cyrus looked thoughtful. "They needed to carry more grain with them. Mules were unsuitable because they ate the bark from cottonwoods, hated heavy loads, and, of course, had bad dispositions. Oxen, on the other hand, could pull more and get along on prairie grass."

"Are we going to carry enough grain for our animals in case we don't find grass?" she asked doubtfully. "We're taking an awful lot of other things."

"You should see the way we're going to pack," Joel reassured her.

Mrs. Cook eyed him distrustfully and demanded, "You aren't filling up the wagons so much I can't ride, are you? I'm not walking to Arizona, and that's final." She tossed her silver-touched brown head indignantly, and her blue eyes flashed.

"No one's walking. Rebecca's already decided to ride Vermilion most of the way. Conchita can walk or ride as she chooses. Cyrus gets the feather bed 'hospital wagon,' and the rest of us will ride and trade off driving," Joel reassured.

Rebecca giggled. "If this were a few years ago, we'd never dare start off with just three wagons for fear of Indians. I'm glad it's 1890 and there's no more fighting."

"Just 'cause Geronimo surrendered four years ago and stopped the Apache raids on lonely outposts an' ranches, even on forts an' towns, doesn't mean that all Arizona Territory's troubles are over," Smokey somberly pointed out. "According to Joel here, his old stomping grounds have got their share of rustlers and outlaws like Hayes."

"That's right. Stockton, whom the Double J boys drove out of the Flag area, has set up business in the Tonto, one of the wildest areas in the whole territory. Gideon says nothing's been proved, but if range gossip is to be believed, Stockton hasn't mended either the fences he tore down or his ways." A frown wrinkled his forehead.

Smokey lounged against the back of his chair. "Men like Hayes an' this Stockton don't last long. By the time we get to the Double J, he may be six feet under." His eyes glittered. "If not, I'll have to have a little confab with him."

"Why yu?" Perkins leaped up, eyes flashing. "Since when d'yu kill the snakes for the whole outfit?"

Friendship warmed in Smokey's voice. "The way I figure, you an' Joel, maybe even Curly by the time we get to Arizona, have womenfolk to tend to." He ignored Mrs. Cook's protest and the red that seeped into Curly's round face. "Now I'm just a free an' riding cowboy whose job is to convince those snakes to rattle elsewhere." A steely glint in his dark eyes showed that beneath the raillery, he meant every word.

"Mercy, let's not be killing rattlesnakes before we ever leave Texas," Rebecca protested, and the tension lessened. But Joel followed Smokey outside with Jim at their heels.

"Killing isn't the way to go," he told them. "Only God has the power of life and death."

"With all due respect, Boss, tell that to Stockton," Perkins said. His face set into hard lines and changed from its usual cast until he looked years older and more rangewise. "A man's gotta pertect his womenfolk."

The stubborn expression on Joel's face showed clearly the matter was not closed.

Bright and beautiful, departure day came. Smokey mounted the horse he'd never called anything except Buckskin, insisting a horse should be given a name that made sense. A little apart, he watched the colorful scene that spread in front of the ranch house. What a picture Rebecca made, mounted on Vermilion, her cheeks redder than his gleaming hide. Tall and golden-haired, Joel sat in Querida's saddle as if he'd been born there. The black impatiently tossed her magnificent body. Again Smokey vowed that one day they must race.

He turned toward Rosa and Carmelita, the tearful servants who had chosen to remain on the Circle S and be near their families, then to the three white-topped wagons. Jim Perkins waved his hat and hollered. Beaming Conchita clung to his arm. Curly sat straight and proud next to Mrs. Cook, her gaze straight toward the west. Smokey grinned. If he knew his onions— and he did—by the time they reached the Double J, there might just be two weddings coming off. He'd seen a fond look in the cook's eyes, and in spite of her protesting, Mrs. Cook wasn't totally immune to Curly's good nature and obliging willingness.

The most amazing facet of the entire caravan was the third wagon driver. Smokey marveled at how fast Cyrus Scott's wound had healed once they reached the Circle S. The cowboy narrowed his eyes as he realized that now, perhaps for the first time in his life, Cyrus had something to live for. If Jim and Curly looked proud, the prodigal son wore pure triumph that dropped years from his visage. Head high, hands strong on the reins, he controlled the horses with a cluck and gentle touch that would grow firm when needed.

Earlier, Smokey had overheard a conversation between Joel and his father. "You're not going to drive, Dad. It's a hospital wagon, a place you can rest. We have a long journey ahead and—"

"And I'm smart enough to know when I've had enough," Cyrus reminded his stripling son with some of the imperiousness that he had shown toward the hands as Samuel Fairfax.

"Promise you'll cry quits when you start feeling tired?" Blue gaze met blue gaze, and Smokey held his breath. He let it out in a sigh of relief when Cyrus flung an arm over his son's shoulders.

"Do you think I'll take any chances on not reaching my father—and Gideon?"

Effectively silenced, Joel said no more, and Smokey stole away. The change in the employer who had once fired him off the Lazy F was even more startling than his physical recovery. Smokey knew it would give him food for thought on the long trip west.

"At least we ain't herdin' no milk cows," Perkins sang out.

Smokey shuddered. Along with the other cowboys, he recognized the need for dairy cattle but secretly held in his contempt. The only true cow critter belonged to the range.

Joel's clear voice broke the hush that had descended. "Father, be with us.

Not just for this journey but always. In the name of Your Son, who came to save us. Amen."

Smokey blinked. How could such a small prayer leave him feeling grateful and at peace with all the hardships they might have to face before they reached the Double J?

Joel raised his hand to give the signal for starting, but a swiftly moving horse heading toward them stilled his motion. "Who on earth—?"

Like statues in a park, the little band froze. Anyone riding like that meant business. Dread settled its blanket over the travelers. Bad news came on racing horses too many times.

As the horse reached them, the thin rider straightened. "Mrs. Baker? Lucinda?" Joel finally asked the panting figure.

Lucinda Baker slid from the saddle and leaned against her heavily breathing horse for support. Her straw-colored hair had escaped its moorings and straggled from under her riding hat. Yet the gray eyes held light and determination. "I heard you were leaving." She marched unerringly toward the wagon where Cyrus Scott sat with a puzzled expression.

"A year ago, I confessed my sins to your son, how all the time I knew the way you had ridden," Lucinda said. "Cyrus, will you forgive me?" She held out a shaking hand. "God has, and I'll never get to Arizona to ask Gideon's forgiveness. Will you give it in my stead?"

Smokey saw the struggle in Cyrus Scott's face, the distaste at being reminded of a painful time long ago. The next moment, pity welled into the blue eyes so like his son's. "I will." He took her hand and said softly, "I'll tell Gideon."

Lucinda's gray eyes softened, and her shoulders squared. "Thank you." She turned to go.

"Wait," Joel told her. "Please go inside and have something cool to drink before you ride back to San Scipio."

Their last picture of home as they pulled over the first hill was of three women, Lucinda's tall figure flanked by the weeping Rosa and Carmelita, their white handkerchiefs waving in the wind.

"That took guts," Perkins murmured to Smokey when he rode alongside the wagon for a minute.

The mounted cowboy tucked the incident away in his knapsack of things to consider later.

A merry-spirited crew gathered around for a bounteous repast Mrs. Cook and the young women prepared for supper that night. "Driving a wagon and taking turns standing night guard are enough," Mrs. Cook ordered Curly in front of everyone. "No cooking for you on this jaunt."

"Yes, Ma'am," he meekly answered, but the secretive glance he shot toward Smokey from under his lowered sombrero was anything but meek. The cowboy grinned in return. Good old Curly had completely succumbed to the buxom housekeeper's charms but was wise enough not to show it. Later that evening, when he relieved Smokey, who had volunteered for first watch, his friend confirmed it.

"No use scaring the bird you want to catch," Curly smugly said, and Smokey laughed until his sides hurt.

—✛—

"This here trip's just one thing after another," Smokey told Buckskin another scorching afternoon. "We haven't had to ford any rivers 'cause they don't have water in them, leastways, not more than a trickle or two. On the other hand, since there's no rain to fill the rivers, green grass there isn't." After that complicated sentence, which made perfect sense to Smokey and probably to his horse, he took off his Stetson, mopped sweat from his forehead, and jammed the hat back on.

The relentless summer sun succeeded in sapping the energy of the once-sturdy travelers. A unanimous vote by the group created the following travel plan: Begin traveling as soon after the first light as possible, and go until it got unbearably hot; if any shade offered itself, stop, rest through the burning afternoons, and go on in early evening. The first day on the new schedule, they realized the folly of continuing once the sun plopped behind the horizon. Trying to care for the stock in the almost-instant darkness proved to be too much of a burden.

Smokey sometimes wondered at the absence of complaining, even in the worst conditions. The day they got caught by a dust storm while miles from any kind of shelter, no one bellyached. They just sat it out, crawled from beneath the covering of whitish gray, did the best they could with a limited amount of water, and hoped for a better day tomorrow.

True to his inner predictions and the entire company's amusement, genial Curly's attentions to Mrs. Cook slowly began to bear fruit. From grudging tolerance to appreciation of his invariable good nature, the motherly woman continued to scold, but genuine regard appeared in her eyes. It changed to frank caring, unashamed and declared, the day she went for water at the rock-rimmed pool that apparently never went dry. Intent on getting her bucket filled, she failed to see the sidewinder coiled on the rocks. Its warning rattle came so close to its strike, she had no time to escape.

She dropped the bucket and cried out. Curly reached her first, in a burst of speed that seemed incredible due to his size. She held out her hand, marred by the tiny dots. "It bit me."

Quick as a heartbeat, Curly sprang for the cooking fire. He snatched a knife and ran back to Mrs. Cook, then grabbed her hand and slashed across the bitten area and the cut. The knife clattered to the ground. Curly jerked the cut hand to his lips, placed his mouth over the bleeding area, and sucked and spat. Again. And again, while his patient stood rigid. He only stopped long enough to gasp, "Bind her arm," then sucked and spat again.

Smokey ripped his neckerchief off and wound it above the wrist. He knotted it snugly enough to prevent the poison from spreading up Mrs. Cook's arm but loosely enough to slip his finger under it and release the pressure for a short time every ten minutes. Perkins ran for soap and water, hot as Mrs. Cook could tolerate. When Curly finally stopped his treatment, Jim quickly washed the wound, and Smokey bandaged it lightly.

"I'm all right," Mrs. Cook protested, but her voice shook. "Is Curly—?" A sob completed her question.

"I'm fine, Ma'am, and you will be, too." Curly turned toward Joel. " 'Twouldn't hurt none for you to make a prayer."

Thanks to the older hand's quick action and the faith of those around her, Mrs. Cook suffered far less than could be expected. When some swelling developed and she felt weak, they made camp for an extra day. By the second morning, she insisted they go on. Smokey noticed a new gentleness in her attitude toward Curly. Now she scolded him for taking such a chance. The rider's keen ears overheard her say, "Why, if you'd had a sore or cut in your mouth, we'd have been missing a driver."

"Would you care?"

Smokey lingered until he caught a low "Yes," then smiled and rode off to watch the cattle and extra horses.

Within a week, Mrs. Cook had taken up the duties Rebecca, Conchita, and Curly shared to give her extra rest. Her friends rejoiced, drawn closer than ever by the near tragedy averted by a brave and loving man.

Now, every day brought them nearer to their goal. While the sun still shone brightly, summer began to wane. Autumn gave its warning with cooling nights and a rainstorm now and then. They reached Phoenix but didn't linger. With more than four hundred miles, they had come two-thirds of the way. Yet mountains and valleys, canyons and rivers stretched before them, to be crossed before a possible early snowfall made the going treacherous.

As Smokey rode his faithful Buckskin, curiosity about what lay ahead and whether it could fill his unspoken longing possessed him. He thrilled at the strange red-rock formations Joel had described, at the deep canyons, brilliant blue sky, and blazing white stars that looked close enough to pick from a tall ladder. He rose to the challenge of climbing from the bowels of the earth, like the swooping eagles, to the heights of stony promontories. With every step of his horse's hooves, Arizona sang a song so beguiling, someday he vowed to claim it for his own.

Chapter 3

Blue shadows lay heavy in the Tonto Basin. Evening had fallen and with it a hush after the warm summer day. Desert birds slowed, then stilled their twittering songs and prepared for the night. A myriad of great, shining stars waited in the wings to be summoned when the shadows deepened.

Blue shadows lay faint but discernible against the translucent skin of a sleeping girl, mute witness that life in her beloved country was not always kind. Her gently rounded cheek, streaked with the dried streams of tears, rested on a pillow of soft moss. The worst outlaw in the Arizona Territory could not help but note the innocence of the sweet face and the helplessness of the slight body.

As a full yellow moon chased away the lingering shadows, creatures of the night yawned and came into their own. Yet neither the scurry of clawed feet nor the distant cry of a coyote wailing for his mate disturbed the sleeper. Not until the stealthy step of something foreign to her surroundings—signaled by the breaking of a twig—did she open her eyes.

A single motion, like that of a frightened doe, brought her upright, crouched, alert for danger. Fair hair, further silvered by the moon, waved back over her small ears, and tendrils loosened by sleep brushed her cheeks. "Who is it?" Her whisper sounded loud in the suddenly silent night.

"Aw, Colley, it's just me." A dark-haired man stepped into the open and doffed his sweat-stained sombrero.

"Hadley, how dare you creep up on me like this!" Fear gave way to anger. Young as she might be, she could handle her stepfather's right-hand man. "And don't call me Colley. I hate it. My name is Columbine, if you must call me anything at all." She turned to leave, moccasined feet quick on the needle-covered ground.

The man stepped in front of her. His eyes looked like dark holes beneath furry charcoal brows. "C'mon, Coll–Columbine, don't get mad. The only way I can see you is like this. That daddy of yores don't cotton to anyone hanging 'round you, except maybe himself." He laughed coarsely. "I'm a heap sight younger and better looking than he is. Why don't we run off and get hitched?"

In spite of her frail appearance, seventeen-year-old Columbine Ames, named for the Rocky Mountain columbine, which matched her expressive blue eyes, possessed the pioneer spirit of her late father. Josiah Ames had traveled with his wife and child to the Arizona Territory from Colorado only to fall victim to spotted fever. Desolate and alone, his beloved girl-bride had to raise their only child in a raw and wild country. Grim determination to hang on saw mother and daughter through until three years ago, when Caroline Ames remarried.

"Zeke is my stepfather," she answered haughtily. "He worshiped Mother."

"And yore the spittin' image of her," Hadley reminded. He took a step closer. "You and yore fancy house he built for you and yore ma, you think yore too good for me. Haw haw, I could tell you things—"

"I'm not interested in anything you have to say," Columbine interrupted. Yet the vague misgivings she had felt ever since her mother died washed over her until she felt weak. No time to consider them now. She had to get away from Hadley. She'd caught a whiff of his breath when he came toward her and shuddered. Men could be beasts when they drank. Her mother had taught her that long ago, carefully protecting the girl from the wild men who lived in the brakes and had secret stills far back in the canyons. Even Zeke. . .

"Move out of the trail, please." Her heart thumped, and she didn't expect her unwilling suitor to obey. To her surprise, he backed away.

"Don't forget what I said about us getting married," he called after her. Her heart beating wildly, Columbine wondered what she would do if he attempted to stop her. Filled with loathing, she didn't deign to reply but instead offered a silent prayer. *I know we aren't to hate others, Lord, but I'm so afraid.* A night bird's plaintive cry sent a pang through her heart. *Why did Mother have to die?* The question persisted, in cadence with her sure feet that barely touched the ground.

Her disquiet grew stronger as she crept into the large, comfortable house Zeke Stockton had built for his wife and her daughter. Too keyed up to sleep, Columbine sat by her window and stared into the night. A crooning wind lulled her, but she refused to give in to its spell or to the hypnotic swaying of the cottonwoods, with their rustling, gossiping leaves.

During the months since her mother's death, something had been growing within her. Until then, she had accepted Zeke Stockton for what he was: a sandy-haired man with rather colorless eyes, fortyish, tall, and heavy-set without being fat. He had been kind to the fourteen-year-old girl he acquired with his bride, and Columbine knew the depths of his love for her frail mother. She had seen it in his face, the way he deferred to his new wife's wishes. But at times, his fierce expression frightened her. Once, one of the mysterious men with whom he had cattle dealings rode in and made the mistake of admiring too openly the fair-haired, blue-eyed Caroline Stockton.

At other times, a kind of anguish filled Zeke's eyes, and Columbine recalled how she had inadvertently stumbled on him a few days after her mother died. The massive shoulders shook. The hard face was contorted with grief. She had made a move to escape, but he had seen her. "It's just you and me now," he said heavily before turning on his boot heel and walking away.

From that moment, a new and disturbing element rose between them. For weeks she had tried to pass it off as shared grief, but more and more Zeke stayed home instead of riding out with the men. He brightened when Columbine entered the room and a dozen times commented, "You're so like her."

Now Hadley's suggestion bit into the girl's mind like salt into a wound. Surely Zeke wouldn't be interested in anyone less than half his age! Did he see in her a replacement for the wife he lost after such a short time? "Dear God, I need Your wisdom," she prayed, glad for the strong faith her parents had instilled in her from the cradle. "If this is true, I'll have to go away."

Where? How? her tired brain asked. Columbine had no answers. She wouldn't be eighteen until July, months away. Even if she were, could she escape if Zeke willed otherwise? The men who rode for him would do as he ordered. Indeed, men like Hadley haunted the trails.

"Why did Father and Mother ever come to this place, anyway?" she despairingly asked the spangled velvet sky. Yet even as she asked no one in particular, she knew the answer. The chance to build a home and life in a new and ruggedly beautiful territory had fired the Ameses with excitement and determination.

Columbine thought of her childhood, a barefoot, happy existence in the poorest of cabins—all her mother could afford—made bright by Caroline Ames's resourcefulness. A single cow, a few chickens, a well-tended garden, fruit trees whose blossoms perfumed the air, and a few beehives spelled home. Mother love and blessings from their heavenly Father overshadowed a lack of things. In time their few books grew tattered; Mother's Bible became worn with hard use. Columbine grew as wild and unspoiled as fragile flowers that bent with the storms and yet continued to glorify the world with their delicate beauty.

She closed her eyes and remembered how things had changed after Zeke

Stockton came riding by one sunny afternoon. He appeared thunderstruck to find a slim, attractive woman and young girl living in the old cabin. Gowned in her favorite sprigged muslin with flowers that matched the blue of her eyes, Caroline Ames welcomed him, made no apology for her humble home, and offered him buttermilk chilled in the brook nearby. He came again and again, spruced up and eager as the cowboys who made eyes at Columbine on the rare occasions she visited the towns of Payson or Pine.

When Caroline Ames accepted his offer of marriage, Zeke promptly made a bold declaration: "I'll build you the finest home in this part of Arizona, anywhere you say." Caroline chose a spot nearby, and the little cabin, just out of sight of the main house, became Columbine's refuge. Off-limits to every rider by the iron order of Zeke Stockton, the cabin became a perfect sanctuary for the girl-turning-woman. Now she had a place to read the books Zeke brought home in his saddlebags from Flagstaff, a spot to dream all the dreams of maidenhood triggered by fairy tales and Bible stories of Esther and Ruth.

Often she wondered how she would meet the man God knew could complete her life. Father had met Mother at a barn raising in Colorado. Zeke, of course, had simply been riding by. Sometimes when lying flat on her back and looking through green tree lace at a sapphire sky or watching a lazy trout reject her bait and retreat beneath a rock in the amber water, she whispered her shy secrets to God.

When her mother knew her time on earth had nearly run out, she called Columbine to her side. "Always remember, I'm just ahead of you on the trail, my darling. Although you will be lonely without me, the years before we meet again to spend eternity together are just a twinkling in God's eyes. Trust Him with your whole heart. Honor and glorify Him in all you do." She raised herself up on one thin white arm, and her eyes glowed. "Above all, never marry a man who doesn't love our God with all his heart."

Columbine lifted her swollen face, and a fresh batch of tears gushed down her cheeks. "But Mother, Zeke—"

"I know." An ineffable look of pain darkened Caroline's tired blue eyes. "He has been good to us both, and I care for him a great deal. My final prayer is that one day he will respond to the love of Christ. Somewhere inside Zeke is the divine spark God has put in everyone. He has given me everything I ever wanted, but he has not turned his heart over to God. Be a witness, Darling."

That night when Columbine kissed her good night, she seemed stronger, and the girl's sad heart rejoiced. Perhaps God would spare her precious mother after all, at least for a few more weeks. Yet a few hours later, death released her undying spirit from its wasted body. Zeke and Columbine buried her on a little slope beneath a tall pine where she had sought shade many times.

Too weary for memories that harrowed her soul, Columbine rested her head on her arms. Trust. Honor. Glorify. Witness. God—and Mother—had laid the path before her. She must travel it warily, triumphantly. She slid into a simple white nightgown and got into bed. That path looked steep and hard, like the climb from the Tonto Basin to the Rim that frowned above it, dark with timber, forbidding and unfriendly. "Dear God, Your Son walked a harder path. Keep my feet, I pray." She fell asleep before she could add, "Amen."

Once suspicious of her stepfather, Columbine took to staying awake nights. Dark riders whose horses' hooves sounded muffled were regular nocturnal visitors at the Cross Z ranch. Zeke had purchased land all around the old Ames cabin and stocked it with cattle and horses, branded with the distinctive Z. Hidden by the thin curtain at her window, Columbine felt no compunction at eavesdropping. A feeling of wrongness had replaced much of the grief and the inner urge to flee from she knew not what.

Now and then heated voices and harsh laughter rose, and she shrank back. Once she heard a shot followed by a cry. The next day she asked her stepfather about the shooting.

Zeke sat still, his eyes blank. "It woke you?"

"Yes."

"One of the boys had a bit too much," he told her nonchalantly. "Fired at an owl."

She said no more, but paralyzing fear swept through her. No owl had made the cry in the night. More than ever, she knew she must find out what was going on. Impulsively, she turned to Zeke and said, "Father, men didn't come in the night when Mother was alive."

A wave of unaccustomed red rose in his face. His lips tightened, then relaxed. "No, Columbine." A strange laugh erupted from his mouth, one that frightened her. "I get lonely. It helps to have the men in." He rose and patted her fair hair with his meaty hand. "You're more like her every day," he mumbled, then jerked his hand away and strode out.

New dread attacked her. If Zeke were confusing her and her mother in his mind, what would happen? She shivered in spite of the warm day. That night for the first time in her entire life, she wished she had a lock on her bedroom door.

Yet as falling leaves changed from green to gold, no further incidents occurred. Zeke was going away on a cattle deal for a few days, to her relief. Mounted and ready, with Hadley grinning from behind him, Zeke said, "Andy Cullen's staying to look after you. He sprained an ankle when his horse slammed him against the corral."

"Wish I'd athought of that," Hadley smirked.

Zeke whirled, his face flaming, voice deadly. "What's that supposed to mean?"

"Not a thing, Boss." But Columbine caught his sideways look and knew he lied.

"It better not." Zeke glanced toward Columbine, his face dark with fury. "She has the deadliest rifle in Arizona and knows how to use it. She won't hesitate, should any polecat or other varmint bother her." Hadley paled and rode off without another word, closely followed by the rest of the outfit.

Zeke lingered a moment. "Yell for Andy if you need to. Otherwise, stay away from the bunkhouse. If something hadn't come up, I'd have found a woman to come in."

Her laughter pealed out unnaturally. "Really, Father. I don't need anyone. I'm almost a woman." She regretted her words the moment she said them.

He paused, rolled a cigarette and lighted it, then slowly said, "I know. When we get back, I want to talk to you." Putting spurs behind his horse, Zeke headed after the others.

Waving good-bye, Columbine clutched at her last shreds of self-control and wondered again what she was going to do.

That evening, Andy hobbled over from the bunkhouse. Not much older than Columbine, he was the newest hand hired and her favorite. The first few months he'd worked at the Z, he showed every evidence of wanting to spark her. Once he'd gone so far as to waylay her outside the cabin and lay his hands on her shoulders. His shock of corn-colored hair tossed in the breeze, and his brown eyes teased. "Miss Columbine, will you be my girl?"

Her first indignant reaction gave way to understanding. In Andy's simple code, both of them were young and unattached. What could be more natural than their drifting together? Yet Columbine's inner sense whispered this nice young man didn't fit the image of her future husband. She slipped from his light grip and looked straight into his eyes. "Andy, I don't want to be your girl, but I do want to be your friend. Will you let me?"

Chivalry of the range had been born and bred into him. His hands dropped to his sides. "I'll be proud to be your friend, Miss Columbine." He couldn't help adding, "Who knows? Maybe someday you'll change your mind."

After a few talks, along with the lack of opportunity to see each other because of Stockton's vigilant guarding, not to mention the arrival of a new rancher with a pretty daughter, Andy slid from would-be sweetheart to staunch friend.

Columbine watched him come, salving her conscience with the fact Zeke had said nothing about visiting Andy on the front porch. "Laid up, I see," she greeted him when he sat down on the top step and leaned back against a post so he could watch her while they talked.

"Yeah." He acted jumpy, not like himself at all. Trouble shone from his brown eyes.

"What's wrong, Andy?"

"I wish I knew." The teasing light she saw so much in his young face wasn't there tonight. "Miss Columbine, have you ever thought of getting clean away from the Cross Z?"

Her face betrayed their kindred feelings. She smoothed the skirt of the simple blue housedress she had made and wore evenings. "Why would you ask such a thing?" She quickly pushed aside the wild notion that perhaps she hadn't succeeded in dampening his caring and this was a hint about eloping. A quick glance under long lashes clearly showed whatever was bothering Andy had nothing to do with romance.

"Sometimes I see and hear things."

"Such as?" She abandoned her rigid pose and leaned forward.

He rumpled his hair until he resembled a wild man in one of Columbine's books. "Little things."

"What *little* things?" she persisted.

He looked at her doubtfully, as if weighing whether to speak or button his lip.

"If I need to know anything, I'd appreciate your telling me," she said quietly.

"I reckon it ain't my place, but you've been so nice and friendly." A wave of red crept into his tanned face. "Uh, has Hadley—or anyone—been bothering you?"

She gasped, feeling someone had poured cold creek water over her. "Hadley followed me once and made some comments about—about—"

"About your daddy who ain't?" The red mounted higher.

Columbine's heart fell with a sickening thud. If Andy had noticed Zeke's interest, the thing she feared must be real.

"I hate like sin asking you," Andy burst out. "But he's too old, and no matter how much he thinks so, you just ain't your mother." Misery filled his eyes.

"Just lately I've wondered." She faltered and could not continue. Her hands nervously pleated and unpleated a fold of her dress. Did she dare ask Andy what she dreaded? Who else could she ask, except God? She bit her lip. "Y—you don't think he means bad by me, do you?" She felt her cheeks go scarlet.

Andy leaped to his feet, white-faced and heedless of his sore ankle. "By all that's holy, he'd better not!" He towered over her, the male protecting the weaker sex. Gradually his body relaxed, and he sat down again and absently rubbed his ankle. "It's more likely he wants to marry you."

"Marry me?" If her heart hadn't felt like lead, Columbine would have screamed with laughter at the absurd idea. "Impossible!"

Andy shook his head. "Any man would be proud to marry you," he said slowly with a twinkle in his brown eyes. "Well, any man but me. Since I done asked you a couple of times and you said no, why, I'm just your friend Andy."

"Besides, you have another girl," she put in, trying desperately to still the trembling of her lips.

A new manliness enveloped his countenance. " 'Course, if it meant getting married in order to save you, that would be a whole new game."

"Andy, Dear," she choked out. "You'll never know how good it is to have a friend like you. I won't take advantage of your offer, no matter what happens, but someday I may have to call on you for help."

He stood, held out a hand, and kept hers when she rose. With a solemn expression in his eyes, he vowed, "It won't have to be more than a whisper, Miss Columbine." With a gentle pressure, he released her hand and went down the steps and across to the bunkhouse, a gallant, limping figure Columbine saw through a blur. Andy was not a storybook knight but a flesh-and-blood cowboy the girl knew had been sent to the Cross Z by a loving God.

Chapter 4

The week Stockton and his men were gone from the Cross Z offered a sunlit valley of peace in the midst of Columbine's mountains of trouble. A strain of music composed by the Master Author ran through the land, played and sung by whispering trees, swaying grass, a multitude of birds, little brooks, and a capricious breeze.

After the first night when Andy promised to stand by Columbine if the need arose, neither said more about it. There would be time enough to plot the future when Stockton and his dark riders returned. For now, Columbine was enjoying the simple pleasures of having her first true friend.

Most of Columbine's life had been spent away from others her own age. Her mother had taught her at home, and visits to Payson and Pine were few and far between. Andy, however, had been on his own since he turned fifteen. Skilled in range lore, he carried his weight on the Cross Z as well as the older men, although he knew Stockton had only hired him because many cowboys wanted to work closer to town.

"Doesn't bother me." He shrugged. "I never cared about drinking and playing cards."

"How can you get along with Hadley and the others?" the curious girl asked, watching the stream ripple over stones at her feet, while Andy lounged nearby, favoring his ankle.

"Mind my own business and keep out of his way." Cullen's boyish lips set hard. "He would have fired me by now except your daddy, uh, Stockton wouldn't hear of it." A glint turned the brown eyes amber. "I heard him tell Hadley to lay off 'the kid' 'cause I could shoot the eye out of a needle and the time might come I'd be handy."

"You would never kill a man, would you?" She shrank from him in horror. "It's wrong to kill. Mother taught me from the Bible that God commanded people not to kill."

Andy sat up straight. "I can tell you this. I ain't going to kill anyone on Stockton's account, even if I do work for him." His eyes turned to molten gold, hard and determined. "I can't say for sure I wouldn't shoot a man if he harmed, uh, someone I cared about."

"Andy," she cried, her blue eyes dark with fear. "Promise me that no matter what, you won't do such a terrible thing."

"Aw, why are we talking about killing on such a beautiful day?" He leaned back against a big rock. "Say, have you ever been to Flagstaff? That place is growing to be quite a town. There's a big department store named Babbitt's. . .might be a fine place for a girl to work, if she ever wanted to." He half closed his eyes and winked at her.

Columbine knew her efforts to make him promise had proved futile. She longed for Andy to know God, but wisely she refrained from preaching. Instead she would pray for him and for God-given chances to speak of Him, "plant a seed," her mother had called it. She forced herself to respond to his change of subject. "Next summer after I'm eighteen, do you think I might get a job at Babbitt's?"

"Why not?" He grinned and ruffled his hair in his typical gesture. "A pretty girl behind the counter would be the best reason in Arizona for cowpokes just aching to spend their money, wouldn't it?"

She laughed and refused to rise to his bait, but long after night fell, the idea surged through her. What if she did go to Flag and get work? What would Zeke do? She wouldn't put it past him to follow her, but once she passed her eighteenth birthday, any claim he made would be worthless. Her spirits rose. Zeke Stockton didn't have a claim on her now; he wasn't blood kin. Too bad she didn't have an uncle or aunt or grandparent somewhere. She'd slip away before Zeke came back. A deep sigh escaped her lips. She didn't have anyone except God and Andy. The next minute, she smiled. With God on her side, how could she fail, especially with Andy thrown in for good measure?

But once Zeke came back, she wouldn't even have Andy. Her stepfather would never stand for her new friend to be hanging around. Her lips trembled. Why must life be so hard? She remembered asking her mother that question long ago. Caroline Stockton's quick answer still burned into her brain as if seared with a red-hot branding iron.

"Sometimes I feel that if everything here were perfect, children of God would grow satisfied. . . . They'd stop longing for their real home, the one He has prepared for us." Her blue eyes so like her daughter's took on a faraway look. "Perhaps we would forget how important it is to live according to His plan, not our own."

The thrum of distant hooves warned the two friends, and Columbine gracefully sprang to her feet. Her heart was pounding. "Go, Andy. If Zeke catches you here with me, he may—"

"I'm not afraid of him." The daring cowboy got up more slowly, his brown eyes blazing.

"Please. Just go. You're the only friend I have except God." Frantically, she pushed him toward the bunkhouse.

Her plea did what fear could not. By the time the band of dark-faced, dark-clad riders swung past the woodsy spot, Andy was lounging on the bunkhouse porch whittling. Columbine had fled into the house, whispered a quick prayer, and seated herself, then snatched up a book, feeling deceitful.

"Ho, where's my daughter?" a familiar voice boomed. "Cullen, do you have any idea where she is?"

"I haven't seen her come out of the house since she went in." His laconic reply floated in an open window, and the girl stifled a giggle. Andy had a knack of clinging to the truth in a way that disclosed nothing.

Heavy steps crossed the porch. The door was flung open, and Zeke Stockton, dusty and trail weary, stepped inside. "Fine thing, when a man can't even get a decent welcome home."

"Hello." She dropped the book and rose.

"Why didn't you come out?" He eyed her suspiciously, and she felt the color leave her face at the half-hidden look in his eyes.

"I don't like to be around the men any more than I have to," she told him truthfully.

"Have any of them dared touch you?" His voice could have been heard on the streets of Payson.

"No." Thank God it was true. Even Hadley hadn't laid hands on her, and she didn't consider the teasing clasp Andy had once attempted important. "I–I just feel uncomfortable around them."

"Did Cullen bother you while I was gone?"

She shook her head violently. "Oh, no." *Far from it*, her heart added. *If he hadn't been here, I would never have felt I had a chance of escape. Now I do.*

"How about a welcome home kiss, Colley?" Zeke laughed carelessly, but again his eyes spoke volumes.

She steeled herself. *God, help me.* "Father." She hesitated. She'd seldom called him that, even when he'd asked her to. "Father, I'm getting too old for that."

He flinched as if struck. "Oh, you are, are you?"

For a moment, she didn't know what he'd do, so she added, "Yes. I'll be eighteen next summer." She hated to remind him after what he had told her when he left but saw no other choice. "I'm not a little girl."

At a loss for words, Zeke regained his composure the next instant by bursting into a laugh. "Spunky, aren't you? Good. Your mother was, too." A peculiar softness stole into his colorless eyes, creating more fear in Columbine than when he raged.

"I'm not Mother," she reminded, forcing herself to be gentle, although her hands were clenched tightly behind her blue-checked gown.

The softness fled, and Stockton's face turned to granite. He abruptly turned. "I have to get cleaned up." Polished floorboards creaked under his weight, and Columbine heaved a sigh of relief as a daring idea hovered and opened its wings. She appeared at supper with her hair in two plaits the way she had worn it as a child, wearing a dress as different from anything her mother had worn as possible.

"What have you done to yourself?" Zeke eyed her with disfavor. "You don't look right. I like your hair the other way."

Because Mother never had plaits. Columbine forced herself to laugh. "I just thought it might be cooler this way."

"I still don't like it." He rested his knife and fork on his plate and continued to stare.

Her plan had failed, but fortunately, after a long time in prayer, another had come. "Father, you'll never know how happy Mother would be that you've always treated me like your own daughter. You've fed me and clothed me, given me books, and made sure no one pestered me." She glanced down and risked a quick glance at him from beneath her lashes. "You're the only father I can remember, and no one could have been kinder."

A line seemed to form around Zeke's mouth, and his jaw set. Would reminding him of Mother and how she trusted herself and her young daughter to his care reach the good in him? Was Zeke's heart waiting to be kindled to the love of Christ?

She played her trump card. "Did you ever think God sent you to us so I could have a father?"

Stockton turned chalky. Suddenly, he leaped to his feet, sending his chair crashing backward to the floor. One great fist slammed into his other hand, and he staggered as if mortally wounded, then lurched out the door.

Columbine heard his unsteady progress across the porch and ran to the window that gave full view of the corral and bunkhouse. She covered her ears at the curses he had never used in front of her or her mother, curses she knew only from overhearing the cruder hands.

"Give me that!" Zeke snatched a lariat from Andy Cullen, who sat perched on the corral fence coiling his rope. It whistled and dropped over a feisty stallion's neck. Iron hands reined in the dancing horse and put saddle and bridle in place. In one fluid motion, Zeke leaped to the steed's back. "Open the gate," he bellowed.

Andy scrambled to obey. Stockton and his wild-eyed mount sprang through and thundered out of sight.

The watching girl felt she had been wrung dry. She groped her way to a chair, and her knees buckled. She hadn't known what to expect, but this? "The way he acted shows he doesn't think of me as a daughter," she whispered brokenly. "He never will again. What can I do?" She rocked back and forth like a grieving child. A dozen plans came to mind, but she rejected them all. If she vanished now, Zeke would know she had realized his feelings for her had changed.

Somehow she managed to clear away the supper neither of them had more than tasted. Listlessly, she washed the dishes and rinsed out her dish towels and hung them to dry. In the weeks after her mother's death, Columbine had sturdily insisted she could keep the house and needed no help. Now she bitterly regretted it. Was it too late to ask Zeke to hire a woman, a motherly soul who could serve as shield and comfort? But who? All the women in that category that they knew either had families of their own or were comfortably situated in Pine or Payson.

"It would take time," she murmured and slowly went to her room. As on other clear nights, she sat by the window for a long time. Unable to sleep, she neither undressed nor thought of going to bed, even when pointing shadows crept into her pretty room. Finally she rose, slipped out of the large house that oppressed her, and fled into the night on moccasined feet. Silent as a mountain lion on padded feet, she wended her way toward her mother's grave. The sight that greeted her froze her in her tracks. Bare-headed, his massive head in his arms, Zeke Stockton was kneeling by the grave.

Columbine sank to the ground, glad for the whispering cottonwoods that would disguise any noise she might make, unwilling to retreat for fear she'd been seen or heard. A prayer for her stepfather formed in her heart, a petition that in his loss he wouldn't turn to the only living part of his beloved dead wife. Perhaps one day, she prayed, he would give his heart to the Lord Jesus Christ, the only One who could heal Zeke's agony.

In the next few days, she sensed the struggle in his soul between nobility—

a strange word to apply to a man such as Zeke Stockton—and desire. If she had seen such a look in Hadley's face, it would have repulsed her and sent her fleeing in horror. Oddly enough, the new understanding Columbine had that Zeke saw her not as a young girl but as her mother blocked hatred. Yet when he rode away for a day and Andy, now healed and back working, managed to talk with her, new worries arose.

"I don't know what's up, but it ain't good," the honest cowboy admitted. He shot a questioning glance at her. "Have you heard anything?"

"I think he's going to have a huge fall roundup and sell off most of our cattle and horses," Columbine said. She wrinkled her forehead, trying to piece together snatches of conversation between Zeke and Hadley, who had become a nightly visitor at the house. Sometimes other men came, too, but Hadley was always there. She had all she could do to keep out of his way, hating the boldness in his face every time she met him.

"Can you stand some bad news?"

Her heart lurched. "Why, yes."

Andy glanced both ways. "The Cross Z ain't got all that many cattle and horses. I've been riding the brakes."

"Maybe he's going to buy and resell." She knew it to be false before he shook his head.

"That doesn't make a lot of sense, what with winter coming on. A roundup's to do just that. Round up critters you don't want to keep over the winter."

"Then how—?" She choked on her words.

"Do you really have to ask?" Andy glanced away.

She shook her head, too stunned to speak. For the first time, she felt fiercely thankful for her mother's death, thankful that her mother had not realized her husband was a rustler.

"I didn't know if I should say anything. It's enough to make a person bawl like a spooked steer." Sympathy darkened his eyes to almost black. "Maybe you think it's pretty rotten of me to squeal, but I promised to be your friend, and one of these days, there's going to be a fight like you never saw before." Gloom laced every word. "Miss Columbine, ain't there some way you can get out of here? I'll take you, if I can. I don't aim to stick around much longer. I'd have gone soon as I heard about the stinking mess Stockton's in if it hadn't been for you."

The truth beat against her like branches whipping in a gale. Her mouth went dry. Columbine Ames, trapped in a nest of rustlers. No wonder Hadley had sneered when he accused her of thinking she was too good for him. No wonder he'd said he could tell her things! Had her inner awareness even then recognized and refused to listen to unspoken evil? "I—I don't think I can bear it," she whispered.

"Aw, sure you can," Andy comforted. "Look how the flowers you're named for bend in the wind. Yet they keep right on blooming and growing, don't they?" He shuffled his boots on the needle-covered ground. "Maybe it ain't as bad as I think, but I'd keep my eyes peeled and ears open." He pressed his lips in a straight line. "And my door locked."

Fresh fear gripped her. "I don't have a lock on my door."

"Then stick a chair under the knob. I don't trust Hadley any more than a polecat." Red rushed into Andy's clear face, but his gaze never left hers.

"You haven't heard anything, have you?" she demanded.

"Just that he's loco over you and telling the rest of the men he'll skin them like rabbits if they get any ideas. Uh, have you had any trouble with Z—uh, with anyone else?"

She knew he had started to say "Zeke." "No."

"Good. Then keep your door locked and your chin up. I'll get you out of here somehow, no matter what it takes." He grinned and headed back to work before anyone could see and suspect him.

That night Zeke Stockton rode in, somber and sullen. All through supper he watched her. To her excited fancy, he appeared to be suspicious of her. Could Hadley or some of the others have reported her talk with Andy? Or was it merely the battle between good and evil waging war in his soul?

She started to rise and clear the table.

"Sit down, Columbine."

She'd never heard him speak in that tone. Tongues of dread licked at her. "I—I just thought I'd get the dishes done before the men come in."

"They won't be coming tonight. Not even Hadley." Light from the lamp she had lit against the early dusk glittered in his eyes, making them more unreadable than ever. "I've thought about it considerable, and I won't wait any longer to speak. Your mother's been gone a year." A spasm of pain contracted the muscles of his face but didn't stop him from continuing. For as long as she lived, Columbine would see his face in the flickering lamplight and relive the gorge that rose within her.

"Hadley's after you. So are half the others. I want you to marry me. You'll be safe, and I'll take care of you." He never took his gaze from her.

She remained silent long enough to ask a prayer for help. What she said now would change the course of her life. She raised her head. "Zeke, you honor me by asking." She struggled to find words that would not antagonize him, her hands clenched until the knuckles showed white against her sprigged gown. "I know I look and act like Mother and—"

"It isn't all that." He leaned forward, hope in his face. "I admire you for yourself, too, Colley. I guess I could even say I love you."

"Thank you for saying that. Father, Zeke, Mother taught me I must never marry any man I don't love with all my heart," she managed to get out.

"You'd come to it in time," he said gruffly. "She loved me that way, didn't she?"

Feeling the ground shake beneath her, Columbine told him, "Yes, she did."

"There can't be anyone else for you," he pondered. "I've seen to that."

"There's no one else. It's just that I know I don't love you in the right way. Zeke, I still think of you as the father who came along when I was a girl. Can't we leave it that way?" Something flickered in his eyes, and she dared hope.

"Maybe all you need is time," he said stubbornly. "What if we forget about it for now and talk again later?"

The temptation to agree nearly overwhelmed her, yet she dared not give in. "I don't think I'll change."

"You might." He stood and laughed. It took every ounce of courage she possessed to keep from shrinking away from him. "I can give you everything you'll ever want," he said, not boasting but stating facts. "If you'd rather live in town, I'll sell out and build there, in Payson or Pine, not Flag." His face darkened. "I'm getting tired of living here in the brakes. How'd you like for me to do one last drive and take you somewhere else, say Colorado or maybe Wyoming?"

Columbine's nails bit into her palms. Andy's direful predictions were on target.

The clink of spurs in the doorway saved her from the need to answer or commit herself. "Sorry to interrupt, Boss, but the, uh, rancher who wants to buy stock's here." Hadley's leer in her direction set the girl's cheeks burning.

"I've told you never to come in here without knocking." Zeke's deadly voice turned even Hadley's face pale. "Now get out."

"Yeah, Boss, but your *visitor* says he's in a hurry." With a last meaningful look, Hadley disappeared into the night.

Stockton followed him, leaving his coveted stepdaughter alone in the room. Columbine knew she must get away, but unless God sent a miracle, she was trapped.

Chapter 5

Several uneasy days passed. Columbine continued with her household duties, unchanged on the outside. Inwardly, she trembled with the growing certainty of her stepfather's crooked dealings. Now that her eyes had been opened, little things she had passed over as insignificant loomed large and frightening. The night visits. The card playing, drinking, and loud voices.

From the fragile safety of her bedroom, chair faithfully propped beneath the doorknob, the girl so like a flower listened and feared, hoped and dreamed, and prayed for the day she could leave. Sometimes she believed Zeke could read her mind. In any event, he assigned Andy Cullen to night guard over the cattle and his henchmen to watch her like a hawk during the day. She had no opportunity for a word with her cowboy friend. Only her strong faith in God's deliverance helped her bear her situation.

To worsen matters, Hadley never missed an opportunity to cast his bold glance her way when Stockton wasn't looking. She refused to let him intimidate her and coolly met his gaze. The biding-my-time glint in his dark, predatory eyes spoke more clearly than words his resentment that a common rustler's daughter should scorn him.

Zeke also bided his time. Although Columbine knew he seldom let her out of his sight except when away on cattle deals, he said no more about marriage. His silence offered no consolation. Each time she passed by, furtively he would reach out and touch her full-skirted gown in a tender caress. Yet her heart sank when more and more often she caught the whiff of whiskey on his breath. She longed to cry out, to remind him how much her mother had hated drinking, but she dared not. Any criticism could shatter the undeclared temporary truce between them.

One night, however, the fragile peace was smashed to smithereens. Columbine had seen the usual procession of evening visitors earlier, heard the too-familiar sounds of frontier mirth and argument, followed by loud voices. Unable to sleep, she huddled by her window. One by one, the riders who haunted her dreams as well as her days rode away. A long time later, she heard uneven steps in the hall outside her bedroom door.

There was a fumbling with the knob. "Oh, God, help me," she whispered. The fumbling continued.

In a frenzy of fear, Columbine snatched a dress, pulled it over her night-gown, and slid her feet into moccasins. She slipped behind the curtains, prepared for flight.

Crash! The door slammed against the wall so hard it shook the floor. A heavy figure stumbled in, groped his way to the empty bed, and fell to his knees.

Columbine seized her only opportunity. Step by cautious step, she inched her way to the open door. Incoherent mumbling told her Zeke still knelt by the bed. Whiskey fumes filled the air. With one hand over her nose, she reached the door.

"Why did you go and leave me?"

Zeke's wild question halted her but only for a second. Pity mingled with fear, and she knew he again had confused her with her mother. With noise-less steps, she went down the hall, her mind strangely clear. Zeke was in no condition to follow her. Even if he called for whatever cowboys weren't on night watch, she still had a margin of time. She hurried to the kitchen, glad for the knowledge that allowed her to skirt furniture and forage in cupboards and pantry. The rest of the supper roast. Cold biscuits. A large chunk of cheese. She would get water from the creek. Into the living room she dashed for a blanket, and her preparations ended. Supplies knotted in a dish towel she could use as a knapsack, blanket over her light dress and fair hair, she reconnoitered at the front door. Not a sound disturbed the stillness. Not the friendly cry of a night bird, not the rustle of small animals scurrying about their nocturnal business. A quick step brought her to the porch, but instead of crossing it and going down the steps, she turned and walked its length and stepped to the ground at the side of the house and thanked God.

Where should she go? Not to her mother's grave. Zeke would look there first. She struck out from the large house toward her cabin refuge. Did she dare go inside, bolt the door, and pray for safety? In spite of his order, Zeke in his alcoholic condition would break his own rule unless he went into a stupor. She walked on until she reached the shady spot by the stream where she and Andy had spent such happy hours. It seemed a lifetime had passed since then, but it had been just a few weeks. Taking advantage of the starlight that cast a dim glow and provided black shadows beneath the cottonwoods, Columbine managed to put a few miles between her and the house. She wondered if her stepfather had missed her. . .perhaps he was still crying for his dead wife. In either case, she couldn't take a chance.

She crept on, not knowing where she could go and be safe. She reached the spot where Hadley had accosted her and glanced fearfully at the bushes as if expecting them to rustle. Her eyes opened wide. Was it her imagination, or had something moved behind her? Too late she whirled. Strong fingers cut off her cry for help, and a steel arm pinioned her own arms to her body. She fought to no avail. The unknown assailant pulled her off the trail into deep shadows. Silently she prayed, *Deliver me from evil.*

"Lie still," her captor whispered. "Hadley's after you."

The throbbing of her heart left her lightheaded. *Andy.* Andy Cullen had snatched her from harm. Too relieved to wonder why or how he'd found her, she sagged against his arm. He removed his other hand from her mouth but only after a low warning, "Don't make a move."

A footfall showed how close behind her Hadley had been. He must have seen her slip from the house. Terror came again, digging claws into her until her body quivered, and Andy gave her arm a reminding squeeze. Long after Hadley's black figure had disappeared and night sounds told them danger had passed, they remained in hiding.

"Come." Andy took her hand and led her back up the trail but cut off in a different direction before they reached the main road to the house. Exhausted more emotionally than physically, Columbine followed, glad for the strong hand that led her. Their strange trek made a curious impression on her. Sometimes she heard the ripple of water and knew they traveled near the brook. At other times they traversed open spaces between clumps of trees, bent low and moving slowly. Hours later, they stopped before what looked like a vast dark hole. "You'll be safe here," Andy told her.

Columbine's sight had adjusted to the starlight. "A cave. How did you find it?"

He didn't answer until they went inside. "Ever since we talked about your having to get away, I've been looking for someplace you could stay if you needed to." His gruff voice couldn't hide his anger. "Here." He took the blanket from her shoulders and wrapped it more securely around her. "There's another on the ground so we can sit."

She gratefully dropped to the cave floor. Enough light came from a small opening in the ceiling to the right of where they sat so she could discern his set face. "Andy, how did you happen to be here when I needed you so much?"

"Maybe that God of yours sent me." He shrugged. "I've been feeling uneasy the last few nights. Tonight when I got the herd bedded down and could see the other night guards were eager to spin yarns around the fire, I said I'd just as lief mosey around and keep an eye out. They called me a fool but laughed and told me some jaspers were suckers for punishment. I've been watching the house, just in case. . ." His voice trailed off. "What happened tonight, anyway?"

"Zeke had been drinking. If he hadn't, I know he never would have broken into my room."

Andy leaped to his feet. "I'll kill him for that!" His low voice rang deadly against the cave walls.

"No," she told him desperately. "He didn't hurt me. He didn't even think of me, just of Mother. Andy, even if it weren't wrong to kill, suppose you shot Zeke? Hadley and the others would either shoot or hang you, and where would I be then?"

"Out of the branding-iron fire and into a forest fire, I reckon." Andy sat back down, breathing hard.

"I need you alive," she told him. "Besides, I honestly don't think Zeke will harm me unless he's so far gone with whiskey he doesn't know what he's doing."

"What are you going to do now?" he demanded.

Her thoughts spun like a singing lariat. "Stay here for a day or two. I brought food. I want you to go back to the herd right away, before someone misses you. Then tomorrow, see what happens at the ranch. The men will be bound to talk. If you can get away tomorrow night for a little while, come tell me what you've learned."

"Leave you here alone? Suppose your friend Hadley finds you?"

"He won't. There's no reason for him to look here, is there? How many of the men know about this cave?" Yet his suggestion chilled her, and she drew the warm blanket closer about her body.

"Any of them could, but there ain't much reason for them to," he admitted. "I stumbled on it by chance when I was chasing a maverick."

"Chance?" her soft, sweet voice challenged. "Or did God lead you here?"

He hunched his shoulders and wrapped his arms around his drawn-up knees. "Might not be such a bad idea at that." With a slight spring, he stood, a lithe defender. "You probably won't need this, but just in case a mean critter wants the cave, I'll feel better if you have it on hand." He pulled something heavy and cold from his shirt and placed it in her hands. "It's loaded. Use it if you have to." A few strides took him to the mouth of the cave. "Stay holed up inside except when you go for water. The creek's straight down and not far. I'll see you tomorrow night or the next at the latest."

She wanted to cling to him, to beg him not to go, but her pioneer stock permitted no weakness. "God bless you, Andy," she called softly. The next moment his dark shape moved, and a large patch of starlight appeared where he had been.

All night Columbine prayed, until sheer fatigue and worry overcame her, and she fell into a deep, dreamless sleep on the earthen floor of the cave. She awakened to the trill of birds and full sunlight, plus the chill of early morning autumn air in the Tonto. Ravenous, hope welling in her heart now that daylight had driven night shadows away, she carefully surveyed the area and satisfied herself no intruder lurked near. The cool water in the stream offered both refreshment and a chance to bathe. Never had food tasted better than the butterless sandwich she made from a cold biscuit, a piece of roast she tore off with her hands, and a sharp, tangy chunk of cheese.

Mindful of Andy's instructions, she stayed near the cave. She whiled away the long hours by seeking out and erasing every footprint that might betray her hiding place. She wished for her Bible, repeating as many promises for deliverance she could remember, and sprang to her feet with a little cry when Andy finally came.

Excitement filled his face. His brown eyes flashed. "Everything's broke loose on the Cross Z," he reported. At the same time, he took from the capacious pockets of his jacket two apples, a chunk of cake carefully wrapped in a clean handkerchief, and two dill pickles. "All I could swipe," he cheerfully told her.

Columbine bit into a juicy apple. "Mmm. Delicious."

"Want to hear what's going on at the ranch?" Andy tormented. His corn-colored hair looked more disheveled than ever.

"Do I!" She finished the apple and reached for the piece of cake.

"First off, I got back to the herd and checked in with the hands around the fire. None of them was any wiser, so I headed for the bunkhouse at first light. Never saw such a sight." Andy slapped his jeans leg in glee. "Place was lit up like the Fourth of July, men running around like scared prairie chickens.

"Hadley comes bellowing up to me with Stockton right behind him. 'Cullen, have you seen Colley?'" The cowboy's open face clouded. "I wanted to poke him one for not being more respectful."

"Don't stop for that," she begged. She could almost see the vivid scene Andy described.

"'Miss Columbine?' sez I. 'I just rode in off night duty.'

"'And yore sure you didn't see her on the way in?' sez he.

" 'Ump-umm.' I *didn't* see you on my way in but on your way out," he chortled. "Anyway, he ups and tells me what he'll do if I'm lying, so I get all wide-eyed and innocent and say, 'She ain't lost, is she, Boss?' I never saw Stockton look so worried as when he barked, 'We hope not. Maybe she just went for an early morning walk, but it's not like her to be late with fixing breakfast.' "

Andy looked disgusted. "I about spilled the beans and said it wasn't any morning walk that made you leave, but instead, I just yawned and said if they needed me to hunt, I'd be glad to. Stockton stared at me for a minute and said no. Told me to get some shut-eye so I could night herd again tonight."

"You said he looked worried."

"Yeah, and dead sober. Your little escapade just about shocked him out of his boots. The way I figure, if you stay out one more night, he will be so miserable and guilty, it will be safe enough for you to go home tomorrow." He scratched his head. "I can't say for how long, though." He hunkered down on his boot heels. "You might want to consider telling him right out he scared you to death coming in your room that way and that you never thought he'd do anything like that."

She rolled it over in her mind, then nodded. "I will." The faint hope that rescue lay in appealing to his better side refused to die.

Andy didn't stay much longer. "Can't let anyone miss me," he explained. "Hadley's sorer than a bear with his paw in a trap, and it wouldn't take much for him to draw on me." He grinned sunnily. "Don't worry. I ain't carrying a gun, and even the Cross Z's hard-nut outfit won't stand for him killing me except in a fair fight. Stockton won't, either."

According to arrangement, Columbine spent the second night in the cave, then met Andy at a prearranged spot early the next morning. Andy could truthfully say he found her on the trail while riding in from his night-herding duties. He reported that most of the outfit had been out looking for her. "Good thing you're going in. Sooner or later some sharp-eyed galoot would spot the cave. We don't want that. It may come in handy again."

Their arrival created a sensation. Andy chose to make a grand entrance and sang out, "Here she is!" before he rode in with Columbine behind him. Unshaven men stared, and Hadley's dark face blackened with suspicion. Stockton sprang from his horse. Evidently, he had been about to begin searching again once it got light.

"Colley? Where have you been, Girl?" Relief, shame, guilt, and anger mingled in his broad face.

"Excuse me, Boss, but she's kind of tired and scratched up," Andy put in respectfully, although the runaway knew he had his tongue stuck in his cheek. "Probably hungry, too. Want me to help her in the house and you can talk later?"

"I'll do it." Zeke lifted Columbine down and carried her inside.

She heard Hadley demand, "Where's she been, and where'd you find her? There's something funny about this."

Andy's quick retort floated to her ears. "Nothing funny about getting turned around in the brakes, is there?"

For the umpteenth time, Columbine bit her lip at his clever habit of answering in truthful generalities. She forced herself to lie limp until her stepfather kicked the door shut, then slid from his grasp. She meant to get in first licks. "Father, I never thought you would degrade yourself with drink until I am not safe in my own home."

He stepped back. His mouth dropped open.

Encouraged by the effect of her first shot, she drew herself to her full height, knowing anger would heighten her five feet and a few inches. "I respected you, considered you my protector against the rough men down here who—who. . ." She covered her face with her hands and produced a convincing shudder that completed the sentence. "Now you burst into my room and frighten me until I must flee into the night, to be chased by your men—"

"What's that?" he roared.

"Surely you know Hadley followed me," she lashed out.

"Only to find where you'd gone." His weak defense poured fuel on the fire of her anger, both real and assumed.

"You promised to give me time to consider marriage. Instead, this." She spread her hands in a helpless gesture, one designed to appeal to any remaining sense of decency.

Zeke cried, "I was drunk! I didn't know what I was doing. You don't honestly think I'd hurt you, Colley. You can't believe that." His face whitened. "Why, you're *her daughter.*"

Drained, she had no need to pretend. "I don't know what I believe." Her shoulders drooped. "Now I'd like to bathe and get some rest." She raised her face and looked him squarely in the eyes. "And I'd like a strong bolt put on the inside of my door."

His pallor almost frightened her. "Of course. You won't run away again, will you?" The muscles of his face convulsed.

"Father." She paused. "That all depends on you."

He gasped, but she ignored him and slowly walked away, wondering if the tearing sounds behind her were sobs. With every step came a feeling of security. She had seen in Zeke's eyes what her flight cost him. But she also knew that God had delivered her this time and only He would make a way if the need arose, using methods she might not even know existed.

From the time Zeke Stockton rode into her and her mother's life, Columbine had never seen him show fear. Now it lurked in his face and in the way he treated her. The mysterious night visitors vanished as if they had never been. Zeke made a trip to Flagstaff and came home with bulging saddlebags filled with dress goods, books, and candy. Further, she no longer smelled whiskey on his breath.

Yet even though she could breathe more freely, she knew things couldn't go on as they were. Her power to stave off Zeke's unwelcome attentions wouldn't last forever.

One sunny afternoon, she walked to a secluded part of the little brook where debris from some previous flood had partially dammed the water into a small pool. Not wide enough to swim in, the water came to her waist and offered a sandy bottom. With the privacy afforded by nearby cottonwoods, she decided to bathe and wash her hair.

Columbine sat on a big rock and removed the pins from her sun-kissed hair. How good the creek flowing over amber stones would feel on her skin and hair. She slid out of her moccasins and wiggled her white toes in the narrow stretch of sand beside the pool. Her slender fingers reached for the top button of her blue calico dress.

A rustle in the bushes stopped her. A roar that split the silence of the little glade followed, then wild thrashing, a heavy *thud*, and a dull moan. Frightened, she stared, her hand at her throat.

As if taking a curtain call, the bushes parted and two men hurled toward her.

Chapter 6

Eb and Lily Sears stepped from the stage at Flagstaff into the warmest welcome either had ever received. All the slender, dark-eyed woman's fears melted in the quick embrace Judith Scott gave her and the strong handclasp from Gideon. Danny, who had been bug-eyed at the sights all the way from Colorado Springs, grinned at the Scott twins. "You're Matt 'n' Millie 'n' Dad says I can have my own pony 'n' maybe you'll teach me to ride 'cause you're three years older 'n' can ride like wild Indians."

His six-year-old hero worship brought instant "Whoopees" from the twins, and they led him to the wagon that would haul them and their parents to the Double J.

As Gideon and Eb joined hands, the long years since their last meeting seemed to melt away. Miles had separated the men as well, since Gideon as a young minister, traveling under his brother's name, rode away from Tomkinsville. He had been cleared of a charge of attempted murder by the man he had outdrawn and whose hand he now held. Eb's face held the eagerness of a boy. "Did you find me a ranch?"

Gideon's blue eyes sparkled in the summer sunlight. "A ranch or a piece of one," he replied. "There's as pretty a little spread not far from the Double J as I've seen. Or you can throw in with the Double J, if you like." Eb started to speak, but Gideon held up a hand. "Don't make up your mind until you see both."

"There's one other thing." Eb glanced at the womenfolk, who had started for the wagon. "Lily has some fool notion she ain't good enough for your wife an' the one Joel's bringin' from Texas. Don't let on I told you, but if you could sorta mention it offhandlike, it'd make everythin' just perfect."

"I will," Gideon promised, and they followed the women. Next to the wagon a fine pair of horses harnessed to a light buckboard pranced restlessly. "Eb, I brought the buckboard in as well as the wagon. How about you and Danny riding in the wagon with me and the twins? Judith can drive Lily and have time to get acquainted."

Lily's dark eyes shone, and Judith's soft smile showed approval of the arrangement. They drove off in the buckboard, and the others waited until the road dust settled before beginning their journey.

At supper that night, Gideon looked down the long table. "Thank God for having family and friends here," he said simply. "This is truly a time of rejoicing. Dad and Mother have chosen to stay in Arizona. Soon Joel, Cyrus, and their wagon train will arrive, and there will be another grand reunion." He smiled at Judith, then turned to Lily. "My wife had a piano hauled in. Will you sing for us?" He ignored her gasp and the way her face paled. "Lily's one of the spunkiest gals I ever knew and has one of the best voices. She earned our respect by taking care of herself after having to go it on her own, then accepting the chance for something better when it came along." His voice lowered. "The first time I ever saw Lily, I couldn't help thinking it could have been Judith if things had been different."

Gratitude dyed Lily's face a rich color. "If it hadn't been for you and Eb and Joel—"

"God often sends help when we most need it," Gideon said quietly. "Now, no more looking back. We've got a growing number of Christian men, women, and children here in Flag, and we intend to make a difference."

"Please, before you seal the past, may I say something?"

"Of course, Lily."

She met his gaze steadily. "Once you asked if that was my real name and I said no. My name is really Lillian. When I left Tomkinsville, I decided to use it. My first husband and his family liked Lily better. I just wanted you to know I didn't lie." She smiled. "Eb likes it better, too. He says if he had to call me Lillian, I'd have to call him Ebenezer and he'd hate that!" The wave of laughter effectively broke the slight constraint that had fallen on the group. "I'll be happy to sing for you if you'll give me a little time to practice. I haven't done much singing since the Livingstons died. They treated me like their own daughter." Tears glistened in her dark eyes. "It's like you said, though. They'd want me to go on and not look back."

Lige and Naomi had remained silent during the conversation. Now the patriarch's blue eyes held long-remembered pain. "Child, we all have many sad things in our lives that are better put to rest. I certainly have. I just thank God for His goodness and mercy and most of all for His forgiveness. As Gideon said, soon my lost son will be restored to me, even as the son I drove away now sits beside me." His great voice rolled out. "Of all men, I am most blessed. Remember the story in the Bible about the two men who received forgiveness, one a little, one much? And Jesus asked which one would love Him most? Once I begged my older son's forgiveness for my blindness that helped make him what he is, even greater joy than being here came."

Never again did Lily Sears feel anything except what she was, a loved member of the community of Christians bound by gospel cords in a raw new land. But Naomi Scott noticed that more and more often a look of longing crept into her husband's eyes, and he turned his face toward the road on which the wagon train would come.

✛

"The last miles are always the hardest," Joel Scott confided in his friend Smokey one late afternoon shortly before time to make up camp. He had ridden Querida alongside Buckskin when Rebecca chose to keep her adopted father company on the high seat of the wagon he capably drove. As usual, Curly handled the second wagon with Mrs. Cook beside him. Pretty Conchita Perkins sat close to her cowboy husband, Jim, on the third wagon.

"It's grand, isn't it?" Joel's voice fell to a hush.

"Yeah." Smokey couldn't put the feast of colors into words: the cottonwood and willow greens; the turning golden aspens and purple-shadowed canyons; the occasional streams that chuckled over amber rocks; the red buttes and cream-and-black-streaked promontories. "Bet there's fish in some of the creeks we've crossed. Once we get to the Double J and unload, I think I'll take me a little vacation an' come back and see." He grinned in his droll way. "Now, if I were like some folks not so far from here, I'd say this whole little excursion had been a vacation. Such as you an' Rebecca, Jim an' Conchita—"

Joel cut in, blond hair flying, blue eyes filled with mischief. "Don't forget Mrs. Cook and Curly. Have you noticed how she keeps on trying to pretend nothing's changed since he acted so quick when the rattler struck?" He inclined his head toward the buxom, round-faced woman.

Smokey snorted. "Talk about opportunity! Better than in some of those stories writer fellers tell. Just his luck. I could live to be older than one of these Arizona century plants an' not have a chance to shine like that in front of a pretty little filly."

"Cheer up, Smokey." Joel's high spirits spilled over in a loud laugh. "You didn't want to spark Mrs. Cook, did you? She's way too old for you."

Red crept into the cowboy's lean face. He refused to dignify the sally with an answer and broke free to herd one of the plodding cattle back in line.

"Smokey, round up Vermilion for me, will you, please?" Rebecca called from her perch. "I'll ride some more."

Rounding up the red mustang stallion he'd hand-broken with love sent other thoughts flying. The frisky Vermilion took his own sweet time coming when Smokey called, then minced toward him like a coquette at a ball. Finally, the horse sidled up to Buckskin and nuzzled her while Smokey expertly threw a saddle blanket over his back.

"Don't bother with the saddle," Rebecca said. She climbed off the slow-moving wagon. Her booted left foot barely touched Smokey's cupped hands before she swung onto Vermilion and smiled down. "Thanks." Her brown hair and eyes held a reddish glow.

A tiny pang crept into the faithful cowboy's heart. He'd long since overcome any remaining shred of jealousy that might spoil his friendship with Rebecca and Joel. More like a reminder, the hollow place inside him still hadn't been filled. Sometimes when Joel spoke of God and His Son, Smokey felt close to discovering what could take away the empty feeling. Yet he hesitated. He could never be as good as Joel or Rebecca. Probably not as good as Mrs. Cook or even Cyrus Scott, who had brokenly confessed his sinful past to them all a few nights ago.

Smokey sighed, remembering the unashamed tears of his former range boss. Anything that could change the hard rancher once known as Samuel Fairfax into this vulnerable, repentant man must be powerful medicine. He had a feeling that one day soon he'd be taking that medicine. Yet when he considered his life and the need for strength to meet the trouble of which Gideon had written, Smokey balked. Joel mustn't betray his calling, even to clean up a nest of Arizona rattlers. That's where his men would come in, and if a feller hadn't accepted Jesus, who said you had to love your enemies? At this point, he always turned his thoughts elsewhere.

At last the thrilling moment came when the three-wagon train reached Flagstaff. Smokey looked around with interest. "Hmm, some little old town."

Jim Perkins echoed his sentiments. "Snappin' crocodiles, no wonder Joel's been itchin' to get here." He nudged Smokey. "Say, Pard, I don't see no p'rade with girls." He guffawed.

"That's because they didn't know for sure when we'd get here," Smokey loftily told him, to the amusement of the others. "Boss, are we going to stop for supplies and the like?"

Joel hesitated, eyes bluer than ever. "No, let's go home."

Smokey turned away from the poignant light in his friend's face. What would it feel like, having a family waiting? Again the vision of a spread, complete with snug cabin, a light in the window, and a girl running toward him when he came home from herding ornery cows danced before him. The same feeling attacked him again when the wagons reached the crest of the rise and the Double J stretched before them. By mutual and unspoken consent, the drivers halted their horses. Those riding reined in their mounts.

"This is where I came to decide whether I should go or stay," Joel said in a voice little above a whisper.

"Thank God you decided not to stay," Cyrus said raggedly, and Rebecca nodded. Smokey wondered if he could ever have left had he been Joel. In all their long miles, he had seen no place that struck a chord in his heart the way the Double J did. He could not single out the reason why, yet the whispering yellow-leafed aspens, the rustling grass, and the sighing pine and cedar spelled home. Soon he would know the forested slopes, the peaceful valley, and the red rimrocked canyons the way he had known northeastern New Mexico. Yet long before he drank his fill of what lay before him, piercing shrieks followed by three horses pelting toward them shattered the silence. Joel slid off his horse and hit the ground running.

"You're here, you're here! Uncle Joel, what took you so long?" Matt and Millie, closely followed by a younger boy Smokey knew must be Danny Sears, slid to a halt. The twins tumbled off and into Joel's bear hug. "We've waited 'n' waited," Danny added, as if he were the twins' brother. He valiantly struggled down from his pony and received a hug.

"Run and tell the others we're coming," Joel ordered. The twins bounded to their horses, but Danny said, "A body's gotta help me. I can get down, not up." Boosted into the saddle, he turned his pony after the others and trotted off.

Smokey glanced at Cyrus Scott, whose hands toyed nervously with the reins. His Scott blue eyes stared at the ranch house visible from where they rested. Smokey turned away, struck to the core of his being. Although he knew the story, he could only guess at what the older man was experiencing. Slowly they started the descent to the Double J. Even Jim Perkins refrained from his joking. As they reached the corral, a group of people stood waiting. The shouting twins and Danny had done their heralding well. Smokey readily identified Gideon, the wronged brother, waiting for Cyrus with the flame of righteousness in his face. Judith, his faithful wife, stood beside him. How would she feel, seeing the man who long ago betrayed her sister?

A tall man and a slim, attractive woman next to him must be the Searses.

No mistaking the older couple who stood rigid. Lige Scott bore a strong family resemblance to his sons and grandson. White-haired Naomi, with her proud carriage and aristocratic features, stood silently with brimming eyes.

Smokey hung back, filled with sudden bashfulness. But he could not tear his gaze from the scene. Joel leaped from Querida and strode to the lead wagon and waited until Cyrus stepped down. "My father and I are home," he said.

Without a moment's hesitation, Gideon limped forward and grabbed Cyrus. "Thank God you live!" Still-graceful Naomi came next, and Smokey looked away, unable to bear the sight of her face. He took a few steps back, intending to slip away. The mighty roll of a thunderous voice stopped everyone in their tracks.

"My son, my son." Lige came into his own. He plowed through the others, little heeding their presence until he stood face-to-face with Cyrus. "Can you ever forgive me?"

"*I*, forgive *you?*" Cyrus Scott dropped to the dusty ground and bowed his head before his father. With strength surprising in one so gaunt, Lige lifted his son and clasped him to his bosom as the prophets of old must have done. "You live. That is all that matters."

Smokey could stand no more. He backed away, mumbling that he'd see to the stock, and made his escape. He found things to do until Joel called him to meet the family. Then he managed to produce enough calm to cover his deep feelings and later went back to the corral where riders had come in from their day's duties.

The quartet of dusty cowhands said they answered to Lonesome, Dusty, Cheyenne, and Kansas. A keen-eyed older man who introduced himself as Fred Aldrich, foreman, took Smokey in at a lightning glance and "reckoned he'd be right useful on the Double J." The newcomer knew, as far as the cowboys were concerned, that remained to be seen. Smokey had ridden for enough outfits to recognize the need to prove himself before the longer-term hands accepted him. He grinned. No slouch at riding, roping, and shooting, he anticipated some fun.

Lights burned in the big ranch house until the early morning hours, but the cozy little cabin the Scotts had delighted in fixing up for Jim and Conchita went dark early. Given a choice of beds in the bunkhouse or a cabin of their own, Smokey and Curly chose the latter. "Although I ain't promising to stay with you any longer than it takes to get a yes out of a certain cook," Curly warned. A gleam in his eye added that his days as a cabinmate were already numbered.

The next day all the hands except those with the herd received a summons to a meeting. Gideon took charge, happiness exuding from every pore. "With all our new friends, we'll need to make some changes," he said simply. "We have the best cook in any Arizona bunkhouse, but with more to feed, Curly can prove invaluable. Mrs. Cook wants to help our housekeeper for a time." He grinned, and the worthy woman actually blushed.

"Smokey and Jim are no strangers to range work, and neither is Cyrus, as soon as he feels up to helping; Dad already is. Mom and Judith and Rebecca can do whatever no one else does." He paused. "Oh, we'll keep on all hands over the winter who want to help build some houses. This place is big enough for now, but by spring, Joel and Rebecca will need their own place."

Curly spoke up like a man. "So will I. Mrs. Cook is going to change her name right soon."

A round of applause greeted the statement followed by congratulations. Smokey slipped away as soon as he could without attracting attention. "More of the two by twos, doggone it," he complained good-naturedly to no one. "Oh, well, I can always slope if it gets too mushy around these parts."

Later that day, Joel sought him out. "Did you mean what you said about wanting a vacation?"

"Sure. I'm hankering to see some more of this country before I settle down chasing cows."

"Then why don't you go anytime? In a week or so, we'll start the fall roundup. I don't suppose you want to miss that."

"Who, me?" Smokey drawled. "Say, Boss, you think you can have a roundup without me? That's like having Thanksgiving with no turkey."

"Settled." Joel lightly punched his friend's arm, then his face clouded over as suddenly as Arizona storm clouds in a clear sky. "The ranchers around here are friendly; so are most of the merchants and people in Flag. If you get down into the Tonto, be careful. Zeke Stockton, whose men shot Gideon that time, lives there. So do a lot of dark-browed riders no one knows much about. Rumors of outlaw gangs float up here now and then. Don't go poking around too much down in the brakes. Those folks are clannish and don't take kindly to strangers. There are stills in the woods and polecats, four legged and two legged. Watch where and how you ride."

"Thanks for the sermon, Boss, but I reckon Arizona bad men can't be much worse than New Mexico ones."

Joel's sharp retort shocked him. "Don't count on it. Other parts of the Southwest are getting more settled, but Arizona's still pretty wild. The way Gideon tells it, a lot of men no longer welcome in Texas, New Mexico, and

Colorado are heading this way." He cleared his throat. "Vaya con Dios, and hurry back home."

Three days later, a rueful Smokey told Buckskin, "I should have listened better about these doggoned brakes. I've never been so turned around since that square dance back in New Mexico." He slid from the saddle and led his horse along a dim trail that must go somewhere unless it petered out the way several others had. He came to a little fork in the path, peered ahead, and caught a glimpse of blue. Then the patch moved. "Good, some feller's up ahead, and we can find out where we are," he said. Buckskin pricked her ears and followed.

The distant patch vanished behind a thicket. Smokey headed toward it. An inner sense of danger warned him. He stepped off the path and held his hand over Buckskin's nose so she wouldn't whinny. A dark figure came into view, bent low and almost creeping forward, as if stalking something or someone.

Smokey felt himself jerk. The figure's stealthy moves meant only trouble for the blue-shirted man ahead. The cowpuncher threw Buckskin's reins down and whispered, "Stand." The stalker had disappeared into the thicket without even a rustle.

Fair play born of an honest soul propelled Smokey after the figure. Inch by inch he followed, then veered a bit to the left so he could see better. He drew in his breath with a hissing sound. A coarse man stood hunched forward, peering through the thick bushes that screened him. His mouth stretched in a leer. His eyes gleamed with excitement.

Smokey frowned. The man made no move to pull a gun; he must not be planning to ambush his quarry. Shifting his position, Smokey let his gaze travel in the direction the stalker looked. Black anger filled him. The blue had not been part of a shirt but a calico dress.

His eyes noted in one lightning glance the slender figure that loosened silvery fair hair until it swung free; the worn moccasins she kicked off; the gleam of a dammed pool; the white face when she half turned before reaching for the top button on her simple dress.

Black rage for any man low enough to spy on a girl launched Smokey forward with a bellow. He landed squarely on top of the crouched dark figure who had been too engrossed to hear his attacker. The element of surprise served him well against the heavier man, that and the intensity of his fury. He seized the spying man by the waist, wrestled with him, then thrust him through the bushes, straight toward the girl.

Chapter 7

You sniveling skunk!" Smokey Travis pushed the hulking lout into the open. With a low cry, the girl leaped to one side. Her defender rushed the spy across the narrow strip of sand and, with a gigantic shove, sent him flying into the pool.

"You lowdown, rotten excuse for a man," Smokey raged. "If I ever catch you spying on a girl again, I'll beat the living daylights out of you an' tell every rancher and hand between here and Flagstaff why. Who are you, anyway?"

Mouth filled with water, the floundering man couldn't answer. He tried to stand but slipped and fell back with a splash.

The cowboy turned to the girl and doffed his sombrero. "Begging your pardon, Miss." His dark eyes twinkled, and his teeth shone white in the tanned face beneath his disheveled dark hair. "Do you know this polecat?"

Color sped into her white face. Her eyes shone like jewels, and Smokey gasped. He'd seen many girls but never one like her. Barefooted, her silvery hair flying, she resembled a shy woodland creature more than a damsel in distress. When she spoke, her voice showed breeding and culture, not what he would have expected from a girl in the Tonto wilds. "His name is Hadley. He's my stepfather's foreman."

The words barely left her lips before an enraged howl from the brook warned that the soaked spy had finally regained his balance. He sounded more animal than human as he splashed toward them, clawing for his low-slung gun.

Before he got the dripping revolver halfway out of the holster, he found himself staring into Smokey's pistol barrel, trained straight at his heart and held in a rock-steady hand.

"Pitch your gun back in the creek," Smokey ordered. "Not that it will fire," he added with a meaningful glance at the Colt. "Then hightail it out of here, an' don't come back. This part of the woods could prove a mite unhealthy for skunks."

Enraged, Hadley lifted his revolver, but instead of obeying, he threw it straight at the cowboy's grinning face and rushed to knock his enemy to the ground.

Nimbly, Smokey leaped aside, sheathed his gun with one hand, and followed it with a punch that sent Hadley sprawling in an ignominious heap. Blood spurted from his nose, and a stream of garbled curses came from his mouth.

Smokey grabbed him by the shirtfront and backhanded him across the face. "Shut your foul mouth, Hadley, if you don't want a pistol-whipping." He gestured menacingly toward his gun. "There's a lady present. If she weren't here, I'd tie you to a tree an' give you what you deserve." He shoved Hadley's chest until the victim fell back to the sand. "At that, it's more than you deserve. Now get up an' get out."

A baleful look on his face, Hadley tramped into the bushes. Smokey called after him, "Don't think you can hide along the trail, either. I'd purely love having a good reason to shoot a hole in you."

A crash followed by a series of diminishing footfalls showed the threat had born fruit, but the foreman had the last word. Safely hidden from sight but still in earshot, he called back, "Columbine Ames, I'll get even. Wait until yore daddy hears about this. He's goin' to be real int'r'sted to know yore a-meetin' a cowboy behind his back." A suggestive laugh preceded running steps.

Why hadn't he killed the yellow dog when he had the chance? Smokey sprang toward the crushed bushes, but the girl, faster than a doe in flight, intercepted him. "Let him go." Scorn flashed in her magnificent eyes. "He's not worth shooting." Her shapely hand rested on his sleeve.

"All right, but I won't promise what will happen if I run up against him again." Smokey's keen eyes saw how her face blanched, and he added hastily, "I probably won't." He laughed cheerily. "Joel Scott said Arizona was full of surprises, but I sure didn't know I'd run into a bad man an' meet a pretty girl before I'd been here a week." The frank admiration in his voice robbed it of any boldness, and after a moment, Columbine laughed.

"I'm glad you came." A rich blush painted her face. "I never dreamed anyone knew I came here to bathe."

"Men like Hadley have ways. Better pick some other place," he soberly told her. "I have a hunch this little event won't make him feel too kindly toward you. A feller never likes to get showed up before a girl, 'specially one he likes."

Her involuntary look of repulsion told him even more than her words when she said, "He's a nightmare."

"Why doesn't your daddy run him off?"

Great tears welled and darkened the blue eyes. "I—I can't tell you." She took a step back. Fear swallowed every bit of color in her face. "Thank you, Mr.—"

"Smokey. Smokey Travis."

Some of her natural dignity returned. She held out a slim hand, and he awkwardly took it for a moment. It lay soft in his, yet he'd bet his favorite saddle blanket strength rested in that hand. "You saved me from an unpleasant time, if not worse, although I don't think Hadley would actually hurt me. He's too afraid of Father." Contempt underlined every word.

"Can he make trouble for you, like he said?"

Her fair head drooped. "I hope not, but Zeke's awfully jealous and. . . I mean, Zeke Stockton. He's not really my father but my stepfather. He married Mother three years ago. She died last year."

Her voice went ragged, and Smokey had the feeling a river of tears lurked behind her shining eyes. He pieced together what information he had: A jealous stepfather, who was none other than Zeke Stockton, and a foreman who sneaked around watching her bathe made Columbine Ames's life no Sunday picnic.

A daring idea slipped into Smokey's brain. "A long time ago something happened an' my pards an' I up an' beat another crooked foreman to the boss. I told him the truth. Wail 'til I get Buckskin, an' I'll take you home. We'll tell your daddy—Zeke—what really happened."

Stark terror swept into her face. "No, oh, no! He'd kill you."

"Who? Hadley? Some chance. Come on, Miss Ames. It's the only way to clear you."

Hope struggled with fear and won, but she still sounded doubtful. "All right. I just don't want killing because of me."

"Some men need killing, don't they?"

"Only God can judge that," she told him quietly. "Promise me that no matter what happens, you won't pull a gun."

He reached for his discarded sombrero and smiled at her. "I won't unless it's to save my life or yours." He saw his words didn't fully satisfy her, so he continued. "Aw, nothing like that's going to happen. Hadley's yellow clear through. He's more likely to dry gulch a man than stand up an' face him."

All the way to the Cross Z ranch house, Smokey kept up a patter of conversation designed to relieve her mind. Twice he succeeded in making her laugh and thrilled to the sound. Long before they halted out of sight of the prosperous ranch buildings, Smokey suspected why he'd come to Arizona.

As Columbine dismounted, a man appeared from nowhere and stepped around a bend in the road. Smokey reached for his gun. "Who're you, an' what do you want?" he barked.

Brown eyes widened beneath a shock of corn-colored hair. The youth's hands shot into the air. "Columbine, are you all right?"

Something in the question caused Smokey to lower his gun. "Andy, this is Smokey Travis. He caught Hadley spying on me," Columbine inserted quickly. She cast an imploring glance at her rescuer. Smokey realized she didn't want to go into any details and nodded slightly. The lithe rider who looked about her age had stiffened at the foreman's name. Hot color poured into his cheeks.

"Put her there," he said and gripped Smokey's hand. The cowboy returned the grip. Something flashed between them, and he felt better about the situation. Unless he were dead wrong, Columbine Ames had a young but true-blue friend in Andy.

"We're riding in so Stockton can learn the truth," Smokey told the other.

"Too late. Hadley's beat you to it."

"Then we'll just have to convince him different." Smokey didn't give them time to protest but coolly marched ahead and around the bend. The house loomed before them. So did a group of hawk-faced riders. No open-faced cowboys here, bent on devilment but basically decent. Smokey thought of Joel's warning about the brakes.

Clannish. . .don't take kindly to strangers. . .a lot of men no longer welcome in Texas and New Mexico and Colorado are heading this way. . . Arizona is still pretty wild.

He could believe it from the looks of the bunch ahead, some lounging against the corral, others astride dark horses. "Which one's Stockton? I don't see Hadley."

His answer came in the form of a door slammed open so hard its bang resounded in the tense, waiting air. A man catapulted from the house. Smokey sized him up in a glance. Six feet, close to two hundred pounds, sandy hair, colorless eyes now blazing hatred and something unreadable. He flung himself across the porch, closely followed by Hadley, whose expression of triumph changed ludicrously when Smokey stepped into his line of vision.

Never one to let another get the drop on him, Smokey halted Stockton's impetuous rush toward Columbine with a clear, ringing call. "Hadley, how'd you have the guts to come back here after I caught you spying on Miss Ames at her bathing place?"

"*What's that?*" Like a tormented bull, the rancher whirled around. "Who the devil are you, and what are you doing here?" Understanding crept into his fury-driven brain. "Say, are you the puncher Hadley told me about?"

"Ump-umm. I'm the one he lied about." Smokey sprang forward. "I never saw your daughter before in my life, Stockton. I did some fishing, got turned around in the brakes, an' run across your foreman peeking through the bushes. He never saw anything. I got him just when Miss Ames had kicked off her moccasins." Truth rang white-hot in his voice.

"It's a lie, it's a lie," Hadley raved. Foam appeared at the corner of his mouth, and his eyes rolled. He reached for his gun and swore when his fingers touched the empty holster. "This cowboy jumped me 'cause I saw him following Colley."

"You told me they were meeting," Stockton roared, his great hands clenching and unclenching.

"I mighta been wrong," he mumbled. Streams of sweat ran down his dark face.

"He's a liar, Father." The bell-like voice turned the players in the scene to statues. Columbine stepped forward. "It happened just the way Mr. Travis said."

Smokey's heart nearly burst with pride. All the girl's earlier nervousness had fled. She stood straight and fearless, facing her enemies, as if protected by an unseen force.

"You—" Stockton snatched for his gun. Hadley's life hung in the balance.

"Hold it!" Smokey drew his gun so fast, a ripple of shock ran through the onlookers.

The rancher's half-raised revolver froze in midair. "Keep out of it, Travis," he roared.

Smokey didn't budge. "You want to kill a man right here before *your daughter?*" he ground out, instinctively hitting Stockton's weak spot.

The big man quivered. With a mighty backhand swing, he knocked Hadley senseless with the hand still holding the gun. "Haul him off the ranch, and tell him if I ever see him again, I'll shoot on sight." Raving, he glared at Smokey. "You ride out, too. If I owe you thanks, this will settle it." He pulled a fistful of bills from his shirt pocket and flung them on the ground in front of the cowboy.

"Father, how could you, after what he did?" Columbine's eyes became grief-filled gulfs; her face went hot with shame.

"Go to your room and stay there," he ordered.

She obeyed but only after saying in a voice that reached every person there, "At least I am grateful."

Smokey tipped his sombrero, kicked the money out of his way, and mounted Buckskin. "Glad to oblige. Adiós, Miss Ames, Stockton." He nodded at the others and winked at Andy, then touched his heels to the mare. But he couldn't resist hollering at the top of his lungs when she leaped and settled into a steady stride, "Yippee-ay!"

A quarter mile down the road, Smokey reined in and hid Buckskin in a cottonwood grove. His senses alert to possible pursuit, he wormed his way back and gained a vantage point from which he had a wide view of the ranch house, corral, and bunkhouse. Columbine and Stockton had vanished. Two disgusted-looking men busily loaded Hadley's limp form into a wagon. Young Andy stood by the corral gazing up at a window Smokey knew must be Columbine's. His hard, young face told its own story.

On impulse, Smokey worked closer, until his low call would reach the lad but not the others. "Andy," he hissed. "Don't turn. It's Smokey."

A convulsive jerk was the only sign the cowboy had heard.

"Start whistling, then kind of easylike walk to the cottonwoods," Smokey directed. He grunted with satisfaction at the nonchalant way Andy carried out his orders. He waited fifteen full minutes, then slithered back the way he'd come.

A white-faced rider stepped from the grove. "Mr. Travis, I—"

"Smokey."

Andy gulped. "Smokey. I 'most choked when you called Hadley." Admiration shone clear and bright in his brown eyes.

Playing on a hunch, Smokey demanded, "Why are you working for Stockton and his rustlers?" He planted his hands on his hips. The reply would help him take measure of the boy's manhood.

He wasn't disappointed. Andy offered neither an apology nor a stammering denial of the charge. "God an' me are the only friends Columbine Ames has. I've stood a lot to stay here for her sake."

"Are you in love with her?"

"I used to be." The steady gaze never wavered. "Who could help loving a girl like her?"

"And now?"

Seriousness gave way to fun. "Naw, I'm her friend. She needs that a heap more than a moonstruck hand her daddy-who-ain't would fire off the place in a minute. I've got another girl. How about you?"

Smokey roared and clapped him on the shoulder. "Never had much time for girls, but I'll be hanged if I've ever seen one like her."

"She's just as sweet and good inside as out," Andy told him. "Her ma

313

taught her the Bible, and if anyone lives it, why, that's got to be Columbine. She tried to make me promise I wouldn't ever shoot anyone, even a two-legged skunk. Says killing's plumb wrong and against everything God intended." His eyes slitted. "I didn't promise, though. If anyone ever lays a hand on her, I'll kill him."

"Can she shoot? Does she have a gun?"

"Yeah and yeah." Andy lowered his voice and repeated the story of Columbine's stay in the cave after her stepfather frightened her. "I made her keep my pistol and got me another one." He sighed, and his shoulders fell dejectedly. "I'm not sure she'd use it, though."

"Then we have to get her away from here."

Andy didn't act surprised that the stranger had pinpointed exactly what he'd decided weeks earlier. "We used to talk, but lately I can't get near her. Trouble is, she won't be eighteen 'til next July."

Smokey pondered. "Since Stockton's no blood kin, by law he has no right to keep her here against her will."

Andy snorted. "Law! In the Tonto? Man, if we had a sheriff, which we don't most of the time 'cept for one that meanders out here from Payson or Pine now and then, more 'n likely he'd be in for his cut." He raised an eyebrow. "How come I'm telling you all this, anyway? Who knows but what you're another Billy the Kid."

"I might be, but I'm not. Besides, look what happened to him," Smokey reminded. "Shot and killed before he was twenty-three. I don't figure on that happening to me." *Especially now,* he mentally added.

"Shh," Andy warned, crouching low. The *clip-clop* of hooves on the road and the sound of voices stilled them until the wagon with Hadley had moved out of sight.

"So what can be proved against Stockton?" Smokey didn't want to waste any time.

"Not a thing so far." Andy grimaced, and a lock of his bright hair fell over his forehead. "I suspect the big roundup he's planning will be the last. He hinted as much to Columbine, said he'd gotten tired of Arizona. I ain't supposed to know this, but I listen real good in the bunkhouse when I'm snoring the loudest." A likable grin lit up his face. "The men are uneasy, wondering what's going to happen, so Stockton ain't told them everything. Say, who're you riding for?"

"The Double J."

Andy let out a whistle. "That's where I aimed to go looking for a job after

I found out there's a lot of shady goings-on down here. Then Columbine needed me."

"There will always be a job on the Double J any time you want it," Smokey assured him. "If we could get Miss Ames there, the Scotts would take her in."

"I figured she could probably get on clerking at Babbitt's in Flag," Andy put in.

"I'm not sure she'd be safe there. She would be at the ranch." A look of complete understanding passed between them, then Andy reluctantly stood.

"I'd better get back. Stockton's suspicious of everyone these days." He cocked his head and grinned. "It would be a fine thing if an upstanding cowboy who doesn't drink or smoke or hang around saloons and loose women fell in love with Columbine and her with him. Of course, he'd have to figure out how to kidnap her and marry her without Zeke knowing it."

Smokey felt red creep under his skin, but he blandly agreed. "A fine thing. If I meet a feller like that, I'll tell him to keep it in mind."

Andy haw-hawed and slipped away. Smokey thoughtfully retrieved Buckskin, who stood grazing nearby, and headed northwest, forgetting that he'd planned to fish some more. Now all he wanted was to get to the Double J and figure out what to do about a slip of a girl with big blue eyes and a flower face who bloomed pure and innocent in the blackest of surroundings.

When he came to the trampled grass and bushes that led to the little pool where he first saw her, Smokey couldn't resist turning out of his way to visit the spot again. How had he missed the beauty of the glade, the shining water in the early evening hush, the white sand and whispering cottonwoods? "Whoa," he told Buckskin and slid from the saddle. He retraced his steps. Here he had seen Hadley, evil all over his face. Fresh rage washed over him, but he shoved it aside and walked into the clearing. His face stared back at him from the still pool. Black eyes blazed; black hair crept from beneath his sombrero. A grim line to his jaw dissolved in a reluctant smile. "If I looked like that when I came bursting from the bushes, it's a wonder she didn't run from Hadley *an'* me," he told his watery image.

A few minutes later, he went back to his horse, wondering why the secluded spot seemed hallowed by the girl's presence, and something more. A sleepy birdsong followed him, the whirr of wings. Unwilling to break the pensive mood that had overtaken him, Smokey rode slowly until he found a good spot to make camp.

After a frugal meal from the supplies he carried in his saddlebags, he stretched out with his head on his saddle, a blanket around him. Great white stars smiled down, mysterious and knowing. A gentle wind rose and crooned through the trees. More keenly than ever before, Smokey realized how right Joel had been. *Arizona did have a music of its own: of good and evil, happiness and danger, beauty and ugliness. But most of all, of love.*

Chapter 8

"Boss, can I talk to you?"

Joel Scott looked up from the bridle he was mending. "Sure, Smokey. What's on your mind?" Dead serious, Smokey lounged against the barn door, his face somber. His tanned cheeks flushed slightly, but his gaze remained steady.

"Do you believe in love at first sight?"

Joel gasped and dropped the bridle. Never in a thousand years would he have expected such a question. "Why. . ." His face showed shock.

"The first time you saw Rebecca Fairfax, did you feel kinda warm inside, that you'd do anything to protect her?" Smokey anxiously waited for the answer. Since he had returned from the Tonto Basin, a fair-haired girl's flower face and blue eyes seldom left his thoughts. Neither did the anger that she lived in a nest of vipers. Cautiously, he had sounded out the hands in the bunkhouse without telling them why. Lonesome, Dusty, Kansas, and Cheyenne all declaimed Zeke Stockton vehemently. As Lonesome put it, his show of respectability "doesn't fool no one."

Foreman Fred Aldrich, who kept the Double J outfit on the straight and narrow, added sourly, "He's pure mean and poison underneath but smoother than cream when he takes the notion."

The peril surrounding Columbine Ames was real, Smokey reflected soberly as he listened eagerly to Joel's reply. The young cowboy minister's eyes glowed like the Arizona sky at its bluest.

"You've hit it square, Pard. And every time I saw her after that, it got worse."

"Ah-uh. That's what I figured."

"Once I knew she cared, too, I felt God had led me to New Mexico so I could not only find my father but meet her and save her from Hayes." Remembrance crept into his face. "It's all I can do to wait a few more weeks until we marry." His expression changed. "Womenfolk need more time to get ready, I guess, but I'm glad we waited until we could be with the whole family." He let out a cowboy yell that startled the horses in the corral and set them to dancing. The next instant, he quietly asked, "Who is she?"

"Who is who?" But Smokey knew his face gave him away.

"The Arizona girl you want to protect." Joel wasn't to be sidetracked.

Smokey gave up all pretense of merely asking for information of the heart. "I ran across a mess down in the Tonto." He described his recent adventure in a few terse sentences. "Columbine Ames looks just like the flower, kinda frail an' delicate. She's not, though. You should have seen her stand up to Zeke Stockton, 'her daddy-who-ain't,' Andy Cullen calls him."

"Who's Andy Cullen?" Joel demanded. "I already know—too well—who Stockton is." The corners of his mouth turned down.

"A shock-haired kid, maybe eighteen. Corn-colored hair, big brown eyes that don't miss much, an' according to him, Columbine's only friend, except God." Smokey noticed how his friend's face lit up, as if someone had set a fire behind his eyes.

"If she knows God, she has a protector," Joel reminded.

"Sure, but doggone it, I hate to think there's no one looking after her here on earth except Andy. He's a hothead, an' sooner or later, Stockton will get wise to him an' boot him off the Cross Z. What'll she do then?"

A little pool of silence fell between them, the silence of range men comfortable with one another. Then Smokey added, "I've seen lots of pretty faces an' lots of good girls, but I never saw one whose eyes are so innocent. You know she's the real thing all the way through. Andy said her ma taught her from the Bible." He shifted his weight and dug the toe of one boot into the dusty ground. "There's something about her that makes a man, if he *is* a man, want to take care of her."

"Is that all?"

Smokey shook his head and looked without fear into his boss's sympathetic face. "Before you rode up to the Lazy F, I never thought no girl or woman could beat Rebecca." He raised his head and watched a hawk sail by. It reminded him of the predatory look in Hadley's face. "I always knew, though, I wasn't the one for her, 'specially when you came. I still think she's pretty close to one of those angels you talk about, an' I'm proud to be her friend all this time." His clear eyes held frank pride.

"I appreciate your honesty," Joel told him.

"Somehow, it's different with Columbine. Don't say anything to Perkins. He's a true an' faithful pard, but he talks too much, an' I don't feel like being joshed. She might never even look at a cowpoke like me. She sure won't if her stepdaddy has his say." Smokey's face darkened, and his hands clenched.

"Stockton about went crazy when his wife died, an' Columbine's the picture of her mother, according to Andy. He thinks Stockton's got them kind of confused in his mind. Anyway, he's bound to marry her with or without her say-so."

"And you aim to stop him."

"I do." Smokey's eyes glittered, and he straightened. "Boss, what I want to know is, are you with me? You saved my life, an we've been comrades ever since. If somehow Andy an' I can smuggle her here, will you back me?"

"With all my heart." Joel's hand shot out, and Smokey gripped it, feeling the depth of commitment in the clasp. "Stockton has no legal claim on the girl. If she needs a place to stay, Judith and Rebecca and everyone else here on the ranch will make her welcome." His eyes sparkled. "At least until you convince her that Columbine Travis is a better handle than Columbine Ames."

Smokey's grip tightened at the idea, and his heart pounded. "An' if necessary, you'll fight for her?"

A shadow clouded Joel's blue eyes. "We'll pray God uses a different way, but yes, we'll fight for her. If she's as sweet as you say, every man on the Double J will defend her."

All during the fall roundup, Smokey went through the physical motions while his mind was far away. Every time he saw Conchita waiting on the little cabin porch for Jim, he smiled and saw himself riding in to find Columbine standing on a similar porch, her blue dress fluttering. Sometimes he called himself loco, but the dreams persisted. They intensified as the day grew closer for Joel and Rebecca's wedding. They'd chosen to keep it simple, with only family and the outfit present. Once when Smokey reported in from the range, he saw Rebecca's bright brown head bent over some frothy white stuff that looked like a waterfall. The happiness in her brown eyes when she looked up brought a smile to his lips. Perhaps someday. . .

Curly and Mrs. Cook had already tied the knot. He drove her into Flag, ostensibly to order supplies. She came back wearing a store-bought dark blue dress with white frill at the neck and a brand-new wedding ring! "We didn't want to take the shine off your and Becky's wedding," the new bride told Joel and Rebecca. "Figured this was best." She cast a proud look at Curly, resplendent in a new cowboy outfit complete with bright scarf and Stetson. "We'd have liked for you to hitch us, but I reckon we're just as married this way."

That night a loud singing rang around the cabin hastily vacated by Smokey. He moved into the bunkhouse with the rest of the Double J hands, all of whom had long since been foiled in their tricks and now accepted him as one of them. His cheerful attitude and willingness to do more than his fair share of the hard work had been his initiation to the ranch.

Smokey also had hours to consider his growing feelings concerning the Scripture Joel used when he preached every Sabbath afternoon. No one on the Double J listened more carefully than the New Mexico cowhand. Not one of the townspeople who faithfully drove out for services realized that in the rough-hewn cowboy's innermost places, the cry for God gradually grew to a shout.

One crisp afternoon astride Buckskin, Smokey opened up to God. "I can see a feller needs the Almighty, but, God, if You're the Trailmate Joel and Gideon say You are, how come You made rattlesnakes like Zeke Stockton?"

Buckskin had no answer, and Smokey rode on, torn between conviction and his determination to serve Columbine. How could he invite the Lord into a heart bent on freeing her from bondage, no matter what the cost?

At last the roundup ended with the herd bunched and ready to drive to the market. As soon as they'd been sold and the cowboys came home, Joel and Rebecca would marry. Smokey began to breathe easier. No more had been heard of Stockton and his crooked dealings or of Hadley. Then Jim Perkins rode in, wearing a bloody bandage and madder than a wet cat. He tumbled off his sorrel mare, blazing eyes showing he hadn't been fatally wounded, and clumped to the bunkhouse porch. "Half the herd's been stolen," he blurted out. "Saddle up." He reeled and would have fallen if Smokey hadn't leaped forward and caught him. He lowered Jim to his own bunk. "Go get Conchita, someone," he barked.

"No," Jim hollered. "It'll scare her to death. Get some of the blood off me first."

"Hey, Aldrich," Lonesome sang out when the foreman appeared in the doorway to see what had caused the commotion. "Our herd's done gone astray with some help from rustlers."

He sprang into action. "Kansas, get Gideon and Joel. Cheyenne, ride for Eb Sears. Good thing his cabin ain't far. Dusty, the rest of you, we're ridin' soon as you can get the horses saddled."

So it had come, the fight the Double J had expected. Smokey hastily removed the stained bandage from Perkins's head, but before he could bathe the slight groove, the women arrived and took over.

"Snappin' crocodiles, the first excitement since I reached Arizona, and here I am weaker'n a newborn foal!" Jim complained.

"Hush." Conchita pushed him back on the bunk. "They can get along without you."

"That's what I'm afeared of," he said comically. "Once the boys find out I ain't necessary, I'll be out of a job."

Smokey laughed along with the others, then hurried out. Buckskin stood saddled and waiting, courtesy of one of the hands. A quick leap into the saddle, a touch of boot heels to her sides, and she responded like the thoroughbred she was.

A long night followed, then a day and another night. The tracks led into the worst part of the brakes. Before the pursuers left the ranch, Jim had admitted he didn't know how long he'd been knocked out, so the rustlers could have had a head start. Yet the unshaven Double J riders kept on. Smokey didn't voice his fear that this was Stockton's doing. He could be wrong. The supposedly honest rancher and his cohorts weren't the only outlaws in the Tonto. Yet from the start, a dozen comments floated to his ears about "Stockton's doings."

Once, a wild idea crossed his mind. This would be a perfect time to rescue Columbine. With Zeke busy elsewhere, Smokey could spirit her away. Yet for better or for what would certainly be worse, his loyalty to the outfit prevented desertion even for a worthy cause.

By late afternoon, they knew they were closing in. Riders outstripped moving cattle even when constrained by the need for caution. Ahead lay a box canyon Aldrich pronounced ideal for rustled cattle: water, plenty of grass, and no way out once they were inside. "Dismount, and don't show yourselves," he ordered. "Duck from the thickets to behind trees and keep low. There's bound to be lookouts. They'll know we had more than one night guard."

Dread filled Smokey at what lay before them. Why did the God Joel preached about let wicked men despoil this beautiful country? Would some of the Double J outfit be killed in the fight?

Grazing cattle filled the canyon. Yellow leaves turned in the breeze and fell. Dark pines and cedar contrasted with the golden world.

"All right, rustlers. We've got enough men to keep you holed in until Judgment Day," Aldrich bawled. His voice echoed against the rock walls of the canyon. "This is Aldrich, Double J."

A string of curses followed, splintering the mountain air. "Come 'n' git us."

"We don't have to," Lonesome yelled.

Have to, have to, came the echo.

"We'll just stick out here 'til you starve," Dusty bellowed, and again it echoed.

Coarse laughter followed. Aldrich and his men pulled back into the mouth of the canyon and made camp out of rifle shot. Smokey pondered the situation and walked to Joel, who stared at the herd with misery in his face. "Think there has to be killing?"

"I hope not. I'm sworn not to kill, but I can't let our outfit be gunned down, and we can't just let rustlers steal our cattle." His still-boyish face looked sick.

"I have an idea that might work. Wait until dark an' let me get the lay of the land," Smokey whispered. The moment dusk fell, he slipped away, worked clear around the herd, and came back grinning. "We can do it an' never fire a shot," he gleefully told the outfit who gathered around him. "Here's my plan. There's no cabin; the rustlers are camped at the far end of the canyon. Only three men are guarding the herd 'cause they can't go anywhere except this way. Now what we do is. . ." He laid it out nice and sweet. "Aldrich, what do you say? Boss? Sears?"

All nodded, and Lonesome burst out admiringly, "Say, you're a smart cuss."

"I will be if it works," Smokey reminded him as he settled his sombrero more firmly on his head. "Remember, don't make any noise until I holler."

"Then all everything's gonna break loose," one of the cowboys chimed in.

"We hope." Smokey raised his hand and crossed his fingers. "I'll give you fifteen minutes to get in your places."

He disappeared back into the welcome darkness. The moon had obligingly stayed behind a ridge, and a few clouds hid some of the stars. Smokey again skirted the herd to the opposite side, noting with satisfaction the way they had bunched together for the night. "All right, Buckskin," he commanded in a low voice. "Yippee-ay!" His shout rang sudden and clear, magnified by the echoes in the canyons and returned by the band of Double J cowboys. Smokey followed it up by shooting in the air and riding straight into the herd.

The pandemonium caused by the echoes spooked the herd. First they milled, then ably assisted by the Double J rider bent low in the saddle, the cattle began to run toward the mouth of the canyon. "Whoopee!" Smokey roared and followed, shooting until his revolver emptied, then reloading while he rode. He could hear Aldrich bellowing orders from one side, Joel on the other. A volley of shots from the upper end of the canyon harmlessly whistled past, and Smokey laughed jubilantly. Yet when his comrades had driven the herd out of the canyon and toward the distant Double J, he couldn't resist the temptation to tether Buckskin at a safe distance and creep back to the rustlers' fire. Like a snake, he slithered on his belly to a lookout behind a small pile of rock that had fallen from the canyon walls.

Carefully he raised his head and froze. *Hadley!* He scanned the other faces, many bearded, all dark and sullen. Relief shot through him. Stockton wasn't among them.

Footfalls a little to his right made him drop his face until the sombrero hid the gleam of moonlight on his cheeks. Three more angry men had joined the little band by the small fire.

"Where in the name of all that's holy were you?" Hadley raged, his face livid in the firelight. A scar on one side of his face, evidently from Stockton's gun, showed clearly. "Fine bunch you are. Let the Double J ride out of here with a herd yore supposed to be guardin'."

"You couldn't a-done no better," one flared. Smokey recognized him as a Cross Z man, one of those by the corral the day he took Columbine home. A little thrill went through him.

"Yore loco. I never shoulda took you on when I split with Stockton," Hadley snapped.

"Quit bellyachin', Hadley," someone called. Smokey turned toward the voice. A dark figure had thrown a saddle over a horse and stood pulling the girth tight. He swung aboard. "The Double J outfit's gonna be back here as soon as they get the herd settled down. I'm ridin' out before they come. This deal stinks like a dead skunk. I wasn't above double-crossin' Stockton, but I ain't aimin' to get killed, 'specially now there's no cattle deal." He spurred his horse and disappeared in the darkness.

Hadley swore and pulled his gun, but a hand next to him knocked it upward before he could pull the trigger. "No use wastin' bullets. He's right. Let's scatter and meet somewheres healthier." A murmur of assent ran through the band of men.

Hadley lowered his voice and gestured, and the men nodded. "Slip past while they're still settlin' the herd," their leader called. "No sense gettin' yore-selves killed. Nobody seen us, so they can't prove nothin'."

Oh, yeah? Smokey grinned in the shadows. *Well, Mr. Rustler Hadley, you're wrong about that. Dead wrong.* His grin faded. This time there had been no killing, but what about the next time? And the next? Soberly, Smokey rejoined his outfit and told them the outlaws had sneaked off. Privately, he wondered why he felt so glad Zeke Stockton had not been part of the raid.

Shortly after reaching the ranch, the cowboys collected the rest of the cattle earmarked for sale and made their drive. "The ones that got stolen dropped a bit in weight," he told Joel. "But that's just so many more that won't be stolen over the winter when they drift down into the draws."

"Right, and we avoided a shoot-out." Joel beamed.

"That's 'cause I wasn't there," Perkins told them. He cocked one eyebrow and flashed the cherubic smile he used on occasion to infuriate his pards.

"At least we're not letting any little old no-'count hurt keep us from working," Smokey told him sarcastically.

"Connie says I can't ride 'til it's healed." Jim smirked. "She's afraid I might get blood poisonin' or sunstroke or—"

Smokey cut off his list of possible maladies by snorting loudly. As he walked off with Joel, he couldn't help grinning at his boss. "Jim's never going to get over missing our raid."

Joel sighed. "I'm afraid there will be more." He shrugged. "Winter should be quiet except for the sound of hammering. There's plenty of room in the ranch house, but I can't wait for Rebecca and me to have our own home."

Days later, the golden-haired man and pretty Rebecca in her white gown stood before Gideon and pledged their love and lives to one another. She looked more like an angel than ever to Smokey, but, to Smokey's amazement, when she lifted her face toward her new husband, her features changed. Silvery fair hair replaced nut-brown. Radiant blue eyes shone instead of merry brown.

He drew in a quick breath. Could a man ask for more in life than Joel now had: a share in a ranch, a charming companion-wife, a God whose presence never faltered? No matter what storms came, the two who had promised to become one could stand.

Words from months earlier came into his mind. . .*after the fire a still small voice.* Joel and Rebecca knew that voice and heeded it. So did Gideon and Judith, Eb and Lily Sears, Lige and Naomi, and even Cyrus Scott, who had ignored it for long years. An unspoken prayer rose in Smokey's heart. *Please. . .* But he couldn't go on. Too many things crowded it out as the wind and the earthquake and the fire had in the Bible story. Smokey sighed. Would he ever come to terms with life and God? The minor strain in the music of the Arizona mountains so often foreshadowed joy. As if on cue, the next day Andy Cullen arrived at the Double J.

Chapter 9

A wide grin lit up Andy Cullen's likable face and set his mischievous brown eyes twinkling. "Howdy." He slid from the saddle of the nondescript horse carrying the Z brand and strode toward Smokey. "What's the chances of a bed and some of that Southern hospitality the Double J's famous for?"

Smokey leaped from his seat on the top bunkhouse step where he'd been waiting for Curly to beat the supper gong. "You're a sight for sore eyes," he told the younger rider. "All duded up, too." His quick gaze took in new jeans, checked shirt, and bright neckerchief. "How'd you get out of jail?"

Andy's grin faded. "It ain't jail for me but—" He lowered his voice and mysteriously nodded his head toward the corral.

Smokey got the message. Together they strolled to the privacy of the corral, empty except for horses. Tired riders had finished their day's work and headed for soap and water before the supper call.

"Is everyone all right at the ranch?" Smokey held his breath.

Andy's steady gaze never wavered. "Sure, if you think being penned up's all right." He then burst out indignantly, "Ever since that business with Hadley, Stockton's been a bear. I don't know how much longer I can hang on. Only reason I got away was 'cause of a sore tooth that needed pulling, so I came to Flag." He gingerly patted his jaw, and Smokey saw the slight swelling.

Andy went on. "Columbine's getting real pale and thin, not that she's ever been what anyone would call real sturdy except inside. A couple of times we got a minute to chat. She doesn't know what to make of Zeke." Andy pulled off his sombrero and tousled his already messed-up shock of hair. "Says he's leaving her strictly alone. I guess he hasn't mentioned you or Hadley or anything except she's not to get out of sight of the ranch house." Andy snorted inelegantly. "It's pitiful. Columbine's always loved the woods and to run free and wild. Once I saw a squirrel a feller had in a cage. It just went round and round. I waited 'til the man's back was turned, then just happened to lurch against the cage. The latch jarred loose. The squirrel took off and never came back."

Smokey caught the significance of the story. He sighed, his dark eyes troubled. "Sounds like Miss Ames needs someone to get her loose, that is, accidentally."

"Just before I rode out, I made so bold as to holler, 'Miss Columbine, you need anything from Flag?' Zeke clouded up like a summer storm, but all his scowling didn't faze her.

" 'Why, thanks, Cullen,' sez she. Zeke hates it if she calls the men by first names. Anyway, she asked me to wait for a minute while she made a list. Her eyes got all shiny, and she said, 'I need white thread and some buttons; I'll give you one to match.'

" 'I ain't in no hurry,' I told her, not being eager to get a tooth pulled. Stockton didn't budge, so I settled more comfortable in the saddle until she came out and give me an envelope." His eyes gleamed. "Funny thing. When I got to Flag and pulled it out, I found a list, a button, and this." He held out another envelope, creased from being folded into a tiny packet.

"What. . ." Smokey stared. Blood rushed to his clear, tanned skin. *Mr. Smokey Travis* in steady handwriting adorned the envelope.

"That's what I thought," Andy explained cheerfully. "When it took longer than I figured at the doctor's—he ain't much better than a horse doctor—why, it got too late to start back today." His voice hardened. "Besides, Columbine Ames gave me a letter to deliver 'cause she trusted me. I didn't want to pass it on to just anybody."

"Thanks, Andy." Smokey still couldn't believe he actually held a message from the girl whose face haunted him.

"Reckon I'll go get some of the trail dust off me," Andy considerately told him and walked back toward the bunkhouse.

Gratitude for the plucky young man's loyalty filled Smokey. He glanced both ways to make sure no one observed him, then took the further precaution of slowly wandering to the shade of a nearby aspen. The greenish-white trunk showed naked now that most of the golden leaves had fallen. He tore open the envelope, noting the lack of any attempt at sealing.

Dear Mr. Travis—Smokey,

I apologize for Father's rudeness. He can be pleasant but lately appears to have a lot on his mind.

Perhaps someday I will see you again. Your actions and chivalry told me you would be a good friend, if circumstances were different. God bless you.

Instead of a signature, a tiny sketch showed a delicate Rocky Mountain columbine waving in a breeze.

If he hadn't adored her already, the brief note would have sealed his infatuation. The words blurred. He, Smokey Travis, considered chivalrous by a girl trapped in the Tonto Basin! He read the message again, rejoicing that it had come, then stuffed it inside his shirt, where it lay close to his heart. Wearing a range-weary look as a mask, he answered the summons for supper when it came.

Known for an open welcome for any drifting cowpuncher who needed bed and board, the Double J saw nothing unusual about Andy's visit. Lonesome plied him with questions about fish in the creeks. Dusty reckoned he'd go catch one soon as the ranch could spare him. The other boys alternately joshed and heckled the visitor.

Smokey barely controlled the urge to knock his comrades' heads together. He wanted to talk with Andy alone. Knowing Smokey's intentions, the young man yawned and stood.

"Me for a little fresh air before hitting the sack. Smokey, you want any?"

"Might as well." Leisurely, he followed Andy out.

"If you happen to want to send an answer, I could smuggle it in to her with the thread and buttons," the go-between tempted.

Smokey's heart bounced. "Are you sure she's safe with Stockton?" he whispered.

"For now."

The sound of steps and Lonesome's plaintive, "I gotta roll out early. Wish a coupla galoots would get in here so we c'n blow out the lamp," ended the conversation.

The next morning, Smokey volunteered to check on a fence in the direction Andy had to take. Out of sight of the ranch, he fumbled in his jacket pocket for pencil and paper and dashed off a quick note. "Here, give her this. An' if she ever needs me, send word."

"I will." The note vanished under the string of a small, brown-paper package before Andy shoved it in his shirt. Moments later, he galloped off, leaving Smokey to watch him out of sight. How he wished he could be the one heading toward the Cross Z and Columbine!

He mulled over Andy's dubious assurance that, at least for the present, Zeke offered no threat. What of the upcoming winter months, months filled with idle hours? Smokey shivered. If only he had a way to get Columbine to the Double J. If he rode in, Stockton would throw him out. If he enlisted

Andy's aid in abduction, the boy would be fired if discovered, no matter how willing the victim was to go. Then Columbine would have to stand off her stepfather alone. Smokey couldn't take the risk.

There on the range, with Buckskin standing quietly beneath him, Smokey bared his head and looked toward heaven. "I don't know You very well, but she does. She trusts an' believes in You. Don't let her down." After a few seconds, he crammed the hat back on his dark hair and goaded the mare into a dead run.

—+—

When Zeke Stockton dismissed Smokey ungraciously, Columbine had fled for the safety of her room. Screened by her window curtain, she watched the rest of the drama. Her keen eyes observed the disdainful way the young man kicked the money Stockton had flung at him out of the way. She heard the farewell, "Adiós," in the clear, carrying voice followed by the wild, "Yippee-ay!"

Her heart thundered in her chest, but she never took her fascinated gaze from the scene. She caught Andy looking up toward her window, and then a slight movement of bushes a little behind the cowboy alerted her senses. "He must have slipped back," she murmured. Fear attacked her. "Please, God, don't let him get caught." There had been one near-killing today. If Smokey returned, tragedy might result.

Heavy footsteps in the hall froze her in place.

"Colley?" A light rap on the door brought her upright and away from the window. She leaped to her bed and called, "Come in."

Zeke opened the door and stepped inside, his large frame almost filling the doorway. "I want the truth. Have you been meeting with Travis?"

"I have not. Everything happened just as he said." She proudly raised her head. "You know me; you shouldn't have to ask such a question."

A subtle change softened the suspicion in his face. "How am I supposed to keep track of what you do?" The closest thing to an apology shone in his colorless eyes. "You're a good girl. Always have been. But you can't trust these drifters. None of them is any good, and they'll chase anything in skirts."

Columbine wanted to cry out in defense of the one who had saved her from embarrassment if not worse. But a look at Zeke's face halted the rush of words. "He isn't a drifter," she instead offered meekly. "Smokey Travis came west with Joel Scott and works for the Double J."

"Wha—at?" There was nothing colorless about his eyes now. They flamed with hatred. A choking laugh came from his corded throat. "Of all the—Travis is with the Double J? That lying outfit that drove an honest rancher out of the Flag area?"

Columbine stifled the questions that surfaced instantly in her mind: *Honest? Were you?*

"If it hadn't been for them, we'd be bigger than the Double J and living in a fine house near Flag," he mumbled. Cunning crept into his expression. He turned to go out, then paused. She had the feeling his mind had been far away from the present. "Stick within sight of the ranch house until I say different."

"But that means I can't ride at all," she protested. "You don't expect me to stay cooped up in here, do you?"

"You'll do as I say." His great fist hit the door frame with a solid thud. "And with no backtalk. I won't have another happening like today. There's not a man on the place who wouldn't do the same, including the Cullen whelp. Keep away from all of them." He stomped down the hall.

"I won't," Columbine rebelliously told the walls that had already begun to close in on her. But in the next weeks, she had little choice. Anytime her stepfather rode out, at least one rider remained, conspicuously perched on the corral fence or the porch of the bunkhouse, his face turned in her direction. Being caught by one of Stockton's men offered no better a situation than living in a cage.

The restrictions made their mark. The face in her mirror became paler than ever, the slim figure more finely tuned. Shadows deepened beneath her listless eyes until even Zeke, preoccupied with many thoughts, noticed. "Are you ailing?"

"No, I just miss being able to ride." She toyed with the delicious food she had prepared and laid down her fork. "I don't have much appetite when I can't get out."

The next day, he tapped at the door of her cabin refuge. "The horses are saddled. Come on."

To her amazement, he accompanied her on the first real ride she had taken since he delivered his edict. He even agreed to an impromptu race, and in his heavy-handed manner, complimented her when she beat him back to the corral by several lengths. From then on, they rode almost every afternoon. Yet the knowledge her freedom had been stolen kept Columbine from fully enjoying the exercise. She couldn't help remembering the way Zeke had insulted the dark-haired cowboy from the Double J and burned with shame each time she remembered it. If only she could make up for it!

Her opportunity came unexpectedly and after much prayer. One morning, she stepped outside to the whinny of horses, the chill of impending winter, and an intensely blue sky. Zeke stood frowning on the porch. Andy Cullen lounged in the saddle of a restless horse.

"I suppose you have to go, but get back immediately," Zeke barked.

"Sure, Boss. Soon as I get rid of this doggoned tooth." Andy touched his scarf-wrapped cheek. He grinned at the girl and raised his voice. "Miss Columbine, you need anything from Flag?"

She started to shake her head but saw the look in Andy's eyes and hesitated. A thrill shot through her. She did need something. Hadn't she been praying about it for days? Scarcely knowing what she replied, she caught Andy's almost imperceptible nod and ran to her room. A list. White thread. A dozen buttons like one she slipped into an envelope. She finished her meager list, dashed off a short note, and without reading it, shoved it into an envelope that folded into the other and tripped lightly down the stairs. "Thanks, A—, er, Cullen." She watched him ride away and forced herself to turn to Zeke. "Breakfast is nearly ready."

Another waiting period began. She mentally rode every foot of the way from the Tonto to Flag and beyond. Andy Cullen rode in just before dusk, cheerful as ever. "Sure glad to get that tooth out, Boss. Here's Miss Columbine's thread and buttons." He handed over a small parcel.

Her spirits sank. Even though she'd tried to tell herself he had no need to answer, her heart protested that Smokey would respond. He hadn't. Never in the world would Andy have entrusted the package to Zeke if it contained anything except her notions. Depressed, she caught the package Zeke tossed and managed to thank Andy. The slight raising of one eyebrow and a quickly hidden grin brightened the evening. Thank God for her one remaining friend on the ranch.

The parcel lay unopened during the hours between its arrival and bedtime. She remembered to take it upstairs with her after bidding Zeke good night. When she shifted it to her left hand so she could open her bedroom door with her right, it crackled. Babbitt's had certainly wrapped it well. Suddenly an idea occurred to her. She stepped inside and felt her way to a table to light a lamp. Taking the precaution of shooting home the sturdy bolt lock Zeke had installed on her door, Columbine ripped open the brown paper. A small sheet of folded white paper fell to the floor. She snatched it up and devoured the contents.

Dear Miss Ames,

You are always welcome on the Double J, whenever you want to come and for as long as you want to stay. I feel sure that one day you will come. Trust in Andy and in that God of yours and in me.

A tiny campfire with a smudge of smoke served as a signature.

Happy tears crowded behind her eyelids. Much of her despair and loneliness subsided. She read it over, feeling a hidden meaning in the first part. When she came to the last sentence, she halted. *Trust in. . .that God of yours. . . .* Disappointment blotted out her happiness. "God, does this mean he doesn't believe in You? If not, why would he write it this way?" Into the dark morning hours, she wrestled with the knotty problem. Her joy had been tarnished by the revealing words.

Before she could fully interpret the letter, Zeke made a surprising move. One night following their supper meal, he said, "Colley, I've been thinking things over. You're young, and you need a husband. No one can give you what I can. There's trouble brewing. Hadley's coaxed off a bunch of our riders. I won't be able to do the roundup until spring." He leaned forward, and the lamplight showed the rigid way he held his body. "I can wait. The winter and next spring are yours to get ready. Next July, we'll head for Flag and the Fourth of July celebration there. You'll like it. Horse races, a picnic, all kinds of goings-on. Your birthday's the tenth, so we'll stick around Flag and be married then. You'll be eighteen and a woman, just like your mother."

She wanted to hurl the lamp at him, to disclaim any intention of ever taking her mother's place in his life. But an inner warning that to do so meant the loss of even those precious months placed a guard on her lips.

"You hear me, Colley?"

"I do." Lamplight glowed on her lowered head.

Evidently satisfied, Zeke leaned back in his chair. From under downcast lashes, she saw the relaxing of his shoulders. She had promised nothing, but he took it for everything. Did she dare tread on the frail foundation of security formed by his decree? She must. To spend months in the imprisoned state of the past weeks would drive her mad.

"May I ride again? If I take someone, Andy, perhaps? Once the men know what you plan, none of them will dare do anything to challenge you."

"You're not in love with Cullen, are you?"

"No. I never have been, and besides, he has a girl." How good to be able to look him straight in the eye, honestly and without guile. "I thank you for riding with me, but you don't really have the time, do you?"

He hesitated, then grudgingly gave in. "No. As long as Cullen keeps his hands off, it's all right."

"Thank you, Father." She rose, knowing if she didn't leave the room, her triumph would give her away. This small concession meant hope for the future.

"I'll announce it tomorrow."

"All right." What did it matter when or what he proclaimed or to whom? She had taken no vows, given no consent.

The next morning, he called in the remaining men and said briefly, "I aim to marry Colley on her birthday next July. Until then, Cullen, you'll ride with her when I can't."

For once even Andy appeared speechless. Columbine saw his look of reproach, and she sent him a signal with her eyes. To her relief, he relaxed and said, "Thanks, Boss. I'll take good care of her."

"See that you do, or you'll answer to me." Stockton turned on his heel and strode back into the house.

For the benefit of the outfit, Columbine called, "Bring the horses up at once, Cullen."

"Yes, Ma'am." Stone-faced but with a wink that threatened to send her into hysterics, Andy headed for the bunkhouse, trailed by the others in small chattering groups.

One more bridge remained to be crossed, and Columbine marched toward it waving banners outwardly and cringing on the inside. Fortified by reading her Bible and strengthened by prayer, she approached Zeke. "Will you do something for me, please?"

"Anything." He threw down a paper on which he'd been figuring, a half smile on his lips.

She stood there before him, young, innocent, wearing unconscious pathos. "This is so different and hard for me to get used to. Will you—can you—I just don't want you to kiss me." She brought out her winning hand. "No one's ever kissed me but Mother. Until I'm a bride. . . ?" She clasped her hands.

A dull red suffused his heavy face. Something flickered in his eyes. If she could win this victory, she thought, surely the months that stretched ahead would be bearable.

"All right, Colley." His husky voice betrayed his feelings and won him more respect than he had ever garnered from his stepdaughter.

"Thank you." She held out one slim hand. He took it, clutched it convulsively, then pulled back. She had won another skirmish, one more battle in her fight for freedom. God willing, she would also win the war.

Chapter 10

True to his word, Zeke made no demands on Columbine. As late fall slipped into winter, she dreamed only of a dark-eyed cowboy. Twice Andy delivered carefully concealed notes to Smokey; by the same means, she replied.

I hate the secrecy, Smokey wrote to her. *I'd like to ride in and tell Stockton I've come to see you, but Andy says no.*

Her heartbeat quickened when she read the simple words, and she wrote back, warning him not to do anything foolish. Just before Christmas, Andy appeared with horses saddled as usual for their afternoon ride. Snow might blanket the peaks near Flag and fall on the Double J, but winters in the Tonto Basin generally stayed pleasant. So far they had ridden every day. Always Columbine felt Zeke's quick survey of her when she came back, but he said nothing. She made a point of acting natural even when her faithful friend sang the praises of a certain Smokey Travis, causing her to blush profusely.

Once out of earshot of the lounging men on the bunkhouse porch, Andy said in a low voice, "I have a surprise for you."

"Really?" Columbine's mouth turned up. Seldom did they complete a ride without his showing her a late flower, a curious rock formation, or an unusual cloud formation. "Will I like it?"

"I should smile." He did and broke into a contagious laugh.

"Is it big or small?"

"Mmm, medium."

"What color?"

"Lots of colors." He laughed again, and his brown eyes twinkled. "Black and tan, mostly."

"A deer like the one we saw last week?"

He nearly fell from his saddle in his glee. "You might say that. Don't ask so many questions."

"Just one more," she teased. "Is it living or dead?"

His corn-colored hair fell over his forehead from under his sombrero. "Haw, haw! Not dead, that's for sure."

"Then it can't be a rock or a tree," she reasoned aloud. Her comment sent Andy into another spasm. She ignored him and obediently guided her horse after him, too intent on wondering what the surprise might be to pay much attention to the path they took. When Andy reined in his horse, she did the same and looked around. "Why, we're at the cave."

"Wait here," Andy told her mysteriously. He dismounted and tossed his horse's reins over its head. "Think I'll go down to the creek for a drink." Without the usual courtesy of helping her from the saddle, he disappeared over the edge of the hill.

"Well, I never." Columbine indignantly clambered from the saddle. "Andy Cullen, where are your manners?"

"Don't be too hard on him. I asked him to bring you and then leave."

She turned. Smokey Travis leaned against the rock wall of the cave entrance. "Why, how did you, Mr. Travis; you know it's dangerous for you to be here. Why did you come?" She valiantly bit back the glad cry that rose within her.

His white teeth gleamed in his deeply tanned face. "I hankered to see you."

She hated the red tide she felt sweeping her cheeks.

"Are you a little glad to see me?"

"Yes." Her heart pounded when twin lamps lit up his dark eyes and he took a step toward her.

"Thank you for writing." He gazed down at her. "Could you—would you—call me Smokey? It's my real name," he added.

"Yes, if you would call me Columbine," she murmured, then thought how inane she sounded. She struggled for her usual calm. "Is everything all right—on the ranch where you work, I mean?"

He unsaddled her horse and spread the saddle blanket on a wide, flat-topped rock. Once seated, he regaled her with the adventures of the twins and their new pard, Danny. He went on to tell how Joel once saved his life and shared scenes of the wagon train trek to Flag from Texas. Laughing uncontrollably, he described Curly's courtship, and almost wistfully, he spoke of Joel and Rebecca's wedding. "Wish you'd been there. I never saw Joel or Rebecca look so happy. You'll like her a lot, an' she'll be crazy about you." His admiring look deepened the high color in her face.

"I hope someday I can meet her."

"You will." Something lurked in the cowboy's watching dark eyes and called to her.

She took a deep breath. "I suppose Andy's told you my—my stepfather says I have to marry him on my eighteenth birthday."

"Saying it an' doing it aren't the same," he told her. His brows came together in a frown. "You don't love him, do you?"

She looked down. "No. He's been kind to me, but I don't love him like Mother said a woman must love a man before she marries." She looked up to see his jaw set in a grim line.

"Then keep trusting in that God of yours an' in Andy an' me," he told her quietly.

Impulsively, Columbine laid her slim hand on his. "Smokey, why do you call him my God? He's yours, too." Earnestness turned her blue eyes almost purple. "Don't you believe in Him?"

"Sure. Who could see a grand country like this and not believe?"

His quick reply didn't satisfy her. She gazed unseeingly at the rock cave, the grazing horses, then back at him. "Are you a Christian?" she asked shyly. "Do you believe in Jesus?"

Smokey looked deep into her eyes. "I can't say I'm a Christian, but I believe in Jesus. I've been around Joel an' Gideon an' the others enough to know what He did for even cowpunchers like me." He turned his hand palm up and grasped hers. "It's like this. Once a man signs on a Trailmate like Him, everything's bound to be different. Then along comes a skunk like Hadley. What's a feller to do? On the one hand, that skunk needs killing. On the other hand, Jesus won't stand for such." Poignancy crept into his expression. "Columbine, do you understand what I'm saying?"

"Yes," she whispered, "but I think you're wrong. I believe when we invite Jesus to ride with us and live in our hearts, He will give us the strength to do what's right, no matter what." She squeezed his hand and realized what she was doing and dropped it.

"If I could believe that, it would make a powerful lot of difference," Smokey muttered.

She wanted deeply to assure him that was true, but a rustling in the woods and the arrival of Andy Cullen forestalled her.

Andy looked apologetic. "Sorry to break up your gab, but if we don't get back to the ranch pretty soon, Zeke will be in a rage."

Smokey stood and helped the girl to her feet. "Before you go, I have something for you." He strode into the cave and came out with a package. "It isn't much, just candy."

"Shall I open it now?"

His face turned crimson. "Why don't you stuff it in your saddle bags an'

open it when you get home?" He spun on his heel. "Andy, you're a real pard."
The younger man reddened with obvious pleasure.

Slowly Smokey turned back to Columbine. "May I come again?"

"How can you?" she asked, afraid but wanting to say yes. "Won't the
Double J think it's strange if you ride off all the time?"

A singularly sweet smile crossed his features. "It won't be all the time.
Besides, now that we're carpentering an' getting houses built, there's little night
herding. After their last try for our cattle, Hadley an' his gang have been lying
low. I put the news out on the range that the rustlers had been recognized, but
I didn't give names."

"Smokey, was my stepfather in on that raid?" She held her breath and
dug her nails into the palms of her clenched hands.

"No!" Smokey immediately answered. "From what I heard, Hadley
talked a bunch of the Z riders into making the raid. Were they ever sore
when it didn't amount to anything!"

She sagged in relief. Yet the memory of Zeke saying Hadley had coaxed
off part of the outfit and that there would be no roundup this spring played
in her mind.

"There's another reason why I might be in these parts," Smokey told them
with dead seriousness. "If the Scotts are willing, I'd like to hole up somewhere
near here an' just keep an eye on Hadley." *And Stockton*, he wanted to add. His
unspoken words hung in the air. Columbine pressed her lips together, torn
between the implication and the delight of seeing Smokey again.

He smiled once more. "If I happen to be riding near this spot in, say, two
weeks, will you be here?" His glance included Andy, but she knew just how
much time that worthy young schemer would spend with them.

"I might." She watched while he resaddled her horse, the years of trail
experience evident in his strong hands. Back in the saddle, she leaned down.
"Be careful."

"I will." He shrugged. "I reckon a New Mexico cowpuncher can be as
clever as one from Arizona." He still stood motionless, arm upraised in
farewell, when Andy and Columbine rode away. The next instant, he dropped
back weakly to the big rock, bare now of the saddle blanket. "Doggone if she
isn't sweeter an' prettier than the first time I saw her." He mopped his hot face
with his neckerchief. "She must like me a little, or she wouldn't have half
promised to meet me. Her eyes showed she didn't like this sort of sneaking
around, but what else can we do?" Deep in thought before heading back to the
Double J, Smokey determined to convince Joel and Gideon a spy in the Tonto

could be real useful in finding what Hadley and Stockton were planning.

Two weeks later to the day, Smokey rode Buckskin to the well-concealed cave. He peered at the trail but saw no fresh tracks other than the small prints of deer. The thumping of his heart sounded loud enough to scare off a mountain lion. A half hour later, his ears picked up the steady beat of hooves. Earlier, he had made sure Buckskin was off the trail. Chances were slim that a rider would be here other than by appointment, but he'd take no risks.

"Smokey?" Andy's cheerful voice brought him into the open. His heart sank. No slender girl rode beside his friend.

"She's here," Andy assured him. "I just wanted to check first. A time or two lately, I've had the feeling someone's trailing us. It ain't one of our hands, but it could be Hadley."

A little thrill swept through Smokey at the sight of Columbine riding toward him, and he had to admit, at the thought of another confrontation with Hadley. If the rustler meant harm to the girl, trouble lay ahead. He smoothed the frown from his face and stepped forward to help her from her horse, but she had already sprung down. He saw the hesitancy in her face, then a flood of color that gladdened his heart. She *did* like him.

—+—

Their strange courtship followed the same general pattern throughout the winter and into the spring. Weather permitting, every two weeks Andy rode with Columbine to the cave. He told Smokey they rode in a different direction each day in case curious eyes took note or plotting men tried to lay in wait. By mid-spring, Stockton had again begun talking of a raid according to Andy, who didn't scorn listening when something interesting was being discussed.

Once, Columbine wandered down to the stream and left the two men alone for a few minutes. Andy whispered, "Hard as it is to believe, I ain't too sure but what Stockton's thrown back in with Hadley."

"Impossible!" Smokey spit out.

"Not permanent-like." Andy tousled his shock of hair. His brown eyes looked worried. "Just for this one big deal. A roundup's likely to include a whole lot more critters than's wearing the Z brand. Shh, here comes Columbine."

Smokey hid his concern and spent the precious time with the one person he had long since realized he wanted for his wife. Reluctantly, at the end of a too-short visit, he watched the two riders out of sight as usual. Once alone, he swung back into the saddle and headed for the Double J, riding all night thanks to a friendly moon that lighted his way. This news had to be passed on.

"Just keep watching and listening," Gideon and Joel ordered.

"What about the girl?" Joel added when he went out with his friend, leaving Gideon behind.

"She's biding her time." Smokey looked deep into the understanding blue eyes. "So am I."

A warm handclasp completed their conversation. After Smokey grabbed a few hours' sleep and packed a supply of grub and clean clothes, he turned south and east. From Flag to the brakes, he had ample time to consider the present and future, to digest what he had learned from Joel, Gideon, and now Columbine.

A slow smile crept over his face. He couldn't help believing she had begun to care. It showed in her honest face, in the little lilt in her voice when she spoke to him, and most of all in the delicate color that tinged her cheeks. An unspoken prayer of thankfulness winged its way from Smokey's troubled heart. The way ahead looked rocky and steep, as tough as any mountain he'd ever had to climb. If only he dared give in to the urge growing stronger every day to turn over the reins to God and His Son. Still he hesitated, every protective bone in his body crying out he must care first for Columbine.

—+—

Never had the music of Arizona been sweeter to Columbine Ames's ears than during the spring of 1891. The laughing brook danced and sang its way over amber stones between new-leafed cottonwoods. Each coyote crying for his mate put an echo in her heart. As if for the first time, she watched birds mating and building nests. Would she one day make a home for the dark-eyed cowboy who seemed to have been part of her life forever? The thought always brought a little gasp. She found herself turning to the Bible's great love stories again and again and then to the New Testament verses that likened the love of Christ for His church to that of a bridegroom coming for his bride. Yet at the same time a little voice warned her Smokey had not yet committed his life to the Lord she worshiped and served. Soon she knew he would; he must. Once he realized the only real strength in the world came from God, the next-to-the-last obstacle to their love would be removed.

At this point, inevitably Columbine sighed. How could she and Smokey find happiness as long as Zeke Stockton coveted her? He would fight to the death before he'd let her go. *So would Smokey*, she told herself. *God, if he killed*

Father, I couldn't bear it. If Father killed him, I wouldn't want to live. The only time she felt strong enough to endure came while she pored over her Bible and talked with the Lord.

Contrary to range rumors, nothing unusual happened at the Z's spring roundup. Hadley had not been present. Andy reported no more than the usual number of mixed-in brands. To everyone's amazement, Stockton kept a careful tally of those and remarked offhandedly, "I'll see the ranchers are paid for these."

"Maybe he's had a change of heart," Smokey suggested in one of their rare conversations when Columbine wasn't present.

" 'Twouldn't surprise me if he ups and goes straight 'cause of her. Too bad he picked Columbine," Andy said soberly, a little crease between his brows.

Yet Smokey couldn't trust Stockton's apparent turnabout completely. He continued to camp out in the Tonto, wide-eyed and alert, all the time aware of how rapidly spring had rushed into summer. Now June lay over the brakes like a wool blanket, and Columbine's birthday and proposed wedding day loomed closer. So far, he and Andy had come up with no way to rescue her. In desperation, Smokey turned to God.

"You can help," he cried one afternoon to a lightning-filled, thunder-heavy sky. "Isn't there some way to save her without bloodshed?" Only another jagged, crackling bolt and a great clash of thunder replied. He waited. Yet the storm passed, and no still small voice came.

Two days later, Andy and Columbine dashed into the clearing in front of the cave. "Smokey, it's here. Our chance." In all his meetings with her, Smokey had never seen such fire and hope in the usually sad blue eyes. Her words hit him the way lightning strikes tall pines. "Father has to go away on business. He will be gone about two weeks, starting the last day of June."

"That's wonderful, but—"

"Don't you see?" Her breath came in little puffs that stirred the silvery fair hair loose from her hat. *"We can't be married on my birthday after all."* Her jewel-like eyes held all the relief Smokey felt in his heart.

"This is the plan," Andy interposed, excitement lighting his face. "Stockton had promised Columbine he'd take her to Flag for the celebration, so ain't it reasonable to say she has permission to go?" He didn't wait for an answer. "The day after he leaves, we'll take her to the Double J. You said she'd be welcome." He grinned. "Once there, if you can't figure out a way to keep her, well. . ." He winked at Smokey. "I'm for a drink from the creek. Why don't you talk things over while I'm gone? It can't be long," he warned.

"Zeke's been complaining our rides take too much time."

The moment he disappeared, Smokey lifted Columbine from the saddle. This time, instead of releasing her, he placed a hand on each of her shoulders. "Columbine, I've loved you from the minute I saw you. How would you like to go ahead and be married on your birthday? To me?" His body rigid, he longed to encircle her with his arms and never let her go. "I'd take good care of you, and Zeke or nobody could ever scare you again." He tilted her chin up with one finger and saw a lone tear seep from between downcast lashes. Humility and a sense of awe overtook him as if he stood on the edge of great understanding.

Her lashes swept up, spiky from tears. Her blue eyes shone tenderly, filled with perfect love and trust. "If you're sure you want me, I'll marry you."

"Sure!" As Smokey's self-control slipped, so did his hands, from her shoulders to her waist. He lowered his head until his lips rested on hers. Her arms tightened. All his wild imaginings hadn't prepared him for the love he discovered at that moment. Instinctively, he knew this was her first kiss; it was his as well.

"Now that's more like it," a laughing voice said from behind them. "I take it there's a wedding coming off? With me as the best man, maybe?"

Smokey freed Columbine just enough so she could lean back, rosy red and smiling. "Not by a long shot! I aim to be the best man at my wedding, but you can stand up with us."

"Andy, we'll never be able to thank you enough." The newly engaged girl faltered. Slipping from Smokey's embrace, she ran to Andy and stood on tiptoe to kiss his lean cheek. A wave of scarlet painted his cheeks as Smokey laughed delightedly.

Andy rubbed his cheek and in his own droll manner retorted, "Say, I can see what they mean about turning the other cheek. This time, it would be a pleasure!" When their laughter died, he reminded, "We have to plan."

Their escape proved so simple that Columbine with all her faith found it surprising, and the two men considered it miraculous. Stockton rode out on schedule. Like many days, the following afternoon, Andy and Columbine mounted for their ride. Their saddlebags, packed in the dead of night, were stuffed to capacity with her clothes and toilette articles. Columbine wore the same outfit for riding she always wore to allay possible suspicion.

Unlike the other days, they did not plan to come back, ever. Before Zeke returned, Columbine would be Mrs. Smokey Travis, and Andy, a valuable part of the Double J.

Chapter 11

S nappin' crocodiles, but yu've gone and done it!" Open admiration for both Columbine's loveliness and his pard's closemouthed courtship shone in Jim Perkins's face.

"This is Columbine Ames," announced Smokey simply at the Double J dinner gathering. "Her stepfather is Zeke Stockton, an' she's running away from him. You're all invited to our wedding on July tenth; she'll be eighteen then."

The chorus of welcomes and warm embraces by the women threatened to undermine Columbine's resolve. Silently, she appealed to Smokey with a fleeting look and five minutes later found herself in a tastefully decorated room.

"Your home until the wedding," Judith Scott told her. "You have nothing to be frightened about." Her eyes filled. "I know what it's like to be alone and uncertain." Another quick hug and she vanished, leaving Columbine to kneel by the spotless counterpane on the inviting bed and pour out her gratitude to God.

Merry-eyed Rebecca Fairfax Scott solved a problem when she drew the newcomer aside. "I'd be proud if you'd wear my wedding dress," she offered hesitantly, her brown eyes shining. "I'm just a few inches taller, and we can take it up and in."

"You're so kind." Still bewildered by the openhearted way the entire Double J had taken her in, she fought tears. "I—I didn't know what to do. I don't have anything suitable with me and somehow. . ." Her voice trailed off.

"You'd rather not be married in something bought with Stockton's or Smokey's money," Rebecca finished for her. "That's what I figured. Now, come see my new home and we'll work on the dress."

So much to see, so much to do! Columbine discovered she didn't have much time alone with Smokey. In a way, she felt glad. The days between her arrival at the ranch and her birthday provided a little breathing space. Soon the white gown hung ready and waiting. The cabin Smokey had shared with Curly received a thorough scrubbing and would house the newlyweds as it had Curly and his wife until their own cabin could be completed. Columbine drifted through the hours wondering if Smokey were thinking of her, of the wedding, *of their future.* Every sight of the dark-eyed cowboy sent a thrill to her heart.

The object of her adoration could barely do the work assigned him for dreaming of his loved one. A dozen times a day he shook himself back to the present from joyful anticipation. Not until Jim Perkins goaded Joel into entering Querida in the annual Fourth of July race did Smokey fire up. "Boss, we've all been hankering for a real showdown between your Kay-reeda an' Rebecca's Vermilion. How about it?"

Joel's blue eyes glistened with boyish fun, then a more mature look came. "Rebecca can't ride him." He flushed bright red, and a delighted grin swept over his face. "There's going to be a little Joel or Becky."

"That's good news, but you can't get out of it so easy. I caught an' broke that red mustang stallion," Smokey reminded. "Besides, it's more fair this way. We're nearer of a weight an' the horses can start even."

The result of the conversation showed up when Flag and half the country reached town the morning of the Fourth. Smokey proudly rode to the starting line. Vermilion glistened in the sun, polished and prancing. His faithful friend Querida's black coat shone as if she'd been oiled. A sigh rippled through the half-dozen riders mounted on the finest horses they could muster, and Smokey's eyes gleamed. He said in an undertone, "Mighty fine nags, but they'll never catch Vermilion. Neither will Kay-reeda."

Joel's teeth flashed white, and his spontaneous laugh turned heads. "Only because she's going to be in front of him. *Way* in front!"

Smokey snorted but contented himself with an answering grin and the knowledge no horse alive could outrun the red stallion, given the same start. He let Vermilion dance a bit more but not enough to take the edge off, then crouched in the saddle, body bent forward. Joel did the same.

Crack! The starting pistol fired. The line of horses leaped ahead. "Yippee-ay!" Andy called. Smokey barely heard him. With his gaze fixed directly between Vermilion's ears, he knew Querida ran beside them, nose even with the stallion's flank. By the end of the first quarter mile, six valiant riders struggled to catch the pair far in the lead. Smokey urged Vermilion into the flowing dead run that ate up the ground. Querida stuck like a leech. At the end of the next quarter mile, they stayed the same. Then with a wild cowboy yell, Joel goaded Querida into a spurt of speed that brought the black mare and her rider slightly ahead of the red.

Vermilion snorted. Smokey knew he didn't like the reversed position. He leaned forward and called in the stallion's ear. Vermilion increased his pace. At the end of the third quarter mile, he ran neck and neck with Querida.

Three hundred yards to go. Two hundred. A hundred. Smokey could hear the deafening roar of the excited crowd. He flattened himself until he almost lay on Vermilion's neck. From the corner of his eye, he could see Joel do the same.

Fifty yards. Thirty. Twenty. Ten. Across the finish line they swept! Had he won? Smokey couldn't tell. He let Vermilion run on and gradually slackened the reins, aware of Querida beside him. Men and beasts came to a stop some distance from the yelling crowd. Smokey shoved back his sombrero and wiped the sweat from his forehead. "Who won?"

"I'm hanged if I know!" Joel burst into laughter. "Shall we go see?"

To the delight of the crowd, they rode back together. Jim Perkins's bellow sounded above the screams. "Snappin' crocodiles, if that ain't the purtiest tie I ever saw!"

"Tie?" Smokey gasped.

"We tied?" Joel doubled over and laughed until tears came. "Put her there, Pard." He gripped Smokey's hand.

"Here's to a couple of grand horses," Smokey told him before bursting at the seams. "Haw haw! If Vermilion and Kay-reeda didn't put one over on us, then I'm a lop-eared mule." He glanced both ways to make sure no one could hear. "At that, I'm glad."

"So am I." Joel wiped his eyes. "If my horse had beaten Rebecca's, she'd never have let me hear the last of it, and vice versa." They walked their steaming mounts to nearby shade and rubbed them down, then rejoined the rest of the Double J for the usual Fourth of July fun.

Columbine's eyes rounded at sights new and strange. Smokey glowed with pride and didn't miss a single envious glance or the way the young bucks "dropped by" to greet him and meet his sweetheart. Good-naturedly, he told them, "Go find your own gals. This one's spoken for by me."

Smokey entered both pistol and rifle contests, outdone by Gideon and Joel in the pistol match but winning first place in the rifle shoot. Andy Cullen came close and took second. His big grin showed how good he felt about being on and a part of the Double J. Jim Perkins loftily informed his friends Conchita had begged him not to enter and show them up. "Anything for a lady," he smirked. When Smokey challenged him to an informal shooting match, he raised an eyebrow, snatched his Colt revolver from its holster, and blazed away at a discarded target with every shot hitting the bull's-eye. Smokey threw up his hands and refused to follow what he called a lucky shooting spree.

As the early days of July crawled by, there was only one bitter drop in the honey of Smokey and Columbine's love: Smokey's indecision to accept Jesus Christ. If he did, he knew he couldn't live up to it, especially if Stockton came calling. Columbine's blue eyes showed how desperately she longed for his commitment, but she said little.

The night before their wedding, he left her and rode out onto the range, the place where he did his best thinking. The midnight blue velvet sky spangled with stars, the pungent smell of sage crushed by Buckskin's hooves, and the whispering aspen leaves left a bittersweet feeling in his heart.

"The one thing she's ever wanted I can't give her," he told the night sky. Buckskin pricked up her ears and slowed her pace. "God, I know it isn't enough if I do it for her. It has to be for me an' You an' because I know it's right." He sighed and shoved his sombrero back on his dark hair. "All those months ago, what Joel said about the voice. Well, I've felt Arizona wind an' the earth shake from thunder an' seen lightning set fires. Why haven't I heard that still small voice?" Restlessness filled him. The void he'd managed partly to fill with love and dreaming yawned deeper and lonelier than ever. "God, where *is* that voice, anyway?"

Only the crooning of the wind and rustling of leaves answered him. He remained silent, slumped in the saddle, filled with the wonder of night. A long time later, Columbine's face flashed into his mind. He recalled her voice and the look in her eyes when she whispered, *I believe when we invite Jesus to ride with us and live in our hearts, He will give us the strength to do what's right, no matter what.* The wind ceased. The rustling halted. But the whispered memory sang on. . .*invite Jesus*. . .*strength to do right*. . .*no matter what.*

On the verge of the most important discovery in his life, Smokey felt blinders being lifted from his eyes. "After the fire," he breathed. Hadn't Columbine passed through the fires of fear and trouble? Their refining process had made her what she was, a witness for her Lord. "God, is the still small voice *You* speaking through *her?*" His heart felt like it might burst. "The same as when You talked to folks in the Bible an' how I feel when Joel an' Gideon preach Your Word?"

Buckskin stopped, and Smokey looked down. Moonlight shone on the fork in the trail. One way led to the ranch, the other to Flag. "Old gal, it's time we—both of us—headed for home." He bowed his head. "The reins are Yours, no matter what." No longer need he search to hear a mysterious voice.

On her wedding morning, Columbine received a gift from her soon-to-be husband: a note scrawled in bold handwriting as black as his hair and eyes. Through wet eyes, she read: NOW HE'S MY TRAILMATE, TOO.

✦

At ten o'clock on her eighteenth birthday, Columbine Ames, a vision in white, became Smokey Travis's wife. The cowboy's open declaration of faith, announced publicly just before the ceremony, left no dry eyes on the Double J. "I asked Jesus to ride with me from now on," he stated. His gaze rested on Jim Perkins, Joel, Curly, and Andy. "I've had a lot of good pards, but He is different. From now on, I'll be heading where He leads me, I mean, us." He smiled at Columbine, whose soft hand lay on his arm. His confession provided the sweetest background music for the marriage vows.

At twelve o'clock, Smokey's newfound faith suffered its first attack: Zeke Stockton rode in. His colorless eyes aflame, he leaped from the saddle before his horse skidded to a stop.

"Where is she?" he roared at Andy Cullen, who lounged on the front porch. "You dirty pup, I ought to kill you."

Andy paled but stood his ground and said nothing.

"What are you, dumb? *Where's my daughter?*"

The commotion brought folks running. They swarmed to the porch, up from the corral and the bunkhouse, until a crowd surrounded the livid intruder.

"I'm here, Father." Columbine, pale as the frail flower whose name she bore, slowly crossed the porch, still gowned in white.

"What the—Colley, what are you doing here dressed like that?" Zeke reeled and rubbed his eyes. "A wedding dress? But you didn't know I could get here in time! Why did you leave the ranch?"

She blanched until her blue eyes shone bright against her face. "I—" She swayed and would have fallen if Smokey hadn't sprung forward to support her.

"You!" Stockton hissed. A hint of foam came to his lips, and his big frame quivered.

"She's my wife, Stockton." Smokey's voice rang loud in the quiet assembly.

"No, no!" The rancher clawed for his gun, but his fingers stilled when Smokey called, "I'm not armed."

"Get a gun, or so help me, I'll kill you where you stand," Stockton yelled. Columbine gave a piteous cry. He ignored her. "Travis, get a gun if you don't want to be shot."

The moment Smokey dreaded and had known he must face was here. *God, help me*, he prayed silently.

"Coward! Skunk!" Zeke fired off every range epithet, his face black with rage, fingers twitching. "Are you a man or a sneaking yellow dog?" He strode toward Smokey, who had come down the steps to face him. "For the last time, will you get a gun?"

The strength to do right, no matter what. Indecision fled. Smokey looked straight into Zeke's eyes. "No."

Disbelief rushed into Zeke's face. His mouth dropped. "You'll stand here and take what no man should and not fight back?" An ugly laugh rolled out. "You, who rode in calm as a summer day, knowing what Hadley had told me? I'd never have figured you for a yellow-belly!"

Smokey said nothing.

Stockton's contemptuous glance swept the crowd. Smokey followed his look. Not an armed man there except Zeke. A thin smile crossed the haggard face. Zeke deliberately drew his Colt and aimed it directly at Smokey's heart. He cocked the gun. "I reckon a dead husband won't stand in the way for me to marry Colley," he taunted.

Smokey didn't move a muscle.

"Why, Travis? Is it 'cause I'm her daddy?"

Smokey squared his shoulders, and a smile creased his face. "No, Stockton. Yesterday I'd have shot you an' felt bad for Columbine. Now I won't. I turned my life over to God last night an' He don't hold with killing, no matter what." He heard a gasp and a rush of flying feet as Columbine swept down the steps to him. She planted herself between him and Zeke. For the first time, Smokey felt fear. The red rage in Stockton's eyes showed he had gone beyond reason. "Columbine, get back!" He grabbed her white-clad arm and tried to swing her out of harm's way.

"No." Her voice rang out like a silver bell. "Father, I love him. The same way you loved Mother and she loved you."

Once Smokey had seen a swooping eagle brought down by a bullet. Columbine's voice had the same effect on her stepfather. He flinched, then staggered. The revolver shook in one trembling hand. "You wouldn't want to live without him?" Deadly earnestness drove every word into Smokey's brain.

Columbine cried out, "I would go on living but in the same way you have since Mother died!"

Pain contorted Zeke's face. The Colt fell from his fingers as he stared at the girl, his face the color of long-dead ashes. An eternity later, he said heavily, "I reckon that won't be necessary." He looked deep into her blue eyes and then at Smokey, who knew his face showed compassion and understanding. The cowboy realized the struggle in the older man's soul between memory of the sweet mother whose love he had hoped to regain through her daughter and the desire to spare Columbine the agony he carried.

Like an aged man, he walked to his horse and climbed into the saddle. He turned to Smokey. "If I ever hear you've mistreated her in any way, I'll kill you, Travis. Armed or not, it won't make any difference." He spurred his horse and rode off before Smokey could reply.

Columbine's high-pitched cry followed him, "Good-bye, Father. God bless you!"

Like animals frozen in a blizzard, the figures in the yard of the Double J watched him ride away, a man beaten by a stripling cowboy with a mighty God. Horse and rider swept around a bend, and Smokey swallowed hard. In years to come, Stockton might look back and curse himself for not killing Smokey and abducting Columbine. Now, however, he had risen to the challenge between good and evil. Smokey turned to his bride, gently picked her up, and carried her away from the sordid scene to the sweet-smelling cabin changed to a bower by loving hands. Once inside, he was about to close the door when Jim Perkins's voice reached them. "Snappin' crocodiles, I never saw anythin' like that before!"

Two weeks later, news of a terrible fight among outlaw bands in the Tonto reached the Double J. At first no one seemed to know who or how many had been killed, but ranchers speculated there'd be a lot fewer missing cattle in the future. Smokey hated to tell Columbine. Despite the great joy their marriage had brought, a shadow lingered in her cameo face and sweet blue eyes.

"There's been trouble," he finally said. "We don't know what men were killed, but Andy and I are riding to the Z to find out."

Every trace of color fled. "Don't go! Smokey, I can't bear it if anything happens to you, too."

"Whoa, we don't know anything's happened to Zeke," he protested, not really believing his words but unwilling for her to worry.

"How long will you be gone?"

"No longer than it takes to—to do what we have to."

Quick understanding filled her eyes.

"Will you stay with Judith or Rebecca?" Smokey wanted to know.

Columbine shook her head. "No. I'll stay here in our own home." She kissed him good-bye and waved from the porch, just as he had pictured her doing all those times in the past when he daydreamed about her. Smokey rode out with Andy, silent and filled with dread. What would they find in the wild, untamed heart of Arizona?

"It can't be much worse," Andy said soberly when they got to the Z. Corrals stood empty. So did the bunkhouse. The door of the ranch house sagged partway open, and when they stepped inside, dust lay thick on the furniture.

The sight of a forgotten apron on the back of a chair made Smokey draw in a deep breath. *Thank God Columbine had escaped before all of this,* he thought suddenly.

A slight sound from overhead sent the riders hurrying up the stairs. Faint moans guided them to a large room. Zeke Stockton, naked to the waist, his eyes dull with fever, was lying in a clutter of crumpled bedclothes. His head and chest were wrapped with blood-stained bandages. As the two men crossed the room, he showed no surprise. He knew who they were.

"Man, you need a doctor." Smokey attacked the bedding. "Andy, heat water. I'll do what I can."

"Too late." Zeke shook his matted, bandaged head. His cough brought blood to his lips. "I'm done for. No," he added when Smokey opened his mouth to protest, "it's all right." He coughed again, harder this time, an effort that seemed to sap his remaining strength. "Tell Colley I was all wrong. Got her and her mother mixed up. Tell her Hadley's dead; the others ran off the rest of my stock. Doesn't matter now."

Smokey caught Andy's pitying look that clearly asked if Zeke's mumble came from fever.

"Her mother used to pray for me. So did Colley. I knew I should listen. Too late to change a lot of things."

"It's never too late to tell God you're sorry." Smokey spoke loudly in an effort to penetrate Zeke's fading consciousness. "Zeke, Jesus died for all of us so our sins could be forgiven." His voice sounded clear and sure in the quiet room.

"Tell Colley to sell the place. Pay back the ranchers I stole from."

Andy's mouth dropped open.

"I'll tell her," Smokey promised. He could see the struggle Stockton was making to get things off his mind. His heart leaped.

"Tell Colley. . ." Zeke's eyes closed with weariness. The next minute, he opened them and stared at Smokey with a look of wonder, then closed them again. A final breath came and with it a look of peace never before seen on the rancher's face.

Smokey and Andy buried him next to his wife. After locking up the sprawling ranch house, they rode away together. For a long time, neither spoke, then Andy said in a gruff voice, "What are you going to tell Columbine?"

"The truth."

"Which is—what? I ain't too sure. There at last, seemed like he did what he could do to make things right."

"Only God knows Zeke Stockton's heart at the moment," Smokey reminded.

He repeated the words to a weeping Columbine after they reached the Double J. He had asked Andy to be present when he broke the news.

"He frightened me, but until Mother died, he was kind," Columbine remembered out loud when they had faithfully given her his messages.

"He died with a peaceful look on his face," Andy put in. For once his hair lay flat without brushing; his brown eyes held no laughter. "I kinda think he really was sorry, maybe even told God so when he couldn't get it out."

"We will never know." Smokey placed his arm around his wife's shoulders. "We do know God forgives even the worst sin. All we can do is hope and leave Zeke with Him."

Columbine nodded, and Andy shuffled off. That evening, she and Smokey walked to a promontory not far from their cabin. From it, they could see the intersecting trails, all leading in different directions. "Like our lives," she observed sagely.

"Yes. It's been a long, hard trail here." Smokey held her close, her fair head on his strong shoulder. "Only God knows what's ahead."

A calf bawled in the distance, followed by the distant sounds of a night herding. The western sky blushed, bathing them in rose and gold and purple shadows. Then as the music of the mountains stilled into the hush of twilight, Smokey and Columbine turned their steps toward home.

Captives of
the Canyon

Author's Note

The legends concerning Dead Horse Point and Dead Horse Canyon are real although unproved. Due to a lack of actual dates other than vague references to "just before the turn of the century," etc., I have taken literary license and fitted these legendary events into the time frame of my novel while remaining as accurate as possible to what I learned in researching the area.

Colleen L. Reece

Chapter 1

Footsore and weary, Andy Cullen paused in the endless pursuit of his chestnut mare, Chinquapin, and, with disfavor, surveyed the world around him. "Why'd I ever leave the Double J ranch?" he complained to a buzzard sailing overhead, bent on its grisly mission. Yet even his sour mood couldn't erase the joy of living that evidenced itself in sparkling brown eyes and a grin like the crack in a cheap watermelon. A lock of hair, darkened by sweat from its normal, ripe corn color, dangled over his forehead. Andy shoved it back under his Stetson, then mopped his hot face with a bright red neckerchief and eyed the crowding red-rock walls that towered above him and offered a million hiding places for a frightened horse. "Chinq, at least they didn't get you." He limped to a nearby boulder the size of a house and leaned against it, glad for the shade.

"Lord, if You're really the way Columbine and Smokey believe, I could sure use a hand. This southeastern Utah ain't no place for a cowpoke on foot a million miles from nowhere. No water. No canteen. Nothing but red and orange rocks." His gaze traveled across the strange, broken land. Great stone arches loomed above him. Formations that looked like petrified giants kept everlasting vigil. Massive rocks that resembled pictures of great cathedrals he'd once seen stood like sentinels. Andy shuddered. Alone, hungry, and thirsty, they posed a serious threat—not only to his quest but to his life.

"I reckon You help those who help themselves," he muttered and straightened. High-heeled boots raised him taller than his five feet, nine inches. He stretched muscled arms. Every sinew in his body ached. Lean, stripling, seasoned, the unaccustomed walking that all riders hated had taken its toll, and Chinq had been missing only since last night.

Andy made a disgusted sound. How could he have been so careless? On the other hand, who'd expect any self-respecting outlaw band to be in a forsaken place like this? His cheerful mouth set in a straight line. "I must be crazy, leaving a good job to chase wild horses. Wild horse, to be exact. I never should have listened to all the stories about Sheik. If I hadn't, I'd be home where I belong."

He thought wistfully of the Double J ranch near Flagstaff. Of Smokey Travis, Columbine Ames, now Mrs. Smokey, and the exasperating but lovable Jim Perkins with his favorite expression, "Snappin' crocodiles." Of Joel, the boy preacher, and all the others. Andy had been welcomed and made part of the Double J family after helping Columbine escape her iron-willed father the previous, fateful summer of 1891.

Most of all he remembered the showdown between Smokey and Zeke Stockton, Columbine's stepfather, who wanted to marry her. Even now his heart broke into a gallop at the memory. When Zeke called Smokey out, Smokey had refused to fight him. Instead, he had chosen to face the inevitable scorn of the range and be branded a coward rather than kill someone, even for Colley's sake.

Andy's big grin spread. If he lived to be older than the red-rock castles around him, he'd never forget his dark-haired, dark-eyed cowboy friend standing in front of the Double J hours after his wedding, his frail, white-clad bride on his arm. Neither would he forget Zeke's charge like an angry bull and what had followed.

"Coward! Skunk! Will you get a gun?" Zeke had bellowed.

"No." Smokey didn't give an inch.

"I'd never have figured you for a yellow-belly. Is it 'cause I'm her daddy?" Zeke stood with his cocked Colt aimed directly at Smokey's heart.

A smile creased Smokey's face. "Yesterday I'd have shot you an' felt bad for Columbine. Now I won't. I turned my life over to God last night, an' He don't hold with killing, no matter what."

A rush of flying feet and Columbine's bell-like voice said, "Father, I love him. The same way you loved Mother and she loved you." That brought Zeke down like a swooping eagle felled with a bullet. To the amazement of all present, he backed off and rode away.

Nothing in Andy's life had impressed him so much as seeing his pard face death rather than go back on his newly found Trailmate. Now Andy soliloquized, "Maybe someday, after I catch Sheik, I'll go back. They said I'll always have a job waiting." He pictured the ranch in his mind. Rolling hills that leveled off in mesas, then climbed until they became distant mountains. Sweet-smelling pine and cedar. Laughter and lighted windows. A pang went through him. The Double J stood for home, the only one he'd known since his parents died and, as a young boy, he had to make it on his own. It seemed incredible that he had ridden away.

"No use pretending," he said ruefully. "Once I turned nineteen in January and stories about Sheik came down from range gossip, I knew I had to track him."

That had been just a few months ago. Andy lounged in the bunkhouse during stormy weather, rode the range when it lifted, but his mind soared north and east. Chinquapin, the mare he'd been given, steadily served his needs and proved herself a satisfying companion. But to own Sheik, the legendary black stallion who fully lived up to his name by stealing every mare possible and driving would-be leaders from his band in fierce battle that boded no good for challengers! Excitement flowed through Andy's veins at the very thought. Couldn't he just see himself riding into the corral on Sheik, hand tamed and glistening ebony!

Reality interrupted his daydreams. "How can it be so hot for spring?" he mumbled. "Summer must be awful." He sighed and increased his pace. "Let's see. I must be a good fifteen miles from Moab. I can't be sure with all these twists and turns. Lord, I reckon You're the only one who knows where I am for sure."

Trailwise, he considered his choices. Trying to travel at night in this unfamiliar country meant the chance of a slip or fall, possibly a broken leg. "Ump-umm." Working his way out of his predicament by day and without water offered an equally unalluring prospect. Best thing to do would be to travel in late afternoon, early evening, and early morning, and hole up during the hottest part of the day. He thought longingly of his well-stocked pack. He'd replenished his supplies in Moab. Now they merrily rode in outlaw saddlebags.

"At least they didn't get Chinq," he gloated. Andy never hobbled her at night; she liked to nuzzle the oats he carried or graze close by when she could find grass.

The other night, though, Andy had been caught off guard. He didn't hear soft footfalls until just before a voice ordered, "Hands up!" When he hesitated, a bullet whistled past his left ear, too close for comfort. His hands shot skyward. Chinq snorted and leaped at the same moment. Her strong shoulder knocked against one of the three dark figures approaching Andy's fire, and a second mighty bound plunged her from the circle of light into blackness.

A volley of yells shattered the crisp night air. A loud "Haw-haw" came from one of the intruders as the fallen one scrambled to his feet and rubbed his arm and shoulder.

"Got any money?" the voice he'd heard earlier asked.

"Not much." Andy tried honesty. "Spent most of it at Moab on supplies." He bit his lip. Of all the stupid remarks, that had to be the worst.

"Good. We'll take them. Traveling men like us can always use more grub." The thieves stepped forward. All that showed between pulled-down hats and pulled-up bandannas were glittering eyes that clearly warned him not to argue. He silently watched them gather his stores, hoping they wouldn't notice Chinq's saddlebags hanging from a small rock outcropping nearby. They contained food he'd need to get back to Moab.

"Hey, Boss, lookee here," one called. He dangled the saddlebags from his hand, and by the flickering campfire light, Andy saw the gleam in his shaded eyes. Strange eyes, almost colorless. If he saw them again, Andy felt he would recognize those eyes.

"What're you doing out here anyway?"

Again Andy resorted to total honesty. "Tracking Sheik."

"Whew!" The man with the odd eyes let out a low whistle.

"You've sure got the right bait," the outlaw who'd taken charge admitted. "What I saw of that mare will be mighty appealing to Sheik, the old robber." He laughed, a surprisingly pleasant sound. "But my pard here got a closer look than I did." He ignored the victim of Chinq's flight when he continued, "You'll find your mare in a day or two if Sheik don't find her first."

For a moment, Andy forgot his loss of supplies and eagerly asked, "Have you seen the stallion and his band lately?"

The masked man shook his head. "Naw. But I heard a few days ago that some rancher was madder than a sore-footed wildcat 'cause Sheik had stolen a couple of his mares." With a swift motion, he turned. "We don't have time to gab, Mister. Thanks for the grub." He raised his revolver and placed a well-aimed shot over Andy's right shoulder. "Don't think about tracking us instead of the stallion." He and his men melted into the dark shadows but not until Andy had caught an unwilling look of admiration in the other's eyes when Andy didn't flinch at the shot.

"Funny galoot," Andy muttered at the memory and walked on in the direction that Chinq's faint tracks led. "If he weren't a miserable thief, I could like the feller. Sure had a sense of humor." He bent his keen gaze to the trail. Here and there, it crossed solid rock and had left no impression. Andy faithfully picked it up again wherever sand had drifted down, yet, by the time darkness had come, he hadn't found his horse. Neither had he seen a jackrabbit, prairie dog, or even a lizard. No supper tonight. He tightened his belt a notch, broke off a few branches from a nearby stunted greasewood, and built a small fire to ward off the growing chill. His bedroll had gone the way of his grub, so he dozed, fed his blaze, and spent a miserable night. Sometime after two o'clock, according to the battered pocket watch he carried, he drifted into an uneasy sleep.

A sound in the night brought him bolt upright. His fire had dwindled and cast only a feeble light. Something in the hovering shadows moved. Andy swallowed and reached for his Colt. "Who's there?"

Nothing answered, but again something moved just beyond the fire's glow.

"Come out, or I'll shoot," he sharply ordered. At the same time, he sprang to his feet and dove to one side, then rolled away from the light into the protective cover of night. If the outlaws had come back, it would be to kill. They knew he had no horse or food and had seemed satisfied as to his state of finances, not bothering to search. They had actually been quite gentlemanly, as robbers go.

Andy's irrepressible grin flashed even while he slithered farther from the fire. The next moment, a complaining whinny sent him into gales of laughter. "Stampeded," he choked when he could speak. "Held up by my own horse!" He stood and crossed to Chinquapin, tossing extra greasewood branches on the fire as he went. "You old fraud. What's the idea of sneaking back here in the middle of the night?" He stroked her tangled mane. His hand felt gritty and showed red dust in the firelight. "A sorry mess you are, but I'll tell the world if I ain't glad to see you."

Chinquapin rubbed her head against his shoulder and moved restlessly.

"Sorry, Girl. No feed for either of us, but tomorrow we'll go into Moab. I still have enough money to get us fed up. May have to look for a job soon, though. I hadn't counted on losing our supplies and my bedroll."

‐‡‐

True to his word, by daylight Andy and Chinq were ready to leave. First he made a trip back to the scene of the robbery. The men had left the cowboy's heavy saddle, and he certainly hadn't wanted to pack it in his search for Chinquapin. Unwilling to put saddle to bare horsehide, Andy used his jacket as a saddle blanket. The corners of his mouth turned down. Smokey and Jim Perkins had given him that blanket for Christmas. "One thing about it," he promised Chinq. "If I see that blanket, I'll know who stole our outfit. Columbine put a tiny *A* for Andy in one corner." He brightened at the thought. Sooner or later, even outlaws had to ride into towns and ranches to stock up. Usually they passed themselves off as strangers riding through or as respectable cowhands, unless they were downright killers, and he had a feeling these men weren't. They could have shot him, dumped his body in a canyon, and never feared being caught in this contorted place. If his remains were ever discovered, the buzzards and coyotes wouldn't have left enough to recognize who it was.

The ugly idea sent sweat to Andy's forehead. "Lord, I guess since I had to meet rustlers or outlaws or whatever they are, I'd better be thankful they weren't any worse." He paused. "Maybe it ain't too respectful talking to You like this, but Smokey says You're a Trailmate, and that's how I'd talk to my best pard." Saying it out loud kind of made it sound better. Andy whistled a cheerful melody and turned Chinq in the direction he hoped Moab lay.

Alas for his plans! When the sun was high in the sky, he found they'd been traveling off course. "Oh, no. That means more hungry, thirsty miles," he told Chinq. "Sorry. I'll make up for it when we get to town."

Once out of the canyon country, they made good time. Andy's growling stomach reminded him how long it had been since supper the other night. Chinq, powerful as she was, was drooping by the time they reached Moab and the livery stable. With the range appreciation of a horse that becomes comrade as well, Andy allowed no one to care for the mare but himself. He fed and watered her, then brushed her chestnut coat to its usual gleam before striding down the wide and dusty main street to a small but excellent cafe. Forty-five minutes later, filled to the brim with tender beefsteak, fried potatoes, too many hot buttered biscuits to count, and side dishes of three vegetables followed by two huge slabs of apple pie, he leaned back and considered his next move.

A conversation at the next table caught his attention. He glanced that way. Four men sat with elbows on the red-checked tablecloth. The one facing Andy looked like he'd just won a bulldogging contest at an annual Fourth of July doings.

"I tell you, it can be done. We'll herd Sheik and his band onto the rock point that overlooks Dead Horse Canyon, barricade it, and have him where we want him."

Andy felt like he'd just swallowed a boulder. Corral *his* wild stallion? Never! He started to rise, decided to be cautious, and motioned for more coffee. Nursing it would give him a good reason to linger and overhear more.

"How come they call it Dead Horse Canyon, anyway?" the broad-shouldered man who sat with his back to Andy demanded.

"There's a rock just below the point that looks like a horse lying on its side. White sandstone. Legend says it's a caveman's horse that fell off a cliff and got petrified."

"I heard it's because someone found a horse drowned in a deep pothole, probably trying to get a drink," another put in. "The sides were too steep to climb out."

The fourth man pounded the table with his fist. "Who cares? What's important is whether it will work."

"It'll work, all right." The first speaker sounded positive. "Mustang herds run wild all over the mesas out there. The promontory's a natural corral, I tell you. The only way on or off it is a thirty-yard-wide neck of land. We can fence it, rope and break the good stock, and either keep them or sell them. There's big money in selling to eastern markets."

"What about the culls, the broomtails?"

"Open the gate. They're smart enough to find their way off the point, ain't they?"

"If we go ahead, one thing's understood." The broad-shouldered man whose face Andy couldn't see spoke clearly and slowly. "If we succeed with this, Sheik's mine. I'll keep him for breeding and get rich."

"No doubt about it," one of his companions drawled. "That stallion's said to be half pure Arabian and half wild stallion. His daddy done stole his mama from George Allen. George sure hated to lose her. Said she was the best mare he ever had."

"Wonder what he'd pay to get Sheik, with the mare to boot? By the way, what happened to Sheik's sire?"

Excitement faded from the first speaker's eyes. "A wild horse hunter roped him, half broke him, and sold him to a rancher who beat the horse and made a killer out of him. One day they found the rancher about dead, stomped." Anger filled his face. "Y'know how they put a price on outlaws' heads? Well, they did the same with that wonderful horse. After the stallion tore down the corral and escaped, some greedy snake killed the stallion so's he could collect the reward."

Andy heard the indignation in the little ripple of protest that ran around the table. Although not bloodthirsty, he could agree to a point when the broad-shouldered man viciously snapped, "Served the rancher right. Might as well kill a mustang as beat him." He shoved back his chair and stood; the others followed. Throwing money on the table, they noisily marched out, leaving Andy shaken.

He paid his bill and ambled outside. All the money he had left must go for supplies. No sleeping in a real bed tonight. He could ride out of town and find a ranch that would give him a place to sleep and breakfast, the usual range hospitality. He shook his head. Chinq needed rest, and he had too much to think about to sleep well. The night promised to be clear, so he headed for the same store where he'd stocked up just days before and entered.

"Back so soon?" The proprietor behind the counter laden with everything from harness to dry goods, canned goods to candy, grinned. "What'd you do, lose your grub?"

"How did you know?" Andy asked.

The deadly words and menacing step that Andy took forward turned the storekeeper's face doughy. "Why, I'm just funnin', Mister," he said.

Andy relaxed and grinned sheepishly. Obviously, the man knew nothing. "Sorry. Three bad men held me up."

Color seeped back into the pasty face. "Sorry to hear it. What can I do for you?"

Andy chose sparingly: flour, bacon, saddle blanket, bedroll.

"Mighty lucky you had some of your money well hid," the proprietor said admiringly.

Andy didn't explain. He still had trouble figuring out why the thieves hadn't made him fork over everything. He merely nodded, waited until the friendly man put everything in an old flour sack, then paid him and walked out, nearly broke but secretly thankful. Strange, how things worked out.

"Might say those scoundrels actually did me a favor," he mumbled. "If they hadn't robbed me, I wouldn't be back in Moab and know Sheik's whereabouts and what those four men aim to do."

A frown marred his smooth forehead. He had to get to Sheik before the quartet carried through their plan, or all his months of wandering and hardship meant nothing.

— + —

That night Andy lay snug and warm on a straw bed. The livery stable owner had agreed he could sleep there for two bits extra. Andy dug deep in his jeans and paid him for the night's lodging plus Chinq's board bill. "I'll be leaving early," he casually said. "Might as well square up now."

"Okay by me, Sonny." The old man grinned. His keen eyes beneath shaggy brows observed his customer until Andy knew that, if he had anything to hide, he wouldn't want this man quizzing him. He hastily bid the older man good night and set about mounding hay into a mattress. He slept soundly after the last two nights of sketchy rest, and his brain awakened him to the sun peeping over the eastern horizon. Before Moab had begun to stir, man and beast had quietly left town.

Once out of sight of possible curious watchers, Andy turned Chinq north and west—straight toward the place called Dead Horse Point. Thirty-some miles lay between him and his destination, and a sense of urgency whispered in his ear, *Hurry, hurry*. Chinq responded to his commands and swung into her easy, tireless stride, which covered the miles and left her rider free to cogitate his next moves.

Chapter 2

When Andy Cullen stood on Dead Horse Point and gazed into the canyon below, he knew he would never forget it. Two thousand feet of red, orange, and rust cliffs, purple-shadowed by late evening, lay at his feet and ended in the curving Colorado River below. Tortuous, twisting, ever cutting, to Andy's trained eyes, it looked a little wider than a rusty ribbon. He had stood on the south rim of the Grand Canyon in Arizona Territory and gazed at the same river miles south and west. Now he experienced the identical sense of awe, of his own smallness compared with the greatness of a God who created such untamed beauty.

He turned away, only to swing back and look again. In those few seconds, the canyon's face had mysteriously changed. Pockets of mist hovered, mercifully disguising the raw, wounded cliffs, softening and draping them until a mere beholder dwindled in proportion to their might.

A verse that Joel, the boy preacher, once quoted in a sermon about David, the shepherd boy who became king, came to mind. *The fool hath said in his heart, There is no God.* Andy shook his head. No man could stand where he stood, see what he saw, without knowing how big a fool one must be to believe such a lie. He bared his head with its shock of ripe corn hair, held his Stetson in one hand, and watched until lengthening shadows warned of the need to make camp. Yet the spell of the canyon, the stirrings within him to know its Creator better, overrode the excitement of his wild horse chase.

—✠—

Morning brought a whole new set of shifting shadows, and again the canyon's face lay changed and appealing. Andy found himself reluctant to ride on, even though he had learned what he wanted to know. The four men in the Moab cafe had been right. The promontory, reached only by that neck of land, offered the finest natural corral in the world once a high fence closed off its entrance behind a band of horses.

"Ump-umm," Andy told Chinq. His brown eyes glistened. "There ain't no man alive who can build a fence high enough to hold Sheik unless he's been tamed." A thrill of pure joy went through him. Every story of the racing black stallion that Andy had unearthed in his search for him made Andy more determined to catch, tame, and own the half-Arabian horse. His quick mind seized on a name used in the Moab cafe. Allen, George Allen. He wrinkled his forehead in concentration and saddled Chinquapin. "I've heard of him, old girl. Runs a big spread near Moab. What's the name of it? Lazy A, Bar A, no. . .Rocking A. That's it." With the toe of his boot, he traced an A in the dust. "If we don't find Sheik before our supplies give out, we'll head for the Rocking A and have a little confab with Mr. Allen. If it ain't too late for spring roundup, he can probably use an extra hand. We're pretty good shakes at cutting and branding, aren't we, Chinq?" A solemn look settled over Andy's merry face. Taking time out to earn money to restock their supplies meant that much time away from tracking Sheik and his band. In the meantime, the Moab quartet would be moving ahead with their plan to fence off the promontory.

He shook off forbidding thoughts, carefully stamped out the remains of his breakfast fire, and stretched his lithe body in a sky-reaching move, then vaulted to Chinquapin's back, young, alive, and hopeful.

The hope ran swift and hot in his veins for a few days, then petered out along with the horse tracks he'd been following. The wily Sheik obviously knew every escape trick recognized by pursuers, and then some. Just when Andy felt he'd catch the band the next day, a stretch of solid rock with tracks that led to the edge and disappeared stopped him short. "Where. . . ?" He peered down, squinted, and looked across the steep expanse of sheer rock. Horses couldn't traverse that, could they? Especially unshod horses, even Sheik. It took Andy's best skills to discover an innocent-looking narrow side trail—one of a dozen like it—with signs of his quarry. "Horse droppings," he exulted. He climbed down from the saddle and examined them. "Yippee! Still fresh." Fired with new enthusiasm, he led Chinq onto the trail barely wide enough for a horse and squeezed between high, jagged rocks. "I wouldn't bring you in here if other horses hadn't come first," he assured his suddenly skittish mare. "There has to be a wide place to turn around, or Sheik wouldn't have brought his band here."

Chinquapin snorted, and Andy laughed. She sounded totally disgusted at the cramped conditions. "If you were Jim Perkins, right now you'd be bellyaching and saying, 'Snappin' crocodiles, where are we goin'?' " he teased.

Chinq shook her head but obediently followed. A right-angle turn took some coaxing before the mare trotted on behind him. How on earth had Sheik discovered the trail in the first place?

"I'll just bet he was being chased. Or maybe his father before him knew the place." He led Chinquapin over a few fallen rocks and shuddered. One good rumbling of the earth would send a shower of boulders and trap any living creatures between the walls that bordered the trail.

Another turn, this time to the left, and—

"My word!" Andy stopped so suddenly that the chestnut mare bumped into him. The trail and rock walls ended simultaneously. A small green valley with red-rock cliffs surrounding it lay ahead, narrow where he stood, widening for about a mile before reaching the sheltering cliffs. A stream ran through it. Lush green grass covered the valley floor, and the rotting remains of an old cabin leaned tipsily beneath the shade of an enormous cottonwood. They vaguely impressed themselves on Andy's mind in his sweeping, lightning glance but slipped into unimportance when he focused his gaze on the far end of the box canyon. A herd of horses stood grazing. Mares, colts, yearlings.

Andy sucked in his breath and strained his eyes to see. His heartbeat quickened. "Where's Sheik?"

Chinquapin tossed her head and neighed. With uncharacteristic independence, she pranced from behind her master and galloped down the valley toward her own kind.

"Chinq!" Andy yelled, more amused than angry.

She ignored him and raced on.

"Great. We've tracked them all this way, are nearly out of grub, and Sheik ain't around. Chinq deserts me, and here I stand like one of them dummies in a store window." Andy shook his head and started forward. His mare had reached the band now. A few of the horses raised their heads; others went on grazing. One old mare nipped at the newcomer's flanks, and Chinquapin danced away, whinnying a protest.

Suddenly tired by disappointment as well as the long chase, Andy headed down the valley. "It ain't reasonable for this band of horses to be here without a stallion," he muttered. "Who led them in here, anyway?" His practiced gaze checked out the colts and yearlings. Not a horse there looked capable of heading up a band like this one. There had to be a stallion with the herd, but where was he?

The horrid scream of a horse in mortal terror split the peace of the quiet valley. Andy's heart leaped until he could barely swallow. He'd heard such screams before, not often, thankfully. Fear lent speed to his booted feet. He veered off to the left, splashed across the surprisingly deep stream and through a clump of screening cottonwoods, aware of pounding hooves behind him as the herd responded to the cry.

A heartrending sight met him when he stopped on the other side of the cottonwoods. A black stallion fought desperately to free himself from a tumble of rocks at the foot of a cliff. Half-buried, his powerful body lunged against the imprisoning boulders that trapped him. Andy saw a dusty trail winding up the red mountain, no wider than the one on which he'd come. So it wasn't a box canyon after all. The trail provided an alternate way out.

"Wrong," he whispered. "No man or beast will get out that way. Sheik— it has to be him—got caught partway up and was swept down." He longed to rush forward but restrained himself. "God, what can I do? If he thrashes around, he's going to either break his legs or kill himself." Tears dimmed his eyes at the sight of the magnificent, losing fight. The black screamed again. Dark shadows blotted out the sun—buzzards, gliding down to perch on nearby rocks and wait.

"No!" Andy could not stand by and see Sheik become buzzard bait. He instinctively reached for his Colt and drew and cocked it. The greatest gift he could give Sheik was instant death. He raised the revolver, aimed. His hand shook until he couldn't steady it. Andy sobbed, all his boyish love for the legendary horse flowing forth in renunciation of his dream. "Good-bye, Sheik."

He took a deep breath and held it. His arm stilled. In a second he would pull the trigger and pray for the first bullet to reach the stallion's brain. If he missed, could he force himself to fire again?

Before Andy could squeeze the trigger, a cold nose poked itself over his left shoulder and against his cheek. Distracted, Andy hesitated and glanced at Chinquapin. She lipped his ear, then stepped away. He tore his gaze from her and glanced back at the black, whose struggles looked feebler, slower. Again he steadied the revolver.

A clatter of hooves. A chestnut mare moving into his vision. "What's going on?" Andy's unshaven, lower jaw dropped. Chinquapin had again deserted, this time to pick her way across the fallen rock until she reached the trapped stallion. Like a slave to her master, she made a beeline to him and stopped only feet away.

"Chinq, come back!"

*Ba–ack. . .ba–ack. . .*came the echoes from the red cliffs.

"Chinq!" Andy implored and sprinted toward her. The cliffside had slid once. It could slide again, trapping her as well as Sheik. Frantically, Andy prayed, "Lord, You made these critters. Please, help me save them." He considered and rejected a dozen ideas. By the time he could remove the rocks, Sheik would be gashed and weakened from blood loss, if it were not already too late. Every ounce of strength would go into fighting man, his long-held foe, should Andy get close. Just now, Sheik lay still, watching Chinquapin—and her master. The cowboy knew it would not last long, yet his only hope rested in that stillness.

"Lord?"

Like a bolt of lightning, a bit of range lore lunged into his consciousness. No one on the Double J ever considered using it; too dangerous, the older hands said. But some wild horse tamers practiced a method hated by most ranchers. They creased a horse with a bullet, not shooting to kill but to stun. By the time horses regained their senses, they had been securely tied.

Desperate men take desperate chances. With a quick prayer, Andy once more raised his revolver. If the bullet went too deep, it meant the end of Sheik's suffering. If not. . . He scarcely let himself hope.

Andy fired. *Spang.* The sound of the shot ricocheted back and forth across the valley, bounced off the walls, and repeated itself a hundred times. The herd, who had crowded close to its fallen leader, reared, snorted, and raced away. All but Chinquapin, who stood looking down at the motionless stallion with great eyes.

Andy leaped toward the horses. If the shot had grazed as he intended, he had no time to lose. He whooped with joy when he saw the rise and fall of breath that showed the stallion hadn't been killed. "Thanks, Pard," he shouted and attacked the boulders with all his might, glad for the muscle and bone and sinew made hard by clean living and excruciating work. Rock after rock he tossed aside, until he'd freed Sheik's front feet. In a twinkling, he tied them together. "Can't take a chance on his coming to and striking out," he told Chinquapin, who had crowded closer to watch. He also blindfolded Sheik with his bandanna.

A shudder went through him when he saw the torn flesh on the black's flanks, but he couldn't stop with his digging. A ripple of movement through Sheik's frame warned that the effect of the bullet had almost worn off. With a last desperate effort, Andy tackled the remaining rocks and firmly secured the wounded horse's back feet.

"Just in time." He mopped his sweaty face. Sheik's body shook with a convulsion that would have brought him to his feet if he hadn't lain bound.

He jerked his head up as far as he could and struggled to stand. Another scream of frustration rent the air.

"It's all right, Boy. You've been hurt, and I helped you. Take it easy. I ain't going to hurt you," Andy soothed.

He might as well have spit against the wind for all the good it did in calming the stallion. Sheik bared his teeth, emitted another full-throated scream, and tried to reach his captor in a mighty bite.

Andy laughed. "I don't blame you. If somebody shot at me and I came to tied like a bulldogged steer, I'd holler, too. Take all the time you need getting used to me. We ain't going anywhere. There's water here, and I'll bet there's game. You and me and Chinquapin are going to get to be real good friends before we leave this hideout of yours."

One of the buzzards let out a squawk, flapped its wings, and flew off. The others followed. Andy's mirth changed to a grim gladness. "No meal for you here, scavengers." He strode to Chinquapin, led her back near the dilapidated shack, and peered inside. "Ugh. Unless it pours, I'll stay outside." Deft hands unpacked supplies, threw off the saddle and new saddle blanket. Free of her burden, Chinquapin danced a bit, then to her owner's surprise, headed back to the fallen stallion.

"Well, found yourself a sweetheart, have you?" Andy grinned and rummaged in his saddlebags. He brought forth soap, a soft cloth, and the extra hackamore he packed for just such an occasion as this. No better time to get it on the black than when he lay helpless. Even so, it took all his strength to avoid the big, vicious teeth and wild turnings of Sheik's magnificent head long enough to get him bridled. He tightened the long loop that served in place of a bit over the stallion's nose. Time enough for that later. Right now, all he wanted to do was to get Sheik used to him and tend to his torn flesh.

It took a full hour to wash the wounds and involved Chinquapin's help in getting the stallion on his feet. Andy loosened the sturdy ropes around Sheik's legs enough to force him to hobble to the creek at the end of a lasso wound around the chestnut mare's saddle horn. "Hold him fast," Andy ordered. Using a cooking pan scoured clean with red sand from the creek bottom, Andy poured stream after stream of water over the black, rejoicing in its chill. His keen gaze had discovered where it gushed from the rocky earth near the base of a cliff. It could be the mouth of one of the many southwestern streams that seemingly vanished into nowhere, then reappeared in the unlikeliest places.

"There, old boy. I've done what I can." Andy eyed the drenched horse, then ordered Chinquapin to haul him out. "Thanks, Lord. No broken legs. He's not even limping; just hating and fighting the ropes. He couldn't have lost all that much blood, either, or he wouldn't have the stamina to keep struggling. Glad he stayed a little dazed until the worst of it got over."

Andy had already selected the spot to anchor Sheik. Two cottonwoods in the grove had grown to massive proportions with only three or four feet separating them. The sturdy chestnut mare, used to planting her feet and staying while her rider worked with recalcitrant steers, proved invaluable in getting Sheik into the proper position. Andy quickly crosstied the stallion between the trees, wisely leaving him blindfolded and hobbled. Tomorrow would be time enough for removing the bandanna. "Okay, old boy, let her rip." Andy slackened and removed the rope that bound Sheik to Chinquapin.

Sheik exploded as much as a horse so bound could do. He neighed and screamed, lunged and fought. The crosstied ropes from the hackamore to the cottonwoods on either side of him obviously infuriated him. So did his hobbled feet. By the time weakness from his ordeal stopped the performance, the stallion stood hot and sweating.

Andy automatically reached for the tin pan to give him water. He stopped and slowly shook his head. Cruel as it seemed to let a horse go hungry and thirsty, if he ever meant to tame the black, he must deprive him of food and drink for a day or two. Nothing else could make Sheik amenable to even the most loving, tender care. He eyed the drooping horse standing exhausted. For a single moment, Andy hated himself. Why should he imprison this animal, any more than he'd clip the wings of a high-soaring eagle? Yet, if he did not, someone else would.

"I guess I'll love you more than anyone else could," he told Sheik. Chinquapin perked her ears, and he hastily added, "Not more than you, Pard. You're the best." The chestnut rubbed her soft nose against his shoulder, then ambled over to stand near the tied stallion, far enough away that if he lunged, she'd be out of striking distance, close enough so her soft whinny reached him.

Andy noticed how the drooping ears lifted and the way Sheik raised his head. An answering whicker confirmed the cowboy's suspicions. If he tamed Sheik, a lot of the credit must be given to his faithful Chinquapin.

All through the night, he heard the restless stirrings of the captured stallion. Andy slept fitfully, yawned himself awake at first light, and built a fire. Hot coffee, bacon, and biscuits from the night before, toasted over the coals, sent new energy through him, although he could barely tear his gaze free from Sheik. Just before he'd opened his eyes, Andy had felt it all a dream. It seemed impossible the black stood securely tied just yards away.

"Sheik, I hate keeping you like this," he told the proud and unbeaten horse who lunged toward the sound of the voice. The crossties held firm, and Andy darted in, snatched off the bandanna blindfold, and leaped back, none too soon. Instead of appreciating the slight freedom, Sheik plunged and tried to rear, acting more enraged than ever.

"At least it tells me you aren't hurt too badly." Relief washed over the slim cowboy. Morning light reflected small gold twinkles in his laughing brown eyes, and his corn-colored hair tossed wilder than ever. "Sorry to do it, but you'll have to go without feed another day. Once some of the ginger gets out of you, we can get on with the business of turning you into a grand saddle horse." He also left the rope hobbles on. Ahead lay the need to check the gashes on Sheik's flanks to make sure they healed without infection, and wicked, flying hooves didn't lend themselves to doctoring.

Bright sun poured into the hidden valley. Sheik settled into an uneasy doze broken by periods of fighting the ropes. Andy took pity on him in late afternoon, snubbed him to Chinquapin's saddle, and let the veteran cow pony lead the black into the creek. He again poured icy water over the stallion's back and sides and grunted with pleasure when he saw how nicely the wounds were coming in the healing air. This time when Andy crosstied Sheik, he left a tiny bit of slack in the ropes, just enough so the horse could lower his head and drink the small amount of water his new master placed in the pan.

"No use trying to get you to drink from my hat," he told the stallion. "Right now you're hating the man smell most as much as you hated the slide. If you behave, tomorrow you can eat."

By the next evening, a vastly subdued horse stood between the cottonwoods. All day he had eyed his herd, grazing in the thick green grass Andy withheld by keeping the crossties tight enough to prevent Sheik's mouth from reaching the ground. He had stayed quiet most of the day, especially when Chinquapin devotedly hovered nearby. Andy noticed how the big black alternated between ignoring his captor and stealing glances at him. He whistled and saw Sheik's ears prick. "Old boy, someday you'll come when I whistle," he promised. "Same as Chinq does." He affectionately pulled the mare's mane, and she rubbed her nose against his shoulder. "With you as stud, maybe I'll get me a little spread back near the Double J, raise horses, and get married."

His eyes opened wider. Not since his early infatuation for Columbine Ames had he dreamed of ever settling down. A slow smile crawled over his expressive face. A boy's shy admiration had been successfully diverted from lovesickness to a staunch friendship. Not a pang smote Andy when he saw Columbine and Smokey Travis stand and take wedding vows. Neither had Andy's frank approval of the girl from Payson he once thought about courting amounted to anything serious. Heart whole, he had ridden away with no regrets.

"Funny, me thinking about getting hitched," he told the quiet valley. Yet in spite of his preoccupation and thrill of the conquest, his anticipation of the days, perhaps weeks he would need to break Sheik, the vision of a snug cabin with a couple of kids playing near its door and Sheik, Chinquapin, and their colt or filly close by, persisted in knocking at his heart's door.

Chapter 3

At the same time Andy Cullen restlessly waited for winter to pass so he could go wild horse hunting, storms beat New England with a vengeance. Linnet Allen, as small and birdlike as the finch for which she had been named, disconsolately stared into a snow-swirled January afternoon from a conveniently placed velveteen settee. Usually she loved the view from her Boston home. Seasons came and went with the same regularity that ruled the eighteen-year-old girl's life with her father.

From the highly polished window glass, a shadowy figure distorted by the snow into a caricature of the brown-haired girl with the soft blue eyes stared back at her. Pale skin gleamed and made her thin face all planes and angles. She raised a frail hand to blot out the sight, then deliberately blew on the chilled glass. A mist rose, obscuring her image. Before it could vanish as her girlhood dreams had done, she traced her name, then the date in the beaded moisture. *Linnet Allen, January 17, 1892.* She stared at the word. If what she felt in her heart came to pass, she wouldn't be there to write the date in 1893.

No tears fell at the thought as they had the first time she realized how weak she'd grown. From childhood, Linnet had been taught the plan of salvation. She had no fear of dying. Her mother already waited in heaven to welcome the beloved daughter she'd left behind years before. Without morbidness, Linnet considered her situation, and when the mist came, she knew that pity for the father who adored his only child inspired her tears.

She hastily brushed them away. For as long as God allowed her to remain, she must play the game with her father, pretending that one day she'd be well and strong. Even when his brown hair whitened and his blue eyes so like hers wore sadness, they continued pretending for each other's sake. Sometimes she wondered if he thought she didn't know how short a time she had left and kept up the game to spare her. Words often trembled on her lips. How much better to bring things into the open! Yet each time, she stilled them. Perhaps her father found comfort in believing she had a future. If so, Linnet must not take it away from him.

Such long years of invalidism, ever since her mother died. Linnet counted them on her fingers. She'd just been seven years old when her mother died giving birth to Judson George Allen, the baby brother who lived only long enough to open his eyes for a single look at the world before following his mother. Eleven years, yet so clearly imprinted on her memory that Linnet recalled each detail with astounding clarity.

"Linnet, Darling, Mother and Baby Judd have gone to live in heaven with Jesus," her father told her, his voice muffled against the little girl's soft hair.

She sat stock-still, unable to comprehend. *"But Mother said I'd have a little brother or sister."*

"You do, but he had to go with Mother."

"Does God need them more than we do?"

The grown-up Linnet still flinched at the memory of her father gathering her close and brokenly saying, *"Perhaps. We still have each other, and someday we'll see Mother and little Judd again."*

The despondency didn't come all at once. A sharp bout with influenza left Linnet weak and subject to grief. Judd Allen did everything possible to help. He called in specialists who examined her, shook their heads, and mumbled platitudes. One forward-thinking doctor declared that the loss of a mother and the baby brother she'd been promised, combined with the high fevers from her illness, had left an indelible mark. In time, Linnet recovered enough to be up and about but with only enough stamina for limited activities. A heart specialist said the muscles of her heart evidently had been weakened and that she must rest and not extend herself.

Linnet docilely followed orders. She ate and drank what the servants brought her, dabbled in the kitchen when she felt like it, and lived life through the wealth of books her father provided. Her keen mind far outstripped her frail body. A succession of governesses and tutors helped her to develop her mental faculties. She not only devoured the classics and romantic novels but avidly read newspapers and delighted her father with her perceptive insight into current problems. By her sixteenth birthday, Linnet Allen had earned the reputation of possessing wisdom beyond her years. She had also made such splendid physical progress, that her father proudly talked of sending her to college.

How her blue eyes glistened! For the first time in her life, she'd be normal, live with other young women her own age, study and make friends, perhaps even fall in love. Pale rose swept into her white skin at the thought. The most beautiful love story she had ever heard came from her own parents. Would God someday send a man as strong and caring as her father to share her life?

A week after her birthday, her rosy illusions shattered. A sudden fluttering of her heart, followed by sharp pains, served notice that the strenuous college life she coveted must forever remain out of reach. A conclave of physicians agreed on that completely.

"Darling, I know how disappointed you are," her father gently told her. His face looked careworn in the dim light of a dying fire. "There's a good side, though. I won't have to be here all alone."

Linnet summoned all her courage, smiled, and gaily told him, "That's right. I'll be here to make sure you take care of yourself."

The attack ended as suddenly as it had come, with no noticeable aftereffects. Still, a change had entered the Allen household. A deepening of the pretend game; an acceptance on Linnet's part of her uncertain life span. If sometimes she rebelled, she reminded herself that God loved her and knew best. Her deepest pain lay in concern for the father who would have no one except God. The depths of his faith would see him through, but how many lonely years would he face before joining his family in a world without tears and sickness and parting?

A heavy step in the hall, quicker than usual, and Judd Allen entered the quiet room. "What? Sitting in the dark?"

"I hadn't noticed," Linnet truthfully said. "I've been watching the storm." She smiled and rejoiced at the look of gladness that replaced the anxious expression he wore when feeling unobserved. A white envelope dangled from his well-shaped hand. "A letter? From whom?"

"Your uncle George."

Excitement lent color to her pale face. "Really?" Uncle George rivaled Sirs Lancelot and Galahad in Linnet's list of earthly heroes. A year younger than his brother Judd, the breezy, tanned man swept into the staid Boston home like a sturdy western breeze on his infrequent visits. He looked ten years younger than Judd, with his sun and laugh wrinkles around the Allen blue eyes. Linnet's greatest dream had centered around growing well enough to one day visit her uncle's Rocking A ranch in far-off Utah.

Judd Allen turned up the gaslight, and the shadows fled from the big room to hover waiting in the corners. Linnet ignored them. Lips parted, she leaned forward.

"Here, little finch, you read it." Her father tossed the letter into her lap.

With eager hands, she tore open the envelope and read the bold scrawled words aloud.

"Dear Judd and Linnet,

I find I won't be able to get back East for a visit this spring or summer after all. Seems like it's getting harder all the time to get good, reliable hands. The sheriff relieved me of three of my newest not long ago on account of their taking ways—taking critters that don't belong to them.

Why don't you hop on the train and come see me? The Rocking A's the best place on earth to get some meat on your bones, Linnet. You can ride and walk and sleep with windows wide open to the fresh air. Best thing in the world for you. You, too, Judd. Last time I saw you, you looked like city death. Come on out here, and we'll fatten you on prime beefsteak.

George

P.S. Better yet, how'd you like to buy half of the Rocking A? Sell home and business, and come live with me. The ranch house is big enough for a dozen. We'll marry Linnet off to one of our Utah or Arizona cowboys and fill the house with their kids. This lonely old bachelor's hankering for kinfolk and someone to carry on the ranch after he's gone."

A peal of laughter came from Linnet's lips at the prospect. Every picture of cowboys and ranches, all Uncle George's stories of the real West with bawling cattle and ornery horses, cliffs and floods and canyons, melded into a colorful, beckoning life that lured with its mystery. The unknown as well as the known tantalized Linnet.

"How I'd love to go!" Her thin face glowed with excitement. "Father, could we?"

The lines in Judd Allen's face deepened as if drawn with heavy black ink. "Darling, I don't see how."

She read the unspoken reason in his face. In her condition, she'd be lucky to get out of Boston before collapsing. Disgust with herself for not fighting mingled with sharp longing. "If I get better, can we go?" She hated the pain in his eyes and bit her lip. Yet rebellion churned inside. She would die soon. She knew and accepted it. Yet must she die before she had ever really lived? Before she saw anything other than Boston and the nearby shore? *Never!*

The little word her heart shouted made her gasp. She willed her body to relax. The one thing the physicians agreed on was her need for peace and quiet. On the other hand, what had they given her except a lassitude that robbed her of the will to walk more than a few steps?

Linnet jerked back from her thoughts when her father lifted one of her pale hands and jokingly asked, "Think these could hold the reins? Or is it that cowboy husband George promised that makes you so eager to go west?"

She tried to match his mood. "Maybe." She forced a grin. "Wonder if Uncle George thinks any cowboy will do or if he has one in mind?"

"I hope not!" Genuine alarm rang in her father's voice. "Think how disappointed the bowlegged specimen would be if he's expecting a bride from Boston and you should arrive, fasten that blue gaze of yours on another cowpoke, then leave Bowlegs dangling!"

What a sport he was. Linnet pretended to wipe her eyes free of laughter to hide the mist. "You haven't answered my question," she accused. "Besides, not all cowboys are bowlegged, are they?"

"I don't know," he admitted. His eyes darkened. "If you get well enough to go by spring or summer, I'll take you." He hunched his shoulders, stood with legs apart and hands on his hips. "We'll fork a coupla hawses an' ride off into the sunset, right, Pardner?"

Her proper Bostonian father looked so ridiculous, Linnet couldn't help laughing again. "Sooo, you've been reading Western novels instead of business reports, have you?"

He haughtily raised his head and looked down his nose at her. "My dear daughter, do try to control your vulgar curiosity. Any well-informed man attempts to become familiar with a wide variety of cultures—"

"Including the American West?" she teased.

"Of course." He looked embarrassed, and his eyes twinkled. "I have to confess, I've always envied George and his life on his ranch."

"Really?" Linnet sat bolt upright. Never before had her father indicated in any way dissatisfaction with his lifestyle. Had he secretly longed to break free of their long line of proper ancestors as Uncle George had done when young? Had he held him back with her invalidism? She winced at the thought. The seed of an idea sprang into her fertile mind. She started to speak, then snapped her mouth shut. This wasn't the time. First she must consider and pray.

"Would you ever think over selling out here and going in with Uncle George as a partner?" She tried to make the question insignificant and felt she'd failed miserably but saw that her father found nothing abnormal in it.

"Depends on what time of day or year it is," he said. He patted his lean stomach. "Speaking of time, isn't it nearly time for dinner? I'd better wash up." He strode to her, leaned over, and dropped a light kiss on her forehead.

375

Linnet noticed the new spring in his step and felt it answered her question more fully than his words did. Uncle George's letter had raised her father's spirits, no doubt about it. The trickle of knowledge fell on the planted seed and watered it.

—+—

The entire dinner table conversation centered around the Rocking A, Uncle George, and his remarkable letter.

"I think he's lonely," Linnet frankly stated while the maid removed the remains of the main course before serving dessert.

"One of the things about remaining unmarried is the lack of someone to grow old with," her father replied. "I know that's poor grammar, but it's true. Another thing. The more years one accumulates, the more important family grows unless there are bad feelings between family members."

"You really miss him, don't you?" Linnet put down the silver spoon she had picked up to use with her fluffy pudding.

"Yes." The simple word held a world of longing.

For the first time, she saw him not as her father but as a man with whom life had not always dealt kindly. Strong, faithful to the God of his forefathers, he kept the commandments learned at his mother's knee and had successfully battled adversity without allowing bitterness to creep in. Yet all these years he must have missed the wife he'd adored and the little son given for such a brief moment. Linnet knew he had poured out all his love to her, never seeming to need other companionship. The warmth of her awareness centered on her rapidly sprouting idea, and by the time she went to bed in her four-poster with the lovely counterpane, that idea had become a bud, then a full-blooming flower.

Wide awake long after she normally slept, Linnet considered every aspect of Uncle George's letter and tried to arrange the petals of her idea in a logical order.

"First, God," she prayed, "Father and I have to speak frankly. Playing our pretend game won't work any longer." She dreaded the confrontation, but it loomed large and was a formidable foe to her rapidly burgeoning plan. Until they faced her health situation honestly and together, nothing else could happen.

"Next, what does it matter if I die here or in Utah? I know You're with me. If I can only grow strong enough for the train journey, it will get Father away from Boston and all his sad memories. He will have that someone to grow old with that he spoke of when discussing Uncle George." A feeling of rightness crept into her heart.

"God, I can't tell him I want to do this for him, or he won't let me take the risk. I have to convince him it's my last wish, and if he takes me west, he's fulfilling it." She sighed in the darkness. Fooling her father wouldn't be easy. Yet, was it really fooling? She *did* long to see something other than the pictures from her window and the sights of Boston in the carriage rides growing less and less frequent, due to her declining health.

"Dear heavenly Father," she prayed just before sleep claimed her. "All of this can only happen if it's Your will, not what I want or think is best." She turned over and knew no more until a light tap on her door announced morning.

"Breakfast in bed, Miss Linnet?" the maid asked as she poked her head through the doorway.

Linnet thought of her new resolve. "No. I'll slip on a housecoat and slippers and come down." She smiled at the maid. "Thank you for lighting my fire. You slipped in so quietly, I never heard you."

"My pleasure, Miss." A flash of friendship passed between the two, one so sturdy and useful, the other, frail and hampered. "Can I help?"

"No, thank you. Just tell Father I'll be down, please."

"Very good."

The door closed. Linnet slid from beneath her covers, quickly washed her face and hands in the bowl of steaming water that greeted her every morning, and donned a warm wrapper and slippers. "Uncle George never said what conveniences his ranch house has. Wonder if I'll have to wash in ice water and build my own fires?" She shivered at the thought. "Well, God, here goes." She slowly made her way downstairs to the pleasant breakfast room.

Judd Allen's blue eyes shone when she came in. He left his position in front of the roaring fire in the fireplace and led her to the nearby table hopefully set for two. The storm had stopped, and pale winter sunlight gleamed through the windows and sparkled off glasses and silver. "How are you this morning, little finch?"

"Hungry." She didn't tell him her long hours of scheming had taken extra energy and left her famished. "What do we have for breakfast, hot biscuits and beefsteak?" She tipped her head in a pert manner.

Judd Allen burst out laughing. "Whoa, young lady. You're confusing this with the Rocking A. I'm afraid you'll have to settle for porridge and muffins or scrambled eggs, bacon, and fruit."

"A buttered muffin, then eggs, bacon, and a glass of milk."

His eyebrows shot up. "I thought you hated milk."

"Milk comes from cows. Cows live on the Rocking A," she told him. "Therefore, I will learn to like milk. Even if I have to hold my nose when I drink it. Milk is good for me," she droned in an imitation of a pompous physician who had thrown up his hands when she said she never drank milk.

Judd stared at her. All trace of mirth left his face. "Linnet, you know this is just pretend, don't you? We can't go to Utah."

His grave manner set her heart fluttering. "Let's talk about it after breakfast, Father." She smiled, and her lips quivered. She steadied them when he nodded, then managed to choke down a creditable breakfast.

Once the breakfast things had been taken away and the maid had shut the door, father and daughter settled into matching chairs across from each other in front of the blazing fire. Its cheery crackle mingled with the sunlight streaming in and added brightness to the small, pleasant room.

Linnet plunged in, taking only a moment for a final, silent prayer for guidance. She leaned forward, laced her fingers together on the soft blue flannel of her housecoat, and began, "We've needed to really talk for a long time, Father."

He didn't pretend to misunderstand. "I know," he said heavily. Despair, along with grief, settled into his face.

"I'm eighteen years old. Before long, I. . .I'll be gone." In spite of her best efforts, her voice broke.

"Linnet, if this is too hard for you, let it go." Judd Allen left his chair to kneel beside hers and take her frail hands in his strong ones.

She shook her head. "No." She looked at him, beseeching him to understand. "It's just that. . .I can't die when I haven't really lived." Words tumbled out, a dictionary of them, spilled by necessity into the quiet room and the ears of a father who loved her second only to their heavenly Father. She told him how she longed to go west, to see the fields and plains, the prairies and rivers, and mountains in between.

"You know the chance you'd be taking?" he hoarsely broke in at one point as his hands tightened on hers.

"I know. I could die on the way, except somehow, I don't think God will let that happen." Assurance she hadn't realized filled her lent credence to her prediction.

"Even if you could reach the Rocking A, all those things George promised are impossible. The riding and—"

"Bowlegs," she finished. A ripple of laughter shook her, but she found her eyes strangely wet. How foolish to weep over a cowboy she had never even met! "It doesn't matter. At least I'll have had that much."

"Don't you want to be, I mean. . ." He couldn't go on.

It took her a few seconds to comprehend. She freed one hand and patted the kneeling figure's brown hair. "I'll be with Mother and little Judd. They won't care about anything else. I think they'd also like my grave to be where you could visit it." She sensed he'd reached the breaking point. "Father, why don't we go? As soon as spring comes? You can do as Uncle George suggested. Sell out here, and plan to stay out west." She played her trump card. "You could keep him from being lonely." *And he will do the same for you,* she knew.

With an inarticulate cry, Judd released her hand and caught her close in his arms.

Linnet's heart leaped. She hadn't won yet, but she would. She must. In no other way could she ensure happiness for the man who meant more to her than anyone else in the world.

Chapter 4

The first discussion began a new era in the Allen household; other long talks followed. In the new atmosphere of honesty with pretense put aside forever, Linnet and her father grew closer than ever. She sometimes felt herself leaving girlhood behind and taking on the maturity of a young woman. She also saw how clearly she had been willing to continue as the pampered, loved child instead of accepting responsibility as a partner, thereby relieving her father of some of the load they now carried on a more equal basis.

Their former adult-to-child relationship changed as well to an adult-to-adult sharing that permitted both of them to open their hearts as never before. Linnet learned the depths of the love that her father still held for her mother. Many times tears secretly sparkled on her lashes. She would never love or be loved in that way. The shadowy image of the man who might have been her husband sometimes haunted her. She could never conjure up a face but smiled when he always wore a wide-brimmed western hat like her uncle George's Stetson. Although it had been several years since Uncle George had visited Boston, Linnet's mind remembered every detail of face and costume, especially the Stetson.

January snowed itself into February. February pouted and dallied between winter and early spring, much like a Southern belle at a cotillion flits from suitor to suitor. Linnet paid little attention. She embarked on a get-better program of her own creation. It included drinking milk and even learning to tolerate it, although her father teased and said the Rocking A ran beef cattle, not dairy cows. She slipped into soft, noiseless slippers behind her closed bedroom door and paced back and forth until her heart twinges reminded her not to overdo it. By the first of March, she had actually gained five pounds and could walk twice as long as before. She didn't tell her father. Raising false hopes would be cruel, yet Linnet couldn't help but know that the results of her hard work gradually began to show. She smiled, comparing her determination with the spirit of her ancestors that long ago fired them to flee religious persecution and settle in the New World a few crossings after the *Mayflower*.

Not until time for her next physician's visit did Linnet allow herself to hope too much. The surprise in his face and his, "Well, Miss Linnet, looks like you're holding your own, at the very least," brought joy to the household. She made a face at the spring tonic he prescribed to "help you continue as you're doing" but obediently swallowed it.

Linnet also secretly opened her bedroom window to the cold air and took great breaths into her lungs, knowing the physician would throw up his hands in disgust at such a practice. She'd read that a new school of thought believed fresh air to be beneficial rather than harmful. It made sense. If God didn't want people to breathe His air, He wouldn't have created it, she firmly told herself.

One evening in late March, Linnet marched downstairs and into the dining room. "Father, I need new clothing. I can barely fit into my old clothes."

"That's the best news you could give me," he told her. His eyes shone. "What kind do you need, eastern or western?"

She impulsively hugged him and felt excitement race through her. "What about simple garments I can wear in both places? May will be a nice time to travel, don't you think?"

"Let's make that in June. Less chance of snow in the high mountains that way." He courteously seated her at the table and sat down across from her.

"You mean we are really, truly going?" Linnet had trouble believing her own ears.

"I promised I'd take you if or when you were able to make the trip, didn't I?" His face wore the biggest smile in the world. It slowly faded when he added, "I have a good offer on the business. Shall I take it? By the way," he added in an offhand manner that didn't fool Linnet one bit, "the buyer of the store also likes this house."

She felt his questioning gaze on her. For a moment, she hesitated, feeling torn between the secure but unsatisfying life she'd known here and the uncertainty of life in the West. A terrible fear smote her. What if she were running before the Lord, arranging her life and her father's on a girlish whim to meet the selfish desire for adventure that dwelled within her? She risked a quick glance at her father. It vanquished fear. He looked even younger than Uncle George on his last visit. Some of the strain had gone from his face. Longing rested in his blue eyes, and eagerness showed in the way he held his knife and fork still, waiting for her reply.

"When do we leave?" she asked.

"I suggest June fifteenth."

Odd how the setting of an actual date made the venture real. Linnet felt a smile blossom onto her lips. "That should give me time to get a suitable wardrobe ready and to sort and pack what we want to take with us." She cast an affectionate look at some of the old, highly polished furniture. "Will Uncle George have room for it?"

"He said the ranch house is big; we'll have to ask how big."

—+—

One by one, things settled themselves into place. Linnet and her father thanked God when the new owners of the house and store eagerly agreed to keep the Allen servants on. None of them evidenced any desire to go west. "Too Boston," Judd announced. A frown wrinkled his broad forehead. "Can you get along without a maid on the train?"

"I can and will." Linnet stood straight and proud. "I'm so much better now, she wouldn't have anything to do."

April passed; May came in a cloud of blossoms. Eager as she was to leave, Linnet had to admit that the Boston spring had never been lovelier. Or perhaps it came with the fact that she now spent much more time outdoors, walking as well as riding in a carriage. A slight cold near the end of May, combined with drizzly weather, dampened their spirits. Surely after selling out and making such careful plans, Linnet's heart wouldn't flare up now. She shivered more at the thought than from her cold and laughed off her father's suggestion that they postpone their journey. Even when she didn't regain energy to the point she had been before the cold, she refused to consider waiting. A feeling of urgency drove her.

"How much strength does it take to sit in a train and look out the window?" she demanded when her father showed concern. "I'm just glad we have the money for first-class accommodations. Ever since George Pullman came out with his Palace Car Company's sleeping cars, transcontinental travel has been a lot more comfortable, at least according to the papers."

"You're right about that." Judd looked amused. "I've seen them. Burnished walnut fittings, heavy damask draperies, and deep plush seats that convert to beds are a real boon. I'd never consider taking you if it meant going coach. The poor folks who ride in them sleep where and as best they can, jammed together in sometimes dirty cars on a first-come, first-served basis."

That night Linnet dreamed of railroad cars. She saw herself running through endless cars filled with a wider segment of humanity than she'd ever seen before: cowhands and schoolteachers; dirtily clad miners traveling to new diggings; farmers and drummers with their wares. Some ragged, some bearded, some wearing revolvers. Now and then a professional cardsharp who gathered his victims in the parlor car and set about fleecing them. Still she ran, searching for she knew not what, until sharp pangs in her heart slowed her feet to a standstill.

She awakened hot and sweaty, tangled in her bedclothes. It hurt to breathe. Fear set her heart pounding. "God, are You here?" she whispered. Gradually her pulse quieted, and her breathing returned to normal. Yet the memory of the dream and its aftermath lived on. At first sign of light, she rose, reached for her Bible, and turned pages, hoping for a talisman to which she could cling. She knew God stayed near at all times. Yet if only she could find a special verse, one she could make her own letter from God along with the Twenty-third Psalm, John 14:1–4, and of course, John 3:16. Twenty minutes later she found it. Psalm 27:14: "Wait on the Lord: be of good courage, and he shall strengthen thine heart: wait, I say, on the Lord." She flipped a page of her well-worn Bible and discovered the same thought phrased a little differently in Psalm 31:24. "Be of good courage, and he shall strengthen your heart, all ye that hope in the Lord."

Comfort flowed through her like an incoming ocean tide. She slipped back into bed, still holding the Bible. "God, I don't know if this promises actual healing, but it says You will strengthen my heart if I wait and have courage. I already have the blessed hope You give through Your Son. Please, help me accept whatever Your will is in my life. In Jesus' Name. Amen."

Soothed, she fell asleep again and awakened to a new day, a new opportunity to wait and hope and practice that "good courage" of which David spoke.

In response to a hearty invitation to "ship any and all of your goods to the Rocking A," the Boston home had been depleted of favorite pieces of furniture. Trunks of her mother's dishes, protected by handmade quilts, had gone ahead, and most of the Allens' belongings would be at the ranch to welcome them. Linnet had patiently stood while a skilled dressmaker took her new measurements and later came back with new gowns, a riding skirt, and waists, undergarments, and petticoats to be tried on and admired. A heavy dark blue traveling costume hung waiting and ready in the closet, along with a matching hat. The private car they reserved meant Linnet and her father would be able to bathe and change clothing whenever they wished.

"And you'll wish real often," the droll railway ticket agent warned. "Even the Pullmans aren't immune from dust."

Linnet decided on the spot to wear the dark blue with several changes of waists on the trip west. "No use getting everything filthy," she announced. "I'll change when we go in the dining car for meals, though."

"You'll be the prettiest young woman there." Judd Allen's pride in his daughter oozed from every pore and brought a rich blush to her normally pale face, which had rounded out a bit under her get-better regime.

The time before leaving dwindled to a few weeks, a week, days. Any time Linnet felt weary, she repeated "her" psalm, took fresh courage, and thanked God for allowing her to make the trip and get her father settled with his brother on the Rocking A. Beyond that, she refused to think. Should, by some miracle, her life continue in Utah, it would bring great joy. For now, she found it enough that they could go.

Of all Linnet's new clothes, she liked her riding outfit best. She pushed from her mind that she might never wear it astride a horse. The dressmaker had cleverly fashioned the divided skirt so that when Linnet stood straight, she appeared to be wearing a full skirt that covered the tops of the boots her father had specially ordered. Nothing could be more modest or more convenient. "Unless I wore boys' pants." Linnet giggled and twirled to show how much freedom the divided skirt gave her. The rich dark green skirt had a pretty vest to match, with a creamy long-sleeved blouse and a clever green cap her father said would blow away in the first wind.

"Then I'll get a sombrero or Stetson," she bragged. "I wish I could wear these clothes all the time instead of my gowns that require—" She broke off and blushed again. Nice girls didn't discuss corsets with their fathers. She had wisely refused to let the dressmaker sew one of the new hourglass styles that demanded tight lacings to make her waist as small as possible. She had tried on such a dress, one ordered and rejected by another customer. She couldn't breathe well and heaved a sigh of relief when she got out of it.

Now she giggled again. The dressmaker had confided from a mouth filled with pins, "Miss Allen, I hear the girls and women in the West don't wear corsets at all. Can you believe that?" She pursed her thin lips.

"Maybe they're too busy being abducted and carried away on racing horses to worry about it," Linnet had said.

"No *lady* would go without a corset, regardless of the circumstances." The woman's look of horror quelled Linnet but didn't keep her from muttering under her breath, "Well, this lady is *not* going to be squeezed to death for the sake of fashion! I can't wait to wear my riding clothes. No one will ever know if I have on a corset or not."

The thought delighted her until she wondered why she hadn't realized how much she rebelled against what "they" say. Perhaps "they" would stay in Boston and she'd be rid of them and what they said when she got out west.

The only hard moment in all their leaving came with the final visit to the cemetery. Judd Allen and his daughter stood by the simple headstones that commemorated wife and mother, son and brother. Hands clasped, each offered a short prayer that they would be true to the God who made them and one day be reunited with Him and the rest of the family. When they turned away, Linnet felt the way she did at the end of a book, even though she knew a sequel was beginning. She looked at her father and, as happened so often, knew he understood.

An ending, a beginning. Then what? How long would Linnet's life last? *"He shall strengthen thine heart."* Her often-repeated verse ran through her mind. She closed her eyes, heart overflowing. Then she silently followed her father to the carriage that would transport them to the railway station. *Good-bye, Boston, with your snow and blossoms, your security and sameness. Good-bye, cemetery, home once happy that became a prison. Good-bye, good memories and sad. I'll take you with me,* she promised.

The carriage rumbled its way over the streets. Judd Allen said nothing. Linnet clutched his hand the way she'd done as a child. Once they left the city, they could relax and look forward. Now was the time to reflect and remember. Somehow, she knew without being told that neither she nor her father would pass through these familiar streets again. A few tears fell, and she surreptitiously wiped them away, knowing she wept for what might have been had Mother and little Judd lived, not for the long years in between.

—+—

America unrolled before Linnet and Judd Allen's fascinated gazes like red velvet carpeting before visiting royalty. Each state added its unique terrain to the great tapestry that made up the land of their birth. Accustomed to Boston and Boston alone, the travelers frankly gaped at stretching fields, hills and valleys, countless rivers, and uninhabited miles. The steady *clackety clack* of the wheels sang them to sleep, and they rolled relentlessly onward. The stopover in Chicago felt endless, and Linnet breathed a sigh of relief when they again took up their journey. Still, she admired the way the city's residents had pitched in and rebuilt their city after the terrible October 1871 fire.

"Did the fire really start in Mrs. O'Leary's barn?" she asked a fellow traveler who sat at the next table in the luxurious dining car.

"Oh, yes. It's a matter of history. A cow kicked over a lighted lantern," the helpful man told her. "The summer of 1871 was exceptionally dry, and in the evening of October eighth, strong winds sent flames racing north and east. They leaped the river and killed at least three hundred people, plus doing two hundred million dollars in property damage. My family and I were among the fortunate." A look of remembrance crept into his eyes. "We shivered in the lake for what felt like hours." He shrugged off unpleasant memories. "But so many fine architects seized the chance to help rebuild, that in less than fifteen years, Chicago became the nation's architectural capital," he finished proudly.

Linnet tucked the information away, as she did whenever she learned new things. All that damage, started by a single cow! Just like sin, starting from a seemingly innocent event, then fanning into a conflagration that destroys everything in its path. Her quick mind made a further connection. Those who escaped the devastating results had taken refuge in the lake. God offered refuge, too, through His Son. Those who came to Him need have no fear of the raging world behind them.

The look of the land changed. Linnet rose each morning and tantalized herself by not flinging apart the rich draperies that curtained her berth and not looking out the window until she had washed and dressed. Every day proved worth the self-discipline. Rolling hills gave way to flatland; farms and cornfields to grasslands. A small herd of buffalo grazed not far from the railroad tracks, and Linnet clapped her hands in delight. Her father's expression told her the sight thrilled him just as much as it did her.

Yet nothing could compare with their first glimpse of the Rocky Mountains. "I used to think the pictures artists painted had to be larger than life," Linnet confessed, face pressed to the window. "No picture can ever do this justice." Jagged peaks serrated the blue sky. Fat white clouds rested for a moment on the tops before scooting away to join their mates. Gigantic evergreen trees stood in sentinel ranks.

"*Semper fidelis,*" Judd softly quoted. "Always faithful."

Linnet could barely tear her gaze away from the scenery long enough to eat. From a full heart, she whispered, "Father, no matter what happens, this trip is right. I've worshiped God since childhood but have never felt His power and greatness so much as right now. It's like having a Best Friend for years and suddenly growing aware of how much more than a Friend He really is."

Her father's sympathetic silence and quick squeeze of her hand showed how deeply her words moved him.

The one bitter drop in the smooth amber honey of their journey west occurred the day before they reached Salt Lake City, where they would leave the train. Through visiting with friendly, congenial people in the diner, they'd heard many of the exciting stories of early railway travel and of how blizzards and spring floods played havoc from late fall to early spring. They rejoiced at their decision to wait. June had been lovely, and outside of a few blinding rainstorms and one thunder and lightning episode that left the Easterners wide-eyed, sunny days prevailed. Neither had they encountered ruffians, as some of the old-timers riding the train said used to barge into the palace cars. "Cowboys thought it fun to do some shooting and see folks duck," one leathery man told them. "Desperadoes held up trains, too, and took money and jewelry. We haven't had any of that for a spell."

"Don't speak too quickly," another bronzed outdoorsman put in. "We aren't there yet."

Linnet's overactive imagination proved her undoing. Sheltered by the damask draperies, she lay awake and nervous. "Don't be a silly goose," she admonished herself. "The man said these things didn't happen now." Yet she uneasily shifted position. What if a marauder burst in and demanded jewelry? Father had advised her to wear none on the train, but a fine string of pearls lay tucked in the toe of a slipper in her traveling bag, and Father's luggage held a small jewel case with a few other choice pieces that had been Mother's. Linnet had kept the pearls close, wearing them only in the privacy of their accommodations and putting them away at night.

Now fear assailed her. Wouldn't robbers look in the bags first of all if they came? The longer she lay there, the more upset she grew. Perhaps she should get up and move the pearls. She could pin them inside her high-necked, long-sleeved nightgown. She quietly sat up so she wouldn't disturb her father and, with one hand, reached to open her berth's draperies. A slight sound turned her to ice. Linnet held her breath and noiselessly slid the draperies open just enough to peer out. Suddenly, she felt faint. In the dim light cast by a one-eyed moon, a dark figure knelt on the floor not more than two feet from where she lay.

Chapter 5

For the space of a heartbeat, Linnet stared at the crouching figure before the words of her psalm rang in her brain. *"Be of good courage."* Anger she hadn't known she possessed raged through her. How dare this creature creep in here to plunder and rob decent people? She sprang from the bunk. "Who are you, and what are you doing?" she demanded.

"Linnet, Darling." The figure straightened.

"Father?" She reeled and clutched the side of the berth for support, keeping her voice low. Relief sagged her knees to the consistency of the pudding served at dinner.

"My head ached, and I thought you might have something in your bag. I didn't mean to frighten you." Remorse filled his voice.

"It's all right." She sat down on her berth and pulled her feet up from the richly carpeted floor. "I guess I just heard too many stories of intruders." She stifled a giggle. "There are some tablets in the small box." She lay back down, conscious that her father had found the tablets and had gone back to his berth. Yet the incident had taken its toll. A faint twinge in her chest reminded her that all the travel in the world, all the majestic mountains and cool, green valleys didn't change the unalterable truth. Linnet sighed and whispered, "God, I bargained with You for enough strength to get me here for Father's sake. . . and mine. Now I'm not content at all. Oh, but I long to ride and run and be free! Must I wait until I reach heaven to do all these things?" More forlorn than she had been in months, she closed her eyes, and for the last time, the clacking wheels sang her to sleep.

―✝―

Uncle George had arranged to meet them in Salt Lake City. "No stagecoach for you," he had written. "I'll be there with the prettiest pair of high steppers you ever saw and a buggy I designed specially for good riding. It's a long ways to the Rocking A from Salt Lake, and we'll take it in easy jaunts. Linnet, wait 'til you sleep with nothing except space between you and our Utah stars."

He was true to his word. Linnet stepped down from the train and into her uncle's waiting arms. He looked even bigger and browner than she remembered him. "Well, Lass, you're here." His keen gaze made Linnet feel he could see clear to her soul.

"Yes." No other words came. She wanted to pinch herself to make sure she wouldn't waken and find herself still in Boston.

George turned to his brother. He slapped him on the back, then gripped Judd's hand with a mighty paw. "Welcome, Pardner."

"Just remember, you're speaking to the new half owner of the Rocking A," Judd told him. His eyes flashed, and Linnet saw how much alike the two were. Except for the gray in her father's hair and his whiter skin, they could be taken for twins. Again, the sense of rightness about their journey warmed her through and through.

"What do you think of the West?" George asked them when they'd stowed away their traveling bags. "Uh, Linnet, don't you want to get out of those clothes and into something, well, a little more rugged? You, too, Judd."

Linnet looked down at her travel-worn outfit. Even the linen duster she'd worn for protection hadn't kept the dust off. "I hate putting on my pretty new riding outfit," she confessed to her uncle.

"You don't have to." George looked sheepish, then produced a large package. "I wasn't sure you'd have the right clothes so I brought some." He undid the string. "These should fit." He held out a heavy shirt, jacket, and jeans to Judd. "They're mine."

"And whose are these?" Linnet bit her lip to keep from laughing when he handed her a matching outfit, only smaller.

"We keep extra clothes on hand in case some ragamuffin cowpoke rides in," George said easily. He took a violently patterned red kerchief from the bottom of the parcel, then an equally bright blue one. "Tie these 'round your neck under your shirt collars. They help stave off dust and sunburn. There's a couple of sombreros in the contraption."

Linnet took the blue kerchief and eyed the curiously constructed buggy. Two-seated, it stood waiting on four high wheels.

"For fording streams," her uncle explained. He pulled a pocket watch out. "I hate to hurry you, but—"

"It's a long way to the Rocking A," Judd and Linnet chorused before repairing to the ladies' and gentlemen's rest rooms to change into western garb.

When Linnet stepped back outside, she felt more self-conscious than ever in her life. She looked totally unlike herself. The dark blue jeans fit as if tailored for her; so did the dark blue shirt. She'd tried on the sheep-lined jacket and knew how comfortable it would be once night fell. Neckerchief tied in a jaunty knot, she practically skipped to the contraption. Uncle George stood talking with a stranger, who turned out to be her father, looking as unfamiliar in his new clothes as she felt.

"Glad you chose the blue scarf," her uncle approved. "It matches your blue eyes." He helped her into the surprisingly soft backseat of the buggy, waited until Judd climbed into the front seat, and clucked to the matched pair of bays. "Giddyap there, David, Goliath." They moved off in perfect unison.

"Why do you call them that?" Linnet wanted to know.

Her uncle grinned back over his strong shoulder. "David in the Bible obeyed God. So does the horse on my right."

"And Goliath?"

"He's inclined to be lazy. He'd go lieth down if David didn't keep him moving."

Linnet started at her father's shout of laughter and the way he slapped his knee. She couldn't help joining in, and she thanked God for the sound. In all their years since her mother and little Judd died, she'd never heard her father laugh like that. Tears actually came to his eyes before he could stop.

"You never did say how you like it out here," George reminded, hands steady on the reins of the trotting pair.

Linnet found herself stammering. "It's big and kind of scary and awe inspiring and. . .and I love it all."

"Good. Now we'll show you some real country."

"I thought that's what we'd been seeing," Judd protested.

"Wait until you see the red-rock canyons and the valleys so green you wonder how the good Lord could make them that way." George's voice lowered. "Or purple and flame sunsets and sunrises, nights darker than black velvet 'til the moon comes out and lights up the world."

He drove on in silence so deep that his guests refrained from questioning him. "It's a grand country, this Utah Territory. One of these days we're going to be a state and the best one in the Union." He warmed to his subject. "It's got everything a man—or woman," he glanced back at Linnet again, "everything anyone could want. A lot of hardworking people have come and put down roots both here and in Arizona Territory, folks like me and now you."

Linnet's heart pounded as he talked. How much she had missed, confined to her velveteen settee, even though the changing seasons from her window offered beauty. It contrasted sharply with the land they traveled toward Moab, this ever-beckoning, protean land of stunted trees, small hills, mesas, rearing mountains, purple-shadowed forests in the distance. "Uncle George, tell me about the ranch."

He remained silent so long that she wondered if he had heard her. Then he quietly said, "Lass, I can tell you everything there is about the ranch and you still won't know it, any more than the folks who know all about Jesus but don't have the smattering of an idea what He's really like. You have to walk and ride the land, sleep out, get caught in storms and by early nightfall. Then you'll know the Rocking A."

"She can't do all those things," Judd reminded in a low voice. His shoulders slumped, and some of his joy left his face.

"Maybe not now. Give this wonderful land a chance. Time and again, I've seen folks come out here to die, then they find themselves made well by the air and peace our Father put here." He broke off, then added, "Of course, there's a lot of hazards. Mean broncs—we won't make you ride them right away—rattlesnakes, and not all of them crawl on their bellies." A thread of steel undergirded his warning. "Worst thing won't be a problem to you, Judd, just to Linnet. Lovesick cowboys aren't worth their feed."

She felt a blush start at the base of her throat and crawl under the blue kerchief and into her face. She couldn't resist demurely asking, "We wondered, when your letter came, if you had a special cowboy in mind for me."

"Naw. And believe me, any hand who thinks he's going to up and run off with my niece is facing two Rocking A owners to please. Right, Judd?"

"Right."

George abruptly changed the subject. "Would one of you like to drive?"

"I. . .I'd better not," Linnet faltered, even though her hands itched to get on the reins. A new and disturbing personality had been donned with her new garb, one who longed to forget heart problems and drink her fill of this strange life.

"I'd love to, if you think it's safe." Judd's glance toward his brother spoke volumes to the young woman watching from the backseat.

"David and Goliath will do what you tell them. Whoa, boys." George reined them in and changed seats so that Judd could easily reach the brake if necessary.

Linnet marveled at how quickly her businessman father had shed eastern reserve. Within moments, he handled the team as capably as his brother and won a covert glance of admiration followed by a canyon-sized grin from George.

Conversation subsided. Linnet realized for the first time how tired she had grown. Excitement had kept her going on the long train trip. Now she felt she could sleep for a month in the pungent, sagebrush-scented air that occasionally held a whiff of clover. She turned sideways, curled up on the comfortable seat, and relaxed, first her body, then her racing mind. She slept, roused to the men's low voices, then slept again. Once she wondered if she'd be the only woman at the ranch. Would she make friends in Moab, the nearest town? She sleepily smiled. Running in on neighbors or to a store out here meant a major undertaking, unlike Boston and its multitude of houses and shopping establishments. She yawned, too tired to pursue the thought.

"Should we wake her?" Her father's question brought Linnet back to consciousness. "She won't want to miss anything."

She started to open her eyes and stopped when George's reassuring, "She won't. These few red rocks are nothing compared with what's ahead. Let her sleep," reached her.

Linnet lay in a cocoon of peace until George said, "Now's a good time to tell me everything. How bad is she?"

She wanted to cry at her father's sad answer. "The doctors say it's just a matter of time. Her heart's been weak for years, and I've had her to every physician I could find."

"Including the Great Physician?"

"Always." Linnet had to strain to hear her father's confession. "I've never been able, at least yet, to tell Him that if it's His will to take her, it's all right with me."

The eavesdropping girl surreptitiously slid a hand over her mouth to keep from exclaiming. Poor Father. Her heart ached for him.

"You will, when the time is right." George's heavy hand fell on his brother's shoulder. "Now, let me make sure I understand. As far as you're concerned, it will take a miracle to save Linnet."

"Yes."

"Will you let me try? I'm no doctor, but if it isn't going to make a difference, I'd like to give it my best."

"What do you propose?"

Linnet lay like one dead. Every nerve end tingled. What amazing suggestions would this hero-uncle have other than the usual orders to rest, take her medicine, and so on?

"Throw away her corsets, first of all."

The subject of discussion found it nearly impossible for her to keep from howling. If the dressmaker could hear Uncle George! Linnet could imagine her face.

He wasn't through. "Judd, it doesn't make sense that women can squeeze themselves into instruments of torture until they can barely breathe and not do harm to their innards. How can a heart be healthy and do its job without plenty of room to beat?"

Linnet wanted to applaud. He'd merely echoed the new sentiments she'd recognized during her final dress fittings.

"She adores you. I think she'll do as you ask," Judd mumbled. "What else?"

"Exercise. Walking every day. Naturally her heart's weak when she hasn't done anything to strengthen it. My finest stallion and filly would soon become useless if not properly worked out."

If he hadn't been dead serious, Linnet's control would have broken. *First, no corsets; second, compared with a fine horse. What next?*

"Have her walk until she starts to feel tired, then not one minute more. My Indian friends have a recipe for living that the white man would do well to adopt. 'Eat before you get hungry; rest before you get tired.' In other words, don't wait until you're starved or exhausted, then try to make up for it by stuffing yourself or sleeping long hours. How's her appetite?"

"Better since we planned to come out here."

George grunted approval. "It'll improve when she exercises. No dainty meals for her, either, but good, honest grub that will build her up. I'm a pretty good hand at cooking, although I've always eaten most of the time in the cookhouse or had a Chinese houseboy. When I found out you were coming, I hired the best cook in the territory. Name's Mrs. Salt, and can she cook? I should smile, she can. Salt by name and salt of the earth, as the old saying goes. She'll mother Linnet to death, of course. Lost her own family years ago in a stagecoach accident. Since then she's been head cook in a Moab boardinghouse, but I offered her twice the wages plus a job as long as she wants it."

"What's she like?"

"About our age." George laughed heartily, and Linnet quickly closed her eyes when he glanced her way before lowering his voice. "If I wasn't a confirmed bachelor, I'd marry her. She's a dandy. Looks like one of those helpless little ladies who can't keep their parasol from blowing away but works like a mule. The ranch house hasn't been this clean since I had it built."

"Does she have a first name?"

"Sure. Sarah. Just don't call her by it. When I talked to her about taking on the Rocking A, she looked at me and said, 'I'll be happy to come, Mr. Allen, and I'll expect to be treated as a lady. That means being called Mrs. Salt.' Well, I'd eaten her flapjacks and apple pie, and I wouldn't have cared if she wanted to be called Queen Victoria. I assured her she'd be well treated, and next thing I knew, she packed her stuff and took over the Rocking A," he ruefully finished.

It also finished Linnet's self-discipline. She burst into laughter.

George quizzically looked back at her. "And just how long have you been awake?" he inquired.

"Long enough to hear all about Mrs. Salt," she told him between giggles. When they subsided, she added, "I actually heard all about your plans for me."

"Do you agree?" His piercing gaze again went to the core of her being.

"With all my heart," she fervently agreed. She saw her father's hands relax a bit where they had tightened on the reins. "I'll be as obedient as David, even if you tell me to go lieth down when I don't feel tired." She felt rewarded for her sally when her uncle bent a mock stern look toward her and shook his head, although his lips twitched. It encouraged her so much, she plaintively said, "It's too late to eat before I get hungry. I'm starving right now."

"Good." His warm look of approval preceded directions for Judd to turn off the road just around the next bend. In the shade of a clump of cottonwoods near a barely moving stream, Linnet watched her uncle uncover a white-wrapped basket and spread the cloth on the leaf-strewn ground. Fried chicken, tiny biscuits, jelly, even chocolate cake followed. Water from canteens provided a drink.

"Manna in the wilderness." Linnet bit into a perfectly cooked chicken breast after her father thanked God for bringing them this far and for the food. "Compliments of Mrs. Salt?"

"No. I had it packed in Salt Lake." George smiled at his pretty niece. "It's good but not as good as my new housekeeper-cook's."

An incredible amount of food later, Linnet stretched, then prepared to curl up for a few moments of rest. Instead, she discovered her uncle had already started to carry out his plans for her when he ordered her to walk.

"You'll have plenty of time to rest in the carriage," he kindly told her. "It's—"

"I know. A long way to the Rocking A."

George's eyebrows rose, but his eyes twinkled. "Has she always been this sassy?" he asked his brother.

"No. It must be in the air," Judd teased.

They traveled until late afternoon. George and Judd spelled off driving the team while Linnet dozed or watched the changing country. It had grown rougher, with steep hills that made even the strong team slow down far before they reached the top and increased their pace down the other side. Rusty-looking dirt had replaced the gray and yellowish soil. Jackrabbits and cottontails bounded through the sage, paused to examine the carriage and its occupants, then went on with their lives. Linnet exclaimed a hundred times at their antics and at the many birds she saw. The only things she hated were the greedy black birds of prey that her uncle called buzzards. "Ugh, they're so ugly." She jerked her unwilling gaze from two of them feasting at the side of the road.

"They're necessary," George said briefly. "They clean up remains of animals that die."

Still, Linnet felt glad when the carriage rolled past and she could no longer see them.

Uncle George didn't allow Linnet to help with camp preparations. "Walk," he told her. "But don't go far. You never know what might be lurking 'round here."

She instantly peopled the quiet spot with a horde of desperate bank robbers, rustlers, and wild animals bent on destruction, then laughed at her fancies. *What a tenderfoot I am! Why can't I be more like Father?* She watched him interestedly while she strolled back and forth in the circle of light cast by the snapping fire that he had helped Uncle George build. One observation and her father duplicated his brother's actions, even taking over and mixing the biscuit dough while Uncle George laughed and watched him. He also helped remove the soft seats from the carriage to make beds.

"What about you, Uncle George?" Linnet asked after the men spread blankets and prepared two couches as easily as the porters on the train whisked seats into berths.

"I'm used to the ground." He threw down a tarpaulin, a couple of blankets, and checked the biscuits baking in a pan he called a Dutch oven. He examined the strips of mouthwatering bacon sizzling on sharpened sticks propped close to the fire, then opened a can of peaches. "Supper's ready."

Linnet couldn't believe how many biscuits she stowed away, along with bacon strips and a large helping of peaches. Under the protection of the carriage top, she changed into her nightclothes. She left her comfortable garb lying smooth for the next day, then slipped into her bed.

"After you've been out here awhile, you'll sleep in your clothes," her uncle George predicted.

"Maybe." She stared at the stars, white against a purplish-black sky. The one-eyed moon she'd seen from her train window had opened its eye a little more and added a sheen to the camp. The fire sputtered and died. A distant owl hooted. Linnet Allen pulled her blankets closer around her and slept.

Chapter 6

Long before the Allens reached the Rocking A, the eastern members of the family were wholeheartedly, unreservedly in love. The wild country that had long since claimed George in his younger days now wove invisible, silken threads of possession about Judd and Linnet. Southeastern Utah's red buttes and cliffs, its arches and twisted formations, held the visitors spellbound—as did the blue-and-purple-shadowed canyons that yawned at their feet.

"Wait until you see Dead Horse Canyon," George promised. "In spite of its gruesome name, it's one of the grandest spots in the state."

"What an odd thing to call a canyon!" Linnet's soft blue eyes opened wide.

Her uncle repeated the same legends that Andy Cullen had overheard in the Moab cafe weeks earlier. He finished by saying, "That trip will have to wait until you're stronger. A man might get a wagon in drawn by mules, but the contraption isn't built for it."

Discouragement dimmed Linnet's anticipation, and she quickly covered a small sigh. Not for anything would she confess how tired the trip had left her. In spite of good food and fresh air in addition to many naps, even the spectacular scenery had begun to pall. She sometimes felt that if she could only get to the Rocking A and sink into a bed, nothing else would matter.

Did Uncle George sense her feelings? Perhaps. In any event, he casually announced, "We can either go clear home tonight or camp out once more."

Judd Allen anxiously looked at his daughter. "Linnet, it's up to you."

"I would like a hot bath," she admitted. "I seem to have accumulated a lot of. . .trail dust, didn't you call it?"

"Home it is." He whistled cheerily and clucked to the team. At the word "home," David and Goliath pricked their ears and stepped out as briskly as if they hadn't already pulled the contraption many miles that day.

Linnet relaxed on her comfortable backseat and let the country flow past until the combination of relief and late afternoon June sun lulled her to sleep.

She awakened to darkness, the whinny of horses, and yellow light streaming into the contraption from a lamp held high.

"Bring her right in, poor thing. She's tuckered out, I reckon," a woman's voice ordered.

Still half asleep, Linnet felt strong arms lift and carry her up shallow steps, across a wide porch, and into a house brightened by lamplight and the flames in an enormous open fireplace. The crisp, kindly voice went on giving directions, and the tired young woman wanted to bury her face in her uncle's shirt and cry. She caught a glimpse of a blue-and-white-checked housedress covered with a huge, spotless white apron but didn't look into Mrs. Salt's face until her uncle gently set her on her feet. Brown hair lightly touched with gray framed a face that showed lines of sorrow but great strength. Compassionate blue eyes as keen as her uncle's peered deep into Linnet's thoughts.

"Run along, Mr. Allen. This young woman needs a bath and bed."

The ghost of a smile trembled on the weary traveler's lips when he meekly replied, "Yes, Mrs. Salt," then beat a hasty retreat. She remembered Uncle George saying that the housekeeper-cook had taken over the Rocking A when she arrived.

"Mercy, Child, you're all bones and no meat," the motherly woman scolded, hands busy divesting Linnet of jacket, shirt, and jeans. She threw a wrapper over the slim, white-clad girl and led her to a nearby bathroom complete with a large tub filled with warm water. "Here's your soap and washcloth and towels. Do you need any help?"

"No." She smiled at Mrs. Salt, who stood perhaps an inch shorter than Linnet's five feet, five inches and outweighed her by about ten pounds. "You are so kind."

"Now, holler if you need me. I'll just warm a gown for you and have it ready when you are." She stepped into the hall and closed the bathroom door behind her.

Linnet wearily let the wrapper slip to the floor and got out of her chemise and long cotton drawers. The warm water and sweet-smelling soap washed away both grime and the terrible, all-gone feeling that had attacked her in the final homestretch. Still tired but feeling better, she washed her hair, soaped it again, then poured clean water over it from a pitcher Mrs. Salt had thoughtfully placed nearby. Then she wrapped herself in a bedsheet-sized towel.

"I'm ready, Mrs. Salt."

The little woman with the big influence bustled in, handed her a fire-warmed nightgown, and considerately turned her head so Linnet could slip into its folds. "Come sit by the fire," she invited, and the new Rocking A resident obediently followed her to a small, padded rocker.

Refreshed by her bath, Linnet took notice of her surroundings, something she hadn't done when she first arrived. "A fireplace in my own room. How nice."

"There's one in each bedroom plus the big one in the living room," Mrs. Salt told her.

"And, why, this is my rocker." Her gaze sped around the room. "And my bed and dressing table."

Mrs. Salt chuckled and vigorously rubbed Linnet's wet hair. "The boys had quite a time of it, hauling your furniture here and getting it set up before you came. Not that they weren't glad to do it," she added smugly. "I just showed them that picture of you that Mr. Allen has on his desk, and you never saw such a hurrying around to offer their services." She took Linnet's comb and brush from the dressing table, and the young woman realized that Mrs. Salt must have unpacked the train bag.

With long, smooth strokes, the woman gently worked out tangles until the brown hair curled just above the toweled shoulders. "We'll turn your back to the fire," she said. "That hair needs to be dry before you go to bed. It's pretty hair. Do you always wear it short?"

Linnet nodded. "The doctors said long hair tired my head, and Father likes the short curls. I feel it makes me look childish, but it's easy to care for."

"Sensible, that's what it is," Mrs. Salt approved. "How do you like your room? We tried to make it as much like yours in Boston as we could but had to depend on Mr. Allen's memory of it, and he isn't much for noticing specifics."

"It's beautiful but different. A nice different. I didn't have hand-braided rugs on my floor or whitewashed log walls, but I like them. They're homey."

"Good. Now I'll bring you some supper, then I have to get the men fed. Mr. Allen will be hungry."

"So am I," Linnet admitted. "I eat a lot more since I left Boston, although I forced myself to eat there when I knew we might come west." She sat perfectly still, content to let the snapping fire do its work.

"In a few weeks, we'll get you built up so you aren't just a remnant, weak and small."

"A *what?*" Linnet roused from the stupor induced by the warm water and fire and stared.

Mrs. Salt raised her eyebrows and looked innocent. "You know, in the song 'All Hail the Power of Jesus' Name.' You're a Christian, aren't you?"

"Yes, but—"

To Linnet's utter astonishment, the amazing housekeeper-cook sang in her rich voice:

"Ye chosen seed of Israel's race,
Ye remnant weak and small,
Hail Him who saves you by His grace,
And crown Him Lord of all."

She ended by saying, "Child, we're glad you came," then she trotted out.

Linnet laughed until the tears came. A "remnant weak and small." Perfect description for a frail person as well as the faithful who followed the Lord. She tipped her head back to capture more of the fire's warmth. God had often taken just a remnant of believers and done mighty things. He could have chosen twelve hundred disciples to carry on His work. Instead, He'd selected twelve—physically strong, many of them, yet subject to spiritual weaknesses. Who knew His ways? She yawned, and Mrs. Salt's entrance with venison stew, hot corn bread, homemade applesauce, and an extra large glass of milk roused her only long enough to eat before tumbling into bed. Mrs. Salt tucked her in the way she'd do a child and swooped down to place a soft kiss on the white forehead.

"Sleep well, Child. God is watching."

Again the urge to cry came, but Linnet successfully fought and overcame it. She would not be a baby, even though this was the first woman's kiss she had received since her mother died.

—+—

Dreamless sleep did what no amount of bathing or good food could. She awakened feeling rested and a little indignant when Mrs. Salt, her father, and Uncle George agreed that a day in bed wouldn't hurt. She had so much to see in her new home. Why, she hadn't even examined the house in which she would live, or the corral or outbuildings or the scenery that lay outside.

"You have the rest of your life to explore," Uncle George told her. His blue eyes like Father's showed how clearly he knew her inner rebellion. "There's just one thing. . . ."

She looked at him inquiringly.

"Lass, everyone here loves you and will do what they can to help. I know you'll cooperate." Not a trace of a smile creased his bronzed face. "Above and beyond all that, your health and life is in the Lord's hands. I'm not a magician or a miracle worker. Neither is your father or Mrs. Salt. We're going to treat you according to plain old common sense, but God will have the last say. If you get well and strong the way we hope, it's because that's His will."

"I know." She took both of his calloused hands in her slim, white ones. "I'll do what you say." A wistful note crept into her voice. "Would it be all right if I lie on a couch instead of the bed? I. . .I'd like to be with you all."

Mrs. Salt wiped her eyes on her apron and took command. "No reason at all she can't rest on that pretty velveteen settee the boys hauled down from Salt Lake. It's by the window in the living room, where she can see what's going on outside as well as into the kitchen where I'm working. Child, can those white fingers of yours do needlework?"

Linnet glanced at them, and red shame crept into her face. "Why, yes. I've embroidered and crocheted and—"

"Ever done any plain hand sewing?"

Her head proudly came up. "I have."

"Good. I've a bundle of flannel that needs finishing into little garments. A family in Moab lost their home in a fire, and they need all the help they can get. I haven't had time to do more than cut them out and pin the seams. If you feel like it, it would help out a lot."

Linnet caught the way Uncle George's mouth opened and felt he planned to protest. Mrs. Salt sent him a quelling look, and he subsided. The same rueful smile that Linnet had seen him wear a few times before returned, and he gruffly said, "Whatever Mrs. Salt says is all right with me."

"Thank you, Mr. Allen." The bland response couldn't quite hide her satisfaction.

Judd Allen hovered over his daughter once she'd been established in the comfortable living room with its sparkling windows, white ruffled curtains, Boston furniture mingled with brightly colored Indian blankets, and more hand-braided rugs on the polished board floor. Finally, she caught his longing look out the window and told him, "Go find Uncle George and get to work. We can't have one owner of the Rocking A do all the work around here, can we?" His face lit up like a child seeing his first pony, and the sound of the big front door closing behind him showed his eagerness to begin his new life's work.

Linnet also started working on the soft flannel clothes for the unfortunate children. Between kitchen duties, Mrs. Salt drifted in and out, once to bring a glass of milk and warm molasses cookies from a recipe she said had been in her family for generations, another time just to see how the sewing was coming. Linnet proudly held up a finished garment and felt an inordinate sense of pride at the good woman's praise. She also discerned exactly what Uncle George had meant about his housekeeper-cook. She never raised her voice or seemed hurried. Yet a luncheon that Uncle George called dinner appeared on the table at twelve o'clock sharp; an equally appealing supper was ready at six o'clock. And each meal had appeared after a deceptively small amount of effort that hid a mountain of work.

By the third day, Linnet felt she knew Mrs. Salt well enough to ask, "Now that we're here, what are you going to call Uncle George and Father? They can't both be Mr. Allen."

"I'll think on it."

Linnet had a feeling she'd hear those words a million times in her acquaintanceship with the motherly woman. They typified the caution inherent in Mrs. Salt of wanting to make wise decisions. Finally, the housekeeper-cook said, "My employer will remain Mr. Allen. If your father doesn't mind, I will call him Mr. Judd."

Both men readily agreed, but Linnet saw how quickly they averted their gaze and suspected how much they wanted to laugh.

Mrs. Salt had a teasing side, as well as her efficient one. Her blue eyes twinkled on a rare occasion when she considered her household duties caught up enough for her to sit with the new daughter of the house and sew. "Didn't I see Reddy Hode and Tommy Blake come in here a little while ago?"

"Yes. They wanted to know where Uncle George had gone. I guess he forgot to give them orders for the day," the unsuspecting Linnet told her. "Charlie Moore came, too."

"Those scalawags. They know perfectly well where they're supposed to be and what they're to do." Mrs. Salt laughed, then frowned. "I suppose it's to be expected. Even rough cowhands like to be around pretty young women, or I should say, especially cowhands. I'll have a word with Mr. Allen."

"Please, don't," Linnet said in alarm. Her heartbeat quickened. "They seem like such nice boys, I wouldn't want them to get into trouble." She shuddered at the thought of being the unwitting cause of young men losing their jobs.

"They're nice enough, I'll hand them that. Not like some we've had." A look of forbearance rested on her face before mirth replaced it. "I'll wager we won't have trouble getting and keeping riders now that you're here. Reddy and Tommy and Charlie won't be the only ones stricken with memory loss that sends them up here to the ranch house. . .not with you sitting there, so dainty and pretty."

"It is pretty, isn't it?" Linnet lifted a fold of her pale yellow gown that looked like a drift of sunlight in the room.

"Yes."

Linnet had a feeling that Mrs. Salt didn't mean the gown. The time since she reached the Rocking A had removed nervous strain from her body and painted a faint pink in the cheeks beginning to round out from good food and the twice daily walk Uncle George insisted she take. True to her word, she stopped the minute she felt tired. Yet each succeeding day found her able to walk a little more without her heart fluttering. She had been introduced to the cowboys, who awkwardly removed their big hats and nudged each other bashfully when she offered her white hand to be swallowed up in their brown paws. She'd seen a parade of horses and longed for the strength to ride. She faithfully thanked God for her progress and refused to look ahead more than a day at a time.

Now, all the talk around the ranch concerned the Independence Day doings in Moab and whether Linnet should go. Naturally, the cowboys loudly proclaimed it wouldn't hurt her a mite. Uncle George and her father reserved judgment, making no decision until Mrs. Salt advised that she didn't see any harm, so long as Linnet took it easy.

On the night of the third, the excited girl had a hard time falling asleep. Visions of bucking horses, expert riding, flags, and fun swirled in her mind. Would all the cowboys be as nice as Reddy, Tommy, Charlie, and the other Rocking A hands? They evidenced none of the uncouthness that many Bostonians associated with their kind, and she knew, without being told, that any one of them would fight to the death to protect her or her good name.

Being placed on a pedestal had troubled her until the frank Mrs. Salt said, "Child, it's good for them to have someone to admire and hold high. Who knows? The way you live your life as a witness for the Lord may be making a far deeper impression on some of our boys than any of us know."

After that, Linnet put aside false embarrassment and simply treated them all the same. Showing favoritism could be disastrous, according to her wise mentor and friend who to some extent had stepped into a mother role.

The mighty Colorado River proved to be disappointing. Due to the hot summer, its wide banks held more red hard-baked clay than sluggish water. "It's a mighty different thing in flood," Mrs. Salt told Linnet from her position next to her in the backseat of the contraption. She pointed out marks showing how high the river had risen, and Linnet gasped, finding it hard to believe the innocuous-looking water could reach that high.

Moab more than made up for seeing the Colorado River's low level. The long main street swarmed with people like ants to a picnic; bright holiday clothing rivaled the red-rock canyons and walls that Linnet never tired of seeing. Indians in buckskin, heavily fringed and beaded, stood aloof, arms crossed.

"Wait until you see them ride." George Allen's eyes glistened. "Some of them have wonderful horses, right off the range. You can't get a finer horse." The corners of his mouth turned down. "I should know. My best Arabian mare was stolen by a wild stallion. I'd give a gold mine to get her back along with the colt sired by the stallion."

Linnet was too intent on the story to blush over the discussion. She'd learned that westerners found nothing objectionable in talking about life and birth among the animals. "Who owns the colt?" she asked.

"Good question. I suppose since his mother's mine, I could make a claim, but first I'd have to catch him." George haw-hawed. "Besides, in this country, a wild horse is considered to belong to the man with grit enough to capture and tame him." He grinned down at the niece who clung to his and her father's arms. "By the way, the boys have Sadie gentled and ready. Soon as we get home from this shindig, we'll try you out on her."

Linnet thought of the white mare who took sugar and carrots from her hand. A thrill went through her. "I can hardly wait!"

"Maybe we should just load up some supplies and head for home," her father teased, looking more than ever like his brother. "What's an Independence Day celebration compared with riding Sadie?"

His daughter squelched him with a reproving, "Father, really," but her laughter spilled over. "It's so good just to be here and be part of all this." Her glance took in everything from the general store to the livery stable. She watched an old man walk from the stable and noticed his keen gaze beneath shaggy brows, the same quality that characterized Uncle George and Mrs. Salt.

"Mrs. Salt, we need more thread," Linnet remembered.

The housekeeper-cook paused in her task of unloading from the contraption a dinner basket, cloth, and a blanket on which to sit. "Run along to the store, Child. Do you need money?"

"Just put it on my bill," Uncle George told her. "I'll be in to settle up later."

Laughing and flushed with the unusual events, Linnet picked her way through the still-growing crowd toward the general store. She held up the skirt of her yellow dress to keep it from dragging in the dust and tried to keep from being jostled by the good-natured throng, wondering if a fish swimming upstream felt this way—pressed and harried. She finally reached her goal, and a surge of humanity swept by. Linnet glanced over her shoulder to wave to Mrs. Salt. She didn't notice that someone had come out of the general store until it was too late. Carried forward by her determination to get the thread quickly so she wouldn't miss anything, she ran full tilt into a solid body.

"Whoa, Miss." Two strong arms shot out and respectfully but firmly kept her from falling.

Linnet felt a warm blush color her face. Annoyance at her carelessness snapped her head back. She looked up, straight into the brownest eyes she had ever seen, sparkling with laughter and the slowly dawning look of one who had waited for this moment a long, long time.

Chapter 7

I s this yahoo bothering you, Miss Allen?" one of the ranch hands asked. The supporting arms fell from her shoulders, and Linnet glanced over at Reddy Hode, his hands on his hips in a protective gesture. Tommy Blake and Charlie Moore flanked him like twin avenging angels. Where had they come from, she had time to wonder before the stranger spoke.

"Sorry, boys. She plumb ran into me, and I had to grab her so she wouldn't fall."

"Is that right?" Reddy assumed his usual role of spokesman for the trio and sounded suspicious.

Linnet's sense of humor saved the situation. "If I'd been walking any faster, I'd have knocked him clear back into the store." Her merry laugh rang out even above the din in the street, and her self-appointed guardians relaxed.

Reddy generously held out his hand to her rescuer. "No offense, Mister. We didn't see her fall. Just saw you grabbing at her." Tommy and Charlie murmured assent.

The cowboy, who topped Linnet's height by perhaps four inches, smiled until his eyes crinkled under the shock of ripe corn hair that sprang into unruliness when he courteously doffed his Stetson. He gripped Reddy's hand, then Tommy's and Charlie's. "I don't blame you a bit. If I'd seen you doing the same, I might have bulldogged you first and asked questions later." His joyous laugh robbed the words of their sting, and the Rocking A hands and Linnet joined in.

"Linnet, haven't you got that thread yet? It's almost time for—" George Allen stopped short and glared at the four cowboys surrounding his niece. "What's going on here?"

"It's all right. I'll tell you later." Linnet urged him into the store. "I almost fell, and that cowboy caught me."

More laughter bubbled inside her like a mountain spring. "I don't know him from Adam, except by now, I suppose Adam would have an awfully long beard if he were still around."

"Oh, the joy of having a pretty niece!" He rolled his eyes. "Get your thread, Lass, before you start a riot."

The Rocking A hands took pains to inform her they'd never seen the stranger before but that they saw him riding out of Moab on one of the prettiest chestnut mares in the country. "Called her Chinquapin," the loquacious Reddy added. "Don't know why he didn't enter her in the race. She looks strong and fast."

Linnet hid her disappointment. In the need to get Uncle George away before he made a scene, she hadn't even thanked the cowboy! Her cheeks felt scorched and not from the weather, hot as it had grown. He must think her stupid and ill-mannered. She couldn't even write a note. No one appeared to know him or anything about him except that he rode a chestnut mare called Chinquapin. She sighed. If he were just passing through, a little splinter of regret would prick her all the rest of her life.

An urchin clad in nothing visible except a pair of bibbed overalls raced toward them. "Didja hear? Didja hear the news?" He ran out of breath.

"What news?"

"There's a myst'ry horse gonna be in the race." He ran on to tell anyone who cared to listen.

"Mystery horse?" Linnet repeated. Not Chinquapin, surely.

Her uncle's tolerant grin settled her down. "Every year someone enters some so-called mystery horse. Usually it's a joke. . .a nag who can barely make it to the starting line." He stopped, raised to the toes of his boots, and stared over the crowd. "Jumping jackrabbits, look at that horse!" He audibly swallowed. "It's the spitting image of—"

The roar of the crowd drowned him out. Linnet clutched her father's arm and tried to see. Why should a horse, even a mystery horse, send such a look to Uncle George's face? For a second, the crowd swayed. She peered through the crowd, and her heart bounced. Not at the proud black stallion prancing down the street but at the rider, whose corn-colored hair fell over his forehead and partly hid laughing brown eyes.

—+—

Andy Cullen had dreamed of this moment since the first time he heard that a black stallion named Sheik roamed the ranges with his band. Now the noise and color faded. In the space of a few moments, the long weeks in the hidden valley returned. He had broken many horses in his years on the range but none like Sheik. He reveled in the magnificent black's spirit and determined to use patience and love rather than the harsh methods fellow horse breakers employed that resulted in a dispirited, cowed horse.

Lack of food but sufficient water aided Andy in his task. He gradually loosened the crossties between the two large cottonwoods enough so that Sheik could eat the grass his new owner pulled and the precious handfuls of oats. It took time for the stallion to reconcile himself to Andy as the source of his food and the tin pan of water noisily slurped. He also grew accustomed to being led snubbed to the faithful Chinquapin's saddle.

Late spring warmed into early summer. Bees droned and staggered drunkenly from an abundance of wildflowers. The valley lay undisturbed except for the band of horses who curiously eyed the goings-on of their lord and master. Time and again, they crowded close but kept a respectful distance from Sheik's lunges against the ropes.

The beautiful June day that Andy first got a saddle on his captive went down in his memory as one never to be forgotten. He'd already tamed Sheik to a point where he unwillingly accepted the feeling of a saddle blanket. The heavy saddle, though, brought out all the fight that made the black horse the king of the range. He kicked up a storm and continued it until he stood dripping wet and exhausted.

"Good boy!" Andy shouted at the top of his lungs. "You'll get used to it. Maybe I'll turn you into a race horse and sell you for enough to buy that spread I want." Yet, even as he said the words, he knew the impossibility of selling Sheik. A pang went through him at the thought of anyone else even riding Sheik, let alone owning him.

Day by day, Andy won Sheik's trust. The stallion suffered the man's touch, although he trembled. Andy instinctively felt the time had come for his first ride. Left toe in the stirrup, he vaulted to the saddle. "Yippee-ay!"

Sheik went into every contortion known to bucking horses, then added a few choice ones of his own. Jolted, hair soaked from sweat, face fiery, Andy hung on for dear life, keeping the black's head up and back. *If he ever got it between his knees, look out, Mama!* What felt like an eternity later, the expert rider gave Sheik just enough slack to stretch out and run. "We're riding the wind, Boy," Andy yelled. Up the hidden canyon they pelted. The horse herd ran for their lives, away from their charging master. Only Chinquapin dared follow, but even her strength and speed could not come close to Sheik's. A wide turn. Back down the valley floor. Up. Back. Andy wondered who would tire first, he or the horse. Just when he knew he could endure little more, the stallion slowed from a dead run to a gallop, then a trot, and at last, a walk. Spent, Sheik stood shaking while Andy rubbed him down. A slap on the rump sent him to his waiting band, Chinquapin still at his heels.

Every day, Andy mounted Chinquapin, cut Sheik from the herd, then lassoed and saddled him. He discovered that the stallion hated the landslide area and maneuvered him in that direction when he could. Every day, Sheik went through the same bone-crunching performance until Andy despaired of ever mastering him.

June waned, and July loomed close. The wild horse hunter lost track of the date. He continued to work with Sheik and one day reaped rich rewards. Sheik had long since learned to prick up his ears at Andy's whistle. On a day that dawned so beautiful it made the cowboy's insides ache, Sheik answered the morning whistle, raced to him, then pranced away like the show-off he had become. His few pitches once Andy mounted were clearly halfhearted, and he settled into the fast rush up and down the canyon that his rider suspected he'd come to love.

"You're broken, you're grand, and you're mine," Andy exulted. He reined in the stallion and rubbed his neck. "Good thing, too. I've been out of flour for two days, and the rabbits are getting scarce. What say we go get some supplies, old boy?"

Sheik whinnied and shook his head before looking toward his band of followers.

"What are we going to do with them?" Andy scratched his head in dismay. "All these weeks, how come I ain't considered your family, old boy?"

Sheik whinnied again.

"Maybe I'd better just leave them here for the time being," Andy mused. "There's plenty of water and grass. The landslide that almost made a dead horse out of you blocked the exit to this hideout of yours. If I roll a few boulders into the trail behind us when we go out the way I tracked you in, they'll be fine."

Chinquapin pressed close to her master, rubbed her soft nose on his shoulder, and looked at him with intelligent, soft eyes that reproached him for transferring allegiance to the stallion.

"Not you, Chinq. Sheik's used to being led tied to your saddle." Yet Andy scratched his head doubtfully. Leading a rope-hobbled Sheik in the confines of the canyon was a far different story than expecting the black to suffer such indignity on the open range, and a lot of miles lay between them and Moab.

"I just can't leave you here, Sheik. What if someone happened on you? Now that you're broken, would you let another cowpoke ride you?" He thought some more and decided the only way out lay in riding Sheik and letting Chinquapin follow. The mare's love affair had progressed at an amazing rate. Andy hoped she'd never have to choose between following Sheik or her owner.

His plan worked beautifully. He filled canteens with water for their journey and picked his way out of the valley leading Sheik and letting Chinq follow down the narrow trail. Once outside the crowding walls, he tied the horses and walked back to the spot where the trail widened into the valley. "Can't let any of the other horses get into the narrow passage and find it blocked at the other end," he reasoned. "They wouldn't be able to turn." Grunting and tugging, he rolled boulders into a rough barricade high enough to discourage a horse from attempting to climb over.

"Wonder what that sharp-eyed old man at the livery stable's going to think when he sees you?" Andy asked his new possession. Every time he thought about riding down the main street of Moab, his funny bone tickled.

"If those four galoots who think they're going to drive you out on Dead Horse Point and fence you in are in town, they'll get the surprise of their lives," he told Sheik. A moment later, Andy's smile of anticipation died. He had caught and tamed the stallion, but the black wore no brand. Horse thieves abounded in southeastern Utah, and Sheik would cause even an honest horse lover's eyes to glisten. On the other hand, no one but Andy had ever ridden the stallion. Ragged and broke, here he had the finest horse in the country and no way to feed it!

His spirits brightened. "Say, old boy, how about our looking up that rancher who used to own your mama. What was his name? Allen? Anyone in Moab will know. I'll bet he will be real glad to hear his mare's all safe and sound in that hidden valley." An idea burst full blown. "All those other mares you stole are like gold dust in a poke. Maybe this Allen will lend me some of his hands. We'll drive the herd out, return the mares to their owners, and dicker for the colts and fillies. You're mine, and I reckon I should have some say about what happens to the family you sired."

The closer he got to Moab, the more the idea appealed to him. With the shrewd knowledge of his kind, Andy decided to stop in Moab long enough to see if the storekeeper would give him a change of clothing on credit, then head for Allen's ranch.

His plans met with an abrupt disruption when he got within earshot of Moab. The village he remembered as quiet and a little lazy rang with noise. Something in it put Andy on the alert. He found a good-sized thicket out of town, led Sheik behind it so he stood screened from the road, and tied him.

"I'll be back. First, I'm going to see what's causing the commotion."

Mounting Chinquapin, Andy rode into town. Bright bunting and flags tipped him off. "Well, if it ain't Independence Day." A wide grin touched his face. "Some goings-on." He finally got through the crowd and took extra precautions with Chinquapin by tying her to a hitching rail near the store. Although trained to stand with reins dropped, she might bolt from the volume of noise and confusion.

Andy hurried into the store, skirted a swarm of customers who filled the place, and strode to the proprietor. "Any chance of getting some decent clothes on credit?" He saw refusal in the man's eyes and leaned close. "Keep it under your hat, but I caught and broke Sheik. I also know where his band of mares is hiding. Is that good enough for you? I plan to—"

The storekeeper's eyes bulged. He kept his voice low and repeated, "Sheik! Cowboy, is he here in Moab?"

Andy nodded.

"Get what you need, then go get him and enter him in the big race. Here's the entry fee." The man peeled a bill off a roll from his pocket and slipped it into Andy's hand. He whispered, "Don't enter him as Sheik if you want to have some fun. Call him the Mystery Horse."

Andy warmed to the man's excitement. At his benefactor's urging, he selected new pants and shirt, gratefully accepted the offer of a razor and the use of the man's living quarters behind the store, and cleaned himself up. "If I win something, half is yours," he told the beaming man after emerging fresh and clean.

The proprietor shook his head decidedly. "You owe me just for the clothes. I aim to collect big by placing some bets."

Andy frowned. Horse races meant betting, and he hated the idea of making Sheik a reason to gamble. On the other hand, though, he wasn't doing the betting. He soothed his conscience, snaked his way to the open door, and strode onto the porch.

A young woman in a yellow dress walked directly toward him, head turned to look back, hand raised to wave to someone in the crowd. Andy had no time to step aside or alert her to the fact that he stood in front of her. Carried forward by her rapid pace, she bumped into him so hard, she staggered.

"Whoa, Miss." Andy's arms shot out to steady her. She looked up with the softest, bluest eyes he had ever seen. Light brown hair worn in short curls peeped from beneath a becoming hat. Rose pink colored her white cheeks, and Andy Cullen temporarily forgot about Sheik, the race, and everything else in the world except the warm feeling that rushed through him.

In rapid succession, three scowling cowboys appeared, Andy released her and mumbled an explanation, and the girl's laugh chimed like harness bells. Andy tore his gaze from her long enough to shake hands with her watchdogs. He laughed away the spokesman's apology and felt an indescribable sense of loss when a big man appeared, to be led away by the young woman he called Linnet. What a pretty name and how fitting! Only after excusing himself, shoving through the crowd, and climbing back on Chinquapin, did Andy remember that the cowboy had called her Miss Allen. Then that big, belligerent man must be her father, probably the same Allen who owned Sheik's mother. Of all the strange coincidences. He firmly pushed them out of his mind and rode back to where he'd tethered Sheik, gave him a quick dusting, and left Chinquapin mournfully looking after them from her secure position.

Back into town, then down the street toward the starting point of the race. Men with startled faces fell back from horse and rider. A ripple of amazement swelled into a roar. "That's for you," Andy told Sheik, whose inclination to show off resulted in a series of dancing steps. "Now, I know you've never raced before, but all you have to do is get out in front of the rest of the horses and stay there. There ain't no fancy footwork required, just the fastest run you can manage."

Sheik snorted and tossed his head. His rider had the feeling the animal knew exactly the part he must play.

"Winning means paying for the clothes plus oats and hay for you," Andy tempted, all the time patting the stallion's neck and keeping a tight rein.

Sheik appeared surprisingly indifferent to the crowd but eyed his compatriots when the ten horses entered in the race lined up, then he tossed his head again.

Crack! The starting pistol fired. Andy's spurless boot heels dug into Sheik's sides. "Go, old boy!"

The stallion's first leap carried him a length ahead of the others and started a volcano-sized roar among the watchers. With the same precision perfected in the long races up and down the hidden valley, Sheik reached the end of the course, wheeled, and headed back far ahead of the swift horses who, by comparison, looked as if they were trotting.

Horse and rider reached the finish line; the roar became a din when they swept across. A hoofbeat later, it changed to horror. A toddling child had somehow escaped her mother's care. She ran on chubby legs into the middle of the street and paused, bewildered by the crowd that had pressed forward to see the finish until only a narrow lane existed.

A flash of yellow brought groans from the watchers. An agonized voice cried, "No!" The next second, the yellow-clad runner flung herself protectively over the child and huddled in the dusty street.

Andy Cullen's range-trained eyes took in the terrible situation. His heart silently pleaded, *Lord, help,* while his cool nerve and iron control screamed he had but one choice. Turning Sheik into the crowd at a dead run meant inevitable death for bystanders. The short distance to the crouched, spread-eagled figure destroyed any hope of reining the stallion in. Sheik's flying hooves would descend like battering rams. Yet the black had not been trained to jump.

The sweat of fear poured down Andy's face. His hands iced but clung to the reins in a death grip. "Now!" He slammed his boot heels into the black flanks and felt the stallion's mighty surge of power. Sheik sprang into the air and over the fallen figures as easily as leaping over a rattlesnake in the trail. He hit the ground far on the other side, still running.

"Thank You, Lord!" Andy cried. Although relief threatened to unseat him, he allowed Sheik to run for a good half mile before pulling him to a walk. "If I never loved you before, I love you now," the disheveled cowboy choked out. He slid from the saddle, put both arms around the lathered horse's neck, and fought the floodwaters gathered just behind his eyelids.

An eternity later, his shaking shoulders stilled. Andy wiped his hot face, mounted Sheik, and slowly rode him back to town. "They can't be hurt," he whispered. "Your hooves didn't even touch her—them." Yet he brushed off the reaching hands and sincere praises of the crowd when he got back to Moab. His gaze turned from side to side, seeking a yellow gown—the right yellow gown, with a laughing face and blue eyes above it.

Andy failed in his mission but at last saw one of the three cowboys who had accosted him earlier. "Miss Allen and the baby. Are they all right?"

Admiration, thankfulness, and gloom filled the tanned face. "The kid's scared but fine." He paused.

"And Miss Allen?"

"Don't know." The cowboy shook his head, and Andy saw misery in his eyes. "They took her to the doc."

"Sheik didn't touch her. Did she get hurt when she threw herself into the road?" A sudden obstruction made it hard to talk. "I never saw such a brave act."

The cowboy squared his shoulders. His jaw set, and he glanced down. His voice sounded hoarse, rough. "A lot braver than you know, Mister. Linnet Allen's the last person in the world who should be pulling stunts like that. Her ticker's no good. She came out to the Rocking A with her daddy from Boston." His face worked. "I hear tell the doctors back East said 'twouldn't make no difference since she was going to die anyway. She's been somewhat better since she came. Now this." He spread his calloused brown hands in a helpless gesture.

Andy felt like he'd been run down by a whole herd of wild horses. That sweet, pretty girl, dying from heart trouble? *No!* He wanted to holler, to grab the cowboy and tell him to stop lying. He could not. The expression on the rider's face showed a truth that could not be denied.

Chapter 8

N o!" Linnet fought the darkness, the thunder of hooves, the great black shadow that swept over her. She felt her eardrums would burst from the noise. Just when it became unendurable, the din lessened, only to be replaced with a mighty roar. Too frightened to care, heart pounding, she felt someone lift and carry her. She struggled against the imprisoning arms. "The baby—"

"Scared but safe," a strange, gruff voice answered. The prick of a needle in her arm stilled Linnet's questions, and she drifted into a noiseless, welcome place.

"Well?" George Allen barked the question hovering on Judd's and Mrs. Salt's lips.

The Moab doctor compressed his lips in a straight line. "Can't tell yet. If you men will step outside, I'll have Mrs. Salt undress her so I can do an examination."

Judd looked down at the slight, pale figure of his daughter. "How could she do it?" he cried. His voice broke.

The crusty doctor cleared his throat. "From what I've seen of the young lady, she couldn't stand by and see a child in danger. I understand she stood closest to the street?"

"We put her there so she could see the race better," George told him. His face worked, but the doctor shooed him out, along with Judd. The brothers didn't talk. Even now Linnet could be dying.

At last, George managed to say, "If she doesn't make it, God forbid, she gave her life to save another."

"Don't!" Judd buried his face in his hands, and his shoulders heaved. George laid a strong arm over them and simply hung on.

What seemed a lifetime later, the doctor jerked open the door separating his little waiting room from the examining area. Mrs. Salt's beaming face told the story even before the worthy doctor spoke.

"I can't see she's any the worse for her little escapade," the physician informed them. His face wrinkled. "I also can't find much that's irregular about her heart. Rapid pulse just now, of course, but that's to be expected under the circumstances." He beetled his brows over keen eyes. "How long has it been since she's been checked?"

"Several weeks, actually." Judd tried to remember. "Once she made up her mind to come out here and gained in strength, she scoffed at the idea of going back to the doctors." His face grayed. "They'd already pronounced her death sentence, so Linnet said she couldn't see that it mattered what she did."

"Hmm." The doctor stroked his waistcoat, then tapped a pudgy finger against his lips. "I don't want to be premature, but. . .what's she been doing since then?"

Mrs. Salt outlined the program of rest, exercise, and good food. "I also keep her busy sewing," she added. Genuine love flashed in her blue eyes. "When a body's working for someone else's good, it leaves less time to think on her own miseries."

The doctor sent her a look of approval. "Keep up the good work," he advised. "Then bring her back to me in a couple of months. Right now I want her to sleep until she wakes up on her own. By the way, who's the rider with brains enough to control his horse? If he'd tried to veer or stop, I'll wager the black would have either trampled her and the child or charged into the crowd and sent me some badly mangled citizens."

George Allen shook his head. "All I know is that his stallion's the mirror image of my Arabian mare stolen awhile back by the leader of a wild horse band. From what I've heard, either the black is Sheik or I'll eat my hat!" He gripped the doctor's hand with his strong paw. "Mrs. Salt, I know you'll want to stay with Linnet. Judd, we have to go find that cowboy and shake his hand." He strode toward the door.

"Thank you." Judd wiped wet eyes and followed, leaving the frankly rejoicing Mrs. Salt and the doctor to tend to their business.

The Allen brothers didn't have to go far to find the hero of the day. A few paces outside the doctor's office, a lithe cowboy leading a black stallion still bearing traces of lather from his magnificent performance hurried toward them. "Mr. Allen, the crowd said your daughter—"

"My niece. This is her father," George interrupted. "She's going to be all right. In fact, she's going to be better than all right unless Doc has taken leave of his senses."

"Thank God!" Andy felt a mountain-sized load slide from his heart. "I knew Sheik didn't touch her, but one of your cowhands said she had a weak heart."

Judd's hand shot out to the young rider whose ripe corn hair hung over his worried brown eyes. "Thanks be to God, the doctor thinks there's a good chance she may recover. It's almost too much to hope for. The only reason we came to Utah was because it didn't matter either way where we lived. Every physician pronounced my daughter's case hopeless."

"Except the Great Physician." Andy looked straight into the distraught man's eyes. A flicker of recognition that a bond lay between them sent joy into the cowboy's heart. He turned to George and said frankly, "Now that I've seen your niece, you may find it hard to believe, but I was on my way to see you when I rode into town and found all the goings-on." He laughed, a clear, ringing sound that tilted the other men's lips up. "I'd been so busy catching and taming Sheik that I forgot the date."

"Where did you find him?" George's eyes gleamed, and he reached out to pat the stallion's neck. Quicker than lightning, Sheik jerked his head back and reared.

"It's all right, old boy." Andy's iron grip brought his horse under control and brought looks of admiration from the Allens, plus Reddy Hode, Tommy Blake, and Charlie Moore, who had followed in Andy and Sheik's wake. "Sorry," Andy apologized. "So far he's only used to me."

"I have a feeling he's a one-man horse and always will be," Reddy ventured. "Good thing. I ain't no horse thief, but that animal's enough to tempt even an honest cowpoke like me." His sally brought laughter.

"Mr. Allen, I'd like to talk with you in private," Andy quietly said. "Begging your pardon, boys."

"Of course. But anything you say should be to my brother as well as me. He's the new half owner of the Rocking A."

"That's swell." Andy could have said a lot more about Judd's pretty daughter and how relief had run hot and swift through his veins when he heard the good news concerning her health. As soon as the three hands ambled off, joshing Andy with remarks about being willing to take Sheik off his hands anytime, the cowboy squared his shoulders and lowered his voice. He told his story well, from the moment he first heard of Sheik and dreamed about capturing him, to the thrilling and terrifying moment when he discovered the stallion putting up his final, losing battle against the slide.

"I never felt sorrier for any critter than that horse, cutting himself on sharp rocks, trying to get free," he said. Without glorifying himself, he hurried over the actual rescue and breaking. His heart pounded with the same excitement he'd experienced when Sheik at last gave in.

"And that ain't all," he finished. "I rolled rocks so the mares—including one that must be your Arabian, Mr. Allen—and colts and fillies would stay in the valley until someone comes for them."

"Where is this valley?" George demanded, then laughed at his own eagerness. "Whoa, first you'll want to be dickering, I suppose."

"I figure the ranchers who get their mares back will be glad enough to have them so's we can make a deal," Andy said. "Sheik's mine, by right of finding and breaking. The colts and fillies sired by Sheik are a bonus. They ought to be worth quite a bit for that reason."

"I can see you've thought it all out." George considered for a moment. "What do you want for them?"

"I need your hands to help me drive," Andy told him. His brown eyes sparkled in anticipation. "I've got one of the best cow ponies in the West, plus having Sheik along will encourage the herd to follow. I know I can trust you. I don't know the other ranchers around here. Once they give their word, will they keep it? I'll return the mares to their rightful owners. Any unbranded animals, and that's all the colts and fillies, will be for sale at the going price."

"That's more than fair," George admitted. He frowned. "Only rancher who may kick up a storm and try to claim some of the offspring is Silas Dunn of the Bar D. He'll be outvoted, though. You found the horses. They're yours. Say, what's your name, anyway, and where are you from?"

"Andy Cullen, lately of Arizona. Rode last for the Double J near Flagstaff."

George grunted. "I've heard of them and all good. How'd you like to throw in with me? Judd and I could use another good rider. Top wages and best food in Utah, as well as one of the prettiest ranches."

"I'd like that," Andy told him. He hesitated, then said, "One thing. It won't be forever. I aim to stash away what I get on this deal and have a spread of my own sometime. Mr. Allen, what's the best way to go about bringing the horses out of the canyon? I've got a feeling it ain't smart to leave them there too long." He repeated the conversation he'd overheard in the Moab cafe weeks earlier.

George acted dumbfounded. "Drive them onto the Point and fence it? Who'd think up such an idea as that?"

Andy faithfully described the three men whose faces he had seen. "I couldn't see the one with his back to me, but he had broad shoulders and spoke clearly and slowly."

George shook his head. "Could be any of a half-dozen ranch owners. Anything to distinguish some of the others? They sound like all cowmen."

"No, but the three scoundrels who relieved me of food and saddlebags and blanket made a deep impression." Andy quickly related the story of his holdup. "One of them had strange eyes, almost colorless. I'd recognize them again, even though the ornery skunk's hat shaded them. The leader had a pleasant laugh. The third got knocked down by my mare, Chinquapin, and it tickled the leader. I guess I should be thankful they didn't put a hole in me and leave me there. Oh, they stole my bedroll, too, and Chinq's blanket. I hated to lose that. It was a Christmas present from my pards at the Double J. The boss's wife put a little *A* in one corner." He grinned. "I got a hunch someday I'm going to see that saddle blanket. When I do, I can track down who robbed me."

George leaned closer, a mysterious glint in his eyes. "Cullen, could the man with the pleasant laugh and the wide-shouldered gent in the cafe have been the same person?"

Andy considered, then regretfully shook his head. "No. Why?"

George compressed his lips. "Just curious. Now, about the horse drive, I suggest we call together all the ranchers around here who have lost mares the last several years. We'll put your deal up to them, tell them we need hands from every spread represented to help drive, and set up a fair way of selling the unbranded stock. Draw lots with number one getting first choice, and so on. Or, don't you want to keep some? Plenty of room on the Rocking A."

"You sure don't want to geld Sheik," George exploded.

"Never!" Andy thought of the proud stallions who had either died or had become spiritless after gelding. "I'll turn him back onto the range before that."

"Don't blame you a bit." George dropped a heavy hand to the younger man's shoulder. "I have a section that's not being used. We'll put Sheik and any unbranded mares in his band there, away from the rest of the stock." He downed the obstacle, and a shrewd expression came to his face. "Reckon it won't hurt none to put on paper exactly how this horse drive and trading are going to be. I'll sign it first, and we won't have any trouble with the others. . . except maybe Dunn, as I said." He shrugged. "He can be sweeter than apple pie sometimes and sourer than green apples others."

Sheik had grown restive during the long confab. Now he tossed his head and shinnied, clearly jealous of these strangers who took so much of his new master's attention. Andy absently patted him. "I'd better go collect my prize money and pay off the storekeeper for my duds. Have to get Chinq, too, before she thinks I've deserted her." He started to move away but stopped when the door of the doctor's office opened. A short, brown-haired woman with blue eyes and a nice smile stood in the doorway.

"How is she?" Judd Allen, who had listened but made no effort to enter the conversation, sprang toward the woman.

"Now, Mr. Judd, there's no need to worry. She's fine. Awake and asking for you. She also wants to see the cowboy who owns the black horse. That's you, I reckon."

Andy felt her single glance had weighed him and learned everything about him there was to know. He rapidly revised his first estimate of her as just a sweet lady. "Yes, Ma'am." He bared his head and held his Stetson in his free hand.

"Well, don't just stand there. Come in."

Andy looked helplessly around. Would Sheik suffer himself to be held by one of the men? Undoubtedly not after his little dance earlier. Andy's quick look spotted a sturdy cottonwood nearby. He led Sheik to it and tied him securely before following the woman inside the waiting room. "I'm Mrs. Salt. Don't stay more than a few minutes," she warned. To his surprise, she laid a hand on Judd Allen's sleeve and said, "Let him go first," then opened the door to the examining room, ushered Andy in, and closed the door behind him.

A keen-eyed doctor with bushy eyebrows stood next to the bed. "You are—"

"Andy Cullen. Mrs. Salt said Miss Allen wanted to see me." He advanced to where the girl lay on a white-sheeted high bed. Her blue eyes looked enormous in her pale face, and short brown curls made a halo around it.

"I. . .I'm glad you are all right," he stammered, twisting his big hat in his hands.

"*You!*" She tried to sit up, but the doctor pushed her back against the flat pillow.

"Just take it easy, Miss Allen," he warned. "You're going to be fine. Your daddy's waiting to come in."

"I didn't know. . .the child, that horse. . ." She covered her lips with trembling fingers. "How did you keep from k–killing us?"

"Sheik leaped clean over you both," Andy told her.

"What a grand horse! May I see him sometime?" Pink banners streamed into her face.

"Of course." He wanted to tell her how he'd caught Sheik, that he'd be at the Rocking A before she reached home, and a hundred other things.

The doctor forestalled him. "Later. Send her father in on your way out, please."

Andy's contagious grin and conspiratorial look brought an answering smile from the patient. "Right, Doc. So long for now, Miss Allen." He ducked his head and marched out but not before he heard the doctor say, "Cocky young rooster, but I kind of like him."

To Andy's everlasting regret, the door closed before he caught the young woman's reply.

"Cullen, do you plan to stick around for the rest of the doings?" George Allen's voice boomed and brought Andy out of his meditations concerning young ladies and yellow dresses.

"Ump-umm. If it's all the same to you, I'll go get my winnings, rub down Sheik, collect Chinq, and head for the Rocking A."

"Good. Soon as Linnet's able, we'll be on our way, too. If you get there before we do, make yourself to home. Most of the boys are in town and will probably stay over, including the cook, but there's plenty of grub, and you look to me like a man who can take care of himself."

"I fry a mean hunk of meat," Andy bragged. "Give me that and a biscuit, and I'm fine." The desire to be totally honest with his new employer made him add, "Besides, now that I won the race, I'll stoke up with a good meal at the cafe. I've been pretty empty the last couple of days."

George's quick grin showed he appreciated the candor. "Nothing wrong with being broke and hungry; I've been that way myself," he gruffly said. "Any chance you want me to carry most of your winnings to the ranch?"

Andy flushed. Anger overcame caution. He drew himself to full height. "I don't drink or gamble or worse."

George's face turned scarlet. "I didn't think you did. The reason I offered is, there's a lot of strangers in Moab and some not so strange. They all saw you win the race."

The significance of it dawned on the new Rocking A hand. "Sorry, Sir. I'll go get the money." He turned away. Even his ears felt hot at the way he'd misjudged the hearty rancher.

"I like a man who sticks up for himself, Cullen. No need to apologize. You might kind of mention around you aren't carrying the prize money."

The veiled warning rang in Andy's brain on the long walk down the main street. Dozens of men had crowded into the saloon where he had to go for his money. A loud cheer rose when he entered. "Hey, Cowboy, that's some horse!"

Andy recognized the storekeeper's voice and quickly located the beaming man. "Thanks," Andy said.

"Set 'em up," the man said. "Drinks on me. I ain't never made such a killing off you boys as today. C'mon, Cowboy, and drink to the grandest stallion what's ever rode down Main Street!"

Andy thought fast, then his wide, white grin appeared. "Sure, if you've got any lemonade."

"Lemonade! What d'you want lemonade for? That's no man's drink," the bartender growled.

Andy stepped closer. A lock of hair fell to his forehead. He grinned again. "That so? Mighty peculiar, ain't it? I'd have bet anything no one but a real man could ride Sheik. . .and win." He clenched his hands, hoping humor would save the situation. It did. First the storekeeper, then the bartender grinned sheepishly and allowed as how he was right. Andy downed an over-sized glass of frosty lemonade and drawled, "Where's my prize money?"

"Right here." The storekeeper handed over a wad of bills, some of them dirty, others wrinkled but big enough to choke Sheik and Chinq together. "What you going to do with it? Order more lemonade?"

The good-natured crowd roared, but Andy laughed, peeled off what he owed for his clothes, took a couple dollars from the roll, stuck them in his pocket, then announced, "My new boss, Mr. Allen, said he'd keep it for me." He turned an innocent face toward the men gathered around him. "I'm just keeping enough out to get me the biggest steak in Moab. Safer, that way. Why, if I kept it with me, I might buy out the store." In the midst of laughter, he escaped, stopped on the boardwalk in front of the saloon, and mopped his hot face. *Whew!* That had been close. His Trail Pard must have kept the men friendly even when Andy refused to drink. He'd seen what booze did to men and wanted no part of it, ever.

A dozen horses hitched to the rail shied nervously when shots came from down the street. *Cowboys letting off steam,* Andy thought. The horses reared again. One in particular acted determined to break free and flee.

Andy stepped nearer. "Whoa, Boy," he told the frightened sorrel. The mare quieted under his touch. Andy's eyes gleamed at her saddle and trappings. Pretty and polished to a high gloss. He leaned closer. Froze. A bit of the saddle blanket hung lower on one side than the other. In its corner was a tiny, telltale *A*.

Chapter 9

H old it!" A voice rang from behind Andy. He felt something hard poke into his back, and he slowly turned. A broad-shouldered man with drooping mustache ordered, "Now suppose you tell us what you think you're doing with that horse."

Steel met steel. "Suppose *you* tell *me* why this sorrel mare's wearing my saddle blanket." Andy's brown eyes darkened, and he crouched a bit.

"Are you calling me a thief?" His opponent sheathed his revolver and doubled his fists. A little ripple of shock ran through the crowd of onlookers who had laughed with Andy and now turned hostile.

"I'm saying three skunks held me up and took my grub and bedroll, saddlebags, and blanket."

"Hey, what's going on?" A burly man elbowed through the crowd. "Dunn, what're you bellyaching about now?"

"I caught this rider examining my horse real careful-like and called him on it. Now, he's accusing me of stealing a saddle blanket." His laugh rang out contemptuously.

Andy caught the glint of a silver star before the newcomer retorted, "Silas, you'd be more likely to steal his horse if you could get away with it. This is the young feller who just won the race on the black stallion that everyone's saying is Sheik."

Dunn's mouth dropped open. He jerked as if hit by a speeding bullet. *"You?"* Greed glittered in his eyes. "What will you take for him, providing he's really Sheik."

"He is, but he ain't for sale." Andy whipped back toward the sheriff. "The sorrel's wearing my saddle blanket. What are you going to do about it?"

The sheriff shoved his sombrero back on his sandy hair. "Well, now, stealing's a serious charge. Can you prove the blanket's yours? What I can see of it, it looks a heap like any other saddle blanket."

"You'll find a tiny embroidered *A* worked into one corner," Andy said quietly. "My pards on the Double J in Arizona gave me the blanket for Christmas, and the boss's wife put my initial on it."

"There ain't no *A* or any other letter on that blanket," Dunn bawled. His face contorted with anger. "Even if there is, and like I said, there ain't, this tinhorn coulda seen it when he was snooping around."

The sheriff ignored the rancher's rantings, strode to the sorrel, lifted the edge of the blanket, and examined it. "It's here all right." He gave Dunn a measuring glance. "And unless a feller knew what to look for, he'd have to have mighty sharp eyes to see it." Dunn bellowed, and the sheriff cut him short with a scathing look. "You just stated clear and positive there was no such thing, so you must never have seen it. Unsaddle the mare and give him his blanket."

Dunn just stood there, speechless with rage. Dark, unhealthy red suffused his face, and storm clouds gathered in his eyes. Andy took an extra long look, expecting them to be colorless. They were not. Dark and dangerous looking, those eyes did not belong to any of the three men who had jumped and robbed him months earlier.

"Move, Dunn, or I'll run you in. Maybe I will, anyway. How'd you get this partic'lar saddle blanket?"

Dunn spat into the dust of the street. "Won it playing poker."

The sheriff's voice turned gravelly. "From a man just passing through, I s'pose."

Sardonic humor ended in a sneer. "How'd you get so smart, Sheriff? That's just who he was. I cleaned him out—"

"I'll just bet you did," the sheriff interrupted.

"Like I said, I cleaned him. He still wanted to play and offered me this blanket." Dunn sent a venomous look at Andy. "I obliged him. Didn't consider it my business where he got it."

Andy accurately gauged the lack of love between the two and tucked the knowledge away. It might come in handy sometime.

"Get that saddle off. Now!" The sheriff's words cracked like a bullwhip. "Cowboy, if I were you, I'd wash it before putting it on a great horse like that Sheik of yours. No telling what kind of vermin it's been around."

The crowd howled, swung into sympathy for the newcomer to Moab who had shown up Dunn in front of his cronies. Evidently, the big rancher was no favorite among them, either.

Andy glanced from their mirth-filled faces back to Dunn, who sullenly marched over to the sorrel. His eyes widened. Those same shoulders had been turned square to him in the Moab cafe the fateful day he overheard the plan to drive Sheik and his band onto Dead Horse Point and fence them in.

Still angry over the saddle blanket business, he opened his mouth to blurt out the scheme but thought better of it. His friend Smokey back in Arizona had once grinned and said, "Pard, the way I see it is like this. The good Lord musta purely wanted us to do twice as much listening as talking, or He wouldn't have given us two ears an' only one mouth."

Now, Andy buttoned his lip, decided he'd keep both ears open, and see what happened.

Saddle blanket over his left arm, aware of the baleful look Dunn gave him, Andy shook hands with the sheriff. "Thanks."

"Who are you, anyway?" the official wanted to know. "All Moab knows about you is that you ride in here on the grandest horse in southeastern Utah, win the race, keep Sheik from killing a mighty brave young woman, and brace Dunn. Oh, yeah, you mentioned riding for the Double J. Most of us in these parts have heard of that spread." He eyed Andy with twinkling, half-closed eyes.

"Name's Andy Cullen, and you know 'most all that's important, except Mr. Dunn's going to be mighty surprised when my new boss, George Allen, fires off our big plan." He chuckled at the sheriff's expression and worked his way through the laughing crowd.

A voice at his elbow drawled, "I sure do admire a feller who stands up for what's his."

A second and third chimed in, "Me, too."

Andy turned his head. The three cowboys who'd leaped to Linnet's defense kept pace with him, grinning like three demons.

"Say, is it true you're hiring on with us?" the leader asked.

Andy stopped short. "Think I should?"

"You bet! Now maybe we can stop some of the—"

Andy's keen gaze saw the quick dig of an elbow in the speaker's ribs and refrained from asking questions. He'd have to prove his trustworthiness by more than winning races and facing Silas Dunn before he could expect the hands' confidences or loyalty. Yet, by the time the quartet reached the cotton-wood where Sheik indignantly proclaimed his displeasure at being forsaken, even temporarily, Andy had sorted out names and faces and suspected Reddy Hode, Tommy Blake, and Charlie Moore to be true-blue to their employer and tickled to death over the events of the day. After he turned over the bulk of his winnings to George Allen, Andy realized his belt buckle felt like it was rubbing his spine from hunger. Still, he took time to conscientiously rub down the black, go get Chinq, and threaten the old man at the livery stable with death and destruction if he let anything happen to either horse.

Less than an hour later, Andy rode out of Moab astride the proud stallion with faithful Chinq trotting close behind. Prime roast beef, mashed potatoes and gravy, hot biscuits, vegetables, and two pieces of apple pie lay tucked in his belly and fortified him for the trip to the Rocking A. Lulled by Sheik's easy motion and the waning heat of the day, he reviewed everything that had happened from the time he first caught sight of flags and buntings. "Seems like a week ago." He yawned. "Not just this morning."

His mind turned to his meeting with Linnet Allen outside the store, and a smile stretched his lips. It died when he relived the chilling moment he saw her fling herself over the toddler directly in his and Sheik's path. Again a wave of gratitude surged through him. "Thanks, Lord." Andy hunkered down in the saddle, alert to anything unusual but comfortable and relaxed.

A thunder of hooves roused him from his reverie. He glanced back. Three men on racing horses pounded down the rutted road behind him, bent low over their mounts' necks. Friend or foe? Andy didn't wait to find out. He leaned forward and touched his heels to Sheik's sides. No horse in Moab could match the black's speed, even after his earlier run. "Go, Boy. Come on, Chinq."

Sheik cannoned into a mighty leap and settled into a dead run. Wind whistled by Andy's ears, yet his excellent hearing caught the steady drum of Chinquapin's racing feet, then a stentorian, "Cullen! Wait up."

Andy laughed aloud and gradually reined the stallion to a stop. He turned and waited for the three riders who had tried so unsuccessfully to catch him. When they pulled up, he laughed again. "What took you boys so long?"

Reddy Hode expertly controlled his fractious horse; Tommy Blake and Charlie Moore did the same. "Why's you running away from us?" Reddy disgustedly burst out. "How are we s'posed to escort you home when you're riding a critter like that?" He pointed accusingly at Sheik.

"How was I s'posed to know you weren't horse thieves?" Andy mimicked. "This *critter* would be mighty fine pickings for a rustler."

"Sure, 'cept we ain't no rustlers. Moab done quieted down 'cause of the near accident. Miss Allen's better, and her daddy and uncle are bringing her home. We figured we'd mosey on back, too." Reddy's crooked grin reminded Andy of himself after he first met Smokey Travis and the Rocking A riders—curious, friendly, a mite cautious.

"I'm sure glad she's all right," Andy said from his heart.

"So're we. Soon as she gets real strong, we're gonna convince her this part of Utah's the best place on earth for staying healthy," Tommy put in.

"Yeah. She needs to settle down, find a handsome cowpoke to marry, and make some feller the sweetest little wife in the West," Reddy added.

"It won't be you," Charlie smirked. "There ain't nothing purty or han'-some about you at all."

"I'm better looking than some I could mention," Reddy said significantly. "And at least I ain't old enough to be her daddy."

"Like the owner of the Bar D?"

Charlie's mocking question snapped Andy's head up. That bullish rancher, courting a delicate flower like Linnet Allen? "Impossible!" he burst out.

Reddy cocked a knowing head. "Naw. I saw him looking at her just before she run out into the street." His lips turned down in scorn. "Sure didn't see him make no effort to save either her or the kid, and he was standing there, bold and barefaced, in the front of the crowd."

"How come you noticed him?" Tommy asked curiously.

"I make it my business to keep an eye peeled toward anyone who might bother our new boss lady." Reddy gave Andy a look of pure mischief and grinned companionably. " 'Course, sometimes things ain't the way they look, at first, but—" He straightened in the saddle. "With Dunn, it's worth observing."

"Let's hit the trail," Tommy complained. "Now that our new hand's decided we ain't no horse stealers maybe we can ride peaceful-like and not have to eat his horses' dust."

"Say, if you don't mind my asking, how'd you catch Sheik?" Reddy, who had crowded in next to Sheik and forced his comrades to drop just behind when the road wouldn't permit four abreast, sounded more eager than curious.

"Talk loud," Tommy pleaded. "So's we can hear. We don't dare get too close to Sheik's heels."

Andy had already decided how trustworthy the three hands were and frankly told them the whole story. Encouraged by their respectful silence broken only by a wild "Yippee-ay" at the end of his recital, he outlined his plan for rounding up Sheik's band and how he planned to return the stolen mares but sell colts, fillies, and any other unbranded horses.

"Did you happen to notice any Bar D brands on them?" Reddy's question sounded just a mite too casual.

"I kept too busy with Sheik to pay attention to brands," Andy frankly said. "Why?"

"Dunn's grabby. Don't let him buffalo you into turning over what ain't his." The next moment, Reddy changed the subject, leaving Andy to ponder the warning.

The riders traveled the last few miles engaged in desultory conversation that ranged from the size of the Rocking A to how well Allen treated his hands. By the time they reached the home corral, Andy felt he had a good idea of what to expect.

"Where can I put Sheik so he won't pick a fight?" he inquired, after tending to his horses. "Allen said he had a section he wasn't using."

"We'll show you." All three cowboys insisted on riding with the new hand to a choice chunk of land that boasted shade and water. "The boss just sold off a bunch of horses and hasn't run others in yet," the loquacious Reddy offered. "Leave that pretty little mare, and Sheik should be all right. There's plenty of space for him to roam and strong fences, although if he took a notion to jump them, he probably could. 'Tain't reasonable he will want to leave feed and water and his girlfriend unless something spooks him. Come on. We can ride double back to the corral."

A quiver of unknown origin flicked Andy. He rubbed Sheik's head, then Chinquapin's. Why did he feel so reluctant to ride off behind Reddy? Realization left him ruefully grinning. Outside of a few short absences in town, tonight was the first time he'd been apart from Sheik since he rode into the canyon and discovered the trapped horse. Andy shook his head at his fancies and chided himself. Yet the same feeling nagged him while he got settled in an empty bunk in the spacious bunkhouse and drifted off to sleep.

Long before daybreak, he slipped into his clothes and, stocking-footed and carrying his boots, stepped outside into a murky dawn. Taking care not to disturb his companions, he eased his way to the corral, snatched a lariat coiled around a post, and snagged one of the horses milling around. Something within shouted *Hurry*, and he urged the horse to its utmost.

When they reached the pasture, Andy pulled the borrowed animal to a stop and peered ahead. Daylight crept over the red rocks that made a natural wall on two sides.

Andy whistled. Waited. No response. He whistled again, then rode forward. "Sheik. Chinq," he called.

Sheik. Chinq, the walls faithfully echoed.

Alarmed beyond belief, he pressed forward, following the uneven fence until—

"No!" The denial thundered back and forth between the cliffs, accusing and confirming the sight Andy longed to shut out but couldn't. A section of fence lay flat, either torn down by humans or knocked over by flying hooves of jumping horses.

Heart in his mouth, Andy jumped from the saddle, secured his horse, and leaped to the outside of the downed fence. He stared at the ground. Some of his dread vanished when he found no boot tracks. Just fresh signs of two strong horses on their way to freedom. He tore his gaze from the ground, heart heavy, remembering how he had hoped Chinquapin would never have to choose between Sheik and her master.

Now she had chosen. Her smaller tracks showed clear, along with the deeper, larger imprints of the stallion.

Andy longed to mount and go after them, then shook his head. Not on this horse. He could never begin to catch them. Better to go back, rouse Reddy and Tommy and Charlie, then get a faster horse. He'd have to let the Allens know, as well. He pictured George's jaw dropping when he heard the bad news.

Andy sighed and followed on foot several paces in the direction the tracks led. Hope refilled his heart. With the unexplainable instinct the Creator had placed in Sheik, the stallion's tracks led straight in the direction of the now-sealed canyon and the band of horses waiting to be freed.

"We can take a shortcut and go directly there," Andy shouted. Moments later, he had remounted and goaded the Rocking A horse back toward the ranch buildings.

—+—

Linnet roused from a deep slumber to a commotion in the corral. She struggled from bed and ran to the window, marveling at how alert and strong she felt. Ever since the doctor gruffly told her he believed that, in time, her heart would be healed, she had thanked God in advance for that day and taken in deep breaths of the clear air. Uncle George had insisted on borrowing a horse to ride home, leaving Judd to drive with Mrs. Salt next to him and Linnet stretched out on the backseat of the contraption. "No sense overdoing it," he'd told her. "What happened today was enough to set anyone back, and we don't want to spoil the good progress you've made so far."

She had actually been grateful and slept a good deal of the way. When they got home, Mrs. Salt ordered her to bed, brought her supper on a tray, and grimly watched her eat every bite. "Thank the good Lord you're here and not trampled under that wicked horse's hooves," she announced.

"He isn't wicked." Linnet put down her fork. "He must be intelligent and wonderful to leap over me like that." She pushed the empty tray away. "Let's not talk about it."

"All right." Mrs. Salt acted subdued. "Did Mr. Allen or Mr. Judd tell you they hired that young cowboy?"

Linnet wondered why the news should make her heart jump. "No."

"Well, they did. And that isn't all." She dropped to a chair near the bed and told the listening young woman how their new hand had gotten away with drinking lemonade in the saloon and making Silas Dunn look like a fool in front of the whole town. "Andy Cullen sure made an impression on Moab today. Got his blanket back, too, and without a killing."

Linnet felt the blood drain from her face. "Surely a man wouldn't kill for a saddle blanket!" Her eyes widened with horror.

"Dunn might. When he comes calling, and he will, keep out of sight as much as you can."

Bewildered, Linnet could only stammer, "But why?"

Mrs. Salt's lips closed in a thin line before she opened them enough to mutter, "There have been stories about him trying to marry every woman in the country, decent or not."

"Is he handsome?"

"Hardly!" Mrs. Salt snorted, and her eyes flashed. "I'd as soon have a loco coyote hanging around as him. He's nearer my age than yours, but that won't make any difference."

Linnet giggled. "Is he bowlegged?"

"Not so you'd notice. Why'd you ask such a question?" Mrs. Salt threw her hands into the air.

Filled with the joy of returning to health and the promise of a future, Linnet told how she and her father had laughed over their coming west and how he predicted a bowlegged cowboy would be her fate.

"My, my, I wouldn't have thought it of Mr. Judd." A smile lurked in the corners of her mouth and softened her eyes. She smoothed the pillows, straightened Linnet's bedclothes, and bade her good night and a peaceful sleep. But just before she stepped into the hall and closed the door behind her, Mrs. Salt fired a parting shot. "By the way, our new hand with the black stallion isn't a bit bowlegged. He walks as straight and proud as your daddy and uncle." The door clicked, and the convulsed girl heard the housekeeper-cook's firm footsteps echo down the hall and fade into silence.

Linnet laughed until she cried, then fell into a sound sleep to dream of powerful black horses, laughing cowboys, and a masked man who came to call and said his name was Silas Dunn.

Now she stood by her window, wishing she knew why cowboys ran to the corral, saddled horses, and called to each other. The Rocking A always rose early, but something in the very air hinted at an unusual situation. Linnet hastily donned a housecoat, thrust her feet into slippers, and stepped into the hall. "Mrs. Salt?"

The good woman appeared as if by magic. Excitement oozed from her. "I knew those pesky men would wake you."

"What's happening?"

Mrs. Salt smoothed her huge apron down over her work dress. "Both of Andy Cullen's horses have bolted. The men are going after them. Cullen should have known he couldn't trust Sheik. This isn't the first time he's run off with a mare, and I'll wager it won't be the last."

Forgetting her attire, Linnet lightly ran down the stairs. Life on the ranch certainly differed from the sheltered eastern existence she had known. She giggled, thinking of the expression proper Bostonians would wear if suddenly awakened by the sound of horses beneath their windows.

Chapter 10

Unwilling to miss the drama taking place in the corral, Linnet hurried to a window and flung it open to the early July morning. She clutched her housecoat close and from the frail protection of a spotless curtain peered out. The clear air amplified voices, and she could hear the conversation very well.

"Wait, boys." George Allen's bellow stilled the hubbub. "There's no sense in rushing off shorthanded." A cry of protest went up from the vastly depleted number of Rocking A riders. George raised his voice to a roar. "Hold it. We know where the horses are headed. It won't take more than half a day to notify the other ranchers of what's going on. They'll be here late this afternoon with as many hands as they can spare. We'll leave tomorrow morning."

"Aw, Boss, it's a pure shame to let Sheik and that pretty little chestnut mare get a day's start," one of the cowboys called. Linnet felt sure it was Reddy who had spoken.

A mumble of agreement ran through the grouped men.

"What's a day?" George asked reasonably, his voice diminished but still plenty loud. "When Sheik gets to the valley and finds he can't get in, he isn't going to up and leave. He'll hang around trying to find a way in. Cullen says there's a goodly bunch of horses holed up in that valley. We're going to need more men than we have here to drive them. The rest of our own outfit will be rolling in this evening, too. We'll head out at daybreak."

"You're the boss, but I ain't too happy about it," the cowboy Linnet had identified as Reddy retorted.

"Everything will be fine, Hode. You boys get some breakfast and start riding to the ranches; one of you swing back by Moab. Better yet, hit town first. You can catch a lot of the ranch owners before they start for home." He turned on his heel and came back toward the house.

Fascinated, Linnet watched his easy stride, then gripped the curtain when a slim rider followed George to the porch.

"Sir, I'd like to go after my horses now and not wait for the others."

Allen wheeled to face his newest hand. "Any special reason?"

From her vantage point, Linnet saw the way Andy Cullen hesitated, then looked square into her uncle's eyes. "I have a funny feeling." His brown eyes pleaded, but he snapped his mouth shut.

"What kind of feeling?"

"I can't explain it, but it has something to do with Sheik and Chinq needing me."

"Go ahead, then. We'll meet you at the valley. Tell me again how to get there."

Andy quickly gave directions. The watching young woman wished with all her heart she could ride out with him to find the black stallion. When the cowboy moved purposefully toward the corral, followed by her uncle's orders to pick whatever horse he wanted, Linnet ran to the front door and confronted her uncle George when he stepped inside. "Could I go?"

"No!" Mrs. Salt whisked into the room, a scandalized expression on her face. "A horse drive's no place for a woman, even one who's a lot stronger than you are."

"Uncle George?" Mutiny rose in Linnet's heart.

"Sorry, Lass." Genuine regret filled his kindly eyes. "Isn't it enough that the doctor's given you hope to get well?"

Shame swept into her heart. Her head drooped like a poorly broken filly's. "I'm sorry. It's just that—"

"That you have Allen blood in you and a pioneering spirit," her father put in from behind her. "I'll stay with you, if you like."

She sensed his longing, even greater than her own. "You'll do no such thing! I want you to help drive the horses and remember all the things that happen so you can tell me. Uncle George will be too busy to notice."

"So you expect me to be a slacker and just watch and let the others do all the work?" Judd drew himself up in mock indignation, and his blue eyes, so like hers, sparkled with fun.

"You know I didn't mean that." The sound of hooves drew her back to the window. This time she dared to draw aside the curtain, heedless of being seen. At that exact moment, Andy Cullen glanced toward the house. Linnet couldn't read his expression, but the wide smile couldn't be denied. He swung aboard the horse he'd just saddled, tipped his hat in her direction, and rode away, leaving her breathless, with a little prayer in her heart for his safety.

✛

The same unexplainable feeling that had urged him to go after his horses and not wait for the outfit sent Andy pell-mell over the range and back the way he had come a few days earlier. The memory of a young woman's sweet face, framed by a window curtain, rode with him, but the frisky horse that had lolled around the corral while the outfit whooped it up in town required attention. Andy had chosen her not only for her spirit but as bait. Another stallion meant trouble, but a mare offered a lure he hoped Sheik would find irresistible.

In a far shorter time than he'd made on his way to Moab, Andy reached the entrance to the hidden, blocked canyon. Sheik and Chinquapin's clear trail showed that in spite of a shortcut Andy took, they remained ahead of him. He reined in and slipped from the saddle. Hope died. A jumble of foot and hoofprints showed clearly in the thick dust of the trail—and the sheltering rocks he had rolled to block its entrance lay scattered into heaps!

Fearing the worst, Andy looped his mount's reins over a nearby rock and ran through the narrow passage. He halted at the valley entrance and stood transfixed. The rock barricade he had so painstakingly built, no longer existed. He raced into the valley and called. His only response came from a winging eagle. The band of horses had vanished as completely as if a giant hand had scooped them up and transported them to another place.

"Sheik. Chinq," he cried in desperation.

Sheik. Chinq, the rock walls faithfully echoed, then silence again reigned.

"Someone must have heard the horses and figured out their whereabouts," Andy surmised. He shoved his Stetson back and stared at the empty valley. "But where's Sheik? And Chinq?" He tried to crawl into the stallion's mind and figure what he'd do in his place. "Track them. He won't stand for his family being spirited away any more than he stood for being corralled with them out here," Andy decided.

He retraced his steps through the passageway and untied his horse. As much as he longed to head after the herd, she needed rest. He led the protesting animal into the valley and let her drink long and graze. She deserved it. Hat over his eyes, Andy lay prone under the cottonwoods where he'd once crosstied Sheik, and he forced his nerves and muscles to relax. Suspicion licked at him, the clear memory of broad shoulders turned against him while Silas Dunn plotted with his henchmen to drive horses onto—

"Dead Horse Point. That's it!" Andy sprang up, galvanized into action.

Hope rekindled. "Come on, Horse. We don't have time to waste."

Five minutes later, they were out of the valley and on their way. Andy's keen eyes didn't miss a sign, and a herd of wild horses being driven left plenty of them. Dusk overtook him and still he pushed on until darkness warned further travel could be disastrous.

He reluctantly made camp, but at first light, he had already stamped out the remains of his small fire and turned the mare onto the clearly marked trail. A passing thought that Reddy and the others would be leaving the Rocking A just about this time crossed his mind. His lips set in a grim line. He couldn't count on their help. Long before they reached the valley and tracked him, he'd be at the Point.

The day wore on, and his sense of urgency grew as well as a restless desire to push his mount beyond her strength. He resisted, and violet shadows lay long on the ground before he reached his destination. With the caution learned as a young lad on his own, especially when he worked on the Cross Z and kept his ears and eyes open to protect Columbine Ames, Andy dismounted when he saw the first flicker of campfire not far from the rim of the canyon. He tied his horse and belly-slid over the ground until he reached the fragile cover provided by a clump of greasewood. When no sound showed he'd been detected, he raised his head and peered through the stiff, thorny branches. He stiffened. Six men hunkered down around the fire. The smell of frying bacon and boiling coffee tantalized him, but after the first sniff, Andy forgot them. He concentrated on the men's faces, one by one.

Unless his eyes betrayed him, three of them were the men from the cafe who enthusiastically endorsed the wild horse drive. He dismissed them and studied the others but shook his head. Two of them could be any dark-visaged rider and might or might not be the holdup men who relieved Andy of his grub. The next moment, one laughed. Pleasant, appealing, the last time he'd heard it, a shot over his right shoulder followed.

Certainty replaced suspicion, and Andy shifted until he could examine the sixth man. Firelight fell on his uncovered face, reflected from his eyes. Weak with excitement, Andy looked straight into the odd, colorless eyes that had gleamed in campfire light months earlier. Any lingering doubt fled forever when Strange Eyes said eagerly, "Hey, Boss, lookee here," and held up a dead cottontail in the exact way he'd dangled Andy's saddlebags at their first meeting.

The cowboy's breath came faster, but cool reason prevailed. One against six meant defeat or bloodshed. Could he lie low until the roundup crew arrived tomorrow? He considered and rejected a dozen plans. First, he must locate Sheik and Chinq. Beyond that, he couldn't plan. He inched his way out of earshot and back to his horse. What if he could find Sheik? He must be tied. Andy's blood boiled at the probable treatment the big stallion had suffered through if captured. On the other hand, just maybe Sheik had been canny enough to keep his presence unknown to the men driving the horse herd, no mean feat for six riders.

Andy's heart leaped. In that event, his own job would be easier than stealing milk from a well-trained cow. If only he had Chinq instead of the mare, whose full capabilities he couldn't count on. "No use wishing for the moon," he muttered. "I have to make do with what I've got."

Tremendous curiosity filled him. Now that he'd satisfied himself about the riders at the campfire, he'd take a gander at the narrow neck of land called Dead Horse Point. A tiny bit of light remained in the sky, just enough for him to make his way to the Point. He guided the mare forward. She acted willing enough, probably caught the scent of horse. It wouldn't matter if she whinnied. One horse among many wouldn't alarm the men at the fire.

In the last gleam of dusk, he saw what he expected. A band of mares, colts, and fillies milled on the thirty-yard-wide neck of land bounded on three sides by canyon. The fourth side boasted a crude fence formed of scraggly brush, lassoes, and a couple of crooked posts fashioned from stunted tree trunks.

Andy grunted and relief washed through him. That so-called fence might discourage mares and young horses from a breakout. Sheik would snort his disdain and leap it in a minute. So would Chinq. Obviously, they were not part of the herd.

He risked a low whistle. Some of the penned horses called back, then off to Andy's left, a familiar nicker sounded. He turned in that direction, spirits rising like the Colorado River in flood. "Chinq?" he called. "Sheik?"

Another nicker. A deeper whinny. A quick rush of hooves, and two horses came to him. The pitch blackness that had fallen couldn't disguise their sounds or the yelling that arose in the horse herders' camp.

"We have to get out of here," Andy told the horses. Leaving the Rocking A mare saddled, he leaped to Sheik's back, hoping the mare would follow the way Chinquapin did. "All right, Boy. Make tracks."

The stallion pranced. Andy gripped the bridle and began the strangest ride of his life. Without saddle or blanket, he pressed his legs to Sheik's sides and prayed the horse wouldn't step in a gopher hole in his wild flight. He heard Chinq and the other mare behind them and made no effort to halt the black until he knew they'd put enough distance between them and the Point so the men camped there couldn't track him in the dark. He also took the precaution, once stopped, to transfer the mare's saddle to Sheik and hobble and tie him. The taste of freedom in the stallion's journey back to the valley might have done irreparable harm to the breaking process. He couldn't chance having a determined horse nosing around the makeshift corral and triggering a panic that would rouse the captors.

Worn out by worry and the long, hard pursuit, Andy fell into a black, dreamless sleep. A wild scream brought him wide awake, and a terrifying sight greeted his unbelieving eyes. He started to leap to his feet. A rope sang through the air. A flicker of time later, he fell, jerked clean off his feet by the lasso. In a twinkling, he lay bound hand and foot, his gaze fixed on Sheik, held fast by a half-dozen ropes and trying to get out from under four men who pinned him to the ground.

"Watch out!" Andy's warning rang just in time. Strange Eyes, who knelt beside the black's head, jerked back, barely escaping Sheik's vicious bite.

His face darkened. "I'll teach you." He cracked the stallion across the nose and just missed losing a hand.

"Stop it!" The man who had bound Andy sprang toward the horse. "You'll make a killer out of him and Du—we don't want that."

Andy warmed to him despite the perilous circumstances. He recognized him as the thief with the pleasant laugh. "Thanks, Mister."

"Say, don't I know you?"

Andy nearly bit his tongue in two to keep back the accusation jammed behind his teeth. "You might," he substituted.

"Hey, you're that feller—"

"Forget it." Andy took a chance and cut off disclosures that could prove fatal. With a quick prayer for help, he asked, "Why the holdup? Watch your hand!" he yelled at Strange Eyes, who had turned his attention to Andy and carelessly leaned too close to the captive stallion.

"Mighty concerned about me, ain't you?" the man jeered.

"More concerned that you'll teach my horse to be scareder of men than he already is," Andy shot back.

"Your horse?" The thief's eyebrows nearly reached his hair. "I don't see no brand."

A sickening feeling attacked Andy. "His name's Sheik. I caught and broke him. He ain't never been ridden by anyone else, and he's mine, brand or no. I found him and his mares—"

"Stolen."

"Sure. Stallions steal mares." Andy twisted against the uncomfortable ropes that cut into his wrists and ankles until he could get into a sitting position. "Allen of the Rocking A and all the other ranchers who've lost mares to Sheik—*including Silas Dunn*—are on their way right now to the valley where I left the band. I aim to return the mares and dicker for the colts and fillies."

"Sure you are." Strange Eyes jumped to his feet, face ablaze. "You've no proof the horses are yours. There's six of us to swear we found them, which we did, freed them, and drove them onto the Point."

"And there's sixty or six hundred to swear they saw me ride Sheik in the Moab Independence Day race and win," Andy flashed back. "We hang horse thieves in Arizona. I don't know what you do with them here."

The enraged man raised a heavy booted foot to kick the tied cowboy, but the leader yelled and told him to lay off. "Fine kettle of rotten fish," he bawled. "Did you know this?" He whirled toward the three guilty-looking men from the cafe who shuffled and admitted they'd heard that a yellow-headed kid won the race.

Sensing a possible split that could only be in his favor, Andy goaded some more. He even managed a cheerful grin. "Getting so you can't trust no one these days. Not trying to tell you your business, but if I were you, I'd hightail it out of here before that roundup outfit rides in. No telling what Allen and his boys will do when they find me trussed up like a Christmas pig ready for the roasting."

The flicker in the leader's eyes showed doubt, and Andy took heart. Sheik lay panting, temporarily defeated but still showing signs of fight.

"We ain't horse thieves," the leader protested. "We could have stole horses lots of times." He pointed his words with a significant look toward Chinquapin, who hovered close enough to see her incapacitated lord and master.

"I didn't think *you* were." Andy left it at that but couldn't resist adding, "What I know is you were hired by Silas Dunn to round up mustangs and drive them onto the Point, then build a corral and keep them there." He forestalled questions by tersely saying, "I heard Dunn and your three friends talking in Moab." His steady glance never left the leader.

The man turned to Dunn's representatives. "Pay up."

"What?" Their faces blackened with anger and surprise.

"Dunn's deal was to drive a herd to the Point, which we did. Me and my boys'll just take our money and vamoose."

Strange Eyes growled low in his throat, but the leader quelled him with a glance. "We ain't having any part in robbing this guy of his horse." He sent a contemptuous glance in his comrades' direction. "Dunn can kill his own snakes when he gets here. We stumbled on the valley, sent for you as agreed on, and made a long, hard drive. Fork over. Now!"

Andy secretly grinned at the results of the innocent-sounding comment. Dunn's men hastily conferred, then one pulled out a roll of bills and sullenly tossed it to the leader.

"Dunn won't like this," he shouted when the trio strode away, Strange Eyes protesting but obviously intimidated by his boss.

"Who cares?" A mellow laugh rang back to them, and the leader tossed the roll of bills. "Me and the boys are tired of Utah, anyway. Think we'll take us a little vacation and try somewhere else. Pickings around here are getting mighty slim."

Andy watched them ride out of sight, again thinking he could have liked the man if he hadn't been a thief and maybe worse. *What causes a fellow with a laugh like that to go bad?*

He didn't have time to consider it. The three men from town stood frowning down at him.

"What're we gonna do with him and the horse?" one asked.

"Leave him here and swear to Dunn he jumped us, tried to run us down with the stallion."

"Think it will hold water?" The third man looked skeptical.

"Why not? Any fool can see the horse's capable of killing a man if he took a notion."

"I don't like giving any horse a bad name," the first speaker complained. "Remember what happened to the black's daddy."

A pool of silence descended. Andy lay perfectly still. Sheik's future hung in the balance.

"Aw, why don't we just tell the truth?" the second man suggested. "We'll tell the boss the big, bad outlaws he hired roped and tied Sheik and his rider, then got cold feet and hightailed it out of here when they heard a bunch of ranchers and hands were on their way." He shot Andy a sharp glance. "Right, Cowboy?"

"That's the way it looked from here. 'Course, I ain't in much of a position to argue. How about untying me?"

"Hold your horses, and I don't mean Sheik. What's Dunn gonna do about those mares and colts and fillies?"

"Let him worry about them. I'm sick of this deal, anyway. I never figured on getting stuck with a band of mostly branded horses," the first man growled. "They were s'posed to be mustangs who belong to anyone, not a passel of already owned nags." He turned on his heel. "Count me out."

"Too late," one of his friends sang out. "A rider's coming and fast."

"*A* rider? Thought you said a whole outfit was heading this way," the first man accused. "What're you doing, trying to make fools out of us?"

Andy slowly shook his head. "They are. I don't know who'd be riding alone." Yet a sneaking suspicion that neither his nor Sheik's troubles were over sent dread through his bound body, and the closer the rider came, the louder the drum of hooves, the more he feared the unknown horseman bearing down on them as if Satan himself followed behind.

Chapter 11

H ow about untying me?" Andy said again. "If our visitor proves a mite unfriendly, I'm pretty good in a scrap."

"Forget it. We can handle a single rider. Besides," he added when a lathered horse pounded around a rock outcropping and slid to a stop in front of them, "it's the boss."

Andy sagged against the ropes. Silas Dunn might be one tough hombre, but he didn't appear to be a killer. His relief proved short lived. The unpleasant smile and hatred in the broad-shouldered man told the hogtied cowboy he hadn't been forgiven for the matter of the saddle blanket. He decided to take the initiative. "Where's the rest of the outfit?" Andy demanded.

"Trailing toward the valley," Dunn gloated. "By the time they get here, my men and I'll have full claim to the horses on the Point."

"Is that so?" Andy set his jaw, hating the advantage Dunn had over him because of the ropes. He expanded his muscles, relaxed them, and silently rejoiced when he felt them slacken. Left alone, he might work free.

"So you got Sheik." Dunn's eyes gleamed, and his face paled with greed. "Best horse I ever saw. Cullen, you should have sold him while you had the chance." He stepped from the saddle of the sorrel mare that no longer wore Andy's blanket and, shaking with excitement, walked toward Sheik. "I'll have him gelded and make him into the best saddle horse in the country."

Andy strained against his bonds. "Then you're the biggest fool in Utah," he hoarsely told the rancher. "Unless you want a poor-spirited nag, ashamed to hold his head up."

"He's right, Boss," one of the men put in. "I'm here to say I ain't gonna stand for any such thing."

"Me, neither," the others agreed.

"So, getting soft, huh? Just remember who put up the money for this deal."

"This deal, as you call it, is over," a cowhand snapped. "Those fancy outlaws you hired to drive the horses have took off. How are you going to take care of that bunch of animals on the Point without them. . .and us?" he added significantly.

Rage turned Dunn's face black. "You yellow-bellies," he bellowed. "I should have known you wouldn't have the stomach for an opportunity like this."

"You said it, Boss. But maybe you'll change your mind when you find out most of the mares are already wearing brands." The rider never budged an inch. "Unless you're considering changing brands, which ain't healthy in these parts. The owners aren't going to stand by with their hands in their pockets while you claim their horses."

"I can claim the colts and fillies."

"How?" Andy asked. "From what I hear, your men aren't willing to lie for you, and my word's better than yours. The ranchers have already learned from Allen who really found the herd."

Dunn speechlessly paced the ground, alternately glaring at Andy and his men and hurling invectives.

"That'll be about all," one finally said. "We got in this 'cause it sounded like an honest way to make some money. I'm dealing myself out now that it's beginning to stink, and I advise my pards to do the same." He backed off a step, then a knowledgeable look crossed his face. "On second thought, maybe we'd better stick around. I'd hate for this young feller to have an accident and then get blamed for it."

"You. . .you. . .cowards." Dunn frothed at the mouth and clenched his fists. With effort, he regained control. "I'll just have a look at the horses on the Point." He leaped into the sorrel mare's saddle, spurred her, and clattered off.

"Thanks, men." Andy let out a sigh of pent-up frustration. "I'd as soon face a wounded grizzly as be left alone with Dunn in this mood. Like you said, I'd hate to have an accident before the outfit gets here. Now, how about letting me up so I can free Sheik."

"Sure." The same rider who'd said he wouldn't stand for Sheik's being gelded produced a knife and cut Andy's bonds.

"Better stand back." Andy rubbed circulation back into his wrists and ankles and stepped toward Sheik, who lunged toward him but only succeeded in falling back because of the ropes. "He's never been handled rough except when I first caught and tamed him."

The men walked away a respectful distance.

"There, Boy. No one's going to hurt you," Andy soothed. Step by step, he came closer to the terrified animal. "Steady, now."

For a time, he didn't think the stallion would let him touch him, but a lot of coaxing later, Andy laid his hand on the black's quivering neck. More quiet talk and the loosening of the ropes that still held, and Sheik stood free. He stood absolutely still for a moment, then shook his head as if coming out of a daze. The next instant he reared, catching Andy off guard.

The cowboy leaped aside but stumbled. Numbness from the tight ropes hadn't completely disappeared. It slowed his actions and made it impossible to keep his balance.

Sheik came down heavily, twisting sidewise in a desperate effort to avoid his owner, but a fraction of a second too late.

Andy, who had hit the ground and tried to roll out of the way, felt a blow to his temple before everything went black.

An eternity later, he roused enough to hear loud shouting and the rolling thunder of many pounding hooves. He tried to struggle out of the terrible darkness clutching at him but could barely give a low moan. His eyelids stayed glued shut, and his weary brain refused to think. An effort to raise his head plummeted him fathoms deep into the smothering night.

⸙

After the outfit had ridden away after Andy Cullen, Linnet Allen spent most of her waking hours aimlessly strolling from house to corral or sitting on the wide porch, watching the road. She'd hidden and watched wide eyed during her uncle's discussion with the ranchers and cowboys who rode in at George's summons. Keen to spot the unusual, Linnet had also caught the quick glance around and shifty way a certain broad-shouldered man's colorless gaze swept the crowded room. In the vernacular of Mrs. Salt, she'd wager anything the man was Silas Dunn. Secure in her hiding place, she shivered. Imagine having that person coming to court a young girl! Unthinkable. The contrast of Andy Cullen's laughing but respectful attitude brought a rich blush to the eavesdropping girl.

After a lot of haranguing, and hemming and hawing on Dunn's part, mostly protesting the fact that the colts and fillies belonged to their finder, the whole bunch of them rode off. Linnet burst from seclusion and ran to the front porch, wondering if the fact that Reddy, Tommy, and Charlie rode grouped at the rear with their heads turned in Silas Dunn's direction held any significance.

"Child, you've been staring down that trail all day," Mrs. Salt complained. "It's been only a couple of days. Give them time."

Linnet turned toward her. "I can't help feeling something is wrong." Even though her good friend and substitute mother pooh-poohed the idea, the young woman couldn't shake the feeling of dread until the morning of the third day following the outfit's departure when she saw a dust cloud far down the road in the direction from which she knew the men would return.

"Mrs. Salt, the men are coming!" Linnet left the porch and hurried down the steps and across the wide space toward the corral, intending to open the gate for the herd of horses. Something in the slow progress of a band of riders far smaller than she'd expected halted her. "Why. . . ?"

Fear lent speed to her feet. She changed direction and flew over the uneven ground toward the snail-paced caravan. Her blue eyes, which had become accustomed to long distances in her time on the Rocking A, widened, and a fresh spurt of terror sped through her when she saw that the chestnut mare called Chinquapin carried a huddled, motionless figure tied in the saddle.

"Father? Uncle George?" Her piercing cry reached the riders before she did.

"They're all right," Reddy Hode called back. "It's Cullen."

A pang went through her. The relief she expected to feel didn't materialize. She ran faster and arrived at the somber-faced bunch. "What happened?" She stared at the quiet figure.

"I'll tell you later, Miss Allen. Tommy, go tell Mrs. Salt to have a bed ready."

"Is he. . .dead?" Linnet managed to gasp. Her heart pounded more from fear than exertion, and she turned back toward the house and the racing horseman.

"Naw, but he needs help. Charlie's already ridden to Moab for the doctor," Reddy evaded.

"Where are Father and Uncle George?"

Hode's eyes glittered. "Rounding up the horses." His lips set with the firmness of a steel trap clicking shut, and Linnet knew she'd hear no more for the moment.

She looked at the dust-stained, quiet figure on the mare he loved. Quick tears crept into her eyes. She scolded herself for them. The last thing anyone needed was a sissy tenderfoot getting in the way. The thought braced her, and after Mrs. Salt and Reddy expertly undressed Andy and put him to bed in a first-floor room, she peeped in.

His fine hands lay curiously still on the turned-back, spotless white sheet. A crisp bandage had replaced the bloodstained one binding his head.

Again she fought tears, then hastened out of the sickroom at Mrs. Salt's peremptory motion and whispered, "All we can do's to wait for Doc." Reddy and Tommy lounged on the front porch but straightened to attention and doffed their hats when she stepped outside.

"Tell me everything." She sank into a rocker.

Reddy took the lead. His eyes flashed when he said, "We've put together bits and pieces. When we got to the hidden valley Cullen described, it lay open and empty." His face darkened. "Shoulda kept a better eye on Dunn." He sounded disgruntled.

"Yeah." Tommy shifted his weight from one foot to the other. "He ducked out on us somewhere between here and the valley, probably when we had to ride single file to get around some rocks next to the trail."

Reddy took up the story again. "I had a hunch and said so. The boss agreed, and we hightailed it for Dead Horse Point. Found a...a mess. Cullen lying on the ground with blood pouring out of his head. Three riders from the Bar D standing over him, and Dunn just sliding from the saddle."

"Did the men *shoot* Andy?" Rage such as she had never before felt brought Linnet out of the rocker and to her feet.

"Naw. 'Cording to the men, they and some others, whose names they kept to themselves, had driven the horses to the Point, split over the deal going sour, and the others rode off, not wanting to meet us when we got there."

"But what happened to Andy?" Linnet demanded.

"I'm getting to that. Sheik and his lady friend, Chinquapin, had followed the horse herd. So had Cullen, who rounded up his horses and put some distance between. Well, the Bar D men ran across them and tied up Cullen *and* Sheik." His clear face flushed, and the corners of his mouth turned down. "Just about scared the stallion to death. When Cullen set him free, he started pitching, and when he came down, his foot knocked Cullen square in the head."

Tommy put in, "Your uncle roared, and some of us were all for running Dunn out of the country. Your daddy said to just let him take a couple of mares wearing his brand and let him go 'cause nothing could be proved against him."

A satisfied smile crawled across Reddy's face. "Dunn won't be pulling any crooked deals for awhile, at least." His grin died. "We talked about sending for a wagon, but Cullen came to long enough to mumble he could ride, so we tied him in the saddle after patching him up until his head looked like one of those quilts Mrs. Salt makes."

"Father and Uncle George should have come with him," Linnet said in an accusing tone.

"No need for that. They figured Cullen'd rather have them bring in the herd." Reddy's gaze wavered.

"What aren't you telling me?" Linnet asked.

He reddened and again avoided her direct gaze.

"Aw, she d'serves to know," Tommy exploded.

"Sheik took off like a scared jackrabbit in front of a pack of wolves." Reddy squirmed. "Cullen's mare went with him but couldn't keep up. We caught her while the boss patched Cullen's head." He heaved a great sigh. "One of the reasons the boss decided to keep most of the outfit and drive the horses back here is he figured Sheik ain't gonna take kindly to losing his herd."

"What if he doesn't come?" Linnet thought of the magnificent horse who had so easily cleared her body in one giant leap.

"I reckon it would 'most break Cullen's heart," Reddy admitted.

"You said that was one of the reasons?" She caught the meaningful look the hands exchanged.

"The colts and fillies aren't branded. If left on the Point, what's to prevent Dunn from showing up after we're gone and burning the Bar D on them?" Reddy shot back.

"Life sure wasn't like this in Boston."

Hode's keen eyes softened. "But you wouldn't trade it, would you? This here place has done healed you. Miss Allen, you sure couldn't have come running to meet us when you first got here."

With a quick prayer for guidance and the right words, Linnet slowly said, "No, I never want to go back, but as much as I've learned to love Utah Territory and the Rocking A, I can't thank them for my health. . .and life." She swallowed hard and felt tears mist her lashes. The cowboys maintained a sympathetic silence. "It's God who healed me."

"No arguing with that," Reddy gruffly said, and Tommy nodded. Linnet thought of what Mrs. Salt had said about the outfit's regard for her. *It's good for them to have someone to admire and hold high. . . .The way you live your life as a witness for the Lord may be making a far deeper impression. . .than any of us know.*

It felt like weeks before the capable doctor who Linnet remembered from her brief encounter arrived in a buggy, escorted by Charlie Moore. He and Mrs. Salt closeted themselves for a long time with the still unconscious cowboy. The doctor had questioned the hands, and according to Charlie, "Had a pure conniption fit," when he found out Cullen had been put on a horse and packed back to the ranch house. Charlie looked awed. "Never knew a man could get so mad, and I've seen plenty of upset fellers." Now he joined Linnet and his two friends on the porch and waited.

Mrs. Salt came out, a troubled look on her face and in her blue eyes. "Wish Mr. Allen were here. Doc says he has to operate; he thinks there's a bone pressing where it isn't supposed to." Her keen gaze traveled from face to face. "I'll help, but he needs one other person. Who's it going to be?"

Reddy turned pale under his tan; Charlie and Tommy just stared. Linnet felt her heart bounce. Sweat sprang to her face. Her hands turned icy. "I'll help."

A wave of protest rang from the cowboys, but she shook her head. "His riding saved me. I want to help. . .if I don't have to look at what's happening." Nausea at the idea attacked her.

"What would Mr. Judd say?" Mrs. Salt expostulated.

"He'd say I must do anything I can to help." The thought steadied her. "Just tell me what to do."

"Get into the oldest, plainest dress you own. On second thought, I'll get you something." She hustled the girl to her room, dug into a pile of clothes she said she'd been keeping for rags, waited while Linnet got into them, then pulled her hair back, fashioned a cap from a dish towel, and led her to the sick room.

"Miss Allen, are you fit for this?" the doctor sternly asked. "I don't want to move him any more. . .even to a table. This means you'll have to bend until your back aches. Mrs. Salt knows enough about my instruments to hand them to me, but I need you to hold the cowboy's head still. I can't be responsible for what happens if he moves his head."

" 'I can do all things through Christ which strengtheneth me.' " The words sprang unbidden from her lips and settled into her trembling, fearful heart. A wellspring of courage, beyond anything she had ever known, steadied her hands and voice, and her mind repeated the familiar words again and again.

Before the doctor directed Mrs. Salt on how to give the anesthetic, he pressed on a spot above the patient's temple. From the depths of unconsciousness came a moan, and the doctor grunted with satisfaction. "Just as I thought."

Every time Linnet knew she could not stay in the rigid position and hold Andy's head steady, she bit her lip, closed her eyes, and prayed—for the doctor, for Mrs. Salt, for herself. But most of all for the valiant young cowboy who, in their few short meetings, had somehow woven himself into the fabric of her life. If anyone had told her in the spring that she would be a crucial part of helping to save a man's life, how she would have laughed. A prayer of thankfulness rose to her lips and hovered over her during the rest of the operation. An eternity later, the operation ended.

"Well done, Lass." The doctor glanced at her. "Are you all right?"

She straightened her back, weary from bending. The room spun. "I. . .I think so."

He pushed her into a chair and told her to hold her head between her knees. The rush of blood to her brain cleared away the dizziness. "Thank you. Will he be all right?"

"He's young, strong. We took care of the problem. I predict that by fall he will be back riding wild broncs." The doctor's eyes twinkled. "In the meantime, he can enjoy a soft bed, Mrs. Salt's good food, and a pretty nurse."

Linnet felt herself flush; gladness filled her. "Thank God."

"I always do." He beetled his brows at her and began helping Mrs. Salt clean up. "Go on outside into the fresh air."

Linnet stumbled from fatigue when she stepped over the doorsill onto the porch. Three guilt-stricken faces greeted her.

"Aw, you're all in." Reddy pushed a chair forward. "We're a bunch of skunks for letting you do it."

"I had no choice." She leaned her head back against the chair top.

"I reckon you didn't, at that. How is he?"

Weariness dropped like a diver into deep water. "He's alive, sleeping naturally, and Doc says he will be okay."

Concern gave way to joshing. Linnet realized it for what it was: the cowboys' way of relieving their worries and frustration at being helpless to aid a fallen companion.

"If you don't need us, we'll ride back out and help bring the herd in," Reddy told her. "Since we ain't lucky enough to live in bed and have you fetch and carry for us."

Banners of red flew in her face. "Go ahead, boys. The more of you there are, the sooner Father will come." She held her eyes wide open to hide the tears that persisted in crowding up at the thought of her father and his strength that she needed. After the trio left, she let the tears spill, then wiped her face and ran upstairs to bathe and change into a fresh outfit.

At Linnet's insistence, Mrs. Salt reluctantly consented to let her take part of the night watch over the patient. Doc had propped pillows on both sides of his head and warned of the need for them to remain in place.

Heart pounding, Linnet seated herself near the bed. A kerosene lamp, turned down until it gave only the faintest yellow glow, cast grotesque shadows on the walls. The even breathing of the patient told his nurse that all was well. Hours later, long after Mrs. Salt had promised to relieve her, Linnet still sat there. The worthy woman must have failed to waken. It didn't matter. Andy hadn't roused.

Contradictory to the thought, a few minutes later, he stirred and tried to turn his head, although his eyes stayed shut. Linnet slipped to her knees and placed a cool hand on his brow. "Don't try to move. You were hurt, but you're going to be all right, thanks to God. Just rest." Her soothing voice went on and on, and he again slept, but when she removed her hand, he turned restless. She replaced it, and he grew quiet, with her still on her knees beside his bed.

For two days they watched him continuously. The second night he talked incoherently, but Linnet caught enough words about "pretty little girl" and "Now, Sheik!" to turn fiery red in the faint light.

"Lord, don't let her die."

She froze at her patient's first complete sentence and wiped sweat from his face. His next words turned her from cold to hot, though she had to bend close to hear them.

"She'll never look at me, Lord, but I love her."

Chapter 12

The next day, the Rocking A riders came home minus Sheik's stolen mares, claimed and driven off by their owners, but with a passel of unbranded stock. Until Andy Cullen regained health and chose which horses to keep and which to sell, the herd would remain intact in the pasture that Sheik and Chinquapin had briefly inhabited on the fateful night such a short time ago.

Linnet formed the habit of visiting the pasture whenever she could, that is, when Mrs. Salt chased her away from the nursing duties she had gladly taken on. Linnet told her father, "I never dreamed what was in me. I hated helping Doc, but I did it." Her blue eyes sparkled; her face glowed. "I also didn't know how easy learning to ride would be."

He looked at her radiant face. "Thank God" was all he could say.

Sadie, the gentle white mare assigned to Linnet, took Linnet on her back as easily as she took sugar and carrots from the hands that had lost some of their delicateness but gained beauty from serving others. The pastured horses learned to know Linnet's call and would come to the fence when she and Sadie arrived. Linnet's eyes glistened at their wild charm, yet most often her gaze would stray to the chestnut mare, Chinquapin, and a slow smile would light up her face. Never in the time following Andy Cullen's return to consciousness had he in word or deed expressed the love he had revealed, yet Linnet's secret knowledge filled her heart, and an answering feeling began. While family and outfit rejoiced over her return to health, she hugged to herself dreams of the future and a devoted cowboy who definitely did not have bowlegs!

Andy daily gained strength; so did Linnet. He chafed under the doctor's restrictions to rest and not take chances; she rode and traded her white skin for a clear tan tinged with red from sun and wind. She and Andy talked about many things: Sheik, Andy's lonely years since his parents died, Linnet's attempt to be courageous in the face of impending death. Gradually, their conversations grew more serious, and they spoke of God.

"Andy," she said one sunny afternoon from the wide porch that overlooked the corrals and range, bathed in summer haze. "You're a Christian, aren't you?" She held her breath, instinctively realizing his answer could make a vast difference in her future.

"I asked the Lord to be my Trailmate, my Pard, after I met Smokey and Joel and the others," he told her. A note of doubt crept into his voice. "I guess that makes me a Christian."

Linnet stumbled for words. "Do you pray?"

"I talk to Him, man to Man, the way I'd talk to Smokey, and He's the Best Friend I ever had, even better than Columbine." He'd long since told of his boyish regard for the girl he considered far above him. "Is that enough?"

Again she sought for just the right thing to say. On impulse, she laid one hand over his that lay on the rocker arm next to her. "I think it's grand that you share that kind of feeling. It's important, though, to know and accept Jesus as your personal Savior. He died in our place so we could have everlasting life."

Andy turned his palm up and gently squeezed her fingers. "Linnet, I would never have dared ask Him to take me on as His pard if Columbine and Smokey hadn't showed me how much God loved a plain old cowpoke and sinner like me," he said huskily.

Glad tears pushed against the girl's eyes. She slipped her hand from his and smiled mistily. "That makes me. . .and Him. . .very happy."

Neither noticed that in that precious moment, Andy, for the very first time, had called her Linnet instead of Miss Allen. Afterwards, she blushed rosy red, and the strong but respectful touch of his work-hardened fingers lingered.

After she went inside, Andy stared unseeingly across the Rocking A he had come to love second only to his cherished Arizona Territory. Linnet's light touch felt burned into his palm. A tide of warmth rose within him, and he thought of the look in her blue eyes when she smiled and said he had made her happy. He pondered, trying to decide whether she'd have felt the same for anyone who loved the Master or if part of the joy was because Andy Cullen hadn't disappointed her.

The longing to be astride a good horse and ride until he felt ready to drop from the saddle assailed him, and his heart leaped. A few more days, Doc had said on his last flying visit. Yet regret blended with the exultation. Once he returned to riding, roping, and rounding up, he'd have little opportunity to see Linnet. No more magical hours of sharing and getting to know each other in the way they had done during his convalescence.

Andy deliberately turned his thoughts elsewhere. *Where was Sheik?* A few times during the weeks he'd been laid up, uncertain reports of a black stallion seen from a distance created interest, but the riders couldn't identify the horse as Sheik. If the horse had visited his family, no sign showed. The thoughtful cowboy wholeheartedly believed he had not. Chinquapin remained in the pasture, more or less content. A couple of times Reddy Hode had driven Andy in the contraption and patiently waited while the Arizona hand petted his mare and took stock of the rest of the horses. The most recent visit had resulted in Andy's pointing out what colts and fillies he wanted to keep. George and Judd Allen put in a bid for the rest of them, and Andy's nest egg made his eyes pop wide open.

"Remember what I said," George told him. "There's plenty of space on the Rocking A, and I wouldn't mind selling you enough to get you started on a little spread of your own."

Andy thought it over. His long-held visions of a cabin and family danced in his mind, but this time he could see the wife who stood in the doorway to welcome him home. She looked amazingly like Linnet Allen.

"No hurry making up your mind," George said kindly.

Andy suspected those shrewd eyes saw clear to the bottom of his newest rider's boots, and he glanced away from the scrutiny.

Now he restlessly stirred and turned to his Trailmate and Savior. "Lord, I reckon if she. . .she cares, I'll stay. If not. . ." His voice trailed off. Where would he go if Linnet didn't care? Beyond recapturing Sheik, he had no ambitions, no desire to return to wild horse hunting. The only reason he'd ever begun to chase mustangs was because of the wild black stallion. Andy heaved a great sigh, then, with the philosophy of the range to deal with one day at a time, he left the future where it belonged—in his Creator's hands.

Fall came stealing on leaf-strewn winds. Peace reigned on the Rocking A, and business went on as usual. Back in the saddle, Andy caught himself peering as far ahead as he could see, no matter where he rode. He discovered that Chinquapin did the same. An obstruction rose to the rider's throat. "Miss him, don't you, Girl?"

Chinq turned her head and observed him with soft eyes, then whinnied and resumed her scanning of the horizon.

Andy finished his day's work, rode back to the ranch, cleaned up, and parked on his bed in the bunkhouse. Reddy, Tommy, and Charlie dragged in, along with a half-dozen other cowhands. Dirty and sullen, they scarcely resembled the merry outfit that argued and played tricks but loyally refused to allow anyone outside the Rocking A to make disparaging comments.

"What's wrong, boys?" Andy asked.

"Aw, you tell him. I can't." Reddy threw his hat on the floor and glowered.

"I'm too mad to talk," Charlie added and flung himself into a chair. "Tommy, you spill the news."

Andy stood up, feeling that whatever was coming required him to be on his feet. "Rustlers haven't stolen horses or cattle, have they?"

"Worse," Reddy ground out. He wiped his sweaty face with a soiled neckerchief.

"Lin—Miss Allen? She's all right?" Andy felt a primitive urge to throttle Reddy and get to the truth.

"She's fine. This deal don't concern the Rocking A 'cept it's so dirty, it's a slap in the face to any decent cowpoke." Reddy straightened from his dispirited slouch. To Andy's amazement, great drops stood on the other's contorted face.

"Reddy, what is it?"

The cowboy mopped at his face again; hatred shone from his eyes. "That skunk Dunn's pulled the rottenest trick ever heard of. It's gonna go down in Utah history as the blackest, meanest thing that could happen."

He paused and, in broken sentences, told the story. "For awhile after that time with Sheik, Dunn laid low, as you all know. Then kinda quietlike, he took up being what he is again. He rounded up the worst men he could find. . .the way I hear it, all his good riders walked out on him after what he did with Sheik."

Andy's nerves screamed. Would Reddy never get the story told?

"Anyhow, Dunn and his outfit went ahead with another horse drive. Sheik ain't the only stallion on the range with a herd of mares and young horses, just the best. Well, Dunn found a wild band. He succeeded in driving them onto Dead Horse Point, same as before." Pain twisted his face.

"What happened?"

Reddy stared into his eyes, but Andy had a feeling his pard was seeing a long line of horses instead. "Dunn and his men half broke the best of the lot, and you can bet how they did it."

Andy flinched, remembering the steel-like grip of some horse breakers he'd known. "It's a pure shame, but that's how a lot of them break horses," he offered.

"That ain't the worst of it," Tommy put in ominously.

A chill ran through Andy, and he jerked as if hit.

Reddy went on. "They drove off all the animals fit to sell and left the broomtails on Dead Horse Point. According to the story Dunn's giving out, the gate they put up was s'posed to be left open so the horses they left could find their way off the Point and back to the open range."

"So?" Andy braced himself.

"So somehow. . ." Reddy's gaze bored into him. "Somehow, no one knows or at least ain't telling, the gate stayed shut."

Andy felt the blood drain from his face, and he took a step back, hating the outcome of the story he already knew.

Reddy made a sound like a sob. "Those broomtails died of thirst, right there within sight of the Colorado River two thousand feet down from where they stood." He turned on his heel and bolted out of the bunkhouse.

The silence of compassion for suffering animals fell. Every cowboy there would shoot down a wild beast in time of danger or put a wounded animal out of its misery. But to leave horses, no matter how poor they might be, corralled on a rock promontory in the hot sun with no water transgressed every law of man and God.

Andy stepped outside and spotted Reddy standing by the corral, his shoulders drooping. He walked over and laid an arm across Reddy's back but said nothing until a new thought caused him to ask, "Does the boss know?"

"Yeah. He told us. For two bits, I'd go call Dunn out." A white line formed around his mouth.

"You don't need to, Reddy. A man has to pay for what he does. Besides, we don't know for sure who shut the gate or who didn't open it when he was supposed to."

"Yeah," Reddy said again. His muscles rippled, then relaxed. "Andy, how come God lets two-legged varmints like Dunn ride around the range pulling shady deals like this one?"

"From what I've seen of Dunn, I'd say Satan's bossing his life right now, not God."

"You sure hit it square between the eyes." The cowboy walked off without looking back, leaving Andy wondering if the seed he'd been able to plant would ever take root and grow.

─┼─

Just before dusk, Andy, on his way to the bunkhouse, passed the wide front porch of the ranch house.

"Andy?" a soft voice called. The patter of feet on boards in a quick rush brought a young woman dressed in white to the top step. "Do you have time to talk?"

He heard tears in her voice and passionately longed to comfort her. His boot heels sounded loud on the steps, and he leaned against a porch post and looked down into her face, shadowed by falling night until her eyes turned dark and mysterious in her pale face.

"Is it true?" she whispered. Her hands clutched his two arms.

Andy suspected that, in her agitation, she didn't realize what she was doing. He couldn't say the same for himself. The touch of her hands sent love and longing through him. "Yes," he told her.

"Dear God, I'd hoped it was a rumor." Her hands dropped, then swept up to cover her face.

Scarcely conscious of his actions and stirred to the depths, he wrapped his arms around her and held her trembling body close. A start went through her before Linnet bowed her head against his chest and wept. In the few moments before she pulled back a little but not free, the last of Andy's boyhood vanished forever, replaced by manhood's strength and the need to care for his womenfolk.

"I. . .I'm sorry." She tilted her head back. Her white face blurred. "I—"

Nothing on earth could have kept Andy from lowering his head until his lips met and clung to hers for little more than a heartbeat. The next instant, he tore free. "Linnet, Sweetheart—"

"Lass, are you out here?"

With a low, incoherent cry, Andy ran down the steps and into the night, running away from the consequences of his actions as well as from Linnet and her uncle. Had he ruined his hope of heaven on earth with that kiss? Yet try as he would, Andy could not regret it. The soft pressure of lips he knew had been unkissed remained.

Unwilling to endure the endless bunkhouse chafing, the distraught cowboy turned toward the corral. Chinquapin no longer roamed in the pasture but stayed closer to the ranch to be more accessible. Andy snatched blanket and saddle from their place in the barn, quickly saddled her, and rode away, pursued by memories.

Hours later he returned, cared for his mare, and crept noiselessly into the bunkhouse, weary from the night ride and able to sleep the few remaining hours until morning.

His heart thudded when Reddy, who had gone out first, shoved the bunkhouse door open and yelled, "Hey, Cullen. Boss wants you."

It could mean only one thing. Linnet must have told her uncle, perhaps her father, of the moment on the porch. Andy considered just stuffing spare clothes into his bedroll and riding out. He could send for the money Allen owed him later. It would save embarrassment all around.

Coward, an inner voice accused. *Be a man and take your medicine.*

He threw back his head and marched to the main house like a gaily caparisoned Arabian on parade.

A court of four awaited him on the porch: Linnet, eyes wide; Mrs. Salt, arms folded across her enveloping apron; George and Judd Allen, who grew more alike every day.

"You wanted me, Boss?" Some of the old insouciance returned to settle Andy down.

"My niece has something to say to you," George Allen boomed.

"Miss Allen?" Andy turned toward her, waiting for his sentence, reveling in her loveliness as she stood there wrapped in a wooly, white shawl against the early morning chill.

Eyes like twin stars looked straight into Andy's brown ones. "Andy, I thought a lot last night after we. . .we talked." A rich blush turned her the same rosy hue as the clouds touched by the rising sun. "If Silas Dunn is out catching wild horses, shouldn't you go find Sheik before that awful man gets him?"

The cowboy's lower jaw dropped. It was the last thing he'd expected.

Linnet rushed on. "Father and Uncle George agree. So does Mrs. Salt." An indescribable look crept into her face, one that needed to be examined in private.

"I'd give anything to go." Andy wheeled toward his employers.

"Take as much time as you need," George Allen gruffly told him. Understanding shone in his eyes. "I remember after Sheik's daddy stole my mare, I spent a lot of days and nights trying to get her back."

If only he could have a moment with Linnet! Yet even if he did, what could he say? Andy hid a small sigh and looked at each of the porch's occupants in turn. "I'm beholden." The quaint expression said what he could not.

"Hurry back, Andy. God go with you." Linnet's benediction rested on him like a poncho, and forty-five minutes later, the bemused cowboy mounted Chinquapin and rode away, remembering the smile on the lips he had kissed and the freedom from condemnation in her eyes. He thanked God he hadn't offended her.

✢

Following a cold trail proved fruitless. Andy spent two weeks tracking down rumors, replenished his supplies at Moab, and went out again. Nights grew chill, and still he found no trace of Sheik. Had Sheik left southeastern Utah and ranged elsewhere, starting over, stealing mares, and building a new herd? Andy shuddered at the thought. It meant he might never again see the black stallion he loved.

Finally, encroaching winter drove him back to the Rocking A. Only the warmth of Linnet Allen's welcome saved him from despair. He'd prayed to find Sheik, and for some reason, the Lord hadn't answered. Or maybe, like Linnet pointed out, God was saying no.

Winter came, warmed and sweetened for Andy by the eastern young woman daily becoming more robust and western. Just before Christmas, he inveigled her into taking a ride. She'd long since graduated from Sadie and often rode Chinq, while Andy straddled whatever horse he fancied. On a rise of land that overlooked the Rocking A, Andy halted and courteously helped the bundled-up girl out of the saddle. He pointed west.

"In the spring, I'll be building a cabin there," he softly told her. "Linnet, will you be my wife and live there with me?"

Straight as a homing pigeon, she came into his arms and turned her face up for his kiss. "Andy Cullen, I'll be proud to be your wife."

Not until the cold day penetrated their warm garments did they leave the spot that would forever be special in memory and the scene of many visits in their life together.

Warm congratulations poured over them when they announced their news to the Rocking A. Andy best remembered Reddy Hode's drawl, "Well, if I couldn't marry her, I'd as soon have you get her as anyone I know."

✢

Spring came with an abundance of tiny desert flowers. A few days before the wedding date, Linnet found Andy standing on the porch, eyes turned toward the distant canyon country. The expression on his face when he glanced at her brought a rush of love and poignancy. She put her arms around him and said nothing, knowing he hadn't forgotten the magnificent black stallion unheard of during all these long months.

"Shall we visit our new home?" she suggested.

Andy nodded. "I wouldn't have believed how skilled the outfit would turn out to be in raising our cabin," he marveled. It stood on a ridge not far away, with a view that took a man's breath away. Barn, large corral, and space for a bunkhouse when needed sometime in the future, the snug spread offered a haven for the couple so soon to be man and wife.

"How does Chinq like her new home?" Linnet asked just before they reached their destination. Her gaze turned from the corral where the faithful mare stood a little apart from the younger horses.

He didn't answer.

She turned back. "Why, where did—" Linnet never finished her question.

A shrill whistle cut the air, followed by a whinny, then the neighing of the horses in the corral. A drooping, dusty horse stood outside the bars, nose extended to a chestnut mare inside.

Andy couldn't move. He whistled.

The strange horse turned and slowly came toward him.

With a wild yell, the cowboy ran toward the limping horse. "Sheik, old boy." He wrapped his fingers in the coarse mane. Tears burned his eyelids. "You old prodigal, where have you been?" Andy tore free and examined the weary black, the lame leg last of all. He whooped again when he found a sharp stone securely wedged in the hoof. Thin and worn he might be, but Sheik was whole, and he had come home.

"I guess we'll never know," he told Linnet after he fed, watered, and rubbed Sheik down. "What's important is, he's back. I opened the corral gate, and he trotted in like he'd lived there forever." He ruefully added, "I hated to leave him for the night, but in just a few days. . . Linnet, it means so much more that Sheik chose to come than if I'd just found him and brought him home." He swallowed hard. "I can't help thinking it's like with God. If He hogtied us and dragged us kicking and screaming, would we ever love Him? Ump-umm. Instead, He gives us all the rope we need. If we're smart, like Sheik, when we get to the end of it, we come back to where we belong."

Andy looked across the top of her head in the direction of Dead Horse Point. A pang rushed through him for the broomtails that had become captives of the canyon. He thought of pardners, trapped by sin, helpless as the penned horses. *Lord, thank You for freeing me,* he silently prayed. *If You can use this plain old cowboy to help round up others, I'll do it.*

Keenly aware of God's love, mightier than creation itself, Andy stood for a long time, the world in his arms, the hope of heaven in his soul. Like Sheik, the bent and weary prodigal, the restless, drifting rider had found where he belonged.

A Letter to Our Readers

Dear Readers:

In order that we might better contribute to your reading enjoyment, we would appreciate your taking a few minutes to respond to the following questions. When completed, please return to the following: Fiction Editor, Barbour Publishing, Inc., P.O. Box 719, Uhrichsville, OH 44683.

1. Did you enjoy reading *Frontier Brides*?
   ❑ Very much—I would like to see more books like this.
   ❑ Moderately—I would have enjoyed it more if _____

   _____

   _____

2. What influenced your decision to purchase this book?
   (Check those that apply.)
   ❑ Cover   ❑ Back cover copy   ❑ Title   ❑ Price
   ❑ Friends   ❑ Publicity   ❑ Other

3. Which story was your favorite?
   ❑ *Silence in the Sage*   ❑ *Music in the Mountains*
   ❑ *Whispers in the Wilderness*   ❑ *Captives of the Canyon*

4. Please check your age range:
   ❑ Under 18   ❑ 18–24   ❑ 25–34
   ❑ 35–45   ❑ 46–55   ❑ Over 55

5. How many hours per week do you read? _____

Name _____

Occupation _____

Address _____

City _____ State _____ Zip _____

E-mail _____